# BIRTH OF A MONSTER

# A.S. COOMER

Grindhouse Press
PO BOX 521
Dayton, Ohio 45401

Grindhouse Press #078
ISBN-13: 978-1-941918-86-9

# BIRTH OF A MONSTER

# CHAPTER ONE
## A MAN'S WORLD

**"SURE SHE'S YER MOMMA," THE** bald man said, "but she's still a cunt."

Jacob didn't miss a step. He wiped the stinging sweat from the corners of his eyes, made sure he didn't trip over the exposed knobs of sandstone and tree roots, and followed the glinting butt of the rifle in the crook of his mother's newest boyfriend Randall Adkins' skinny, tattooed arm up the ridgeline.

"One day, when you're older, you'll understand," Randall Adkins said, slowing long enough to release a strand of dip spit onto the sandy path. Jacob watched the congealed mess turn end over end as if in slow motion. "It's not a personal thing. Not something they can help. They're just hard-wired that way, women are. Cunts."

Jacob paused over the glistening hunk of saliva and chewing tobacco, noting the way the edges of the goo were slowly absorbed by the thin, gritty soil. The viscous glob had mostly held together to form a slanted cross in the center of the path between two large rocks. Jacob stopped and watched as it slowly faded into a dark, dry stain, the tobacco already looking dehydrated and wasted and waiting for a good rain to carry it down the steep slope of the mountain.

"Keep up, shit ass," Randall Adkins called over his shoulder. "I ain't trying to lose yer dumb ass out here."

Jacob stepped over the evaporating cross and followed the bald man up the path and back into the woods.

-

They found a rocky perch overlooking a small, flat clearing.

"Here," Randall Adkins said, slipping the frayed pack off his shoulders. He shoved the pack roughly into Jacob's pudgy chest, nearly knocking the breath out of him. It was heavy and Jacob held it awkwardly with both of his hands as Randall Adkins worked at the broken zipper until it opened. The first thing he brought out of the bag was a pack of cigarettes. He put one in his cracked and chapped lips but did not light it.

I

# BIRTH OF A MONSTER

Jacob tried not to breathe in the man's sour smell by inhaling through his mouth. Randall Adkins removed a square chunk of white salt and the bag became nearly weightless in Jacob's small, dirty hands. The cords in Randall Adkins' neck and arms bulged with the weight of it.

"Stay put," he said, spinning quickly on his heels and surefootedly descending the rocky terrain to the clearing.

Jacob watched the man for a moment before sneaking a peek into the bag. He found a long-bladed hunting knife, three packs of bargain cigarettes, a leather pouch, something wrapped in cut and duct-taped tarpaulin, a rust-freckled handgun with the word *Specialist* written above the trigger, and a roll of cash tightly rubber-banded together. His stomach fluttered. He ran his shaking pointer finger along the cold metal barrel to the point where it touched the wad of money. He snuck a quick glance down the mountain to see Randall Adkins carefully making his way down the treacherous rockface. He worked several bills out of the roll, wadding them tightly in his sweating hands then stuffing them deep into the back pocket of his pants.

The bald man hopped off a rock into the clearing. He dropped the salt block onto the patchy grass in the middle of the space.

"See it alright from up there, shit ass?" Randall Adkins called up.

The man's gruff voice scared up a pair of rock pigeons from a low-lying branch. The sudden beating of their wings caused Randall Adkins to jump and half-turn, the blue ink of jailhouse tattoos on his neck shining with sweat. He aimed the rifle at the fluttering gray specks as they took to the air but did not fire. He lowered the rifle, watched the birds disappear, then lit the cigarette still cradled between his lips.

Jacob took a last glance at the roll of money, thought it looked as it had before he took the bills, then let the bag drop to his feet. He leaned backwards and stretched the tired muscles of his back.

"You better not be tuckered out yet, shit ass," Randall Adkins called up. "We've got another stop to make before hunting."

Jacob didn't reply. He unslung his own pack, retrieved the hot bottle of Mountain Dew and drank half in three long swallows. The burp that followed brought tears to his eyes. He watched the bald man climb back up the rockface in quick, assured movements, the thin wisps of his cigarette smoke looking like steam in Jacob's blurry eyes.

They followed a steep animal's path off the hunter's trail down into an overgrown valley thick with mosquitos. Thorns snagged Jacob's pack and pricked his bare arms and legs, the bright red of blood running alongside the salted smears of sweat. He swatted at the constant biting of the bugs. He wiped at the endless stinging in his eyes.

Though his body was slick with sweat, Randall Adkins did not appear the least bit tired. He whistled faintly as he strode with wide, stomping steps.

"Cain't believe you ain't been hunting before now," the bald man called over his shoulder. "Damn shame. But yer mother isn't the brightest bulb in the tanning bed, is she?"

Jacob didn't think he was supposed to offer a reply, so he didn't.

"Hunting is righteous. Hunting is sacred. Hunting is man's safety valve, shit ass."

"Shit ass" was the only name Randall Adkins had ever called Jacob, but he was used to being called names. No one but his teachers called him by his actual name and then only when calling roll; he never spoke up in school.

"A man has to hunt," Randall Adkins said. "It's in our nature. If a man doesn't go out and shoot and kill something, then he'll go crazy and kill in other ways."

The path ended at the banks of a trickling stream, mostly exposed stones lapped smooth and circular from years of spring and summer showers. Randall Adkins stopped long enough to put another cigarette in his mouth, light it, and inhale before crossing the small stream on the exposed, dry stones.

"If a man doesn't kill something—a deer, a wildcat, a hog, whatever—" the bald man exhaled a blue-gray plume of smoke, "he'll carry that bloodlust with him. See, a man is born with bloodlust; it's in our nature. We're programmed to kill. We're natural born hunters, shit ass."

Jacob followed Randall Adkins into a dense thicket of brambles and honeysuckle. The path was so small and overgrown he didn't see it at first. The foliage was thick and close, encasing the dirt path like a shroud. Jacob fought against the stabbing thorns and slapping branches, keeping the slick, pockmarked surface of the back of the bald man's head in view.

"Thick as flies on shit in here, ain't it, shit ass?" Randall Adkins laughed.

The path took an abrupt, sharp right turn around the trunk of an ancient hemlock. A branch whipped back and slapped Jacob fully in the face, the soft, feathery needles doing nothing to blunt the force of the branch.

"Pay attention, shit ass," Randall Adkins laughed.

Jacob felt the welt rising under his right eye. His upper lip felt bruised and swollen.

In an instant, Jacob knew Randall Adkins had pulled the branch back and sent it smashing into his face on purpose. He didn't get angry. Jacob was hit too often for that. He chided himself on not expecting it.

Jacob pushed through the hemlock and found himself standing next to the bald man and a strange looking science experiment. An overly large bronze kettle was hung over a small, smoldering fire. What appeared to be an aluminum pot had been welded onto the kettle and a series of tubes and pipes connected it to another aluminum pot. A small trickle of white liquid dripped down into a nearly full mason jar.

Randall Adkins bent down and picked up the mason jar. He held the jar under his nose and smelled deeply.

"Ah," he exhaled, smiling around his cigarette. "Straight from the teat."

He removed the cigarette from his lips and took a long pull from the jar.

Jacob knew of moonshine stills. He'd heard talk of family stills hidden throughout the hills and had even seen a historic still from the pioneer days of the long hunters on a field trip but he still found himself fascinated by the setup. He stepped to his left for a better look at the strange mix of copper and aluminum.

"Whew," Randall Adkins exclaimed. "That'll get ye right. Here. Put a little hair on that flabby chest."

The jar was shoved into Jacob's chest, soaking his shirt in the warm pungent liquid. He took the jar with both of his hands and stared down into it. The sharp odor of alcohol prickled his nostrils and made him blink back burgeoning tears.

"Go on then, shit ass," the bald man said. "Don't be afraid. It's a man's drink but you're on yer way to becoming one."

Jacob looked up from the mason jar at the bald man. The still and the small clearing around it shielded the two of them from the harsh sun. The slanted light that found its way down cast strange shadows on Randall Adkins' scarred, ugly face. His crooked nose and yellowed teeth loomed large and sinister in the relief of shadows cast across his smiling visage.

Jacob raised the glass to his lips, hesitating as the smell brought more tears to his eyes.

The bald man's smile stretched, encasing the lower half of his head in a wolf's grin.

"Drink up, boy," Randall Adkins said.

Jacob let a trickle of moonshine spill onto his tongue. His taste buds rebelled but he knew better than to spit the liquid out. He squeezed his eyes shut against the tears and quickly swallowed it down. A rush of heat followed the moonshine as it traced the outline of his throat into his stomach. Jacob saw the flashing splash of napalm and agent orange in a grainy replay from the Vietnam documentary they'd just watched in American history class in his head.

His body rocked, spasmed, and, despite his best efforts, Jacob sputtered and coughed. He nearly dropped the glass jar as his body revolted against the spreading burn in his mouth, throat, and trunk.

The bald man took the mason jar back, laughing. He slapped Jacob's back hard enough to send him lurching forward into the low-lying boughs of a hemlock tree.

"There ye go," Randall Adkins said. "That'll cure what ails ye. Maybe burn out some of that priss ye cunt mom's instilled in ye too."

Jacob fought for air, coughing and wiping at the tears on his cheeks with hands already slick and grimy with sweat, grit, and blood.

-

The hike back to the rockface overlooking the clearing where Randall Adkins left the block of salt was filled with a buzzing quiet. The blood rushed high up in his neck and face. His ears felt burned and tingly. His temples throbbed with the frantic beat of his pulse.

Randall Adkins had filled his pack with several jars of the shine. He'd drank nearly all of that first jar, forcing Jacob to take four more drinks from it.

"More than a sip now, shit ass," he'd said. "I'm trying to show ye how to be a man, not the fairy ye mom's turned you into."

Jacob's feet felt like wooden blocks. When he looked down he expected to see those funny Dutch shoes Sandra Vandercamp brought to Ancestor Day back in fourth grade. He slowed his pace but did not stop when he saw the shape of his pants, which were frayed, ripped, stained with blood and grime, and covered in cockle-burs.

*Mom's gonna pitch a fit,* he thought.

They were one of the three pairs of pants he had. His mother had taken him to the Goodwill in Pikeville just a few weeks back to get him "new" clothes for the school year. The battered pair of women's K-Swiss shoes, which had earned him the nickname "Little Miss K-Swiss," had come from that shopping trip as well. The already off-white and scuffed tennis shoes were hopelessly stained and ripped from the rugged mountain paths.

"We're all killers, shit ass," Randall Adkins said, his voice strangely hushed, not quite a whisper.

The abruptness of the statement after so long a silence startled Jacob. He'd been lost in the hazy motion of drunkenness and worn expressions of exasperated anger he foresaw from his mother when she saw the condition of his clothes.

They made it back to the spot overlooking the clearing with the salt block. He followed the bald man's gaze down to a young buck steadily working the white block of salt with its tongue. Jacob was surprised to see how long a deer's tongue was.

A thunderous crack sent him stumbling backwards on his un-steady feet. It was followed, in rapid succession, by three more thun-derous bangs. Jacob crashed down into an elderberry bush, the breath knocked out of his heaving chest. He floundered in the shrub, open-mouthed and gaping like a fish out of water, for an agonized few moments before air trickled back into his screaming lungs.

"That'll happen, shit ass," the bald man's face loomed over Jacob like a craggy, smiling moon. "You'll get yer sea legs. It comes with practice."

Randall Adkins yanked Jacob out of the shrubbery and onto his feet. A jar of moonshine was thrust into his hands. He squeezed back fresh tears as he took another gulp.

Down in the little clearing, the young buck, as well as two small does Jacob hadn't seen before he fell, lay dead in a small semicircle around the block of salt.

The bald man took the jar from Jacob's shaking hands. He smiled down at the boy before raising the glass to his mouth and gulping around upturned lips.

"There ain't nothing like taking a life."

Jacob stood over the young buck. Its tongue hung limply out of its open mouth. In all the photos he'd seen of his classmates and their fathers with the bucks they shot, the antlers were grand protruding crowns, branching off to several shoots before pointing skyward. The antlers on the buck at his feet had no branches. They were barely more than forehead nubs.

The bald man lit another cigarette, sucking the smoke in, holding it, then exhaling with a sigh of contentment.

One of the does wasn't dead. It shook and tried to rise to its feet but couldn't. The doe's coat was matted and covered with ticks. It looked old and frail and close to death even without the dime-sized hole pumping blood from its neck.

Randall Adkins stood over the dying doe and exhaled smoke into the late afternoon sun.

"Ain't a thing in the world like it, shit ass," he said, stepping down onto the animal's neck.

The doe struggled, but weakly.

The bald man reared up and brought his heavy boot down onto the doe's head. The crunch of splintering bone sent Jacob's stomach roiling. He spun away as Randall Adkins stomped the deer's skull again. His vision blurred and heat swept up his throat into his face. Jacob dropped to his knees and vomited as the bald man continued to stomp in the animal's head.

-

"Well, we better be getting on," Randall Adkins said, his voice dreamy and far away. "We got one last stop 'fore home."

Jacob rose on shaky legs, using the inside of his sweat drenched t-shirt to wipe spit and puke from his chin and mouth.

The bald man didn't wait on him. He swung the pack back over his tattooed shoulders and started down the path. Jacob watched the pack bounce softly against the man's lower back, the glass mason jars clinking against each other within.

Jacob took one last look at the three dead deer around the salt block. He'd always heard that death could look peaceful. There was nothing peaceful about what he saw.

He turned back to the path but before he started after his mother's new boyfriend, he plugged each of his nostrils and blew clinging strings of snot, acidic bile, and blood from his nose down into the dirt.

-

"I've got a little something to show ye," the bald man called. "It ain't much further."

The trees were scarcer and sickly on this part of the mountain. Jacob felt he was entering some alien moonscape: crags and the burnt, hollowed out remains of skeletal trees. There wasn't much grass and the few blades growing were yellowed and stunted.

Randall Adkins whistled as he walked, his steps jaunty things that sprung off the tips of his worn-out Justin steel toe boots, some nearly tuneless melody punctuated by the clinking of the mason jars in his pack.

Jacob wasn't exactly scared of the bald man. Not more than Gerry or Richard or Fats or Jeremiah. He didn't beat Jacob any worse than the others, it was just that his eyes promised worse yet. Jacob wouldn't allow that he was fearful. So, he was . . . wary.

The bald man, momentarily, couldn't contain himself. He snatched the cigarette from his lips and growled up to the glaring sun, "Goin' down, sweet little one, oh. I'm going down, sweet babe. The night's almost ended, our bliss's been spent. If I use it anymore, I'll owe a doctor money for a ten-inch splint."

The way Randall Adkins laughed sent little goosebumps prickling up Jacob's sweat-slick ribs.

"Ever been down in a mine, shit ass?" the bald man asked.

He didn't wait for a reply.

"Dark as a dungeon it truly is. I lost a dog, among other things," he shot a slick grin over his shoulder at Jacob but did not slow his stride, "in this very one a few years back."

Jacob tripped and had to awkwardly run a handful of steps to avoid falling flat on his face. Half a brick lay in the middle of the small but worn path, its jagged, broken interior sun-bleached but sanguine. He walked back to it and knelt down.

The sun slanted and reddened as it sank closer to the hills across the valley.

One side of the broken brick was scorched. He leaned forward and slid his left pointer finger in a mostly straight line down the middle of the blackened surfaced. The greasy ash rolled up against Jacob's already filthy fingernail like the folds on the back of Garth Brooks' neck, reminding him the little shit had snapped at him three times since Wednesday, when it drew blood from his left big toe. His mother always named her pugs after country singers.

Kneeling down, Jacob noticed how weird the ground was. It

looked like it had been pan-fried decades ago. Eerily, ghost-like weeds fluttered in some unfelt, unseen breeze. Jacob thought it a glimpse of winged angels in one of their ritual dances. He followed a steady line of the swaying forms to a rockface rising fifteen feet into the purpling sky.

"I want to show you something, shit ass," Randall Adkins' voice reverberated.

A heavy blackness yawned open at the cleft of the slight incline: the burnt brick and splintered wood remains of a building buttressed against the exposed sandstone.

The path led up into the opening left by an exploded door, a chasm bordered by broken brick and stygian scorches. Though Jacob remained frozen, waiting for the bald man to speak again, he knew that was where his voice had come from and why it sounded so disconnected.

"We already spent the day, shit ass." The bald man's lips stretched and curdled into a smile as he spoke. "Let's not squander the night."

-

Jacob stepped into a profound darkness. He expected to be hit for making Randall Adkins wait, but he figured rushing into a thousand-foot hole was the greater of the two evils. He carefully searched the shadowland beyond the setting sun's last rays with the scooting tips of his little miss K-Swisses.

Jacob heard the flick of a lighter and the bald man's face was illuminated by the flickering flame that lit another cigarette.

"Watch yer step, shit ass."

In the shifting shadows, the bald man's face appeared as still and revealing as an oil painting not five feet in front of Jacob.

The flame disappeared, coating the small enclosure in a gauze-like darkness. Randall Adkins' face glowed oily and watchful with each of his drags.

"Ye almost found the drop-off," he said, flicking the lighter to expose an impenetrable darkness staring upward from the earthen floor.

Jacob staggered backwards and crouched lower, suddenly unsure of his balance. When he looked up into the bald man's eyes, Randall Adkins' made a show of squeezing them closed and smoking half the cigarette in a spasm of feigned ecstasy. The bald man unslung the pack from his shoulders and removed the wrapped bundle. He tossed it into the hole.

Jacob was shocked at how fast it disappeared. He listened for it to hit the bottom.

The bald man held the glowing tip of his cigarette under Jacob's face. Jacob watched as the man slowly made exaggerated circles with it over the hole between them.

"Here's a magic trick for ye," Randall Adkins said, letting the cigarette slip from his fingers.

It turned end over end in a long arcing twirl until it hit the side of the hole, which sent exactly three sparks bouncing off the worn sandstone.

From his periphery, Jacob saw the bald man leap into the shadows deeper in the building and was just in the beginning phases of recalling his wariness of his mother's boyfriend when a great sigh belched up from the hole. It knocked the air from his face with the heat of an oven and the percussive force of the massive gong they kept locked in the band room at school.

Jacob's pack cushioned his back from the fall, but his head wasn't so lucky. He felt the back of his skull crash against the brick wall then everything was fuzzy and buzzing. In the great sea of sputtering darkness, a swarm of static bees strutted and jerked. Jacob watched them, dumbfounded, for some time before realizing they were floaters. He pushed himself up on his elbows until he could rest his back against the greasy brick wall. He touched the back of his head with fingers he barely felt in control of.

*This is gonna be one hell of a goose egg,* Jacob thought.

"Whewee!" Randall Adkins cackled.

The floaters were dissipating one by one, but a steady ringing filled Jacob's ears. The bald man's voice, though audible, sounded muffled.

"Learned the hard way that ye gotta be careful how you use this 'ere hidey hole."

The nearness of Randall Adkins' voice brought Jacob's eyes back into focus. Though he could admit to himself he was out and out scared now, Jacob took a prideful pleasure in the overwhelming drowsiness pulling at his eyelids.

"If yer thinkin' I'm gonna carry yer shit ass home, boy, you are mistaken."

Jacob blinked once. Twice. He couldn't keep them open. The last time he opened his eyes before sinking into an exhausting, dreamless sleep, Jacob thought he could make out a bouquet of angels dancing. If he had enough strength to squint, he knew each of the rotten teeth in the sparsely populated bottom row was a pedestal, the glowing tip of the bald man's cigarette a fading signal for the coming curtain call.

It felt like another party he hadn't been invited to.

-

He woke up sweating, drenched in the light of midmorning.

Jacob moaned at the pounding in his head. His neck screamed with a sudden cramp when he made to lift himself from the dirt. Every muscle in his body went rigid with the flaring pain. He kneaded the bulging muscle with desperate hands until it relaxed enough for Jacob to realize, at some point in his unconsciousness, he'd not only pissed himself but had also coated the front of his shirt in whiskey-tinged vomit. His tongue found several thick chunks of what felt like the instant grits he'd had for breakfast dried to the roof of his mouth and the backs of several of his teeth.

His stomach roiled and Jacob knew he wouldn't be able to make it back to the trailer before he'd have to shit. He brought his knees within grasping distance of his hands and used them to pull himself as erect as he could manage. His pulse beat a frenetic beat at the corners of his raw eyes. He sucked in gulps of foul air until enough of the shakiness had gone that he could climb up to his hands and knees.

Jacob vomited in two rapid expulsions and felt the hot kiss of diarrhea fill his underwear.

"Oh god," he moaned, crawling on all fours toward the blistering sunlight.

Just outside the opening where a door used to hang, Jacob felt hot, shameful tears splash down onto his filthy cheeks as he blinked and blinked, willing his eyes to adjust to the dazzling brightness.

The heat sent the competing odors rising up into Jacob's nostrils. He gagged, then began to weep.

-

When he could stand, Jacob made his way over to a burnt stump. He pulled down his pants and underwear in one motion and eased himself down onto it. He shifted his weight until he could sit on the stump and shit off the back end onto the burned earth. After the heaviest period of the shitstorm, Jacob lifted himself enough to drop his pecker off the stump so he could piss.

His head felt overly large and heavy on his shoulders. His neck was of no use; it'd been craned at an unnatural angle for far too long. Jacob panted through his open mouth. He swore he could almost taste the shit from the overwhelming smell. He opened his eyes and saw the mess inside his threadbare underwear. He kicked off his shoes and socks, then slowly, careful not to slip off his precarious perch on the stump, he lifted his left leg and slid the pant leg down. He shifted his weight and repeated the action for the right leg. He leaned forward and tweezered the baconed waistband of the briefs between his left thumb and pointer finger, pulling them free from the pants then tossing them a few feet away.

His anus burned and spasmed with wet, coughing farts. He held his breath and squeezed out a particularly painful ball of pressure from low in his stomach, then he picked up his pants and examined the interior. He saw only a smallish splotch of smeared shit, which he ground into the dirt between his bare feet.

Jacob remembered the stolen bills. He hastily brushed bits of dirt, cinder, and weeds from the inside of his pants then flipped them over onto his naked lap. Stale piss filled his nostrils, sending his stomach turning over and another bark sounded from his stinging asshole.

Something about the piss on his pants was strange.

*What's stranger than waking up covered in piss?*

He shoved his hand into the back pocket but found nothing but soggy lint. Jacob straightened the left leg of the pants, stretching it out completely before him. The piss stain ran down the side of pants.

*I couldn't have done that.*

He saw it in his head as clearly as if it were an instant replay. Randall Adkins knowing Jacob took his money, then finding it in his pocket, then leaving Jacob a golden reminder of his crime.

Jacob gagged. He fought against it but couldn't stop from vomiting into his mouth. He spit and had to cleave the clinging strand from his lips and wipe his hand onto the side of the stump. He whimpered but did not allow himself to out-and-out cry when he used his shirt to wipe.

He was startled by the beating of wings overhead. He gripped the shirt to his chest in an instinctive move to protect his trunk and nearly fell off the sooty stump flinching at the sudden sound. A large raven slowly lowered itself onto the remnants of what must've been a towering oak. It turned its inky eyes on Jacob then cawed shrilly three times.

*Caw caw. Caw.*

Jacob couldn't stand the intensity of the bird's gaze. He looked down at the dripping brown mess on his pale freckled chest. He felt his chin stick to the slickened skin and realized he had his own shit smeared on his face.

"Fuck you!" Jacob screamed, leaping to his feet and charging the bird.

The raven took flight long before he had a chance of reaching it, which caused Jacob a great deal of unease when he discovered he was laughing in a voice he barely recognized as his own.

-

Jacob watched the bird diminish into the cloudless sky, the sound of his breathing punctuated by the ragged beating of his pulse in his temples. The black, insulting speck's arc shifted upward and disappeared into the blinding fury of the sun. Out of a sense of spiteful defiance, Jacob squinted into the effulgence for as long as he could stand it, his raw eyes spilling hot, comfortless tears onto his windburnt cheeks.

He closed his eyes, his shoulders slumping with a nearly overwhelming tiredness.

When he opened his eyes some time later, Jacob's nakedness was startling. The pale length of his inner thighs were two white cavefish frozen in sudden luminance. The freckles peppering his trunk were just discernible from the flecks of vomit, shit, and trail grit.

Jacob turned away from the sun and retrieved his pants. He used a stump for balance and inserted each of his legs. He shivered at the cool wetness inside as he zippered and buttoned the pants. He stared at his stained miss K-Swisses and longed for a hot shower, then remembered the hot water tank had crapped out last week. Another in a long line of things going wrong in the many rented trailers his mother moved him in and out of on a semi-monthly basis.

*Or was that the last place?* Jacob couldn't remember. *The one up Black Dog Branch?*

He couldn't keep them all separated sometimes.

Jacob picked up his shirt, saw that it was hopelessly stained, and tossed it onto the blackened ground. He looked back to the brick building at the foot of the mountain. Nothing about its construction spoke of professionalism: the bricks did not match, the space between each row was great and varied, even the three hinges left in the scorched doorjamb were mismatched.

# BIRTH OF A MONSTER

The sun slanted through the doorless opening, exposing the gaping hole of the mineshaft. Jacob was captivated. It was not a perfect circle, not even remotely. The light fell away, dropping off into the darkness below in strange rolling waves as if it had been hollowed out by some slow, sad song instead of the plunging of bladed drills.

Jacob stepped into the building, trailing the fingers of his left hand along the roughened soot-covered bricks, his eyes never leaving the hole. He inched his bare feet to the opening, crouching low on his knees and holding each of his shaking arms out like a tyro tightrope walker until he could curl each of his big toes around the cool edge, sending crumbling bits of formerly packed earth dropping into the chasm.

Jacob crouched lower, the seat of his pants nearly brushing the ground, narrowing his eyes and cocking his head slightly to the right. He waited but did not hear any sign of a bottom. He pulled his eyes from the hole long enough to scan the small interior for something to drop. He picked up the broken corner of a brick, carefully studied its weight, then held if over the hole. He took in a deep, slow breath, holding it for as long as he could then letting it out through pursed lips. He repeated this until his breathing was slow and regular. Then he dropped the brick.

Jacob closed his eyes and held his breath. A robin tweeted from somewhere outside the building. A hawk screeched from high above. The brick never made a sound.

-

The growling of his stomach pulled Jacob away from the hole. He carefully scooted away from the opening on his butt, his legs sliding up and over the edge back onto the dusty earthen floor, his eyes blinking away a blinding darkness as they filtered in the light of early afternoon. He rose on popping joints, holding his breath to yawn and stretch. His stomach churned and he thought about deserts and seabeds. The sun and the bottomless hole. Hunger and nausea.

Jacob walked out of the building and found his shoes. He plopped down onto the stump he'd used for a toilet and slid his feet into the women's tennis shoes. He looked at the descending fall of the path to where it slipped seamlessly into the forest. The notched spine of the ridgeline gradually turned eastward, leading, after nearly five long miles, to the unpaved loggers' road that almost connected with the twisting county road after another four miles. A great chunk of the loggers' road had fallen off the side of the mountain years ago and thick vegetation had reclaimed the small portion of mountain, creating a blind from any passersby. Randall Adkins had parked the beat-to-shit F-150 he was buying in installments there. Jacob didn't expect it, or the bald man, to be there waiting when he finally made it. From there, it was three miles to Thompkins' Hilltop Trailer Court and the salmon-colored singlewide his mother was renting on a month-to-month lease.

Jacob craned his head without turning his body and took another long look at the hole before starting the considerable walk home.

He ate the entire bag of beef jerky, two chocolate chip granola bars, and a roll of Life Savers at the beginning of the second mile. He was ravished by the end of the third.

With every blink of his tired eyes, Jacob saw the staring blackness of the hole. He remembered the force of the hole's fury, the bald man's painful magic trick. Though most of the path was blanketed by a canopy of trees, Jacob felt the exposed skin of his neck, back, arms, and ears burning. He hated his red hair and pale skin. He hated his downy freckles and sausage-like moles. He hated his hairless upper lip and soft voice.

He paused, hidden behind the face of a moss-covered boulder, and watched seven ragged elk slowly pick their way across the path. The buck leading the elk was ancient. His gnarled rack rose like a pagan crown from his matted head. He had wary eyes that often flickered in Jacob's direction as if he could sense Jacob's presence.

When the elk disappeared into the overgrown valley below, Jacob stepped back onto the path. The elk had spent several minutes at the foot of the largest pawpaw tree Jacob had ever seen. He reached up and pulled a greenish yellow pawpaw off a nearby branch. The fruit gave slightly as he squeezed it in his fist.

*That bull practically knew I was here*, he thought. *He didn't really give two shits either.*

Jacob let the pawpaw drop onto the path.

He saw the bald man's cigarette slip soundlessly into the hole. He saw the white-lined eyes of the wary buck glance momentarily over his own. He saw the hunk of broken brick turn end over end in slow freefall, the eye of the doe burst from its socket.

Jacob felt new grooves form as his teeth ground together painfully in his skull. His muscles sang in rigidity as he lifted his foot over the underripe pawpaw. He watched the yellow meat of the fruit spill out from under his miss K-Swisses, wondering what it'd feel like to fall forever.

-

Dusk brought gooseflesh rippling across Jacob's blistered back and ribs. His right ear was wet from the sweat that had oozed from the burst blister topping his right ear, which had erupted with a soft pop when he brushed against it, wiping sweat from his stinging eyes.

Thompkins' Hilltop Trailer Court was alive and moving. Lights burned from nearly all eleven mobile homes, the salmon-coated singlewide Jacob and his mother shared no exception. His feet sank into the gravel that had been unevenly distributed not three days after they'd moved in. A week later and only Randall Adkins' pickup had driven over it. Jacob's thighs twinged with the extra effort.

"I'd find somewhere else to stop 'fore home," a gruff female voice said.

Jacob stopped and turned toward it, his shoulders drooping, his sweaty palms gripping the fabric at his knees.

"Huh?" he sighed.

"You don't hear 'at?"

The shape of the voice stepped out from behind Mitch Huff's purple and rust Pontiac LeMans, revealing itself as belonging to Stacie Q, from two trailers down. Her eyes were shiny and red under the yellow security light.

Jacob didn't waste his ragged breath with a reply. He sucked in five more mouthfuls of humid evening air and listened.

"Nope," Stacie Q said before sucking on a hand-rolled cigarette. She pulled in the air slowly and held it for a long time, her eyes squeezing shut.

"Stupid bitch!" the bald man's voice was loud even with the aluminum shell of the trailer encasing it.

The sound of glass breaking was followed by a muted cry from Jacob's mother and a dull thud. The brightness of the recently painted trailer's pink was evident even in the darkening evening. Jacob could see it shaking with the violence inside.

"Jesus," Stacie Q whispered, sending a cloud of thick smoke billowing around Jacob.

*Marijuana*, he recognized. *Better than what mom smokes too.*

"Sorry," she coughed. "Does it get worse 'an this? When will we know we should call the law?"

"How could ye be so goddamn stupid?" Randall Adkins yelled.

"I'm sorry!" his mother pleaded.

He'd hit her before. Most of 'em hit her. She'd probably deserved it most times too. He waited for the sound of his mother's voice, knowing by experience how to gauge the situation by the tremor of her tenor was a skill learned long ago.

"Hit this?" Stacie Q asked.

Jacob looked down at the woman's extended hand. Her fingers were skinny but wrinkled with overly large knuckles. Even in the dim light Jacob could see more dirt than polish on her yellowed fingernails.

Smoke swayed upward, wafting into his sniffing nostrils. It smelled sweetly sour and strong. Jacob took the joint from his neighbor and turned back to the pink trailer. He put the joint to his lips, feeling damp weed crumbles mash against the paper and his chapped lips, and watched the shadowplay on the closed blinds of his living room. A tall fin paced the length of the little room, disappearing from the confines of the window momentarily before returning and stomping in the direction in which it'd just come.

Jacob inhaled the smoke and closed his eyes.

"How could ye be so fucking careless, ye cunt?"

He heard the open-handed slap as clearly as if he were sitting on the couch in the living room. Jacob did not cough when he let the smoke slowly trickle from his open mouth and nostrils. He kept his eyes closed, extending his left hand, the joint nestled between his index finger and thumb, blindly in Stacie Q's direction. Jacob felt her fingers brush against his and carefully lift the joint away.

"Okay, goddamn it!" his mother screamed. "Ye've already bloodied my lip and busted my eyes up. Ye gonna break my fucking nose too, you bastard?"

Jacob heard Stacie Q take another drag.

"Thanks," he whispered, putting his tired body in motion.

She exhaled quickly and tried to speak but couldn't make an intelligible noise except a fit of coughing.

Jacob's thighs screamed as he took the cinderblock steps one at a time.

"Anytime," Stacie Q called from several trailers away. "Take care now."

Jacob put his hand on the doorknob, trying not to hear the pity in her voice, and held his breath. Every time it was a climactic event; every time it was a recycled memory. Fists and ashtrays. Lipstick and bruises. Bottles full; bottles empty and lined with the bloated stubs of cigarette butts. Curses and insults. Caresses and squeezing, twisting pinches. Blood and spit and snarling teeth. Jacob felt the flare of the cigarette tip, the scream of the belt, the bite of the belt buckle. He tasted copper and felt fuzz in his thirsty mouth.

He wanted to disappear. He wanted to explode. He wanted to kill the bald man. He wanted to kill his mother. Desert. Seabed.

The wetness of his mother's crying was the first thing he could focus on. It came from behind the couch, which was flipped over on top of her huddled form. Her crying was wet and sticky: slurping sucks of air followed by coughing sputters of snot and whimpers.

Pathetic. Helpless. Pitiful.

"Well now," the bald man said, his voice hoarse but amused. "Look who finally turned up. Ye spend the whole night up on that mountain?"

Randall Adkins was barefooted in his bib overalls, using one hand to lean against the wall, the other to raise the tallboy to his sneering mouth. Jacob could see the raised welts burning red and swollen on the knuckles gripping the beer can.

"See any good magic tricks?" the bald man asked.

He leaned backwards and belched loudly.

The black hole stared out, unblinking. The doe's eye exploded into smashed pawpaw pulp.

"Go on back to yer room, Jacob," his mother said.

Jacob couldn't find her face in the huddled mass half-hidden under the upturned couch.

"Best he learn now," Randall Adkins said.

His eyes locked onto Jacob's and held them as he drained the can in four long swallows. He crushed the can in his hand and threw it at Jacob's mother.

"Learn that women are stupid, careless cunts," he yelled. "Best he learn that his mother is just another stupid, careless cunt in a world chockful of stu-pid, id-iotic cunts."

The bald man kicked Jacob's mother twice. Jacob heard the breath leave her lungs and finally caught a glimpse of her face in the tangled mess of her dyed black hair. Her eyes were molded potatoes slit with fear and inebriation, smeared with cheap makeup and snot flecked with blood and crushed Xanax.

*So that's what this is about*, Jacob thought. He'd seen his mother snort pills all his life. It was a near nightly occurrence. He'd also seen her beaten for snorting drugs that did not belong to her or that she had yet to pay for or work off.

He'd seen his mother punched before. He watched her get punched again.

"This is what happens when yer not careful," Randall Adkins used his left hand to grab a handful of his mother's stringy hair. He pulled her out from under the thrift-store couch. "This is what happens when ye trust a woman, a *cunt*, to be careful."

He ended the sentence with a quick jab to her forehead. The knock sounded hollow and, somehow, dry to Jacob.

*What is this about?*

The bald man dragged Jacob's mother to her knees and twisted her around until both of them faced Jacob. His mother's tiny hands clawed at the hand fisted around her hair. Her face was twisted in agony, covered in sweat-matted strands of her lank hair and running smears of blue snot.

"Like I told ye yesterday, shit ass," Randall Adkins said, the black holes of his eyes wet and hard but there was a smile on his face, "this is a man's world. Ye ain't a man yet, but one day ye'll be one and I hope to God you don't have to put up with a miserable cunt like yer whore-mother."

The bald man jerked her hair upward and twisted his hand. Jacob's mother gasped then cried out pathetically.

"Ye know what she done, shit ass?" the man's smile faded. "She went and got herself in trouble."

*Trouble?*

She was really blubbering now. Her thin t-shirt was soaked with sweat and stained with drops of blood from her face, her nipples standing erect and lopsided. She tried to speak, shuddered, and fell back to blubbering. Her eyes were crazed and unseeing, flying across the room but focusing on nothing.

Jacob wanted to hit her. He wished she'd shut the hell up. He wished his own eyes weren't so raw and tired and stinging so much. Jacob wished he could disappear. He wished his mother would disappear. He wanted the bald man to fall but not forever. He wanted him to hit something far down and very hard. He wondered what it looked like from where the bald man was standing right then.

"In a *family* way," Randall Adkins said, jerking a handful of hair from her head.

Jacob's mother screeched. Jacob saw the blood and the patch of pale whiteness on her scalp where the hair used to be. The bald man flicked the clump of hair, little balls of skin and follicle clinging to the naturally red ends, to the floor and kicked her in the stomach.

"Cunt!" he bellowed. "Stupid cunt!"

Randall Adkins leaned over Jacob's mother and spat.

"I'm sorry!" she cried. "I'm sorry, Randall! I'm sor—"

With the sudden ferocity and speed of a cottonmouth, the bald man sent his huge right fist crashing into Christy Goodman's forehead. Jacob watched his mother's head bounce off the threadbare carpet. Her closed eyes slowly opened, revealing more white than not.

"Come here, Jake," his mother whispered.

In the suffocating darkness, Jacob couldn't tell where it came from. He squinted and stilled his shaking body, straining with all his being to hear her again, but the shifting void confused him. Indefinable shapes loomed and disappeared. Something unimaginably long and heavy moved silently overhead. Jacob held an invisible hand before his own eyes.

"Jake," her voice, though no louder than a prayer, filled his being. "Come here."

His mother was the only person that consistently called him Jake.

"Where are ye, Momma?"

"I'm right here," all of the space around him answered in his mother's voice. "Cain't ye see me?"

## CHAPTER TWO
## FALLING FOREVER / THE GREAT GAME

JACOB WOKE EARLY. THE BLUE-BLACK sky was cloudless through the cracked blinds. The sun was a hint of warmth in the east, a gentle curdling of black to blue to purple. Jacob knew the quiet of the trailer would not last. He also knew that some hangovers were violent. He dressed in the weak light from the shadeless lamp atop his scuffed dresser, careful to make as little noise as possible.

All the lights were on in the small kitchen. Jacob's eyes skipped across the empty beer cans, the broken plates, the overturned trashcan. He took his steps carefully, avoiding several mysterious wet spots and chips of broken ceramic and jagged glass. He shielded his body behind the thin paneling of the doorframe and peered into the quiet living room.

The bald man was asleep on the couch, which had been set right-side up but in the exact center of the narrow room. Randall Adkins was crumpled over the length of the argyle couch like a stained cloth left out to dry. The straps of his bib overalls hung loosely at his side, the flap covering his trunk pulled low on his hairy stomach. His strangely waxen skin shone with a damp sheen of sweat reflecting the yellow light of the kitchen. The man's face was completely slack. The pockmarks marring the skin looked craggy and deep in the dimness of the room. Jacob stared at the closed lids of the man's eyes for a long time, waiting for signs of a pretense.

Jacob looked to the front door on the other side of his mother's sleeping boyfriend. He steadied his breathing and resolved that each of his steps would be silent and swift.

The bald man's mouth hung open, the peering, blackened spots in his sparse collection of teeth seemed to follow his movements like eyes. Jacob choose the path on the backside of the couch for the protection it afforded, squatting below the bald man's sightline on very sore legs. He half-expected a charley horse. Jacob turned on his heels and, holding his breath to keep from moaning, rose to his feet. He studied the bald man, one hand ready to rip open the front door with the first hint of suspicion, but saw no sign of wakefulness.

With one last look over his shoulder, Jacob turned to the water-logged front door but hesitated with his sweating palm on the plastic knob. He closed his eyes, slowing his breathing as best he could, and turned his head slightly toward the darkened hall ending at his mother's closed bedroom door. Jacob heard nothing. He opened his eyes and saw only more darkness in the uneven space between the thin carpet and the bottom of the particleboard door.

He opened the door just wide enough to slip through.

The woods were always a comfort. The hills rolled on for miles, sometimes obstructed by home or farm or business, but mostly it was wood and rock. Jacob walked for hours, miles and miles of not seeing a solitary person. It was easy to avoid people in the wilderness. Most folks he encountered in the woods, even those wearing expensive hiking gear, were obviously unaccustomed to relying on quiet for survival. They stomped and thrashed, snapping branches and kicking stones. They belched and farted, echoing things that often preceded laughter, and breathed like they'd just run a marathon or were more hog than human.

*Least hogs don't have no fists*, he thought.

The only fists he saw were his own or the tiny ones holding acorns or thimbleberries and attached to creatures as wary of Jacob as Jacob was of others. Though his mother's child-sized knuckles often struck the top of his head, as well as his chest and upper back, it felt better to be hit by her than by some man who wasn't even kin. The bald man slapped Jacob across the back of his head on the first night they'd met. Randall Adkins hit Jacob so hard little white pinpricks had blossomed in his eyes like the visual mix of a kaleidoscope and a snow globe. His aunt owned dozens of gaudy snow globes, wishing anyone who'd care to look a "Merry Christmas" as well as listing the year of celebration. She used to whip Jacob with a candy-striped extension cord (that she'd fold lengthwise exactly twice. Every, single time.) back when the old social worker made him live all the way out there in Wheelwright when Momma was at Step-works Recovery Center, the first time. There were vines in the woods he frequented three times as thick as that.

Jacob saw next to nothing that wished him harm in the hills. The sounds he heard felt unrelated to him, allowing him a nameless an-onymity. No guilt by association. No *Refuse to Serve* Notices at the corner store. No pink notices of eviction. No *Lacks Improvement* teacher comments on any of the trees like there were on his last two report cards. No epithets or insults or undisguised pity existed out there. The only screams Jacob heard were of the Great Game, as he'd come to call it. The call of the hawk and the wails of the cottontail. The coyotes' howl and the panicked gobble of wild turkey. Jacob watched the happenings of the woods with a splendidly detached fascination, getting as close as he could without spooking hunter or prey.

"Your middle name is Hunter and you ain't never even shot a squirrel?" Rodney Tackett's laugh was an abomination that often found its way to Jacob's thoughts. "Why, I think Mrs. Horace's Word of the Day fits you like a glove, Jacob Hunter Goodman: *Misnomer*. You know what that means *Hun*-ter?"

In the woods, Jacob's feet were sure, even when clouded in suffocating memory; he stepped over a small buttonbush nearly covered in butterflies.

He'd tried to close his locker and walk away but Rodney Tackett had caught it before it latched.

"Maybe we can edify ye a bit, huh?" he sneered, digging his hand into his pocket and retrieving a Sharpie. "We all know how much ye need the help."

All six of the boys, as well as some of the growing crowd in the hallway, erupted in squealing laughter.

Jacob felt hot blood rush up his neck.

"Here now," Rodney Tackett said, uncapping the permanent marker. "M-I-S-N-O-M-E-R."

Jacob's insides seemed to sag lower in his gut as he watched the much larger boy carefully spell out the word which Jacob, indeed, remembered seeing on Mrs. Horace's small decorative chalkboard she kept just outside her classroom door.

Rodney Tackett said each word in the monotone of concentration, after writing it on the metal door of Jacob's open locker.

"A ... wrong ... name ... or ... inappropriate ... desicknation," he said, turning his smiling face back toward Jacob.

*Des-ick-nation*, Jacob saw. *Designation, you idiot.*

Jacob could see that some of the other boys had noticed the error as well.

"I think calling you a *boy* is a misnomification too," Rodney Tackett said, using the hand not holding the Sharpie to grab and squeeze his crotch.

"Misnomer," somebody corrected him.

"Whatever!" Rodney Tackett shot back, grabbing Jacob by the already stretched-out collar of his t-shirt. "I think calling Jacob Hunter Goodman a *boy* is a *mis-gnome-er*. Don't you all?"

Jacob wanted to disappear. He'd been goaded into a tussle with Rodney Tackett before, an embarrassment nobody seemed able to stop reminding Jacob about. Rodney had nearly ripped Jacob's underwear out of his jeans when he'd lifted Jacob helplessly into the air by them. Jacob remembered looking down at his childish, kicking legs and hating himself for being so small and redheaded and unwanted. Jacob held his arms as limply at his sides as he could, his dirty nails etching little half-moons into his sweating palms.

"Maybe we should help him out, huh?" Rodney Tackett half-turned to ask the crowd.

He didn't see Jacob anymore; Jacob could see that clearly. He read it in the steady growing of the buck-toothed smile, which Jacob noticed was haloed by a thin and uneven but quite visible mustache. Rodney Tackett was playing for the crowd like he did on the basketball court at all those idiotic pep rallies.

Time stretched out an unwelcomed, halting hand. It was hard to catch his breath. The sound of his labored heaving was deafening in his ears. Jacob's vision dimmed in rhythm with the pounding of his pulse, constant earthquakes with twin epicenters at his temples. He saw the marker coming but knew he would do nothing to stop it. He saw all possibilities as useless. If he struggled, he'd be beaten. If he tried to flee, he'd be even further humiliated. He'd be beaten when he got home regardless.

Then, Rodney Tackett seemed to see Jacob as if for the first time. Rodney Tackett's green eyes were wide and excited. Jacob could see little flakes of a yellowish crust sprinkled about his dark eyelashes as well as at the corners of each eye. The larger boy hesitated, but only for a moment.

"Let's give him what all those silly bitches on teevee call a make-over," Rodney Tackett said, lifting the marker to Jacob's quivering face.

The ink was cold and pungent, just under Jacob's dripping nose. He squeezed his eyes and mouth closed but kept his arms at his sides. The sound of the slanted tip of the permanent marker roughly running the length of his upper lip was grating. It was louder than

Jacob's whimpering. It was louder than Rodney Tackett's open-mouthed huffing.

Jacob opened his eyes.

"Comin' in thick now, boys," Rodney Tackett announced.

The boy's face was contorted in concentration: his lips were bunched together at the left side of his mouth, the pink tip of his tongue poking out like a spit-up winter strawberry, his eyes narrowed slits directed downward with a shining glint. There was one small dimple marring the suntanned smoothness of Rodney Tackett's chin. Jacob stared at it.

He wondered if people could disappear.

*I bet it feels just like falling forever.*

The marker outlined a triangle under Jacob's bottom lip, then colored it in with much more ink than was necessary.

"Well, that's about all I can do for ye," Rodney Tackett said, taking a half-step away from Jacob, his fist still loosely holding the t-shirt's collar.

Jacob watched the boy's green eyes sweep the bottom half of his face. Rodney Tackett smiled toothily at his work then crashed backwards into the adjoining lockers, doubled over with high-pitched cackles. His back was slapped, his hair tousled, his name cheered.

Jacob suddenly knew people could disappear. The surety was followed by a wave of nausea and understanding.

The doe's eye. The crushed pawpaw. The desert. The seabed.

His middle name was Hunter.

The overbearing sun and the unblinking eye of the bottomless mineshaft were the same thing.

In the woods, Jacob could remember and see.

-

Jacob leaned against the dying sycamore, shielding himself from view behind the patchy, hollowed-out trunk, and watched an ancient, mismatched pickup putter by. He heard the far-off wail of a train whistle and the lessening grumble of the truck heading westward but the faint rustling of the leaves above and behind him were loudest.

The little stream he'd been following dropped down a man-made face of crushed rock, cinderblocks, and wire mesh into a drainage tunnel that ran under U.S. Route 23. Jacob could see a similar embankment across the four lanes, where a near-mirrored image of the stream he stood beside rose up into the blanketing forest of the mountain beyond.

Jacob looked both ways then half-slid, half-fell down the steep hill. He hit the road running, his head swiveling from left to right for oncoming cars, and crossed to the other side. He chose his foot and handholds with care as he climbed up the wire mesh-covered debris. The shade of the forest was welcoming and hushed. Jacob followed the trickling water and spongy moss along a worn animal's path and hummed softly to himself.

*He's got the whole world in His hands.*

Jacob wasn't sure how long he'd been walking. Several hours, probably. He knew his mother wouldn't have his whereabouts at the forefront of her concerns. The bald man probably hoped Jacob would run away. He had no friends to visit or invite over. And it was Sunday, so he didn't have anywhere to be.

A car horn honked nearby. Jacob stopped to wipe the sweat from the corners of his eyes with his shirt and heard a child's plaintive wail from somewhere below.

The path climbed until the increasing spaces between branches revealed the tops of several houses and buildings clustered together, then it ended abruptly in a small clearing cloistered by white pine trees. There were several empty beer cans and bottles, as well as cigarette butts and wrappers in the small space.

"You're late," a man said.

Jacob spun around but found the small space empty. He carefully moved one of the white pine's branches and looked for the sound of the speaker.

"I know, I know," the man said, "but I got us two hours, alone. I bet Sither tries to push himself in, but I've kept the door locked."

A man leaned against the brick building, the sole of one tennis shoe parked on the red brick, the other supporting his weight. He held a cellphone cradled in the crook of his left shoulder and a cigarette pressed to his lips, one hand shielding the raised lighter, the other flicking the spark wheel. It took four flicks for the flame to catch and light the cigarette.

"I know you don't mind him," the man said, dropping the lighter into his scrub pocket, "but I think he's an absolute twat."

Jacob was close enough to see the tension lines along the man's forehead ease as he inhaled the smoke.

The man stood just outside a slate gray door marked "No Entry." The door did not have a handle or knob but was propped open with a rusted coffee can.

The man sighed and rolled his eyes.

"Listen, you said you'd help me out with the uterine tubes and the infundibulum of the uterine tube, the cervix, and all that," the man said. "I've got the key. The cadaver lab is mine for the next . . ."

He took the phone in his left hand and held it out to read the screen.

"Hour and a half," the man said. "I'm going back in there now. Block is coming up and I can't bomb Reproductive Systems. You can come help me or I can call Stovak. Either way, I'm getting back to it."

The man ended the call, sliding the phone into his stained scrubs.

"Asshole," he said under his breath.

Jacob watched the man finish the cigarette and snub it out against the brick wall. The man leaned forward and pushed the butt into a small slit on top of the coffee can. He then leaned backwards, stretched his back, and farted. The man slid the coffee can away with his foot then stepped into the darkness inside. The door clicked shut.

Jacob pushed through the pine needles and stepped out into the empty parking lot. He could hear the traffic on the other side of the building droning below. He looked around and saw that he was alone. There was a dumpster on the far side of the parking lot encased by a recently painted wooden fence. The buildings higher up on the mountain were dark and quiet but Jacob never felt truly alone around things man had made.

*That man said he had a key,* Jacob thought, *to the . . . what did he say? Body room? No.* Cadaver *lab. That's it. The cadaver lab.*

He put one foot in front of the other until he was pushing the unlocked door of a fence open. There was no overbearing stink inside the close, fenced-in area, but a dumpster sat still and shiny, the letters of the company name crisp and legible. It was unlike any dumpster Jacob could recall.

*What in the blue hell is a cadaver lab?*

Jacob walked the tight perimeter of the dumpster and found a stack of three cardboard boxes. They weren't sealed, just folded closed, so Jacob leaned forward and opened the box on top. Pale and butterfly-shaped, the upturned smile that greeted his eyes was coolly comforting. The box was filled with textbooks. Jacob saw what he'd at first mistaken for a smile was actually a detailed ink drawing of a human pelvis. For an instant, he saw both the ghostly smiling visage and the bleached, sterile bones, then he could only see it as a man's drawing.

He kicked the top box off the stack, then opened the box below.

More books. He picked up the one on top, needing both hands due to the book's heft, and flipped it open. The outline of an angel raising robed hands upward sent invisible spiders racing across the back of his neck and arms. A fleshy halo outlined her featureless head while a curtain of flesh encased her floating, supple body.

Jacob felt the air catch in his throat. Sweat trickled down the curve of his spine and began to collect in the waistband of his underwear.

He felt confused, like the pictures and text on the glossy pages were being transmuted on a schizophrenic television: it was the Virgin Mary; it was human flesh; an angel; meat.

Jacob closed his eyes and shook his head. He blinked his eyes several times then tried again.

"External genital organs in the female," he read aloud. "Anterior aspect. Labia reflected."

*Desert. Seabed.*

Jacob closed the book in his hands and read the title: *Color Atlas of Anatomy*.

The next book in the box was upside down, so Jacob knelt, set *Color Atlas of Anatomy* down at his feet, and turned it over.

*Essentials of General Surgery.*

The book underneath that was Beckmann and Ling's *Obstetrics and Gynecology*.

Jacob realized he'd walked all the way to Pikeville, the county seat of Pike County, the next county over, and was now standing beside its medical school's dumpster.

*Cadaver lab. That guy smoking the cigarette was studying to become a doctor.*

Jacob had been to see a doctor exactly three times he could remember. The first had been when his tonsils got infected and had to be removed. The second was when both Jacob and his mother had nearly puked and shat themselves to death with the stomach flu. The third was hazy but still sucked the spit from Jacob's mouth when he thought about it.

He was five years old. His mother had sat him at the little plastic table, handed him Blake Turner's keys, and told him to "be good for a minute," before disappearing into the back bedroom area of the little RV with Blake Turner, who had a thin mustache, patchy sideburns, and a funny way of smiling at Jacob. Jacob played with the keys and the Velcro of the wallet while his mother and Blake Turner made an awful racket behind the closed door, cussing and crying and hollering "Oh God" and "Sweet Jesus." After a while, Jacob was bored with the wallet and keys and small cramped table, so he climbed down and started exploring the RV's cabinets. He found matches and bottle caps and forks and sugar. In the last drawer he opened, Jacob found a bundle of photographs rubber banded together. He pulled a photo free from the stack and wondered why Blake Turner had a photo of a naked little boy crying. Jacob let it fall back into the drawer and pulled another from the stack. It was another child but this one had on a wig, a sequined bikini, and a clown's makeup on its face. The next photo confused Jacob. Blake Turner was wearing a baby's diaper and was hanging from a rope in a small closet. A dainty silver chain stretched from metallic clothespins attached to each of his nipples. Blake Turner's eyes were closed and his mouth was making a nearly perfect "O" shape.

Jacob didn't like the photos, so he put them back in the drawer and closed it.

"Momma," he called. "I want to go home, Momma."

Blake Turner called from the back of the RV but Jacob couldn't understand what he said.

"What?"

His mother cried out like she did when she bumped her shin into the coffee table at home.

Jacob stood outside the bedroom, his little ear and palms on the cool, wooden door. On the other side, he heard lots of loud breathing. It sounded like somebody was jumping on the bed. When he closed his eyes, Jacob could feel the slight shaking of the RV.

"Momma?" he called.

He put his hand on the knob but didn't open it. She'd told him Blake Turner had some work for her to do. Jacob knew his momma didn't like him bugging her when she was doing a job for a man.

"Oh fuck yeah," Blake Turner cried.

It sounded like his momma was doing a good job, so Jacob didn't open the door. Instead, he decided he'd see what was outside the RV. He pushed the door, but it didn't open. He tried again, this time twisting the handle and putting all his weight behind his shoulder and pushing. The door flew open, sending Jacob crashing down into the sunlit gravel. He pushed himself up and felt hot tears well in his eyes. He looked back to the RV and remembered that Momma was working. He made sure his hands and knees weren't bleeding, wiped his nose, and stood.

The little RV was rocking. Jacob could see it now that he was outside.

*Must be working hard.*

Jacob saw a little bicycle lying on its side next to the Lincoln Momma borrowed from Uncle Phil, who wasn't really Jacob's uncle but somebody Momma wanted him to call "Uncle." Jacob picked it up and pushed it along for several steps. Everything seemed to work properly. Jacob looked around, then hopped on the bike. He started peddling as fast as he could. The little bike picked up speed readily. He felt the wind pull at his cheeks and hair. He closed his eyes and smiled. He felt the cut inside his mouth—Momma had slapped him harder than she meant to after he had cut his finger opening a can of beans—pull then rip, filling his mouth with the coppery taste of blood.

Then the truck hit him.

That's what they told Jacob when he woke up at the hospital in Prestonsburg. The nice doctor there told Jacob he was a lucky boy. The doctor said the little bike crumpled over him and shielded his body from most of the truck's weight when it dragged him across the county road into the steep gulley on the other side. The only lasting injury he'd have from the accident, the doctor told him, was a broken right thumb; the concussion and cuts would heal with time, but his right thumb would remain crooked and never regain full dexterity. Jacob thought the doctor's face lit up like a Lite-Brite when he told the doctor he was left-handed.

"Well, that's great, Jacob," the doctor said. "The Lord gives us no burdens we cannot carry."

Jacob didn't know what the doctor meant. He was just getting ready to ask the doctor where his mother was when the doctor told Jacob a police officer needed to talk to him. Jacob was taken to a little room and told his mother was in jail. The police officer said a nice lady called a social worker would be helping to find somebody to take care of Jacob while his mother was away. They didn't listen to him when he screamed, or when he cried. When Momma finally took him home, he'd had two birthdays, one with his cousins and aunt and uncle, the other with a foster family.

The next book in the box was the *Textbook of Family Medicine*.
*Trouble*, Jacob remembered, *in a family way*.

Jacob put all the books back inside the cardboard boxes, forcing his thoughts away from that statement.

*They can't throw these away*, he decided.

He bent down and picked up the box he'd kicked over. It was heavy but not impossibly so. He pushed open the fence, made sure the parking lot was still empty, then slipped back into the cover of the pines.

He decided the little clearing fenced by white pines wouldn't do as a safe place for the books. The litter on the patchy, matted grass made him uneasy. He carried the heavy cardboard box a few dozen yards farther down the path, where he found a buttonbush. He sat the box down and pushed it under the green, glossy leaves.

Back behind the dumpster, Jacob picked up the second box. It was heavier than the first. He had to set it down to readjust his grip. He straightened his back and relied on his thighs to hoist him back to standing, his arms shaking with the weight of the books. He hadn't taken two steps before the bottom of the box gave out. The books plummeted to the ground, spines and covers bending, pages fluttering and ripping onto his feet. His left foot took the worst of it; three books fell together, crashing down on the stained laces of the women's K-Swiss shoe and sending air hissing through his gritted teeth.

Jacob sank to the ground, clutching his throbbing toes through the thin, worn leather. When the pain ebbed, he looked around at the scattered books. Most of them weren't really of much interest to him; titles included the *Encyclopedia of Intensive Care*, *Biochemistry with Clinical Correlations*, *Pathophysiology of Disease*, and *Basic and Clinical Pharmacology*. A breeze ruffled the open pages of a book at his feet. He saw no exposed muscles or organs. No network of veins or arteries. Not the muted shine of a cleaned fingerbone.

He pulled back the flaps of the third box. An alien entity floated languidly in a warm red light, its head elongated and smooth. The strange, hairless creature was staring down with over-large, pupilless eyes at a fleshy tether protruding off the book's cover near the spine. He read the title out loud, "*Medical Embryology*."

*It's human*, he realized, picking up the book for a closer look. Sure enough, there was the miniscule slit of a mouth, the budding protrusion above that would form the nose, and the faintest hint of the unformed ears on the side of the head. The little arms led to little hands, the fingers barely differentiated from the hand.

*Everyone that's ever lived looked like this at one point,* he thought. He flipped open the book to the middle but nearly dropped it when the sound of a car door slamming shut startled him by its nearness.

Jacob crouched and snuck around the dumpster to peer through a crack in the fence. A man leaned against the hood of a Camry, his arms folded across his chest, a cigarette lit between his lips.

The door marked "No Entry" opened and the man Jacob had seen earlier stepped out, propped the door open with the rusted coffee can, and greeted the man smoking against the Camry. He lit up a cigarette of his own, taking his place leaning against the building as he had earlier. They spoke of tests and study aids and flash cards and after-boards-drinking.

Jacob thought doctors, even those studying to become them, should sound smarter. These two young guys seemed to only care about getting drunk after their test. Jacob eased the gate open as the first of the two men stepped into the building. He was running across the parking lot, holding back the slap of his feet as best he could, when the second guy disappeared into the darkness inside. Jacob flung the embryology book forward and caught the door just as it was sliding soundlessly shut. He reached in with the hand not holding the book and took hold of the door. Using the tips of his fingers, Jacob let the door ease closer to the frame until it was nearly closed. He stood along the crack, blocking as much of the space between the door and its frame as he could. He silently counted to ten, carefully enunciating each of the four syllables of "Mississippi" in his head, hoping the men wouldn't notice the door hadn't closed behind them and that he'd given them plenty of time to get farther away, then pulled the door open.

The hall was dark and quiet. After he ensured no one was around, Jacob stepped inside and pulled the door closed. He stood blinking for several moments as his eyes slowly adjusted to the dimness of the yellow lights overhead. The building looked old and outdated on the inside and smelled weird.

To his right, Jacob heard a toilet flush and the muted voice of the two men talking. He turned and strode down the hall in the opposite direction at a pace just under a run. The strange smell intensified with each step. He sniffed and sniffed but couldn't place the smell. It smelled vaguely chemical and moldy at the same time. He stopped in front of a closed door. The smell was even stronger here. There was a sign on the door, but he didn't have time to read it. He heard a door open down the hall and the sound of the men's voices was no longer muffled.

Jacob opened the door and slipped inside.

-

He pulled the door closed as quickly as he could without slamming it, then took two steps backwards, listening. The voices were getting louder as the men made their way down the hall. Jacob was in a storage room. There were bankers boxes stacked several feet into the air throughout the little space, as well as a series of shelves stacked with labeled boxes. The men passed by the door without stopping.

Jacob opened the door and peeked out into the hallway. The two men stood by a door near the end of the hall. One of them pushed some buttons on a keypad and the door opened.

"Shit," one of the men said. "I left my notes in the car. I'll be right back."

"The door'll lock behind you. I'll go with you."

Jacob ducked back inside, pulling the door closed and keeping his hand on the knob. When the two men passed the door again, he slipped out into the hallway and darted down the hall. The strange smell grew in intensity. He threw a quick look over his shoulder and saw the two men slowly walking down the hall, none the wiser to Jacob's presence.

The sign on the metal door read: "Cadaver Lab." It was cracked. Jacob put his sweaty left palm against the cold metal and pushed the door open.

One of the two men opened the door to the parking lot, sending a rush of fresh air whipping down the dim hallway. Jacob took one last look in their direction, then stepped inside the cadaver lab.

-

The smell was terrible inside. The room was rectangular and lined with tables, a walkway splitting the room down the middle. A black bag sat on top of each table.

*Body bags*, he knew. *There is a dead person in each one of those.*

Jacob felt goosebumps ripple across his arms and sunburnt neck.

*Holy shit*, he thought, his eyes bouncing from bag to bag. *There must be fifteen dead bodies in here.*

# BIRTH OF A MONSTER

Near the far side of the room, on the second to last table, one of the bags was unzipped. A bright fluorescent light hung above a pale, naked woman. Even from this distance, Jacob could tell she was elderly. He walked across the room, his eyes never leaving the waxen skin.

*Oh, Jesus, look at her titties.*

The woman's breasts were long and tubular, the nipples flattened, featureless saucers.

A long incision ran the length of the woman's trunk. The beginnings of the woman's interior glistened red and dark under the flap of flesh. He wanted to know what it felt like against the tips of his fingers. He wanted to know what it looked like under the flap of skin.

The woman's age disgusted Jacob the more he noticed it. He cringed at the folds of wrinkles lining the woman's neck. He hated the thin white hair lining her small head. Her hands were gnarled claw-like things that curled upward as if in agony. He could smell her. A stink you could almost miss if you focused on the chemical smell.

*Formaldehyde*, he recalled. *That's what it's called, the stuff they preserve bodies with. Formaldehyde.*

Though the smell was strong, the smell of the decrepit woman was stronger. Jacob wanted to open her stomach and see her rottenness. He pictured a shapeless mass of green and black, slippery with pus and mucus.

There were several instruments on a small tray beside the woman's body. One of them, a metallic blade, looked wet.

He wanted to know what it felt like to cut human skin. He imagined his fingers gliding along, the hiss of scissors slicing wrapping paper.

The black bag had been zippered to the woman's waist. Jacob tasted sour milk when he noticed the tangle of salt and pepper pubic hair well below the woman's bellybutton. It didn't look much thicker than the white hair on her head.

Jacob took hold of the metal zipper and slid it to the woman's knees. He couldn't make his eyes focus on one thing. They darted around frantically, trying to see everything in great detail at once: the purpled, curdled veins, the patches of thick leg and pubic hair, the off-red and black bumps, a painful looking rash of some sort littering both legs. The folds of wrinkled skin were the same as Uncle

34

Martin's upper lip: stretched out, thin, and the blue-black of a five o'clock shadow. It purpled like a cat's tongue near each awkward folding of the skin.

He felt light-headed. His stomach twisted painfully, and he felt a heat deep in his bowels and groin. He wanted to squeeze the tip of the waxy skin. He knew it'd feel like putty or taffy.

It felt harder to breathe; there was a tightness in Jacob's chest and throat. He lifted his hand and reached for the sagging skin of the woman's crotch. The tips of his ring and middle fingers brushed the skin but before he could grasp it between his thumb and fingers, he heard the men outside the door.

His stomach dropped.

*Oh God, where do I go?*

There were windows lining the wall. They looked too small and awkwardly placed to quickly climb through.

*Shit.*

He spun on his heels and scanned the room behind him. There was a closed door. Jacob bolted across the floor. Ten feet to go and he heard the metal door open, the two men laughing really hard at something, both gasping and snorting.

Jacob grabbed the handle.

*Please be unlocked.*

He yanked the handle, felt it give, then threw himself against the door. He fell into darkness, scrambling wildly on his sweat-slickened hands across the linoleum until he could reach the door, which he gently pushed until it was nearly closed. He collapsed forward on his knees, pressing his forehead between his thighs and sucking in long swallows of air.

One of the men regained control of himself long enough to whisper, "That's some nice pie."

Jacob looked out through the cracked door. One of the men waved his arms in front him, begging the other man to stop. Tears ran down his cheeks.

Sweat trickled down Jacob's brow, stinging his eyes. He moved a little farther back into the shadows, then used the inside of his shirt to wipe his face.

*What do I do?* he wondered. *What if they come in here?*

He tried to peer into the darkness around him. The slit of light coming from the cadaver lab, from which the snorting of both men reverberated, was as thin as sandwich meat and illuminated next to nothing.

Jacob rose slowly to his feet, using the inside of the doorjamb for balance. He positioned himself for a better view. The two men had finally made their giggling way over to the naked elderly woman's body. They both wore white jackets over their scrubs now. They each stretched latex gloves over their hands, both of them letting the elasticity slap the gloves against their wrists.

The Camry man picked up a metal blade.

"Well, let's get at 'er, huh?"

Jacob watched the gloved hands take hold of the flaps of skin. He wished it were his hands. The two men opened the old woman's trunk, the cut skin were the blossoming petals of a daylily forced into bloom. If he stood on his tippy toes, he could see a little bit of the old woman's insides. Glistening tubes of purple and blue, knots of a yellowish white, all highlighted by a general red.

The two men talked as they worked. Jacob heard the babble of their voices but couldn't make out a single word. Their gloved hands darkened and shone wet and slick under the bright lights.

He watched them work in quiet fascination. He studied the way they held their instruments, the way they moved around the opening for a better view, the way they ignored the woman as a person, focusing instead on what could be gained from her presence there in the black bag on the raised table.

*This is what happens when you donate your body to science.*

Jacob wondered what he looked like on the inside.

*Am I as rotten as her?* he wondered. *I bet I am. I bet everyone is.*

He thought of death as something everyone carried around with them, a silent, nearly invisible appendage waiting for the right opportunity to bring it all screeching to a sudden, irrevocable halt.

One of the men set down his instrument. He leaned over the opened woman, his white coat dipping into the cavity with his hands, and reached inside. Jacob's view was blocked as the other man shifted his stance for a better look into the woman.

Jacob fought the urge to throw open the door for an unobstructed view.

"Easy."

"I got it."

The man came out of the woman's lower stomach area holding a piece of her in his gloved hands.

"Name?" he asked.

The other man bent in for a closer look. He then turned back to the body, studying the area the reddish-brown mass came from.

"Sigmoid colon?"

The other man sighed.

"Other side, Trevor."

The man went back to the body, then the organ in the man's hands.

"Ileum?"

"It's the cecum, man." Disappointment in the voice. "See?"

Both men turned back to the body. The man holding the cecum sat it back inside the woman and then Jacob's view was obstructed again by the men's backs.

"Oh. I see now."

"Uh-huh."

"Listen, I know you're just trying to be helpful, but we really need to focus on this next block."

"Sure. Okay. Sorry."

*Can't see. Move!*

"I really appreciate your help, man. I can't bomb Female Urogenital."

"Gotcha. Let's go over to the sigmoid colon and work our way down then."

Frustrated, Jacob turned away from the crack in the door, determined to see if the little room had an exit. He stepped farther into the darkness, blinking his eyes rapidly, forcing them to adjust. Gradually, the room presented itself. There was a little table in the corner, papers and boxes littering the surface, several long shelves lining the walls, and a row of filing cabinets.

Jacob walked over to the desk, saw a lamp, and, after a moment of hesitation, switched it on. The light from the small bulb was weak. It barely reached the slit of light emanating from the crack in the door. It was bright enough for a look around the small room but not bright enough to tip off the medical students that an intruder was in their midst.

The papers on the desk did not interest Jacob. He moved over to the boxes on the shelves. There were several stacks of them, each small and labeled. He took one of the boxes down at random and opened it. It was filled with individually wrapped pencil-like shapes. He removed one, setting the box down on the desk, and slowly tore open the wrapper. There was a plastic handle Jacob used to slide the utensil out of the paper wrapper. The other end was capped with clear plastic. He removed the cap and held the shining blade underneath the glow of the little desk lamp where the tip of the blade looked thin enough to separate a single strand of hair.

Jacob stared dumbly at the blade. He picked the box back up and read the label: Disposable Stainless-Sterile Scalpels, Size 20, Box of 10. At least twenty of these little boxes lined the shelves. He reached down and angled the light of the lamp upwards at the shelves. There were boxes of latex gloves, boxes of trauma shears, clinical penlights, forceps, arrow needles, angular needles, mall and probe seekers, and more.

*I'm in the supplies closet.*

He slid a handful of the individually wrapped scalpels into his front left pocket. He opened another box of them, then filled his other front pocket. He opened the box labeled "trauma shears" and took out a pair of the funny looking scissors. They looked as if they'd been partially stubbed out like a cigarette.

*If they're good enough for doctors, I shouldn't pass up a pair*, he thought, stuffing the trauma shears into his back pocket.

Jacob stood still and held his breath. He hadn't heard the voices of the two men for some time. He couldn't hear them over the rush of blood in his ears. He inched toward the cracked door, straining to listen.

When he placed his burning cheeks to the cold frame of the door, he saw the two men huddled over a thick binder, their white-coated backs to him.

"Hmm. Meghan must've borrowed mine and not put it back."

"I've got my lecture notes in the car."

"Smoke break?"

"Sure. A short one though."

The two men degloved. Jacob watched them take off their white coats, which they laid on the zippered bag on the table beside the exposed elderly woman. They walked up the center aisle toward the metal door but stopped near the front of the room. The sun shone in through the windows like a spotlight.

"Did you see what Banks did?"

"No. What?"

The Camry man unzipped the bag on the table. It was a black man of about forty or fifty years old. Half the skin on his face was missing, the stringy lines of muscles dully red like boiled meat going bad.

"You know he's a big hunter, right?"

"Who doesn't? Aside from Alabama football, that's the only topic of conversation with that guy."

"Well," the man reached under the table and came back with two latex gloves, "check out this guy's right hand."

Jacob watched the man put the gloves on, letting the elastic pop back against his wrist. He then reached down, grasped the dead man's left forearm and raised it up for closer examination.

"Wha—"

The man gasped.

The other chuckled.

"No."

"Yep."

Jacob watched the man pick at the tips of the cadaver's fingers.

*What is he doing?*

The skin lifted from the hand.

*What?*

"Jesus."

The two men were shaking with silent laughter.

The man removed the dead man's skin. It twirled in the light of the sun, looking vaguely translucent and paper-like.

"Put it on," the Camry man said.

The other man shot him a shocked look.

"Seriously," he nodded. "That's what Banks did."

Jacob watched the man take the skin carefully between the gloved fingers of his right hand and separate the sticking skin then insert his gloved left hand into the skin. He worked it down over the blue latex carefully, the way Jacob had to put on his "nice clothes" from last year: in little tugs and caresses. The man held the hand up into the air, turning it slowly in the sunlight.

"Jesus Christ," the man whispered, his eyes wide and staring. His mouth hung gaping, a gold crown reflecting the dazzling sun across the cadaver lab into Jacob's eyes.

As he blinked away the sunspots, the negative image of the man with the raised hand that flashed with each of Jacob's blinks looked like it was falling. Forever.

## CHAPTER THREE
## SUCH A HAPPY BOY

**HE CROUCHED LOW, CAREFUL NOT** to brush up against the noisy petals of the magnolia he was hiding behind. Using the tips of his fingers, Jacob parted the leaves just far enough apart to see between. The fawn was nearly within arm's length of Jacob, nibbling at the ground, its mother about ten feet farther along the ridge; neither had heard him approach.

*I'm getting better at this*, he thought.

He'd lost track of how many animals had eluded him already. Dozens. He'd catch glimpses of them from his place in the towering tulip poplar, follow their path as best he could, and as soon as he was in position to strike—he'd stolen a very nice hunting knife from the Walmart in Prestonsburg—some little thing would give him away: the snapping of a twig, the wind's sudden change of direction, an unstoppable sneeze, a bird's alarm bell chirps.

He adjusted his grip on the hunting knife's handle. It felt light but solid.

*Mine*, he thought, rocking back on his heels, readying himself to spring.

The fawn flinched, jerked its head toward its mother, then bolted down the hill where it fell in step with its mother and fled off into the forest below.

Jacob screamed in fury until a muscle twinged painfully in his neck. He dropped to his knees and the knife went skittering off the sandstone and into a briar patch.

-

Jacob found the little hunter's cabin following a possum in the deepening purple of dusk. He thought he'd seen a little head or two peeking out from underneath her ghostly fur. He could do so much with their little bodies.

*Plus, a mother might be a bit easier to pick off if she's trying to defend her babies.*

The last he saw of the possum was the thick hairless tip of her tail slipping under the ancient wooden cabin. He stopped dead in his tracks, scanning the area around him. Thankfully, it was abandoned. He'd chased the possum for so long he wasn't really sure where he was.

Jacob pushed in the crooked door, which screamed on rusty hinges until he stopped it.

The cabin was a one-room-one-window affair. It had a little cot in the far corner, an ancient wood-burning stove, and a farmer's table under the cracked glass of the little window. There was animal shit all over the place.

Jacob took the five steps to the window slowly, breathing through his open mouth. Though the view wasn't spectacular, the window looked out onto a small copse of white pine partially destroyed by some disease or infestation. He found his face twisted upward into a smile at the image of a place all to himself. He saw himself alone and at ease on his own, high up here in the hills. He leaned forward, studied the latch, then opened the window, which screeched nearly as loudly as the door had.

The cool night breeze smelled of honeysuckle and clover. Jacob closed his eyes and breathed it in.

When the chipmunk reached forward, sitting back on its hind legs, for the hunk of peanut butter in his left palm, Jacob grabbed it. It fought and squeaked, trying to bite his fingers and flailing about wildly. He adjusted his grip until his hand covered the soft, warm throat.

The chipmunk's eyes were frantic, bulging drops in the brown and red stripes on its head. Jacob felt it's little throat work to swallow. He squeezed his hand tighter, trying to capture the air pocket or spit under his thumb. He felt something shift under the soft fur. The animal shook and redoubled its fight to escape.

"We both know it's pointless, little guy," Jacob said. "Yer mine now."

He upped the pressure of his grip slowly until he was sure the little thing couldn't breathe, then he squeezed just a little bit tighter. He felt the little bones and tendons of the chipmunk begin to jostle against the softer tissue and flesh. He watched it open its little whiskered mouth to scream a soundless scream.

There was something so funny about it. Jacob relaxed his hand enough for the chipmunk to breathe again. He watched it suck in air, squirming and pissing under his grip.

*Mine*, he thought. *Mine.*

With a sudden jerk, Jacob squeezed his hand together as hard as he could, seeing a desert pool reflecting the midnight sky in each of the furry creature's little glassy eyes.

-

He grabbed the possum by the tail before it even knew Jacob was there. It felt rubbery and wrong, but he did not slacken his grip. He lifted the animal off its feet and sent it hissing against a sandstone boulder. The first dull thud silenced the panicked screaming. The second knocked the thing into unconsciousness.

Jacob stood still, his arm outstretched, dangling the inert possum away from his body, just in case. It did not move. The quiet of the night returned after a few minutes.

The possum was heavier than it looked. Jacob held the limp white creature higher and stepped out of the tree line into the crystalline moonlight for a closer look. It was still breathing. He could hear the suck and push of air steadily moving in and out of its lolling mouth; the pale pink tip of its tongue hung outside its exposed white teeth. He'd counted 48 teeth in the last one he took. A thin network of blood slowly worked its way out of the creature's ears and mouth.

*Mine*, he thought.

Jacob slung the possum over his shoulder and started back toward the hunter's cabin, which he now thought of simply as "the hideout."

-

He set the possum on the table next to his collection of paws and claws. He hovered over it for a moment, watching the steady rise and fall of its trunk, making sure it wasn't playing dead, then he turned around, shut the rickety door, and stripped off his clothes.

Jacob, though the teachers had said he was a slow learner and held him back twice in elementary school, didn't make the mistake of wearing his clothes when he was conducting his experiments. His mother had backhanded him when she saw the stains that first time.

"Ye think money grows on trees?" she asked him. "Ye think you can go and just splash whatever on your clothes and I'll jus', what, swoop down and buy ye more?"

Jacob knew better than to offer up anything other than "no, ma'am" and "yes, ma'am" when his mother took up that tone, which was the only way her voice sounded when she wasn't crying. The bald man had been staying elsewhere with an increasing frequency. First, he was gone two nights in a row, then four. Now when he was around, he was drunker than a skunk and full of barbs pricklier than a honey locust.

"Ye get yer little problem taken care of yet?"

"Ye know I'm waiting to hear back from Courtney, Randall." Jacob hated the pleading in his mother's voice.

"Wait any longer and ye'll be rounder 'an a watermelon," the bald man said. "It's already hard enough to look at ye with them puffy cheeks. Why do ye think I've been gone so much, you cow? How ye gonna sell it with an extra twenty pounds, huh?"

*Trouble*, Jacob thought, *in a family way*.

His mother didn't reply. She lifted the nearly empty bottle to her lips, twin tears racing each other down the powder on her cheeks. She was really caking it on these days. She tilted her head impossibly far back on her neck, opening her throat and taking huge swallows of the cheap bourbon. Jacob could see she'd been at the pills again; little clumps of blue were smearing her nostrils.

The little crow on the label seemed to be smirking at what it saw.

"Jesus H," Randall Adkins spat, his words on the cusp of slur. "Ye fucking drunk."

His mother's eyes were closed, her head still sitting far back on her neck, her mouth hanging partially open. Jacob watched the bottle drop from her hand and hit the stained carpet with a hollow thunk, the last bit of amber liquid sloshing around but not spilling out of the bottle.

Jacob tensed, seeing the cords standing in the bald man's neck, knowing the hitting was about to start. He crouched lower on his little corner of the couch, squeezing the handle of his hunting knife in the pouch pocket of the Kentucky Wildcats hoodie he'd stolen from the Lost & Found at school, wishing he'd stayed out in the woods or in the hideout. He hated his mother but didn't think he could sit through another beating.

The bald man lifted his hand to slap her but seemed to think of something at the last moment. A crooked smile spread across his pock-marked face. He leaned forward, picked up the nearly empty bottle of bourbon, and held it out to her.

"Ye know what?" he asked. "Go on, girl. Ye might not need Courtney to steal you those abortion pills after all."

Jacob's mother opened her eyes for the first time in a long, long time. They fluttered, blinking through clumping mascara, then found the bald man's hoovering over her. Jacob watched his mother slowly process the scene: the smiling man who'd just been screaming, the extended bottle of bourbon, the abrupt change in tone and tension in the singlewide's close living room.

"Wha?" her voice sounded fuzzy, far away.

"Go on, Christy," Randall Adkins cooed. "Have a whittle drinky-drink. Wet that puffy whistle of yer'n."

Jacob watched the slipping gears in his mother's head click into place. Her eyes flicked between the bottle and the grinning bald man, at first weighing the threat, then the reward. Jacob watched her accept the situation, embrace it, a sweeping, lopsided smile blossoming on her face. She took the bottle with clumsy hands and drank, little rivulets of bourbon spilling around her cracked lips.

"There ye go, ye dumb cunt," the bald man's voice was soft, purring. "Drink and be merry."

Jacob watched his mother finish the bottle, which she'd opened as soon as she woke that afternoon, in three, languid swallows.

"Ah," she sighed, reaching out to set the empty bottle onto the crowded coffee table. Her aim was off, and the bottle clanked against the edge of the table before rolling under the couch.

The bald man was smiling at his mother. Jacob didn't understand what was happening. The beating would've at least been predictable.

"I think ye'd better find a friend to stay with tonight, shit ass," Randall Adkins said, his eyes never leaving Christy Goodman's. Jacob watched the man undo the Confederate flag buckle at his hip. "Yer momma and me have a little *bidness* to attend to."

Jacob didn't know what to do. All the muscles in his body felt like live wires, shooting buzzing jerks down his legs and arms. His left hand clenched the hunting knife, his right pumped into an unsteady fist.

"Go on," the bald man whispered.

Jacob leapt from the couch, throwing open the front door and slipping into the warm night without a single look back.

-

The penlights he'd stolen from the medical school in Pikeville came in handy on his near nightly prowls. They were small enough to slip in and out of his left front pocket quickly and easily. The bulbs were bright enough to illuminate the immediate path in front of him but not large or powerful enough to alert his presence beyond a few yards. Plus, their nearly inaudible click on and off barely registered in Jacob's forest-sharpened ears. On nights with the moon shining down like an ancient nightlight, he hardly even used them, as accustomed to the rolling hills as he'd become.

Something rustled in the underbrush ahead. Jacob quietly moved into the shadows of a sugarplum tree, the smell of the ripening berries strong and pleasant.

*They'll be ripe within a week*, he guessed.

Jacob rested back on his haunches, watching the white flowered heads of the hydrangea bush bounce and sway as the small animal moved about within it. He thought he could make out some dark fur between the leaves, but he wasn't sure.

*Rabbit? Possum? Raccoon?*

He hoped it was a raccoon. They had the most interesting hands; tiny, softly padded things that could almost pass for those of an old black woman. Jacob had started his collection not two months ago and already had three complete sets and one partial; he'd nearly taken the thing's left forepaw off at the wrist when it swiped at him. Not to mention the squirrel skulls and tails, the possum teeth and tails, and other assorted bones.

Jacob was good with the scalpel now. He could cleave off the smallest tip of a baby raccoon's pinky finger, if he felt like it. He'd shaved the bridge of a pregnant possum's nose down to the bones in minute layers with it. He'd even gotten a bit of the bone to come off before dulling too many of the disposable blades to warrant anything but smashing them with the clawhammer he'd stolen from Ace Hardware. Inside the bones he cracked or hacksawed—a very useful instrument Jacob had stolen from the Glenn's camper two Sundays back—Jacob was astonished to find a whiteish semi-solid tissue, which a library internet search revealed to be *bone marrow*, inside the long shin bone of a squirrel's left leg. Jacob put a bit of it on his tongue and moved it around in his mouth. It hadn't tasted bad at all.

The animal moved out of the hydrangea into the shadows farther down the mountain. Jacob crept over to the bush at a crouch. He tapped on the penlight and examined a surprisingly large pile of shit at his feet. It was still warm; flecks of partially digested serviceberries dotted the curled logs.

*Definitely a raccoon*, he decided. *Mine.*

Jacob flicked off the penlight, returned it to his pocket, then wiped his hands on the soft blue petals of the hydrangea bush. He listened to the raccoon chitter, snuffle, and forage until he was sure it hadn't detected him, then he followed it.

Hunting, what Jacob was doing, stalking and tracking prey, not setting up a saltlick and shooting the licking creatures as they came, was all about timing, something Jacob was steadily improving on. His misses were few now. He waited, followed, waited, followed, and waited and followed some more until his undetected proximity nearly ensured the prey's kill or, more recently, its capture.

Jacob saw this raccoon already bound in the stolen chicken wire and hung from the planter hook he'd screwed into the wood next to the windowsill, which he'd also taken from Ace Hardware. He saw another set of beady eyes wishing him harm. He saw another puddle dried on the floor. He planned on stealing kitty litter to help soak it all up by wearing his camo cargo pants to the grocery store and filling all six pockets with handfuls of the expensive brand.

*Mine.*

Jacob stepped onto the pavement of the medical school parking lot looking all around for people. There were three empty cars there; none of them ticking from recent use. The door marked "No Entry" was partially cracked, the rusted coffee can propping it open.

He saw his dwindling supply of stolen disposable scalpels sitting on the blood-stained farmer's table in his head as he walked across the parking lot. He pulled the door open, stepped over the coffee can, nearly three-quarters full of stained cigarette butts, then eased the door back against the can.

There was no one in the hall. Jacob turned left and made his way to the closed door of the cadaver lab. He pressed his left ear to the cold metal but heard nothing. He tried the knob and wasn't surprised to find it locked.

*How do I get in?*

He heard a voice from the other side of the door. It quickly grew louder. Jacob sprang away from the door, his heart fluttering in his chest. He sprinted the short distance to the end of the hall, sliding to his stomach on the waxy linoleum until he was completely under a wooden bench.

"Hang on, hang on," a woman said, emerging from the cadaver lab, a cellphone held to her blonde head by her hunched left shoulder. "I'm leaving the lab now. I'll be there in fifteen minutes. Stop crying. I can't understand you, honey. Where's your brother, Rebecca?"

Jacob scrambled out from under the bench as the woman strode down the hall in the opposite direction, her white coat fluttering like a flag of surrender. He raced down the hall and managed to catch the heavy metal door of the cadaver lab before it closed by jamming in his left foot. He pushed the door open and stepped inside.

He ducked low and scanned the room. After he was sure he was alone, Jacob saw one black bag unzipped, the pale, milky skin of a redheaded man shone bright under the lowered lamp over the table. He went straight to the supplies closet. He flipped the switch on the wall and set about reading every labeled box.

He filled his bag with scalpels, opening each box and dumping the individually wrapped containers inside, then closed the boxes and set them back on the shelf. He opened the box labeled "Single-Use Curved Mayo Scissors" and studied the stainless-steel instrument. They were, indeed, curved but seemed to be of very sturdy construction. The blade felt sharp. Jacob put all ten pairs in his bag with the scalpels.

He needed sutures. All the pictures in the medical books showed wounds and bodies closed up with sutures. A suture looked like glossy, hooked thread in the color photos and just thinner twine in the drawings. Jacob found the boxes in an unlocked storage cabinet and stuffed the sutures into the remaining space of the bag. He returned the boxes empty.

He flipped the light switch as he stepped back into the cadaver lab but nearly screamed when he saw the blonde woman hunched over the red-headed corpse. He stood, rigid and still, afraid his panicked breathing was going to alert the student-doctor to his trespass. Jacob slowly lowered himself behind the zippered body bag nearest to him. He pressed himself against the cold floor, bleach and formaldehyde filling his nostrils, until he could see the blonde's feet under the metal legs of the tables.

He quietly tightened his bag's straps, then began crawling along the wall toward the metal door, keeping his eyes on the woman's Nike tennis shoes. She rocked on the balls of her feet as she worked, leaning in for a closer examination.

When he'd made it to the metal door leading out to the hallway, Jacob rose to a crouch just high enough to reach the doorknob. He turned it slowly, his eyes on the blonde bun shining under the hanging lamp. He got the door open without a sound and slipped noiselessly into the hall. He turned the knob completely, then inched it closed. He slowly allowed the knob to return to its normal position. He stood completely still and listened.

Nothing.

In one fluid motion, Jacob spun on his miss K-Swisses and bolted down the hallway.

-

Farmers left stuff lying around. All the time. Jacob found the barbed wire, auburn with a thick layer of rust, already rolled up and ready for the taking. He'd carried it on his shoulder, setting his jaw as the barbs bit.

*Shit*, he remembered thinking. *They'll never miss it.*

He paused, reached his left hand over his right shoulder and scratched at the drying blood clots dotting his back. He'd already had the chicken pox, but this was worse. He thought he could feel his blood turning the same color as the rust on the wire. He opened and closed his jaw repeatedly, knowing each time that it wouldn't open, or it'd stutter on its hinges, the lockjaw, bloodrustin', or tetanus beginning to kick in.

With the needle nose pliers, Ace Hardware, Jacob bound the unconscious cat with twisted barbed wire to the wall of his hideout with three bent but sturdy nails. Little droplets of blood bloomed like dehydrated tulips where the brittle metal tips of the wire slipped between the white and black fur of Cleo, according to the tag on its collar.

As he worked, he turned over image after image of the experiments: the hissing possum he'd skinned alive; the amputated turkey's caruncles jiggling wetly in his shining, red hands; the young squirrel that lived for almost three hours after he'd clipped off its arms and legs with the trauma shears; the eyeless rabbit, metallic camping spork from Walmart, he threw outside the hideout being lifted back into the air then into the tree shadows by a huge, graceful owl, almost immediately; and, now, with the most delicious relish, the desperate raccoon he'd trapped.

Jacob guessed it'd been there half a day or more. The plated-steel jaws of the trap, also Walmart, had snapped its left arm just below the elbow. The thing was steadily working at the place where the trap met the broken arm, gnashing and gnashing. Jacob watched it for ten minutes before the thing noticed him, and then it was only because he farted. On purpose.

It spun around, the trap refusing to move with it, then the raccoon bounced around in this hilarious hissing-pain-dance that looked like the tapes Jacob liked to put in the VCR on Fast-Forward X2 Mode, those movies the bald man brought over. His mom didn't like them, Jacob could tell. She wouldn't say anything to him unless she got ahold of more blue bars. He'd heard her asking around in that sing-song tone she used, but she didn't like to watch what was happening on the screen when Randall Adkins got drunk, which was every night he stayed at the trailer, and put them on.

"Not in front of the kid," she'd whined that first time.

The bald man just looked at her. He hit the play button directly on the VCR—there wasn't a remote—then turned to Jacob.

"Pay attention, shit ass," the bald man said, his face the pock-marked surface of the moon; the desert, the seabed. "Ye might learn somethin'."

*More Whores Volume Ten.*

Jacob forgot to notice his mother's discomfort. He'd muted the television, long after Randall Adkins had slapped his mother and stormed out of the trailer, and watched all three tapes, twice, in the fluttering beauty of Fast-Forward X2 Mode.

His cum glinted in wet, ropey clumps on the filthy carpet in the golden light from the television. Jacob left it there but turned the television off.

The raccoon jumped up and down, hissing then screeching, hissing then screeching.

Huge, bulbous titties waved up and down, up and down, from the softly pixelated static of Fast-Forward X2 Mode.

Jacob stiffened, felt himself vibrating in every atom of his being.

In a sudden burst of fury, the raccoon started tearing into the red wreck of its broken, trapped arm. It screamed wetly while it worked. It wailed twice, tried to continue, then passed out.

Jacob laughed until he had tears in his eyes.

He tested the barbed wire attached to the wall. It held. He tested the twisted and pinched wire binding Cleo's front paws together. It, too, held. He smiled at the craftsmanship of his work. With more force than he intended, Jacob threw the unconscious cat against the wall. It thumped against the hardwood and hit the floor. It didn't wake up. Not right away.

Jacob was fascinated by their little hands; *raccoons and their little old lady hands*. He practically skipped back to the hideout. Caught himself about to whistle when it came into view. He had the sudden urge to use the hacksaw for an air-guitar solo but resisted.

It woke as soon as Jacob started, screeching and wiggling under his foot. It tried to curl its other hand and both of its back legs around Jacob's shoe to stay the saw steadily working in the space where the wrist of the broken arm joins the hand. Then the tendons, muscle, flesh and fur on the other side.

The raccoon passed out, whimpering lightly as it snored.

Jacob held the hand up in the white light of the moon. The deep blue horizon was littered with the twinkling eyes of stars. He twirled the hand, still warm but cooling, until it didn't seem out of place in the night sky.

-

The cat was awake when Jacob returned. It hissed and yowled at him before he'd even opened the door. He'd given it only three and a half feet of barbed wire leash-space, but he cracked the door open slowly, just in case.

Twin gleaming eyes and an angry mewl, surprisingly loud in volume for such a little housecat, greeted him.

"I see yer awake," Jacob said.

The cat hissed in response. Jacob listened to the tiny beast struggle against its rusty, barbed shackling, panting and moaning in quick bursts.

He clicked on the penlight as he pushed open the door.

He smelled it then, the cat shit and, worse, the cat piss. It hung like a sin aired in weakness.

"Ye pissed on my floor?"

The cat renewed its hissing, snarling, too, in fits, at Jacob's voice.

He felt he should've been angrier than he was. He felt less the man because of it, but he didn't much care for anger. The world was angry enough. He was, in fact, angry. And quite often too. Right then, though, he wasn't. He was intensely curious. He wondered just exactly how long the cat, Cleo, would live if he poured some of Patrick DeLaney's old diesel oil on it, then set it on fire.

Farmers were always leaving stuff lying around.

-

Jacob twisted the cut ends of the barbed wired together, four times, then tugged on the improvised collar. The squirrel's head lolled on its neck, its eyes open but unseeing. He then unspooled a bit of clear fishing line, Walmart, and knotted it around the collar. He tested the line by jerking the squirrel on the end of about six inches of it, lightly at first, then with more force when he was sure it'd hold. The Trilene was Professional Grade Line composed of 100% fluorocarbon with a breaking point of eight pounds. The squirrel couldn't be much less than five pounds.

The Trilene was nearly invisible in the dim lighting of the hideout. He tilted his head slightly backwards so the penlight he held between his teeth was fully on the knot in the fishing line he was working on. He pulled it as tight as he could manage with his fingers, then a few millimeters more with the needle-nose.

Jacob stepped back, removed the penlight from his mouth, and tossed the pliers onto the farmer's table.

*Perfect placement*, he concluded. *Just to the left inside the door. Won't hit it when the door is open. Won't run into it if I forget it's there. Not close enough to use the wall to pull itself up.*

He knew the squirrel was alive, despite hanging completely still from the Trilene knotted around the stainless-steel head of the 1 3/8-inch carpenter nail, Ace Hardware, he'd hammered to the ceiling. He bound the tiny gray hands—he already had two sets of squirrel hands in the collection—together with loop after loop of the fishing line and closed it off with a Palomar knot, which he'd learned how to tie on the internet in the library.

If he squinted, he could see the squirrel steadily breathing, but, when he turned around from the bright moon hanging like a drain in the star-speckled, cloudless sky, it looked like it was the released spirit of a squirrel that had just kicked the bucket. Jacob smiled.

He planned on seeing how many days it would take for the squirrel to starve to death.

The rabbit had lasted a measly two days. Two. That's it. And it had been on the stickiest part of the floor too, not even *in position* like the squirrel. It had gnawed at the dried and scorched blood and fur, then the floor itself, then at its own feet and legs. It would've kept trying to eat itself if it had had the energy. Instead, it turned on its side, shat and vomited for a time, then stopped moving. Its little chest rose and fell, and its eyelids opened and closed, but that was all. This lasted a long time.

Jacob encouraged it.

He cussed it.

He even spat on it.

Finally, it died. He knew it was coming; it'd been steadily approaching for the past thirty minutes, its breaths ragged, wet things torn with increasing effort. It couldn't even spare a moan.

Little wheezes now.

In.

Out.

Desert.

Seabed.

Jacob had to keep his hands on his knees to stay his greedy feet from stomping on it.

The squishing meat of the under-ripened pawpaw.

The rabbit sucked in air. That was it. Nothing ever came back out of its yawning mouth. Jacob had strained his ears, recognizing the moment immediately, but heard only the intake.

The last breath had gone inward. He felt that was an important thing to know. He'd stolen a few of those Cambridge quad-ruled notebooks and retractable ink pens from the bio lab supplies room to help him keep track.

*It's time I got serious about it,* he thought. *I'm just about lethal now. Steady enough for lab conditions, anyhow.*

Jacob thought his biology class was a joke. He'd heard other kids saying they got to dissect stuff—a cat, a rabbit, a frog, or an owl pellet, by the various accounts he'd overheard on the bus, in the lunch room, or in the hall—but since they started three days ago, the teacher just wheeled in a projector and screened films with impossible to hear narration from an old, spitty-mouthed man with an indecipherable English accent of tiny circles dividing into more tiny circles, and scientists, men with mostly masked faces and clipboards that studied boiling liquids or peered upwards into M. C. Escher-like structures of interrelated tubing culminating in a dripping beaker of neon fluid, the women usually white-toothed and smiling, more curved than you'd expect to notice in an educational film, always directed by the brusque men to correct their own or another woman's mistake, "get me that beaker, miss" and "quick, lower the Bunsen burner by a quarter turn now, miss" and "make yourself useful and fill the sink up while I go over The Lab Clean-Up Protocol on the board over here."

*Women are so stupid,* Jacob thought. *Nice to look at it, but that's about it.*

He decided they might even be too much trouble to warrant keeping around. He didn't want to be shackled to an imbecile, handicapped; life was already hard enough. It didn't need help being any harder was what he figured, and he swore he'd keep his path clear of them.

Jacob reached forward and poked the inert squirrel with the penlight. It swung within a few inches from the wall but did not touch it. He fought the giggly shaking feeling rising up from his stomach every time the swinging squirrel glided out of the darkness like a somnambulant dream rider.

"M-M-Mine," he teetered.

He shook his head, forcing the smile off his face, then cleared his throat.

"Mine," he whispered. "Mine."

Jacob knew he was smiling, but he couldn't help it. He was such a happy boy sometimes.

"I've got work for ye," the bald man said through a mouthful of SpaghettiOs. "Sherman Alexander is comin' by tonight."

Jacob watched his mother's face drop. She opened her mouth to complain, but he cut her off.

"Don't give me any of that, now," Randall Adkins said, lifting the spoon from the plastic bowl and pointing it at her. "Word's gotten 'round about yer being knocked up. Not too many guys are gonna hook with a girl that's preggers, but Sherman . . ."

Jacob's mother looked out the small kitchen window, masking a shudder by running her nicotine-stained fingers through her unwashed hair.

"Money's a bit tight while I get the operation off the ground, Christy," Randall Adkins said, punctuating the sentence by slurping more soup. Twin streams of tomato sauce trickled from the corners of his mouth, giving the pockmarked face the air of a hillbilly vampire. "'Bout got the recipe worked out."

His mother's eyes hardened, but only for a moment.

"You know he ain't got the ticker to go all night anyway," the bald man said. "Too much blubber. It'll be an easy buck."

She looked like she wanted to say something but didn't.

Jacob lifted the plastic bowl to his lips, wishing he were back at the hideout, and swallowed the last bit of his clam chowder. He'd wanted the SpaghettiOs, but the food pantry had only one can and the bald man claimed it. Jacob made a mental note to snag a few things from the corner store or the Food City to keep out at the hideout. He hated clam chowder.

His mother pushed herself up from the table, taking the sweating glass of bourbon and sweet tea to the sink. She raised the plastic cup to her lips, the ice tinkling inside sounding hollow and mostly melted, and drained it.

"There ye go, girl," the bald man laughed. "Bottom's up. Sherman said he'd be by within the next hour or two."

Jacob took his bowl to the sink and found a place near the top of the pile to set it. His mother stood next to him, staring out the window at the trees dancing in the breeze. Jacob could smell the bourbon on her. It was the cheap stuff, more yeast and alcohol than smoke and barrel.

"Ye do these dishes 'fore you go," she said, her voice steady but quiet.

Jacob turned to her briefly, saw the spiraled veins spiderwebbing her dull eyes, the thin line of her unpainted lips stretched long and straight.

"I'm sick of livin' in a goddamn pigsty," she said, turning away from the window and pouring more of the bourbon into her cup.

Jacob watched his mother's reflection in the smudgy window over the stinking sink. She raised the plastic cup to her lips and drank, her fingers trembling, a single tear running down her cheek when she squeezed her eyes closed.

"Can I do it tomorrow?"

His mother didn't reply. She took another swallow, her sallow cheeks momentarily bulging, the wrinkles etching through yesterday's makeup like pressure cracks or stress fractures, but kept her eyes closed. Jacob thought she was holding her breath.

The bald man chuckled behind them. Jacob turned around just as Randall Adkins set the empty mason jar on the Formica table. He swallowed the last of the moonshine and exhaled.

"Ah," he said, a crooked smile and growing redness spreading across his stubbled face. "Ye'll probably want to be elsewhere for the next few hours, shit ass. Go on and get."

He turned back to his mother. She hadn't opened her eyes yet. She stood completely still, part of her weight leaned against the cluttered counter, both of her hands now holding the sweating cup. She looked like she was asleep, sleepwalking through some bad dream, the desperation of wanting escape but not trusting that she'd wake to something better slapped on her pretty but bloated face like a child's finger-painting.

*This is what happens*, he thought, *when you're not careful.*

He wasn't sure what that meant, it'd just popped into his head, but it felt very adult. He felt mature for having had it, even if he didn't fully grasp it yet.

The bald man bellowed a wet-sounding burp. Jacob watched him swallow-battle for a few moments, then belch again, smaller and gurgled.

"Whew," Randall Adkins laughed. "She'll get ye right, now. Right!"

*At least the bald man is doing what he wants*, Jacob thought, watching the man light a thin, uneven joint between his knobby knuckles.

He turned back to his mother, her eyes now open but empty, and watched her for a long minute. She took little sips from her drink as she stared. It didn't take him long to see she was lost in her smudged reflection in the thin glass.

Jacob wanted to feel sorry for her or, better yet, knew he should *want* to feel sorry for her, but he didn't. The bald man was right; she was Jacob's mother, but she was still a cunt.

Though it was empty, Jacob made sure Randall Adkins didn't see him take the mason jar with him when he walked out into the night.

-

The squirrel wasn't dead yet, but it'd ceased fighting its predicament. Its beady little eyes followed Jacob when he was within sight, but it didn't fight against the spiraling motion of the Trilene when it spun him around.

Jacob walked over to it, slipping the penlight between his teeth. With deft fingers, he grabbed the squirrel's skull firmly with his right hand, ensuring no bucktoothed bites, then set about picking off the bulging ticks from the panting but compliant squirrel and dropping them into the mason jar nestled in the crook of his right arm.

When he'd picked the last of the ticks, he released the furry skull and held the mason jar up into the penlight.

*There must over thirty of the little bastards in there*, he thought. *Most of 'em are alive still too.*

The tick experiments were still being sorted out in his head. Jacob knew he needed to collect them. He enjoyed keeping them in the mason jar and letting them feed on whatever animal he had *on display* and had that falling forever look about them.

Jacob guessed the ticks, and tick parts, ringing the bottom of the mason jar must've been undernourished at the time of their imprisonment. He wondered if this was the sort of thing he was supposed to feel deeply moved at upon understanding. He should shed big, wet tears with snot streaking from his freckled nose. But he wasn't *moved*. He didn't really think he even understood what that meant.

He thought about the ticks gorging themselves on the starving rabbit from a few weeks back. Jacob understood at once the ticks knew the rabbit was dying. They were rushing to get what they could, make the most of the situation.

He screwed the lid, Walmart, on the mason jar, the bald man, then set the ticks on the farmer's table under the window. He slung the tactical bag, Freddy Little's Army Surplus, over his shoulders, stepping out into the fog knowing the tick experiment would sort itself out. He'd keep collecting them in the meantime.

"Where ya coming from?"

Jacob stopped walking, standing stupefied for an embarrassingly long moment.

She chuckled, freeing Jacob from whatever strange paralysis had temporarily plagued him. He turned toward the voice, squinting into the shadows on the other side of the yellow security light.

"Over here," she said, stepping into the light. "Boy, you look like a deer in headlights."

She was his age, maybe a little older, it was hard to tell. He wiped the sweat and grime from his face with the inside of his shirt but felt fresh sweat already spilling from his pores like an overfilled basin.

"Well just look at you," she laughed, sidestepping to Jacob's right for a better view in the security light. "Uh, uh. You are filthy. Here I was gonna offer to share this joint with you as a token of my newness to the trailer park, but if your outside looks like that—"

She waved a lit joint, Jacob could smell it now, in his general direction.

"—there's no telling what the inside of your mouth looks like." Her green eyes twinkled as she took a quick puff on the joint. "So that's out of the question."

Her voice was pinched with the intake of smoke. A fuzzy smile spread across her puckered lips. Her shoulders shook once, twice, then she snorted, smoke spilling out of the button of her nose. She closed her eyes, the tears spilling down the long, light lashes. Smoke surrounded her as she hacked.

He thought about leaning forward and patting her back with his hand but, eventually, decided against it.

"Here," she whispered, extending the joint.

She was wiping tears from her face with the sleeve of a green sweatshirt, though she was wearing volleyball shorts, he saw.

Jacob accepted the joint, took a long drag, then sputtered and coughed.

"Damn," he said, after a time.

"Right?"

He passed the joint back.

"I'm Maggie."

"Hi, Maggie."

She smiled, nodding her head as she smoked. As she blew out the smoke, she said, "This is where you tell me your name."

Jacob was surprised she got it all out before the next bout of coughing.

"Jacob," he said. "Jacob Goodman."

*Hunter.*

"Where ya been all evening, Jacob Goodman?" she asked, snickering when he nearly dropped the proffered joint.

He looked at her, once, then down at his stained sneakers. He put the joint in his mouth, taking the longest pull he could. Jacob closed his eyes, blindly extending the joint out. He felt her small, moist fingers pluck it from his grimy, calloused hand.

He swore he could feel the smoke slowly twirling in his lungs and throat. He felt the tips of their wispy heads and raised hands tickling the roof of his mouth and his phlegm-coated throat. He saw the desert and the seabed; the smoke a fuzzy sandstorm in one, a misty, rain-flecked fog in the other.

He exhaled, coughed.

"There you are," Maggie cried.

When Jacob opened his eyes, he saw the gentle, pale curves of Maggie's butt cheeks. She was bent over a small pug, cooing and babbling things in a higher pitched voice.

Jacob wondered what Maggie would do if he reached over and slid the dirty tip of his left pointer finger inside those volleyball shorts.

*If she was smart*, he thought, *she'd ask me for five bucks.*

"That yer dog?" he asked.

"This is Martin," she said, scooping the hideous creature into her arms. "Martin's such a good boy. Aren't you, Martin? Aren't you?"

Jacob watched Maggie kiss the dog, Martin's wet nose. He wondered what the dog's skull looked like.

*Is it sloped funny in the front?* he wondered. *Is that why its nose is all fucked up?*

Jacob hated the sound of the dog, Martin's breathing.

"You go to Floyd County or Prestonsburg?" Maggie asked.

"Floyd County."

"That's where I'll be going, I guess."

She set the dog, Martin, back on the ground.

"Some bald guy came by your place earlier," she said, putting the tip of the remaining joint in her lips. Jacob waited while she flicked the lighter until it caught. After she got the joint going again, she continued. "He was drunk and yelling. I'm not trying to butt in, but I think I heard him hit that woman. She your momma?"

Jacob nodded.

"She came out later, after he'd gone in that beat-to-shit F-150." Maggie took another hit of the joint after Jacob declined. "She was higher than a kite, man. She-et. Your mom and my mom are gonna be best friends, I'm telling you now."

The dog, Martin, stared up at Jacob with shining, blank eyes.

-

Jacob hunched over the front door of the pink trailer, his body shielding his empty hands from view, and pretended to unlock it. He didn't have a key for the pink trailer. He didn't remember owning a key in his life.

"Act like it," his mother had told him. "Just make sure they cain't see yer hands, then act like yer unlocking the door."

He remembered her stepping back, making a show of reaching a hand into her jean shorts, her hand closed, a shielded fist around an imaginary ring of keys. She'd showed him how to hunch over a doorknob and pretend.

Jacob had learned early on you don't keep your important things at home, where you slept. His mother and her endless string of friends and boyfriends had taught Jacob many things, even when they hadn't meant to.

"It's best for everybody if they think the door is locked," Jacob heard his mother say as he pushed open the unlocked door.

The overhead light in the kitchen was on—the weak, yellowed glow of the single exposed bulb—but the living room was etched in deep pools of darkness. The couch had been knocked over earlier in the night. After a few tense moments of holding his breath and squinting at unmoving shadows, Jacob decided he was alone in the living room and flipped the light switch by the front door.

The place was a wreck. There were empty beer and soda cans everywhere. Jacob saw three empty bourbon bottles too; the beady-eyed crows staring up from the stained carpet like fallen sentinels. The window blinds had been broken; several slats reached out toward Jacob like skeletal fingers.

The VCR and TV seemed to be alright though. He could see the black plastic tips of the bald man's tapes behind the composite wood stand.

Jacob felt himself stir at the thought of the muted tapes in Fast-Forward X2 Mode.

*If she's good and gone*, he thought, *I might not even have to mute them all the way.*

From what Maggie said, Jacob figured his mother would've gotten absolutely blitzed after the bald man left.

The hallway was still; Jacob could see only darkness under his mother's closed bedroom door. He had just about decided to see what was in the fridge when something in the hall caught his eye. He turned his body fully toward the hall, unsure what he was looking for.

He saw the faintest flicker of light, a fluttering of shadows really, from under the master bedroom door.

He tiptoed down the hall, the soles of his miss K-Swisses nearly inaudible on the thin carpet. As he neared the door, Jacob picked up the unmistakable dance of flame in the shadowplay under his mother's closed bedroom door.

Jacob pressed his left ear to the cool door but heard nothing. No television or radio static. No drunken snoring. He cleared his throat, preparing himself to call for his mother and knock on her door, but the distinct *plink* of a droplet splashing into a pool of liquid stilled him.

*Is she taking a bath?* Jacob wondered, seeing the interior of the master bedroom's bathroom, the gaudy, soap-scummed seashell bathtub dripping from the crooked faucet, in his mind. *She never takes baths.*

Jacob carefully wrapped the fingers of his left hand around the doorknob and turned it, slowly but steadily, until it clicked open, unlocked. He held the doorknob, fully turned, for a shaky moment before sucking in a mouthful of air and gently pressing his right shoulder into the thin, pressed wood and easing it open.

His mother's room was a disaster in the faint flickering candle-light coming from the opened bathroom. Jacob made it a point to avoid the room. He had mingled ideas about the room that confused him. She worked back there, slept back there, bathed and dressed and put on makeup back there, kept the pills and other drugs back there, so Jacob simply did not go into his mother's bedroom. It took him a minute to acclimate to the disarray of the room. Her dresser was overturned at the foot of the bed. At least one of the drawers had splintered into cheap wooden shards in the fall. Clothes and shoes littered the floor, a collage of black and red bra straps, silk bows on lacy satin, stained and faded jeans and shorts, floral printed sundresses, the worn cotton softness of old band t-shirts.

*Plink.*

Jacob could just make out the beginning of the porcelain bathtub in his mother's bathroom: the dull pink glow of a tealight candle's flickering tongue on the tub's edge. He stepped over the dresser and around the unmade bed. The closet door had been knocked off its hinges and, not for the first time, he expected this to be the time he found her dead.

"Mom?"

Jacob cringed at how child-like his voice sounded. He cleared his throat and tried again, in a lower register.

"Mom?" he called, louder. "I'm home."

There were drops of something dried and nearly black on the carpet leading into the bathroom. Jacob saw the same drops on the laminate flooring of the bathroom.

"Mom," he said, "I think yer dripping wax."

The sound of the leaked droplet splashing down into the pink seashell bathtub was louder than Jacob thought it should've been. He stepped into his mother's bathroom, his chest feeling bound and tight, and saw her there, in the tub.

"Mom?"

Despite the blue and purple bruises, Jacob could tell his mother's eyes were closed. Her lumpy face was turned toward the shadows dancing on the water-stained ceiling, her unpainted and swollen lips parted, a strand of saliva hanging from the right side where it traced the outline of a handprint that spanned the entire side of her face before dropping to the knobbed paleness of her exposed collarbone.

The still water of the tub was not clear, nor was it lined in suds of the fragrant soap his mother used, lavender and chamomile and honeydew melon. It was tinged in red. Over the initial shock of his mother's naked form, Jacob registered something as out of the ordinary, wrong. It looked like she was wearing a diaper, some water-logged swaddling stained a red that was nearly black.

"Mom?" Jacob whispered.

*Plink.*

The ripple of the water droplet cascaded across the tinged water inside the pink seashell. His mother did not move. Jacob leaned over the tub for a closer look.

*Those are her bedsheets*, he saw.

The white sheets had been wrapped around her waist like a towel, tucked in near the gentle rise where her stomach met the left side of her hip, and they were bloodstained. His mother's groin had been cut or injured.

The sheets had been used to catch the blood. He followed the red stains on the bathroom floor and traced the path back to the bed, which was bloody as well.

Jacob thought he was going to faint. The room quivered for a second, then he caught his breath and leaned back against the vanity. He squeezed his eyes shut, rubbed them with the grimy knuckles of his hands, and slowed his breathing.

*You knew it'd happen one day*, he told himself, realizing that knowing this didn't make the situation any less overwhelming.

"Hurts."

Jacob hadn't even seen her move, but his mother's soft voice reverberated in the stillness of the bathroom. Jacob could see the disturbed water around her breasts, though her blackened eyes remained closed.

"Mom?"

"Tired," Jacob's mother croaked.

She moaned, a quick, light murmur deep in the back of her throat, but said no more.

Jacob thought she looked ready for death. She could've been asleep, more tired than tired had any right of being, but not quite dead.

*Not yet*, he thought.

Jacob didn't know what to think or feel or do. He thought she'd been dead. When she spoke, he acknowledged relief as well as disappointment roiling about in his stomach.

*Stupid*, he thought, *cunt*.

Jacob felt his face erupt in red as he came to the realization that his mother, who was not dead though obviously beaten badly, was completely naked in his presence. He couldn't help but see the darkened nubs of her nipples, the tuft of pubic hair just visible around the wrapped bedsheets, the little scars on her stomach.

Jacob turned away from the tub, hot tears blurring his vision. He slapped on the hot water of the sink and hunched over it. It took some time for the water to get hot, but when it got there, he rubbed the grime off his hands as best he could, then splashed water onto his burning face.

Through his closed eyes, Jacob saw the negative of his naked mother in the seashell bathtub interrupted by the bouncing bodies from the bald man's tapes played in Fast-Forward X2 Mode. Jacob clenched his teeth together, trying to force the nude image of his mother out of his head.

*Fuck*, he screamed in his head. *Fuck!*

He opened his eyes and saw himself in the flicker of the bathtub tealights in the toothpaste and pimple-stained mirror. His eyes were wide, mostly white with the twin holes of his pupils glaring up like black fires, like reflected voids, like the open hole of the mineshaft the bald man had shown him.

Desert. Seabed.

*I could do it*, he realized.

Jacob didn't turn away from the mirror. He swiveled his head so he could see his inert mother in the mirror over his shoulder.

He knew it wouldn't take much: two hands pressed to her damp shoulders. One push down, some holding. He knew it wouldn't take long either, he'd seen the movies. Some splashing, some thrashing, but it'd all be over in under three minutes.

Jacob closed his eyes.

*You can do it. You can.*

He opened his eyes to his unsmiling reflection and knew he couldn't.

Yet.

## CHAPTER FOUR
## THE BONUS ROUND – CRYSTAL CUBISM

*DEAR EDITOR,*

*We've all seen the posters: Reward! Help! Lost! Pictures of little furry faces smiling up from the taped fliers. Names and numbers and addresses and favorite foods listed.*

*We all know somebody with a missing pet: four out of the six houses on my street are missing cats and/or dogs; six dogs are missing the next street over; or, like myself, are missing your own furbaby (Momma misses you, Button).*

*There's too many of our pets, our dear, little loved ones gone for it not to be noticeable.*

*What is happening, Prestonsburg? Who is taking our pets? What's being done about it?*

*Melissa W.*

-

Jacob looked down at the orange tabby licking at the open can of cat food below. From his place on the branch in the black oak, ten feet above the cat, Jacob could just make out the pink tip of the cat's tongue as it worked at the gravy covered gelatinous goop.

The cat wore a red collar with yellow polka dots. The cat's tags jingled against the collar as it worked at the Fancy Feast Jacob had stolen from Walmart. The cat sneezed into the food, then went right back to eating.

Jacob sneered.

It hadn't even lifted its head from the can.

A noisy pickup backfired nearby. Jacob was sure the cat was going to bolt at the sound of it, but it didn't.

*City cats*, Jacob smiled to himself.

He eased some slack into the rope, watched the hanging metal cage drift a few inches closer to the distracted cat.

-

The sky's depth drained steadily with the coming sun. Jacob watched the last of the stars slip from the horizon through the leathery fingers of a raccoon hand, one of sixteen strung along the length of the windowsill like chimes. It'd been a most pleasant evening. He'd hunted, killed, experimented. He'd prowled.

That was the word for it.

*Prowled.*

Long after he'd tracked some animal through the woods, or checked one of his many traps to find one waiting, or happened by a stray dog or collared cat, or saw the outline of a sleeping form within a doghouse, long after Jacob had killed that small creature, he prowled the sleeping houses of Prestonsburg. He wore his darkest clothes, though he didn't think it really mattered, everyone was fast asleep, and circled darkened houses. Jacob tried every door and window he came to until one opened.

One always opened.

It was the hunt after the hunt. The bonus round. The victory lap.

Jacob never really thought he knew anybody. He'd never known his father; his mother hadn't even bothered with a lie.

"Don't know. Could've been a few guys I knew around that time."

The shrug of her bare shoulders, a smooth roll that alerted anyone with open eyes to the fact she was braless, told Jacob all he needed to know.

*She doesn't know*, he saw, *and she doesn't care.*

Jacob had come to learn more on his near nightly prowls than he ever learned from a conversation. Going into sleeping houses, opening their closed drawers and unlocked doors, tiptoeing around their snoring bedrooms, peering into the corners of their cracked closets and cobwebbed attics, showed Jacob who the people of Prestonsburg were.

They were vain, wasteful, insecure, and feckless, Mrs. Horace's Word of the Day earlier that week. Keeping meaningless things: dusty porcelain plates commemorating one disastrous celebrity death, military victory, or president of the United States or another; boxes upon boxes of mostly Christmas decorations; brittle, ornate furniture unfit for use, whole rooms of it entirely for show. Then they threw out perfectly serviceable milk crates and only slightly rusty knives, nice bookshelves only a little scuffed and sticky and stickered with ponies and dolphins, kerosene heaters that only needed a good cleaning with a toothbrush and some gasoline.

Then there were the secrets. The little hidden treasures stuffed in the back of underwear drawers and nightstands, tucked under moldering sweatshirts in the tops of closets, under the beds in which they slept open-mouthed and drooling, in thick metal safes that more than one person didn't feel the need to even close, much less lock.

Polaroids. Over-exposed photographs. Rolls of undeveloped film. Magazines. Flipbooks. VHS tapes and DVDs. Pen and ink drawings and velvet paintings. Paperback books musty to the touch. The bottles of lubrication and packages of condoms. The vaguely weapon-like toys people, somehow, used for sex that smelled, strongly.

The portable, handheld vagina.

The blow-up lady with an open mouth, spread legs, and straw-like hair clumped together in several places.

Jacob learned to smell the panties and bras. He saw it on the television in some late-night movie. A teenage boy at a friend's house sneaks up the stairs into his friend's parents' bedroom. He opens the top drawer of a dresser. Wrong: tighty-whiteys. The next dresser's top drawer is the one: full of soft, silky panties and supple, curved bras. The boy's eyes nearly glaze over. He slaps a pair of black panties over his nose and mouth and inhales.

Jacob couldn't stop himself when he found the woman from Highland Avenue's small blue dildo sitting upright like a plastic cactus. He could see the damp ring near the base, a few short and curly hairs on the little nubby arm-like extension, when he picked it up and held it under the moonlight pouring in from the window above her bed.

*Got one out 'fore she went to bed.*

It was in his mouth before Jacob knew what he was doing. It tasted vaguely soured, but not in a bad way. The smell and taste felt disconnected somehow.

He stared down at the woman from Highland Avenue as his tongue explored the crusty ring of her dildo. He worked at one particularly thick section until it broke free and clung to his tongue. He removed the dildo from his mouth, set it silently back onto the nightstand, then carefully bent over her pillow until he could smell her dyed, blonde hair as the bit of her dissolved in his mouth.

The victory lap became more fun than the hunt. On some nights, Jacob thought it even rivaled the kill.

He carefully ran his left index finger along the small, papery raccoon palm hanging just above his forehead from the nearly invisible

# BIRTH OF A MONSTER

Trilene, Walmart.

*Nearly ready*, Jacob decided.

He had an idea for a new creation, had trapped a young, fat groundhog earlier in the afternoon for it, and needed the raccoon hands to be a little more dried out than last time.

Jacob didn't know how long he'd been standing in the window of the hideout, rubbing small, soft concentric circles into the raccoon palm, but he realized his neck and back were aching. He lowered his arm and felt the muscles around his left shoulder twinge and nearly seize up in a cramp. Then he felt the strangeness of his face. He could barely feel anything there when he lifted his filthy fingers up to the twitching skin. It felt like a meaty mask had been super glued over his own, which, for some reason, was comforting.

*I've been smiling for hours*, Jacob realized.

He saw the rugged moon through the tips of his fingers; it, too, was smiling.

*I am the desert*, Jacob thought. *I am the seabed. I am such a happy boy.*

-

Jacob had many visions for his experiments. Sometimes, when he wasn't paying attention to himself or the steadily turning cogs in his train of thought, he got lost in smeared images of quilted animals, so much like some of those surrealist paintings Mrs. Vance told them about on Tuesday that he stole an awkwardly sized book from the Floyd County Public Library about Crystal Cubism.

A perfect pattern of interlocking square patches of the meat from a squirrel's hind quarters, the in-toed angled front hoofs of a white-tailed fawn, the clawed C's of an adult male raccoon, the long gracefully curved neck and skull of a swan, the slick black beak and bright red eyes of the canvasback duck he'd beaten to death with a rock, all surrounding a furry figure eight, a cocky, slanting thing sliding leftwards across the canvas of Jacob's mind, the comforting yellow of Little Richard, the golden retriever from the gently rocking houseboat on Dewey Lake.

Jenny Wiley State Park had a marina and a small amphitheater. The night Jacob took Little Richard, the golden retriever, there'd been a performance of *Little Women* by the University of Pikeville's minoring theater students; Jacob read the big sign they put out near the visitor's center parking lot. The place was packed. The graying lesbian couple—at first he thought they'd been sisters but a month of nights peering into the parted curtains of the teal houseboat's windows showed him they weren't sisters—slid the glass door of their houseboat shut, patted Little Richard on his upturned, smiling head, then walked up the dock toward the amphitheater.

Jacob got up from the couch of the houseboat he'd been watching from, *another locked door*, and stepped out onto the dock.

Little Richard, the golden retriever, lifted his head, and Jacob smiled at the steady thumping of the stupid animal's tail.

In one hand: an open can of solid white albacore, Save-A-Lot. The other: a hunk of grippy sandstone the size of a softball.

"That's right, you dumb fuck," Jacob cooed around the upturned corners of his lips. "Want some nice smelly fish from a can, mister yellow dog, whittle bitty Little Richard?"

In one corner, Jacob saw the whites of Little Richard, the golden retriever's, eyes as he felt more than saw Jacob's sudden move.

*Too late*, those eyes sang. *Too late and oh no.*

Jacob stepped away from the hanging hands in the window to study a page he'd torn out of *Crystal Cubism* and tacked to the wall above the farmer's table. He'd ended up needing three boxes of tacks, two from Ace Hardware and one from Walmart, to hang up all the paintings he liked … nearly all of them. Something about the disjointedly straightforwardness of Juan Gris' *Harlequin with a Guitar* drew him.

Jacob pictured all of his experiments as his own spin on Juan Gris' *Harlequin with a Guitar*; each death a varied texture, each creation a section of canvas, another layered canyon of the character: obstructed, but in view.

Jacob saw each hunt, each capture, each kill, each experiment through the lens of the paintings of Crystal Cubism: writhing, stinking, bleeding, pissing, yowling works of abstract genius. Each one a revelation. Each one a snapshot of dozens of nights, dozens of experiments.

Next to Juan Gris' painting was Pablo Picasso's *Harlequin Playing the Guitar*. Gaping human mouth and pyramid nose a kaleidoscope of crushed, splintered squirrel skull fragments. The curled hand wrapped around the neck of the violin the black tail of Margaret Cat Fulkerson, as the tag had read on the fluffy black and white cat he'd killed at Middle Creek National Battlefield just outside Prestonsburg. The sheet music was comprised entirely of teeth; squirrels', raccoons', rabbits', gars', cats', dogs', possums'. He stared at the interlocking shapes, the jagged juts of splintered calcium, the stained

# BIRTH OF A MONSTER

splotches of blackened rot and discolored food. The mass of veiny, purpled gums was implied beneath the gentle sweep of teeth, these darker and gnashing, serving as the shadow of the thumb holding the blurred sheet music. The painting in Jacob's head, his quilted copy, experiment upon experiment upon experiment, of Picasso's *Harlequin* was so *engrossing*, another of Mrs. Horace's Words of the Day, one Jacob couldn't help but think of when he thought about the experiments, that you could almost hear it as you looked at it. Crisp nibblings. The wet plop of fresh meat slapping sandstone. Fat bubbling alongside the hissing, stringy muscle of the dead-eyed puppy; he'd found that chubby mutt up the Levisa Fork—everyone said "La-Vees-ah"—near the sleeping community of Emma. The brittle pop of raccoon finger bones snapping, one after the next, until he'd run through all four limbs: dried kindling tossed onto the billowing flames; the negative image of the sheet music as shadow.

*The Harlequin Playing the Guitar of Experimentation,* Jacob named the floating vision, his mouth gaping, but smiling.

The first rays of morning cascaded over the ridgeline, spilling into the hideout, onto the *Guitar of Experimentation*, the black body of which was comprised of the soggy pelt of Button, the mostly black Boston Terrier he found sniffing shit on the one-lane bridge at Archer Park and killed with a golf club, Paul Hunt Thompson Golf Course. He couldn't imagine anything more beautiful.

Tackett's Jewelry & Watch Repair was a prefab building Rodney Tackett's father, Johnnie Floyd Tackett, built the year Jacob had transferred from Osborne Elementary out near Wheelwright to Prestonsburg Elementary School, where, right off the bat, Rodney Tackett had begun to pick on Jacob. The Tackett family lived in town. Johnnie Floyd's shop was metal-topped, metal-sided, and metal-doored, located at the end of a steep gravel driveway off Hyden Branch, all on its own. The nearest house was almost a quarter of a mile on down the road.

Jacob wondered what it sounded like in the building during a hailstorm.

It was a cloudy night, but not even threatening to sprinkle.

Jacob tried the door and was not surprised to find it was locked.

This didn't matter. He'd staked the place out, three nights in a row, and saw Rodney Tackett sneak into the building late one night, unlocking the door with a key hidden under a rock and leaving

# BIRTH OF A MONSTER

a

short three minutes later, quickly tossing the key onto the ground and nudging the rock only partially over it with the white tip of his clean, definitely not thrift store Nike Air Maxes.

Scrubbed as he did, Jacob could see the bloodstains from the possum on his miss K-Swisses quite clearly, even in the dark of after midnight. Jacob bounced his eyes from splatter drop to splatter drop with each steady clap of Rodney Tackett's footfalls.

Step. *Drop.*

*Drip.* Step.

Step. *Drop.*

*Drip.* Step.

The dead winter grass around Jacob's feet was in a similar hue as Little Richard, the golden retriever's, fur had been.

*Is,* Jacob thought. *I left Little Richard, the golden retriever, strung up in the top of that old poplar looking over Sugarloaf Branch.*

Baking in the winter sun, Jacob planned on using Little Richard, the golden retriever's, hide as a rug for the hideout.

*Might be ready to work on tomorrow,* Jacob thought, stepping out of the woods now that Rodney Tackett's footsteps were so far away that they could no longer be heard. He turned over the rock, picked up the key, then opened the front door of Tackett's Jewelry & Watch Repair.

Jacob needed a few things for the hideout, some supplies for the experiments. He wanted to see smaller things with greater detail; a jeweler and watch repairman's magnifying glasses, which a library computer search revealed was called a loupe, would be perfect for some of the experiments Jacob envisioned for hand and finger and claw bones, which Jacob found *engrossing.* He craved more *precision, thanks again Mrs. Horace,* for his next experiments. Some of the work on display now at the hideout could be improved with a more precise snip here, there.

Jacob found what he was looking for. There wasn't much to the place: a few shelves and display cases of shiny rocks and gleaming metal. In the little backroom, Jacob found a monitor and recording setup for a security system. He could tell it wasn't turned on; the screen was dark. The console of the recording thingy wasn't lit up either. Jacob saw that the surge protector housing all of the electronic equipment was also dark and not plugged into the bare socket on the wall.

In a drawer of the desk the security stuff was sitting on, Jacob found a porno magazine called *Slant-Eyed Whores Love Hard Black Dicks*. He folded it, twice, and stuck it in the right back pocket of his pants, the pocket without the gigantic hole in it. He'd put it in his pack, but he didn't think he'd make it back to the hideout before he'd have to click on the penlight, put it in his mouth, and beat off to Johnnie Floyd's exotic porno mag.

Jacob had heard Rodney Tackett tell more than one racist joke, a common pastime on long bus rides or between classes. He found the magazine intriguing; he wondered vaguely if Asian women had different looking pussies, though he doubted it.

"They're all just cunts, shit ass," the bald man had told him.

Jacob, though he didn't like Randall Adkins, believed he was right in this regard.

He found the magnifying glasses, the loupe, on a workbench. Jacob flicked on the lamp hanging above the desk, then put on the glasses. He was immediately disoriented and had to close his eyes. He decided to study the back of his left hand, then opened his eyes again. The desert of his skin looked parched and etched with lines like the broken glass-like mud clumps of the dried-up seabed.

Jacob took off the glasses, smiling. He put them in his pack, along with batteries, a collection of watchmaker screwdrivers of various sizes, all small and very small, and an unopened jar of pickled bologna.

-

Jacob had burned through the surgical sutures much quicker than he'd anticipated. Before he knew it, he'd run out and found himself making the long walk to the University of Pikeville Medical School through the night shrouded hills to steal some more. He'd wasted more than he cared to admit learning how the sutures worked, what he could do with them, which of his limited tools worked best with the different types of flesh, how much weight they could hold. No telling how many he'd wasted before he noticed the little needle nose plier-like apparatus in several photos in the books he'd taken and learned a needle driver was handy to have around when working with sutures. He stole several pairs from the medical school soon after.

Jacob slept during school these days. He spent the nights haunting the hills, he felt; a pale ghoul stalking and killing the animals he needed for the experiments, preparing the parts of them he needed, setting traps, opening doors and windows. His mother had missed the second parent-teacher conference that Wednesday.

"Shit," she'd said when he reminded her that afternoon. "Slipped my mind."

From the slur of her words, Jacob could tell most things were slipping his mother's mind. She'd been different since the night he left her in her bathtub. He'd spent the night wide awake, listening for the sound of wet thrashing, knowing she'd slip below the surface of the water and be too weak to pull herself out. Jacob remembered gripping his hands together, the muscles of his forearms knotting, his knuckles blanching white from the strain, unsure if he'd be able to pull himself from his sleepless bed to pull his mother from the cold bathwater. He wasn't sure he'd even want to.

School no longer mattered, not that it really ever did before. Jacob went, though he was sure he could skip if he really wanted to, simply because he was used to going. He spent his school days in a fog, a hazy series of naps and punishment and undercooked pizza and powdered potatoes. A few of the teachers scolded Jacob. He was written up, given warnings, put in detention, forced into meetings with the school counselor and assistant principal. Jacob's Kentucky history teacher, Mr. Burkhart, an earnest, well-meaning man, had even pulled Jacob aside and asked if "everything was alright at home."

Jacob smiled as he stepped over the rotting trunk of a fallen black gum tree, the sutures already put to use in his mind. Hobart, the Tackett family's cat, had finally starved to death yesterday while on display. Jacob planned on removing the cat, Hobart's front two limbs, and replacing them with those from the gigantic female raccoon he'd hung from a redbud twenty yards or so outside the hideout. He saw both creatures as he'd left them: Hobart strung from the hideout's roofbeams by Trilene and wide gap fishing hooks, Walmart; the raccoon gutted and decapitated, the skull buried a few feet in the dirt not far from the hideout, its arms carefully tied together and protected from breakage. The T-Rex-like creation would be further altered when Jacob found the right possum head.

For now, he planned on using a set of small metallic storage hooks, Ace Hardware, as anchors for the arms; the hooks were the kind with a screw built into one end, so all you had to do was screw it into the spot where you wanted it. After Jacob set in the raccoon arms, he planned on suturing them to Hobart's trunk, doing his best to hide all trace of his work, which was often the hardest part of the process.

Jacob crossed Route 23 just outside Pikeville. A small herd of deer, not a buck among them, were picking at the dead grass just off the shoulder; all of their heads lifted up from the ground and followed Jacob as he slipped past them into the thin copse of trees higher up the mountain. He followed the path until it ended in the small clearing hidden by pines and littered with cigarette butts and empty beer cans. He moved a needle laden branch just far enough to peer through. The parking lot was empty. The door marked "No Entry" was shut.

Jacob had figured it would be. He ducked low as he crossed the parking lot.

*I'll get in through one of the windows lining the cadaver lab*, he thought.

He slipped between the fence of the dumpster and the brick of the medical school building, breathing steadily through his smiling mouth. He was excited about getting more of the sutures, which he now saw as essential supplies; Jacob had tried using variously sized needles and thread, Walmart, as well as ten different sizes of Trilene and other fishing line, Walmart & Yates' Bait & Tackle, and from several unattended fishing and houseboats around Dewey Lake, but nothing worked quite like the surgical sutures.

Glimpses of a new experiment had been flickering through the static in his head most of the day. Bits of fur, muscle and tendon, an assortment of bones, layers of crushed teeth and cartridge, dozens upon dozens of sets ground into sand and stone and trunk; the flayed flesh of Barnie, the hulking boxer from Happy Hollow in West Prestonsburg, melding, there, with the skinned flesh of two dozen possums, boiled and sun-dried, diverging there into feminine stretches of the de-furred skin of the very large, exotic-looking dog Jacob had poisoned outside a large house up the Big Branch of Abbott Creek. He'd forgotten to read the name tag on the expensive-looking collar. Now, the dog's skin was pale but speckled and spotted with textured patches of green and black and dark-blue mold, the places where the most blood had pooled and, in his haste for a new display, Jacob hadn't allowed to fully dry out in the weak but steady winter sun. The new experiment would be a study, but in Jacob's own style and distinct medium, of Jean Metzinger's *Two Nudes, Two Women*.

*I've got a lot to learn about preserving hides*, he thought, making a

74

# BIRTH OF A MONSTER

mental note to do some research at the Floyd County Public Library. *They're bound to have books on taxidermy too.*

Jacob spent the daylight hours after school staring at the fluttering pages tacked to the walls of the hideout. Interspersed among the glossy color photos from *Crystal Cubism*, Floyd County Public Library, Jacob put up several pages from the *Color Atlas of Anatomy*, University of Pikeville Medical School. The dissections and landscapes did not clash in any way Jacob could see. Nor were the musicians and models at odds with the sectioned-off human joints and vertebral canal and spinal cord photographs they were tacked beside. The wall, as a thing in itself, was close. Jacob moved the inferior aspect of the arteries of the brain to the upper left-hand portion, then he switched a squishy looking shot of the coronal section through the thorax with Albert Gleizes' *Horsewoman*.

*Closer.*

The sketchy outline dancing in the last rays of the setting sun gave him visions of the next creation. He'd dragged two wooden pallets, Dollar General, to the hideout; he planned on attaching them together with the 2 x 4 whitewood stud and sixteen-gauge steel finish nails stolen from Jason Hughes, a self-employed contractor, according to the tacky graphic on his silver Silverado, which was parked outside the reach of the security light zip-tied to the base of a satellite dish on top of his trailer on Blue River Road.

Jacob kept walking over to the middle of the wall, where he hung *Two Nudes, Two Women*. He'd stared at it until the sun had sunk below the ridgeline to the west, but he remembered now as he remembered it earlier that afternoon: perfectly formed in its seemingly incomplete presentation. When he envisioned the two pallets attached, Jacob could already see the cascade of lines he'd use for the outline. He'd raise the pelts and skin and bones and other parts with hooks and trunnels and nails, Ace Hardware, Walmart, and Jason Hughes, making Metzinger's curtain-like effect by draping the prepared flesh across Trilene or suturing it together in weaved strips of fur and skin to blur the distinction between the woman on the right's limbs and the tanned trunks and branches of the forest beyond.

Jacob didn't see the security guard. He would have continued walking along the bushes until he found the windows looking into the cadaver lab, where he would have gone about getting inside, by any means necessary, if the guard hadn't choked on the cigarette smoke he'd just inhaled when Jacob had come into his view.

Jacob spun on his heels, saw the black and orange gold cart and coughing security guard down on the street below, and froze. He couldn't breathe. He couldn't move. He stood and watched the pudgy, uniformed man double over his knees, hacking. For an enticing moment, Jacob was sure that if he stared at the choking man hard enough, he'd help to make him die.

The man began retching.

*He's not going to die*, Jacob realized, coming back to himself. *I gotta get outta here!*

The security guard found enough breath to yell, "Stop!"

Jacob didn't look back.

-

He slowed to a trot, shot quick glances in each direction, saw no approaching cars, as he crossed back over Route 23. Jacob was furious with himself. He shouted names and hurled unintelligible insults at himself in his head and wished the herd of deer had still been there.

*Idiot.*

*Amateur.*

*Child.*

Heard Rodney Tackett's voice twanging, "*Hun*-ter. *Mis-gnome-er.* *Hun*-ter."

*Retard.*

*Faggot.*

*Shit ass.*

*Squirt.*

He heard sirens, back in Pikeville behind him, and felt a new weight on his chest, a soured taste coating all the phlegm in the back of his throat.

*Failure.*

*Failure.*

Jacob caught his breath.

*Failure*, he thought, breaking into a run he knew he'd regret at school in three short hours.

-

Jacob dreamed when he slept, but he dreamt plenty when he was awake too. Practically the entire time Jacob was out of the woods he was on autopilot, envisioning his experiments and creations and the studies from *Crystal Cubism*, reliving kills as if they were his first, each and every one.

*Long limbs.*
*Pale skin.*
*Breasts.*
*—Somebody's pet. Anybody could be somebody's—*
*Fur.*
*Always blood.*
> *Shit; Piss.*
> *Desert; Seabed.*
*Long, silky blonde hair*
*the flake / the taste of      // Highland Avenue*
*Purpled intestines / curling kielbasa*
> *veined in blue and red.*
*Tooth powder.*
*Blurring distinctions with braided pelts.*
*Ritualistic quilting / animalistic torture*
*Marrow.*
*A dead cat / Hobart*
*Maggots,* faggot.
*Ghosts*

-

In his distracted state, Jacob carried the voices he hadn't registered as coming from inside the hideout over into his semi-dream-state.

# CHAPTER FIVE
## STARS STRUTTING IN STRANGE CONSTELLATIONS

**FUCKING PSYCHOPATH.**

Weirdo.

Told y'all he's a faggot.

Sicko. Psychopath.

Fucking faggot-queer.

Shh-shhhhh.

What?

I heard it too.

There.

Him?

A brief flight when the realization hit him, both quick things, lightning instances of hot fright coupled with cold, steady aversion.

*Ho*bart.

What the fuck is wrong with ye, queer bait?

You goddamn sick homo-perv.

*Hun*-ter.

Flashes of white. Pain, pain, pain, and more pain.

Rodney Tackett.

-

Jacob opened his eyes, knowing immediately he was going to puke.

"He's wak—"

Rodney Tackett's cheeks were red, his eyes wide, more white than pupil. Jacob saw him clearly before he spewed vomit from his mouth, then from his mouth and through both of his nostrils, which got the tears flooding his eyes. He forgot about everything but not squirting hot shit into his pants as he vomited.

When his stomach lapsed into angry roils and rumbles, Jacob tried to wipe his mouth with the sleeves of his shirt, but found his arms locked behind him.

"Ye fucking asshole!" Rodney Tackett shrieked, his voice high and hysterical.

"He got ye good, Rodney," a familiar voice laughed from behind

Jacob.

"Shut the fuck up, Patrick," Rodney Tackett screamed, "or I'll beat yer mother fucking pussy ass!"

*Knock*, the feeling like the word. *Knock*, hard and hollow and reverberating around in his head like a marble slowly rolling around the world's largest metal trash can.

*Knock*.

A dent in the can.

The swinging of a foot.

Knock.

The snake-like fists, looming into view for only the briefest of moments, struck with a speed Jacob saw and felt slowly deteriorate as it progressed.

Knock

Faggot.

Jesus.

Bam, man. Again. Bam.

Give me that.

What.

That.

This?

That.

Why you want a bunch of screwdrivers for, Rodney?

Shut the fuck up and give them goddamn motherfucking screwdrivers to me, Pat-trick, or I'm gonna fuck yer sister until she cumshits my babies, you fuck.

Jesus, man. Here.

Fuck.

What the fuck.

Fuck ye.

*Knock*.

"What're ye doing?" Jacob asked.

He tasted blood in his mouth, heat and copper, and hated the pleading sound of his voice as he heard it. Jacob was having great difficulty getting his eyes to focus. They felt loose in their sockets, crossing and uncrossing in blurred smears, as several shapes moved about the hideout.

Jacob could tell he was in the hideout by the smell.

"What have ye done to Hobart?" Rodney Tackett asked.

81

Jacob could hear the clenched teeth in the question, the hysteria and anger vibrating like a live wire.

"Ye fucking psycho," Rodney Tackett said, spitting each of the words. "What did ye do to my cat?"

The question was punctuated with a punch. Jacob felt a hollow crash near his left temple and a cascade of fuzzy stars blanketed the room in static white.

-

Jesus, Rodney. Ease up.

Fuck ye.

You're gonna really hurt him, man.

He killed my fucking cat.

Yeah, but . . .

He killed. My. Fucking. Cat. My *mom*'s cat.

White hot stars danced in the blurred room. The morning sun slanted through the window. Jacob blinked and blinked, trying to focus on the fluttering, tacked pages on the wall in front of him. In a flash, he saw the outline there: a great shape hulking behind the glossy photographs of paintings and bodies. Something large and waiting and beckoning.

Jacob tried to get his eyes to focus on it but another punch sent the stars strutting in strange constellations.

-

He couldn't tell how long his eyes had been open. Jacob tried to blink, thought he'd sent the appropriate signal to the right place, but the morning light stayed steady: white but unfocused. For a long time, he couldn't remember where he was or what he was doing there.

After a time, he became aware of a boy's voice. At first, it sounded tinny and far away. Then it seemed to squeeze through some long, soup can tunnel, coming out the other side blood red and belonging to Rodney Tackett.

"This screwdriver set came from my father's shop, *Hun*-ter."

The morning light disappeared; Rodney Tackett's wide-eyed face loomed over Jacob. Jacob traced the cracked red veins in his class-mate's eyes; the image of dried-up desert riverbeds vibrated into running streams of hissing lava.

"How the fuck did it end up here?" Rodney Tackett asked. "Not in his shop, but out here in the middle of the goddamn woods? In your . . . creepy . . . fucking . . . cabin?"

His voice broke.

Jacob watched great root systems bloom on his classmate, Rodney Tackett. The first appeared under the streaking beads of sweat on Rodney Tackett's forehead, slanting leftward from just under the brown widow's peak. The second pumped fiercely up his neck, a mountain stream gushing with sudden spring rain. The third was the heartwood of a black walnut spiraling around Rodney Tackett's pupils: hard, split and splintering.

Jacob realized he was in serious danger.

The face jerked backwards, twisting in rage. Jacob watched the wind-up, knew what was coming, but could do nothing to stop it. There was a beautiful stillness in the fleeting moment: Rodney Tackett's crooked, bared teeth seeming to pull in the skin and muscles around them, the heartwood walnut hatred lining his eyes, the right arm rearing backwards, the elbow a shark's fin breaking the surface.

It was so beautiful Jacob no longer cared if he lived or if he died. He felt strange. His head was the crisp clearness of a full moon but insulated in dense wisps of cotton. The desert radiated heat in dancing shimmers; the kelp and fish tails undulated as the current tickled the seabed.

Just before the punch landed, Jacob closed his eyes, seeing the desert and the seabed at the same time.

To see the sea / in 3-D.

Hold him.

Come on, Rodney. This isn't cool, man.

Cool? Not *cool*?

Come on.

He killed my mom's cat. My cat. He killed it. Look at it.

I know. I do. It's awful.

Real fucked up, Rodney.

Sorry, man.

Look at it. Look. At. It.

Jacob couldn't open his eyes. In the silence, pages fluttered in a quickening wind.

Hobart is dead. This creepy fuck killed him. Poisoned him or something.

Jesus.

Rodney.

What're ye going to do with that?

He also likes to steal. Don't you?

A hot bite of pain tore into Jacob's right bicep. He screamed before he knew he was going to, but bit it off as soon as he was capable.

Holy fuck, Rodney.

Shit.

Oh god.

What about that? How'd ye like that? Huh?

Rodney, stop it.

This is too much, man. Too much. Too much.

Too much? He killed Hobart. Killed him.

Jesus, take it out of him, man.

Oh god.

Pull it out.

Jacob's arm swam in fresh agony.

Fuck, he's bleeding.

Oh god.

Of course he's bleeding, Rodney fucking stabbed him. Ye stabbed him.

Holy god.

Stop it. Stop.

This time Jacob felt the bite on his upper left thigh, but his pants helped cushion the force of the blow and it wasn't as deep.

Shit.

Stop it, Rodney. This is insane. Yer crazy.

I'm leaving.

No yer not. What did we say when we set out this morning? Huh? Jesus.

What did we say? We all said we'd search for the missing pets together, right? Said we'd find 'em together, split the money together.

Rodney.

Did we not say we were in this together? Did we? Huh?

Yes.

What?

I said yes. Fuck.

Uh-huh. Well, this is part of it now, Kyle.

I didn't—

Shut up. Shut the fuck up. We're in this together. This creep-o killed my mom's cat. Ye've seen the posters same as I have. We all know how many pets are missing. This fucker.

Jacob felt the next bite near the first and equally as painful. He howled, then clenched his teeth together, shaking and moaning. He was in a river of misery, carried from barb to burn, flay to throb.

Hold him.

Wha—

Hold him. Now. David, left. Left.

Jacob was moved farther down the stream, his limbs heavy, useless, his head a stomped-on wasp's nest, his eyes twin holes of empty sky.

What're ye doing?

Rodney.

Jacob bobbed, sucked in air, but choked and sputtered. He fought for air.

Stop it.

Holy shit.

Quit.

Though he strained against it, the stream held Jacob down. He coughed again, clearing something wet and lumpy from his windpipe.

What're ye doing? What's he doing, y'all?

Rodney.

Ye like to steal stuff, huh, thief?

Fuck.

Jacob drifted into cooler water.

Why'd he take his pants off?

Fuck.

Take things that don't belong to ye?

Cold spring water merged with the warmer, slower river.

He just pulled his pecker out. Rodney just pulled that kid's pecker out. What're ye doing, man?

Rodney.

I don't know what that whore mother of yours has taught ye about taking things that don't belong to ye, Hun-ter, but I'm going to leave ye with a little lesson, Hun-ter.

Don't. Don't.

Don't.

Stop.

God.

Hold. Hold him.

Don't do it.

# BIRTH OF A MONSTER

Please, god. Don't.

Jacob would've screamed but the pain was too great.

*Waterfall.*

An empty, vast expanse /

// Unseen currents pulling like spectral hands.

Holy shit.

There. That'll teach ye.

Fu—

A live wire of terrible pain hit him at the same time as the sound of vomit splashing onto the floorboards, then nothing.

Get back here.
    Footfall.
    Kill ye.
    Crying.
    Moaning.
    Nothing.

From the swaying bottom, Jacob came to rest among the smooth stones of the drying riverbed.

## CHAPTER SIX
## WHAT RODNEY TACKETT DONE

**JACOB WAS ON THE HUNT.** The forest warm and breathing right alongside him, a gentle breeze cooling the sweat on his naked body. The full moon filtered down through the treetops in straight shafts of pale white light of various thicknesses.

No, it wasn't *all* light. Jacob could see that some of the shining pillars of light were folded lengths of luminous extension cord. His back, ass, and thighs erupted in remembered welts and fresh goosepimples.

*Hun*-ter.

The soured, pungent musk of an animal's den hung in the air. Jacob followed the smell deeper into the pulsating forest.

Great forked tongues of lightning flashed nearby, followed quickly by a rush of cold, booming thunder and the brisk scent of ozone.

A woman was moaning, hurt or "*working*"—*rusty bed springs, quick, shallow breathing, yes, god, yes*, her voice frustratingly familiar. The live wire jerked, sending a spray of sparks onto Jacob's penis.

Yes. No. God. Jesus. Harder. Oh.

Electric pain.

*Hun*-ter.

The forest shimmered, then settled. Sweat prickled his upper lip, salty and warm. His bare feet sunk into the moist earth, slowly squishing between his toes.

It was hurt; Jacob listened to it whimper, hiccup, then softly moan.

He slowed to a creep, taking each step carefully.

Yes. Yesyesyes. Oh.

The woods were vibrating, greens, blacks, blues, browns, humming with the climax of the hunt: the kill.

It's coming.

He felt his penis stiffen painfully.

I am the desert.

I am the seabed.

It was unlike anything Jacob had ever seen. It had the tufted chest of a mourning dove, the gray furry arms of a squirrel, the black, leathery hands and long, bushy tail of a raccoon, the head of a possum, the eyes of a housecat.

Harder, god. Yes. Fuck me.

*Working.*

Jacob saw its mouth move with the woman's words. He saw that the possum's ears were actually the beaks of two Canadian geese.

I'm coming. Baby, I'm coming.

Fast-Forward X2 Mode.

Electric pain.

Soundless but percussive thunder.

Smashed pawpaw meat.

The stream rushed by overhead, heavy and impending like a looming supercell. It pressed down against every part of his body. It cupped unseen hands over his mouth, his throat, his chest, his throbbing, hurting penis.

Jacob was going to ejaculate glass shards. He knew it in the same way he knew he was going to throw up just before he did when he was sick.

Yes. Oh. Oh, god.

Jacob also realized he didn't want to die, not exactly; no, he only wanted to keep on falling. Forever.

Jacob opened his eyes to blue darkness. The wind, somewhere nearby but shielded from directly hitting him, howled, fluttering some pages. His head hurt. His mouth felt stuffed with thick river mud. He hunched his shoulders to help himself sit up, but a hot, angry pain paralyzed him. He squeezed in breaths between his clenched teeth and tried to figure out where the pain was located; it'd been so blinding all he could focus on was getting through it.

He tucked his chin toward his chest, squinting into the darkness.

*Stomach?* he wondered.

He sucked in his gut, slowly, waiting for the pain to strike. It didn't.

*Please no.*

He squeezed his butt cheeks together. Pinpricks of pain fizzled across his groin, sending ripples of nausea lapping low in his stomach. His eyes adjusted slowly until he could make out the pale, white skin of his exposed stomach, thighs, crotch.

He looked at his dick. Something about it was wrong. It was standing at a straight angle from his nearly hairless body, but it didn't look fat and solid like it did when he had an erection.

Electric pain.

Clouds parted in the night sky outside the hideout, sending revealing moonlight through the windows. Something rounded and metallic glinted in the pale light.

Jacob knew what it was immediately: the bottom end of the 1.00mm screwdriver from the set he stole from Tackett's Jewelry & Watch Repair. It was the only one in the set that didn't have a hexagonal-shaped base.

The folded skin of his penis looked like a deflated scarecrow draped over the screwdriver, strung out in a pale desert seabed.

Jacob blacked out.

Jacob dreamed of a great, gaping hole; bones; teeth; dripping, red hunks of meat; tufts of fur and hair and feather. His mother's voice, disembodied and drifting, laughed, tonelessly, heartlessly from somewhere below him, echoing off some great empty expanse, bouncing off unseen edges until Jacob was sure he was inside it, a part of it. He opened his mouth to laugh, to cry, to scream, and found he was falling.

Jacob knew he should be afraid, and a part of him was, but most of him wanted to hit the ground.

The creaking of the hideout's front door woke him. Jacob opened his crust-coated eyes and watched the thin wooden door slowly swing in, then out, stopping each time with a hollow pop before groaning back into motion and repeating the process over again.

For a moment, Jacob was fine. He watched the door, his mind hazy and empty, a drowsy hive of smoked-out bees, unsure why he was on the floor, why the hideout's front door was open, why he couldn't figure out what was wrong with the entire situation.

Then he moved.

Great leaping currents of pain riptided up from his crotch, sending greasy cold tendrils of nausea radiating up his stomach into his throat. Hot bile, acidic and tear-inducing, filled his mouth. He tried to keep his lips from parting, but the rush was too sudden, too powerful, and he vomited onto himself before he could turn his head away from his body.

Jacob choked and coughed, spitting clinging strings of mucus and puke between his stomach's involuntary heavings.

When he was empty and able to control himself enough to examine the source of the pain, Jacob nearly passed out again. His penis was skewered around the needle-like screwdriver; the folds of his skin inflamed and a particularly angry shade of red. The rounded bottom of the screwdriver shone bright in the morning light. Dried blood along the grooved surface of the handle looked slicker, less dry as it descended into Jacob's body.

*Oh God*, he thought.

His vision sank away. Twirling glints of floaters and black spots swam at the edges of his vision, crushing his sight into a narrow tunnel; he nearly passed out again. All Jacob could see was the screwdriver sunk deep into his pee hole, vignetted and hazy with shock and confusion; all Jacob could muster his mind to produce was one floating question: Does pain have a point of diminishing return?

Jacob very nearly believed the screwdriver was electrically charged; even the briefest of brushes of its metallic base sent currents of alarming pain up from his crotch. He kept his ass planted as firmly in place as he could, every movement of his hips or legs stretched the aggravated skin of his penis, which he could see was in the beginning phases of bruising. Purple and black splotches were blossoming in the puffy folds of red and white.

*Do it*, a voice in his head demanded. *Do it or you're gonna just lay on the floor like some useless wart until you starve to death like Hobart, like Muffy Muffintop, like all those squirrels, rabbits, possums, and raccoons, like those lizards and snakes and spiders, like those baby cardinals. Are you a wart? Are you a cardinal?*

He remembered Darrel Honaker, four or five of his mother's boyfriends back, using the needle nose plyers to pull out two of his teeth. Darrel Honaker was so drunk he pulled the wrong one out before Jacob could stop him. He'd distracted Jacob with some words of advice that came back to Jacob then, "Ye just gotta yank the fucker outta there real quick, like one of those got dam Band-Aids."

Jacob sucked in a slow chestful of air through his clenched teeth, then he positioned his left hand above the bloody 1.00mm screwdriver.

*Do it.*

# BIRTH OF A MONSTER

Jacob pinched the 1.00mm screwdriver between his thumb, index, and middle fingers, seeing the quick blanching of his fingernails with the pressure, then squeezed his eyes shut and flung his arm upward, away from his body.

There was a pressure like the pull of a great tub being suddenly unstopped. Jacob was sure his very being was going to be removed along with the 1.00mm screwdriver. There was a moment where the resistance to his arm's outward motion seemed like it would be too strong for the screwdriver's removal. Jacob's eyes cracked and he thought what he saw could easily be someone making taffy. Then the resistance broke like a rubber band's twanging snap, and everything went black.

-

Jacob's own moans woke him. They were pitiful things, the moans, *his moaning*. Jacob had heard the tone of the sound before. It was the sound of hopeless desperation. It was the fifth hour before starving to death. It was the beaten howl of surrender.

He saw the yellow meat of the pawpaw oozing out from under his foot.

*Get up*, the voice inside his head said.

*You never will if you don't right this instant*, it said without words.

Jacob pushed himself up with his elbows, hurling his heavy head forward without opening his eyes. He thrust himself up onto his knees, then his feet. Only then did he open his eyes. He nearly fell over when he did: the room was swimming and doubling, smeared with tears and whiteish eye-sludge, stuttering to the left then resetting itself several feet to the right without warning.

Jacob steadied himself on the doorjamb, squeezing his eyes shut again and shaking his head, hoping it'd clear.

*Look at it.*

Jacob opened his eyes, the hideout, bright in the light from the afternoon sun, was steady. Not three feet from where he stood with his pants and underwear around his ankles, slightly swaying, Jacob saw the 1.00mm screwdriver, blood-caked and inert. The blood looked nearly black near the grooved handle and rounded bottom.

He remembered the pull and the resistance met, then the break.

*Look at it.*

Jacob kept his eyes on the screwdriver.

*The one-double-oh-m-and-mmm.*

Jacob blinked, swallowed, then looked at his ravaged penis.

*Look at what Rodney Tackett did to you.*

He didn't put on his pants, or underwear, which he saw were now streaked with little clumps and splotches of shit, until he reached the edge of the forest looking down into the little valley and Thompkins' Hilltop Trailer Court. He didn't have to squint hard in the darkening dusk to see the salmon-pink singlewide; the trailer park's lone security light was shining. Though yellowed and dim, it'd be light a-plenty for an eyeful of Jacob's swollen dick and, within the last twenty minutes, his balls, as well.

Jacob had wiped his underwear as best he could along the smooth surface of a birch, but they'd been a lost cause. He tossed them into a myrtle bush near the hideout, knowing he was down to only two pairs of bacon-waisted Fruit of the Looms. Stepping into his too-small pants, Jacob knew he wouldn't have been able to get the underwear on anyway.

*I'll steal some new ones from Walmart*, he thought, trying to distract himself, to little effect.

Jacob was hunched forward, both of his hands squeezed into white-knuckled fists around the waist band of his dirty pants just above his dry, shaky knees.

*Ye just gotta yank the fucker outta there real quick, just like one of those got dam Band-Aids. Just like that. Do it.*

Jacob bent forward, angling *what Rodney Tackett done* directly over the open hole of his pants. He slid the pants slowly, carefully up his pale thighs. He paused for a shuttering moment at his hips, jerking his head to the right and left, looking for any snags the pants might find. Sweat dropped down onto the place where Jacob knew he should've had hair by now, and he feared he'd lose his resolve if sweat stung down onto *what Rodney Tackett done*.

Jacob eased the pants all the way up. He zipped them up very slowly, turning his body so the direct rays of midday sunlight highlighted the process.

*Like that game, Operation*, he thought, again trying to distract himself from the pinpricks of pain: each an electric flash, a constellation of neon blue bolts.

*Does pain have a point of diminishing return?* Jacob wondered, easing the copper-coated button through the hole.

Jacob remembered playing Operation at Aunt Teresa's. He'd been so lost in the careful extraction of a white, plastic slice of bread from the stomach of the pudgy man, that he didn't see or hear his aunt's approach. There'd been dishes in the sink, or crumbs on the counter, or a bagful of trash in the can. Of course, there'd been something, but Jacob couldn't recall what it'd been that time when he was playing the game, Operation.

She'd hit him with the candy-striped extension cord, folded lengthways, twice, then started in with the dressing down.

The game buzzed as the tweezers fell from Jacob's little fingers.

"Eatin' up my food like a little piggy."

*Thwack.*

"Shittin' and pissin' all over the got dam commode."

*Thwack.*

"Ye think all these lights are free? This air conditioning?"

*Thwack-Thwack.*

"Ye think batteries are free?"

*Thwack.*

*Buzz* went the game, Operation's battery-powered board.

Jacob tried to ease himself into standing erect. The constellation all went supernova at once. Jacob nearly fell to his knees. He hunched forward and unbuttoned the pants. He carefully lowered the zipper, ensuring the pull tab was on the outside, resting flatly on the grimy fabric.

*Just hafta hold 'em.*

Jacob took ginger but quick steps out of the forest, across the county road, and into Thompkins' Hilltop Trailer Court, hoping Maggie or Stacie Q, everybody was either inside their trailers, preoccupied, or, better yet, gone out partying at some other trailer park on the other side of the county. The whine of a small engine, Jacob guessed dirt bike or four-wheeler, busted that bubble. He crouched lower and moved with more pace and less precision, making the decision that his feet could withstand more pain than his throbbing crotch could.

*Does pain have a point of diminishing return?*

"Jake!" Maggie whispered from behind him. "Jacob!"

He didn't stop. He took the salmon trailer's three cinderblock steps in three quick bursts, a moan breaking free from his heaving chest and sounding strangled, low in his phlegm-coated throat.

Jacob removed his left hand from his waistband and used it to open the trailer's front door.

"Hey, Jacob!" Maggie called.

In his rush to enter the trailer and with his limited range of motion, *what Rodney Tackett done*, Jacob tripped; the toe of his right miss K-Swiss caught on the lip of the door. He fell forward before he could even lift his hands up, the right side of his face smashing down into the dirty, threadbare carpet.

All of the air was knocked out him.

Lightning strikes of white-hot pain sent Jacob rolling onto his left side, then his back. Floundering for air and relief, he rocked from left to right, his mouth working and working but making only dry lip noises.

His head was filled with alarm bells and the *buzz* from the battery-powered game, Operation's board.

*Buzz.*

A trickle of air entered his lungs, he clawed at his throat and chest. His neck felt filled to bursting with trapped screams and cries and curses.

*God.*

*Fuck.*

*Thwack.*

*Shit.*

*Kill me.*

"Jay'ke? Zat you?" his mother called from the back of the trailer. "Wha' th' *fuck?*"

The air was returning to his lungs, but the pain showed no signs of letting up. Hot blue and white bolts of lightning made Jacob wish his dick and balls would just fall off already. He wished he didn't have them anymore.

Jacob turned his head to the right and vomited onto his mother's feet.

-

"I'm just sick is all." Jacob wiped spit and bile from his sticky chin.

"No shit," she said, snorting twice. "Ye don't say."

His mother tended to speak in exaggerated twang when she drank. "Shit" came out as "She-hit," while "You" became "Ye" and "don't" slurred into "dote."

"I ain't cleanin' this got dam mess up," she said.

Jacob tried to sit up, but the pain in his crotch was too much. He sat rigid and still, holding his breath until the electric bolts receded to a duller, aching rumble.

"Ye really sick, huh?"

He nodded his head, very slightly, very slowly, tears escaping the confines of his raw eyes.

"Got dam it, Jake," she whined. "Ye know we cain't afford no doctor bills right now."

Jacob found he could breathe, a little.

"I'm sorry, Momma," he whispered, easing himself forward, testing movement.

"Well what's wrong with ye?"

His swollen testicles brushed against the bottom of his pants, sending more electric pain flashing up into his penis and lower gut.

"Stomach," Jacob moaned.

"Did ye eat something?"

Jacob shook his head, a slow, careful process, ensuring nothing moved more than was necessary for the gesture.

The pain resided a bit. Jacob took a shaky gulp of air, then noticed his mother's scrutinizing eyes.

"What's really wrong with ye?" she asked, her voice hard.

His mother was closer now, hovering over him with narrowed, bloodshot eyes. The ice in her cup tinkled; the paper towel, folded hotdog-style, once, wrapped around the glass was nearing the point where the cheap pulp paper began to clump and disintegrate. Jacob could not count all the glasses his mother had broken when the paper towel neared or passed this point, even if he used all the toes on his feet along with the ten fingers of his hands. Drops, bumps, tosses, throws, kicks.

"Jacob," she said, her voice low, near to quiet.

He'd tell her. He knew it as sure as he knew she wasn't quite drunk yet, but she would be. She always would be.

*Sure she's your momma*, the bald man had told him, *but she's still a cunt.*

"They hurt me," Jacob said, hating himself and his mother. "They found the hideout, the creations, everything. Then they hurt me, Momma."

The ice tinkled, so Jacob looked up. His mother's face was cloudy, unreadable. She swished a mouthful of bourbon, her cheeks rounding out then deflating. She swallowed.

"What did ye do, Jake?"

Jacob was worried by the tonelessness of his mother's voice. Through the pain, flashing like heat lightning, he felt the goosebumps spread across his arms. He looked up, twin tears spilling over his raw eyelids, and watched his mother take another cheek-puffing drink from the glass. Like an ice floe, Jacob watched the bottom corner of the folded paper towel break away and begin riding the condensation down the sweating glass.

"Don't ye even think 'bout lying to me, boy," she said.

The television was muted but on, Jacob saw when he looked away from his mother. There was a man sitting behind a desk in an ill-fitting suit looking directly into the camera and talking seriously. His hair was parted awkwardly, slightly forward and to the left. His red checkered tie was crooked. The man tried out a smile, abandoned the effort halfway in, then Jacob's mother's glass smashed into the control panel of the television, exploding into a spray of strong-smelling bourbon and shattered glass.

"An Appalachian family living with snakes," the man's calm voice boomed from the television's speakers.

"Got dam it, boy," she screamed. "What the fuck did ye do, Jacob Hunter Goodman?"

*Hun*-ter. Hun*ter*.

"Holiness or insanity?" the man's voice filled with buzzing static as the television's little speakers began to fail. "You decide after this message from our sponsors."

The screen was a flickering blanket of snow. The dull outline of a man behind a desk faded into flashing pixels.

She'd hit him soon, he knew. It didn't matter if he spoke now, lied like a lawyer or told it like it'd been, because the glass was broken. Probably the TV too. The glass was broken, and she wasn't all the way there yet. That's always when it got bad.

He thought about it: *there* is a place and *where*'s a when.

Miss Roe told them to treat some poems—they were talking about free-verse— as if they were mosaics, composed of tiny sharp pieces, or collages, two-dimensional assemblages, he'd looked this word up in the library later on, carefully placed to create something new.

*Poetry is easy / the red tie is crooked / the screen?*
*a blanket of static snow / the hands are now empty*

He shook his head at the wrong word choice.

*unburdened*, Jacob corrected himself, *and ready for to blow*

There was an overly loud clicking noise from behind the television followed closely by a small *hiss*, then the television faded into a quiet darkness.

"They found 'em, Momma," Jacob said into the pulsing quiet of the salmon trailer.

Those words were in there too.

*they found 'em, Momma / tied up or sewn / the carefully crafted experiments showing what's there to display / they found me, Momma, distracted, deaf and dumb*

She was breathing harder.

*Picking up steam.*

The phrases, words became clearer to Jacob as he set them into the inky type in his head, envisioning the line breaks with more ease:

*what strange images come from new focus*
*the hurried man picked a patch of steam*
*a self-contained bushel no larger than a dinner plate*
*tucked it carefully under his arm & waited to disintegrate*
*singing, "what does it feel like to fall forever, Momma?"*

"They found 'em and then they beat me up," Jacob said.

The breath caught in her throat.

"Why?" she hissed. "What did ye do?"

*how many times has she asked that question?*
*I don't have the fingers or the toes*
*lord knows the rose grows crooked in the long, dark land of shadow*

Jacob saw a scarecrow blowing in the headwinds of a thunderstorm.

Lightning pain flared in his groin. Jacob gagged at the sudden rush of nausea it rushed up from his stomach.

His head jerked painfully upwards and his mother's perspiring face loomed into view.

*The moonscape of her face showed neither smile nor snarl.*

He let that sentence have its punctuation, proud of the way it felt flickering around the forked tongue of his mind.

She twisted her fingers tighter around Jacob's hair.

"Tell it."

He felt the roots pop free in several places. One of his mother's chewed on fingernails bit into his sunburned scalp.

"I killed a cat," Jacob said softly.

His head hit the blank television screen. Jacob smelled the bourbon as he registered the cut beginning to bleed on his cheek. Her fingers were gone from his hair. Little flashing floaters danced across the stained carpet.

*the angels flutter across the shattered glass of night*

*twirling bravely on ballerina's legs*
Jacob looked up to see his mother leave the room.

He tried to shower, even though the little shower next to his bedroom had no soap or shampoo or washcloths. His mother had forgotten again.

He'd nearly shit himself from the pain.

When he looked into the bathroom mirror, Jacob saw that he'd blown the blood vessels in his left eyeball. There wasn't a stitch of white left to be seen anywhere there.

"Son of a bitch," he whispered.

*the son of a bitch softly swore*
*taking his mother's name in vain*
*Cut her veins / smash her brains / bring the rains, o' mighty rainmaker /*
*send the reins of pain to shackle on & claim the remains of the blood-dried day*

He pissed a few painful drops of blood-tinged piss. He had to sit down to do it. He shat a hot mess of acid immediately afterwards. When he wiped, there'd been blood there too.

*the boy died to be born an exposed nerve*
*there is no heaven, just the falling forever, just the fall*
*surely you can't fall through the same space twice*
*on the same fall / can you?*

Jacob looked at his unrecognizable dick and knew he needed to see a doctor.

He'd just about fallen asleep when his bedroom door flew inward; the faux brass doorknob implanted itself into the paneling of the wall with a hollow crunch.

"Killed a cat?" his mother screamed. "Why on earth would ye kill a cat?"

The glass exploded against the wall over his head. Bourbon splashed down onto the covers and his third copy of the *Color Atlas of Anatomy*, University of Pikeville Medical School. Jacob scrambled to save the book, both from the pungent bourbon and his raging mother. He crouched over the thin comforter and dabbed at the pages of the open book.

In dismay, Jacob watched the main branches of the internal iliac artery in the male, a schematic drawing but one which Jacob found fascinating and textured, curl up around the edges then blur as the ink began to merge with the bourbon.

Her tiny fist, composed of nothing but skin and bird bone, bounced off the back of Jacob's head, driving his forehead onto the damp pages of the *Color Atlas of Anatomy*.

"What the fuck is wrong with ye?" she screamed, her voice breaking on an extended hold on the "o" in "wrong."

The tears were coming, he knew. He wasn't out of danger yet, there still could be a final bonanza of fury or two before the squall finally broke, but he could see the gray of steady rain not too distant on the horizon.

"I had to, Momma," Jacob said, closing the book.

He shoved the *Color Atlas of Anatomy*, University of Pikeville Medical School, under the covers, then wiped at the stinging in his eyes.

*Stall*, he thought. *It's almost over.*

Jacob watched his mother's droopy face twist into confused agony.

"Why?" she cried. "Why, Jacob?"

*Hun*ter.

"For the experiments," he said, raising his arms toward his head, just in case.

His mother looked *confounded*, another of Mrs. Horace's words: *1: confused, perplexed 2: damned*.

*Both usages*, Jacob thought, *apply*.

His mother moved much faster than Jacob expected. He threw up his arms to shield as much of his face and head as he could, but the blows did not come. Instead, a rush of cooler air flooded over his naked lower half, then an electric current of pain lit up his grotesquely swollen genitals.

His vision swam into murkier waters, nearly dissipating into the deeper darkness of the current.

"Oh my god," his mother said.

*an eddy pool / near to still*

Jacob's penis was bleeding; a thin trickle slowly ran down the inside of his thigh onto the rough bedsheets and tacky plastic bag of the nearly room temperature tater tots, the only frozen food in the freezer. His mother taught him not to use her ice a long time ago, *the fist & the lesson learned*. Jacob became aware that one edge of the Extra Crispy Tato Tots was tucked up into the crack of his ass. Slowly, using his elbows, Jacob slid himself into a semi-sitting position onto the sheets. He hunched forward, doing his best to shield his throbbing privates from his mother.

*a reflection pond / shimmering shame*

"Oh my god," she said again.

*a prayer / a refrain*

Jacob watched his mother's face change from pitying disgust to spiteful exasperation. He followed the path her eyes took, down from the discolored blooming of his crotch to his hairless, white ankles, and saw that the *Color Atlas of Anatomy*, University of Pikeville Medical School, had been flipped open.

He cringed, snapping his eyes closed; he knew the page.

## Female External Genital Organs

*External genital organs in the female (anterior aspect). Labia reflected.*

*Female external genital organs in relation to internal genital organs and urinary system (isolated, anterior aspect).*

Jacob flinched at the force of his mother's laughter.

*mother's laughter / mother slaughter*
*power of syntax / the taxing power of sin*

"I shoulda named ye John, boy," she spat. "One in a lo-*o*-ong line of 'em."

*her laugh / broken glass*
*interrupting / the quiet night*

Jacob counted all long pauses as stanza breaks.

*confounded / like mother like son*

He opened his eyes, leaned forward to grab the book, the *Color Atlas of Anatomy*, University of Pikeville Medical School, but the bright electric pain immediately stilled him.

"I would be blessed with a got dam J-ohn," her laugh was derisive, Mrs. Horace's Word of the Day, and her slurred pronunciation of "John" included several *s*'s before ending on a pouty "n" "uh."

She reached for the book, a white woman's vagina opened like a beaconing angel, and Jacob could do nothing to stop her; the pain was leeching up into his stomach again and he feared he might shit himself if it got much worse.

*external genital organs in the female (anterior aspect)*
*the angel in supplication / the drowning woman waved*

Jacob watched his mother raise the book for a closer inspection. "F'ck kind of porno's this?"

*the current pulls / it all can't help but go downhill*
*More Whores Volume Ten / Fast-Forward X2 Mode*

Jacob couldn't remember if Rodney Tackett and the others, *who all had been there?*, had left the wall alone. The hulking outline beginning to take shape; *definition: 3b(1): clarity of visual presentation : distinctness of outline or detail*.

He couldn't quite put it together, but it was getting close.

*clarity through experimentation / clouds on display*
*repulsion pulsing through some woman's glassy-eyed stare*

"Another f'ckin' John," she said, "always havin' ta buy what ye don't even un'erstan'."

She let the book plop onto the thin carpet. Jacob thought the floors sounded even thinner in the salmon trailer than the baby blue one the social worker made them leave up a windy dirt path in Dorton.

"Or want, even," she said, hiccupping to a stop. "John's don't even really want it. Nope. Y'all don'."

Jacob watched his mother, dark purple bags sagging under her bloodshot eyes, lines gaining definition along the smile lines of her cheeks, shake her head like a child.

*left to right / left to right*
*shake years like dandruff*

"Payin' for power is all," she said, her shake effortlessly becoming a nod.

*the same sloppy enthusiasm / a beckoning angel*
*anterior aspect / labia reflected*
*Sure she's your momma / but she's still a cunt.*
*the grinning saint / shining baldness*

"So's you's kin say you *fucked* her," his mother screamed. "Fucked her! Fucked her! Fucked her! Fucked *me*! Fuck you too!"

Jacob barely covered his face in time. His mother's open right hand glanced off his right forearm and smashed into Jacob's left ear. The loudness of the blow was nearly as electric as the pain in his crotch from the motion it'd caused. She punched him again, but he was mostly covered up, and he felt his right upper arm take the brunt of the blow.

*a lessening fury*

Jacob kept his himself huddled forward, tucked over his exposed penis and testicles, his eyes shut in expectation of at least one more punch, maybe even a half-hearted kick or two.

"Why the cat?" she asked, startling him.

"Which one?" he asked before he could stop himself.

He cringed at his haste, *rash or headlong action*, Mrs. Horace, and sent more electric sparks spilling out of his genital region. Stars danced in the narrowing confines of his vision.

"Why?" she asked.

"I needed it for the experiments," he said.

*/ showing what's there to display*

"Fuck," she hissed.

She burped, a wet fizzing sound, lower in her throat.

"Shit," she said.

Jacob watched his mother swallow back a mouthful of vomit.

*/ violence is thirsty work*

Tears streamed from her closed eyes. She held one finger up in Jacob's general direction, as if directing him to pause while she gathered herself. Her other hand was clasped around her chin, her palm acting as a seal over her smeared lips. She almost staved it off.

Jacob watched the puke mist through his mother's tight lips and

# BIRTH OF A MONSTER

fingers down onto the floor. She swung her body away from the bed, puke arcing along with her. For the second time in the same night, Jacob sat in agonizing pain and watched his mother desert him.

*desert / pain*
*electric / seabed*

# CHAPTER SEVEN
## IT ALL CAN'T HELP BUT GO DOWNHILL
## (THREE WAYS TO SUNDAY)

**HE STOOD OUTSIDE HIS MOTHER'S** door for some time, wanting desperately to knock and for her to be sober enough, and willing, to take him to the hospital. Jacob raised his left hand to knock at least a dozen times but couldn't do it. He knew she was passed out by now. Oblivious to any but the most extreme of wake-up calls. He could smell the vomit and bourbon from behind the closed door, but he wasn't sure if it was tonight's or last night's or the night before that's.

Jacob slowly made his way back down the hall to the bathroom, pulling the door closed behind him, just in case the bald man showed up. He opened the mirror quickly, avoiding his reflection, found the acetaminophen and took four of the gel caps, cupping his hand under the sink for water to wash them down with.

He knew he should feel weird about walking around naked from the waist down, but any look at what he had going on downstairs showed exactly why he was uncovered.

He kept looking at his penis and testicles, hoping against hope with each glance they'd returned to their pre-screwdriver insertion size and condition.

*They look fake*, Jacob thought. *Horror-scene props.*

He couldn't help it; Jacob cried.

-

When he could stop crying, Jacob resolved to ask Randall Adkins to take him to the hospital, on the off-chance he should stop by the pink trailer. He cracked the window of his bedroom to air out the smell of bourbon and puke, then eased himself onto the dry half of his bed.

He looked down at his uncovered penis, enshrouded in extra folds of shadows in the light from the desk lamp on his nightstand, and remembered the student doctors in the cadaver lab taking turns trying on the hand-skin of the dead man. Jacob thought his dick could be that of some pathetic radiation monster.

107

*zombie dick only wants relief*

Jacob, despite the never-ending flashes of pain, felt immensely tired. His eyelids began to slide lower and lower and, before he could even think to turn off the desk lamp, he was asleep.

-

His mother's loud vomiting woke him. Jacob found her slung over the toilet, her right breast fully exposed. Her eyes were squeezed shut, her mouth hanging open and shaking in fits of little tremors, so Jacob stared at the breast.

*round & bronzed like a pressed penny*
*dark around the edges / wear 'n' tear*

White-hot, electric pain erupted in his groin. He moaned and lurched forward, steadying himself with his hands digging into the skin around his knees.

"What the fuck?" his mother whined. "Oh my god."

Jacob stared at the shit-stains dotting the toilet like a rash. His mother's hands were wrapped around the lip of the commode, thick veins bulging from her neck as she gurgled up bubbly spit and stomach acid.

Jacob was dripping blood from his penis onto the bathroom rug. He unspooled several handfuls of toilet paper from the roll as his mother groaned and retched. He cleaned himself up as gingerly as he could, pausing frequently to make sure his mother wasn't watching.

"What happened to your li'l pecker?" she asked, wiping her mouth with the outside of her left hand.

Jacob could see smudges of shit on her palms and fingers.

"Oh," she said. "Oh."

Jacob watched her piece it together.

*the quilted memory / shreds of time sutured into place*

"A cat," she said. "Ye got beat up because ye killed a cat."

A collage of cat deaths shone in Jacob's frazzled mind like early morning light through stained glass.

*witch cat / which cat / which one / served me best*
*mine / own / prey*

Jacob couldn't remember why his head was filled with word associations.

*Was I working on a poetry assignment?*
*a sign? / assign / assassinate*
*asses and breasts bouncing on a pixelated screen / Fast-Forward X2 Mode*

Jacob's ears felt hot: two burning irons squeezing his head inwards.

*Strange*, he thought. *I don't ever remember feeling like my ears were hot.*

"Ye sick little freak," his mother whispered. "Why'd ye kill their cat? What did ye do to it?"

She was crying. He watched her, wishing he could make himself feel bad about the sight.

"Ye didn't . . ." She couldn't hold his eyes. She saw the toilet seat and cringed.

"Fuck," she said, stepping over to the sink and turning on the hot water.

Jacob watched his mother wash her hands, over her shoulder, in the toothpaste and pimple-stained mirror. He could tell she knew he was watching her. He could also tell she was avoiding his eyes. She was pale and sweaty; Jacob could smell the bourbon slowly coming out of her pores.

"Did ye fuck a cat?" she said.

She turned off the water, grabbed the crusty towel and dried her hands, still avoiding his eyes.

"No, Momma," Jacob said.

"Well, that's good news," she said, "boy."

"Yes, Momma," Jacob said.

"Why'd they . . ." she searched all over the room for the words, including a probing few moments in the direction of his naked genitals, "hurt ye . . . down there?"

"I'm not sure, Momma."

*I bet he fucked it / a standout from the choir*
*a hand in the refrain / refrain from mishandling the refrain*

"Don't lie to me, boy."

Her eyes found his, held them.

"Why'd they hurt ye down there?"

*what Rodney Tackett done*

"They didn't understand," he said.

                    */ nobody does*

"What's there to understand?"

*Show / what's there to display*

"Life," Jacob whispered.

*Death.*

Again, she fled. This time, Jacob followed her.

"Momma," he called, moving with as little motion as was

possible. "Momma, wait. I need to go to the doctor. Momma."

"Get away from me," she yelled. "Yer a freak."

Jacob cringed, hearing the same name hurled at him from voices other than his mother's.

*Freak. Weirdo.*

He rounded the corner of the hallway into the living room, doing his best to walk slowly and cover himself as best he could. Jacob looked down. The swelling was making this a nearly impossible job.

She was in the kitchen, arms and head in the stained yellow interior of the freezer, rooting out ice cubes for her first drink of the day. The television set was dark, a rare thing, but Jacob could just make out the top half of one of the bald man's VHS tapes beside the Goodwill VCR.

*Jungle Booty 10 / Fast-Forward X2 Mode*

Jacob looked away, shuffling across the cluttered carpet, empty beer cans and bottles and cigarette butts scattered anywhere and everywhere.

"Momma," Jacob called, cringing again, this time at the tone of his voice. "Can ye take me to the doctor? Please? It hurts."

And it did. It hurt so much he couldn't force his voice to sound manly and controlled. With the continuous lightning flashes of pain, Jacob couldn't feel embarrassed about being half-naked in front of his mother. It hurt so bad he thought he might scream.

"Good," she said, slamming the freezer door shut. "It should hurt. It should hurt. I hope it does. It serves ye right. Killing a cat. What the fuck is wrong with ye?"

"Momma," his voice broke as he stepped onto the dirty linoleum. "Please. It hurts. So bad."

She didn't look at him. She unscrewed the plastic cap; Jacob saw that it was "fresh," what his mother called all unopened bottles, with the shiny black crow staring at Jacob from across the small kitchen with beady, watchful eyes.

Jacob watched his mother steal a sideways glance over her shoulder at him, naked below the waist, standing just inside the doorway, then take a cheek-filling mouthful straight from the bottle. It was a long, slow drink.

*the crow sees / a single, unblinking eye*

The mostly green tie-dyed Grateful Dead shirt his mother wore was as thin as cotton could get before it transitioned back into raw material or became a shroud.

He watched her throat move as she swallowed. Christy Good-man, her eyes squeezed shut, poured several ounces onto the counter beside her sweating glass.

"Shit," she hissed, snapping her eyes wide and redirecting her aim.

The pain was beginning to burn blue. His weight felt tripled with the charged electricity of it; he shifted his weight continuously from the balls of his feet to his toes, from his left foot to his right.

His mother finished pouring her drink, returned the cap carefully to the bottle, then sipped.

Jacob could just make out the outline of the same nipple he saw earlier.

*strange / how many days you can squeeze into a handful of hours*

"Momma," he said, before he even knew he was going to speak. "Please, Momma. It hurts, Momma."

*Momma. Please. Please, Momma.*

The kitchen was spinning, but not completely.

*It was a jerky thing,* Jacob thought, *what the room's doing.*

*Acts like it's gonna spin smoothly on leftwards and upwards like a ball on a string, then* ERK *it stops abruptly and restarts at the same low spot, but shifted over a few degrees.*

*ghost dance rituals / with each pass the specter expected less*

*& shifted along the spectrum / electric blue*

*pain pain / & more pain*

"Sounds like ye got what ye deserved, boy," Christy Goodman told her son.

Jacob thought he hadn't heard her, then it hit him right alongside another electric shot of a blue so hot it was nearly blindingly white.

"Momma," Jacob moaned through his aching, grinding teeth. "Please."

"This'll teach ye," she said, swinging her hips so she could lean back against the countertop, "to play around with dead things. To not have any friends. For going outta yer got dam way to fuck up my life! Over and over again! Three ways to Sunday and beyond, Christ!"

He watched three mirrored images of his mother take long pulls from their glasses, which now had the customary hotdog-folded paper towels wrapped around them.

*When did she do that?*

He missed it somehow.

Jacob forced himself to blink several times, keeping his eyes closed a little longer each time.

His stomach was roiling, though there wasn't a thing in there left to disgorge.

Expulsion, Mrs. Horace, *the act of expelling: the state of being expelled.*

"I ain't ruinin' what I got left of my credit cos yer a fuckin' freak!"

She'd started the sentence off with a low, quiet voice, something between a whisper and a warning, but ended it in a hoarse screech.

"Fuck!"

Jacob slowly learned forward, resting his hands on his knees. He wasn't sure if he'd leaked shit during the last lightning strike of pain, or if the sweat, that he now noticed coated his entire body, had begun pouring down the crack of his ass. He craned his head upward and watched his mother take another closed-eyed drink.

*freak / fuck / fuckin' freak / fuck you / freak*

*White pain now,* Jacob realized, right before he hit the floor, retching.

"For fuck's sake," his mother's startled voice bounced around, echoing like thunder chasing every strike in the storm.

Jacob couldn't see right. The kitchen was gone. All he saw was light and the spaces where the light was.

Flashes so bright, Jacob was sure he was being electrocuted in Old Sparky, the electric chair he saw on the social science field trip to the Kentucky State Penitentiary in Eddyville.

He tried to call out for his mother. He didn't think she'd help him, but he didn't know who else to call out to.

"M-mmm," Jacob moaned.

"I ain't fuckin' cleanin' this shit up," she said, snapping each word off the same way she did those gas station jerky-sticks she loved so much. "Fuck!"

Jacob drifted back into the current, the white-hot background fizzling into the afterimages of the kitchen in the pink trailer.

*thompkins' hilltop trailer court / salmon pink don't blink*
*don't think / just fall. forever.*

Jacob felt the restraints around his wrists and ankles. His head felt hollowed out, liable to float off into dust at the slightest burst of air, held in place only by the straps affixing him to Old Sparky.

*the current quickens / the night comes*

"Sit up," she demanded, "got dam it, sit up."

The straps were gone but a new weight had settled around his frail bird bones.

*heavier than sin / heavier than life*
*death, freak / this is death*

Jacob felt every bit of his being being strangled, suffocated slowly but steadily.

The swirling eye of the hole, the belching maw on the mountain the bald man had shown him, blossomed with a darkness eclipsing all traces of light.

*has there ever been / a light?*

His mother's face was suddenly before him.

"Here," she said, her eyes not on his but a bit lower, "open up. Open. There."

Something was in his mouth. He tried to get his tongue to explore, but his mother poured cool liquid into the back of his throat, nearly choking him. Jacob began swallowing, reflex, until whatever she'd put in his mouth had several more swallows of what Jacob could now taste as flat Diet Mountain Dew on top of it.

"That'll help with the pain," Christy Goodman told her son, not without some warmth, "and the swelling."

Her eyes found his. She did not smile.

Darkness spread across the narrowing confines of his mother's face.

*the current pulls / it all can't help but go downhill*

-

"Wake up, Jake. Take this."

Slight shifts in the ever-changing current jostled Jacob but did not interrupt his journey downstream.

"Shit."

*She-it.*
*It hurts so bad.*

-

*Here's another, Jake.*
*Another.*

-

*Nigh'c'p, Jake?*

-

Jacob opened his eyes, saw the vaguely familiar outlines of the water-stained ceiling and wondered how, and when, he'd gotten back to his bed. The steady light on the small black specks of mold beginning to show showed Jacob it was late in the morning.

*Probably on towards afternoon*, he saw.

Jacob balled his sweaty hands into fists and used the middle knuckle of each of his index fingers to break off clots of crust and goo from his eyelashes.

He blinked, then rubbed some more.

Jacob tried to sit up but yelped and froze instead.

*Oh god!* his mind screamed. *Lightning just struck my dick!*

He expected charred remains but was even more *dismayed*, Mrs. Horace, at what his eyes saw.

Purpled veins and angry red lines. The skin stretched tight around curdled-looking flesh. Several lumps, the size of grapes, around the base of his unrecognizable penis. His testicles were angry hornets' nests, billowing lines of creased, inflated agony.

*pain pain & more pain*

He saw a gooey line stringing from the head of his penis down a yellowed-white streak to his pale thigh, where it was tinged with red.

"Holy shit," the bald man said.

He was standing just inside the open bedroom door, Jacob's mother peeking around his bare, tattooed left arm.

"You dumb, stupid bitch," Randall Adkins said, turning to Christy Goodman. "The kid don't need no *Roxi*codone. He needs some got dam *penny*-seal-in."

Jacob watched the bald man slap his mother with the outside of his huge right hand. It sounded like meat hitting countertop.

An oval confusion bloomed across her face.

*Does the truth always shock / & confuse?*

*Sure she's momma but she's still a cunt.*

"Got dam it, Randall, I got a date tonight."

"Ye dumb bitch," the bald man yelled, much louder now. "Ye think I don't know that. Ye honestly think I don't know when yer workin'? When yer workin' for me. Ye think I don't know?"

Randall Adkins knocked Christy Goodman to the hallway floor, kicking her low in the stomach before she curled herself into a quaking ball.

"Now the social workers are gonna come pokin' 'round," the bald man yelled, driving the right steel toe of his shitkicker into the exposed flesh of her thigh. "And the boy's dick is fucked three ways to Sunday."

He reached down and took a handful of her hair between the

heavy knuckles of his left hand, lifting her head awkwardly.

"Ye dumb bitch," Randall Adkins said.

Jacob watched the bald man spit directly into his mother's open-mouthed face of despair. Then he watched him punch her into unconsciousness.

It took six swings.

Jacob let his head fall back onto the pillow.

The water stains, though familiar, were of no comfort.

*pain pain / & more pain*

Jacob closed his eyes and didn't have to wait long for the current to take him. His mother's wet snoring sounded like a paddle gingerly breaking the surface of a river with no end.

-

*the current beckons / the current pulls*
*the darkness is enfolding / something beyond cold*

-

A loud banging woke him, just not fully.

*an eddy pool / near to still*

He heard muffled voices, motion. The sound of something glass breaking, then something wooden snapping.

"Quit!" a panicked male voice yelled. "Stop!"

Jacob's eyelids were too heavy to hold back; they slid closed.

"No! I told ye," the man's voice was scared, pleading. "God! I cain't!"

*voices fade off the gently rocking waves*

"She don't have to be awake, you fuckin' pussy!"

-

*Crying's bad enough*, Jacob thought, *but the shame that comes with it is worse.*

Still, Jacob wanted to cry. He woke early in the morning, the sun warming the horizon, slowly draining the deepness of the blue but not yet cresting the eastern ridge, with a pain he'd never thought possible. Jacob opened his eyes expecting to see some great monster leeching the life from his body. He expected to see he was cut in half at the waist.

Jacob reached over, clicked on the desk lamp on his nightstand, and saw that his penis was even more swollen; he hadn't thought it possible it could stretch the bruised, aggravated skin any further. His testicles, also larger, were lined with red, angry troughs. Jacob, with a sinking feeling in the pit of his stomach, saw that the unmissable red lines on his testicles were popping up around the base of his penis as well as both of his upper thighs.

*Infection.*

The word felt like an infection in Jacob's head, arriving uninvited and immediately overstaying its welcome, and promising the worst was yet to come.

*Does pain have a point of diminishing return?*

Though he doubted it, Jacob hoped so, feeling the sting of tears in both eyes. He forced himself to sit up and not cry. The motion sent more ripples of pain up from his groin; Jacob closed his eyes and focused on breathing slowly and steadily until it receded.

He opened his eyes and saw that his bedroom door was still open.

He listened; the trailer was quiet.

A coal truck rumbled by on the county road outside.

He wanted to call out to his mother.

*What if she doesn't answer? What if she can't?*

Jacob wasn't sure how he felt about that. He chose to ignore the questions, not call out into the quiet morning, and, instead, to gingerly get out of his bed and onto his feet.

*I need to shower. It's going to hurt, but I need to clean . . . this.*

Jacob watched his penis slowly, painfully swing from left to right.

He couldn't remember if there was any hydrogen peroxide in the pink trailer or not. He did see a clear bottle marked rubbing alcohol, but Jacob didn't think he'd be able to stomach putting rubbing alcohol on his penis or balls. He feared he'd black out again.

For a paralyzing moment, Jacob thought he might cry despite his best efforts not to.

*Start with Tylenol and a shower*, he told himself. *Cleaning it may be enough.*

He shuffled his feet in stretches of six inches, not daring to spread his legs any further. Already the skin of his upper thighs was pulled tight, like bunched underwear two sizes too small, and felt much warmer than usual.

In the hall, Jacob paused to listen: the trailer was quiet.

*not a creature was stirring / not even a mouse*

Jacob had mousetraps, Ace Hardware, all along the perimeter of the hideout. Most of the mice were killed instantly or died slowly from their injuries before Jacob found them, but sometimes there'd be a live one, only wounded and caught. He thought about one such mouse he'd picked apart like petals from a daisy then slowly squished its head with a hand vice, Ace Hardware, positioning his left ear as close as he could, the sounds sending waves of goosebumps across his arms and neck.

He closed the door of the bathroom quietly, then tried to turn the cheap plastic lock on the worn doorknob, but it was broken. He looked around the cramped bathroom, saw the cheap carpeted mat, and wedged it between the bottom of the door and the floor. It wouldn't stop anybody from entering the bathroom of the pink trailer, but it would make it more difficult.

Jacob started the shower, then stood at the sink looking down at his injuries. The two exposed bulbs above the mirror were the brightest in the house. He carefully lifted his penis until he could see his pee hole.

*a canyon cleaved & left unclean / carved of my flesh, purpling in decay*

A cloudy substance was slowly dribbling out of his penis. Jacob sent the signal to his bowel muscles to clench, but the leak continued, his pain flaring from a dull ache to a staticky cluster of electric blue.

His head thumped at his temples with the rapid beating of his heart.

*God please be the infection,* Jacob thought, catching a bit of the fluid with his left pointer finger, *and not my dissolved insides.* He eased his penis back down and studied the sticky drainage under the bathroom lights. He smelled it and cringed, wiped his finger on the outside of his stiff t-shirt.

*That is not a good smell,* Jacob thought, taking his shirt off and tossing it on the floor.

Jacob stepped into the shower and turned his back to the uneven stream of hot water. He reached up and directed the showerhead at the wall, then turned around carefully, ensuring his dick didn't brush up against the floral-printed shower curtain or catch any splashed water.

*This is gonna hurt.*

Jacob moved the showerhead until he could direct his face into the steaming stream. The water broke crust from his eyelids. He felt them tickle free then get carried off his chin. He felt grime dislodge from his left arm and when Jacob opened his eyes and looked down at his feet, the dingy white of the tub was now mostly brown and dirty gray.

*filthy or pure / i'm a sore, an infection laid bare*

Jacob used his hands to wipe clean his neck, shoulder, arms, chest, then stomach. He stood, shaking in the anticipated pain, the water splashing off his chest onto his penis.

*Do it. Do it.*

Jacob eased one hand around the base of his penis, taking hold of the showerhead with the other.

He sucked a breath in through clenched teeth, feeling every muscle of his body go rigid and alert.

Jacob lowered the shower head, directing the hot water directly onto his penis.

A bright flash of electric white blinded him, feeling like the percussive sucker punch of a soundless sonic boom.

Jacob heard himself squealing from somewhere in an electrical storm of lashing pain. He thrust himself forward, out of the water's stream.

His penis was an unappealing red sausage, overfilled and well-past ripe. A burning yellow fluid, thicker than what had been leaking from it a few moments ago was roping out of his pee hole.

*Oh god.*

Jacob was shaking, sweating in the hot shower but covered in goosebumps, his scuzzy teeth rattling together like a jerky, dying engine, his jaw screaming out for the immediate release of the constant tension.

He felt like he had to piss but, when he tried, hot streaks of pain flashed and no urine flowed. He held his penis with his right hand, the fingernails of his left hand digging into his right forearm.

*fruitless diversion / pain, pain, & more pain*

It felt like something was lodged inside. Jacob squeezed a little higher and, with lashing bolts of whitish-blue pain, felt it move farther along his piss-canal before becoming lodged again.

His breath whistled through his clenched teeth.

*It feels as big as a marble!* Jacob thought. *What is it? A ball of pus? The tip of the 1.00mm screwdriver?*

*Tackett's Jewelry & Watch Repair*

*what Rodney Tackett done*

*Rodney / Tackett*

Jacob pinched his penis between his fingers and slid slowly, painfully forward, dislodging a bloody clot that clinked off the rim of the tub down into the wet filth, spiraling toward the hairy drain. He wasn't sure it was the tip of the 1.00mm screwdriver he'd stolen from Tackett's Jewelry & Watch Repair until it came to a momentary pause on the edge of the rust-flecked drain.

*four paths terminating at a single point*
*a set of crosshairs or the head of a crosshead screw*
*screwed either way / three ways to Sunday*

Jacob let out a rush of held breath and accidentally farted. The sudden rush of air through his wet butt-cheeks amplified the sound and gave it a wetter note than it warranted.

Jacob felt his body quake. He wasn't sure what was happening— *Am I gonna throw up? Shit the shower?*—until the sound of his laugh began echoing around the small bathroom with tinned reverb.

The motion was enough to nudge the bloody tip of the 1.00mm screwdriver, Tackett's Jewelry & Watch Repair, down into the drain with a muted *clink*.

Jacob sat on the closed lid of the toilet, a cotton ball coated with rubbing alcohol in his left hand, his pecker in his right.

*Do it*, he told himself for what must've been the hundredth time. *Do it, got dam it. Do it, you pussy. Do it, faggot. Do it, boy. Do it, now.*

His shoulders were shaking with tired tension.

*Do it.*

The slit of his pee hole, normally something that could be missed if you weren't looking for it, was now an angry, bulbous divide; the shot of a volcanic valley blossoming into molten lava.

The liquid had trickled out, along with some clotted blood, for a few minutes after the 1.00mm screwdriver's tip went down the drain, then stopped, leaving the burning need to urinate in its place.

Jacob felt exhausted.

*And the sun's not even up yet.*

His testicles looked less swollen, but the red lines were still there and very much visible.

*Look at what Rodney Tackett done*, Jacob told himself, resting his naked back against the porcelain chamber of the toilet. *Look at what Rodney Tackett done and clean yourself up so you can get rid of this infection, so you can* get him back. *Yes. Make him pay for* this.

Jacob rested his penis on the cold plastic toilet seat, spreading his legs until he was straddling the seat more than sitting on it.

His breathing was rapid. He sucked in five quick wisps of breaths, then pressed the alcohol-soaked cotton ball onto his pee hole.

Hot, blinding pain.

A thick pulse of blood and a snot-like jelly shot out from under the cotton ball onto the toilet seat. It quivered to a rest but something was wrong with the room; it slanted off to the left, almost imperceptibly at first, but picking up speed until everything was an impressionistic painting of the pink trailer's bathroom.

*painpainandmorepain / painpainpainpainpain //*

-

Jacob woke up, a stained pair of his mother's satin panties partially covering his left eye. He pushed himself up onto his elbows, pulled the panties, which had a musty, mushroom-like odor about them, off his face and yawned.

He was still naked. His penis, though tipped with blood and something vaguely yellowish, wasn't as swollen as it had been.

*Holy shit!*

Jacob sat up, gingerly took his bruised penis into his left hand, and examined it for a long time.

*It's getting better*, he finally decided. *Thank God, it's getting better.*

His testicles were still lined but the redness had definitely lost its brightness. They weren't as swollen as they'd been earlier either.

Jacob knew he was smiling, but he couldn't help it. He was such a happy boy sometimes.

## CHAPTER EIGHT
## FREE DRINKS AT PISS BAY
## (DIE, HALLELUJAH)

**HE SAT DOWN TO PISS.** He knew if anything else was left inside were to dislodge, he'd pass right the fuck out again. Jacob rocked back and forth in fraught little jerks, each of his shaking hands gripping a kneecap with as much force as he dared.

"Okay, okay, okayokayokay," he whispered, rocking faster as the pressure of his full bladder intensified.

*It's going to be fine*, he told himself. *Just go ahead and piss.*
*like the little girl you are //*

He clenched his eyes shut and let go.

Nothing happened at first. Then, out of the cloudy but non-threatening sky: a thick bolt of blue lightning punctuated by a sudden splash. The flare of pain faded, and Jacob found he could piss more freely, though not completely free, as there was the rumbling of more pain rising every time he tried to open his flow.

It was the longest piss of Jacob's life.

Floaters danced in his eyes for some time before Jacob realized he was holding his breath.

*Idiot.*

He released the air in his lungs, refilled them, again and again, forcing himself to slow the process with each renewal.

He finished pissing, gently shook a few clinging droplets of urine from his dickhead, then stood up. He examined the contents of the toilet.

*blood swirls / crimson tornados*
*hurricanes of decay / free drinks at piss bay*

He was smiling again, holding his penis in his left hand, his right cupping both of his sore testicles, jostling them back and forth gently. He flushed the toilet with his right hand, then returned it to his ball sack.

He walked out of the shower naked, not bothering or caring if his mother saw him.

*sure she's your momma / but she's still a cunt*

# BIRTH OF A MONSTER

There were moments when Jacob could forget about his physical pain. He opened his bedroom window and stared out at the happenings of Thompkins' Hilltop Trailer Court. The next-door neighbor, a haggard coal mine foreman who appeared to only come home to bathe and sleep, had a gigantic Ford pickup truck backed up to Jacob's bedroom window, but the truck's front and back windshields weren't tinted very dark and Jacob could see through them just fine.

Stacie Q smoked half a joint sitting spread-legged on the cinderblock steps of her faded baby blue single-wide, then carefully extinguished the tip, slipped it into a pocket of her denim shorts, and walked out of Jacob's view toward the county road.

Mitch Huff's purple and rust Pontiac LeMans fired up, after three tries, but did not leave the park. Jacob couldn't tell who was behind the wheel, the miner's rearview mirror was in the way.

A wild-eyed, shirtless man on a bicycle made two circuitous rounds of the park, a black trash bag thrown over his shoulder. Jacob watched him go through the few trash cans in the park—"Most everybody uses the corner store's dumpster on Tuesday evening. Wednesdays are trash days."—Dave Gimar, park supervisor, told them on the day they moved in.

*hillbilly santa's on a borrowed bike / picking empties out of trash cans at the trailer park*

Jacob's penis was beginning to ache, a deep throbbing that slowly expanded with the steady pumping of blood. He grabbed it with both his hands and squeezed, the pressure both electric pain and a pleasure that was sickly sweet. He squeezed until he couldn't take any more of the pain, then relaxed his grip until the ache returned. Then he squeezed again.

Jacob didn't realize how much time had passed or how long it'd been since he'd last eaten until the rumbling of his empty stomach grew too loud to ignore. He let go of his penis, then got out of bed.

He was halfway down the hall on the way to the kitchen to see what he could find there when he realized he still hadn't seen or heard hide nor tail of his mother. He stopped his awkward shuffle halfway through the living room and listened.

Another coal truck barreled by the trailer park outside. A lawnmower was misfiring somewhere near.

But the pink trailer was quiet.

His head felt fuzzy. His stomach roiled with cold, greasy waves.

*When did the bald man beat her up? It's all blurred together.*

Jacob tried to focus but couldn't. His thoughts bounced and skipped across the frozen surface of his mind, impervious and echoing.

*god i cain't / quit*
*she don't have to be awake / you fuckin' pussy*

"Ye fuckin' pussy," Jacob whispered, catching the wisp of a memory like a familiar scent in the wind.

Six swings. The blue-ink of tattoos stretched over working arms. The sound of heavy knuckles on thin skin.

"Momma?" Jacob called, his voice hoarse and high.

*the crinkling of autumn leaves / leaving and cleaving are ways of being free*

"Momma, where are ye?" he called again, forcing his voice into more surety in a lower register.

Stacie Q started coughing outside the pink trailer. The walls were so thin, Jacob could hear her wheeze "holy shit, that got me" in a tiny, gasping voice between sputtering coughing fits.

Jacob crossed the living room, heading for his mother's bedroom, but stopped at the TV. He looked over the stand at the small stack of the bald man's VHS tapes, then back at the television. The screen didn't look broken, so Jacob tried the power button. There was a buzzing, something flickered low and off-center on the screen, then it hissed into silence and stillness.

*Fucked,* Jacob thought. *Stupid cunt broke another TV.*

"Momma!" Jacob yelled.

He had both his hands on his penis, squeezing, trying to stave off the building pressure, abuzz with increasing lightning strikes, as he shuffled toward the pink trailer's master bedroom.

"TV's broken!"

Her door wasn't closed, but it wasn't quite open neither. Jacob could see only a few feet into the shadowy bedroom: three empty beer cans on a carpet almost completely covered by laundry.

"Momma," Jacob yelled, "ye broke the TV again."

He paused at the door, let go of his aching penis after another firm squeezing, then used his right hand to push the door inward and his left to rap his knuckles on the cheap pressed-wood three times.

"Momma!" he yelled, pushing the door with increasing force as it encountered what Jacob assumed was more clothing on the floor. "Jesus!"

123

# BIRTH OF A MONSTER

The door opened only about halfway before stopping and refusing to budge, which pissed Jacob off. He barely contained his first impulse, which was to rage on the door, fling both his fists and elbows and knees and feet at the door until it splintered. His vision went so far as to give him a snarling glimpse of himself sinking his teeth into the cheap wood in blind fury. His throbbing penis and testicles prevented this.

"Mom-*ma*!" he screamed.

Jacob stepped into the darkness of the pink trailer's master bedroom furious, his chest heaving trying to contain it all, his eyes peeled into slits trying to adjust to the gloom of the room.

"Wake up!"

Jacob squinted at the bed but could make out only indefinite lumps, folds, and shadow. He huffed, slowly spun around, then flipped up the light switch.

"Momma!" he said, squeezing his penis again. "Ye need to wake up!"

The room was a wreck, even by Christy Goodman standards. The dresser was upended, perched at an awkward angle by a partially open and broken drawer, spilling multi-colored t-shirts onto the floor. He shuffled over to the bed, his eyes on the nightstand, drawn to a strange leather case sitting partially unzipped but closed. There was a small white cross on its cover.

"Momma!"

Jacob unzipped the case, then opened it. Inside he found a white pocket Bible, four thin hypodermic needles, three small plastic baggies, two lighters, two Dollar General brand cough drops, and a burnt metal spoon.

*Oh no. Not this*, he squeezed his penis tighter. *Not now.*

Jacob turned to the bed below him. He slowly lowered both of his knees onto the mattress, which sat on the floor, unsupported by either box-spring or bedframe. He reached his left hand down to the biggest of the lumps under the crumb-covered covers. His hand sank into empty space. He felt another lump: a buried pillow.

In a sudden frenzy, Jacob ripped the comforter off his mother's bed. She wasn't there and the violence of his movement had him doubled over with electric blue flashes of pain deep in his penis, on the inside, well out of reach for his frantic, squeezing hand.

*Ohgodohgod*

Jacob's penis felt on fire. He envisioned those screaming, grainy

Vietnamese from the video in school coated in napalm or agent orange when he tried to put his physical pain into type in his head. The outside of his body, the inside of his head, and, especially, his entire groin felt coated in burning, clinging napalm.

*Oh god / thought rocks skip / scatter, shatter the frozen tundra of my m—*

"Momma!" his voice broke and for a fleeting second, Jacob felt slightly embarrassed at the textbook nature of the cracking.

*boy / child / kid / babybabybaby*
*sure she's yer momma but—*

The bed was empty. Jacob turned to the bathroom and saw that the door was closed. There were three fist-sized holes in the flimsy wall to the left of the bathroom door.

"Momma."

Jacob meant to scream, push his voice off into the red of unthinking rage, but only that soft murmur came out.

*Momma.*

He pushed himself up from his mother's bed, crossed the room in his slow shuffle, and pressed both his palms against the tacky surface of the door. He became aware he was drenched in sweat.

*I think I have a fever,* he thought, pressing his hot forehead against the cool door.

It smelled strongly of stale beer.

Jacob saw the tallboy can of Miller Lite slam against the locked, closed bathroom door in a flash.

*stupid whore / family way*
*know what she done, shit ass / went and got herself in a trouble*
*whatrodneytackettdonewhatrodneytackettdone*
*she don't have to be awake / you fuckin' pussy*
*man has to hunt / go crazy*
*it's in our nature / kill in other ways*

He tried the door. Locked.

*she's still / a cunt*

"Momma," Jacob whispered again.

*/*

Jacob was slowly crawling across his bedroom floor. He felt a dull sting and looked down to see a piece of glass sticking out of his right index finger, just underneath the nail.

*How'd I get here?*

He looked around.

*bedroom / mine but where*

*Nothing's making sense*, Jacob thought, feeling fresh sweat break out across his naked body.

*sense sensors for sensory detection / sense censors for serial reduction*

He watched goosebumps ripple across his arms. He knew, with sudden clarity, that he was going to vomit. He also knew that he was going to shit himself.

*what's it like to fall forever? / ¿is there even a bottom?*

Jacob woke up on his stomach, his neck craned painfully to the right, his cock and balls squeezed even more painfully with both his hands.

He rolled over onto his side and vomited off the bed. He felt a hot, wet shart bubble out between his legs.

*Kill me*, Jacob thought.

He felt the squishy pawpaw meat of the doe's smashed head between his toes. His tongue felt thicker and coated in bristles. He just knew he had a slowly burning hole where his pecker and balls used to be. He could smell the charred skin.

Jacob tried to roll off his side onto his back, but both of his arms were beginning to tingle with stinging needles from where he'd lain on them. He flopped back onto his stomach, his arms fussing for a moment then rumbling to an uneasy stillness.

He felt the current pull him.

Jacob drifted back into the void.

-

His aching penis woke him. It was swollen and red again, though not anything like the monstrosity it'd been. He sat on the edge of the bed, his left foot sinking into a puddle of cold, mushy puke, and squeezed it, his penis.

The pain didn't really go away when Jacob did this, but instead, would mutate into a hot, sugary burning.

*pain of a different sort / the poisoned, cat tongue flicker of flames*

Jacob envisioned a heap of flesh burning under a starless sky.

*Animal?* he wondered, sniffing.

*dead is dead is dead / is dead*

He realized he hoped it was human flesh burning. It felt like such a natural desire.

*naturally ripened / purpled with decay*

A coal truck rumbled by.

Jacob lifted himself off the bed enough to angle his penis under his bare ass. He slowly settled his weight down onto his still-aching penis.

*sweet tooth / baby's got a sweet tooth*

Jacob leaned into the sickly-sweet pain until his open mouth was salty with his tears, then he leaned forward, thick vomit rushing up from the carpet between all five of his left toes. He thought he could make out the smell of cooking meat. His mouth filled with saliva and he clenched his feet and hands involuntarily. He thought he might shit or laugh.

*that sweet tooth pain receded like an unstoppered drain*

Strange pinpricks of ice prickled his naked, sweaty body. Jacob expected to see a cascade of rays shining out of him from the stabbing pricks. He saw *what Rodney Tackett done.*

"Cunt," he whispered, easing himself backwards in the slowly rising current of electric pain.

*dead is dead is dead / pain, pain, & more pain*

-

Jacob woke in dimming light. He felt light-headed and weak.

*stale tea that's me / i smell pee pee*

Jacob looked down, *what Rodney Tackett done*, and cried out at what he saw. His bruised penis was lying on the inside of his left hip. There was a thick puddle of yellow pus tinged with blood clumped on his pale skin. There was blood, too much blood.

Jacob let the current take him back under.

-

A bold voice, brassy, huge and echoing, filled everything. It was commanding, a steady influx of trumpeted declarations. Jacob couldn't understand a single word.

*Are they words?* He couldn't tell.

He tried to open his eyes, sent the appropriate signals, but nothing happened; everything remained absolutely black, inky, and empty, save the voice. He felt every fiber of his body vibrating with the reverberations of the unintelligible voice like a tightening guitar string, slowly lifting toward the same note, the key of the great, commanding voice.

*What is this?*

From the absolute darkness came the flickering of a tiny flame, twisting and turning, twirling in a flit and flutter to the tune of the great, commanding voice.

Jacob was fascinated, *transfixed*; he'd never seen fire behave so strangely.

Transfix, *Mrs. Horace, 1: to hold motionless by or as if by piercing; 2: to pierce through with or as if with a pointed weapon.*

After a time, minutes were hours, hours, days, Jacob could tell the flickering flame was getting larger. The dancing tongue of fire looked hairy in sizzling spits of electric white and blue; the red and orange glowing steadily deeper, hotter, but buzzing with a growing electricity.

The tone of the voice shifted suddenly, dropping into an angry rumble that beat against Jacob's naked body like wind-driven waves, *another nameless 100-year flood*, against a failing levee. The handless arms of white-hot lightning reached out of the lapping tongue of fire, extended with pulsating slowness across the great void, and brought every strand of hair on Jacob's body upright. He could feel the tingle of static electricity brush against goosebumps on his arms as it sparked and slowly grew, encircling him like a human plasma globe.

Jacob was filled with a terrific doom.

*It's finally over.*

The fire drew nearer. Jacob was already connected to it by electric tethers, the sloth-like bolts of white and, now, neon blue lightning.

He couldn't get enough air into his lungs. His mouth tasted bitter and metallic.

Cataclysm, *Mrs. Horace, 1: flood, deluge; 2: catastrophe; 3: a momentous and violent event marked by overwhelming upheaval and demolition; broadly: an event that brings great changes.*

*It's finally over.*

Jacob felt hot, wet tears spill out onto his cheeks. He didn't fight the next set of them, or the ones after that. He didn't bother to wipe them away either.

*the great, commanding voice is a whisper / sent sailin' through fall's brittle leaves*

*those flickering flames flutter & flit / shootin' static-tongued licks across the void at me*

*i get to die, hallelujah / i get to die.*

He felt the punctuation mark, the period, *finally finale, an end to the pain, pain / & more pain*, jut out into the void, push the space into an absolute ball of white, hot light, felt every bit of himself no longer just of himself but mashed into liquid cohesion with trees and dirt, grass and beetles, the leaning post of the security light outside the salmon pink singlewide at Thompkins' Hilltop Trailer Court and Stacie Q's canoeing joint, all of it.

*hallelujah* hall*elujah hallelujah / hallelujah hallelujah hallelujah*

Then the voice laughed, the first out-and-out emotion Jacob was able to detect, and everything exploded from a great, commanding palm of fire. He saw each of the fingers, long pillars of flame wreathed in jolts of electricity, and the supple curve of the arcing thumb, thrust open as he flew by.

"No," Jacob screamed, watching the great hand of fire shrink as he barreled through the void on a stream of screaming gas. "I was dead. I was dead . . . is dead is dead is dead . . ."

Jacob woke screaming, bolting upright, and panted for some time before he could get control of himself.

*I've never been that scared in my life*, Jacob realized.

He brushed sweaty hair from his damp forehead, then put both palms down onto the mattress and made to push himself backwards against the headboard but hot bolts of pain crumpled him over his covered knees, gagging. He had nothing in his stomach to vomit, so he just floundered in carp-like dry heaves until the pain receded some.

"Holy fuckin' shit," he moaned.

Jacob eased the covers off his naked body and instantly smelled something awful. He gagged again when he saw the mess.

*wet / dream*

*Oh god, it smells like rancid cream of mushroom soup*, Jacob thought, leaning forward for a closer look and smell. There was one large puddle on the bedsheets as well as several stains on the insides of both of his thighs. It was thick, just beginning to dry, and the color didn't look right.

*Why's it yellow?*

There were streaks of green too.

*Oh god.*

His testicles were more swollen than they'd ever been. His penis was dark purple and throbbing with each beat of his heart; Jacob watched in muted horror as it pumped, feeling a painful pressure steadily growing.

He reached down with both hands and squeezed.

*There's something in it*, he felt, moving the index and thumb of both hands slowly upward from the base.

He screamed when he felt it, just below his pee hole.

*pain / a hot knife*

Jacob had to pee more than he'd ever had to pee in his entire life.

*Oh god, the pressure*, he wanted to scream.

*pain, pain / & mo—*

Jacob thrust with all his might and felt something tear through the swollen passageway onto the bedsheets.

"Oh," he moaned. "Ohgodohgod."

When he could open his eyes again, Jacob saw two different types of blood on his bed and crotch: a dark, thicker blood, a yellowed crystalline rock sitting in the middle of it like a river pearl, and thinner red blood, which he saw was still slowly coming out of his dickhead.

*i was / dead.*

Jacob woke up hungry. His stomach felt painfully empty, like it was contracting in on itself, *intestinal cannibalism.*

Jacob felt like an old, bleached dishtowel hung out on the line. He let himself slowly wake without moving, eyes glazing over the water spots in the ceiling.

*Okay. Look.*

His penis, though horribly bruised—bits of yellow and green were spotting it now—and his testicles were less swollen. He sat up and saw the mess he'd made of his bedsheets and cringed. He could still smell the fecund odor of rotten mushrooms.

He had a fading vision of a great hand made of fire, but it slipped out of his mind before he could fully register it amongst the stink, pus, and blood. He rubbed the crusted sleep from his eyes and the corners of his mouth.

*It's early*, Jacob thought, seeing the dim yellow glow of the security light outside losing prominence to the rising sun.

He got out of bed and shuffled into the hall. The trailer was quiet. His mother's bedroom door was closed. He walked down the hall, across the living room, into the kitchen.

A small cockroach scurried across the floor, dropping into the floor vent beside the sink.

*Seen bigger*, Jacob thought.

He opened the cabinet most likely to have food and found two packages of cherry-flavored off-brand Pop-Tarts and one bag of low-calorie Food Lion popcorn. He took both packages of cherry pastries to the toaster, opened both packages, dropped one set into the toaster and stuffed a third of one of them into his mouth. He chewed, feeling the granules of flavored sugar crunch under his scummy teeth. He finished the Pop-Tart, ate the other, then hit the Cancel button on the toaster, sending the half-cooked Pop-Tarts partially into the air. He took both of them out, and set them onto the counter, where an ant immediately beelined for the steaming rectangles. Jacob smashed the ant then stuffed more into his mouth, not bothering to wipe the crushed ant pieces from his fingertip.

"Momma!" he called with a full mouth. He swallowed then called again, "Momma!"

Something thumped onto the floor back in his mother's bedroom.

"Momma! Wake up!"

He heard his mother's muffled moan.

"Why?" she called out weakly a few moments later.

"I need ye to take me to school," he called, finishing the last bit of off-brand Pop-Tart as he shuffled toward his mother's bedroom.

*I don't think I could manage it,* Jacob thought, fearing the nearly constant bouncing and jostling.

"Ride the got dam bus," her voice was still weak, like she was talking in her sleep.

Jacob turned the doorknob and eased the door open.

"I can't, Momma," Jacob said into the darkness. "I think it'll hurt too much to ride the bus."

"What?" her voice was passively confused. "Hurt?"

"My penis, Momma," Jacob said. "Remember?"

*what Rodney Tackett done*

"Penis?" his mother asked, then she laughed. "It's always about a dick, isn't it?"

Her voice was different.

*It's her, sure,* Jacob thought, *but she sounds airy. Distant.*

He flipped on the light and his mother groaned, disappearing under the covers before he could get a good look.

"Okay, okay, Jake," she said. "Turn the light off and I'll take ye to school."

"Promise?"

She groaned.

"Yes, got dam it, now shut off them fuckin' lights."

Jacob flipped the switch.

"I'm gonna take a shower. I messed my sheets, Momma."

"Jesusgod."

Jacob thought, though his mother sounded more disgusted than angry at this, she didn't really sound like she cared.

*not here / anymore*

He blinked his eyes in the darkness and had a brief vision of a quilt made of fur and skin and meat swaying stiffly in a hot breeze. He smelled the rotten mushrooms, felt the pawpaw meat of a doe's brains between his toes, and thought he was going to shit or ejaculate. He closed his eyes, stood as still as he could, and breathed slowly, in through his nose, out through his mouth.

"Momma?" he said, opening his eyes to the darkness again.

He didn't expect her to answer; in this, she didn't let him down.

Jacob turned to leave the room but paused at the door and flipped the light back on.

"Off," she said from under the covers. "Turn it off."

Jacob didn't slow his shuffle at any of his mother's curses. He closed the bathroom door behind him, hearing glass shatter and rage fill the emptiness of his mother's husky voice.

-

The shower wasn't as painful as he expected. He squeezed a bit of green and yellow pus out of his penis, then ground his teeth as he soaped and rinsed under the burning water.

Jacob slid on a pair of gray sweatpants so stained you'd miss the Kentucky Wildcats' logo if you didn't know where to look. He didn't even try underwear.

-

"Ride the bus home," Christy Goodman told her son, bringing the rattling Cavalier wagon to a stop in the grass of the teachers' parking lot.

"But it'll hurt, Momma," Jacob said, his right hand frozen on the handle.

"I don't give uh flyin' fuck," she said, staring straight out the cracked windshield. "It might just teach ye to play with dead things, huh?"

Jacob looked at his mother for a moment longer, saw it was useless, *what isn't / useless*, then opened the passenger side door.

The car was already moving when it clicked shut again.

## CHAPTER NINE
## ENGINE OF PAIN

"*HUN*-TER," THE FAMILIAR VOICE JEERED. "Welcome back to school, *Hun*-ter."

Jacob watched his mother turn left out of the parking lot, cutting off a mini-van without so much as a glance in its direction. The van locked up its brakes with a squealing of tires and the blaring of its horn. A pickup truck behind the van nearly rear-ended it, swerving partially onto the shoulder in a skittering of loose gravel.

Jacob watched the driver of the van, a youngish mother, throw her hands up in frustrated exasperation, then after a few deep breaths, continue on into the morning traffic.

"Hey, fuckhead!"

Something bounced off Jacob's backpack. He turned around, saw the group of boys leaning against the brick wall then the banana peel on the sidewalk beside his miss K-Swisses. He felt a pressure begin to build, low in his stomach.

"Hi, Rodney Tackett," Jacob said, his voice flat, low.

"Hi, *Hun*-ter."

The boys laughed as if at a new joke. Their heads jerked backwards; the bowed brims of their hats jutted toward the morning sky.

Jacob felt like he always felt around other people, especially other kids: confused, but he also felt a prickle of fear, and with it, shame. The tip of Jacob's penis was burning, not pain with a capital "P" but the pressure was growing and he could already sense the buzz of electric pain building.

*what Rodney Tackett done*

Jacob ducked his head and made for the door.

"Yer not gonna offer the pervert the goods?"

Jacob didn't place the voice, but the word "pervert" slapped him like a wet towel, then bounced around the hollowed-out drum of his skull, coming back with memories.

*pervert / creep / weirdo / goddamn sick homo-perv*

Jacob was breathing fast. He felt light-headed and nauseous.

133

"Hey, Hun-ter," Rodney Tackett pushed himself off the wall and stepped away from the group toward Jacob. "Ye like titties and pussy? Or are ye just into dead cats and raccoons and other creepy faggot shit?"

Jacob felt his face flush as he cringed away from the larger boy, who prodded Jacob's heaving chest with his pointer finger after the words "pussy," "cats," and "faggot."

The pressure in his stomach dropped fully into Jacob's groin. He felt unsure if he was going to discharge something painful and messy from his penis, piss himself, or shit his pants. The pressure fluidly transmuted into pressure, briefly into pleasure, then back into pressure.

Jacob saw the pus-covered tip of the 1.00mm screwdriver, Tackett's Jewelry & Watch Repair, in the dirty bottom of the bathtub back in the pink trailer.

*what Rodney Tackett done*

Jacob wanted to wrap several lengths of the thicker Trilene XL, Walmart, around Rodney Tackett's throat and pull as hard as he could. He wanted to cut his fingers in the process. Jacob wanted his blood to slide down the line until it met the blood coming out of Rodney Tackett's neck. He wanted to pull the line with so much force Rodney Tackett's head would cleave free from his body. He wanted to hear the sound it made hitting the wooden floor of the hideout.

Jacob's jaw popped as he fought back a sudden burst of vomit. His eyes blurred with tears as he swallowed back the acidic bile.

"Oh, my," Rodney Tackett cooed. "Is our whittle *Hun*-ter frightened of women? Does the word *pussy* make you cry, pussy?"

Jacob wanted to piss and shit all the pressure and pain out of his body at the same time. He felt tainted, poisoned, curdling with equal parts shame and fear and hatred.

He waited for Rodney Tackett to start in on another rotation around him, then tried to break for the door again. Jacob was jerked backwards by his backpack's straps. He nearly fell, but Rodney Tackett kept this from happening by yanking the backpack upwards until Jacob was forced onto the tips of his miss K-Swisses.

Rodney Tackett had twisted the straps of the backpack around Jacob's arms in a tightening vice. Jacob realized the other boys had fallen silent when he could clearly make out the whistle of a booger in the larger boy's nose behind him.

"Uh, Rodney," came one of the other boy's voices. "Don't ye think you should . . . I don't know . . . maybe go easy on 'em after . . . you know."

The whistling intensified as did the straps. They dug deep into Jacob's armpits.

"No, I don't know, Marcus," Rodney Tackett said. "I don't know at all. Why don't ye tell me what, huh? Go ahead. Tell me *what*."

Jacob saw in a flash that existence was circular. He saw the gleaming tip of the 1.00mm screwdriver, Tackett's Jewelry & Watch Repair, standing straight up from his body, his penis stretched out and draped around the metallic tool like a scarecrow. He saw himself in his current position as if from above: Rodney Tackett, child-farmer putting up another scarecrow, this one named *Hun*-ter.

Jacob's earliest memory was the glowing tip of a cigarette slowly ground out on the right side of his pudgy toddler's stomach.

For a second, it all made painful, perfect sense to Jacob: *the world's an engine of pain*. Birth is pain. Living is pain. Dying is pain. *pain pain / & more pain*. The circle goes round and round and round; the snake eats its own tail, begets itself, births itself, kills itself, then starts again.

Jacob felt tired.

*kill / me*

"Th'as what I thought," Rodney Tackett said.

Then he released his grip on Jacob's backpack.

Jacob slouched on weak knees, tucking his fingers into his smarting armpits. He felt drained of nearly everything; a dried-out husk left on the stalk far too long; an unseen flag of surrender, smoke, smoke, and more smoke; a limp scarecrow slumped over the farmer's corpse, the crow-covered, barren field.

*dead & getting deader*

"I'm not a bad guy," Rodney Tackett said. "Hunter, here, has no problems with me. Do ye? He knows he fucked up."

Jacob was spun around by his shoulders.

Rodney Tackett's crooked teeth, uncleaned, Jacob could see in the bright sun, were exposed like a wound out to dry as he drew back his chapped but mustache-lined lips.

"Don't ye?"

Little droplets of spit clung to Rodney Tackett's crooked teeth like oil on water.

*grater grated on grating its way towards the twin gates*

Jacob's face felt numb. He lifted his hands and explored his cheeks. They were wet. He could feel the tears on the tips of his fingers, but he had no sensation anywhere about his face.

*my face / a desert*

Visions flashed across his mind, slipping over what his eyes broadcasted to his brain like undeveloped film.

*the desert / an overflowing sewer drain*

*the rivers pouring from my eyes / drain the river, drain the ocean*

*let the electricity jolt new sanctity / into the old ritual*

"I said," Rodney Tackett's crooked yellow smile faltered. "Don't ye, *Hun*-ter?"

*the desert presents a sewer / filled to the brim with dessert / / pain*

Rodney Tackett had a handful of Jacob's pants as well as the tip of his swollen, burning penis in his right fist.

*desert / pain*

"No," Jacob cried out. "No, no no. No, Rodney Tackett. No."

*electric / seabed*

"Good," Rodney Tackett cooed, letting go. "See, boys? No harm, no foul."

Jacob dropped to his knees, his eyes squeezed shut against the world's disconcerting tilt and spin.

*let the seabed be oasis / let the wind be breath*

*let the end come / let the end come*

*Why'd I come to school?*

"Here, see," Rodney Tackett said. "I'm not such a bad guy. I'll give him first dibs of the product, because it is real, really is for sale, really is sexy as hell."

A glossy photograph was shoved into Jacob's face: a blurred female form. Jacob tried to reach up and take the photograph from Rodney Tackett but the larger boy slapped the smaller boy's hands away.

"Keep yer filthy pervert fingers offa the product," he said, holding the picture up again, this time a little farther back.

It was a photograph of a beautiful young woman in the shower. The angle was looking straight down from a few inches above the showerhead. Water droplets and streams sat perfectly still between the supple curves of pale breasts. One of the girl's eyes was closed, the other slanted at a drunken angle; she'd been photographed in mid-blink.

*product / stolen photographs*

"Who's that?" Jacob heard himself ask.

"That, my sick-faggot-perverted friend, is my cousin," Rodney Tackett said, pocketing the photograph while simultaneously pulling Jacob to his feet. "Tanya Miller. Total fox, huh?"

Jacob blinked rapidly, tracing the gently sloping lines of the girl, Tanya Miller, in his memory.

*Fast-Forward X2 Mode / Tanya Miller*

There was a knot the size of an egg in Jacob's throat. He thought he was going to choke on it when he nodded his head at Rodney Tackett's question.

"I've got nine choice shots, boys," Rodney Tackett said, reaching his right hand into his back pocket and returning with a handful of glossy photographs.

Jacob was forgotten in the sudden rush toward the photographs.

"Easy!" Rodney Tackett shouted. "Easy!"

Jacob walked over to the door, the side entrance to the cafeteria, as quickly as he could. He felt his penis swelling, a painful throbbing increasing right along with his heartrate. He waited for Rodney Tackett to shout at him again, *Hun-ter*, beat him up again, shove something else metallic and sharp inside him.

Jacob pushed open the door with too much force; it barreled inward causing him to lose his balance. He crashed into the cafeteria, throwing his right elbow up at the last possible moment before smacking into the polished tiles.

All of the air was knocked out of his lungs. Jacob floundered on the tiles, his mouth working but not able to get his lungs to accept any intake of air.

He saw himself from above: a fish out of water on a sun-cracked riverbed.

*desert / seabed*

-

Just when he was sure he was going to pass out from oxygen deprivation, Jacob managed to suck in a mouthful of air. He pushed his pelvis and stomach up with the effort of breathing. He breathed in more and more and more until he could sit up.

Tanya Miller was standing over him.

"Uh," she said, her open eyes sparkling and clear, not the awkward, drunken things from the glossy photograph Rodney Tackett had in his back pocket. "Are ye alright?"

Jacob thought he could just make out the shape of her dime-sized nipples under her green t-shirt.

"Hey, weirdo? Ye okay?" she asked. "Want me to get ye a teacher or somethin'?"

Jacob shook his head, smelling her for the first time: vanilla and lavender. He watched her eyes narrow, the brows pinching in a bit as they knitted into a frown. She shook her head in return.

"This fucking school," she said, giving Jacob one last look into her eyes before she walked around him and out into the bright morning light.

When he heard the locker room door squeak open, Jacob lifted both of his feet off the water-stained floor, placing the smooth bottoms of his miss K-Swisses against the locked stall door, and held his breath. He heard the clank and jingle of Mr. Cottrell's infamous University of Nebraska Cornhuskers Football lanyard, which hung from his neck like a medieval torture device and culminated in a massive keyring stuffed with keys since Mr. Cottrell held two positions at Floyd County High, full-time janitor and part-time substitute teacher, then the overbearing overhead lights clinked off and the locker room door squeaked shut.

Jacob let out a soft sigh of relief, easing his feet back to the floor. *Second period gym's not gonna be that hard to get out of after all*, he thought.

It was the day before the timed one-mile run. Jacob didn't think he could complete a single jumping jack—his penis was indeed swelling again after *what Rodney Tackett done* but nothing like before—much less run an entire mile.

He lowered his pants, took his penis in his hands, and examined it. The head was swelling more than the shaft and mostly around his pee hole, which had puffed up like a busted lip. Clear fluid hung around the slit opening, which made Jacob think about the wet, button nose of fluffy little Muffy Muffintop, who he'd starved to death hanging from the rafters of the hideout by her two back paws. Her nose had been moist the first few days, but like the other dogs and cats and raccoons and possums and others, it'd dried up like the rest of it without water.

*Tanya Miller.*

Jacob put his penis back in his pants, then unlocked the stall. He eased the door open, poked his head out and made sure the locker room was empty. He walked over to the three benches, clothes and backpacks and shoes all over the place, and sat down in front of the locker Rodney Tackett always used.

He opened the shut door, none of the lockers' locks actually worked, and looked down at Rodney Tackett's backpack, shitkickers, oversized Jason Aldean t-shirt, and Wrangler jeans. He picked up the jeans, found the right back pocket, and took out the small stack of glossy photographs.

*Tanya Miller.*

Her eyes closed.

Her eyes open, but unfocused.

*hazy-eyed woman / give yourself to me*

Her mouth framing a nearly perfect, lower-case "o"; the pink tip of her tongue a blossom above the twin blooms of her breasts.

Jacob looked at each photograph quickly, devouring each slice of Tanya Miller's shower *as shot / from above* then looked at them all over again.

*left breast / wet, blonde hair*
*the tips of ten painted toes / left nipple*
*a migrating glacier of sudsy soap / lavender and vanilla*
*right nipple / eight glorious fingers w/ creamy purple painted nails*
*left thumb / the slope of slopes*
*right thumb / curve of curves*

Jacob was glad he was sitting down. His penis was painfully erect, a wetness spreading on his pants around his dickhead. He had the immediate need to piss, shit, and cum all at the same time.

*lavender and vanilla / vanilla and lavender*

*Those painted nails*, Jacob thought, looking at the single photograph in which all ten of Tanya Miller's creamy purple fingernails were visible. *Oh yes. Oh god!*

Jacob went through all ten photographs, *Rodney Tackett's a liar, big surprise*, again, even more slowly, each photograph seeming to vibrate in his tremulous hands.

*Tanya Miller / Fast-Forward X2 Mode*

-

*How long've I been sitting here staring?* Jacob wondered, sucking in air through his open mouth.

His shirt stuck to his back, sides, and stomach with sweat. His pants were too tight, but they were loosening up with each slowing beat of his pulse as seen in the throbbing, swollen outline of his penis.

*I just came without even touching it.*

He saw the dark stain spread around his already stained pants. He sniffed, frowning immediately when he smelled the pungent odor: hot, decomposing mushrooms and expired mayonnaise.

"Jesus," he whispered. "God."

The smell was somehow sinister. It reeked of a deeper decay; it was the smell of the rotten spirit. Jacob set the photographs, *Tanya Miller / Tanya Miller*, down on the bench beside a pair of neatly folded Adidas break-away track pants, matching zip-up, and t-shirt, and shuffled to the nearest of the three small porcelain sinks in the cramped, musty locker room.

Jacob pushed down the small circular button for hot, it stayed depressed for a brief moment, then slowly began to slide upward, keeping the water continuously streaming for about five seconds before the button would have to be depressed again. He ran one cycle of hot water through, knowing the school was old and badly in need of update and repair or replacement, while he slid his pants down to his knees, rose to his tippy toes, and held his penis above the sink.

Jacob was inching forward to secure a gentler entrance into the stream when he heard the voices of several boys echoing in the gymnasium down the short, dark hall from the locker room.

*Oh shit!*

Jacob hopped out of his craned position over the sink, twinged at the electric flash that motion ignited, then pulled his pants around *what Rodney Tackett done* and up onto his waist.

"Seventeen years old!"

"Holy fuckin' shit, she's a fox!"

"'N only ten dollars apiece."

"Look at those tits!"

"Two for twenty."

*They're in the hallway,* Jacob realized, spinning away from the locker room's door.

He ran directly into the bench he'd been sitting on, his right shin now shooting off lightning strikes to flash alongside the ones shooting out of his dickhead. His stomach felt loaded with napalm, *slowly goes, slowly goes / slowly along, the lava flows*, and a pressure was building somewhere deep inside him, between the bones of his hip.

"Mother. Fuckin'. Landin'. Strip, y'all."

"Why's she stayin' with y'all again?"

"Yeah, I forgot too."

"Whorin', was it?"

Jacob bounced on his left foot, reaching down to, alternately, grab and rub his shin along the length of the locker room toward the three stalls.

"Ye stupid assholes, listen when I's talkin' so we don't have to keep doin' this."

*what Rodney Tackett done*

Jacob pushed in the middle stall door, but with too much force; it banged into the rubber stopper, echoing briefly in the cave-like room.

*They've had to have heard that!* Jacob thought, throwing himself backwards onto the toilet, hoping the seat was down.

Jacob smiled as he lifted his miss K-Swisses up onto the closed stall door, thankful not to have plunged ass-first into toilet water.

The locker room door squeaked open much faster than it had when Mr. Cottrell had opened it earlier. Jacob eased the stall door closed, then slid the lock in place.

"Whorin', right, Rodney?"

Rodney Tackett sounded distant when he began his sentence, but his voice was echoing off the walls of the locker room by the time he finished it.

"As I said earlier," he said, his voice dripping exasperation, but also tinged with a bouncing excitement, "CPS tol' her momma, my aunt, Helena, and her boyfriend, some pillbilly from up Johnson County somewheres, that they's the unfit parents they is and placed her in our home until they's completed parentin' classes and su'stance abuse re-treatment."

"That yer momma's sister or yer daddy's sister?"

"What?"

"She your cousin on yer momma's side or yer daddy's?"

"What's it matter?"

"Well, I guess it don't matter much, just 'as wondering is all."

Jacob heard the sound of several boys moving in tandem down the narrow locker room.

"My momma's sister," Rodney Tackett snapped. "Now ye'ns wanna buy a picture or not?"

"Okay, okay," Stevie Risner said, his squeaky voice nearly breaking. "Here's the twenty, here. Here. I get to choose which one."

"Sure. First come, first served."

"I'll take one too."

"I ain't got it on me. Can I pick one out now and pay ye

tomorrow?"

"No moolah, no pic'ure."

"My mom owes me ten for rubbing her feet."

"Faggot."

"I get first look cos I already paid ye."

"Aw c'mon, Rodney, you know I'm good f—"

"What the fuck," Rodney Tackett shrieked. "Which of ye thieves?"

Jacob heard a commotion: grunts and squeaking tennis shoes, startled yelps and the slapping of skin on skin. Then the banging of something striking a locker; Jacob guessed Rodney Tackett's fist or foot.

"Which one of ye thieves took 'em?" Rodney Tackett yelled.

Another hollow crash against the metallic locker.

"Wha—"

"Who took the fuckin' pictures?" Rodney Tackett screamed, his voice breaking on the "c" of "pictures." "I'll fuckin' fuck ye up motherfuckers!"

Jacob listened to Rodney Tackett's voice rise in pitch and volume.

Hysteria, *Mrs. Horace, 2: behavior exhibiting overwhelming or unmanageable fear or emotional excess.*

"Pussies," Rodney Tackett yelled. "Who took 'em?"

The locker room door squeaked open as Rodney Tackett's voice bounced off the cinderblock walls.

"What's the problem, Mr. Tackett?" Mr. Cottrell asked.

Jacob heard the slight jingle of Mr. Cottrell's keys on the Cornhusker lanyard and, Jacob assumed, Rodney Tackett's heavy breathing.

After a long moment, Rodney Tackett mumbled something Jacob didn't understand.

"What was that?" Mr. Cottrell asked.

"No problem," Rodney Tackett said.

"Huh," Mr. Cottrell said. "That's funny cos I heard a whole heck of a lot of hollerin' 'n' carryin' on comin' from inside here just a few seconds ago. What about that?"

No response.

"Nothin', huh?" Mr. Cottrell said. "Figured I'd miss ye zigging when everybody else zagged? Huh?"

Mr. Cottrell's lanyard jingled.

"I see," he said. "Y'all think that because I'm just the substitute teacher that ye can do whatever ye want? Rule the roost like a red-headed banty rooster?"

Rodney Tackett said something under his breath. Jacob slit his eyes and cocked his head, but he couldn't make out what the bully said. There was a ripple of noise among the boys; Jacob couldn't tell if it was snickering or gasping or a combination of both.

"What did ye say?" Mr. Cottrell's voice was loud, not far from yelling. "What did ye just say?"

"I said," Rodney Tackett said, "ye ain't no substitute teacher. You're just the janitor."

There was a moment of absolute silence. Jacob listened but only heard the rushing of blood in his ears as he strained to keep his feet from sliding down the stall door. With a sinking in his stomach, Jacob realized his feet were sliding and there was nothing he could do to stop them. The downward motion, inching steadily along, brought increasing flashes of pain.

From the sound of his keys, Jacob imagined Mr. Cottrell was flailing his arms or bouncing in place.

*the substitute janitor's lanyard was a cacophonous tolling of cheap bells*
*cacophony / mrs. horace / 1: harsh or jarring sound / 2: the sound of life*

Jacob's left foot plummeted off the stall door, sending him dropping off the seat of the toilet. He tried to catch himself on the toilet paper dispenser, but it was plastic and quickly wrenched free from the stall's wall to fall on the dirty tile floor beside him.

"Wha—" Mr. Cottrell stammered. "Wh-What? Who's in there?"

Hot flashes of white and blue pain flared in Jacob's groin. He'd hit his elbow on the floor too. It throbbed somewhere nearer the surface; Jacob felt temporarily in the current's grip, unable to move until the electric pain lessened.

The stall door rattled, but Jacob had locked it.

"Open this door," Mr. Cottrell demanded, the keys jangling against the plastic stall door.

Jacob tried to focus on his breathing, hoping the pain would lessen.

*Does pain have a point of diminishing return?*

Jacob envisioned the flashes of pain over a great, flat desert nightscape. Roiling clouds curdled overhead.

He tried to sit up and felt the percussive burst of thunder; pain flashed a blinding light blue.

"Jacob Goodman," Mr. Cottrell said. "Ye open this door right this instant."

The electric pain revealed the desert as an arid seabed.

"Told ye I didn't have 'em!" a boy whispered.

*Tanya Miller / Tanya Miller*

"Give me those," Rodney Tackett hissed from somewhere farther away.

"What're y'all doin' over there?"

*Tanya Miller / Tanya Miller*

A chorus of nothin's.

The lanyard clanged against the door right before Mr. Cottrell began open-palm slapping the locked door.

"Open this door right this instant, Jacob Goodman! I ain' playin'."

"They all there?" Stevie Risner asked.

*Tanya Miller / Tanya Miller*

"Right now, Goodman!"

"Yeah, *Hun*-ter. Open the door."

*misnomer mrs. horace / desert / seabed / hun-hun-hun-ter*

*what Rodney Tackett done / what Rodney Tackett done*

Jacob gritted his teeth and forced himself back up onto the toilet.

The pain was receding but it'd left an awkward pressure deep in his testicles.

"I'm on the toilet," Jacob said, forcing his voice to come out flat, expressionless.

"Baloney!" Mr. Cottrell yelled. "Ye were just on the floor. I seen ye."

"I'm on the toilet," Jacob said again.

"Open. This. Door."

"I can't right now, Mr. Cottrell," Jacob said. "I'm on the toilet."

The boys in the locker room erupted into riotous laughter. It bounced around the echoing room until it sounded like horse laughter.

Jacob closed his eyes and saw the desert / *seabed* / the flashes of lightning reduced to distant rumbles on the storm-shrouded horizon. He saw wild horses galloping, but not all of them were alive; some of them were shredded things, meat and bone and tendon.

"Ye lookin' to add peeping tom to yer resume?" Rodney Tackett said, mispronouncing the word.

"Résumé," somebody corrected.

"Whatever!" Rodney Tackett shouted. "Ye tryin' to add watchin' kids use the bathroom to yer job description, Mr. Cottrell?"

*more / horse laughter*

*more / bones dancing in the night*

*desert / seabed*

"Goodman, I'll be seeing ye," Mr. Cottrell said, "after class."

"Yeah," Rodney Tackett said. "I'll be seeing ye too, Hun-ter."

*what Rodney Tackett done*

"Tackett. Outside. Right now," Mr. Cottrell said. "Now!"

Jacob heard the jingling of keys, a small cry of pain, then the squeak of the locker room door opening, then again as it slowly swung shut.

There was a brief moment of silence, then a hurried flurry of whispers.

"Jacob?"

"Holy shit!"

"What do ye think Mr. Cottrell's gonna do to 'im?"

"What can he do? He's just a substitute."

"Not even that! He's just a janitor!"

"Substitutes can still give ye detention."

"Jacob! You takin' a dump?"

Jacob could see it: the desert; the seabed. He could see the shadow figures running soundlessly across the great empty expanse. Each flicker of the heat lightning showed the pale glow of the sun-bleached bones frozen in mid-stride. He could sense a great hulking shape looming somewhere just out his line of sight, something impending, unseen but watching.

*I will have Tanya Miller,* Jacob decided, *for what Rodney Tackett done.*

# CHAPTER TEN
## THE QUILTS OF FAILURE & A PALE WIND

*IT'S AMAZING HOW CLOSE YOU can get*, Jacob thought, *if you're quiet.*

He couldn't count how many times he'd had this exact thought. He smiled, his teeth feeling thick and unclean but strong, and pulled the tripwire, which sprung the spring, taken from Old Man Humphrey's new riding mower's seat, and sent a sharpened camping stake, Ace Hardware, plunging into the fluffy housecat's face.

Jacob forced his eyes to remain open at the suddenness of it. He flinched, of course, *instincts can't be helped*, but he did not close his eyes.

The quick punch of the stake into the cat's startled, stupid face. The rigidly regal way the animal held its self for the quickest of moments, then the blood mist, the little coughing noise, the gurgled cries. The end.

Jacob smiled, despite the pressure and the pain from lying on his penis for the past forty-five minutes. He smiled because he'd found a way to hunt without being able to hunt the way he wanted to. He smiled because he wasn't sure it'd work for him like the other ways did, but it had. He smiled because he had warm, wet blood on his filthy face. He smiled because he didn't know the name of the cat he'd just killed. He smiled because Tanya Miller had cheerleading practice after school on Wednesdays, which meant he could watch her sneak off with Rebecca Pinwheel, Sarah Smothers, and that pudgier one Jacob could never remember the name of to smoke cigarettes behind the dumpsters behind the gym. He smiled because he thought he'd found a way to get into the ceiling of the girls' locker room. He smiled because he was just such a happy boy sometimes.

*There you are*, Jacob thought. *Mine. You're mine.*

From his place in the underbrush, Jacob could see the top half of the east wing door. The top of Tanya Miller's blonde hair bobbed briefly into view before turning left toward the parking lot. He shifted his weight, then lowered himself down a branch for a nearly unobstructed view of the mostly empty student parking lot. Tanya Miller, dressed in the navy blue and white skirt and sleeveless top of the Bobcat Cheer Squad, swayed across the asphalt to a small cluster of cars parked in an odd circle in the far corner, near the entrance to the football field. Three of the five cars had been modified by their teenage drivers: grossly oversized rims, bumpers and glass tattooed with player numbers, deer racks and skulls, band logos, and scuff marks, and the buzzing thump of bass from one of the stereo's was counterpointed by the searing scream of a metal band.

A group of teenagers, Jacob recognized only Robbie Farmer, a tall varsity basketball player who's sweat-streaked face often graced the front page of the *News-Enterprise*'s Sports Section, were huddled between the cars, punching each other in the arms when not scratching or preening themselves. Tanya Miller cupped her hands around her mouth and yelled something at them. Jacob saw five male heads look up, in syncopation, in her direction.

*Deer. Sheep. Cattle.*

Jacob felt the pawpaw meat of their smashed heads between his toes.

*Meat. That's all they are: meat.*

"Made the first cut, bitches!" Tanya Miller yelled.

There were several whoops and hollers in response.

*Just like the gorillas from that documentary in Mrs. Millsap's class*, Jacob thought, watching the older boys ogle Tanya Miller in her skimpy cheerleader uniform. He could hear the narrator's earnest, quiet voice, "The males of the troop attempt to solicit the female by making interested, loud noises."

Jacob watched Tanya Miller skip the last twenty feet of blacktop before disappearing into the tinted interior of a Mustang. The outline of her shadow glinted in the sun as the car peeled out of the parking lot and onto the county road.

For a second, Jacob could see the skeletal horses racing across the desert seabed. He saw a great quilt of fur and meat and hair and skin. Then the pressure in his groin forced him to slowly, carefully climb down the tree. Jacob thought he had to urinate, but when he tried, he only managed to squeeze out a few oily drops of what was mostly blood.

-

Jacob took the cat with the crushed-in face back to the hideout. He set it on the table, after moving the raccoon ribcages, then used the hatchet, Walmart, to remove the cat's head. The blood was thick and not as warm as the mist had been. He slid his fingers into the space underneath the cat's skin. He moved his fingers slowly, feeling every hair on his body stand as air popped and sucked in behind his fingertips, making a crackling noise he wanted to hear forever.

When he could, Jacob palmed the top of the cat with the crushed-in face's skull; it was slick but small. He could feel the smile on his face spread as he slowly smashed and ground the animal's head. He scooped out the broken bones and brains and eyes until he was left with what he thought looked like a strange, fur sock.

*Or mitten*, Jacob thought, seeing the student-doctor slide his gloved fingers into the skin of the black bag cadaver.

He looked at the rounded, bloody stump on the end of his left arm.

*Nah.*

The cat's face had been wrecked by the camping stake, Ace Hardware, and Jacob's frenzied need to hollow the thing out had obliterated the animal's head fur. He looked at the headless body on the table.

*Looks as good as new*, he thought. *Just missing a head.*

Jacob had a vision.

"A quilt," he whispered. "A quilt."

-

The Tackett's cracked and peeling white house was near to ramshackle. The front porch, which lined the entire front and right side of the house, slouched and sagged with rot. A single bare bulb illuminated a bloated argyle couch to the left of the door, mold-speckled stuffing spilling out to be picked up by the wind or nest-building animals. Several of the front windows were cracked but had been repaired with duct tape and clear plastic.

Jacob, carefully tucked behind a copse of sassafras trees, watched the Tackett house for a long time, taking note of where each member of the house moved and, eventually, settled down for the night. When the last light blinked out, Jacob stepped out into the small, overgrown yard, moving slowly, his left testicle and penis aching, beginning to swell.

*what Rodney Tackett done*

Jacob circled the house twice, hunched forward, moving slowly and quietly.

*No security lights.*

Jacob stepped up onto the rickety backsteps and looked into the darkened kitchen, feeling the crash of his quickened pulse in both of his ears and, with increasing flashes of electric blue, the head of his penis.

*I am the desert*, Jacob told himself. *I am the seabed.*

Jacob turned the doorknob, unlocked as he knew it would be, as far as it would turn, then eased the door inward.

*Do it.*

Jacob felt a sudden rush of adrenaline. The dark, silent house seemed to welcome him with open arms. Come inside, he thought he heard. See what I'm hiding. See what it's like here. Come see Tanya Miller. Maybe she sleeps naked.

Jacob couldn't remember what Rodney Tackett's mother's name was. He couldn't remember what she looked like either.

*If Johnnie Floyd's looks are a predictor . . . woof.*

Jacob lifted his left miss K-Swiss to step inside the Tackett house, but a tearing white rip of pain struck somewhere in his groin. It hurt so badly he couldn't tell exactly where the pain was coming from. He fell to his knees, squeezing himself.

Even in the fog of pain, Jacob heard the dishes on the counter rattle when he dropped to his knees.

*Shit! I gotta get outta here*, Jacob thought, unable to move.

*the pain magnet / the pain receptor*

Jacob saw his crotch as a lightning rod for pain.

*pain pain / & more pain*

But the storm was moving on farther into the barren wastelands.

*desert / seabed*

Jacob heard a door open in a nearby room.

*Move.*

Jacob pushed himself to his feet, biting his lip to keep from crying out at the blue and white pain and turned to flee but stopped himself.

*Close the door*, a voice in Jacob's head told him. *Leave no trace. It'll just be another bump in the night. Nothing to get yer guard up fer.*

The voice was familiar, but Jacob couldn't place it.

*Am I going crazy?*

*No, sir.*

Jacob grabbed the doorknob, pulled the door closed as quietly as he could, then leapt over the three slanting stairs onto the dew-slickened grass. Hot pain and a budding pressure erupted in his crotch and spread back to his anus and up into his stomach.

*Run.*

Jacob ran.

-

He didn't stop running until he was high up on the ridgeline overlooking the little valley where the hideout was nestled. Panting, both sweaty palms trying to slide off his knees, Jacob thought about that voice he'd heard in his head. It was infuriatingly familiar, but still, he couldn't assign it a name or a face.

*the moon's just a sliver / a nervous nail chewed off & spit out in haste*

His penis and, now, both testicles were swollen. He could feel them pressing painfully into his black sweatpants, Walmart. He'd stolen the blank, black hoodie from there too.

*I was inside,* Jacob marveled.

A taste of that ecstatic adrenaline came back to him.

*I was inside. Oh god, I was inside.*

Jacob could just see Tanya Miller in her bed on the second floor, her eyes closed, the pink petal of her mouth partially open.

*a rose in bloom / a bride for her groom*

"I was inside," Jacob told the swaying heads of dogwoods and poplars below.

He started down the steep slope to the hideout, knowing he wouldn't be returning to the salmon trailer anytime soon. He could tell by the position of the moon he had a good three or four hours left until sunrise.

*I'll work on the quilt,* Jacob decided, a smile already on his face.

-

Tanya Miller could kick her legs above her head. Jacob, from his vantage point under the visitor-side bleachers in the gym, could see the delicate fold, the place where both of her long, tanned legs almost met. On a particularly high kick, that Tanya Miller held for a long, long time, Jacob thought he could make out the impression of her pubic hair under the shiny satin.

*The landing strip,* Jacob had heard it called.

He pressed himself with increasing force against the cool wooden bleachers.

Tanya Miller was sweating. Her arms, legs, and neck were glistening. He could see little beads on her smooth, acne-free forehead. Her breasts bounced heavily under the embroidered F and H.

Wednesdays were dress practices, Jacob knew, meaning the cheer squad wore their uniforms and went through their routines as if a varsity basketball game was being played in the gym at that very moment. Jacob loved their uniforms. He also loved the cheerleading coach and home economics teacher, Mrs. Martin's, attention to detail; for every dress practice, all of the cheerleaders had to wear navy blue or white nail polish. Jacob couldn't help watching Tanya Miller's hands, the nails of her left blue, her right white, as she went about the routines. He imagined those hands caressing the warm, wet body under the uniform.

He pressed himself even harder into the dusty bleachers.

*Just look at those nails*, Jacob thought. *Just look at those hands.*

Tanya Miller was sitting on a quilt—Jacob involuntarily cringed at his own embarrassing failures at quilting—in the only section of the Tackett yard that had been mowed, which faced the tombstone-pocked descending slope of Richmond Cemetery. She had on orange cat-eye sunglasses, even though it was cloudy and had been all afternoon, and Jacob could see her lids getting heavier.

Jacob move farther into the woods, making a wide, slow arc around Tanya Miller until he was crouched behind a huckleberry bush only a few feet behind her. He watched the back of her blonde head bob down once, twice, then, after the third time, Tanya Miller set down Joseph Conrad's *Heart of Darkness*. She was in Mrs. Davis' junior-year CP English class.

Jacob watched her lift her tanned, slightly muscular arms and rub her eyes. She stretched, yawned, then settled onto her back on the quilt.

*the quilts of failure / broken sutures*

In a flash, Jacob saw the dissolution of the skin and the pelts and the fur. Again, he held the limp, smelly "quilt" in his twisting, rage-filled fingers.

His face flushed at his failure; his jaw tightened, his teeth gnashed.

*Stupid fuckin' animal skin won't hold together.*

Jacob forced his fists to relax.

*Look at her.*

She was wearing a t-shirt so thin from wear that it was shiny. Jacob could make out the twin peaks of Tanya Miller's nipples through the thin cotton.

# BIRTH OF A MONSTER

*Oh god.*

Jacob squeezed himself. He watched the slow, even rise and fall of Tanya Miller's chest and saw her as she was in Rodney Tackett's photograph: naked, wet, unknowing.

*Oh god,* Jacob thought, squeezing his painful erection. *Oh god.*

Tanya Miller rustled, trying to find a more comfortable position. Jacob could make out the pout of her open mouth after she covered her eyes with her right forearm. Her nails on that hand, though chipped and cracked in places, were painted a bright, blinding white.

-

Jacob had moments, beginning to happen more and more often, where he felt invisible—*a pale wind across the barren desert / seabed / desert / seabed*—not just stealthy, he often felt this, but completely unable to be seen.

*I am the predator,* Jacob thought, envisioning himself as if shown in the movie, his new favorite, stolen from Walmart and secreted in the AV Club room at school, moving with surety and purpose, just the outline of himself wrapped in that alien invisibility cloak.

*A pale wind,* Jacob thought, watching himself climb up the wooden frame of the porch onto its roof. A predator. A hunter.

Jacob crouched low and peeked inside Rodney Tackett's bedroom window, *hun-ter, hun-ter.* He could see the outline of the bully's body under the navy-blue comforter.

*oh god / her nails / the outline of her landing strip / her open pouting mouth*

He moved farther along the top of the porch, making his way to the front side of the house, taking his steps carefully on the sagging wood. He passed two more windows, a bathroom, a narrow, shadow-laden stairwell, before he crouched at Tanya Miller's cracked bedroom window.

*pale wind predator / precious sleeping prey*

Tanya Miller was sleeping in an oversized NASCAR t-shirt and panties. The quilt, Jacob cringed, was in a heap on the floor beside the bed.

*She's hot,* Jacob thought.

There was no air-conditioner unit in the window, like those on Johnnie Floyd and Marie's—Jacob had opened their mailbox on every nightly visit and learned her name—and Rodney Tackett's bedroom windows. Jacob didn't see a fan in Tanya Miller's room either.

*Good.* He liked the thought of her wet.

152

He eased himself down onto his stomach on the cool, soggy wood. He pressed his nose through the four inches of space left between the window and the window seal and sniffed. He smelled stale cat piss, *Hobart*, the evening's meal, *Hamburger Helper, by the smell of it*, and there, just under the smell of stale sweat, was vanilla and lavender.

*Oh yes.*

Jacob spent four straight nights silently haranguing, *Mrs. Horace*, himself, *hun-ter hun-ter hun-ter hun-ter*, for not sliding open Tanya Miller's cracked window. She cracked it each and every night until, on the fifth night, he crept across the porch roof to find her awake. He'd been deep in himself, imagining how easy it would be to pop out the air conditioning unit from Rodney Tackett's window, which he crept by each and every night, sneak in and remove his scalp with the fileting knife, Roger's Bait 'n' Tackle, when he'd nearly gasped out loud at the sight of light spilling onto the roof of the porch from Tanya Miller's open bedroom window.

*Leave*, one voice told him.

He dropped to his hands and crawled noiselessly toward the yellow pillar of light, taking the advice of the other voice in his head.

*Look. See.*

*look / see*

The light came from a shadeless lamp sitting on the writing desk to the left of the bed. Tanya Miller was propped up against the wall, the white nails of her right hand glistening as they rubbed the outside of her panties, which were pulled tight, revealing more than just the outline of her landing strip. Tanya Miller's eyes were closed, her front two teeth biting hard into the pale pink of her bottom lip, her left hand slowly tuning the reddened dial of her right nipple.

*look / see*

Jacob began to slowly move himself up and down the roof of the Tackett's front porch, syncopating his pace with the painted white nails.

*In.*
*Up.*
*Out.*
*Down.*
*Desert.*
*Seabed.*

Jacob watched the Tacketts, dressed in the navy blue and white of Floyd County High for the game, plus Tanya Miller, in a mostly baby blue floral-print sundress, climb inside Johnnie Floyd's lifted Dodge Ram from his hiding place behind the patch of young sassafras trees. He watched Tanya Miller's blonde bun bob in the rear window as the truck bounced down the descending gravel drive toward the rows of mostly white tombstones gleaming in the orange light of the setting sun.

Jacob had nearly mistimed the hike to the Tackett's, guessing the Tackett's would leave early for the game against Magoffin County since Rodney Tackett was on the team, but he'd ground his teeth and pushed himself through the swelling and pain to make it just in time to watch Rodney Tackett, tight white pants, cleats and all, toss his gear into the bed of the truck then stick both hands down his baseball pants and readjust his cup.

*I hope that cup gives you cancer,* Jacob thought. *I hope it malfunctions tonight and you lose a testicle.*

They were discussing consumerism and safety in Mr. Burkhart's class and it seemed to Jacob that most companies got rich on products or services that killed or maimed its employees or customers: all sorts of cancers and diseases. Black lung. There was a whole wing at the hospital in Pikeville devoted to coal miners and black lung. Black lung felt like such a natural death to Jacob. You go that deep underground you're bound to get into the kind of stuff that'll kill you.

*from earth / we return*
*ashes to ashes / & dirt to dirt*

Jacob smiled as Johnnie Floyd's Ram turned onto South Lake Drive, disappearing into the dusk, envisioning himself as the creator of cancers. He saw himself as a grinning puppet master, expertly pulling string after string, exerting minimal energy but maximum control. Jacob wanted to open a mine and fill it with asbestos then shove all the miners in eastern Kentucky deep into the hole. He wanted to include a broken stitch in every seatbelt. Jacob wanted to hide a screw in every tire, microscopic shards of glass in every bottle of drinking water. He wanted the brakes to fail on every school bus.

Jacob rose and stretched. He readjusted his swollen testicles in the black sweatpants, Walmart, then turned to the Tackett house. The single exposed bulb next to the front door was on, but the rest of the house was dark and still.

*Empty*, Jacob thought. *Empty and waiting and welcoming and mine. Mine.*

# CHAPTER ELEVEN
## STINK

**THE FRONT DOOR WAS LOCKED,** as was the back, but Jacob had expected this. People sure made a fuss to say how you didn't have to lock your doors in the country, but most folks tended to lock their front and back doors. He climbed up onto the roof of the rickety front porch with an injured grace that felt second-nature to him after so many ascents. He hunched low and moved quickly, knowing the black he wore made him hard but not impossible to see. Jacob peeked into the glass over the air-conditioning unit into Rodney Tackett's window out of habit, then moved around the corner to the front.

Tanya Miller's room was empty. Jacob looked at the rumpled sheets of the unmade bed and saw the painted fingers of her right hand glistening as they rubbed the satin-clothed mound between her legs.

*Oh god,* Jacob thought. *Those nails. Those hands. Those fingers.*

He put both of his hands on Tanya Miller's bedroom window and tried to slide it open.

*Shit, it's locked.*

Jacob sat back on his haunches in thought, staring into the darkened room. He had to know what the sheets smelled like, what they felt like. He needed to smell Tanya Miller's pillow and clothes. Had to.

*I'm shaking,* Jacob realized, raising his left hand up to his eyes and noting the tremor. *I need to calm down. I need to—*

*Get inside,* a commanding voice finished. *Get inside. Now.*

Jacob did as he was told; he climbed off the front porch's roof, then started checking each of the windows on the ground floor until he found one unlocked. He slid the window up—it screeched on rusty tracts—saw that it led to a small, cluttered bathroom, then lifted himself inside. He turned to close the window, but hesitated.

*Leave it open,* the voice commanded.

Jacob left the window open.

156

*I'm alive*, Jacob thought, *for the first time. This is it.*

His body tingled like he'd rubbed every nerve, every fiber of his being with IcyHot. He could hear the air rushing in and out of his lungs, the blood pumping through his expanded veins and arteries. His arms and legs felt suffuse with an energy that was not his own. He squeezed his hands and shivered at the raw strength he felt in them: so capable of destruction.

He didn't turn on the light. He stood upright in the middle of the bathroom for a few moments, letting the air rush in and out of his open mouth and his wide eyes adjust to the darkness, which didn't take long. Jacob smiled at the crispness of his vision.

*pale wind / predator*
*hawkeyed / & taloned*

Jacob had the funny thought that if he jumped at that moment, he'd crash through the ceiling into the second floor. He felt so tall that when he left the Tackett's first floor bathroom, he ducked, needlessly, as he passed under the doorway.

-

The place smelled like burnt hot dogs and mold. Jacob felt he could smell every little thing in the house: the laundry on the floor of the bathroom he just left, the dust on the rug lining the hallway outside the bathroom, the faint floral scent of detergent as he passed the laundry room.

*This is what having superpowers must feel like*, Jacob thought, stepping into the darkened living room.

The couch was old and long, taking up most of the space. Blocking the front windows, which looked out onto the front porch and Richmond Cemetery beyond, was a bulky, pressed-wood entertainment center. Jacob walked over to it and examined the spines of the VHS tapes on display under the battered old television, but after a blank period of time, *Fast-Forward X2 Mode / Rodney Tackett's collection of photos of Tanya Miller*, he couldn't recall a single title he'd read.

He turned toward the stairs.

-

He could smell her, Tanya Miller, even from outside her room; vanilla and lavender. Jacob forced his hand not to crush the doorknob as he eased the door open.

He closed his eyes and breathed in the smell of her, Tanya Miller. He saw the painted fingers caress the mound under her satin panties.

157

# BIRTH OF A MONSTER

He saw her exasperated expression the day he saw her in person for the first time, looming over him just inside the door at school.

Jacob opened his eyes, seeing every aspect of the room in detail all at once. He felt dizzy, thought the room was vibrating, pulsating under his gaze.

*pale wind / predator*
*hawkeyed / & taloned*

He walked over to the unmade bed, sniffing hurriedly, and sat down. The sheets were cheap and rough—*K-Mart or Walmart or Big Lots*, Jacob thought, knowing the look and feel all too well—but smelled like her.

*Tanya Miller / Tanya Miller*
*Mine.*

He lifted the pillow and buried his face into it. He breathed in the smell of her until his face began to sweat. He reached over to the writing desk and flipped on the shadeless lamp. Little golden strands, *thicker than the first few boxes of Trilene*, Jacob saw, were stuck to the pillow. He carefully removed the blonde hairs and held them up before the exposed bulb.

*the halo shines / the angel leaves her mark*

Jacob turned back to the mattress. He looked at the spot where her head went, then slowly moved down the length of the bed until his eyes rested on the spot where her painted fingers had glistened and kneaded. He knelt and smelled.

A strangled moan sounded deep in his throat. Jacob heard it, knew it as himself, but still jumped at the urgency of the sound. He tried to pull himself from the spot in the sheets—he could just make out the oblong oval patch, a shade darker than the gray cotton—but couldn't. He smashed his face against the crusted cotton, licking and sucking and biting and tasting.

*Mine*, he thought.

*Mine*, the voice in his head echoed. *Mine.*

-

Jacob opened the top drawer of the little dresser and gasped.

*Panties.*

Jacob slipped his fingers into the sea of red and pink and blue and black and purple and cream like he was breaking the surface of a warm, still pond. He half-expected to hear the sound of water disturbed.

The pressure and pain intensified as his penis hardened, shooting off blue and white streaks of electricity. His fingers buzzed with it as they brushed the soft fabric, *so weightless, so delicate.* Jacob lifted an especially silky pair of green panties from the drawer and covered his mouth and nose with them.

He explored the stitching with his tongue. He tugged at the little purple bow, just below the elastic waistband, with his teeth, exploring its strength and feel, but did not tear it from the panties.

The pain was excruciating. Jacob braced himself against the dresser with his right hand, shoving his left, along with Tanya Miller's panties, down into the black sweatpants, Walmart, and grabbed himself. He felt his pulse beating in his erect, throbbing penis. Each heavy pulsation was a sonic flare of static pain. He wrapped his fingers around himself, feeling Tanya Miller's soft panties between his hot, inflamed foreskin and his hand.

*pain pain & more pain / does pain have a point of diminishing return?*

Jacob envisioned a flipping coin, as if in slow-motion, and knew by its color it was a dime.

*both sides of the coin are silver*

The voice in his head was talking again.

*pain is pleasure / pleasure is pain*
*the snake eats its own tail / the tail eats its own snake*

Jacob went through Tanya Miller's room in the Tackett home thoroughly. He felt every item of clothing, pressed most of them to his face, breathing in the vanilla and the lavender and the sweat and the other smell, the smell lining the inside of the panties in the pile in the corner of the room, the smell lingering in the clean panties in the top dresser drawer.

*Cunt stink.*

*Cunt stink* is what the bald man called it.

"Some love it," Randall Adkins had said over his shoulder during that hunting trip.

*Hun-ter / shit ass*

"Some hate it," the bald man's laugh was a trill, discordant tangle of sharps, "but every man knows it: cunt stink. Ye ever smelled it, shit ass? Huh?"

Randall Adkins stopped dead on the little ridgetop trail and turned around, smiling that shark's smile of his, devoid of warmth and, Jacob had seen, most of his teeth.

"Ye even smelled a pussy up close?" he'd asked. "Aside from yer momma, I mean."

Jacob remembered pretending to watch a lone hawk circle, almost at eye-level where they'd stood high on the ridge, unable to meet the bald man's eyes. His face felt hot and he couldn't stop recalling the hairy slit in his mother's crotch. How many times had he seen it? He wasn't sure. How many times had it creeped into the back of his mind?

Jacob cringed.

"Ye never eaten a pussy?" Randall Adkins was faux-incredulous. "Ye never tasted that sweet and sour, juicy cunt stink b'fore?"

*That's cunt stink*, Jacob thought, practically sticking the green panties into his nostrils. *Cunt stink.*

-

Jacob forced himself to leave Tanya Miller's bedroom. He didn't know how long he'd been in there, but he knew it was a long, long time. He pushed himself off the mattress, picked up the small pile of hair he'd collected from her pillow, sheets, and clothing, and held it under the lamplight, carefully studying the way the light hit the bland, vaguely yellow strand and blossomed into something else: a golden amber glow.

Jacob thought this must be innate in all women, this refraction, the deception that must be a natural trait, a reflex.

*You think they're one thing,* Jacob thought, slowly rolling the strands between his thumb and forefinger, *then, upon further examination, you see they're something else entirely.*

He put the hair deep into his left pocket and left Tanya Miller's bedroom.

*The bald man was right,* he thought, *they're all cunts.*

-

At first, Rodney Tackett's room was a bit disappointing to Jacob in a way he couldn't quite understand. The bully had a lot of baseball crap: posters, cards, gloves, bats, helmets, uniforms. There were a few action figures on the little desk and a few more in the closet.

There was a dusty ceiling fan, the air-conditioning unit in the window, a brass-framed twin bed, a dresser, a door to the second-floor bathroom, a closet. The space felt empty to Jacob, where it should feel threatening. He expected the room to punch him, spit in his face. Jacob expected Rodney Tackett's room to grab him by his infected penis and call him a "faggot."

When it didn't, Jacob got pissed.

160

*what Rodney Tackett done*

The panging lightning flared inside the black sweatpants, Walmart, and Jacob felt his pulse quicken.

*what Rodney Tackett done*

Jacob wanted to hurt the room. He wanted to maim the space somehow, punch it, bruise it, scar it. He paced the length of Rodney Tackett's bedroom, feeling as strong and hateful and *ominous*, Mrs. Horace's Word of the Day the day before, as the cougar he'd seen on the sixth-grade fieldtrip to the Cincinnati Zoo. He stopped suddenly, overwhelmed by hatred, and threw his head back on his neck, hocking the biggest loogie he could and spit it onto Rodney Tackett's Cincinnati Reds pillow case. He smiled at the gleaming snot island, which was quickly surrounded by a spreading stain, *the pulling current returns / lapping clean / clapping mean.*

*The pictures*, the voice told him. *Find the pictures.*

*Tanya Miller / Tanya Miller*

Jacob could still smell her, her *cunt stink*. He could still taste the tangy crust he'd licked and sucked off her bedsheets.

He went through the bully's dresser first. Then the desk. Then the closet. Then, just when he was getting ready to lose it and start breaking Rodney Tackett's stuff, Jacob thought to check under the bed. There, inside a rusted chocolate tin, Jacob found seventeen photographs of Tanya Miller showering.

-

Jacob was looking down at her eyes, *closed slits / pouty, parted lips*, but he couldn't help but notice the sudsy titties and wet pubic hair, *hairy slit / landing strip*. He could smell the shower, feel the steam rising up and blanketing his face in the mingling scents of vanilla and lavender / *& cunt stink.*

*You even smelled a pussy up close?*

*sweet / sour*

Jacob could taste her, Tanya Miller. He could feel the liquid of her body as separate, distinct from the water falling out of the showerhead. He could feel it rolling around the tip of his tongue, little beads of her spilling down his burning throat.

*Mine.*

His eyes slowly slid up from her cunt, along the landing strip, the flat, smooth stomach, the perky, small titties, the long, upturned neck, the gentle slope of her pointy chin, the parted, pouty mouth, the closed slits of her eyes, her blonde hair foaming with shampoo, then, at last, both of her hands, painted *painted / painted* painted nails, fingers like snakes, working *working / working* working. The navy blue. The white. The peach skin and lines, hinting at the flexibility of the joints. The moist little webbing, stretched and glistening, connecting her left thumb to her pointer finger. The slim, ornate quality to the hands, *so fragile, so beautiful.*

"Oh," Jacob gasped, "god."

Jacob heard the tires on the gravel and realized he was back on Tanya Miller's bed, part of her bedsheets, the oblong, crusty spot, inside his mouth, his teeth painfully grinding the cotton back and forth, the muscles of his throat working, swallowing, gulping.

*How long have I been here?* he wondered.

*Get out*, the voice told him. *Get out now.*

Jacob saw the twin beams of Johnnie Flynn's Dodge Ram break through the warm yellow lamplight on the ceiling as the truck pulled up onto the ascending gravel driveway. He flung himself off the bed onto the floor.

Electric pain.

Jacob felt a wetness in the crotch of the black sweatpants, Walmart, so he lifted the waistband. A vile smell unlike anything he could ever recall coming from his body hit him in the face like a sudden slap.

Jacob nearly gagged. He saw a thick, green and yellow and vaguely white mess around his penis and testicles.

*Oh god.*

*Get out of the house*, the voice demanded.

Jacob let the waistband of the black sweatpants, Walmart, slap shut. He pushed himself to a crouch and slunk to the window. He saw the red of brake lights, then heard the closing of a door, before realizing the lamp was still on behind him. He ducked down, banging his forehead on the windowsill in the process.

"Shit," he hissed, rubbing the already rising welt on his forehead.

He crawled across Tanya Miller's bedroom floor to turn the lamp off but hesitated, his thumb hovering over the switch.

*They'll notice*, the voice said. *Leave it on. Go out the window. Now.*

Jacob did as he was told. He unlocked Tanya Miller's window, climbed out, and closed it quietly behind him just as the front door below him rattled shut. He smiled when he heard the noisy lock slide into place.

Jacob climbed off the Tackett's front porch without issue, though he felt the black sweatpants, Walmart, bunch and twist painfully around his penis and swollen testicles. He crouched low, stuck his left hand inside to readjust himself and felt something foreign, aside from the pungent mucus, bunched up and partially twisted around the head of his penis. He removed it, with difficulty and gritted teeth, and pulled it out.

*Mine*, he thought, holding Tanya Miller's green panties in the moonlight.

A long glob of the smelly goo dropped off the soft satin and floated toward Jacob's feet like a spider on a web.

*Mine*, the voice echoed. *Mine.*

-

Jacob felt himself wake, as if from an absurdly deep slumber, with an onset of dizziness, *vertigo, Mrs. Horace, 1: a sensation of motion in which the individual or the individual's surroundings seem to whirl dizzily; 2: a dizzy confused state of mind,* and the dancing of floaters all across his vision, no matter where he turned his head. He eased himself down onto his hands and knees, feeling his body jerk and shake, out of his control. It felt like a vice was squeezing his chest, the clamps biting deeper with each turn of the handle. Electric flashes of white and blue stabbed and jolted. He was sure the pressure at his temples would force his brain to blow out the back of his head at the next moment.

He tried to open his mouth to scream but couldn't even manage a moan. Instead, he vomited.

-

Slowly, lazily, *in little pirouettes of flit and flutter / a shutter's staccato stutter*, the floaters winked out of existence like snow in sudden sun, leaving Jacob blank-eyed and gaping. His head felt like a scooped-out pumpkin, *a hollow-headed jack o' lantern / all tricks & no treats*, echoing with a fuzzy, persistent pain.

*pain pain & more pain / does pain have a point of diminishing return?*
*rain rain, keep the sun away / what the light doesn't blind, it cleaves away*
*It's raining*, Jacob realized.

He felt the droplets, large, hot, and halting, at first, but intensifying toward a real downpour with each passing second, at the same moment he realized the floaters were gone and he was sitting on the edge of the rocky bluff on the eastern ridge looking down some one hundred and fifty feet or so at the hideout, the stained and torn miss

# BIRTH OF A MONSTER

K-Swisses dangling in the brisk, predawn wind.

Needles prickled the bottoms of his feet, spreading like a virus up his legs, into his groin, stomach, chest, arms and hands, neck and head.

He shoved himself backwards, dragging his legs up over the rough lip of the rocky cliff and ripping both legs of the black sweatpants, Walmart. Something crashed out of his pocket and shattered on the sandstone at his left side. A small pile of black specks was scattered in the shatter; some remained where they fell, to be jostled by the wind, but others began to scurry in all directions.

*Ticks.*

Jacob didn't remember putting the mason jar, nearly a third full, in the large, left pocket of the black sweatpants, Walmart, but, with a dumbfoundingly vivid clarity, he suddenly remembered having the mason jar in the bully's room. He saw himself as the star actor in some black and white movie on the AV Club's Sony television at school.

*the hero / the villain*
*the only character / in the whole play today*

Jacob felt unmade. He watched the ugly, young actor, *the star / the star*, smile as he twisted the lid off the mason jar. He heard the rising tremor in the string section score; the tension building *building / building. Fraught,* Mrs. Horace's Word of the Day, *1: full of or accompanied by something specific; 2: causing or characterized by emotional distress or tension.* Jacob watched himself sprinkle ticks into Rodney Tackett's pillowcase, bedsheets, underwear drawer, in every pocket of his backpack, and under his bed.

Jacob watched himself stare into the lidless mason jar, face expressionless, for a long, long time. Just when he thought he couldn't stand to watch his own idiotic spacing out a moment longer, he watched a guileless smile blossom across his face like monsoon desert deltas in flood and couldn't help it, he smiled too.

*God*, he thought. *Despite it all, I'm such a happy boy sometimes.*

-

"I don't feel good, Mr. Cottrell," Jacob said, his voice blank, toneless.

The janitor jingled his keys.

"Mr. Goodman, this is the third day in a row that ye 'haven't felt good'," Mr. Cottrell said, sticking the needle into a dodgeball and allowing some air to hiss out.

164

Jacob smelled the rubber and thought of the long, black gloves he'd seen advertised by Ace Hardware in the *Floyd County Times*.

"I don't feel good, Mr. Cottrell," Jacob said again, trying to force some emotion into his voice but failing.

The janitor sighed.

"To the nurse's office, Goodman," he said, tossing the ball onto the hardwood floor and pulling another from the mesh bag. "I'm going to call ahead too. Tell them a call should be placed to yer parents to make sure you get the proper medical attention for . . ."

Jacob felt, simultaneously, as if he were sleepwalking and as if he were watching himself sleepwalk on the A.V. Club's Sony TV in an eerie black and white movie.

*I should answer him*, Jacob thought, but he didn't. He just stood there, looking down at the gleaming hardwood of the auxiliary gym. He was the stock image of dejection. He was the kicked dog, tail shaking between its legs.

His mother's voice narrated the inane sequence of Jacob walking down the long east wing of Floyd County High.

*Quit lookin' like that.*

*What do you have to be so got damn unhappy about?*

*The things I have to do for ye, ye little twerp. If you only knew.*

His arms felt twice as heavy as they should. His legs were cheap prosthetics in poor fittings. Jacob was sure his testicles, purpled and red the night before, were swelling again. He could feel the hot skin sticking to the thin underwear. He didn't even bother looking before sinking his left hand into his pants and gently readjusting himself.

He opened the thick door into the nurse's office without looking at the person behind the desk.

"I don't feel good," Jacob said.

-

Jacob was amazed how easy it was to blend in sometimes. He found he could watch Tanya Miller in between almost every single class. He could get close enough to hear her voice, see the way the light blazed when it struck the golden strands of her hair, smell the vanilla and lavender, if he just kept steadily moving along with the rest of the continuous flow of students and teachers and school staff clogging the hallways like ant farm tunnels. Jacob walked a pace just under that of those around him, kept his head slightly downward, his face turned partially toward her, Tanya Miller, his eyes darting and alert and careful.

# BIRTH OF A MONSTER

Tanya Miller wasn't talking to Dennard Taylor anymore. He just didn't understand her.

Tanya Miller wasn't content to be a base for every routine. She was going to be a top, a floater.

Tanya Miller thought her creepy asshole cousin stole a pair of her underwear.

Jacob reached out a stray finger and felt the soft place just above her elbow on the back of her arm. A gentle brushing, not even a baby's breath of pressure, but a touch. He put his head down and shuffled farther along down the hallway, undetected.

*Mine*, Jacob thought, bringing his left index finger to his mouth and sucking. *Mine.*

The cardboard box was sitting just off the shoulder of Route 23. Jacob saw it from the ridgetop, knew it wasn't far from the place where he crossed the highway, and decided to check it out, if the coast was clear.

The cloudless sky was glittering with stars, planes, and satellites. The angle of the ridgetops lining this portion of Route 23 blocked the moon and sent darker shadows farther into the woods in patterns that tricked depth deception. Jacob stood behind a rough blue oak, shielded from both sides of the road, and waited, listening.

Everything was still and quiet.

Jacob hadn't been sleeping much, again. He half-hoped a car or coal truck would pass by so he could allow himself to skip checking out the cardboard box without internal shame about his cowardice, but the highway was empty and dark.

Jacob stepped up onto the rocky shoulder of the road but, in the misleading shadows of the curvy valley, he caught the toe of his right miss K-Swiss on the lip of the pavement and tumbled forward. He threw his hands out to catch himself and felt the bite of little rocks and other sharp debris in the palms of each of his hands. The jarring motion sent an eruption of hot pain flaring up from his groin into his lower stomach.

Jacob held every muscle of his body rigid, putting all his effort into not shitting himself. He sucked in air through clenched teeth until he was sure he was in complete control of his faculties, then he spat out an oily loogie that had the lingering aftertaste of spoiled milk and pushed himself back to his feet.

*I gotta get some sleep*, Jacob thought, feeling the tiredness in his very bones. The light's always so strange in this spot.

The moon was nearing the top of the ridgeline, bending and stretching the shadows further. The forest on the other side of the highway seemed to reach out to him.

Sound from the cardboard box startled Jacob; he turned away from the reaching trees toward it. He could hear movement, little scratching and whimpering sounds, coming from inside. He watched his elongated but nearly translucent shadow reach and blanket the cardboard box.

Jacob knew what was in it before he looked inside. He could feel the skin of his cheeks pulling tighter with another smile.

*Such a happy boy.*

The moon crested the ridgetop, God's forgotten toenail upturned and glowing.

*The moon's smiling too*, Jacob saw, letting his beaming face turn upward into the pale, white light.

For a time, Jacob lost himself in the beautiful luminance of the moon's wan smile, Mrs. Horace's Word of the Day winking in his mind like a neon sign: *Providence: 1: divine guidance or care; 2: God conceived as the power sustaining and guiding human destiny.*

The moon was nearly behind the opposite ridge when Jacob came back to himself on the shoulder of Route 23. He looked down into the box of wet-eyed puppies and felt suddenly connected to everything: the rough bark of the blue oak, the smiling, toenail moon, the soft fur on the little wriggling puppies, the filet knife clipped onto the waistband of the black sweatpants he stole from Walmart, even the whistling whimpering one of the little mutts kept sounding.

*a place for everything / everything in its place*
*pain is pleasure / pleasure is pain*
*desert / seabed*

Jacob looked down at the crying puppy, saw the curve of its ribcage at each of its shaking sides, and heard his jaw creak as his smile stretched even further.

*Patches*, he thought, *for the quilt.*

Jacob knelt down, gritted his teeth against the pain, the smile firmly in place, unwavering, and carefully closed the top of the cardboard box.

# CHAPTER TWELVE
## PAIN / PLEASURE

**TANYA MILLER WAS ACTING FUNNY.** Jacob watched the way she held herself, usually so straight and lithe, today: as rigid as a board.

*As rigid as rigor mortis*, he thought, averting his eyes and passing by her, Tanya Miller, in front of her locker, where she was pretending to be normal in a small cluster of popular kids and jocks.

Jacob had been having a reoccurring daydream: every animal he'd ever killed, dozens upon dozens, stacked up, horizontally, stretched upward to the sky; a corpse ladder, where each rung, each step up, or down, is a victim, a night or early morning spent hunting, catching, killing, experimenting. In the dream, Jacob was climbing and climbing, rung by stiffened, stinking rung, reliving each moment with the animal, smelling its smells, feeling its fur or feather or scale, stretched tail and leg, claw and paw and hoof and talon, and the blood, always the blood. He passed hours of his school life climbing that ladder.

There was a tightness in her face, Tanya Miller's face. Jacob could see it clearly as he passed by her locker again.

*So much is there*, Jacob thought, *if you only opened your eyes and looked.* So many people walked around with open but unseeing eyes.

*all the world's asleep / everyone a sleepwalker*

Robbie Farmer, eyes like a trusting puppy, navy and white lettermen jacket spotless, bent forward, leaned down from his exceptional tallness to kiss her, *Tanya Miller / Tanya Miller*, Tanya Miller. The starting forward for the Bobcats was much taller than Tanya Miller, Bobcat Cheer Squad base, and both she and Jacob had time to see the kiss coming. Jacob watched her, Tanya Miller, watch him, Robbie Farmer, with a strange look on her face, her eyes suddenly flashing, suddenly brighter, the smooth skin of her forehead and cheeks pulled tight, hinting at the worry lines to come.

Often, Jacob felt he saw too much and had to look away.

-

168

Tanya Miller walked home to the Tackett house from school. Jacob followed behind her, in plain sight so long as there were other students, then from behind buildings and vehicles and shrubs and trees, watching the way every piece of her body moved in tandem. Her feet planted each step firmly, without hesitation, the muscles of each muscular leg thrusting the body forward in a jellyfish's hypnotic glide. The swishing sashay of her ass. The bouncing under her shirt. The tanned arms wrapped around two textbooks and a Lisa Frank trapper keeper, a hummingbird comprised and surrounded by overly bright colors.

Jacob saw all of this, from his varying vantage points, but his eyes, drawn as if by magnetic force, kept returning to Tanya Miller's glitter-painted nails. They caught, held, and reflected the light, even under the low-hanging gray clouds.

*Those hands*, Jacob kept repeating. *Those nails.*

He watched her, Tanya Miller, glide up the rickety porch stairs and disappear through the Tackett's front door from his place behind the sassafras trees. The slim fingers of her right hand wrapped around the old-fashioned brass doorknob sent sparks of hot white shooting off from his groin.

*pain / pleasure*

*pleasure / pain*

Jacob couldn't tell where she was in the house. The cloud cover was gray, which reflected off the dirty windows and made him uncomfortable. He slipped deeper into the woods surrounding the house, moving toward the side of the house where he climbed on and off the rickety front porch.

He pictured those glittery nails exploring the supple folds and curves of her body, stepping out into the overgrown side yard. Jacob saw the sparkling tip of her right thumb kneading the top of the hairy slit between her legs. He saw the glittered nails of her right fingers glint as she pinched and pulled and twisted the dark circles of her nipples.

Jacob saw her, Tanya Miller, from the overhead perspective of Rodney Tackett's shower photographs, her hair wet, sudsy, the tips of her glittered nails slipping in and out of water and blonde hair. He saw the closed, horizontal slits of her eyes, the hairy, vertical slit between her legs under the landing strip. He saw the open, pouty mouth and water-slickened breasts.

*Those hands*, Jacob thought. *Those painted nails.*

# BIRTH OF A MONSTER

Jacob nearly fell when the Tackett's front door opened and she, Tanya Miller, stepped onto the rickety front porch. She didn't see him, as she quickly spun on her heels, her straight back facing him, to lock the door. Jacob, on swift, nearly noiseless feet, dropped to a crouch and ducked down at the side of the porch. His breath rushed in and out of his mouth and he took the gulps as quietly as he could without passing out.

Jacob watched Tanya Miller, walking with a purpose, a sweatshirt tied around her waist, from the side of the porch, his chest heaving, needles pricking the undersides of his feet and the palms of his hands. With each step, she shrank in size until she was a stray piece of food along the earth's lower jaw, gliding down the Tackett's descending gravel drive toward the rows of tombstones.

*tombstones as molars / tombstones as incisors*

Jacob, watching her, Tanya Miller, slip between the tombstones, walking straight through the graveyard instead of around it, was positive the world was a great hunter too.

*the chewer of men / spitting out only to swallow again*

He was sure of it. He was but a cog in some great masticating beast.

*A fang of the beast*, he thought. *First to strike, first to bite, first to rend & tear.*

He forced himself to stand just as she, Tanya Miller, turned right onto the sidewalk lining South Lake Drive.

*This is unusual*, he thought, taking to the woods to follow her.

-

At first, Jacob wondered where Tanya Miller was heading. To a friend's house? Robbie Farmer's?

After a time though, he fell into sync with her steps, *the rhythm of the world / the teeth & the gnashing*, and the question slipped from his head as he watched the cleft of her perfect ass rise and fall, rise and fall.

The pressure in his groin built. The static humming of electrical pain hissed and crackled.

Tanya Miller walked the nearly three miles past Archer Park, through Prestonsburg, to the Walmart without so much as a single glance over her shoulder. Jacob trailed her from the woods for as long as he could, then took to the sidewalk, allowing ample space between them. Stealing glances at the houses and businesses they passed by, but no one seemed to take notice of him.

170

*Why would they?* Jacob thought, watching Tanya Miller's right hand pick a wedgie from the form-fitting shorts. *When Tanya Miller is snapping the ass of her panties on the sidewalk?*

Jacob followed Tanya Miller across the road into the little shopping center. The asphalt parking lot was littered with trash and vehicles, most of which had seen better days. Tanya Miller walked straight by the McDonald's, the Goodwill, and the Big Lots and headed for the entrance to the Walmart. She stopped momentarily beside the cart corral, untied the sweatshirt around her waist, and pulled it on over her blonde head, leaving the hood up despite the warm weather.

Jacob walked through the automatic door twenty-five seconds after her.

-

The elderly greeter's back faced Jacob as the automatic door slid open. He watched the white-haired woman in the blue vest follow Tanya Miller's covered head as it bobbed over the half-aisle of potato chips and soda. She raised the radio to her wrinkled lips just as Jacob was walking by.

"Black sweatshirt, looks blonde, high-school age," the greeter said into the walkie-talkie. "Probably headed for cosmetics."

Jacob didn't understand why everybody was so driven by the need to be seen. The best experiences of his life had come about by his ability to hide, often in plain sight. Jacob saw the way the kids who weren't popular looked at the kids who were, that desire to be seen, to fit in while simultaneously standing out.

*Wanting to be worth something / for nothing*

*But it doesn't work that way,* Jacob thought, adjusting his pace and furtively scanning for more blue vests. Everything from his past told him there was a cost, "there're no free drinks," as his mother always said, for everything. Mrs. Wallers told them all the mass and energy in the universe was constant. Jacob, exhausted from his quilt work—he added one dog, two cats, and a possum late into the early morning hours—understood her to mean everything that ever was is, and everything that ever will be, is as well.

Jacob thought about the past. It seemed to him most people saw the past as recollections of how they felt about events at the time processed through their need to be needed. Trivial. Meaningless. He didn't want to be needed anymore. He didn't think he ever really was.

# BIRTH OF A MONSTER

He thought about his past, *sixteen years of heavy cringing*, and felt the immediate need to break something, to lash out at anything and everything. His hands tightened into fists. A weight settled onto his chest. His jaw worked side to side, his teeth grinding.

*Stop it*, the voice in his head demanded. *Stop it right now.*

Jacob took in a deep breath, held it, let it out.

*There*, he told himself. *Find her.*

Jacob was approaching cosmetics when he saw two blue vests rounding the intersecting aisle, clearly headed in that direction as well. Jacob turned toward a pair of athletic shorts on a rack of workout clothing marked CLEARANCE BLOWOUT and pretended to examine the fabric's elasticity until they'd passed. Then he casually followed them, examining endcaps and display bins along the way.

*Where is she?*

The nearly blinding aisle of makeup and facial soaps and scrubs and assorted beauty products was empty, save one middle-aged woman fretting between two boxes of red hair dye.

Jacob saw the cleverness of the bright lights in the beauty aisles immediately and, for the *n*th time, thanked God he wasn't a girl. All the things he stole weren't anywhere remotely as difficult to take without detection.

The two blue vests, a middle-aged man with an enormous beer-gut and a tall, lanky pimple-faced older boy, stopped in their tracks at the same time. Jacob, unconsciously, stopped too; he watched Beer-belly lift the handheld walkie-talkie to his ear then turn and offer a quick look at Pimples. The two blue-vests turned back the way they'd come and walked with looks of determined purpose on their doughy faces.

*Move*, the voice told him.

Jacob picked up the product nearest him and pretended to study it. His stomach dropped when he saw he was holding a cardboard carton labeled: Equate Ultra Thin Pads with Flexi-Wings for Overnight. He felt his red, Judas-blood blanket his face in shame and embarrassment.

He turned his back partially to the quickly approaching blue vests, setting the box of Equate Ultra Thin Pads with Flexi-Wings for Overnight back on the shelf. He hoped neither blue vest noticed he'd put the product in the wrong place; they were so close. Jacob picked up a green bottle and forced himself to read the title:

Renewing Argan Oil of Morocco. Vaguely, he wondered what this argan oil would feel like on his pubic hair. He wondered if Tanya Miller ever used it. What it would smell like in her hair. He wondered what it would taste like on her landing strip.

The blue vests passed Jacob without so much as a glance.

Jacob set the bottle of argan oil back on the shelf, turned on his heels to follow them, but stopped again when he didn't see them anywhere down the aisle in front of him.

*Where'd they go?*

Three families with three carts stuffed to overflowing were visible but not blue vests and no Tanya Miller.

*Where is she?*

Jacob turned around and looked back down that end of the aisle, but in vain.

*Why's she even in here in the first place?*

Jacob heard the crackle of a walkie-talkie to his left. He listened for a moment, heard it again, this time a little farther away but definitely coming from the other side of the aisle he was standing in front of, which he saw was filled with hundreds of bottles of fingernail polish and fingernail accessories. Jacob walked down the aisle, his head cocked to the right, his left ear angled slightly upwards and toward the sound, his mouth hanging nearly as open as his greedy, darting eyes.

So many colors.

*Red & green / blue & purple*

So many variations.

*Bruises in bloom / intestines removed*

So many flavors.

*Raspy raspberry lemonade / Mindy Chocolate Milk Robertson, the choy from S. Lake Dr.*

The aisle ended abruptly, and Jacob found himself dazedly staring at a rack of pale pink grannie panties. He jerked his head to the left and saw another rack of elderly women's underwear.

More Judas-blood flushed his face.

Images of folded, wrinkly skin flashed in his head. He smelled sour cheese and tasted soured milk in the back of his phlegmy throat.

He spun away and down the feeder aisle, shaking his head in disgust.

*Keep it together*, the voice said. *Act right.*

Jacob peeked around the corner of the aisle and saw them. The blue vests were slowly walking toward her, Tanya Miller, who was looking at rows of white and light blue and pink boxes with unmistakable anxiety on her partially obscured but still obviously beautiful face.

*What's she doing?*

The two blue vests were literally creeping toward her, Tanya Miller.

*She doesn't even know they're there,* Jacob saw.

The blue vests looked to be about fifteen feet away from her, Tanya Miller, who reached up and brought down one of the boxes from the shelf for a closer examination. Jacob saw the nails of her right hand, the slim fingers grasping the blue and white cardboard box with lithe speed, were glitter-coated; the harsh fluorescent lights overhead sent a cascade of shimmering sparks trailing behind each of her, Tanya Miller's, fingernails as they glided up to the box, then back down with it in tow. She flipped it over, the nails of her right hand sparkling with even the subtlest of her, Tanya Miller's, movements.

*Those nails.*

Jacob watched the change come over her, Tanya Miller. At first, he was just focused on her hands but the voice in his head made him pay attention and he watched the way her shoulders suddenly hunched, the way her head craned side-to-side on her neck, trying to see without seeming to be watching. Jacob watched her, Tanya Miller, and knew she was getting ready to try and steal that pregnancy test. He knew before she even lifted the baggy sweatshirt up and stuffed the box inside.

The two blue vests also knew. Jacob knew they knew and watched them watch her, Tanya Miller, as she lifted up the bottom front of her sweatshirt, nails glittering, and drop to a near-crouch.

Her thin white hand looked porcelain under the harsh lights, topped by her sparkling, marvelous fingers. Jacob felt time stop at the sight of them.

Transfix, *Mrs. Horace, 1: to hold motionless by or as if by piercing; 2: to pierce through with or as if with a pointed weapon.*

Just as the last bit of blue and white disappeared into Tanya Miller's sweatshirt, Jacob saw the tower of women's shaving cream cans. He threw himself at the stacked cans before he even realized what he was doing. He had just enough time to reach down and cup his privates before the loud crash and thump of the fall.

Jacob went sprawling alongside the clanging, rolling cans. Foam exploded onto the tiles and onto the lower shelves. Most of the air had been knocked out of him, but not all of it. He tried to push himself up, but slipped in the white, fragrant foam back onto the tile. His right shoulder hurt from both of the falls. He rolled over onto his back, groaning.

The two blue vests stood over him.

"You okay, kid?" Beer-belly asked.

Jacob threw himself forward, rolling between the blue vests, then scampering to his feet and into a full-on run.

"Hey!" the blue vest yelled.

"Stop!"

He nearly fell again when he slipped in a puddle of foam, but he caught himself on a shelf, knocking over several boxes and bottles, and kept running.

-

Electric pain flashed with each step, but Jacob didn't stop running until he was nearly to the front of the store where he ducked into the candy aisle and saw Tanya Miller slip into a door marked WOMEN not fifteen feet away.

Jacob heard the crackle of the blue vests' walkie-talkies and bolted upright.

*Follow her*, the voice said.

Jacob did as he was told.

-

He kept his head down, his pace steady as he neared the door.

*I can't—*

*Do it.*

Jacob reached out his shaky left hand and pushed in the door marked WOMEN.

-

The door swung shut behind him. There was no one at the wall of sinks and mirrors. He spun around and slid the bolt shut.

He took a few quiet steps into the bathroom, then stood still, listening. He heard her sniffling almost immediately. She was in one of the stalls. There were only stalls in the women's restroom and Jacob chided himself at how childish this thought revealed him to be. Tanya Miller was near the far wall, softly crying like a pitiful puppy.

Jacob didn't like puppies, but he had killed lots of them. He

175

preferred killing older dogs, they were harder to trick, but, mainly, because puppies were too stupid to realize what was happening to them. He often thought dogs could smell something on him, some pheromone of danger, the sickly-sweet scent of death, and this made killing them much more fulfilling.

Jacob walked to within three stalls of the one she, Tanya Miller, was in, silently pushed in the door, then dropped to his hands and knees once inside. There were her Sketchers, her ankles, shins, calves.

Jacob sank to his stomach and inched toward her.

"Please, God," Tanya Miller moaned. "Please, please. Please. God."

Jacob stopped his progress when he heard the sound of liquid meeting liquid. He lifted his chin up and sniffed as quietly as he could. He could smell piss alright, but he wasn't sure if it was her piss, Tanya Miller's. He thought he could just whiff her; vanilla and lavender.

/ *& cunt stink*

He felt himself harden painfully against the bathroom floor imagining the landing strip just mere inches away.

"Wait five minutes," Tanya Miller mumbled. "Five minutes. Jesus. What am I supposed to do with this thing in the meantime?"

Jacob watched her Sketches shift from side to side as she moved.

"There," she said.

She sat there silently for a time. Jacob knew she was going to hear his breathing, the pumping of the blood in his temples and crotch.

"No," she moaned. "No. No, no, no no!"

Jacob heard cardboard tear open. Then he heard Tanya Miller make a series of odd grunting noises, the toes of her tennis shoes grinding into the tiles.

He heard a squirt of water, another grunt, then a trickle more.

"Five minutes," she whispered.

She sounded like a woman in church.

"God, please," she whispered. "Please, God. God. Oh."

The pressure in his groin worsened, shooting off little flares of electric blue and white.

Jacob watched her, Tanya Miller, rock back and forth on the toilet, whispering and muttering and moaning.

Jacob had grown accustomed to the nearly silent half-breaths he sucked in through his gaping mouth, his anxiety about being heard momentarily forgotten, as he felt flooded with sudden clarity. He could see the little flecks and streaks of piss and shit on the toilet beside him. He smelled the soured mixture of lemon-scented disinfectant just before the awful smell of human waste and imagined a clean cherry sitting on top of a steaming pile of shit. An overly long pubic hair, wavy at odd angles like a wire-brush on its last leg, hung, somehow, from the bottom of the stall wall just to his left.

*How did it get there?*

*How's it even hanging there?*

*Focus*, the voice said.

Jacob inched a little closer to her, Tanya Miller, feeling his swollen genitals mash and drag on the cool floor under him.

*Mine.*

"Shit!" she cried, startling him.

Jacob hadn't expected the noise and couldn't stop himself from jerking backwards at the sound of it, banging the topside of his head against the stall. The force of the blow rattled the doors on several stalls, they were all interconnected, including hers.

"Wha—" she cried. "Who's there?"

Jacob rubbed the smarting top of his head with his left hand as he awkwardly tried to scoot backwards on the floor. In his haste, he misjudged the height of the stall bottoms and banged into one with the small of his back.

"What the hell?" Tanya Miller shouted. "What're ye doing over there?"

*Shit!*

Jacob wasn't sure if he should bolt out the stall door and make a run for it or try his hand at a polite lady-like cough and hope Tanya Miller bought it. He was still in the throes of coming to a decision when the stall door above him flew open. Tanya Miller stood looking down at him, both her supple, glitter-tipped hands on her slender hips, her cheeks wet and reflecting the overhead lights dully.

Jacob watched the rapid changes on her face, thinking how like a kaleidoscope emotions were.

Just a turn of the dial and one blends fluidly, hypnotizingly into the next, then into the next, the next, until you're back where you began and hardly recognize it. Jacob was glad he wasn't a woman. They had too many emotions and too little control over them.

She was frightened, at first, then she was confused, then she was shocked, then she was angry.

"Yer the boy who tripped in the door at school," Tanya Miller said. "What're ye doing in here?"

Jacob was still processing the gentle cascade of facial expressions that had come and gone across her face. He opened his mouth to respond and stammered something incoherent.

"What?" she said. "I cain't understand ye. Speak up."

All he could do was stare up at her. He knew how idiotic he looked—wide, dazed eyes, open, soundless mouth—but he felt paralyzed just the same. *Transfix, Mrs. Horace, to hold motionless by piercing / pierce through with a pointed weapon.* Her eyes, Tanya Miller's eyes looked him over then returned to his, yet another emotion rising to the surface: disgust.

"Ye fuckin' creep," she said, lifting her right hand from her hip and pointing it at him. "Ye like to watch girls use the bathroom? What kind of fucked up shit is that? Ye sicko."

*She's working herself up*, the voice in his head told him. *Ye gotta stop 'er 'fore she gets a head full o' steam.*

The extended pointer finger of Tanya Miller's right hand jabbed accusatorily at him as she spoke, her little, frenzied stabs serving as punctuation for her tirade.

"Jesus fuckin' Christ but this is a backwards place; everybody's so fucking weird and stupid in this county," she said.

Jacob could hear it as she spoke like a steady tightening of already overwrought strings.

*I don't know what to do.*

"Everyone's either fuckin' their cousin or brother or workin' on fuckin' whoever's around," she said. "Or fuckin' ye after promisin' it'd be nice and not like those other times, but it was. Exactly like those other times. And then actin' like nothin' ever happened! Or . . . or . . ."

The glitter-painted nails were shooting stars, constellations of super novas, sparkles and glimmers leaving tracers and trails glittering into shadow, ripples in the rising water, the current just beginning the pull. Those nails were blackholes, pulling Jacob into their terrific and all-consuming beauty.

*Focus*, the voice commanded.

". . . or spy on girls in the bathroom!" Tanya Miller's voice broke and her face crumpled.

She sank to her knees, sobbing. Jacob watched the sparkles shine as Tanya Miller covered her face and wept.

"Oh, God," she cried. "Oh. God."

-

Jacob couldn't look away.

*oh god / those hands*

"Oh, god," she kept crying.

*oh god / those pretty, pretty nails*

Tanya Miller gulped for air; she was bawling so hard. Her glittery nails shook with her wracking sobs, wet tears and snot spilled through the open spaces between her long, slender fingers.

Jacob had seen his mother lose it like this on several drunken occasions, twice screaming that Jacob was her biggest mistake.

She was so overcome that she was completely at his mercy, he realized.

Jacob forced himself off his stomach onto his knees, flashes of electric blue and white leaping to the forefront of his mind for the briefest of instants as his swollen crotch was jostled by his movement. His eyes squeezed shut automatically, his face a gritting grin of pain until it passed. When he opened his eyes again she was looking at him.

There was a mingling of emotions there now: shame, sorrow, desperation, and, swimming at the forefront of them all, pity.

*Pity, Mrs. Horace, sympathetic sorrow for one suffering, distressed, or unhappy.*

Tanya Miller looked at Jacob the way his mother looked at puppies: doe-eyed and wanting. Something in him desperately needed to remove that look from her face. Jacob wanted to reach over and take ahold of her pretty blonde hair and yank that pitying face upward toward the sky. He wanted to lean over and spit into those sympathetic eyes, that pouty, pitying mouth, he needed to.

*Focus*, the voice said. *Control yourself.*

"What're ye even doin' in here, boy?" Tanya Miller asked. "Jesus, I'm so tired."

The optical illusion of her face changed again and Jacob knew he didn't have to answer. The voice in his head reaffirmed this.

*There ye go*, the voice said. *Just go with it. Yer in like Flynn.*

-

She didn't stop talking. Jacob knew, from his constant passing by and hiding in plain sight nearby, that Tanya Miller talked a lot, but he had no clue a person could literally, continuously speak. There didn't seem to be a filter between the confused tangle of thoughts and feelings in her head and what ceaselessly poured out of her mouth.

"I cain't believe I'm pregnant," she said. "I mean I know everybody said I'd be, like, by the start of last year, jus' like Momma was, but I didn't think it would actually happen."

She'd moved from the floor in front of the stall across the long room to the row of sinks and mirrors, where she turned on the hot water and studied her face under the bright lights, talking all the while.

"I mean, we were careful. Capital 'C,' you know what I mean?"

She shot a look over her shoulder in the mirror at Jacob.

*Nod yer head*, the voice said.

Jacob nodded his head.

She surprised him by laughing, which although a very musical and melodious sound, something akin to lots of ringing bells and bottles clanging together in the gathering wind of a summer thunderhead, deeply infuriated him. Jacob felt a bitter green rage rising up from his chest into the back of his throat, felt his hands tighten into claw-like fists, his fingernails digging into the sweaty palms.

*She's laughing at me.*

Jacob saw her, Tanya Miller, with open, unseeing eyes. He saw the front of her face bashed in, her teeth broken, gleaming bits of fine china protruding at all angles from the decomposing bud of a poisoned rose.

"Of course ye wouldn't know what I mean," she said. "What're ye, twelve?"

At first, Jacob was too overwhelmed by this vision of her, Tanya Miller, a thing of beauty brutally unmade, destroyed, to reply to the question. It looked so real he half expected to smell the iron pang of blood. He felt the blood pumping from his heart down into his crotch. He opened his mouth, wanting to warn her, to tell her, Tanya Miller, what he saw as clear as day.

"Huh?" she asked. "Cat got yer tongue?"

A sudden bolt of anger rose up and Jacob found his voice.

"Sixteen," he said, his voice breaking on the second syllable.

It echoed around the empty stalls and gleaming sinks of the bathroom, *the women's restroom*, for a moment, pumping more scarlet into his cringing face.

Her laugh was clear, swift water running down the side of a

mountain. It grabbed his full attention and rattled him, opened a
well-spring of confusion. There was something so simply beautiful
about the laugh; the tone, the tenor, and the length of it all co-min-
gled into a symphony of expression. Jacob could hear so much in it
that he couldn't figure out how to take it. There was scorn, relief,
sorrow, and other emotions Jacob couldn't place or properly recognize sliding in and out, *turning the dial / on the kaleidoscope*. It didn't feel
or sound like she was laughing at him, not really, not completely.

Then, to complete Jacob's confusion, Tanya Miller began to cry
again.

"I jus' don't know what to do," she cried. "I mean, I don't. This
wasn't supposed to happen. I mean they all said it would but it I—I
. . . I jus' don't."

Her glittery nails were fretfully working at the tears and the snot
and the puffy circles budding under each of her blue eyes. She
worked in fraught little circles, starting with the tears, dropping to
the leaking nose, then back up to the eyes.

"It's positive," she cried. "I cain't believe it's positive. I took it
twice, too. What am I supposed to do?"

Jacob didn't know what to say, so he didn't say anything, just
kept watching those glittery nails and slender fingers.

Such pretty hands.

"There's no tellin' what Johnny Flynn will say," Tanya Miller said.
"And Marie! Oh, God!"

She looked out from behind her working, glittery fingers at Jacob, her face red from crying and her restless hands, shooting quick,
strange looks at him. He didn't know what was in them; there was
so much.

*the kaleidoscope flicks like a Bic / changes again & again & again*
*fear, sadness, commiseration, confusion, askance*

Jacob worked at keeping incredulity off his face, worked at keeping it blank, worked at keeping the rising flush from returning. He
worked at understanding what was happening. *What does she want from
me? What am I supposed to do? Why did I see her face smashed in?* He worked
at shifting himself subtly on the cool tile floor, his swollen testicles
pressing uncomfortably against the underside of his penis and his
pants.

"I haven't heard from Momma in almost two weeks," Tanya Miller nearly wailed. "She missed her court date and the social worker

won't tell me shit! That cunt jus' stops by to make sure I ain't starvin' to death. She don't give a shit about me, not really. Or Momma!"

Her beautiful hands were shaking fists now. Little shooting stars striking the air, wiping away a tear or her nose, then flashing out under the fluorescent sky once again.

"I think she wants her to keep failin' her drug tests, ye know that?" Tanya Miller said. "I can see it in the cunt's eye, like a gleam or dirty look, ye know? She acts so got dam above it all. Little Miss Perfect. Little Miss College Degree. From Money."

She was pacing the length of the bathroom now.

*Not quite like that cougar from the Cincinnati zoo*, Jacob thought. *More like a pissed off house cat.*

Jacob saw the feral tabby cat from last night: flayed and dripping and covered with ticks.

The pressure in his groin worsened. He could hear the static hum of the building blue and white, *the flares to come / pain pain & more pain.*

"And she won't . . . let . . . me go home," she hiccuped back into sobs, the "o" of "home" stretched into a held moan, *the backbeat of the song.*

When she was finished, Tanya Miller looked up from her glittery hands and smiled.

*sun / after the rain*

"I'm sorry," she said. "I don't even know yer name. I'm Tanya. Miller."

She did something then that Jacob never forgot; she stooped down, slowly, in front of him and reached out with the porcelain beauty of her right hand, the shooting stars of her nails a triumph under the harsh fluorescent sky, and smiled down at him.

*an angel descends / enshrouded, blinded by kindness*

*as defenseless as a puppy / a kitten a possum a squirrel a fawn a coon a groundhog a . . .*

Jacob took the hand without hesitating.

"Jacob," he said, "Hunter—"

*Mine.*

"Goodman."

## CHAPTER THIRTEEN
## TROUBLE / IN A FAMILY WAY
## (PRAIRIE DOGGIN')

**"HERE," SHE SAID, STOPPING SUDDENLY** on the sidewalk.

Jacob, dazed from the inundation of Tanya Miller's ceaseless, animated talking, took three steps before he even realized it.

He turned around just as Tanya Miller dug out a stick of tinted lip balm from her pocket.

"Give me yer—"

*lungs*, the voice said, *thumbs / spleen / liver / scalp / heart*

"—arm," she said, taking Jacob's arm. "I gotta get scootin'. Cheerleadin'."

Jacob watched those glittered hands slide the sleeve of his shirt up to his elbow. She moved a half-step closer to Jacob, then tucked his hand between her trunk and left arm.

*She's warm.*

Then he saw the gentle curve of her left breast resting on the space just above his wrist.

*Oh.*

The growing pressure almost drew a wince, but Jacob forced it down.

"Here's my number at Johnny Flynn 'n' Marie's," Tanya Miller said, the nearness of her voice shocking him.

He jerked his head up, but smelled her hot, slightly soured breath for a lifetime before his hazy eyes found the smiling, partially open lips. He breathed her in through his nostrils.

*Oh God!*

Jacob watched as Tanya Miller wrote out seven numbers in dark pink lip balm, the curve of her slender fingers dotted with so many shooting stars. He smelled her again, slowly.

*Vanilla and lavender and . . .*

He couldn't quite place the other odor.

*Vanilla and lavender and . . .*

183

# BIRTH OF A MONSTER

It was on the tip of his tongue and in the bridge of nose like a stinging sneeze delayed.

*Vanilla and lavender and . . .*

"We've got an away game tomorrow in Letcher County," Tanya Miller said, "but how 'bout you show me yer little 'hideout' Saturday mornin'? It'd be a godsend to get outta that house for a bit."

*Cunt stink*, the voice said.

Jacob readjusted his swollen testicles with the numb fingers of his left hand. His whole body felt asleep, full of needles, smoky, slumbering bees.

*Cunt stink*, Jacob echoed, closing his eyes and sniffing again.

Jacob wanted nothing more than to leave the pink trailer, but the swelling in his left nut and the painful throbbing on the bottom side of his dickhead made this an impossibility. After he walked home, he didn't have one single memory of the nearly three-and-a-half-mile trek. He'd masturbated, twice, into the bathroom sink.

Electric white and blue pain and a pressure that changed into a different kind of pressure each time he came had him doubled over the running water, his left hand wrapped around his throbbing penis, the other flattened against the mirror, supporting what felt like the weight of the universe on his heaving shoulders. He could hear the air wheezing in and out of his lungs but he felt like none of it made it past his choked throat to his lungs.

After a long moment—Jacob was sure he was going to pass out more than once—he eased his green and purple penis into the steaming stream.

*pain pain / & more pain*

He turned his head as far to the left as it could go, feeling and hearing the crack in his neck in a slightly delayed break with continuity, seeing the bathroom door standing wide open—*Did I even bother to close it?*—and his disgusted mother, dressed in shiny black panties and not a stitch else. He heard the crack before he felt the extra give after the pop.

How many furry little necks had he made sound so much worse than that? How many times had he felt the click of the crack like a key in a lock?

*Not enough*, the voice said, just as Jacob ejaculated a glob of yellowish-green and white into the crusty sink.

*Why are my hands numb?* Jacob wondered.

His mother was no longer in the doorway, which stood open and empty and swaying, lined with shifting shadows from the security light outside. Jacob knew he was going to vomit but didn't bother moving to the toilet. He stood naked and trembling, puking into the sink.

He didn't bother knocking on his mother's door to tell her he didn't feel well enough to go to school. He didn't think she'd be up for hours anyway. She'd had "an old friend" over late last night and they'd pissed and moaned and cussed all night long. His mother's full-throated demand for "the motherfuckin' money" had infiltrated his dreams. Jacob had been a diseased version of Winnie the Pooh, all veins and lesions and pus, trapped in a bank vault with a rotten but hornet-filled hive stuck on his cock and balls. When he woke up, he couldn't believe the itchiness and burning underlining the now nearly constant pressure and pain in his groin.

Tanya Miller would be at school. She'd be in her cheerleader uniform or matching cheer squad sweat pants and zip-up too. They had an away game in Letcher County, Jacob remembered. Tanya Miller would be at school and Jacob wouldn't.

His heart beat frantically in his chest as he made his way to the kitchen for something cold to drink. Jacob looked down and, without real shock or concern, observed that he was completely naked. The living room shifted oddly from the right to the left then shifted several feet in another direction before starting the whole process again every three seconds. He thought he was going to throw up, but he was so thirsty he didn't care. His throat felt coated in crushed glass, his ears burning with fresh coals, his stomach wet and hot and soured.

Tanya Miller was at school in her cheerleading uniform. Tanya Miller, who had talked to Jacob, a lot, wrote her phone number on the inside of his arm with her pink lip balm, and Jacob couldn't remember feeling worse in his entire life. He found a cup, not bothering to see if it was even clean, which he doubted, and knocked over a stack of dishes in the sink to get to the faucet.

The water smelled hard and bad. He couldn't taste it, so he downed an entire glass. He held it back under the water, gulping and burping and keeping his eyes closed because the room was shifting and spinning faster and faster every time he looked, until it was full, spilling hard water onto his shaky fingers, then he drank it again.

185

# BIRTH OF A MONSTER

Jacob slept.

When he woke, it was dark and he'd somehow made it back to his bedroom, though the last thing he remembered, and this not very clearly, was getting a drink of water from the kitchen sink. His head hurt, but it wasn't like any headache he'd ever had. He could feel and hear the beating of his heart, which he was certain was the darkest, blackest substance on earth, in his head, / *a marble the size of the sun rattling around a soup can universe.*

He thought he heard his mother's voice raised in anger, in drunkenness, in drunken anger, in surprise, in anger again, then Jacob thought he heard his mother softly crying his name, over and over.

He wanted to get out of his bed and investigate but couldn't. His stomach was swollen, distending outward the lower it went, the closer it got to his groin. Jacob lost time looking at *what Rodney Tackett done.*

He slept without meaning to.

He woke without realizing it.

He looked at the photograph Rodney Tackett had secretly taken of Tanya Miller from a little attic space above the Tackett's second-floor shower, remembering what Tanya Miller smelled like up close, seeing the nails in the photograph as the nails on the slender porcelain hand writing out the seven digits of the Tackett's phone number on his arm in pink, seeing the jagged juts of the white, broken teeth protruding up from the slanted lower jaw of her smashed-in face, the smell of vanilla and lavender and *cunt stink.*

Jacob woke and whispered it.

"Cunt stink."

He woke and realized he'd been awake a long time, watching the water stain on the ceiling shift and flutter with his unsteady, swimming vision.

*Cunt stink*, the voice confirmed. *Uh-huh. Cunt stink.*

The dream was blue. The sky, of course, when he could see it through the trees, which were blue, was blue. He wasn't a body, he was just a collection of wet spots in the air, suspended blue. There was a loud echoing wailing coming from another part of the blue forest and this, too, was blue. It was round, like Jacob, and blue, like Jacob, but it was a different temperature of blue, much, much hotter than any blue flame Jacob had ever been close enough to experience.

He could smell the fire, a pungent, brimstone-like odor, and it was blue, but Jacob nearly mistook it for green.

He laughed at this. Maybe he laughed at it for too long.

Jacob thought laughing in a blue world was the only thing to do. Besides, he was such a happy boy. Blue was his new favorite color.

-

When he woke up again, his head felt empty, the way tires looked after you blew out the innertube. There was a strange taste in his mouth he couldn't place, something rancid beyond the weeks without brushing his teeth and the vinegary remnant of vomit, and he found his vision had steadied enough for him to make it down the hall to the bathroom to brush his teeth.

He didn't bother looking at himself while he brushed his teeth, which took a long time because there were three places, two upper teeth, one lower tooth, that hurt like hell when he tried to clean around them. When he finally spit into the sink, still flecked with vomit and stained a bit green from his cum, he saw that his gums were bleeding. Jacob looked into the mirror for a long time, processing what the empty-eyed reflection looking back from there meant.

In the end, he didn't know, but he still felt strong enough to shower, so he did.

-

Jacob stepped out of the shower onto the pile of dirty laundry that nearly covered the bathroom floor in its entirety. There wasn't a clean towel. The pink trailer had no washer or drier and his mother hadn't done laundry since they'd moved into Thompkins' Hilltop Trailer Court, so Jacob slowly bent down, careful not to jostle his swollen, aching groin, and picked up a red sweatshirt, one of his mother's, and used it to dry off.

Steam hung around the cramped little bathroom but was leisurely making its way out of the open bathroom door into the hall. If there was one thing to be said about the pink trailer, it was that the hot water heater worked, and worked like a charm. His skin felt slightly scalded; Jacob had turned the plastic nozzle as far to the left as it would go and forced every bit of himself under the burning stream until his skin prickled with sweat and pinkened like ground round just beginning to brown.

He felt like he'd been out stranded under a relentless Death Valley sun for a week or more. His eyes felt dry and raw and shaky. His lips were cracked at the corners and chapped. The skin of his body hurt all over, like the time he got sun poisoned, but the pain and pressure, which was a pain of sorts, one with entirely different parameters of uncomfortableness, in his penis and testicles, had receded a great deal since the previous day.

*Or was it the day before yesterday?* Jacob wondered, knowing he slept for a long, long time but not sure exactly just how long.

*Is it Friday?* he wondered.

His memory was the empty, shadowed interior of a metal bucket in a wintry dusk.

*No*, he decided, *it's Saturday.*

He'd had no memory of it, but, apparently, he'd told Tanya Miller about the hideout and agreed to take her out there and show it to her to boot.

The hideout with the fourth attempt at the quilt strung up by Trilene, Walmart, and curing in the little window. The hideout with the stained, sticky floor. The hideout with the pregnant raccoon currently on display, strung up on large fishhooks by its shoulder blades, slowly starving to death. The hideout where he'd killed countless animals.

*Including Hobart*, the voice said, *Tanya Miller's relatives' pet. Rodney Tackett's cat.*

Jacob saw *what Rodney Tackett done* in the hideout as if from a decaying movie montage, the tape hissing and garbling the edges of the moving pictures it showed.

He looked down at himself, saw that he was purpled and green with bruising but the swelling had receded greatly.

*This'll teach ye*, he heard his mother scream, *to play around with dead things. To not have any friends. For going outta yer got dam way to fuck up my life!*

*What Rodney Tackett done looks to be on the mend*, Jacob thought, prodding the area with careful, unsure fingers.

*what Rodney Tackett done / what Rodney Tackett done*

Jacob was in his room. He didn't remember getting there, but he didn't dwell on this. Instead, he hunted around the clothing strewn all over the floor until he found a pair of boxers that looked relatively clean, and slid them on, careful the elastic band didn't catch.

*Make 'em pay for it*, the voice said. *Make 'em pay.*

Jacob was nodding along with it the way people did at a bit of information they'd heard a hundred times before.

*Make 'em pay for what Rodney Tackett done.*
*For not understanding.*
*for fuckin' up my life / for not having any friends*
*For not seeing the beauty and skill of what you're doin'*, the voice said, *what we're doing.*

"Yes," Jacob whispered.

Hearing his voice in the quiet of the pink trailer sent a tingle racing up the length of his spine.

"Make 'em pay. Yes."

-

Jacob was sitting on the couch in his boxers, the corded telephone receiver cradled between his shoulder and his ear, punching out the seven numbers, the phone number Tanya Miller had written on Jacob's forearm in tinted lip balm, her number at the Tackett's, on the dial pad on the phone's base.

As he heard the ringing through the static, Jacob examined both of his forearms and saw that the shower had removed Tanya Miller's number. He tried to recall the numbers he'd just jabbed out, but couldn't.

"Hello?" a woman's voice.

Jacob couldn't speak.

He couldn't tell if it was her, *Tanya Miller / Tanya Miller*, or Marie Tackett, Johnnie Flynn's wife, Rodney Tackett's mother.

*what Rodney Tackett done/ what Rodney Tackett done*

"Hello?" the voice was irritable now. "Hello? Is anybody there?"

"Yes, uh," Jacob stammered, seeing Marie Tackett's face in his head. "Uh. Hi."

There was a brief pause, then Marie Tackett, in a flat, unamused voice said, "Rodney or Tanya?"

*what Rodney Tackett done/ Tanya Miller / Tanya Miller / make 'em pay*

"Tanya," Jacob whispered.

"What?"

He coughed into the crook of his arm, then spoke again.

"Tanya," he said, smiling. "Tanya Miller."

"Tanya!" Marie Tackett yelled in the background. "Phone!"

-

"What's up?" she said.

*Tanya Miller. Mine. Make 'em pay.*

Glittered nails slipping through suds of shampoo in her blonde hair.

189

*vanilla and lavender and / vanilla and lavender a—*
*as shot from above / Fast-Forward X2 Mode*

Jacob was sweating. His throat was dry but he spoke.

"Hi, Tanya," he said.

"Jacob, hi!" she squealed.

Jacob felt his chest tighten.

"I've been waitin' fer ye to call all morning," she said. "What took ye so long? When're we goin' out to see this little 'hideout' of yours?"

Jacob recalled the vision of Tanya Miller's destroyed face and felt very scared and tired suddenly.

*Pussy*, the voice said. *Gonna pussy out, ye pussy?*

*No*, Jacob told the voice, *I'm not.*

"I'm ready whenever ye are," Jacob said.

She squealed again.

"Meet me here?" she asked.

He could hear her moving, pictured her in her room, opening the drawers of the dresser he'd touched, retrieving a shirt he'd touched, a pair of pants he'd touched, a pair of panties he'd touched, *but not the green pair, no not those.* Jacob felt his face smiling as he tried to remember if the Tackett family had a cordless phone. He assumed so and couldn't tell if it were his voice or the other voice in his head that chided him for being so unobservant.

Jacob didn't remember getting off the phone with Tanya. He was back inside his room, easing himself into the cleanest pants he could find on his floor.

*Tanya Miller is waiting on you.*

He felt slightly stunned at this realization, and finding a clean t-shirt took some time. The first few he picked up, which would've been fine to wear any other day, now seemed too dirty. Many were now blood-stained, or gave the wrong impression, like the South Floyd Elementary PTA shirt from his mother's brief attempt at direct involvement with Jacob's education. He'd ended up held back a year anyway and both he and his mother got some interesting stares when they saw anybody from Hi-Hat and South Floyd Elementary. Vice Principal Harold dropped the charges against Jacob's mother almost immediately, but Bernice Harold, owner of Look Hair! Day Spa and Salon and Vice Principal Harold's wife, never forgave Christy Goodman, scowled at Jacob whenever they crossed paths, and made a stink big enough to get them to move, again.

Jacob found a gray shirt, only a little ripe around the arm pits, and put it on. Then he found two dry socks, one a dingy, formerly white tube sock, the other a brown, woolen hiking sock, and eased himself down onto his bed to put them on. Something crinkled under him. Jacob scooted away from the spot and rooted around in the tangled blankets until he found the source of the sound: the photograph of Tanya Miller in the shower of the Tackett's second-floor bathroom, the stolen snapshot shot from above by the bully who shoved a 1.00mm screwdriver, all the way to the handle, into Jacob's penis.

*what Rodney Tackett done / the pitiful scarecrow of draped and folded skin*
*You took his cat and he found it.*
*They don't understand; no one understands.*
*What's to understand, you sick little freak? Why'd you kill their cat? What did you do to it?*

In his own voice, a strange question occurred to Jacob, out of the blue, *an unknown shape floating by in the rising waters*, for the first time.

*Does it matter*, Jacob wondered, *what you've done after you've gone?*

He thought of all the awful things he knew about, all the awful things he'd seen people do to each other, the awful things they did to themselves. He thought about all the nights and the men and then the two men that locked his door shut and didn't unlock it until they were done doing what Jacob hadn't understood then and disappeared back into his mother's party.

*I mean, just what can you do with all that?* Jacob didn't know. *There can't be enough punishment in all the universe, even just for the sins of Floyd County.*

It felt paramount that he know the answer to this question, but Jacob couldn't decide just which way he felt about it.

*Paramount*, Mrs. Horace's Word of the Day some time recently, but Jacob couldn't recall exactly when, *superior to all others.*

He didn't mind the thought of dying. In fact, Jacob had found the thought of his own death a comforting thing. He wouldn't hurt all the time if he were dead. He wouldn't be confused or scared or hopeless or numb. He wouldn't feel like a wrinkled scarecrow. He hoped death was just a cessation of being, an empty blank in place of troubled, troubling substance.

*If God is real*, Jacob thought, slipping his feet into the miss K-Swisses, *like they all say, then Heaven must be real too. Angels and trumpets and clouds and the pearly gates. Some bearded guy with a clipboard and a list.*

# BIRTH OF A MONSTER

*Hell, then.*

As he shuffled through the pink trailer, his mother's door was closed, but he could hear water running, faintly, back in the master bathroom.

*trouble / in a family way*
*probably trying to get rid of it / cunt stink*

The bald man's voice, unattached to his shark's eyes and wolf's grin, clanged and chimed like some hellish pipe organ in Jacob's head.

He opened the door to brightness, taking the steps with slits for eyes, then walked up the gravel drive of Thompkins' Trailer Court as fast as the pain and pressure in his groin would let him. He didn't slow down until he was deep into the woods and climbing up the ridge, the ridge that would look down on little Prestonsburg. The glinting white heads of the tombstones of Richmond looked like shattered teeth, *clawhammer / clawhammer clawhammer* clawhammer, Ace Hardware, the sweat stinging his recently scrubbed skin.

He'd dreamt of raccoon skulls in tube socks, four of them so small, tiny almost, two of them not, and the clawhammer, Ace Hardware, and the sound, *the / sound*, the sound.

Jacob saw himself, wide-angle from the front, walking up the Tackett's ascending drive. He saw himself jump first, then felt the push and momentary weightlessness of his apex. He watched the stained women's tennis shoes his mother had bought him at the Goodwill in Pikeville last April smack down into the clear puddle of water in the pothole. Jacob watched, in detailed slow-motion, as the water shot upward in turgid white boils until it was a splash, then he heard the sound of it, but more like the sound of it as replayed in a broken speaker in a gigantic, hollow box.

Jacob watched as the camera zoomed in from its wide-angle shot of the awkward kid jumping into the puddle, the splashing water no longer the focal point, no longer of interest, at least visually. The stretched sounds of the disturbed water were still bouncing around his skull. He felt his face tighten, swore he could hear the sound of his lips cracking from it over the slow-motion water as he saw himself smiling stupidly under the cloudless sky.

Jacob understood he was waiting for the title screen to appear. He also understood he already knew the title.

*Such A Happy Boy*, it'd say, his dolt's grin artfully enhanced by each letter's careful placement.

"Jacob!" her voice squealed from the open window above the rickety front porch. "Hi! I'll be righ' down!"

Jacob felt cheated out of something, but he wasn't sure what. He shook the cobwebs out of his head and looked up just in time to see her, Tanya Miller's, blonde head bob back inside the window, which slammed shut, and disappear.

Jacob looked down at his soaked feet.

*What the fuck is wrong with me?* he wondered.

The childish jump into the puddle had jarred his privates. He felt the oily roil of pain and pressure deep and low in his stomach and forced himself to take his steps to the front of the Tackett home slowly, planting each heel firmly onto the gravel, *what Rodney Tackett done / step / what Rodney Tackett done / step*, until he was knocking on the hulking door.

Johnnie Flynn opened the door almost immediately. He looked Jacob up and down, twice, before speaking.

"Rodney or Tanya?" he said.

*what Rodney Tackett done / Tanya Miller*

"Tanya Miller," Jacob said.

One of Johnnie Flynn's eyebrows lifted.

"Tanya!" he hollered without turning around, his eyes locked onto Jacob's.

*Why didn't you just wait for her to come down?*

"How do ye know Tanya, boy?"

"School," Jacob said.

His dickhead was burning. He shifted his weight from foot to foot trying to generate some sort of friction. The itching was getting ready to start, he knew. The itching that burned the more you scratched and itched the more it burned. He'd scratched and rubbed and scratched until his penis was as hard as a cinderblock and burned and itched and was as raw as if he'd been beating off with gloves made of stinging nettle.

"Uh-huh," Johnnie Flynn grunted.

Jacob heard Tanya Miller's pounding footfalls on the stairs.

"Tanya!" Johnnie Flynn shouted, his eyes still on Jacob. "A quick word."

Her blonde head poked over Johnnie Flynn's shoulder.

"Hi, Jacob," she said.

"Hi, Tanya."

"Kitchen," Johnnie Flynn said, turning away from Jacob and

brushing by his niece. "Now."

Tanya Miller's face looked only slightly annoyed.

"Okay," she shouted. "Jus' a minute."

"Now!"

Jacob had been in that kitchen. He could picture Johnnie Flynn looking down the short hall into the living room and front door, Tanya's blonde head a-glow in the sunshine.

"He thinks he's my dad," Tanya Miller whispered.

"Now, got dam it!"

Jacob felt the air in his lungs disappear along with Tanya Miller's pupils as she rolled her eyes into the back of her head. Jacob wanted to make her, Tanya Miller, do that. He wanted to make her eyes roll back into her pretty head.

"I'll be righ' back," she said, spinning around into the darkness of the Tackett home.

"Shut the damn door, boy! Were ye raised in a barn?"

Jacob didn't know whether to step inside the home or wait outside on the porch. He eased the door shut, deciding the front lawn was the best choice. As he turned to walk down the porch steps, he slipped his left hand into the pants and squeezed the tip of his burning, itching penis. He felt a piercing stab of pain, then a hot wetness as pus was shot out into his pants, then a warm, half-satisfaction, an itch temporarily relieved. He pulled his hand out, saw the yellow goo on his thumb and forefinger, and did not resist the urge to smell his fingers.

It wasn't long before the Tackett's front door sprang outward and Tanya Miller burst out of the darkness onto the porch. Jacob heard the wood groan under her quick motions. She turned, slammed the door shut, cupped both hands around her mouth—the nails were painted a creamy white with navy blue polka dots—and shouted, "I'll be ho— back, I'll be back later!"

She was going to say "home," Jacob knew.

Jacob didn't think he had a home. The pink trailer at Thompkins' Hilltop Trailer Court for damn-sure wasn't it. The place up Wheelwright hadn't been either; nor the house up Teaberry, definitely not his aunt's.

*Have I ever had a home?*

"Come on, Jacob," Tanya Miller said, flying by him, an angel in daisy dukes nearly running toward the graveyard ahead. "Let's get outta here."

"He's such a fuckin' prick," Tanya Miller huffed. "'Let Tanya do the dishes. Let Tanya do the laundry. Let Tanya clean the bathroom, it's the least she can do. Gotta earn her room and board like the rest of us, huh?'"

Jacob was amazed at how much she could talk.

*It's like she can't stop*, he thought.

"And Marie jus' gives me these mean looks all the time," Tanya Miller was huffing with the climb, but she hadn't slowed down a bit during the hour-long hike. "When she sees my underwear, when she sees my bras, when she sees my tank tops, my cheerleading outfit, anything! It's like she cain't stand that I'm young and she's not any-more."

Jacob felt the panties, the green ones he'd stolen from her drawer, tingle the bottom of his nose, smelled the vanilla and laven-der and / cunt stink.

"How much further is this place anyway?" she asked.

Jacob held a branch for Tanya Miller to step under, then pointed at the little cabin, the hideout, sitting in the clearing in the center of the valley.

She squealed and clasped her hands together.

"Oh, wow!"

Jacob could see the quilt curing in the window, nondescript cur-tains from this distance but Jacob thought he could see the line sep-arating the skins and pelts and furs. He thought he could hear the thin, hollow rattle of ribcages he'd strung along the rafters. Jacob could feel the wonderful tacky floor under his miss K-Swisses.

"I can't wait to show you," he said.

Jacob could see the nondescript shapes of the other boys fleeing the open door of the hideout. He could see the sinister smiling moon shine down its pale baleful luminance on Rodney Tackett slowly walking out, his face working and working.

Jacob tried to swallow but couldn't find enough moisture in his mouth to complete the action.

Rodney Tackett and the 1.00mm screwdriver, Tackett's Jewelry & Watch Repair.

*what Rodney Tackett done / make 'em pay*

*There. That'll teach ye.*

Jacob's penis was burning again. He could feel both of his testi-cles swelling. He wanted to puke, knew he couldn't, and felt cheated again, angry even.

"Earth to Jacob," Tanya Miller laughed. Jacob thought the sound of her laughing was a pleasant sound, but he thought the sound of her screaming might be even better. "Come in, Jacob!"

*Does it matter*, Jacob wondered, *what you've done after you've gone?*

"Sorry," he said. "I was just thinking."

"Be careful with that," she said. "That'll always get ye into trouble."

"I think ye might be right."

Jacob made sure Tanya Miller made it down the steep, narrow path to the hideout without a single scratch, and though she talked the whole way, he didn't really hear a word.

-

"Why're ye walkin' like that?"

Jacob tried to stop in mid-stride and nearly fell over.

"What's wrong?" Tanya Miller asked.

Jacob slowly turned to face her; the blood drained from his face. The descent to the hideout had been slow and painful; he could feel both his swollen testicles pressing uncomfortably against the pants, another Goodwill purchase and a bit undersized to begin with, as well as the underside of his burning dickhead.

*The itching's gonna start soon.*

"I . . . I, uh," Jacob stammered.

Her eyes were looking him up and down in much the same way as Johnnie Flynn had earlier.

"Ye prairie doggin'?"

It took him a second to process the question and realize she was asking if he had to poop before Jacob felt his entire face and neck flush a bright, hot red.

"No!" he nearly shouted.

Jacob flinched, then coughed and cleared his throat.

"No," he said in a firmer, more quiet voice. "I don't have to . . . I'm not prairie doggin'."

Tanya Miller's face, which had clouded over with concern, suddenly erupted into a bright smile. Her laughter trilled off the ridge-tops on both sides of the little valley.

*clear swift water running off the top of the mountain / unmuddied by the dark current*

Jacob saw the doe's head smashed under the bald man's foot.

*sure she's your momma / but she's still a cunt*

*I shoulda named ye John, boy / one in a lo-o-ong line of 'em*

Jacob saw a crystalline stream abruptly turbid, felt the meat of the pawpaw between the toes of his left foot. The pressure in his stomach seemed to quadruple.

*what Rodney Tackett done*

Jacob tried to breathe but found he couldn't get enough air to his lungs.

*Calm down*, the voice said. *Stay ca—*

*what Rodney Tackett done / Wha—*

Tanya Miller's face, sharp blue eyes and just the faintest kiss of river birch freckles dotting her smooth cheeks, eclipsed Jacob's vision. The mirth was gone; concern tilted the slant of her eyebrows and the corners of her lips.

"Jacob, what's wrong?" she asked.

*What isn't? What's right?*

*Stay calm*, the voice said, a broken record, one for inducing hypnosis, trapped in the drivel of filler, pleasantries, before or after but not during. Stay calm. Stay calm.

*What's up? What's down?*

*Wrong? Right?*

*Does it matter what you've done after you die?*

"I think I'm going to be sick," Jacob said, just before jerking his head to the left and puking onto the sun-bleached grass.

"Uh."

The pressure was as bad as it had ever been. Jacob could think of nothing but making it stop.

"Uh, Jacob?"

*in / out*

*blue skies / rain*

*in / out*

*Stay calm*, the voice said. *Calm.*

Electric blue and white pain.

Jacob took all of himself in both of his hands and squeezed. For a blinding second, Jacob was sure he'd passed out, then hot, burning pus dislodged from his penis.

"Oh," Jacob sighed and moaned simultaneously. "Oh."

"What're you doing?"

Jacob opened his eyes, saw he was lying on his side, facing away from her, Tanya Miller, saw that both of his hands were sunk into the front of his pants, saw the dark stain blossoming in the cotton fabric. He slid his hands out, smelled the pus instantaneously, and cringed.

"Jacob!"

"Uh, sorry," he said, angling his body so Tanya Miller could not see the wet spot.

The smell was terrible. Jacob saw the thick yellowish white on his fingers and quickly wiped them on the grass around him.

"I, uh, I . . ."

*Did I cum?* he wondered. *No, but it feels just like it does just after I cum and still work at it anyway.*

"What're ye doin' with your hands?"

Jacob pulled his knees to his chest, hoping to shield his crotch from view, and almost screamed out at the near ecstasy he felt at the friction of his pants against his dickhead.

"Nothin'," his voice broke, a sharp squealing even sharper.

*I must've just came,* he decided and he had to clear his throat before he could try again.

"Nothin'," he said.

"What's wrong?"

Tanya Miller was right there, blocking everything from his view but herself.

*Inches.*

She reached down and put both of her hands onto his trembling shoulders.

Oh.

"What's the matter with ye?" Tanya Miller asked.

*Don't,* the voice said. *Stay calm. Stay*—

Then she smiled, *warmer than the summer sun / smiling completion before work's even begun,* and Jacob knew he'd tell her, knew he couldn't *not* tell her. No one had ever looked at him and smiled like that.

You can tell me anything and I'll believe you, those eyes said. Whatever you need to tell, I'll listen and believe you.

Jacob thought that, if she'd asked him the right questions, he would've even told her, Tanya Miller, about the two guys, friends of friends of Momma's, and the locked door at the party, even though Momma told him "no locked doors" and he hadn't locked it himself.

"What's wrong with ye?"

*what isn't / wrong with me*
*you sick little freak / what did you do to it?*

*freak / weirdo*

"My dick," Jacob said, swallowing the sticky "k".

He cleared the phlegm from the back of his throat.

"And balls."

---

For a long moment, her bright blue eyes bounced back and forth between his.

*flick / right*

*flick / left*

The corners of her mouth wrinkled a bit, like she'd just plopped something tart under her tongue.

"Ye fuckin' with me, Jacob Goodman?"

*Hun-ter.*

Tanya Miller decided he wasn't, Jacob saw it; it was like flicking the switch of an overly bright light.

"Oh, man," she cooed. "Ye poor thing."

Jacob waited for the unsuspecting backhand, the blow that always came at the brink of affection, *oh Jake*, but it didn't come.

"Ye poor, poor thing!"

---

Tanya Miller's sweat was slippery. Jacob wanted to lean even further against her as she helped him hobble across the little clearing to the hideout and scoop up some of it with his tongue. There was the vanilla; there was the lavender.

"Did something happen to ye, uh, it, I mean?" she asked.

*what Rodney Tackett done*

They were twenty feet from the windowless side of the hideout.

His cock and balls were feeling better after that last expulsion, but the nearly painful pleasure the friction of walking, not to mention the friction between her body and his own—he could feel the soft fat of her right tit bounce against him with each step—was quickly becoming too much.

"I need to sit down," he said, his voice just barely above a whisper.

"Oh, okay," she said. "Here, there. Okay. Are ye okay, hon?"

*hon / honey*

*bear, my / tear, me*

"Yes," Jacob said, closing his eyes, too aware of how hard he was breathing.

*Calm down.*

*down / down*
*what's it like to fall forever?*
"Have ye been to the doctor?"
Jacob opened his eyes.
*Concern, Mrs. Horace, 1: to relate to; 2: to have an influence on; 3: to be a*
*care, trouble, or distress to.*
*I ain't ruinin' what I got left / of my credit cos yer a fuckin' freak*
*minimal energy / maximum control*
"No," he said.
*I ain't ruinin' what I got left / of my credit cos yer a fuckin' freak*
"Can't afford to," he said.
"Oh, hon," Tanya Miller cooed.
Then, to Jacob's shuddering wonder, Tanya Miller wrapped Jacob in her arms and hugged him. His wide eyes and open mouth filled with her warmth, with the soft, damp cotton of her t-shirt, the tickling blonde locks of her hair, the smooth firmness of her belly, the soft, plump squish of her titties against the bottom of his chin, all punctuated with the smell of her, Tanya Miller.
*vanilla and lavender and / cunt stink shit ass*
*landing strip / freak // weirdo*
"Oh, Jacob," Tanya Miller cooed, gently patting Jacob's back with one hand and running the glittered nails of her other through his greasy hair. "Oh, honey."
The floodgates opened; Jacob wept like he'd never wept before. He hadn't heard such a soothing, motherly voice. Something wrestled itself free from his inner grasp and writhed to the surface. Jacob saw himself as shot from above; he could almost picture Rodney Tackett secreted in a branch of the loblolly yonder with his camera trained and zoomed and readying the shot. Yet he could do nothing to stop himself. His shaking was so violent he feared injuring her, Tanya Miller, at one point. She must've considered just this same thing because she drew Jacob even closer with firm, sure arms, her breath hot, sourly sweet in his right ear and cheek.
"There," she cooed. "There. Tha's it. Tha's it."
He cried and cried and cried.

-

"Well, then," Tanya Miller said, her voice still as soft as feathers. "How 'bout we do a lil' talkin' now, k?"
Jacob nodded, wiped great globs of clinging snot from his nose on his hands, his pants, then the grass, and nodded again.

"Okay," he said.

"K."

Jacob went on nodding and wiping the snot onto the grass.

"Jacob."

He changed the intensity of his nodding.

*more force / minimum control*

*No, that's not it. I can't think. Why can't I think?*

Jacob was sweating. He became aware his head was pounding, probably had been for some time now. Not a normal headache. No, this was that fever, that hot dragon's breath working like a plume for the night's cooking fire.

*minimal energy / maximum control*

"Jacob!"

He opened his eyes. Jacob didn't remember shutting his eyes. Tanya Miller stood in front of him, looking concerned.

*Genuinely concerned*, Jacob marveled.

He was in the little valley near the hideout. He turned his head around and saw it, the hideout, sitting there, the side without the window facing them.

*The quilt's curing at that exact spot*, Jacob thought, *but on the other side. I bet she'll understand the quilt. I bet she'll appreciate it.*

"Do you like quilts?" he asked.

"Quilts? What?" she leaned down and put the underside of her forearm against his forehead. "Jesus! Yer burning up!"

He was, too, Jacob knew. He may have dislodged the most recent batch of pus, but there'd be more.

*pain pain & more pain / does pain have a point of diminishing return*

"What happened to ye?" Tanya Miller asked.

Jacob couldn't look away from her eyes.

*Transfix,* Mrs. Horace's Word of the Day, *1: to hold motionless by or as if by piercing; 2: to pierce through with or as if with a pointed weapon.*

"Rodney Tackett done it," Jacob said.

## CHAPTER FOURTEEN
## GRADE A HUN-TER

**HE DANCED AROUND IT, THE** full telling; the steps were easy once he got into the swing of it. Gentle deflections, startling redirections, phantom pains and pressures when he felt backed into a corner.

*Gotta be careful with that one*, the voice told him. *Options get scarcer once that bridge is burned.*

"He thought ye killed Hobart?" she asked.

"But I found 'im that way," Jacob said, quickly. "Dead, I mean. I found him already dead and I, well, I figured, he's dead and that would just hurt everybody if they knew. I figured it'd be better if they just thought Hobart ran away and never came back or got lost or something."

At first, Jacob didn't think it'd work, that Tanya Miller knew exactly what he'd done to Hobart, that she'd seen the Tackett's housecat strung up by the Trilene and fishhooks, Walmart, on display, starved to death, *does it matter what you've done after you're gone?*, but she was nodding along before he knew it and he didn't waste a second with relief.

"Plus, I was lookin' for animals for the creations I was telling ye about," Jacob said. "I figured people give their bodies to science all the time, and Hobart was dead already, so I just took 'im."

"And Rodney found Hobart here," she pointed over Jacob's shoulder to the hideout. "And thought ye killed him, so, he beat ye up."

She was looking at him again.

"And he . . ." Tanya Miller looked very uncomfortable. "And Rodney stuck a screwdriver up yer pee hole?"

She squirmed, grimacing and sneaking looks at Jacob's crotch.

Jacob nodded, smelling the pus inside his pants and on his hands faintly as the wind changed directions.

"With the 1.00mm screwdriver."

*Tackett's Jewelry & Watch Repair.*

"That ye stole from Johnnie Flynn's shop."

"Needed it for the experiments," Jacob said, "and the creations."

"Jesus," she said, slowly shaking her head. "Rodney is such a fuckin' asshole."

Jacob smiled a smile that showed too much; he forced it back to a grimace.

"Yes," he said, "he is."

"A real asshole-perv."

She was smiling with her eyes, Jacob saw.

*How does she do that?*

"A real asshole-bully."

-

"Ye know, I'm almost positive he stole a pair of my underwear?" Tanya Miller said. "And one of my favorite pairs too!"

She laughed, even with the disgust plainly apparent, it was a beautiful thing, a clear chime from a solid bell.

"No!" Jacob said.

*Too loud*, the voice said. *Take 'er back another notch.*

"I'm sure he did!" she said. "Ye know, sometimes I feel like he's been snooping around my roo— my things."

She seemed to catch on nearly saying the word "room." Jacob saw the sudden dulling of her eyes, like a reflected light winking out, and rushed to steer her back into the rising current.

"Snooping?" Jacob said.

*Good*, the voice said.

Her eyes returned to his, *blue blue / blue blue*, and Jacob felt little bubbles, like ginger ale, *like kisses from a green spring mist*, as they rose up from the top of his stomach, settling in his chest with a crackling warmness. He knew it, even if it felt so fresh, so new at that moment, this feeling, but he couldn't quite place it.

She, Tanya Miller, nodded her head and Jacob thought about the way some horses gallop, that full extension, completely outstretched, none of their legs touching the earth, flying for the briefest of seconds, and knew what they must feel.

*what it's like to fly / to fall forever*

"Yeah, he's totally goin' through my stuff," she said, nodding right along. "I can jus' tell, ye know?"

"Yep."

"Some of my stuff jus' feels like it's been . . ." she looked up into the blue for the word, "*handled*. I can almost feel his greasy, dirty little fingers on my clothes, my bed even!"

She shivered.

"Grosses me out," Tanya Miller said, her lips puckered, her brow scrunched. "I can almost smell him in my room sometimes. Rodney is such an asshole perv."

"Yep," he said.

*Mine*, he thought.

"Ye know I catch him lookin' at me," she said, "all the time. Seriously. I'm like, 'we're cousins,' and he tries to act all offended, like I's the one doin' all the lookin', all I wasn't lookin' at ye, ew, gross. But, yeah right, I've seen 'im."

Tanya Miller gave Jacob a knowing smile, which he did his best to mirror.

"Yeah, I've seen 'im," she said, a secretive smile spread across her face. "I think he tries to see me in the shower sometimes."

Jacob initially fought the shock he felt, then he thought about how odd this must look to her, Tanya Miller, so he let it show.

"I know!" she said, smiling even further and shaking her head. "I get the feelin' that he's trying to watch me in there though. I'm not sure how, I lock the door, shut the curtains, everything, but I can feel it, ye know? That feeling that somebody's watchin' ye. Makes the hair on my arms and neck stand up jus' thinkin' 'bout it. Creepy, ain't it?"

Jacob watched Tanya Miller shiver.

*Like a cardinal in a birdbath*, Jacob thought, *and, boy, do I feel like the patient cat.*

So close, watching, feeling he could see almost every detail of Tanya Miller's being, *show / what's there to display*, smell every competing scent on her, *vanilla and lavender / and cunt stink*, Jacob finally placed the feeling he was experiencing. It was the same feeling, the very exact one, he got just as the hunt was nearing its conclusion, *stomp the head / feel the meat of the pawpaw / the shatter of bone on rock / fur & skin & tendon / & breast & landing strip & / you never eaten a pussy? / you never tasted that sweet and sour, juicy cunt stink b'fore?*

Jacob couldn't stop looking at her hands.

*They're birds too*, he thought, watching as they worried a loose strand on the bottom of her t-shirt, then dug around in the pockets of her shorts, then flicked a stray blonde hair from her forehead, then swatted a mosquito.

The glittered nails did something magical when the sunlight hit them. There was a silent explosion of stars, a universe exploding, birthing a cascade of shimmering universes-to-be, leaving floater-like streaks that dissipated somehow always a moment or two before you could even tell they were gone.

*She could write out her name like with a sparkler*, Jacob thought.

*If she could see them*, the voice said.

Jacob could smell woodsmoke on the breeze.

*Maybe you could help her see them*, the voice said, softer, the sound of scale on reptilian scale. *Everyone deserves to see the stars, right?*

"Yes," Jacob said.

Tanya Miller reached down her glittery, open hand.

"Feelin' up to showin' me yer little fort?"

"Yes," Jacob said, lifting his hand and letting those supple, slender fingers, that hand of fine china, enfold his own. "The hideout."

"Right," Tanya Miller said, helping Jacob to his feet. "Yer hideout."

*the sun's a brittle banana chip / a neon dream*
*the wind carries ash / fire blackens after the blast*

Jacob's vision swam; he felt unsteady on his feet.

Tanya Miller caught hold of his arm before he could topple back down onto the grass, then slipped her shoulder into his armpit, her slim arm cupping his back, glittery fingers pressing into the thin skin above his heaving ribcage, *the perfect fit / feels so good / never let it quit*, and the smell of her nearly bowled him over despite her support.

*Vanilla and lavender and //*

They were in the hideout. Jacob didn't remember leaving the clearing.

*the potato chip sun / the holy gun*

Had he fallen? He couldn't remember.

*Doesn't matter*, a voice Jacob understood immediately to be only audible inside his own head said and Jacob knew this was a *true statement*.

*is there only one truth? / does it matter what I did to Hobart now that he's dead?*

*if you weren't supposed to flay and string up animals, why did it feel so good, so right, so true? Killing is a true statement, that is true a statement.*

Jacob heard something. Was it a gasp?

It almost sounded like a punctured lung, as soothing as silky mud from the creek that sound was, a gentle hiss best achieved with a flathead screwdriver, Ace Hardware.

# BIRTH OF A MONSTER

He was looking at the long, straight curve of her spine, the blonde hair seeming to quiver a bit in the hazy light coming in the window, the little bit of it, that is, that made it past the curing quilt, the wind-chime-like bundles of raccoon hands and squirrel feet and possum jaws, trembling like a black-eyed Susan overburdened with *green / green / green /* green dew. He couldn't see her hands, *those glittered nails / those long, slender fingers*, her arms were bent at the elbow, her body shielding them from his view.

He followed her gaze to the collage, the outline, the blueprint, the hulking shape comprised of bits of the *Color Atlas of Anatomy*, *National Geographic*, Beckmann and Ling's *Obstetrics and Gynecology*, *Cosmopolitan*, *Hustler*, *Medical Embryology*, photographs, illustrations, cartoons, and advertisement clippings from the *Floyd County Times*, and, recently, his own drawings. Jacob'd only been able to stay awake at school by the constant motion of his pen these days, but he was careful not to let anybody see what he drew. No need for misunderstandings.

*they wouldn't understand / nobody does*
*what's there / to understand?*
*show / what's there to display*
*Pay attention*, the voice said, and Jacob knew this direction, too, was true.

Tanya Miller was definitely looking at the outline, but Jacob couldn't tell if she was really *seeing* it.
*She has to see it*, he thought, *to understand it.*
*See: the desert is the seabed.*
*See: the seabed is the desert.*

Jacob stepped into the hideout, the sticky floor's slaps and sucks a welcoming, an embrace.

Tanya Miller spun around at the sound, *shrieking / at the window dressing*, and nearly fell. She caught herself on the farmer's table, her chest heaving, rivulets of sweat running down her long, long neck, disappearing into the soft, fragrant cotton of her thin t-shirt. He could smell her. He could taste the salt of her on his tongue.

"Jacob," she panted. "What? Jacob?"
*Hun-ter.*
"Tanya," he said.

-

"What is this?" Tanya Miller asked, holding one palm turned toward the exposed beams of the hideout's slouching ceiling, the glittered nails leaving a trail of sparkles in their wake as they slowly, shakily circled the single room.

*home / is where the heart is*

She moved to the farmer's table, her hands wrapping around herself at the chest—how many animals had he watched unconsciously do just this same thing?—her eyes seeming to bounce off everything at once, a pinball ricocheting beyond the player's control, her blonde head jerking and bobbing to try and keep up, trying to see all there was to see and all at once.

The quilt gleamed wetly in the sunlight. It was a soothing sight, on one hand, the smoothness of the whole was deeply satisfying to him, but it also made Jacob begin to grind his teeth in frustration. The polyurethane varnish, Walmart, was taking much longer to dry than he had expected. He was beginning to think the varnish would never dry and was going to be a failure in the same throbbing vein as the model cement he'd applied to bolster the sutures of the first quilt; the stuff had made the quilt a brittle, clumsy mess. He had ripped it apart with his hands and teeth, screaming and wheezing and crying hot tears of shame and rage.

"Are those . . ." she didn't finish.

She was looking at the ribcages and paws and hands twirling from the Trilene, Walmart, on both sides of the quilt. Her pouty mouth was hanging open. Jacob imagined brushing some of the polyurethane varnish onto the little cracks and dry spots on her lips. He could hear the air rushing in and out of Tanya Miller's mouth in rapid bursts.

Fear. Excitement.

*She understands*, Jacob thought. *She's in awe.*

Tanya Miller made to reach up and touch one of the dark raccoon hands hanging in front of the window but pulled away from it still four inches away.

*See, she doesn't want to interfere with any of the work.*

"Those are . . ." Tanya Miller leaned a little closer to the red and white and yellow of a dachshund's ribcage, "rib bones?"

Tanya Miller turned and faced Jacob.

"Jacob," she said, "this is all . . ."

Exciting. Fascinating. Enthralling.

*Enthrall*, Mrs. Horace's Word of the Day, *1: to hold in or reduce to slavery; 2: to hold spellbound.*

Didn't he feel enthralled? How many times had the

understanding that he was doing something others would look at as weird or odd or disturbing crossed his mind? *Does it matter what you've done after you're gone?*

Jacob looked at the smooth, black raccoon fingers, their palms lined and papery now they'd been dried in the sun, then at the clear, sure cuts he'd made removing the dachshund's ribcage, and, finally, at the quilt shining like a recently completed canvas.

A failure, sure, but he'd learned something from the painting, Jacob knew.

*Yes*, he decided. *Yes, it does matter what you've done after you're gone. Or, at least, I can see how it* could.

He smiled.

"Enthralling," he said.

She started with the talking again. Nonstop. Describing how *this* made her feel *that*. *That* made her feel *this*. And on and on. Jacob watched her mouth move but didn't focus closely on what she said. He moved with her as she went about the place commenting on this and that and her feelings.

Jacob wondered what she'd look like on display. He doubted Trilene, no matter the test, made fishing line strong enough to hold up a hundred and ten pounds or so.

*Not any I could steal this far away from the ocean anyway.*

Tanya Miller moved to the corner of the room where Jacob had moved several of his older creations. He'd made a pedestal out of milk crates, the BP station, and arranged four of his better creations on top of them. She bent low for a better look and Jacob watched her shirt ride up her smooth white back with the motion, exposing the bright tops of her pink and red panties.

"Oh my god!" she squealed. "Is that a raccoon hand?"

Her head swiveled, her bright blue eyes lighting on his for just a moment, long enough for Jacob to know she knew it was, indeed, a raccoon hand at the end of the grizzled black and gray squirrel's left arm, before snapping back to his creations.

She gasped and squealed as she noticed more of the details.

"How did you get the beak on it?"

Jacob didn't answer, didn't plan on answering, but Tanya Miller hadn't waited for a reply anyway. She moved on with the constant chatter and exclamation.

She moved away from the rabbit with the turkey vulture's head after a shudder.

Jacob smiled; he was particularly fond of that creation. He'd found the fluffy little vulture, *an ugly, black-faced reptile / in stolen, downy feathers*, not five minutes after killing the rabbit; it'd just been hanging around an old log by itself. *Some things are just meant to be*, Jacob had thought, scooping up the squawking baby bird and shoving it into the black backpack, Walmart, with the dead / *dead* rabbit.

"You didn't?" Tanya Miller nearly screamed. "You didn't!"

Jacob felt jolted awake.

She was facing him again, her blue eyes wide and white and waiting.

"Jacob," she said, the corners of her lips quivering. "You did not paint those tiny little nails with glitter polish? Oh. My. God!"

That bell tolling laughter. That echoing tinkle of chimes.

Jacob smiled back, he couldn't help it, before nodding.

"Yep," he said. "Used that pair of watch repairman's magnifying glasses and a brush from a model airplane kit."

*Tackett's Jewelry & Watch Repair. Hobby Lobby.*

She laughed even harder. Jacob marveled at the chiming notes and the way they became slightly distorted as they increased in volume.

He tried to match the sound with his own laughter, softly, mostly to himself, but gave up quickly and smiled his happy boy smile.

"Would you paint mine?" she asked.

His stomach dropped.

"I would love that."

Bells. Chiming.

Jacob was on his knees.

*/ exultation*

He was on his knees, her porcelain right foot, slightly crimpled from her sock and boot, resting on his left knee, both of his hands touching the tougher but still smooth and relatively soft skin there, hearing the gentle chiming of her talk, understanding not a word, desiring to understand not a word but wanting her to continue on for a time longer just the same.

*John 13 / wrinkled veiny feet shoved up & dripping into my face*

". . . and I said 'I know what ye did' and, get this, he . . . looked . . . scared and guilty!"

*Black Branch Baptist Church Friday Communion / these aren't the*

# BIRTH OF A MONSTER

*apostles Christ*

". . . he jus' said, 'I dunno wut yer talkin' 'bout' then scampered off like a shittin' kitten."

*the bell tolls / the chimes ring*

Jacob put on the watch repairman's magnifying glasses, Tackett's Jewelry & Watch Repair, picked up the glitter nail polish, Walmart, and smiled.

*Tanya Miller as shot from above / suds and sparkles and nipples and landing strip*

*wet / wet / wet / wet*

The pressure was starting to build. Little sparks were shooting off, brightly blue and white and signifying the strike to come. Jacob felt it, hated it, chose to ignore it, stretching the skin of his face to pull tighter; his smile grew.

"If I catch ye snoopin' 'round my room again I'm uh tell Aunt Marie, I shouted at 'im. Ye could nearly see the tail between his legs, I swear!"

His penis was stiffening, smashed between his thigh and the stretched pants, and he tried to casually readjust his position to shield himself from her view.

"Yer not gettin' off on touchin' my feet are ye?" Tanya Miller asked suddenly.

Jacob nearly gasped. He thought he'd done a good job at keeping shock from his face but Tanya Miller's eruption into a fit of giggles dispelled that.

"Oh, Jesus," she laughed. "Ye shoulda seent yer face."

"It hurts is all," Jacob said.

She stopped laughing.

"Oh," she said, her blue eyes round and wet. "Oh, Jacob, I'm sorry. I didn't . . ."

"It's okay," Jacob said, taking the opportunity to adjust himself, on the outside of the pants, to a more comfortable position.

He felt her watching him do this and didn't know exactly how he felt about it. He let himself go after a few exploratory tugs and looked up her long legs then her crotch, landing strip, her smooth, flat stomach, her titties, her neck, her chin, her pouty lips, her darting, averting eyes. He watched her cheeks redden.

"I'm sorry," she said, rising up from the farmer's table she'd been sitting on, removing her foot from Jacob's hand. "Why don't we . . ."

She looked around the hideout, her eyes pinballing around once

210

again, seeking something she wasn't finding anywhere in the little room.

"Why don't we go out, outside," she said, moving toward the door, her steps sucking and farting in the muck. "Yeah, and ye can show me how ye . . . hunt. Yeah."

She was lost in a blaze of sunlight.

Jacob looked down at the stained crotch of his pants, smelled the pus, saw his half-erect penis, and sighed. He pushed himself to his feet, looked at the outline on the wall for a moment, then followed her, Tanya Miller, out into the little clearing outside.

-

Jacob squinted and limped into the light. The pressure was steadily increasing, even though his penis was no longer hard.

"Sorry," Tanya Miller said. "It's cool, yer hideout, I mean, but I jus' had to get out. Get some fresh air, ye know?"

Her voice was excited, fast, but Jacob sensed something underlying it. Something he was having trouble placing.

"Plus, with all those animals in there—"

Jacob's eyes had adjusted enough to see her point behind him, back at the hideout. He didn't turn to follow her finger.

"—it's obvious yer a Grade A hunter," Tanya Miller said.

*Hun-ter.*

"And it's absolutely beautiful out here." She was smiling, but it was a bit off.

*a smudge mark / on a masterpiece*

*What is it?* He still couldn't quite place it.

"So, why not go out and do a little huntin', huh?"

Her eyes found and held his.

*blue / wet*

"Okay," he said.

## CHAPTER FIFTEEN
## IN LIKE FLYNN
## (DESERT / SEABED)

**THE SQUIRREL WAS BARKING HALFWAY** up a black oak not thirty yards ahead of them.

"There," Jacob said, his voice low.

"Why's it makin' that noise?"

Jacob shrugged his shoulders before turning back to watch the little furry shape jerk and twitch with the strains of its aggravated shouting.

"Little fucker jus' won't let up," Tanya Miller said.

Jacob turned back to her, placed the index finger of his left hand to his lips, and voiced the faintest whisper of a shush.

"Sorry," she mouthed.

Jacob turned around to see the talons of the biggest chicken hawk he'd ever seen rip into the squirrel and clamp down. The squirrel opened its mouth to scream but no sound came out. The hawk lifted the squirrel into the air with three swooping beats of its black and brown wings and disappeared into the tangle of branches.

He wanted to scream. He wanted to cuss. He wanted to thrash and tear and bite. He could feel the green and red of failure beating raggedly in his temples and in his groin. But he didn't. He turned around, slowly, his face as blank as stone, and looked at her. She was knelt forward, picking the petals from a black-eyed Susan.

*She didn't even see.*

"He sure shut up quick," Tanya Miller said, looking up and seeing Jacob turned in her direction. "Oh shit. Did I scare 'im?"

Jacob smiled.

"No, no," he said. "Would ye like to learn how to set up a simple trap?"

"Oh, okay," she said. "Sure."

Jacob pulled down the hickory sapling, knotted on the rope, Ace Hardware, cut it with the Buck hunting knife, Roger Dunnham's unlocked garage, then checked the pressure.

"And what's that gonna do?"

She wouldn't stop talking; she'd talked the entire time he'd been setting the snare up. Jacob was almost positive they'd have to wait the rest of the afternoon into early evening before any animal with ears would come back after the amount of noise Tanya Miller made.

"Oh, I see," she said, ending the sentence on a rising note, nearly turning it into a question.

*No, you don't*, Jacob thought.

"Now, I take the notched stake I made earlier," he said softly, reaching down and picking up the sharpened stick, all the while keeping the sapling bent over, "and tie it on like this."

Jacob knotted the rope, Ace Hardware, around the top of the stick.

"Now we notch 'em together," he said, pushing the hickory sapling down until he could slip the notches in the sticks together. "See?"

Tanya Miller was nodding her head but Jacob thought she looked like a deer in headlights.

"The notches hold the sapling down until something messes with our noose here," Jacob knelt down at the two twigs supporting the rope noose. "When the animal touches it . . ."

Jacob picked up the stake that had splintered during the notching process and thrust it into the open "O" of the rope noose. The sapling snapped upward, yanking the stick from Jacob's hand and slinging it into the cloudless afternoon blue for a split second before smacking it onto the ground. The sapling stood straight and swaying, the failed notch stake hanging four and a half feet off the ground, securely snared.

"Holy shit!" Tanya Miller said. "That's crazy!"

Jacob made the shushing signal, but not the sound.

"Sorry," Tanya Miller mouthed.

Jacob worked the slipknot loose, then tossed the stake into the brush.

"Let's hook 'er back up," Jacob said, bending the hickory sapling back down to the notched stake he'd planted firmly into the ground, "and see what we catch."

Jacob could feel her watching him as he worked. He tried not to show the discomfort he was in—his testicles were aggravated and swollen—but gave it up when the hickory slipped from his grip and slapped him in the crotch before slinging upward, the rope popping like a wet towel.

It wasn't much more than a passing glance, but the pain was dizzying. Jacob clenched both his hands around himself and tried to hold perfectly still, his eyes and jaw clenched tightly shut.

She was giggling. Jacob could hear it despite the inarticulate screaming in his head. It sounded muffled and Jacob guessed she was doing her best to control herself, covering her mouth with her slender, glittery fingers. This did little to assuage his rage.

*Shut up*, he wanted to scream. *Shut your cunt mouth.*

"Oh," Tanya Miller laughed. "I'm so sorry. I cain't he'p it. It jus' shot up and thwacked ye. . ."

*bells / chimes*
*muted / by rope*

Jacob opened his eyes, saw he was on his knees with both of his hand in his pants, and flinched. Hot, red shame washed over him. He carefully let go of his throbbing cock and balls, then tried to stand up.

"Oh," she said again, more in control of herself. "Are ye okay?"

Jacob nodded his head, tasting soured milk but willing himself to swallow it back down. He tried again to stand up.

"Here," she said, then he was awash in the smell of her. "Let me he'p ye."

He closed his eyes, breathing deeply through his nostrils.

*vanilla and lavender / vanilla and lavender and //*

Her hair tickled his face as she slipped under his right arm, her skinny but strong arms wrapped around his sweat-drenched back, and hoisted him to his feet.

"'Eir we are," Tanya Miller said. "Ye okay, Jake?"

*Jake.*

Jacob turned his face toward her voice, then opened his eyes. Tanya Miller was all he could see, *blue eyes, pouty mouth / a faint spray of freckles / the tiniest, finest blonde hair on the far side of her cheeks / beside her peach, perfect ears,* and imagined this was what seeing a movie in one of those IMAX theaters they advertised on the TV all the time was like.

*vanilla and lavender*

"Yes," he whispered. "I think so."

"Alrigh'," Tanya Miller said, her straight white teeth gleaming in the sun. "Well then."

She seemed to hesitate and that strange look crossed her face again, momentarily darkening her eyes.

*Move*, the voice said. *Get to moving; she sees you. Move: Hide and wait.*

Jacob still couldn't place it, that expression, that *look*.

"Thanks," he said, "let's find a good place to wait 'n' watch."

*wait & watch / watch & see*

*come a little closer / closer to me*

"K," she said, the smile all but faltering now.

Jacob forced himself to gently push himself away from her, Tanya Miller, but not before one long intake of her smell. His muscles contracted, his eyes closed, and he breathed in.

*vanilla and lavender and*

*Pity.*

*That look, that sound, it's pity*, he realized. Pity!

*No, she understands! It can't be pity. You misunderstood*, Jacob thought, *just like always.*

He opened his eyes and, sure enough, it wasn't pity he saw on Tanya Miller's face. No, not pity, something closer to disgust.

"What're ye doin'?" she asked.

*Be quick*, the voice said.

"I don't feel so good," Jacob said.

It wasn't exactly a lie, he couldn't ever recall feeling completely "good" in his life, but it almost felt like one. Not that he had any trouble lying. His mother taught him lies were only important if you were bad at them. Jacob pushed the feeling away.

Her expression changed with a quickness rivaling the beat of a hummingbird's heart. It was wary, then it wasn't; it was concerned. Genuine; concerned.

Jacob didn't know what to feel. His mother had so rarely revealed this much of herself to him that Jacob sometimes seriously doubted he'd ever really experienced it. Concern not tied to the apron of a lesser but more pressing need was the way their quilt had been knitted.

*You know we cain't afford no doctor bills right now.*

Jacob felt stunned. *I ain't ruinin' what I got left of my credit cos yer a fuckin' freak. Stun*, Mrs. Horace's Word of the Day, *1: to make senseless, groggy, or dizzy by or as if by a blow; 2: to shock with noise; 3: to overcome especially with paralyzing astonishment or disbelief.*

Jacob wondered what would happen to blood if he put it in one of the decorative ice cube trays he saw at Walmart. He could do a pumpkin or a pineapple or a perfect square, yes, a square, a cube of blood like a slab of meat. He could put it in Jimmy Wilcox's deep freezer overnight and check in the morning. Jimmy Wilcox and his family had left two days ago for Florida. He'd watched them go, then opened their backdoor with a screwdriver.

Jacob blinked, hard.

*Focus*, the voice said.

"I don't feel so good," Jacob said again.

His voice sounded toneless, robotic to his own ears.

*Am I even alive anymore?* he wondered. *Was I ever really alive?*

How many times had he felt like the butt of a bad joke? How many times had he felt invisible? Or, how many times had he been seen and seen with disdain? Disgust? Hatred?

"Oh, Jacob," Tanya Miller said, her voice low.

*Motherly?*

"I'm sorry. Le's find us a place to set a spell."

*Us.*

Jacob relaxed, smiled, and felt the current pulling him a little farther along the edge of some drop-off. He could almost see the line separating him and some deeper, fuller understanding of things. He swore he could almost feel the updrafts of the cooler stream trickling up the backs of his legs.

*us / mine*

-

"Here," she said, pulling him against her warm body, "I think there's a lit'l rise this a'ways."

Tanya had enough time to clip the sentence off before sucking in a mouthful of startled air from her sudden gasp as the hickory sapling flew upward and something small and screaming went streaming after it.

*Mine*, Jacob thought as the screaming crunched into twitching, swaying silence.

-

"Holy shit!" Tanya Miller kept saying. "Holy shit. Holy shit! Holy shit."

Jacob used the Buck hunting knife, Roger Dunnham's unlocked garage, to cut the rope ten inches above the noose. The rabbit wasn't moving. Jacob saw blood slowly trickling out of both its ears, as well as its nostril.

*Killed it with one quick SLAP!*

He clapped his hands together loudly, but just one time.

216

Jacob smiled at the blood dotting the fine, tiny hairs near the rabbit's mouth, thinking, *That book was right: hickory really is the perfect wood for twitch-ups.*

What had it been called? He couldn't remember the book's title.

The little hairs weren't absorbing the blood, not at first. It beaded and balled on several hair follicles.

*How did I just clap?*

Jacob saw he was holding the rabbit by the noose in his right hand, the Buck hunting knife, Roger Dunnham's unlocked garage, in his left. His black backpack, Walmart, was open at his feet. He did not recall taking it off his back or opening it.

*Focus*, the voice said.

*flips & dips / pages rip*
*blood it boils / blood it drips*

Jacob needed to know if blood would freeze into the shape of a pumpkin or a pineapple, no, a cube. Jacob needed to see blood frozen into a cube.

He blinked, forced his eyes away from the blood on the rabbit's fur. Tanya Miller was staring at him.

Pity.

Disgust.

Suspicion.

All those dancing in Tanya Miller's bright blue eyes, but concern, genuine concern, was there too, Jacob saw.

*she understands / in like Flynn*

Jacob saw the squirrel as they were nearing the last rise to the ridgetop overlooking the hideout. He stopped, held up his hand, waited for Tanya Miller to stop, then pointed it out.

"See it?" he whispered, leaning his body toward hers while extending his arm in the squirrel's direction.

It took her a few long moments before she did.

"It's distracted," Jacob said. "I cain't tell what it's got, but I know I can sneak up on it."

Her eyes widened.

"Ye wanted to see me hunt?" Jacob smiled. "I need another animal if you want to see how I make them, the creations."

She nodded her head, just a little, but a nod.

Jacob knelt down and picked up a stick about the size of a t-ball bat. He hefted it several times, gauging its weight and strength, found it wanting, and picked up a piece of sandstone about the size of a brick instead.

He thought he heard her gasp as he dropped to a crouch and tiptoed toward the squirrel. Its back faced him and he couldn't tell what it was so absorbed in eating.

Jacob was three feet away, lifting the stick above his head, ready to bring it smashing down on the back of the squirrel's head, when he finally had the angle to see what it was eating: a baby robin.

"Don't do it!" Tanya Miller gasped. "I'm sorry, I know it's jus' a stupid squirrel but please don't!"

The squirrel dropped the bloody chick and bolted, but not before Jacob saw the blood smeared across its twitching nose, the blood dripping from its open little mouth, the blood coating its claw-like hands. He saw it a long time after it'd gone, went on seeing it the way you went on seeing the camera's flash after the picture's done been taken, a silent, static afterimage shifting, disappearing, reappearing.

"Yer not mad are ye?" Tanya Miller asked.

She was behind him. Jacob did not turn to answer.

"I'm not mad," he said.

"Good! I know ye need animals for yer experiments but I couldn't watch ye brain that little thing to death. I jus' couldn't," Tanya Miller said. "Not a cute, furry little squirrel."

She came around and saw.

*show / what's there to display*

"Oh," she gasped.

"Come on," Jacob said, blinking away the last of the static blood from his eyes, "we're almost there."

-

Jacob used the serrated side of the Buck hunting knife, Roger Dunnham, to saw into the shallow skin under the rabbit's fur just above its paws. He was aware of Tanya Miller's gasp on some level, but he was deep into the work now. When he made it to the dull white of the bone, Jacob shifted his weight and positioned himself over the blade, then crunched through to the farmer's table underneath.

He heard her strangled moan, then the gagging, then the vomit hitting the sticky floor. He heard her crying as she stumbled out into the fading light of late afternoon. He heard her crying and gagging more outside the hideout, and he continued the work.

Jacob was working the sutures into place, still on the first hand, the first paw, when he heard her tentative steps back into the hideout. He didn't stop his work when he felt her breath on the back of his neck, or when her sweet scent, *vanilla and lavender / and*, filled each of his nostrils, whisking over the smells of blood and vomit and the rabbit's bodily fluids and making butterflies fill his stomach.

He could feel her eyes, *blue blue / blue blue*, on the side of his face, on his glistening, working hands, on the work, on the budding creation.

Jacob heard and felt but pushed her, Tanya Miller, to a back-burner, a dish to simmer, and focused.

-

*stitch to stitch / patch the pieces in place*
    *give him a hand / give him another*

-

When he'd finished with the rabbit, Jacob started on the squirrel, using just one of the rabbit's paws. For its left, he opted for one of the dried and waiting raccoon hands dangling in the window.

-

"Ye were praying for it, weren't ye?" she asked. "When ye were jus' holding it, the bunny I mean, weren't ye?"

Jacob stilled his hand and tried to remember.

"Jus' after the trap flung it into the ground, ye cut it down," she said. "And ye held it up and jus' stared at it, but your eyes were all blank, cloudy. Empty-like."

Jacob had no recollection of this exact moment, but he could envision it. He saw himself holding a dead rabbit, its neck broken, its skull misshapen, saw the blank look on his face and decided it could be a sort of prayer. It was a communion of sorts.

*Does it matter what you've done after you're gone?*

*Of course, it does,* Jacob thought. *She'll never forget that moment, the sound of one, little death. A crunch. Could've been something as little as a snapping a twig on yer knee. Could've been, but wasn't. Death, it was death: the only thing that matters, the only thing you can really take, the only thing for certain.*

Jacob went back to the work, but slowly, savoring even the slightest of his movements. The feel of the congealing blood, the smell of it, the bits of tendon and gristle stuffed under his fingernails, all coated in the smell of her, Tanya Miller, like the scene had been shot in monochrome and touched up in vibrant streaks of purple.

"Yes," he whispered.

219

"I knew it," she said. "At first I completely wigged out. I mean, shit, this is weird as all hell, but I think it's different now. It's special. Like, uh, like it's yer callin', ye know? Watching ye, I see that."

*She understands.*

Jacob pulled the two skins together, then drove the suture, first, into the squirrel, then carefully stretched the dried skin of the raccoon until he could puncture it with the suture, University of Pikeville Medical School, and pull the Trilene, Walmart, through.

*No, she doesn't, not really.*

"I can tell it's like, uh, a religious experience for ye," Tanya Miller said.

Jacob smiled, slowly.

"Yes," he said. "It is."

-

The work focused him. Jacob stretched the squirrel's broken neck—the noise was delicious—until he could get the Buck hunting knife, Roger Dunnham, in and sever the spine several inches below the head. Jacob moved the headless body, one raccoon hand and one bunny paw ending both its little arms, to the edge of the farmer's table to let the blood and spinal fluid leak onto the floor.

At some point, Jacob had removed his miss K-Swisses. He didn't remember doing this, but he must've because he felt the warm blood oozing between his toes. He felt other things in the blood too.

*That's torn skin*, he thought. *There's fur from the rabbit. Some from the squirrel. That must be a bit of bone. Wrist? Hand? Can't tell.*

"Oh, Jesus," she whispered. "I-I, oh, I cain't."

Jacob had started sewing the head of the squirrel onto the rabbit's neck, a slippery, difficult task, which he didn't look up from to see her flee.

*I told you she wouldn't understand.*

*No one ever will.*

Despite these thoughts, Jacob did not even think of stopping the work.

-

*leaving / how can they leave if they were never really here*
*she was / there*
*was she? / . . . yes*
*remember those eyes? / blue blue blue kind*
*genuine / concerned*
*but she fled / they all leave*

*Mom / Aunt Teresa*
*Grandnanna Sheryl Lee / Debbie Sue his foster mother*
*if they were ever really / really there*

Jacob hated himself for it, felt the hot flush of shame burning his ears and cheek and throat, but he wanted his mother to hold him. Right there, right then.

*wishes like fishes / fishes we eat*
*dreams on bobbers / dreams in nets*
*love spilling out / holes in yer boots & chest*

Jacob wanted her smell, cheap bourbon, *more yeast & alcohol / than smoke & barrel.*

*Momma.*

He wanted her to hold him, just him, and be there. Really be there. Not thinking about bills, or pills, or refilling her drink, getting ready for a visit from her friend John, they're all named John, *shoulda named ye John, boy / one in a lo-o-ong line of 'em,* just being there. With him.

*sure she's your momma / but she's still a cunt*

When was the last time his mother had held him like that? Jacob couldn't remember. *Had to have been years and years ago.*

*did she ever / ever really?*
*Yes!*
*No?*
*I don't know.*
*Does it matter what you've done / after you're gone?*
*I don't know.*

-

Jacob put the two new creations on the floor beside the others, which he rearranged on their pedestals.

*show / what's to display*

He placed the squirrel with the rabbit head and the rabbit with the squirrel head on opposite sides of the display. Jacob moved a few steps back, took a quick cursory look, then made some minor readjustments to the squirrel with the rabbit head.

*There. Finished.*

*Yer improving,* the voice said.

*Yes,* Jacob agreed, readjusting his swelling testicles.

*She fled.*

*Yes, she did.*

Jacob closed his eyes. He could smell the faintest remnants of her smell amongst the blood and the gore.

*vanilla and lavender / and cunt stink*

Jacob's penis was throbbing now. He could feel the burning that always came just before the unbearable itching, the itching that always got him partially hard, a painful yet pleasurable state.

*pain pain & more pain*
*what Rodney Tackett done*
*Tanya Miller / as shot from above*
*Fast-Forward X2 Mode*
*blood blood / blood blood*
*red red / red red*
*blue blue / blue blue*

Jacob started knowing there'd be pain, knowing there'd be pleasure too.

*desert / seabed*

*The bald man was right*, Jacob thought. *When ye hear 'em say, "One day, when you're older, you'll understand," and you think that, yeah, sure, there's probably some truth in the experience, there's time for lessons, hard and soft, but I didn't expect to get it so soon.*

Randall Adkins' voice replayed in his head: *One day, when yer older, ye'll understand. It's not a personal thing. Not something they can help. They're jus' hard-wired that way, women are. Cunts.*

Jacob nodded, rolling the word around on his dry tongue: *cunts.*

*She just up and ran.*

*I thought she'd understand.*

*I thought she was understanding.*

*No one does / understand*

Jacob had cleaned himself up with one of the Scott Shop Towels, Walmart, much better than the cheap stuff his mother picked up at Dollar General, surprised at the coloration of the mess, swirls of red and green and yellow and chunky white.

*They can't help it,* he realized, *they're jus' hard-wired that way, to be cunts.*

Jacob looked up from his filthy, bare feet, saw he was deep in the woods, not even on a trail, and continued on. The sun was rising behind him. He could feel the perspiration beginning to dampen the grime on the inside of his shirt and pants as more and more light found its way over the knob and through the tangle of trees. He could smell himself but didn't think it could be as bad as cunt stink.

*No, cunt stink carries something heavier with it,* Jacob thought, but he couldn't quite put his finger on what it was.

*Fear?*

*Allure?*

*Lust?*

That all felt a part of it but not the thing complete.

Jacob closed his eyes, trying to recall the smell of Tanya Miller's green panties, that faint hint of the real thing. The way parts of her sheet, near the middle, tasted when he filled his mouth and sucked.

*Ye never tasted that sweet and sour, juicy cunt stink b'fore?*

The bald man had asked, but he knew the answer.

*Ye never eaten a pussy?*

She didn't really see, Jacob now knew. He'd thought she'd seen the work, the quilt, the creations, what was on display, *show / what's there to display*, saw all of it and understood, got it, got his genius, saw the way he could make and do and make do and realized the potential of it, of him. They were so wrapped up in their meaningless little lives; games, all of it, baseball games, basketball games, school was a game, work was a game. They all played and tried to get ahead, to win, or, at least, not lose. They were all so blind to what was real. They didn't see. Jacob had thought she was different, that she'd see, *show / what's there to display*, and understand, *really understand* him. But she didn't.

*Of course* she didn't.

Jacob was angry and hurt and alone. He didn't know where he was, not exactly, but that didn't concern him. He found he was good at finding his way. He'd walked the hills long and often enough. But he still felt hunted, followed. Jacob knew now he'd been mistaken when he'd come to see the mountains as his place. He'd let himself grow comfortable, *at home / ha ha ha*, in a dangerous place; how could he have been so stupid, so naive?

He hated himself, felt the hot flush of embarrassment in his wet cheeks—*why were his cheeks wet?, it wasn't raining*—but he couldn't help it, he wanted a nightlight. He wanted a nightlight and a bed of his own, under a roof of a place he could call "home." He wanted to feel his mother's arms around him. He wanted to feel loved. He wanted to sleep. He wanted to stop walking. He wanted to find a fawn and stomp its head in. He wanted to eat pussy, Tanya Miller's pussy.

*Shame.*

That's what cunt stink carried with it: shame. Shame for being so unlucky to be born a woman, a girl.

*They can't help it,* Jacob repeated, *they're jus' hard-wired that way, to be cunts.*

-

"Get up," she said. "Yer gone be late fur school."

Jacob opened his eyes. That was his mother's voice. He was home. He didn't remember going home. For a moment he couldn't remember where home was, *Virgie / Teaberry / Weeksbury / Johnson-ville / Prestonsburg / Wheelwright,* before the color pink filled his head and he remembered Thompkins' Hilltop Trailer Court and the salmon-colored singlewide.

"I said git yo ass up!"

Glass shattered on the wall above Jacob's bed. His eyes flew open but slapped back shut as bourbon and glass shards splashed down.

Jacob's bedroom door slammed shut, rattling the framed painting of bigfoot off the wall onto the floor, where it cracked with a plasticy *clink.* He sat up slowly, careful not to let any of the broken bits of glass get under the covers.

*Why don't I remember getting into bed?*

The sunglass-clad bigfoot, painted on velvet, stolen from an un-attended booth at the fair, was looking up at Jacob from a skewed angle and his face seemed more snide than comic now.

*Letting a woman scare ye like that,* it smirked.

*Letting that cunt stink get ye.*

Jacob threw the covers off. He nearly gagged as the smell of his infected penis mixed with the cheap bourbon, *maggots / crows.* He saw chunks of drying pus strung a good ten inches from his crotch and legs to the crusty blankets before snapping like an old rubber band.

*Look at what they did to ye,* Velvet Bigfoot smiled sadly.

-

Jacob forced a hard ball of what he thought was crystalized pus out of his penis. He was sure it didn't take nearly as long as it felt like it took, but he'd also tried to masturbate afterwards. *Why waste a har-don?* Besides, the hurt was kind of good just afterwards, but Jacob couldn't get all the way there no matter what he saw in his head, and his mother was waiting for him in the living room after he'd finally given up, sweating and hurting and refusing to acknowledge the hot tears in his eyes.

"Well," she said, startling him.

*Be careful,* the voice said.

"Rise 'n' shine, mornin' glory," his mother said.

*Sure, careful,* Velvet Bigfoot smirked. *Careful and controlled and cowering. C for Coward.*

*C for Cunt.*

Jacob walked by the couch to the kitchen as quickly as he could without out and out running. Experience taught him she was still fast when she was as hammered as she seemed now. It was her aim and precision that got drowned in the corn.

He made a bowl of stale off-brand Honey Smacks, careful not to keep his back to her for long.

"I got a phone call the other day," she said.

She sipped from her drink the way she did when she was drunk, a loud, crass sound, overindulgent and wet.

"Know what they wanted?"

*She didn't ask if he knew who had called.*

*It's the school.*

*It's the social worker.*

*It's the court-appointed.*

Jacob filled his mouth and shook his head.

She crossed her right leg over her left knee on the second attempt. Even in the murk, Jacob could see his mother's humorless smile.

"They want me to take time away from my biz e schedule," she paused long enough to burp softly, "to go down to the got dam school fer uh p'rent teacher conference."

*Uh-oh,* Jacob swallowed the partially chewed mass of sugar, scratching his throat and bringing fresh, hot tears to his raw eyes. The last parent-teacher conference held him back a grade, got him suspended a week, in-school detention for one week, after-school for two, almost got his mother arrested (again), and nearly resulted in his being removed from his mother's care by state social workers again.

"Say ye've been missin' quite a bit of school," she said.

*I went to school last week,* Jacob took another bite. *Two days, I think. Whole days too. Didn't I? What's today?*

He didn't know.

*Focus,* the voice said, *on the problem at hand.*

"So much school tha' they want me to come down there," Christy Goodman uncrossed her legs, "and tell 'em why."

Jacob watched his mother lift the sweating glass to her lips and drink. Jacob saw she'd put on makeup. Her closed eyes looked like a child's outline of a mountain range, the mascara ran in jagged juts, straight and in-line with her lashes in very few intersections. There was a deep gouge of red on her cheeks that was not even nor even remotely symmetrical. Her hair, stiff in places, greasy and dandruff-flaked in others, was pulled back in what was supposed to be a high and tight ponytail, but her slouching position on the couch had pushed it off-kilter and pulled a lot of it free or mostly free. She drained the last of the bourbon from the glass, her eyes still closed, and burped, a sound that seemed to take place mostly deep in her throat. She thrust herself forward, using her forward momentum and two hands on the frayed cushions to push herself, *a drunken top / a twirling twit-twat*, to her feet.

"Why ain't ye bin in school, Jake?"

She bent at the waist, picked up the bottle of bourbon, *maggots / crows*, from the coffee table, and sloshed some more into her glass.

"Come here."

Jacob set the bowl on the counter, his eyes never leaving his mother, watching as she threw back another mouthful of the pungent bourbon, *maggots / crows*, seeing her crash her right shin into the coffee table.

"Shit!" she hissed. "Got dam it!"

Jacob moved silently across the little kitchen into the living room where Christy Goodman was back on the couch, the drink spilling over the sides in her shaking right hand, her left kneading the angry knot growing on her shin, which Jacob saw was shaved, but nicked and cut and patchy. Tears ran down her painted cheeks, a great blurring of black and red and sallow white. He moved across the living room, his back to the door, his eyes on his mother, waiting on the attack that would be fast and brutal and unexpected.

Always unexpected.

*Sure, she's yer momma but she still's a cunt and all that*, Jacob thought, *but she's also got something on me, over me, some power over me, some spell or voodoo*, cunt stink / Transfix, *Mrs. Horace, 1: to hold motionless by or as if by piercing; 2: to pierce through with or as if with a pointed weapon.*

His mother was across the room, seeming to float over the coffee table, this time without even touching it, before Jacob could find the front door with his blind, groping hands. She wrapped one hand around his throat, the other took a handful of his hair and twisted, hard enough that Jacob thought he could hear the follicles popping across his scalp like bubble wrap.

"Why ain't you bin in school?" she asked. "Huh?"

Her grip was tremendous. Jacob couldn't have answered her if he'd tried. He simultaneously hated her touch and craved it, felt warmed by it, even this, pain, and more pain to come.

*pain pain & more pain / Does pain have a point of diminishing return?*

The pressure was growing; little flickers of static electricity began to flash.

She let go of his hair long enough to slap him across the face, then she had it knotted between her fingers again.

"What am I gonna tell these people, huh?" she asked. "You bin out killin' cats and dogs and experimentin' on 'em?"

Her eyes changed. Jacob watched it happen the way it happens on the TV. They were hard and fierce and shiny in a glassy way, then, poof, all of a sudden it was like a light went off behind them. Christy Goodman looked more hungover than drunk. She looked more asleep than awake. She looked unhappy and she looked away.

Then she slapped him again, this time with the back of her hand, mostly her bony knuckles. Lights flashed in Jacob's eye.

*Always unexpected*, he chided himself. *Expect the unexpected.*

Jacob opened his eyes in time to see his mother's fist, a blur of pale white, smash into his face, then everything was really bright, but only for a second.

-

He kept his mouth closed. He saw them talking, their old people's wrinkles and dour lines of disapproval, heard the noise of their tired voice boxes working, stacking up the ways Jacob was fucking up.

Jacob kept his face passive, blank, empty. In his head, he outlined the next quilt, the one that would click, the quilt that would look and feel and be what he envisioned, what he had to see done.

His mother said something—she'd stopped at the Pump 'n' Pay for cigarettes and Red Bull and Jacob couldn't help but feel a bit proud she was able to sound almost sober—then all four of their heads, Vice Principal, Counselor, Teacher, and Mother, swiveled in his direction.

*Did they ask me a question?* he wondered.

*Stay silent*, the voice said.

Jacob did.

-

His head ached dully as he walked up the empty hallway from the vice principal's office. He felt along the lumpy ridge of his right eye-brow and winced.

His mother packed a wallop of a punch for someone her size, that was for damn sure. He'd never tell a soul about it, or anything else for that matter, but for one horrible-yet-alluring moment, Jacob was sure he was going to open his mouth and start blabbering. He couldn't remember just what it'd been, the look on the counselor's face maybe? She was so young compared to the other adults in the room—*hell, in the entire school*—and there was so much longing to make him *okay* in her eyes. He could almost reach out and touch it, that need to fix, that desire to comfort.

It was like a sickness, Jacob saw. It had nearly infected him. He'd nearly talked. Talking to people was something you don't do. Ever.

He opened his locker and got out his books, still ashamed at his near breaking.

*Maybe she rattled something loose in my head this morning*, he thought, swinging the flimsy metallic door shut.

Tanya Miller was standing there.

Jacob nearly leapt out of his skin.

"Sorry," she said, smiling. "Didn't mean to scare ye."

"Ye didn't," Jacob said immediately.

"Okay," she said. "I want to, uh, apologize."

Jacob looked at her. She was serious, those bright blue eyes holding his, her mouth smiling but demurely, apologetically.

"I didn't mean to run away like that," Tanya Miller said. "It was jus' . . ."

She leaned her weight on her left hip and seemed to search around the empty hall for what exactly it had been. She gave up, shook her head sadly, then started again.

"I've never seen nothin' like that before, is all," Tanya Miller said, beginning to blush. "I guess I'm jus' a wussy or whatever, but I saw all that . . ." She didn't finish her specification. "I jus' didn't know how to feel." She leaned in very close to Jacob. "I think it's my hormones."

Tanya Miller gave Jacob a knowing look, the smile slipping from her face for a moment before returning to its demure state.

"From my . . . condition," she said, her face in full flush.

*Trouble*, Jacob remembered, *in a family way*.

"Anyway, I'm really sorry if I hurt yer feelin's," she went on quickly. "I didn't mean to. I jus' don't know how I feel all the time these days. Seems like it changes from one minute to the next. Shit, one second to the next."

She laughed and Jacob heard the bells, the chiming, but the tones sounded brittle, a different sort of hollow.

"I'm sorry," she said, looking into his eyes again. "Still friends?"

Tanya Miller held out her right hand, the colors of her fingernails alternating, navy blue and white. He took her hand, forcing himself to look back up into her expectant face, and smiled.

"Friends," he said.

-

Jacob floated through the rest of the school day, not even bothering to try to skip gym. Even as Mr. Cottrell yelled and stomped around the baseball diamond at Jacob's refusal to run, jump, kick, or move in the least bit athletically. Jacob thought that, if he had to, he could've run, jumped, kicked, or moved athletically—the swelling wasn't as bad today and the pressure was nearly nonexistent—but he didn't see the point in poking the sleeping lion. Not for gym class. Not even after Mr. Cottrell reminded Jacob his mother had been in that very morning for a parent-teacher conference on Jacob's behavior and complete lack of motivation.

*Fuck 'em*, the voice said.

*Fuck 'em*, Jacob agreed.

Jacob found himself walking slowly, setting the pace as slow as he could without actually stopping, his head a dull, buzzing ache. He felt like he'd just woke up from a deep, unexpected nap. He lifted his head, saw he was in the woods, and smiled. He had the whole afternoon and night to work on the new quilt. He knew this one would work out the way it was supposed to. He'd make it.

-

Jacob looked down into the little valley and saw her blonde head against the faded grain of the hideout's rear wall.

He blinked once, hard, and realized he'd just come out of a pleasantly empty blank space. He couldn't remember where he'd been, what he'd done, what he'd seen; nothing.

Jacob felt the extra weight and looked down to see he had a red fox, two squirrels, and a possum, all obviously dead, nestled against his shirtless chest, cradled in his blood-stained arms.

He let the bodies drop to his feet, which he saw were bare too.

A mockingbird called from the pines above him and Jacob suddenly knew where he'd find his shirt and his miss K-Swisses. It didn't matter how he knew if he had no memory of even taking them off. He saw himself rinsing the congealing blood from his pale, dirty body, saw himself splashing water on his face, rinsing the gristle and bits of meat from his mouth, saw himself spitting it back into the clear, swift water.

Jacob approached the hideout at a saunter. He has washed the blood from his body. He wore a moderately clean shirt he doesn't recognize. His miss K-Swisses were soaked but as clean as they could possibly be for as hard used as they'd been; parts of them are nearly white in the brilliant afternoon sun.

"There ye are!" Tanya Miller squealed.

Jacob found himself smiling. It wasn't much effort to continue, so he did.

"Where've ye been all day?"

"Out 'n' 'bout," he said. "How are ye?"

She smiled, a solid thing, a brick of warmth, affection, a cinderblock of it even, *i am the deer / here are the headlights,* then hugged Jacob before he even saw it coming.

*This must be what it feels like*, Jacob thought, *to be hit by the truck.*

*expect / the unexpected*

*vanilla and lavender*

*/ and*

Then she was a blonde whirl of receding warmth and Jacob felt dizzy. He had to stand still and focus on his breathing or he thought he might have to sit down.

*Focus*, the voice said.

Jacob blinked slowly, taking in air through his nostrils, holding it, then blowing it out of his slightly open mouth.

She was talking.

*When was she not?*

A chittering hummingbird, constantly in motion, or directing those piercing blue eyes, *transfix,* Mrs. Horace's Word of the Day, *1: to hold motionless by or as if by piercing; 2: to pierce through with or as if with a pointed weapon*, at him while remaining perfectly still. Jacob found her unnerving, but he didn't want her to be anywhere else but right there, with him. The more he thought about that, about Tanya Miller being elsewhere, with other people, boys, older boys, boys with cars, the more he felt short of breath and agitated. *That can't be, that can't be*, he kept telling himself.

*Focus,* the voice said.

Jacob opened his eyes.

"Jacob? Are ye alright?"

She was right there when he opened his eyes.

*Tanya Miller / Tanya Miller*

The pressure was back. How had he not noticed that until now? It was nearly overwhelming. He could see streaks of white and blue pain and had to fight the burgeoning need to vomit.

"I don't feel good," Jacob said.

He knew speaking had been a mistake as soon as he started. The muscles he used to speak, apparently, were needed to clench in vomit. He spewed hot, wet chunks of he knew not what over the dried grass. He tried to close his eyes but the force of the expulsion was so great his eyes felt like they were bulging from his head, his eyelids felt stretched to the point of tearing. Drops and flecks of his vomit splashed onto his pants and miss K-Swisses.

A vein burst in his right eye. It sounded like a toothpick snapping, felt like one broken off into his eye.

He heaved for another minute or two before turning away from her, Tanya Miller, and sinking to his hands and knees.

His body was coated in sweat.

*Fever's back,* Jacob knew. *Motherfucking fever's back.*

Jacob had to shit but forced it back. He hoped against hope he could continue to hold it. He didn't think he'd be able to live with himself if he shat his pants in front of Tanya Miller.

"Oh, Lord," Tanya Miller cooed. "Ye needs to see a doctor."

*I do, too,* Jacob knew.

She helped him to his feet, talk-talk-talking, and got him into the hideout.

*What did I do with that fox, possum, and those two squirrels?*

He didn't know.

He didn't remember what he was thinking about.

*What is wrong with me?*

"There ye go," Tanya Miller said, easing Jacob onto the rickety, blood-stained chair. "Jus' sit thair 'til ye feel a bit better. Think ye could drink a lil water?"

Jacob did. He smiled. He was quite thirsty.

-

Jacob couldn't dream of himself dancing, couldn't see his awkward body moving with anything remotely resembling grace, but he found this was a dance he could perform, and with minimum effort too, this talking with her, Tanya Miller. He didn't even have to really listen to a thing she said either. She was definitely the leader in this dance, but that felt just fine with Jacob. All he had to do was wait for the pause, note the look, process it, nod or shake, smile and wait, dancing the dance like all the rest.

"I mean I'm not real sure how preggers I am, ye know?" she said. "How long do ye reckon it'll be 'fore I start showin', do ye think?"

Jacob shook his head and smiled, the dance still easy enough.

She tried to account for the time in events, each and every one. Jacob watched her mouth as she talked, thought about her hands and imagined what those painted nails would look like snaking down that landing strip.

*vanilla and lavender*

*Robbie put the baby in her*, Jacob heard.

"Robbie doesn't even live in Kentucky no more neither," she said.

"Fuck 'im," Jacob said.

She gave him an absolute sunbeam of a smile. It opened the way the flowers on the nature documentary had opened in Mrs. Clark's class. Jacob was, again, transfixed.

"Yeah!" Tanya Miller said, after what felt like a very long time. "Fuck 'im!"

In the end, she guessed a month and a half to two months or so had gone by since Robbie had put the baby in her.

"What am I supposed to do?" she asked.

*trouble / in a family way*

Jacob heard it like a coda, she'd said it so often. He heard it like punctuation, the question instead of a pause, the question serving as the pause.

*This is what you get*, Jacob thought, *for letting it go.*

Jacob knew she knew it.

*they can't help it / cunts*

"What am I supposed to do?"

Jacob looked at her eyes and knew what the bald man must've felt right before he stomped on that doe's head. It made his stomach and skin crawl and hot, burning pain lash out from his swelling testicles and penis. He could feel the pressure like an inflating innertube in the thin space between his hip bones. He wanted to lash out and destroy. He didn't care if it was beautiful or not his property. He didn't give a fuck about anything but death—black, forever death, the wind howling, the bark peeled off every branch in the naked screaming night.

It felt like the most uncomfortable shit of Jacob's life, but it didn't come from his anus: it came from his dick. A burning, clawing mass slowly made its way down the length of his half-hard penis before popping out into his pants.

Jacob moaned and groaned and drooled and, despite the very best of his efforts, shat himself too.

-

She helped him across the dried grass. She held him up when the pressure and electric pain paralyzed him, despite the smell, the sweat, the shaking, and got him over to the place where the little stream frothed white from the sudden change of direction. She helped him down to the edge of the shallow pool, then she turned her back but didn't leave.

Tanya Miller had, of course, talked the entire time. Jacob found her voice much like the bubbling stream, a pleasant thing if you ignored all that it was saying and listened to the round, continuous sound of it, the consistency of gentle tones an audible tonic.

"Ye jus' take all the time ye need now," she cooed. "Don't ye worry about nothin'. Just get yourself cleaned up 'n' we'll get ye back home alrigh'."

*Home is a bitter word*, Jacob thought, slipping his shirt over his head.

His skin was slick with sweat, but what he smelled was the liquid shit in his pants, and, just under that, the smell of the infection.

Tanya Miller had known he'd shit himself. There was no way she could've missed that fact, yet, she'd helped him anyway.

Jacob eased the pants down to his knees, keeping his back to her. The head of his penis was a mushroom from a witch's pantry, purples and greens and off-white all tinged with yellow and red. His stomach turned over at the sight of it. Seeing it made the smell worse somehow.

"I cain't believe this all happened to ye," Tanya Miller said. "Rodney is such an asshole."

Jacob stepped out of the pants bunched around his ankles and into the cold water. All the hair on his body rose to its full height, brimming with static expectation atop little goosepimple mountains. He took hold of his genitals and eased himself down, a task

233

completed in little dips like tea steeping, until he was sitting, the frigid water lapping at his little tuft of pubic hair, bits of gravel and silt tickling and poking his ass cheeks.

"I'm embarrassed to be related to that asshole, I swear," she said.

Jacob gently uncupped his hands and looked at what Rodney Tackett done. His penis half-floated toward the surface of the water, undulating in the rocking waters, the head swollen, grotesquely shifted to the right side like something overturned then melted.

*see / what Rodney Tackett done*

The cold water was numbing the electric pain. It seemed to keep the pressure somewhere just at bay.

"Anyway, take yer time," she said. "Hey, guess what? I think I might've found a solution to my little problem."

*trouble / in a family way*

Jacob watched a thin stream of blood trickle out of his penis and muddy the water before being swept away and dissipated like smoke in a summer's breeze. Then he felt a sharp pain and the immediate need to piss overtook him. He clamped his teeth together and squeezed out what he hoped would be just a small bit of infection followed by a stream of sweet relief, but that's not what happened. To his horror, Jacob watched what could've passed for a creamy spaghetti noodle worm its way through the thin line of his pee hole. It swayed like a hula dancer's grass skirt as it slowly worked its way free.

Jacob had popped pimples on his nose and chin like this, little things on the surface but when you started squeezing it just strung out like an oily rope and kept coming.

"We've been makin' out after I get outta practice," Tanya Miller said, "and I think I'm gonna let him feel me up tomorrow after the game."

The infection worm ended in a cloud of blood and soupy pus the cool running water swept away. The worm seemed immune to the pulls of the current. It drifted languidly away, but not downstream, back toward the bank, back toward her, Tanya Miller.

Jacob wanted to drink for the first time in his life. He didn't know why but he suddenly wanted, needed, nothing more on the planet than three long swallows of sour mash straight Kentucky bourbon.

A crow cawed high overhead. It was immediately answered by another, more talkative crow.

*Jokerman*, Jacob thought, hearing the first crow's cackled laughter.

"By homecomin' I'll let him go all the way," she said, "then it'll look jus' like it should, ye know?"

The crows fell silent, as did Tanya Miller.

He felt her eyes on his back and, instinctively, covered himself, cringing at his water-numbed hands' clumsy touch. His splashing hands disrupted the worm's gentle hula motions and Jacob felt his face contort into a grimace as the worm separated into oil and pus.

He forced himself to slowly nod his head.

Up.

Down.

Jacob squeezed his penis, just under the witch's mushroom, and forced out what he hoped was the last of the infection, then nodded again.

Jacob assumed she felt the weight of the silence too heavy.

*They are weak*, Jacob realized, *women are.*

*It's not a personal thing / not something they can help.*

*They're just hard-wired that way / women are. Cunts.*

"He seems like he's not an asshole," Tanya Miller blurted out. "He's a good kisser, isn't a complete horse's ass, somewhat intelligent, and is second-string quarterback. Not bad prospects, right?"

*The bald man was right*, Jacob decided.

Her laugh was a bird's nervous twitter.

Hawks about. Hawks about.

Jacob could tell she was facing away from him by the sound of her voice. He stood up, dripping and shaking, covered himself with both hands, and got out of the water.

# CHAPTER SIXTEEN
## CHOKE ON IT AND DIE
## (ALL THE GOOD YER WORTH)

**THEY WERE BACK INSIDE THE** hideout. The comforting suck of the sticky floor brought Jacob back fully awake.

*Was I sleepwalking?*

He couldn't tell.

The blank periods, *black patches of another kind of quilt entirely*, were so frequent Jacob was becoming accustomed to them, the way you can get used to just about everything.

*So long as you make allowances*, he thought, *and only allow yourself realistic expectations, you can get used to just about anything.*

"Ye poor thing," she cooed, shuffling him to the lone chair.

The bloodstains were a sight for sore eyes, Jacob felt.

*She understands*, Jacob thought. *She cares, actually cares, and she understands.*

*Be careful*, the voice said.

Jacob refused to acknowledge it.

He smiled up at the leathery little raccoon hands dangling in the window. More light was coming in now that he'd destroyed the most recent quilt failure.

Jacob smiled at the memory of the third quilt. It had seemed like such a sure thing at the outset but had deteriorated as it neared the finishing line.

*It'd been close though*, he thought. *The next one is The One.*

"I know it's weird," Tanya Miller said, "but I think ye should at least let me see it. I mean, if yer not gonna go to the doctor, I mean, cain't go to the doctor, then you need to show it to somebody. Why not me?"

Jacob felt his stomach drop through his body without a sound. He almost looked down to see how it'd look next to the stains and gristle.

Her eyes were serious. Her smile was gone. But Jacob could still tell she cared. He could see she just wanted to make sure he was alright.

For a paralyzing moment, Jacob was sure he was going to burst into tears.

*Focus*, the voice said.

*Fuck you!*

Tanya Miller leaned forward and put her little porcelain hands into his rough, calloused ones.

"I care about ye," Tanya Miller said. "I know we only jus' met a li'l bit ago, but I feel like yer ma li'l brother."

Jacob thought he heard someone laughing, would've looked away to see who was spying in on them if her blue eyes hadn't been so hypnotizing, so *transfix*ing, *Mrs. Horace's Word of the Day, 1: to hold motionless by / or as if by piercing; 2: to pierce through with / or as if with a pointed weapon.*

"Jus' think of me like I's yer mom or something," she said, dropping onto her knees on the sticky floor. "Or yer sister, yeah, yer sister."

She slipped her hands from his, the way raindrops slide off hostas in a downpour. Jacob watched the blue and white tipped fingers disappear inside his waistband and hesitate, just for the briefest of moments, before gently sliding his pants down.

He closed his eyes and wanted to swallow but his throat was too dry.

Jacob opened his eyes and looked down.

Her painted hands now covered her mouth. Her eyes were wide and shocked. She seemed to be vibrating on some frequency making her just visible to him, like she was glitching in and out of projection. He blinked, slowly, and tried again.

Now Jacob read something else on her face, something else entirely.

*Disgust.*

She took in one shuddered breath, then turned her head to the side and vomited onto the bloodstained floor.

-

*See?*

*No.*

*I told you.*

*No.*

She turned back to his witch's mushroom, sniffed, gagged, then puked some more.

*disgust / ringing like a cracking bell*

# BIRTH OF A MONSTER

*Don't need Mrs. Horace's chalked Word of the Day board to tell me what that one means*, Jacob thought.

*disgust / off-key like a dropped piano*
*curdled milk / trashcan juice*

She wiped her mouth with the back of her porcelain right hand.

Index finger: blue.

Middle finger: white.

Ring finger: blue.

Pinky finger: white.

Thumb: half blue, half white.

"Oh," she whined.

Jacob watched her run out the open front door of the hideout this time. He saw it all with a painful, slow-motion clarity too: the bits of granola she had for breakfast roping up to her chin, the faintest hint of a red pimple nestled in all that smooth white skin, the blue eyes clouded over, *a winter's sun / shrouded in cloud*, then the turn and jerk, an awkward scamper at first, a fawn trying to run instead of learning to walk, then the muscled legs pumping and finding sticking purchase, the way her ass bounced, not a fat jiggle but a muscle-bound bounce, the way her elbows V'd and pumped right along with her legs, her painted nails becoming glints in the sun, then a blur of blue and white, then gone.

-

Jacob showered when he got back to the salmon trailer. When he'd finished and dried off, he squeezed a bit of blood and pus from his penis and rubbed it with a sock soaked in rubbing alcohol.

His mother wasn't home. He could tell as soon as he stepped inside. The place felt empty.

Hollowed out was how Jacob felt. Something in much worse shape than the pink singlewide.

That night Jacob did two things he'd never done before: he got drunk and he read the Bible. His mother had left just over a quarter of the bottle of the old crow's bourbon whiskey and Jacob couldn't get the picture of the pus worm out of his head. He saw it dancing there, suspended as if in one of those lava lamps he'd been meaning to steal from Walmart. It had come out of him, out of his . . .

Jacob started with careful, exploratory sips from the bottle. It tasted like liquid fire, something you put in a car engine, or used to start the kind of bonfires teenagers were always having in music videos and movies on the TV, but he found the more he drank it, the

238

more he found he could tolerate the taste. Eventually, he came to think he even liked it.

*It doesn't lie to you*, Jacob thought, taking another mouthful of the Old Crow. *At least the bourbon doesn't lie to you. Ye get the burn right up front. BOOM, baby!*

He was spinning, sweating and not caring about how sweaty he was, which was a nice change, somewhere in the salmon singlewide in Thompkins' Hilltop Trailer Court, but, for the ever-loving life of him, Jacob couldn't tell which room's ceiling he found himself staring at.

*Damn thing is spinning*, he saw.

He thought about the story he'd read, while he still could read, the lines kept drifting into each other when he last tried, from the Bible the foster mother, Debbi Sue Owsley, who gave her love out like a Pez dispenser in equal, little portions, who'd given all the foster children bibles when they arrived, right off the bat, the story about Lot's wife becoming a pillar of stone.

*Stupid. All she had to do was run* / not run away//*away. That's it. Run away and not look back.*

*run away* / *and don't look back*

Jacob replayed the scene from the hideout earlier that afternoon in his head again. He envisioned the ending differently: this time when he'd finally made it to the open door of the hideout, after carefully tucking his swollen privates back into the filthy pants, Tanya Miller was there, on her knees like she'd been on the sticky, stained floor, but with palms upturned, nails facing away from him, transformed from a porcelain beauty into a pillar of salt.

He meant to snort but hiccupped instead.

*Stupid cunt.* Jacob hated them all: women. *What good are they? They're rotten mothers. Terrible friends. They lie, trick, hurt, confuse, and all just because they can. Just because they have some power over us, men.*

*transfix* / *pay for power*

Jacob felt so confused, so sad. He hated it. The bourbon seemed to help, but he was so sad, there didn't seem to be enough to make it all go away. He hated them, but why'd they have to have such pretty hands?

-

When he woke up, Jacob wanted to die. Someone had scooped out the inside of his head like a pumpkin while he was asleep and didn't even bother placing anything but pain in its place. He tried to sit up, but there was a serious imbalance between his ears. He felt like he'd slept on driftwood, not his smelly but stable single bed. The water-stained ceiling was shifting and swaying then righting itself, only to shift and sway.

*shift / sway*

Jacob threw up while still lying flat on his back. His vomit rose about six inches, a sad, foul Old Faithful, before splashing back into his open mouth and everywhere else. He felt it slip into each of his ear canals. It stung into both of his clenched eyes.

Jacob rolled over onto his side for his next bout of puking. He quickly found out he failed at this too; the vomit hit the paneled wall and splashed back, startling Jacob so much he both shit and pissed himself.

-

Jacob woke, but didn't open his eyes. He hadn't meant to fall back asleep. He was going to shower. He couldn't remember why, but he'd planned on showering.

He opened his eyes to blinding pain. He squeezed them shut again, both of his hands automatically pawing away the crusted gunk.

*What—*

Then he remembered, and with that, came the smell.

*Thank God*, Jacob thought, after the dry heaves passed, *there's nothing left in me to expel.*

*Expulsion, Mrs. Horace, the act of expelling: the state of being expelled.*

Jacob had to grit his teeth at the pain beating like a hammer in his temples, behind each of his eyes, his cracked lips, and raw throat.

*everywhere / pain pain & more pain*

He had to grit his teeth at the way his stomach lurched up and down without his consent or control. He felt a hot trickle stream out of his ass and had to grit his teeth at the shame and embarrassment and anger that came with it.

*Shower*, the voice said.

*Yes*, he replied, gritting his teeth at the floaters dancing in his peripheries that swelled and receded.

*visual / tidal*

Each step: quicksand.

Each beating of his heart: a *(claw)*hammer's unkind kiss.

Each step an unanswered prayer for death.

Each step a reflexive response to the tragedy of life.

Jacob collapsed into the bathtub, sucking in ragged gasps of air, drooling bubbly strands of sticky spit onto his bare, hairless chest, sure as shit his heart was going to explode with the next breath.

*This one.*

*This one.*

Jacob craned his left leg to the side and pushed in the stopper of the drain with his heel. He shifted his weight upwards from his middle, then lifted his left leg high enough to toe on the hot water before collapsing back onto the scummy tub.

*This one.*

Water slowly filled the tub, cold, at first, but scalding after no more than half a minute. Jacob didn't bother moving his feet, bottoms pressed together like an inverse prayer, *as above / so below*, even when he looked down and saw how tomato red his skin had become. He could see that through the shit and filth steadily muddying the steaming bathwater.

He watched the swirls as long as he could.

Jacob woke when the warm water filled both of his nostrils. He splashed forward, sputtering on both the terrible smelling water and the clinging clots of phlegm coating the back of his throat.

Once he had control of himself, Jacob reached forward into the murky water and popped up the drain, then shut off the water. He pulled his knees up to his chest, wrapped both of his arms around his legs, and knew he would've cried like a little bitty baby if he hadn't been so tired.

*So goddamn tired.*

Jacob worked himself into starting his jaw. He got his teeth to meet, then to squeeze together, finally to crush and grind.

Something about it caught a portion of the pain, the pain he knew was coming, the pain that was already there, the pain that never left.

*There's no end*, Jacob realized, not surprised by the hot blurring in his eyes, but ashamed of it just the same. *There's no way out.*

Jacob rose up on dripping, shaky legs, using the shower handles to keep from tumbling into the stained tub, caught his breath, then stepped out onto the mounds of discarded clothes. He stepped over to the mirror, his head still empty but filled with something like a spider's web, but more sad than sinister, *not quite black / but blue.*

Jacob looked up into the mirror, steamed at the four corners like a vignette or the fake old-timey photographs you could pay to take at the fair and Hillbilly Days, and felt watched by eyes other than his own frightened pair. The feeling was so strong Jacob spun in a hesitated, jerky circle, seeking out the observer. He felt his gaze linger on the little bulb outside the tub on the ceiling. He could envision how it would look from that angle, if someone climbed up on the pink trailer and popped off the fan cover. Jacob could see the angle with absolute clarity, but he found no one watching him.

As he dressed, in the cleanest clothes he could find in his bedroom, Jacob kept waiting for the feeling to go away. It didn't. In fact, Jacob felt the hair on the back of his neck and arms stand up as the feeling got even stronger.

*What the hell? What's happening?*

"Who's there?" Jacob asked.

His voice wasn't loud, but it felt like it ricocheted around the pink trailer like a tooth rattling around a drain.

"Who's there?" he screamed. "Answer me got dam ye—"

Jacob cut off abruptly as a violent tinge rocked the right side of his neck and clamped his mouth shut. Cool pinpricks began rippling down the back of his neck.

He moaned in pain and confusion, sure this was finally death, this breath, this one, this, *this*.

-

Jacob had both of his hands on his knees, panting for breath.

*the sun's an oven / set too high*
*the sun's a glimmer / in the reaper's eye*

Sweat stung down into his eyes but he saw the hideout sitting in the little valley below. He didn't remember leaving Thompkins' Hilltop Trailer Court and the salmon-colored singlewide. Then, against all fathomability, he *did*. He did remember leaving, saw, in fact, himself doing so, in wide, wide pan-o-ramic, nodding at the man from 3F who, Jacob saw with detail, had patchy facial hair, coarse black hair on the bologna-like tumor hanging over the left-side of his mouth, saw the growing pile of rusted machinery and ancient tools in the back of the man's rust-bucket pickup, saw the look of distant surprise and furtive aversion cross his face like a veil. Jacob saw himself wave dismissively at Maggie, the cause of his facial expressions, who seemed oddly let down Jacob didn't stop and talk. Jacob saw himself cross the county road and slip into the woods as if stepping behind a curtain.

"What the fuck is wrong with me?" Jacob asked, feeling dizziness like a hot summer breeze.

*Focus*, the voice said.

*Go see.*

"Go see what?" he asked, closing his eyes for a long moment. "Where? There?"

The hideout looked like a boil in the tawny grass. He saw the door standing open but only shadows within. Shadows on shadows.

*Show / what's there to display*

His breath was coming in easier now, but it felt like somebody was sitting on his chest, squeezing his lungs like beanbags. Jacob started down the mountain path with a sense of dread that was alien and bitter.

*What is this?*

He had no idea. He'd never approached the hideout with anything in him but expectation or hope.

Until he'd agreed to show her, Tanya Miller, his "little hideout." Why had he done that? Why? Sure, she was a girl, a friend, a beautiful friend, but a friend, a friend that had showed him care and concern, but why had he taken her to the one place that was *his*? Why? And why was he suddenly so afraid to go to his place, his little hideout?

"What does it all mean?"

*see / what you've done*

"What Rodney Tackett done?"

*Yes*, the voice said, *and what ye done.*

He saw himself trip on dozens of rocks on his descent, saw himself in closeup, wide-angle, overhead, the whole nine yards, watched himself bounce like a golf ball, saw his head burst like a watermelon on sandstone, saw his neck extend too far, then at too sharp an angle. He saw all his deaths, but he didn't fall. He stepped into the dried, brittle grass, the weight on his chest even heavier now he was back on relatively flat ground.

There was something on the floor of the hideout. He could see the vague outline of something, but the shape or shapes were so vague he couldn't even venture a mental guess. He started across the grass, staring down at his feet, wondering when he'd put on his miss K-Swisses, waiting, in vain, for the memory to return.

-

She was on the floor, the sticky, stained floor, bits of red polka-dotting the strands of her blonde hair and smooth, perfect face.

*Tanya Miller / Tanya Miller*

But when Jacob heard and felt the familiar, comforting suck of the hideout's floor, he also saw her at a different angle. He saw that only one side of her face, her head, was smooth, was perfect.

The other side . . .

Jacob shuddered, then he remembered.

*Oh god.*

-

The clawhammer, Ace Hardware, was a red so dark that, at first, Jacob mistook it for black, and, therefore, not his. The memory of what he'd done was a montage of smells and tastes and other sensations. Jacob saw, felt, tasted, breathed it all in again. The experience was so overwhelming he collapsed onto the sticky floor beside her, Tanya Miller.

*My friend,* Jacob thought bitterly. *My friend,* genuine / concern*, who I beat,* use yer skull / as a drum*, to death.*

*clawhammer / Ace Hardware*

*Right here,* Jacob watched dust motes float in the sunlight. The weight in his chest, he was sure, was slowly, brutally crushing him to death, suffocating him invisibly.

*her / Tanya Miller*

Jacob watched himself bash her head with the hammer. First, he saw the disgust in her eyes, the appearance of slanting lines on her cheeks, the downward curl of her usually pouty lips. Then she had to go and throw up. Jacob watched himself recoil at the slap of embarrassment, saw the disappointment, recalled the lone wail only he could hear: *I thought she understood!*

*She didn't.*

*I told ye so.*

Jacob flinched at each of the hammer's blows. He stopped counting them, but he couldn't, and didn't want to stop watching. It was a lava lamp. It was a train wreck. It was the quick and ugly dismantling of something beautiful.

*life / death*

*living / dying*

*desert / seabed*

Jacob felt the smile on his face, hated himself for it, but couldn't remove it. He felt absolutely helpless, pitiful, useless. The smile was bitter. The smile was mournful. The smile was appreciative in a connoisseur kind of way. The smile was an embarrassed reflex.

*Piece o' shit,* he heard his mother call him. *Little piece o' shit. Shoulda jus' flushed ye. All the good ye've brought me.*

Jacob heard the sucking sound the clawhammer made when he pressed the sole of his left miss K-Swiss to Tanya Miller's sunken head and yanked free.

*All the good yer worth.*

He knew he was screaming but couldn't decide if it was then and in his head or here and now and in the hideout. He didn't wonder long though. The weight on his chest finally cut off all of his air supply and he plummeted into darkness with his eyes wide but unseeing.

-

The movie started.

*An empty, vast expanse /*

*// Unseen currents pulling like spectral hands.*

-

The blackness was everywhere, but Jacob knew there was sky and water, though he couldn't see a distinction. He could see himself, a pale, lumpy dot in an ocean of absolute darkness. Could see the slow arc of the current through his slow but steady progression. After a while, Jacob became unsure if he was watching himself drift or if he'd finally stopped moving; it was infuriating.

*You can choke on nothing.*

*high & low / far & wide*

*nothing nothing nothing*

*You can choke on it and die,* Jacob understood.

The shot somehow dissipated into a closeup of Jacob's tired, hopeless face, little droplets of absolute black dripping onto his brow from his hair and running the length of his dirty, but very pale, face. He looked at his bad teeth hanging out of his gaping mouth, his lips like the dried scales of discarded fish. His nose was bleeding, not a lot, just a little trickle from both nostrils. Both of his eyes were purpling, bruising like a crocus in blossom, but that's not what alarmed him most.

His eyes were different, Jacob saw as the camera slowly directed all of its focus there.

*There's not a lick of white in them. No color neither.*

It was as if his eyes were all pupil, completely black. It was unnerving.

Jacob didn't want to watch this movie, but that didn't matter. He was going to watch it, had to.

There was a long, breathless scene of just the twin holes of his eyes, black, depthless eyes, the lashes gray in the monochromatic cinematography, the skin pale and oily. The eyes did not move, nor did the lids blink or flinch. The skin stayed still. The inky blackness seemed to be roiling but on a level of subtlety nearly impossible to catch. It reminded Jacob of the video of the Great Red Spot on Jupiter the sub had shown them twice last week—*or was it the week before?*—a violence so immense it could not be seen or understood in real-time by any human means, just the slow, steady swirling in pixelated shades of gray and darker gray.

Jacob couldn't look away from his own eyes that were just like that.

After a time, he became aware of a changing in the eyes. It started with a few movements just under the surface at seemingly random places in each of them, like a large fish, or a school of smaller ones slowly approaching the surface of the blackness but not quite breaking it. It happened again after a few moments, then again, and again. With each swell—they were gentle at first, but grew to whitecapped waves breaking hundreds of feet tall—a bit of change occurred to the dark.

Gradually, it lightened.

Gradually, it became the hideout.

The camera work and editing were truly tremendous. It filled Jacob with a sense of wonder that momentarily eclipsed the clinging doom.

*See*, a voice said.

*Show*, Jacob answered.

*what's there to display* shimmered across the screen like heat dancing on a desert highway and Jacob wanted to applaud, envisioned himself as eight years old, beaming and slapping his hands together like there was no tomorrow, then it faded like the languid smoke from incense.

Jacob stood next to the farmer's table, his back to the camera, looking down at Tanya Miller, who was on her knees on the sticky floor at his feet, his miss K-Swisses unmistakably not the shoes you'd expect to see on a boy—*a young man*, Jacob corrected—such as this.

It could've been the beginning to a hundred different porno tapes—*Virgin Trim Volume 10, Slant-Eyed Vixens, Beaver Fever 6: Cabin Fever / Fast-Forward X2 Mode*—but something about the charged stillness of the moment seemed to vibrate with a hum you felt more than heard, something just under an alarm, not quite a bell, not a chime.

Jacob watched Tanya Miller, her eyes big, bright, upturned like the saucer under fancy coffee cups, slip her porcelain fingers, oh god those blue and white painted fingernails, into the waistband of his pants. He watched the last bit of their eye contact linger for a hair's breadth of a tick. With the tock, Jacob watched as his pale, pimply ass was slowly uncovered, *sunset / moonrise,* then his nearly hairless legs, the backs of his thighs so pale they were nearly blue.

The camera began a long, slow zoom into Tanya Miller, kneeling there on the stained, sticky floor. At first the only change Jacob could register was the simultaneous rising of her eyelids and her eyebrows, like a twitch, then they rose again and, this time, they didn't come back down until she started vomiting, and Jacob, despite the dread coating every square inch of his insides, watched the movie as if for the first time, as if he didn't know how this particular scene played out. Then something jerked in her long, tanned throat, so supple, so smooth, and both corners of her pouty lips suddenly turned southward in a textbook frown, *the clown cries / his mask now vertical & blue,* but she swallowed it back down.

He watched tears fill her large blue eyes as a knot raced up and down her throat in quick jerky starts and stops. The eyes darted from one aspect of what was not shown on the screen to the next in rapid succession five or six times before slowing down and really seeing what wasn't a foot away from her and at eye-level. The frown stretched beyond the confines of that expression, and—Jacob had never felt so entranced by camerawork in his life—became Horror. Capital H, terrified horse, slasher-flick closeup, blanching of all color from the young face, even the pouty lips, now stretched thin and white from the perfect oval of her soundless scream, like the withering of a jack-o'-lantern Horror.

Her nostrils flared and it was like she'd been socked in the belly. She seemed to double forward, even though she couldn't have moved forward very far without bumping into the source of all her discomfort, which Jacob was glad did not appear on the screen.

Then Absolute Aversion flashed across her face like a projectionist's soft refocusing. It could've been a scene on any daytime soap opera, the gentle haze of the shot; it reminded Jacob of a dream sequence scene and he felt the urgent, competing needs to laugh and to cry. He couldn't breathe all that well, the haziness on the screen felt like a shroud over his face; he could feel his hot, soured breath too close on his cheeks.

*a dream of a dream / of a dream*
*he he / ha ha ho*

The camera angle suddenly changed; it now looked up and over Tanya Miller's round, perfect ass—both her feet nestled under it reminded Jacob of the way cats folded into themselves sometimes—at Jacob.

Seeing himself on the screen, every bit of his being vibrating from an alarming sense of capital D Dread, Jacob wished he could turn it off. He wished somebody would change the channel. He didn't want to see what happened next. He especially didn't want to see himself and what he was getting ready to do from this angle.

Tanya Miller's blonde head jerked up, then down, then to the side, her eyes squeezed slits, tears spilling from both eyes, a thin trickle of snot wetting the bottom of each of her nostrils, and started puking, exposing Jacob's infected penis and swollen testicles on the screen for the first time in excruciating detail.

Jacob felt his stomach turn over. He swore he could smell it.

He wanted to cry.

Laugh.

He felt a giggle escape his lips like a burped hiccup, but he didn't think he heard it, not really. Maybe he felt it. He couldn't tell.

Jacob saw his face twist as if it were a mask and instead of a face on the other side somebody shoved their hand in and gave it a good wrenching. Then it went blank, seemed to hesitate, sway there for a moment before a bright, unnerving smile stretched the skin tight on his dirty face. Jacob saw the smile reach the eyes he knew were his own but looked so inhuman, so very animal-like.

The Dread broke like a dam. It rocked him. After the initial torrent, Jacob felt it slow, running through him like the last suds down the drain.

Jacob watched Such A Happy Boy pivot his hips so he could reach over to the farmer's table without moving his feet. He watched him lift the clawhammer, Ace Hardware, from the table and pivot back around on his hips like a deranged funhouse animatronic Pinocchio.

*i'm a real boy / such a happy boy*

He raised the clawhammer, Ace Hardware, above his head, his whole visage a smile now, and waited for her to finish picking at the strand of vomit connecting the sticky, stained floor to her smooth, gently rounded chin.

The camera angle was above SAHB's shoulder, the raised arm and held hammer more outline and shadow then fully realized image, Tanya Miller's dulled eyes looking up from *what Rodney Tackett done* to SAHB's beaming smile to the raised arm and waiting hammer.

Her mouth had enough time to round into the "O" of "no" before SAHB sank the polished forged head of the clawhammer, Ace Hardware, into the apex of her high, perfect cheek bone.

Jacob's ears filled with the first sound of the movie.

Such a Happy Boy lifted the clawhammer, Ace Hardware, up, then he brought it down. Sometimes he was able to jerk it free from the ruins of her face; sometimes, he had to plant a firm foot on Tanya Miller's skull or throat and really yank at it to get the clawhammer, Ace Hardware, to dislodge.

The camera wasn't hazy now. There was nothing soft about the shots. They came in different angles and with increasing rapidity, the only sound being the thwacking of steel on flesh, the crunch of steel on bone, the splat of deeper, softer matter. The slant of his smile was sharp, angular, wolfish.

*Such a happy boy*, SAHB thought.

Jacob saw she was still breathing. Despite the cratered moonscape of one entire hemisphere of her head, bits of jawbone oozing blood and marrow, pink brain exposed in a tear through the blonde, Tanya Miller still breathed.

SAHB dropped the hammer onto the farmer's table, then collapsed into the chair, his smile still there but now the strain apparent wasn't from holding back but from keeping up. Jacob saw that, he could understand that feeling. He felt it again.

The camera showed the uneven bulge in SAHB's pants, showed the exact moment SAHB's breathing slowed enough for him to fully take stock of himself, see, and feel his painful erection. His left hand went about pushing and pulling as if charming a snake.

Jacob saw SAHB's mouth open, watched his blood-speckled face tighten with effort and focus.

*Focus*, Jacob could hear the voice saying. He heard it again.

A chime clanged in his head, which was aching like an over-used muscle.

Tanya Miller did not move an arm, a leg, a finger. Her chest rose and fell rhythmically. Jacob saw this but couldn't hear it while SAHB got up from the chair, retrieved a bag from behind the open door, then upended the contents onto the farmer's table, next to the gleaming clawhammer, Ace Hardware. There was rope, Walmart, duct-tape, Ace Hardware, rat poison, Walmart, bolt-cutters, Ace Hardware, a sock stuffed with two handfuls of smooth river pebbles, Levisa Fork, and some more rope, Ace Hardware.

Jacob watched him drag her, *Tanya Miller / Tanya Miller*, into a sitting position, her right arm folded over her left, both behind her back, then SAHB tied her, Tanya Miller, up with the rope Jacob had stolen from Ace Hardware.

-

The movie was straining. Jacob could almost hear the reels of film struggling in the projector as the image before his eyes seemed to pull tighter, first into clearer focus, then into the realms of the impressionistic, great smears of colors and shapes giving just the general appearance of things.

All that blood, Jacob saw.

Her hands were untouched snow; how had the artist kept them so clean, so pure, so white, with all the blending and mixing and smearing? Jacob could make out a smidgen of blue, a tuft of a bright white, the alternating pattern of her painted fingernails.

*Those . . . painted . . . nails.* Jacob tried to swallow, but it felt like a cocklebur the size of a walnut had lodged itself inside his Adam's apple.

Jacob wanted to blink, knew he couldn't, but the images on the screen gained definition as if he'd willed it. It made him feel slightly giddy. The word "powerful" kept rolling around his tongue like a lemon drop in his cotton mouth.

There seemed to be the beating of a heart. Nothing on the screen showed this, but Jacob felt it, a low thumping, something at an inaudible frequency, felt more than heard in his prickling ears, a *thump-thump, thump-thump* that very gradually grew in volume as Jacob watched himself needlessly tightening the ropes around her, Tanya Miller.

She still wasn't moving, not really, just the steady rise and fall of her chest. He couldn't see any air passing in or out of her ripped-open mouth or ruined nose, but the *thump-thump, thump-thump* kept on getting louder and louder. The rhythm of the heart was at ease, at peace, but there was something absolutely sinister about the sound just the same.

SAHB needlessly tied more rope, Walmart, around her, Tanya Miller. Though the camera didn't zoom in, Jacob could see the grotesque erection oozing, not a lot but continuously, as he finished the last knot.

He let her slump over onto her side on the floor, his left hand now gripped around himself and steadily working, up and down, up and down. Jacob watched as he walked around her, Tanya Miller, alive somehow but bleeding and bleeding and bleeding on the stained floor, his left hand never stopping, though he bends in for a closer look here, there, there again.

The camera shifted to Tanya Miller's bound hands, her fingers looked relaxed, as perfect as a doll's, the blue and white painted nails somehow untouched by blood or hammer.

-

The sound of something wet splashed in Jacob's ears.

The camera was a liquid smear, as shot from below, then the shot whirred upwards and around, a closeup, looking directly down at a puddle of viscous, off-white streaked with dirty yellow and sinus infection green. And blood.

The kaleidoscope of images was a moment of bliss, even if it was tinged with nausea.

-

Such a Happy Boy had the trauma shears in his left hand, the denim folds of Tanya Miller's thin shorts in his right. Her plump thigh dimpled with the pressure of SAHB's knuckles. Jacob saw he was still smiling, still erect. His eyes were twin beads of hard black sunk back in the head, so familiar, so alien, dressed up with purpled bags hung like musty drapes or rotten plum flesh.

Jacob followed the trauma shears, Pikeville Medical School, as they sliced their way toward the ropes. The camera rode the blade like a flea on a cat's tail; Jacob marveled.

SAHB stilled the shears at the ropes, Ace Hardware, Walmart, set them aside, his left hand working at the throbbing, infected penis until they were needed to untie the knots they'd knotted a little bit ago.

*Such a short time*, Jacob thought, *for so much to change.*

After untying her, Tanya Miller, SAHB cut a pretty straight line up the middle of her shirt, making sure to snip the peach-colored bra at the thin place it attached between the titties. It made him think of the hideout, *yer "little" hideout*, sitting in the valley between the two knobs, then he set the trauma shears, Pikeville Medical School, onto the sticky, stained floor.

Jacob watched him open her clothes, the smile on his face making it look like Christmas morning, like he was unwrapping presents: this one, the revered landing strip; this one, the flat, gentle expanse of her belly, the belly button nothing more than backroad pothole; this one, the pale, round clouds of her titties, the nipples not as hard as in the shower shot but definitely the same ones.

Jacob thought about that story from English class. It told them the ending right off the bat. The story kept going though. Jacob remembered not having high expectations for a story that told you how it ended at the beginning, that just seemed like the exact opposite way you were supposed to tell a story, but Jacob found himself fully engrossed all the way through to the ending, the same one he knew at the outset was coming, but now felt important and final in a new way, a different way, a more fulfilling way. This movie felt like that to Jacob.

The camera made it look like the opening of the body Jacob had seen at the medical school, folds of flesh opened like a meat-book, like the opening of a crocodile's mud-covered mouth from TV, the exposed peapod slit and bristle-like hair of the landing strip like the blossoming of a cherry zinnia.

The dread was a thing of beauty too, Jacob knew. He felt it right alongside the knowing of what came next, felt it in that strange, new, fulfilling way from the story.

He watched his failed attempt at entering her, Tanya Miller. He watched himself push, prod, finger, lick, bite, sniff, then prod some more, the laugh track more *Fraiser* than *Roseanne*. He'd just about had it started when the electric flashes of pain, bright neon buzzes he lashed across the screen like perfect whips, became too much and he had to roll off her, Tanya Miller, onto the sticky, stained floor, panting, sweating, steadily working at his inflamed penis.

Jacob saw he was still smiling, but a grimace flashed across this face, once, twice, then became a candle's steady flicker, *a static whisper / a smile upside down*, and oily sweat beaded across his upper lip and dripped down his pimple-covered forehead and upturned eyebrows.

The beating of her heart, *thump-thump, thump-thump*, was so loud in Jacob's buzzing, prickling ears it distorted into a mountainous bass, crushing, squeezing.

He studied her vagina. Jacob watched him.

*Just like the gorillas from that documentary in Mrs. Millsap's class*, Jacob thought, feeling a shiver run the length of his spine, wondering where it'd come from.

He picked at the folds, the hair. He sniffed, licked, nibbled. He put the index finger of his clumsy right hand inside her, Tanya Miller, and felt around, his right hand rubbing around his swollen, burning dickhead.

There was a wobble; Jacob felt it in his head like the rumble of thunder just overhead.

The screen showed her perfect white hand, palm turned upward, the golden, slanted light of evening ending at the burning tips of each of her fingers, then, in another awe-inspiring visual, the painted nails glittered in a brilliant luster, despite the fact the nails weren't facing any light, little pinpricks of it seemed to tear holes in the hideout, illuminating paler pinpricks.

Jacob watched him use her left hand, watched him hunker over her on his knees on the stained, sticky floor until the angle was right and the palm was where he needed it to be, the fingers wrapped around him, his around hers, the nails just a-gleaming and a-glittering in the last rays of day.

Jacob held her small, beautiful hand in his. He was speeding up; the need overbearing, overwhelming. He wanted to lean down and bite her arm, leave little holes of himself there. He forced himself to lean back a little, so the light coming in through the window would hit her painted nails, *Oh God her painted nails*, and the burning, the need, would end.

*They're glittering*, he marveled.

The blue and white tips of Tanya Miller's fingernails were shooting off golden sparks and shimmers.

The pressure came to a climax.

There was another wobbling in his head, this one sounded like a failing motor.

Pain erupted with an immediacy that sucked the breath from his lips.

Jacob felt his entire existence pressed down into a white-hot ball of complete and utter emptiness for twelve and a half seconds. He heard her, Tanya Miller, suck in a whistling breath, *sweet static whisper / singing so long*, that seemed to stretch on and on like the last chord of a bawdy ballad, *overindulgent deaths / uninvited, lingering guests*, before Jacob found himself straining and wondering if he could even still hear it.

*That was it*, he realized, a smile gripping his face like a vise, *her last breath*.

Then it all sputtered, gasped, gushed, then throbbed, dully, and Jacob came back to himself, saw that he was in the hideout, that he was sitting on a thin, tanned arm, his knees on the stained, sticky floor, his left hand pressing the perfect porcelain fingers around himself. He knew they were hers, Tanya Miller's, but he also knew that was a fiction, a *farce, Mrs. Horace's Word of the Day, an empty or patently ridiculous act, proceeding, or situation*.

He saw his puddle on the floor, all that blood, all that infection, discoloration, *wrong yellows / hard greens*, and had to look away.

-

The screen went dark, just winked out like a prolonged blink, and the next thing it showed was Tanya Miller's smashed in face. One of her blue eyes, *no longer bright, no longer genuine,* was hanging from a pale bit of gooey stuff not two inches off the floor, not really swinging, but not really still either.

*The way a river is*, Jacob thought, *in the middle of August*.

# IN UTERO

## CHAPTER SEVENTEEN
## HEAVIER THAN HEAVEN

*I'M IN IT NOW,* **JACOB** thought. *Jesus Christ, but I'm in it now.*

She looked like a body then, a pale blueness settling in, marring the healthy tanned skin, making it seem polluted somehow.

*All them movies make it out like there's beauty in death*, Jacob thought, forcing his eyes to follow the sunken skin of Tanya Miller's crushed-in face, *but there ain't nothing pretty about this.*

Jacob wanted to believe those words, but he crouched down on his haunches and saw the ragged skin, bits of sinew and cartilage jutting out exposed and gleaming in the strange light coming in through the hideout's sole window, and felt the air still in his lungs.

*Real beauty*, he thought, leaning in to study the blue eye hanging just above the stained, sticky floor, still attached to Tanya Miller's head. *Real beauty.*

Some period of time had passed with him staring fixedly at Tanya Miller's unmoving body. He could smell her now, Tanya Miller. It was a sweet stink and Jacob marveled in it.

*You really do shit yourself when you die*, he saw. *You piss and shit yourself just like a little baby.*

He stepped out into the burgeoning night, his face hurting from smiling.

-

The tarp, Ace Hardware, was blue and spotless. Jacob carefully unfolded it on the filthy floor of the hideout beside her, Tanya Miller. It wasn't quite as long as she was, but it was nearly four times as wide as her thin frame.

Jacob stood looking from the tarp to the unmoving body of Tanya Miller. It felt like a math problem just out of his solving ability. He forced himself back into motion, knowing he'd slip back into the blank space of unknowable time lost if he didn't keep himself in motion.

Jacob slowly cut off her clothes with the trauma shears, Pikeville Medical School, stopping to savor the exposed flesh of her genitals as well as the creamy white of her smooth belly.

*Focus*, the voice said.

Jacob saw the hatchet, Walmart, in his head and a plan began to take shape.

He felt the percussive belch from deep within the earth again and began to sweat.

*Learned the hard way that you gotta be careful how you use this 'ere hidey hole*, the bald man had said.

Jacob looked from the nude, bluing body of Tanya Miller to the blue tarp.

*Cut her up*, the voice said. *Use the hatchet.*

Jacob retrieved the hatchet, Walmart, and got to work. He knew he was smiling, but he couldn't help it; he was such a happy boy sometimes.

-

He'd carefully arranged each bit of her, Tanya Miller, in the center of the tarp, Ace Hardware, until there were just the gooey leftovers from the inside of her head that slipped through his grimy fingers left. He figured something would come a-sniffing if he left the hideout's door open. Jacob brought each of the four corners of the tarp, Ace Hardware, together and hefted the bundle over his left shoulder.

*Not so bad*, he'd initially thought.

The way to the mineshaft from this side of the entrance was difficult in the best of times. Hauling one hundred and ten pounds of extra weight made the going slow and *arduous*, Mrs. Horace's Word of the Day, *1: hard to accomplish or achieve; 2: hard to climb*. There were thick patches of cockspur hawthorns all over the mountain and the bundled tarp, Ace Hardware, got stuck several times. He'd lost his temper momentarily the last time he'd had to stop and ripped a dollar-sized hole in the tarp, Ace Hardware. From then on, he'd had to drag her, Tanya Miller, up the last half-mile of the ascending trail.

Somewhere distantly, his penis and balls ached and throbbed with a dulled fury.

*what Rodney Tackett done / what Rodney Tackett done*

Jacob hated her, Tanya Miller, and himself with each step.

*You knew this would happen, didn't you?*

*You freak.*

*Sicko.*

*Couldn't even fuck her pussy could you, shit ass?*

Jacob let the tarp, Ace Hardware, drop at the dilapidated brick entrance to the mineshaft.

*No but I sure tasted it, didn't I?*

Jacob wiped sweat from his brow and smiled up into the moon.

*This'll teach him*, the voice said, *for what Rodney Tackett done.*

It felt more than that for Jacob but he couldn't translate his feelings into words. It was like the nails on her hands, Tanya Miller's. He'd carefully cleaved both her hands just below the wrist bone and spent a considerable amount of time, of which he could not specifically account for, staring at the slender fingers and painted nails. Fondling them. Using them to fondle himself.

*blue / white*

He wanted to keep both her hands, but only one would fit snugly in the bottom of the tacklebox he'd stolen from an uncovered johnboat at Jenny Wiley State Park. He'd kept her, Tanya Miller's, one good eye on the top shelf, where it sat atop a pile of sinkers and spinner-baits.

*She's jus' a disposable cunt, shit ass*, the voice said.

Jacob found he was nodding his head.

*Jus' another in a long line.*

"Yes, she is," Such A Happy Boy replied.

*Rodney Tackett did this.*

*what Rodney Tackett done / what Rodney Tackett done*

"Yes, he did," SAHB whispered back.

Jacob saw the long trail leading up to the tarp, Ace Hardware, and wanted to kill her again.

*Another mess for me to clean up*, he raged as he kicked the sodden bundle.

When it'd passed, Jacob was squatting next to what remained of her, Tanya Miller, on the open tarpaulin, Ace Hardware, her head and torso, which he'd left connected, having no recollection of moving inside the burnt-out remains of the brick building housing the mineshaft. The dropping of the parts replayed in his head in Fast-Forward X2 Mode. The camera angles were off-center and each frame seemed more exposed than the one before until the morning light was all Jacob could see.

He blinked, bringing his left hand up to shield his raw eyes.

Jacob stood just outside the doorframe of the mineshaft, the blue tarp, Ace Hardware, carefully folded and tucked under his right arm. He could feel the damp stickiness of it through his shirt. He shivered under the impending sun.

He turned back to the dark, yawning hole in the ground and tossed the tarpaulin, Ace Hardware, down.

*Better safe than sorry*, he thought. *I don't want to pay for what Rodney Tackett done more than I already have.*

He set about walking back to the salmon pink trailer in Thompkins' Hilltop Trailer Court more exhausted than he could ever recall being. With each step, Jacob was sure he couldn't possibly take another.

He was surprised to find the pink singlewide's flimsy doorknob in his hand.

The last thought Jacob had before slipping into a troubled sleep was that Tanya Miller now knew something Jacob didn't: what it felt like to fall forever.

-

*You didn't even feel a thing*, Jacob told himself in the bathroom mirror. *You squatted down there on the stained, sticky floor of the hideout and you hacked her to bits and you didn't feel a thing. Not a single thing.*

There was something faltering in the voice in his head that didn't translate to the image his eye saw in the pimple-squeezings covered mirror. His eyes were the eyes of the voice, the flat, expressionless eyes of the taxidermized black bear at Breaks Interstate Park, the eyes were the bottomless hole just inside the blown-off door of the brick building.

*What have I done?*

*what Rodney Tackett done / what Rodney Tackett done*

*What does this make me?*

*blue / white / white / blue*

*Nothing. You are nothing.*

Jacob was at school, his eyes heavier than Heaven could ever dream of being. He let his head sink down onto his curled arms on the desktop.

*You tossed her, Tanya Miller, down into that bottomless hole, bit by bit, piece by piece.* Jacob saw them in a stilted Fast-Forward X2 Mode—forearm, darkness, other forearm, darkness, thigh, darkness, foot, darkness—until she was gone and not a sound to answer for her.

*Watch yer step, shit ass*, the bald man had told him. *Ye almost found the drop-off.*

*Is there a drop-off? Did I find it?*

*Is this what it feels like to fall forever?*

An alarm was sounding: loud, brassy, abrasive.

Jacob woke to the shuffling of his classmates leaving the classroom. The bell rang again.

"Good morning, Mr. Hunter," Mrs. Horace said. "So good of you to finally join us."

Jacob rubbed his burning eyes. The classroom seemed too full of light. His head felt stuffed full of raw cotton.

"Let's have us a little chat with Mr. Harold, shall we?"

Hearing the vice principal's name should've brought fear or panic into Jacob, but it didn't. He knew if he got into more trouble at school his mother would be notified and he'd catch a beating. He knew it all as sure as he knew he'd tossed her, Tanya Miller, into the mineshaft Randall Adkins had shown him, but he still had a hard time incorporating this knowledge into his current scheme of things.

Knowing isn't always understanding.

Jacob didn't listen to anything else from Mrs. Horace. She talked the whole walk down the east wing.

*Women sure love to talk*, Jacob thought. *That's all they seem to do, unless you shut them up. I sure shut her, Tanya Miller, up.*

For a panic stricken second, Jacob was absolutely sure Mrs. Horace knew everything. She knew about the animals, the bodies in the Cadaver Lab at Pikeville Medical School, the quilts, the outline, and, of course she knew, everybody had to know about her, *about Tanya Miller, didn't they?*

Jacob stopped walking and threw up in the middle of the hallway. It hit the floor and splashed onto Mrs. Horace's leather loafers and khaki pants.

She hadn't looked or felt or smelt or tasted like anything but meat.

*just meat / another animal*
*sinew & bone / bone meal & stringy fat*
Jacob puked again.

-

Swirling darkness. The water deeper and more sinister than Jacob had imagined. It sucked and pulled at every inch of his being. He gasped for breath, felt the water, cold and alarmingly thick, fill his mouth, his nostrils, his eyes.

-

He was in the nurse's office. He felt shaky and cold. Jacob didn't remember coming to school, much less why he was sitting on the crinkling paper-covered bed staring out at a cloudless blue sky. He could hear the murmur of adult voices coming from the other side of the closed door.

There was a commotion and one of the adult voices, a strident male voice, called out harshly four times, four harsh syllables that Jacob heard clearly despite the closed door.

"Rodney Tackett!"

Jacob pushed open the door without meaning to leave his perch on the paper-covered bed. He saw Vice Principal Harold, red-faced and sweating, holding Rodney Tackett by the back of his shirt, and another student in the same manner. There was a small crowd in the little office room section of the Student Health office with Rodney Tackett at the center.

"There he is!" Rodney Tackett shouted. "The little faggot! Ye did something, didn't ye?"

"Watch your mouth," Vice Principal Harold barked.

"He killed my mom's cat!" Rodney Tackett screamed, his eyes more white than not. "He killed it and he probably fucked it too!"

Vice Principal Harold pulled Rodney Tackett with him as he strode to the door.

"That's it," he said, pushing the door open.

Jacob saw he'd left the other student with the little crowd. It was Milton Bradley and Milton was bleeding from a busted nose, which he wasn't handling very well.

*He's bawling and carrying on like a stuck pig*, Jacob thought.

Jacob realized he wanted to quiet him. He stepped back into the little room and pulled the door closed. He walked over to the window and looked out. What he thought was a speck on the window slowly, majestically turned into the gracefully floating visage of a turkey vulture. Then he saw another, then another, and another.

*Something's dead*, Jacob knew.

-

The days stacked up like the garbage bags just outside the pink trailer.

-

"She was whorin'."

"Doesn't mean she was a whore."

"You better not let Rodney hear you sayin' that."

"You gonna tell 'im?"

"Nuh-uh."

"Best not."

Jacob heard all the talking as he made his way invisibly through the halls.

"Heard she got knocked up."

"Then they shipped her off to an orphanage for preggers."

Jacob felt the delicate skin behind his ears prickle at each utterance of her name.

*Tanya Miller / Tanya Miller*

There was an announcement through the school's intercom system during first period that asked any student with knowledge or information about the whereabouts of Tanya Miller to come forward and tell a teacher or faculty member.

"I bet she jus' ran away."

"Me too."

"She didn't seem to like it here too much."

"Who does?"

Jacob walked by her locker, Tanya Miller's, a part of him expecting to see her there, surrounded by the popular kids and jocks, and was let down to find it closed with a piece of paper taped to the front. A black and white photograph, Tanya Miller smiling at the camera in her light and dark cheer squad outfit. There was a typed physical description of her just below the photograph, which didn't show Tanya Miller's fingers at all.

After the third day of what the TV called Tanya Miller's "disappearance," there was a candlelight vigil held in the student parking lot. The dozens of students, parents, and school faculty formed a clumpy circle around a dumbstruck looking Johnnie Floyd and Marie Tackett. Their faces flickered with the glow of the tealight candles each of them held and Marie's eyes were puffed into slits from her steady tears. Marie Tackett wiped her red, raw nose, seeing the tip glisten under the yellow lights. Johnnie Floyd shifted his weight from foot to foot as if the weight of his being was steadily increasing and becoming uncomfortable to hold upright.

"Where's Rodney Tackett?" Jacob wondered as he moved away from the Tackett's and farther into the crowd.

Someone handed him a little tealight candle on a dark plastic saucer. Another set of hands held him still long enough to light the wick. The flame flickered and nearly went out. Jacob had to stoop a bit until the faltering fire burned through the thin layer of wax on the wick.

Each of the faces looked ominous in the glow of so many candles. Jacob felt his skin prickle with unseen eyes. He felt people watching him, but when he scanned the faces around him, a few returned his glances, most completely ignored him.

*They know*, a voice whispered in his mind.

He shook his head, twice, to clear it, then began to make his way to a better vantage point of Johnnie Floyd and Marie Tackett. He felt drawn to their long, tired faces. The saggy yellow crags of their faces held traces of her face, Tanya Miller's, there. Jacob could see the family resemblance in this strange lighting. It was the general shape of their faces: Tanya's had been smooth and without the tired failure painted on Johnnie Floyd and Marie Tackett's.

*It would've been though*, Jacob thought. *She was pregnant.*

*trouble / in a family way*

*They know*, the voice repeated. *All of them know.*

Jacob began to sweat. He wanted to run away but knew it would look suspicious if he left now.

*How could you be so stupid*, Jacob chided himself, *to come here knowing what you done.*

*what Rodney Tackett done / what Rodney Tackett done*

Jacob half expected to see blood on his hands when he looked beyond the tiny flame he held near his chest with his left hand and the red glow from the tealight candle nearly tricked him into seeing it. He was focused on moving toward the fringe of the crowd, the side nearest the forest beyond the parking lot, cupping the flame from the motion of his movement to keep the flame from extinguishing when he heard the squealing tires. He stepped out from the circle of bodies and saw the Camaro barreling toward them.

His first instinct was to drop the candle and run for the woods. He envisioned the green hood smashing into the circle of flesh and cleaving through like a knife through butter. He saw the smashed plastic bend and break bones. He heard flesh tear and blood gurgle.

The driver revved the engine three times before coming to a screeching halt some fifteen feet away from the crowd. The passenger-side door opened and Rodney Tackett lurched out, leaving greasy handprints all over the window of the door he leaned on for support, holding a MegaGulp Styrofoam cup above his head like he was in high water.

"I's made it here," Rodney Tackett called out.

There was a collective whisper.

*He's drunk,* Jacob realized.

Rodney Tackett balanced himself on two feet spread more than a shoulder's length apart and took a wet gulp from the cup. He made a pained face, swallowed, then burped.

A shadowy arm reached across the interior of the Camaro and pulled the passenger door closed. The engine roared again and the car was a green blur whizzing across the parking lot toward the county road beyond. The brake lights blinked and blinked and blinked until they shrank away, hidden by the bend of the road and the full darkness that had steadily descended on the candle vigil.

"I made it," Rodney Tackett told the quiet crowd, which parted as he entered. "Give me one of them got dam candles."

There was the sound of cheap plastic meeting pavement as Rodney Tackett stumbled and nearly fell, knocking the candle from a student's grip. Jacob heard some of the liquid splash down.

"Jesus Christ but I'm a bit on the drunk-end," Rodney Tackett said, his voice loud enough for everyone to hear.

Someone snickered.

Someone else cleared their throat in a disapproving manner.

Jacob tried to blend back in with the crowd but it was too late.

"You!" Rodney Tackett shouted. "Ye fuckin' sicko!"

Jacob tried to will himself into invisibility. He closed his eyes, hard, and thought only clear, see-through thoughts, but when he opened his eyes a new tunnel had opened in the crowd and Rodney Tackett was weaving and stumbling toward him.

"Ye fuckin' pervert," his words were slurring together.

Jacob watched Rodney Tackett pick up steam as he bounced off each waiting, outstretched hand. Rodney Tackett knocked another tealight to the pavement, stopped long enough to stomp on the plastic plate, then pointed at Jacob from less than five yards away.

"Ye killed my fucking cat, ye sick motherfucker."

Jacob felt blood rush up from his stomach into his neck and face. He felt like a squeezed bottle before the eyes of the crowd.

Rodney Tackett seemed to take stock of the crowd for the first time then.

"Tha's righ'," he said. "This motherfucker right here killed a cat. He probably killed all y'all's pets too. All those that went missing? Yeah, that's this sick fuck right here."

Rodney Tackett directed his right index finger at Jacob.

Jacob felt all the heads simultaneously turn toward him.

"This fucker here—" Rodney Tackett was abruptly cut off by the strongarm intervention of Johnnie Floyd, who pulled the drunk boy into a sort of headlock-hug and began angrily whispering in his ear.

At first, Rodney Tackett tried to fight off his father but he was overpowered and quickly submitted to the terse whispering.

Jacob took the time to slip off unnoticed into the woods.

Jacob ran to the hideout, unheeding the branches lashing and whipping at his face and arms. He felt panic clenching every artery and vein.

*They know*, the voice said. *They know. Everybody knows.*

Jacob kicked open the door and came tumbling down onto the sticky, stained floor. His chest was heaving with the effort to get air into his lungs, which felt constricted, stuffed full of barbed cotton and rubber-banded together.

Jacob closed his eyes and brought his knees up to his chest. He focused on slowing his breathing. He clenched his hands together then forced them apart as he pressed his face against the inner sides of his knees.

*They know.*

He slapped the floor with the bottoms of each clenched fist. He raised them and felt the suck and pull of the stained, sticky floor.

*They know.*

He opened his fists then brought his palms down in a stinging slap.

*You cut her up right here.*

He saw it in Fast-Forward X2 Mode.

Jacob slapped the stained, sticky floor.

*They know.*

*Get rid of it.*

*What?*

*Anything that leads them back to you*, the voice said.

Jacob opened his eyes and saw the interior of the hideout. The blood and specks of gristle lining the walls. The infantile raccoon suspended from the ceiling slowly turning round and round in a graceful twirl. The rows of little raccoon hands strung up in the lone window like showy curtains. The squirrel skulls and tails beside them. The pedestals of his creations in the corner. The little works standing *on display*.

*show / what's there to display*
*Get rid of it*, the voice said, *all of it.*

-

Jacob took each of the six current creations—how many dozens had he made in all this time? *strange / how many days you can squeeze into a handful of hours*—to the mineshaft and, after careful scrutiny, studying his failures and his successes, his artistry and his greenhorn fumblings, dropped them down. He slitted his eyes and strained his ears but did not hear a single one hit the bottom.

-

Every time they flashed her bright smile across the screen, Jacob pictured her from above as shot by Rodney Tackett in Johnnie Floyd and Marie's upstairs shower, her hair sudsy, her fingers painted.

*blue & white / blue & white*

*Oh those hands.* Jacob still had the left one, her left hand. He kept it the bottom of the tacklebox, Jenny Wiley, in an old catcher's mitt he'd stolen from the storage closet in the back of the auxiliary gym. He'd wired the glove, Floyd County High School, with galvanized steel wire, Ace Hardware, so he could slip the disembodied hand in and out despite the rigidity of the fingers. He'd molded the position of Tanya Miller's left hand to perfectly fit his erect penis. He'd lost track of how many times he'd used the hand, her hand, Tanya Miller's no longer quite perfect left hand.

*Get rid of it*, the voice said.

Jacob didn't want to. The hand helped him remember. The hand made him feel good. The hand reminded him he wasn't as weak and pitiful as everyone seemed to think he was.

In the daytime quiet of early afternoon in Thompkins' Trailer Court, Jacob eased the pale hand from the catcher's mitt, Floyd County, and masturbated with hatred pushing against the insides of his red, raw eyes. He felt his hatred, *what Rodney Tackett done / what Rodney Tackett done*, burn bright red as he squeezed out a painful ejaculation. He stared at the bubbling cum as it dripped onto the floor through Tanya Miller's painted fingers knowing he'd have to get rid of the hand too and hating Rodney Tackett even more for it.

-

Jacob put the hand, Tanya Miller, and the wired catcher's mitt, Floyd County, in the tactical backpack, Freddy Little's Army Surplus, and walked the four and half miles from the hideout to the mineshaft Randall Adkins had shown him. He saw the burnt-out brick building and remembered the fiery blast that had knocked him off his feet and probably given him a concussion, *learned the hard way that ye gotta be careful how you use this 'ere hidey hole.*

He remembered waking up with a pounding headache and his mother's boyfriend's piss all over him.

Jacob ground his teeth, felt the dead grass crunch under his feet, and wished he could throw Randall Adkins down the hidey hole. He wished he could throw his mother and Rodney fucking Tackett down there too.

*Shit,* Jacob thought, feeling an uneasy slipping in his head. *I wish I could just throw myself down.*

He felt like a chickenshit standing above the unblinking hole looking down.

*Do it,* he told himself. *Jump. Take the step and fall. Fall forever.*

Jacob held out the wired catcher's mitt and let it fall from his right hand. It disappeared much quicker than he expected it to. He did not hear it hit bottom.

He held her pale left hand, Tanya Miller's, up in the poor light from a partially covered moon. It looked pale and beautiful now that he couldn't see the way it'd aged so quickly after he'd hacked it off her arm, Tanya Miller's.

He couldn't help himself: he used the hand one last time, standing there above the gaping hole in the ground. He inched himself to the edge and shot his load into the maw of darkness. As he wilted in her hand, Tanya Miller's, he decided Rodney Tackett wasn't taking everything from him. Jacob felt he couldn't allow this to happen. He couldn't allow Rodney Tackett, the bully, to dictate anything anymore. He wouldn't keep the hand, that wouldn't be smart, that was how he'd get caught, the voice in his head told him, but he'd keep the painted thumb nail. He'd keep it as a reminder, as a talisman, as a trophy.

Jacob approached the darkened house at a crouch, stealing glances as he went. He knew no one was home but he couldn't help but feel unseen eyes follow his path through the woods, across the overgrown yard, around the side of the house to the back door. He figured it was a good thing to still feel fear. It was how he avoided being caught.

He put his hand on the knob, his breath shaky and excited, heard no sound from within, and turned it. It wasn't locked. He pushed the door inward and stepped into the darkened kitchen of the Tackett house, smelling the fried bacon he'd watched Marie Tackett distractedly make from high in an oak in the woods. His stomach turned over, empty and growling. He stood still for a few moments, letting his eyes adjust to the darkness, then crossed over to the stovetop and ate a piece of the burnt bacon from the congealed pan.

Jacob fingered several dishes on the counter around the crowded kitchen sink, picking up a gleaming steak knife and running his grimy fingers along the sticky, serrated edge. There were at least four casserole dishes on the counter. He expected there was more in the fridge. He hadn't eaten all day and briefly considered fixing himself a plate. Instead, he walked back to the stovetop and ate another piece of cold, blackened bacon.

Jacob left the kitchen, took the stairs from the hall up to the second floor, and eased her door, Tanya Miller's, open. He stood completely still, his eyes clenched into slits, and breathed in the smells of her. He crossed the little room to the bedside and turned on the lamp. He sat down on the edge of her bed, Tanya Miller's, moving slowly so as to not disperse the last of her smell. He picked up one of her pillows and covered his entire face with it and breathed her in, Tanya Miller.

Jacob watched himself toss each piece of her, Tanya Miller, down into the mineshaft in Fast-Forward X2 Mode, his face flush with sweat and a cockeyed smile spreading up and up.

*The Cheshire cat ain't got nothin' on me.*

Jacob shook and gasped for breath, pulling the pillow away from his face before he passed out. He set the pillow back carefully.

Jacob felt *vindicated*, Mrs. Horace's Word of the Day, but only the second usage definition: *avenged*.

*what Rodney Tackett done*

He blinked back tears.

*what Rodney Tackett done*

Jacob saw a tilted shot of Such A Happy Boy swinging the hatchet, Walmart, there in the hideout. He saw each splatter and spray as fireworks in the night sky.

*Oh God.*

Jacob felt eyes on him again. He spun around, scanning the room, but saw no one else there. A red-hot ember of anger flickered into flame in his chest.

*what Rodney Tackett done*

# BIRTH OF A MONSTER

He left her room, Tanya Miller's, and stalked down the short hall to the bully's room. He pushed open the door and smelled him, Rodney Tackett, the bully. He wanted to set the room on fire. He wanted to rip down every stupid baseball poster. He wanted to piss on the bully's bed and shit in his pillowcases. He felt the rage boiling in his stomach and chest. He forced himself to close his eyes and take several long, slow breaths.

When Jacob opened his eyes again, a plan began to form in his head. He walked over to the small, cluttered desk and opened the top drawer. There was a shoebox inside. Jacob lifted it from the drawer and set it on the desktop and opened it. The box was filled with baseball cards.

*Rodney Tackett's secret stash.*

Jacob picked up several cards at random and saw faces and names he didn't recognize or care about. There were more cards of Kevin Youkilis, a third and first basemen, than anybody else.

*Must be his favorite player*, Jacob thought, turning over one of the cards and scanning the information on the back. *Played for the University of Cincinnati in college, then spent most of his career with the Boston Red Sox. There's his rookie card. Another. And another.*

Jacob dumped the cards onto the bully's desk and removed each Youkilis card and set them aside. Once he was sure he had every Youkilis card, Jacob bent and scratched each of them. He used the dirty nails of his forefinger and thumb to completely obliterate the baseball player's head and face. Jacob peeled the top layer off the embossed cardboard on several of the more elaborate cards then returned all the cards to the shoebox and slammed it back into the top drawer.

*There*, he thought. *There.*

Jacob waited behind the little copse of sassafras trees until Johnnie Floyd's lifted Dodge Ram had descended the drive past the cemetery and turned right, heading toward Prestonsburg. Jacob climbed up onto the rickety front porch and made his way around to the bully Rodney Tackett's window. He unslung the backpack, Freddy Little's Army Surplus, from his back and unzipped it. He took out the squirrel and raccoon intestines and arranged them along the vents of the window air-conditioner unit. He felt his face smiling as he worked, his hands slippery with the blood and stomach juices.

*Such a happy boy sometimes*, he thought.

He stepped away and admired his handiwork.

-

Jacob waited behind the sassafras trees bouncing from foot to foot for hours, but the Tackett family did not leave their home. A wild part of him wanted to climb the porch and enter her room anyway. He had to fight against his desire to keep himself planted firmly out of sight.

-

Jacob watched the police cruiser, the lights and siren off, pull up to the Tackett house. He knelt closer to the ground, ensuring no part of him was visible, and watched the short, squat police officer get out and walk up the steps to the rickety front porch. The door opened before he could knock and Marie Tackett stood there, her hair in a messy bun, her face working and working as if she had something sour and hot under her tongue.

Jacob couldn't hear what either adult said. Marie Tackett stepped aside and held the door for the policeman to enter the Tackett house. The door closed behind them.

A few minutes later, with the sun beginning its descent behind the ridgeline, the light came on in Tanya Miller's room. Jacob could see the outline of the policeman and Johnnie Floyd and Marie Tackett in there. The light was on for some time before it winked back out.

Jacob wanted to run across the yard and climb up the porch and see.

He felt sick with anticipation.

*What do they know?* he wondered. *Do they know? They can't possibly know.*

The Tackett's front door opened and the policeman stepped out. He turned and spoke with Johnnie Floyd and Marie briefly before taking the stairs down to his cruiser. Jacob watched the Tacketts, now joined by a sheepish looking Rodney Tackett, watch the patrol car leave.

Jacob closed his right eye and held his forefinger and thumb up before his face and squished Rodney Tackett several times before the family went back inside and closed their front door.

-

He opened the door of the pink singlewide as quietly as he could. He stepped into the living room and found his mother passed out on the argyle couch. Each of her nostrils were coated with white and blue pill residue. There was a small china platter on the table littered with pills, crushed and whole, and a five-dollar bill rolled up into a miniature straw.

Jacob stood over his unconscious mother for some time willing her to die. He almost thought he could force her to stop breathing if he thought about it hard enough.

He bent over the plate and carefully picked up four of the white pills and three of the blues.

The Tacketts were asleep. He was sure of it. He'd waited hours, watching the lights blink off one by one until the entire house, save the exposed bulb hanging by the front door, winked out. Jacob stepped out into the bright moonlight and crossed the yard at a trot. His heart hammered like a misfiring piston in his chest as he climbed up onto the Tackett's front porch. He smelled the rotting intestines before he rounded the corner to the front of the house and saw them gleaming on the air-conditioning unit hanging out of the bully's window.

Jacob slid open Tanya Miller's window and slipped inside.

His breath sounded overly loud in the quiet of the house. He moved quietly, taking each step carefully, ensuring his weight remained centered for maximum control. He carried the knife, Ace Hardware, just in case. He'd had daydreams about using it on the bully, Rodney Tackett, and couldn't talk himself out of carrying it with him into the home.

Jacob walked over to Tanya Miller's bed and carefully laid himself down. He closed his eyes, holding himself with the hand not holding the knife, and breathed in the fading smell of her. He wished he could turn on the light and find a strand or two of her hair. He wished he could take her pillow sheets back to the secrecy of the hideout and masturbate with them.

After a time, Jacob got up from the bed and snuck out into the darkened hallway. He made his way carefully down the narrow staircase to the first floor and stepped into the little laundry room. He fumbled with the dirty clothes in the hamper until he found a pair of Rodney Tackett's baseball pants. Jacob reached into his front pants pocket and took out the pills he'd taken from the pink singlewide in Thompkins' Trailer Court and put them in the right back pocket of the baseball pants and returned them to the hamper.

Smiling, Jacob exited the house the way he'd entered.

Jacob watched the police car pull up to the Tackett's house. A gray sedan pulled up behind it, parking in the yard beside Johnnie Floyd's lifted Dodge Ram. A smartly dressed woman got out of the sedan and met the policeman, the same squat man Jacob had seen the other day, at the steps to the Tackett's front porch. Marie had the door open and met the two before they'd ascended the stairs.

Her face was stricken, her features contorted. She asked a shaky question Jacob could not fully catch from his place behind the sassafras trees. The woman from the sedan shook her head and with a sweep of her arm indicated they should converse inside the home. Marie turned on her heels and jerkily walked back inside, leaving the door open for them to follow.

As the Tackett's front door closed, the term "social worker" popped into Jacob's head.

*That's Tanya Miller's social worker,* Jacob thought.

He remembered she had a mother, also on drugs from what he'd heard, in another county that didn't have custody of her.

*No one has custody now.*

Jacob felt a great mingling of emotion well up inside him. Tears stung his raw eyes yet his lips were curled upward in a broad smile.

He nearly jumped when he heard a baby's cry sound from the woods behind him. He spun around and scanned the forest around him but saw no child. He waited, panting, for the cry to sound again but it didn't.

Jacob took one of the blue pills. He didn't want to snort it like his mother did, so he just put it in his mouth and swallowed it.

His mother was asleep back in her room. She'd given herself fully to drug use these last three days. Jacob watched her crush pill after pill with her lighter. She thinned and straightened the pill powder into lines with an expired credit card and snorted them with the five-dollar straw.

She said nice things to him from time to time after she got high.

Jacob almost didn't hate her, then she started asking questions.

"Where do ye go all day?" she asked. "I don't mean school neither. Ye ain't been goin' but some days. I been getting' calls."

"Nowhere," he said.

She snorted at him and he thought he'd hit her. It took everything in him to stay his hand.

# BIRTH OF A MONSTER

Christy Goodman snorted a blue line then spoke to him while working on lining up her next hit.

"Ye listen to me now, Jake," she said. "I don't want no more calls from the school. I don't want no more parent-teacher conferences. I don't want no more truancy worker callin' and threatenin' to get the social workers back involved. I don't need any more shit in my life. Ye understand me?"

Jacob hated himself, but he nodded.

*I hate you*, he told her with his mind. *I hate you, you bitch.*

-

Jacob began seeing her face, Tanya Miller's, on telephone poles and student lockers. He saw her face on the television and heard her name wrapped up in hushed whispers and pleading tones.

*Missing*, all the signs read.

*Missing*, all the people said.

Jacob wanted to laugh at it all but he was afraid they'd know. The halls seemed stiller and more watchful at school. His cohorts passing by with eyes that did not meet others. Jacob was afraid it showed on his face somehow, a mark or stain of a darker knowledge not meant to share.

He imagined **KILLER** embossed on his forehead like a neon stain, visible to anyone that looked close enough. He especially avoided adults, fearing they were attuned to problems with children so more likely to find him out.

Jacob saw Rodney Tackett at school and avoided him. It was easy at first, avoiding the bully, but as the days passed so did Rodney Tackett's quiet, stunned demeanor.

"Fucking freak," he hissed at Jacob in the hallway one day.

"Faggot sicko," he barked the next.

Jacob kept his head down and shuffled his feet, keeping his left hand in his pants pocket wrapped around Tanya Miller's blue and white painted thumbnail.

-

"I'm talkin' to ye, faggot," Rodney Tackett called after him.

Jacob didn't stop walking. The final bell had finished its second repetition and the halls were nearly empty of students.

Jacob was too far from the double doors to escape the bully without an out and out run, so he stopped and slowly turned around to face him.

"Ye know what happened to my cousin?" Rodney Tackett asked,

his red cheeks twitching uncontrollably under the burning twin flames of his eyes. "Huh? Answer me, ye sick freak."

Jacob shook his head and lowered his eyes. He felt heat flush his neck and hated his Judas blood for the betrayal.

"Ye hear me, freak?" Rodney Tackett asked, shoving Jacob against the row of lockers.

The bang of Jacob's elbows and upper back and head hitting the locker echoed down the halls.

"Answer me!" Rodney Tackett hissed through clenched teeth. "Where's my cousin?"

"What's this?" an adult voice asked.

Jacob and the bully turned in unison to the voice.

Mr. Blevins, a seventh grade English teacher and track coach, stood just outside his room about ten feet down the hall.

Jacob took the moment to slide along the lockers on his back, away from the bully, Rodney Tackett, closer to the exit.

The bell rang a third and final time. Jacob turned on his heels and ran down the hall to the exit, hitting the doors with both of his extended hands and bursting out into the sunshine, his name reverberating after him.

-

*He knows. He knows. He knows.*

Jacob felt panic seize his throat and begin to slowly choke him.

*He knows what I did.*

*What Rodney Tackett done.*

*They'll all know. They'll all know and hang me.*

Jacob remembered talk of lynching from history class. They used to hang black people in the south for no other reason than their skin color.

*What'll they think once they know what I did?*

Jacob saw SAHB hacking and sawing. He saw SAHB drop piece after piece of her, *Tanya Miller / Tanya Miller*, down into the open mineshaft. He saw SAHB using the hand, Tanya Miller's cold, stiff hand with the painted nails. He saw the smile on SAHB's face and knew his countenance was not matching it right then.

Jacob raced across the nearly empty parking lot toward the tree line. He heard the bully's voice trail after him on the wind.

"Freak! Sick fuck!"

Jacob entered the forest at a run he did not slow until he was at the hideout.

Jacob pushed open the door to the hideout and felt a little more at ease. His feet plunged into the muck, sticking and popping with suction sounds. He wished it were the bully's blood on the floor.

*what Rodney Tackett done / what Rodney Tackett done*

Jacob sank to the floor, pulled both of his knees to his chest, and held his breath as the pain in his crotch slowly worsened. He repositioned himself so he sat on his swollen penis and testicles and leaned farther onto them.

Jacob witnessed no confrontation about the pills he'd hidden inside the bully, Rodney Tackett's, baseball pants. He'd watched the house long after each member had gone to bed. He tried to will Johnnie Floyd into beating his bully son, but it did not happen.

Jacob climbed the porch slowly, his groin buzzing with infection and pain, and put a handful of squirrel guts on top of the bully's air-conditioning unit. He stood on his tippy toes and peered into the darkened bedroom. He could just make out the shape of the bully under the covers of his bed.

Jacob envisioned himself pushing the air-conditioning unit into the room and leaping inside. He saw himself smiling, *Such a Happy Boy*, gleaming knife in hand, blood flying and spraying, a darker darkness in the shadowy room.

*Sicko. Freak.*

Jacob forced himself to climb slowly back down from the roof of the front porch. He took another look up at the darkened bedroom window and offered up his middle finger.

*Pervert. Faggot.*

*I showed ye,* Jacob thought. *I took her away from ye. Y'all'll never have her back neither.*

Jacob smiled despite the growing pain in his crotch. He could feel the fever returning along with the deep burn that he knew meant another explosive mess in his near future.

*For what Rodney Tackett done.*

Rodney Tackett was staying over with the team after the game. Jacob took to listening under the Tackett family's windows at night. He heard most everything. All the laments about the missing niece, the court proceedings and the social workers and the state police. The whole community involved in the girl's disappearance now.

Johnnie Floyd still adamantly thought Tanya Miller had run off "with some boy or other." Marie didn't think so but she wasn't convinced one way or the other. They both hated the stink Marie's sister was making about the girl's disappearance in court. She blamed the Tacketts for not caring enough to take better care of Tanya Miller.

Johnnie Floyd was pissed, calling his sister-in-law all sorts of names. *Cunt. Bitch. No-account hussy.* There were several Budweiser-fueled "apple" and "tree" invectives. Johnnie Floyd told his wife her sister "was no good" at least seven different times.

Jacob heard all this with a smile, waiting the long evening crouched along the cool brick and siding listening, waiting. When the last light had long since been extinguished, Jacob climbed atop the rickety front porch and made his way around to the front of the house and entered through Tanya Miller's unlocked window.

The house felt stifling in its quietude. A waiting meanness. Jacob picked up her pillow, Tanya Miller's, and filled his nostrils with the fading smell of her. He set it back on the bed and went over to the small dresser. Jacob opened the top drawer and rifled through the panties and bras. He picked up a pair of pale pink panties and stuffed them completely inside his mouth. He let his tongue explore the soft fabric. He then opened his mouth and leaned forward over the drawer, letting the spit-dampened panties back down. He put another pair in his mouth and repeated the process.

He remembered her smell and what SAHB had done, what *he* had done. The frame by frame retelling of it flashed in his head in Fast-Forward X2 Mode.

Jacob found he was shaking. At first, he thought it was fear or tears but the shaking was working its way to being uncontrollable and he realized it was laughter he was barely stifling down.

He made his way to the bully's room and quietly closed the door behind him. He retrieved the jar of ticks from his backpack, Freddy Little's Army Surplus, and unscrewed the lid. He then released the starved ticks throughout the bully's bedroom.

When he was finished with this task, Jacob went over to Rodney Tackett's bed and knelt down. He retrieved the chocolate tin and opened it. There were the photographs of Tanya Miller in the Tacketts' shower. He counted them slowly, savoring each of the images of the naked girl, especially the few that showed her hands, *oh those painted nails*, in greater detail.

Flickers of building pain lashed across his crotch. His pee hole was burning and he could feel the beat of his heart painfully throughout his groin.

Her face was so pale in the dim lighting she looked ghostly. Jacob could still hear the ceaseless prattle of her voice if he tried hard enough. He counted seventeen, just like last time, and decided he'd take two of the photographs. He slipped one of the photographs into the tactical bag, Freddy Little's Army Surplus, and pocketed the other.

Next, Jacob went into the upstairs bathroom and pulled the door gently closed behind him. He flipped on his penlight, Pikeville Medical School, and quickly found the toothbrushes. There were two of them, each green and white. He took the toothbrushes to the toilet and began brushing the interior of the bowl with each bristled head.

He then set the lid down carefully. He pushed his grimy pants and stained underwear down to his ankles and sat down on the toilet. He eased his swollen penis downward and waited for the burning piss to flow. He gritted his teeth against the pain and shot a wad of infection out before the thin trickle of hot piss. He leaned over on one side, allowing his left hand to dip the two toothbrushes into the bloody piss. He then reached across the sink and set them back down in their containers.

He rose, pulled his clothing back on as carefully as he could, then closed the toilet seat cover.

Jacob made his way down the narrow staircase to the first floor of the Tackett house slowly. He took each step first with the toes of his miss K-Swisses then shifted the weight to his heels. The stairs groaned once, but the house remained still and quiet. Jacob made his way into the little laundry room and found a pair of the bully, Rodney Tackett's, Wrangler jeans and slipped one of the photos of Tanya Miller in the shower into the back pocket.

He stopped at the open door of Johnnie Floyd and Marie Tackett's bedroom. He could see their twin shapes under the quilts and had the vague urge to take his fileting knife, Roger's Bait 'n' Tackle, and stab each of them until they were dead, until they were mush, *paw-paw meat*. Jacob hesitated there in the doorframe for some time feeling a strange power tingling his every last nerve ending.

*I could*, he thought. *I could.*

He could almost see it in his mind.

*Not tonight*, the voice said.

Jacob nodded, turned on his heels, and quietly made his way up the stairs and out of the Tackett home.

The walk back to the hideout was painful. Each step seemed to turn some vise in his groin. He knew he'd have to rub out another clot of infection; he could feel the hard ball of crystalized putrefaction near the base of his penis.

*I need to see a doctor.*

Jacob tried to piss three times on the way back to the hideout but managed only a thin dribbling.

*What if this causes permanent damage? What if I can't get hard again? What if this makes me sterile?*

Another voice answered his questions.

*Does it really matter? Who are you getting hard for? Nobody loves you.*

Jacob pushed in the door of the hideout and was struck by the absence of his creations. He hated getting rid of them but it'd been the right decision and the voice in his head, the one that seemed to have his best interests considered, had told him to do it. So he'd done it. Now, in the nearly empty hideout, he wished he'd at least kept the hanging row of raccoon hands.

He looked down at the stained, sticky floor and saw her blood there, Tanya Miller's. It was a bit darker, a bit thicker than the stains of lesser beasts. He toed it with his miss K-Swisses and smiled at the stickiness.

*Still fresh*, a voice said.

Jacob knelt down and put his index and middle fingers against the tacky surface. They came away smudged but not wet. He smelled his fingers for a long time before placing them inside his mouth and sucking.

There was a sound on the wind outside the hideout. It almost sounded like a baby's cry. Jacob broke out in gooseflesh and rose up on unsteady legs.

"What the hell?" he wondered at the sound.

It was definitely a baby's cry he heard off in the distance. Jacob listened to it for a long time, eventually taking a seat at the farmer's table, staring out the single window of the hideout at the coming morning, tears running unheeded down his dirty cheeks.

*She was pregnant*, the voice said.

*trouble / in a family way*

*She was pregnant and you killed her.*

The sentence clanged around his head like a golf ball in a metal trashcan, sending hollow thumps and crashes echoing off into oblivion.

He tried to answer each repetition but his thoughts felt jumbled and confused.

*what Rodney Tackett done / what Rodney Tackett done*

Jacob was in the pink trailer, he discovered. He had no recollection of the hike back to Thompkins' Trailer Court. He was naked and didn't remember de-clothing. He watched his hairless chest rise and fall rapidly. He was having trouble breathing, feeling the weight of some unseen body on his chest, crowding out his lungs.

*What's happening?* he wondered. *What is this? A heart attack?*

His mother stood in the doorway. Jacob nearly fell out of bed when he finally noticed her.

*How long has she been standing there?*

"Ye sure are naked a lot," his mother said.

Her voice was a soft singsong, gentle coos and slurred consonants. Jacob could see the unnatural color of her mucus trailing down onto her smiling upper lip.

"Why were ye making baby cries?" she asked. "Ye ain't still sick, are ye? We cain't afford no doctor bills right now."

Jacob looked down at his exposed genitals and knew he should feel embarrassed, but he didn't. The head of his penis was lopsided and burning. He could tell he'd have to work out a ball of infection in the next little bit.

Jacob saw SAHB trying to insert the swollen, painful erection into her, Tanya Miller, there on the stained, sticky hideout floor. He watched himself use the dying girl's left hand to satisfy himself.

*Does it matter what you've done after you die?*

Jacob wondered if this moment meant anything. Did it matter he was completely naked in front of his stoned mother? He couldn't remember a moment of his life that actually mattered until he killed Tanya Miller. That felt like a watershed moment in his meaningless existence.

*I changed the world when I did that,* he thought. *There was a person and then there wasn't. I did that. I changed things.*

"What's so funny?" Christy Goodman asked her son.

"Not a damn thing," Jacob said, turning away from her to face the stained wall.

# CHAPTER EIGHTEEN
## TROUBLE, TROUBLE, & MORE TROUBLE

**JACOB DREAMED OF A CRYING** infant. He was in a long, dark cave illuminated as if by gaslight though he couldn't see a single flame anywhere. The cries echoed from farther down. He walked for hours but came no closer to the source of the cries. A sense of panic welled up within him and he soon found himself running, his bare feet slapping the smooth rock flooring.

"Where are ye?" he yelled, which was answered by the wailing child somewhere deeper in the cave.

Jacob stopped with a sudden halt, knowing he was hearing the cries of Tanya Miller's child. He began to shake uncontrollably and felt a great rending scream build up in his overwrought chest.

The child continued to cry.

-

Jacob woke covered in sweat and goosebumps. He could feel the fever pounding in his head again. He looked down and saw he'd tucked his genitals underneath himself. He shifted his weight and blood rushed painfully back to the region. He nearly threw up from the pain that made him feel like he was buoyed in a sea of nausea.

He forced himself to sit up in the bed, swinging each of his bare legs over the side. His left foot found a cold, greasy puddle of his own vomit.

"Jesus," he hissed and nearly threw up again.

He pictured the child, Tanya Miller's, clawing its way out of her dead body, Tanya Miller's. He saw the child turn its angry face upward, taking in the dime-sized sun that was the hole's beginning up in the burnt out remains of the mineshaft.

The child opened its tiny mouth and wailed.

Jacob jumped at the nearness of the cry.

-

He showered in a daze. When he stepped out onto the piles of dirty laundry on the bathroom floor, he saw he hadn't rinsed the shampoo from his head. He turned the shower back on and got back inside.

Jacob's shoulders were roughly shaken. He pushed up from the tabletop, groggy and numb.

"Huh?" he murmured.

"Wake up, Mr. Goodman."

Jacob rubbed the crust from his eyes. The classroom was empty save Mr. Roberts and a police officer. He blinked rapidly several times and sat up straight in his chair.

"Jacob, this is Detective Thomas of the Kentucky State Police," Mr. Roberts said. "He wants to ask you a few questions, okay?"

Jacob wasn't given time to respond. Mr. Roberts turned on his heel and headed for the classroom door.

"Bring him down to the front office when you're all finished here, okay?" Mr. Roberts said over his shoulder.

The door closed with a click behind him.

Jacob felt the cop's eyes on him and squirmed in his seat. His head pounded with fever. He wondered vaguely if any of the different colored pills his mother had would help.

"Jacob," the cop began. "Can I call you Jacob? Or do you prefer Jake?"

Jacob shrugged his shoulders and avoided the cop's intense eyes.

"Jake, then," he said. "You can call me Kevin."

There was a pause and Jacob knew he was supposed to say something but he didn't know what, so he stayed quiet and looked out the window at the clear, cloudless sky.

"Do you know Tanya Miller?" the cop, Kevin Thomas, asked.

Jacob forced himself to sit absolutely still. He wanted to scream and run and hide.

"Jake?" Detective Kevin Thomas asked. "Are you alright?"

Jacob felt the sweat break out across his entire body. His stomach roiled and felt full of old cooking oil. He felt the intense need to shit and puke.

"I don't feel so good," Jacob said.

"You don't look too good," the detective, the cop, Kevin Thomas said.

Jacob hated him.

"Well, this won't take too long and I'll get you down to the nurse's office directly."

The cop pulled out a chair at the table and sat down. He was a short, wide man and he spilled over both sides of the plastic chair.

"Tanya Miller is new here, right?"

Jacob nodded his head slowly, feeling something akin to motion sickness.

Something whimpered just outside the classroom windows. Jacob turned his head quickly in that direction and nearly vomited from the intense vertigo.

"Did you know her well?" the cop asked. "Were y'all friends or anything like that?"

Jacob shook his head slowly, returning his gaze to his hands, clasped together and wringing, in his lap.

The whimpering grew louder.

His head pounded with each frenzied beat of his heart. Jacob saw a static snow dancing pirouettes in his peripheries. He watched his vision slowly narrow until he could only see what was directly in front of him: his restless, sweat-slickened hands.

The whimpering turned into an out-and-out wailing.

"Are you okay, Jake?" the cop asked.

Jacob shook his head and instantly regretted it. He leaned over, away from the detective, the cop, Kevin Thomas, and threw up onto the floor. He felt something in his stomach tear free and he vomited some more. When he was finished, he used the sleeve of his sweater to wipe his mouth clean. He used the other to wipe the sweat from his forehead and cheeks.

"Jesus Christ," the detective, the cop, Kevin Thomas, said.

Jacob had pissed himself. His penis felt strangely pleasant in the hot wetness. The stain in his pants, Goodwill, grew darker and darker yet. He could smell the infection more than he could smell the urine. He leaned back in the chair and gulped in air.

"You stay put," the detective, the cop, Kevin Thomas said. "I'll go get the nurse."

As soon as the door shut behind him, Jacob rose on unsteady legs and made his way over to the window. He looked down onto the playground and faculty parking lot but saw no child.

*It's hers,* the voice said. *Sitting at the bottom of that bottomless hole.*

*Oh God. What have I done?*

He pulled on the waistband of his pants, Goodwill, and looked inside. There was dark blood staining his legs, his threadbare underwear, and the Goodwill pants. The smell was heady and strong.

*I need to see a doctor.*

The door opened and Mr. Roberts came in looking worried.

"Jacob, are you okay?" he asked, then he saw the vomit and his face changed. "Let's get you on down to the nurse, okay?"

The child cried and cried as Jacob let the geography teacher lead him away. He couldn't help but flinch at the loudness of it.

-

Jacob was in the nurse's office. He sat on the crinkly examination table and listened to the nurse try to get ahold of his mother on the phone. When the nurse finally gave up, she called in Vice Principal Harold.

"How you doin', Jacob?" Vice Principal Harold asked.

"I don't feel too good," Jacob said.

He could still taste the vomit and opening his mouth seemed to upset his stomach again.

"Well, we cain't seem to get ahold of yer mom," Vice Principal Harold said. "Is there another number where we can get her?"

Jacob shook his head slowly.

The baby cried.

Jacob felt fresh sweat drip down his forehead onto his eyebrows, then down into his raw, aching eyes. His vision had narrowed considerably. He tried to keep his eyes closed but he felt dizzy and everything seemed to spin when they were closed for any length of time.

"Well, we're really concerned about ye," Vice Principal Harold said.

The nurse was standing next to him nodding her head.

"We think ye need to see a doctor right away," Vice Principal Harold said. "We're gonna get somebody to come get ye. That okay with ye?"

Jacob nodded his head. He felt something, piss or blood or pus, drip out of his swollen penis, sending shivers of revulsion rippling up his spine.

*It's down there all by itself*, the voice said. *Listen to it. Ye did this.*

Jacob felt tears crowd his eyes.

"It's goin' to be okay," Vice Principal Harold said. "We've got an ambulance coming for ye now."

*Mom is going to shit a brick*, Jacob thought. *Fuck her.*

-

The ambulance came with lights and sirens blaring. Jacob was seated onto a gurney and wheeled down the halls and through the front door, which Vice Principal Harold held open.

"Chin up," he said as the gurney passed him. "Ye'll be back to feeling better in no time. Don't ye worry none."

Jacob felt the eyes of the school on him as the EMTs rolled him across the entrance pavement to the waiting ambulance. He heard the cries of the child he'd abandoned in the mine and began to cry. He felt pitiful and hated himself for it but he couldn't stop it.

The ride to the Highlands Regional Hospital was a blur. He watched the trees and cars shrink and grow through the back windows.

"Did something happen to ye?" the EMT in the back asked.

Jacob couldn't have answered if he wanted to. He was crying so hard he was incapable of speech. He sobbed deep and shuddered but couldn't seem to get his lungs to fill with enough air to properly breathe.

The doctor was young and Jacob wondered if he'd studied at Pike-ville in the Cadaver Lab. He came into the room and sat down in a little swivel chair beside a computer.

Jacob's clothes were drenched and clinging. He could smell his unclean body under the smell of the infection.

"Let me take a look," the doctor said.

Jacob leaned forward on the hospital bed and eased his pants down to his knees.

The doctor, his hands in green latex gloves, leaned in close from his perch on the little chair and took hold of Jacob's swollen penis with his right hand, making a sound in his throat Jacob did not catch the meaning of.

"This is quite an infection," the doctor said. "Could you tell me a little bit about what happened, Jeffrey?"

His hands were careful but the pain was enormous. It brought Jacob out of his head and back into the hospital room.

"It's Jacob," he whispered through clenched teeth.

"Sorry, Jacob," the doctor said, his eyes not leaving Jacob's gen-italia. "When did this start?"

"A while ago."

"Uh-huh. Can you tell me about how it started?"

"No."

The doctor looked up into Jacob's eyes for the first time.

"No?"

"No."

The doctor went back to his examination. After a long, painful

285

time, the doctor pushed himself away from the examination table and wheeled his chair back to the computer. He was engrossed in typing and clicking for some time.

Jacob was thankful the baby had stopped its crying for the time being but his dick and balls were hurting worse than ever before.

"Well, we'll get you started on some antibiotics and keep you for a while to see how you do," the doctor said, his eyes returning to Jacob's exposed privates. "We'll get you a gown that'll be a bit more comfortable for you. Do you have another contact number for your mother?"

Jacob shook his head.

"What about your father?"

Jacob shook his head again, closing his eyes and instantly feeling dizzy.

"Well," the doctor said. "We'll keep trying to get ahold of her."

-

Several different nurses came in and out of the room. He was stuck with a needle and an IV was put in his left arm. Before long, he was sleeping deeply.

-

Jacob was falling down the mineshaft. The air was hot and humid against his bare skin as he plummeted down. He wanted to scream but the fall was so long his fear gradually transmogrified into a kind of dumbstruck wonder.

The child's cries sounded from all directions at once: deafening and demanding. The wordless cries bounced off the rock walls of the mineshaft, doubling back with increasing volume.

Jacob tried to cover his ears with his hands but the cries only intensified.

He woke just before he hit the bottom.

-

"Git yer goddamn hands offa me!" his mother screamed.

Jacob blinked several times and had to rub the crust from his eyes before he could see anything.

His mother was at the foot of his bed wrestling with a heavyset man in scrubs.

"Calm down, lady!" the man huffed.

They were struggling against one another.

"I'll fuckin' kill ye!" his mother screeched. "Git offa me! Let me go, got damn ye!"

Jacob could tell she was drunk by the sound of her voice. He wished he felt embarrassed at the scene his mother was making in the hospital but he wasn't. It just made him hate her even more.

He wanted to scream at her but he felt too tired to raise his voice. He blinked and the next thing he knew, he was dreaming again.

-

Jacob didn't stay asleep long. He sunk back into the mineshaft, heard the echoing cries of her baby, Tanya Miller's, but was still unable to find the child.

-

"I cain't be here," the bald man whispered. "I got warrants."

"Come on now," his mother whined. "Ye know I cain't do this alone."

"Ye'll have ta."

From somewhere just beyond wakefulness, Jacob heard his mother crying. A while later he heard her sniffling. Then he heard her snorting and sniffing.

-

"Ma'am, he needs his rest."

"Yer gonna wake him up."

Jacob opened his eyes to a smeared room.

"Why don't we step out in the hall so you can talk to Mrs. Dennis."

"I don't need to talk to no fuckin' social worker!" Christy Goodman screamed.

"If yer gonna start acting up again, I'm gonna have to ask ye to leave, ma'am," a man's voice said.

"Fuck you! I ain't leavin'," Christy Goodman shouted. "Tha's my son y'all got in that hospital bed. He's my son and I ain't leavin'."

On one level, Jacob thought he should feel a sense of pride in his mother's obstinacy, but all he actually felt was revulsion. His mother was drunk, probably high on her pills too, and making a scene in the emergency room.

"Mom," Jacob said.

Christy Goodman did not hear her son.

"And I didn't authorize no ambulance ride!" Jacob's mother yelled. "I cain't afford no ambulance bill. I would've taken him my own self if y'all'd given me the chance."

"We tried calling you several times, ma'am."

"My ass!" she hollered. "I've got my phone righ' here. Look and

287

see! Nary a one missed call. Nary a one!"

Jacob could see the bald man's phone in his mother's hand. He wondered if she even knew where her phone was. It was probably disconnected anyway.

Jacob rubbed the sleep from his eyes and sat up in the hospital bed. The uncomfortable hospital gown crinkled when he moved.

"Ma'am. Ma'am!" the man's voice grew hard and stern. "Yer son is awake. He's awake. See?"

Jacob watched his disheveled mother turn from the door to face him. He saw the way her stomach protruded and, for the first time, fully realized his mother was pregnant.

*trouble / in a family way*

The bald man, Randall Adkins's, words came back to him.

"Sure she's your momma," he'd said time after time, "but she's still a cunt."

"Shut up," Jacob said.

His mother didn't hear him.

"Jake," Christy Goodman slurred. "How're ye feelin'?"

"Fine," Jacob said.

"Let me take a look at ye," his mother said, crossing the room on wobbly legs to sit on the edge of the bed.

Jacob could see she was putting on a show for the three people standing just inside the room, putting on a more nurturing tone of voice and smiling a great deal.

She took his right hand in hers and held it, alternately patting it and rubbing at it as if it were a stain needing removal.

"How're ye feelin'?" she asked in a voice too loud for their close proximity.

Jacob answered before actually taking stock of himself.

"Fine," he said.

He could see a bit of white in one of her nostrils and a bit of blue in the other.

*blue / white*

*Just like her painted nails, Tanya Miller's.*

Jacob flinched, felt his penis constrict painfully, and knew something was inside it. He threw back the rough hospital sheets and lifted his papery gown to find a thin plastic tube protruding from his dickhole.

"Leave that alone now," a woman's voice called from the door.

Jacob looked up to see his mother looking down at his crotch with her eyes and mouth wide open. Two of the three adults at the door had turned away from the bed and huddled together.

*Cop. Social worker.*

The nurse stepped away from them and closer to the bed.

"That's your catheter, Jacob," she said. "You got to leave that alone now. It'll come out in a few days. Maybe tomorrow even. But for now you got to leave it alone. Okay?"

Jacob wanted it out of him, but he recalled the pain and burning and misery, *what Rodney Tackett done / what Rodney Tackett done*, and noticed the absence of the terrible infection smell and decided to trust this woman in green scrubs, this nurse.

He covered himself back up.

"You've got a pretty nasty infection that spread up from your privates into your bladder," the nurse said. "We've got you on antibiotics and steroids and you should be out of here in no time."

She smiled at Jacob, but he saw the way she sidestepped his mother and avoided looking directly at her.

*Trouble*, Jacob knew. *Social workers and cops and nurses and trouble and trouble and more trouble.*

Jacob stole a glance at his mother and saw her eyes had become heavy lidded, nearly closed. Her mouth was partially open, she was breathing through it alone, and Jacob could see all the black spots of rot and decay like black holes made visible in the night sky.

*Stoned out of her mind. Oh Jesus, she's stoned out of her mind.*

Jacob made like he was adjusting himself in the bed and bumped his knee against her to wake her back up. She stirred, shook her head, and blinked several times in slow succession.

"Ms. Goodman," the cop had crossed the room and was standing at the foot of the bed. "I need to get some information from ye. Jacob looks like he could use a little bit more rest, so why don't we step outside and talk. Maybe Nurse Berkshire here can find us a quiet place to talk."

The nurse, Berkshire, nodded her head and made her way to the door.

"If you need anything, Jacob," she said, "just hit the button there on the bed beside you."

"I don't need to talk to ye fuckers," Christy Goodman said. "Not at t'all."

Jacob could see her working her anger up. There was a vein in her forehead that bloomed upward like a lava rock from the sea when she got angry. Jacob saw it pumping furiously now. He could also see the color in her face steadily turning a tomato red.

"Now, come on now, Christy," the cop said. "There ain't no need for that kind of language. Yer gonna upset yer boy and ye don't want to do that, now do ye?"

"Fuck you," Christy Goodman yelled suddenly.

Jacob flinched at the violence of his mother's movement. She flung herself up from the bed and kicked over one of the chairs at the bedside. It clanged into the one of the machines at the head of the bed and shattered something made of glass.

"Fuck ye and all ye fuckin' fucks!"

The cop, Jacob now saw it was the same one that had come to school to talk to him, wrapped his muscular arms around his mother. He leaned backwards on his short but stout frame and lifted Christy Goodman off her kicking feet. He shuffled backwards, carrying the screaming, kicking woman out of the door and into the hallway, out of Jacob's sight. He heard the commotion, strangled cries of anger and pain from his mother, and the squawk of a nurse shouting, "Code Green! Security!" over and over again.

After a few short moments, he heard his mother's strangled shouting.

"Yer hurtin' me, ye fuckin' pig! I'll fuckin' gut ye like the pig ye are! Fuck you!"

Jacob felt torn. He wanted his mother to hurt and he didn't. Jacob wished he was the one with the power to hurt or to not hurt her. There was a heaviness on his chest as if some unseen weight had been placed there.

*The stupid bitch,* he thought. *Why didn't she just stay home?*

*Why didn't she just take me to the doctor when I asked her to?* he thought. *All of this could've been avoided.*

The policeman, the detective, Kevin Thomas, strode by the open door with his mother, handcuffed, in tow. The nurse went by a second later, looking white-faced and shaky.

*Trouble,* Jacob thought. *Trouble, trouble, & more trouble.*

He remembered the last social worker and the last foster home. He remembered living with his aunt and the candy-striped extension cord, folded lengthwise twice, and the welts it left.

*Ain't no help for it,* the voice said. *Just keep yer mouth shut.*

He knew that rule well.

"Don't talk to nobody about what happens in this house, ye

hear?" his mother always said. "Don't talk to no teacher, no social worker, no cop, nobody. Ever."

Jacob realized he was sitting up rigidly in the bed and forced himself to sit back and take a gulping, shaky breath. Then another. And another.

*Jus' keep your mouth shut,* the voice said. *Don't say nothing about nothing. Jus' take yer medicine and get better.*

Jacob fell back asleep and didn't wake until the following morning.

—

"Good morning," the social worker said.

She was in jeans and a blouse. Jacob guessed she was somewhere in her early forties.

"I'm Melissa Atwell," the social worker said. "I'm a social worker. You know what that is, don't you?"

"Why didn't they send the one from last time?" Jacob asked.

She'd been easy to lie to.

"I'll be here to work with you and your mother," Melissa Atwell, the social worker, said. "Is it alright if I pull this chair up to your bed?"

Jacob didn't respond.

The social worker pulled the chair up to the bed and sat down. She had a small briefcase with her. She set it on her lap and opened it. She took out a manila folder, a legal pad, and a pen.

"I want to start by saying I'm sorry you're ill," the social worker, Melissa Atwell, said.

Jacob almost believed her.

"I'm sorry you're ill but I'm glad you're here and getting better. The nurse said you already look worlds better than you did when you came in."

Jacob nearly threw off the bedsheets to look for himself.

"I'm glad you're getting better but I'm concerned about how this happened. Do you want to tell me a little bit about what happened?"

Jacob turned away from Melissa Atwell, the social worker, and looked out the window at the gray, cloud-covered morning.

"Jacob? Jacob?"

There wasn't a bird in the sky. Jacob wondered vaguely if birds could see when they flew through the clouds.

*Or is it like driving through the fog in the mornings and at night?*

"I know this is a difficult time for you," the social worker said.

"I do. I work with families and children in situations like yours every day."

*Do you?* Jacob doubted it.

"You can talk to me. I'm here to help."

Jacob looked at her then. She had small brown eyes set too close together but she seemed to mean what she said and, for a moment, Jacob wanted to tell her everything: about the hideout, about the experiments, the creations, the quilts.

*Tanya Miller / Tanya Miller*

Jacob blinked and was shocked to feel tears drop onto his cheeks.

*Keep it together*, the voice said.

Jacob swallowed and wiped the tears off his cheeks roughly with the palms of his hands.

"I know you must be scared. I would be if I were sitting there in your bed and saw what you saw with your mother. You're scared, and that's okay. Okay?"

Jacob wanted to nod his head but didn't.

"I work with families every day to make sure children just like you are safe," Melissa Atwell, the social worker, said. "I'm an investigative social worker. That means I go in and make sure children and families are safe, and, if need be, work with the families to ensure safety. Once I'm done with my investigation, I'll introduce you to your Ongoing Social Worker who'll work with you and your momma toward reunification. I worked with your mom last night to make a Safety Plan for you."

"Where is she?" Jacob asked.

Jail, he knew.

"I'm not going to sugar-coat it for you, you're a big boy," the social worker said. "Your momma is in jail right now. She's in for a few days, but she won't be in forever and, like I said, she worked with me last night to make a Safety Plan for you, to make sure you're taken care of. That's because she cares about you."

Jacob wanted to laugh.

"Now, I've talked with your Mamaw and Papaw and they'll be here directly to see you and make arrangements for you to go stay with them for a while once you're well enough to leave here. Not for long, now, don't you worry. We're working with your momma to get you back home with her, safely. We all want to make sure you're safe."

*Safe?*

The only safety Jacob knew was the safety of the hills, of the hideout. He wanted nothing more than to be sitting at the farmer's table working on another creation.

"We've worked out a safety plan with your Mamaw and Papaw to make sure all of your needs are met," the social worker said.

All of them? Jacob felt a strong need to hunt, to kill. Would this be provided for?

*Yes*, the voice said, *if yer careful and keep your mouth shut.*

"Would you like to go stay with your grandparents for a while?" Melissa Atwell, the social worker, asked.

"Yes," Jacob said.

He was already calculating the distance between his grandparents' house up Black Branch and the hideout in the little valley just outside town.

The social worker smiled and said, "Good. Good."

Jacob wondered what she looked like when screaming.

The social worker's phone rang and she answered it.

"Oh yes," she said. "Hello, hello. I've got him here now."

She covered the microphone with one hand and leaned over toward Jacob.

"It's your Mamaw," she said, smiling.

The last time he'd seen Mamaw and Papaw, his mother's parents, Jacob's mother had tried to steal their guestroom television and kicked Chester, their obese Jack Russell Terrier. She'd been snorting pills for at least two weeks at that time and didn't make rent as a result of it, so they'd stayed four days and nights in Mamaw and Papaw's double-wide up Black Branch. His mother kept up her drug use, sneaking off to her junk Buick or the bathroom to use, and eventually ran dry. That's when she tried to steal the television, telling Jacob she was just going to put it in pawn until she could "get back on her feet."

Papaw Russell must've expected something of the sort because he was sitting up in the living room when Jacob's mother had rounded the corner to the front door, lugging the heavy TV in front of her.

"Chris," Papaw always called Jacob's mother "Chris." "What in the hell are ye doin'?"

She started crying immediately. Pitiful blubbering that made Jacob embarrassed for her at the time. Looking back on that moment now, Jacob figured the tears were mostly sincere.

"I'm sorry," she kept saying.

How many times had he heard his mother apologize in slurred words?

The social worker gave Mamaw Melinda Jacob's hospital room number and hung up.

"I'm sorry this is happening," Melissa Atwell, the social worker, said, "but families go through hard times all the time. Things happen and sometimes people make decisions they wouldn't normally make. You're not alone."

Jacob would've laughed if he was sure his laughter wouldn't end in sobs.

"This is only a temporary thing," the social worker said. "Just long enough until we can make sure everybody is safe. That's why I'm going to work with y'all and make safety plans so we can get y'all reunited again soon. That okay?"

*Like I have an option.*

Jacob absently nodded his head thinking about the fluttering pages of the outline tacked to the wall of the hideout, envisioning them in his head as if he were standing there. He could see something new taking shape amongst the human anatomy photos ripped from *The Color Atlas of Anatomy*, University of Pikeville Medical School, and the colorful paintings from *Crystal Cubism*, Floyd County Public Library, and the women's lingerie cutouts from the JC Penny catalog; something sinister and domineering.

At first, he thought it was the shape of a monstrous multi-faceted face. He saw the profiles of several smiling faces, smiling the way skulls grin, then, he saw a larger face obscured by the images of which it was comprised staring blankly back at Jacob. You couldn't look at it directly to see it. Jacob could only see it if he imagined looking at the wall as a whole. The eyes followed him in every way he imagined it, just like the Mona Lisa they'd talked about in art class. The Mona Lisa Effect is what the teacher called this unnerving feature of the painting.

*A hand*, Jacob saw. *It's a gigantic, upturned hand.*

As soon as he glimpsed the outline as a whole, it was gone. He tried to bring the wall, the outline, to the forefront of his mind with more detail but the social worker wouldn't stop talking.

Jacob wished the social worker would hurry up with her questions and get him on to his grandparents' house. He needed to get back to the woods and hunt. The hand, *it was a hand*, would take all the kills he could get. Jacob saw it rising high off the ground, perched on a wrist of stone. He'd have to find wood or metal to support it, the fingers curled up as if poised to crush whatever was in its palm.

There was a knock at the door of the room and Jacob's grandparents entered looking flustered, ancient, and annoyed.

The social worker crossed the room and shook each of their hands.

"Hi, Melinda," she said. "Hi, Russell. Thank you for coming."

"Didn't have much of a choice, did we?" Papaw Russell said.

He harrumphed; his face twisted in a soured smile.

"I appreciate it," Melissa Atwell, the social worker, said. "And I'm sure Jacob here appreciates it too."

All three adult faces turned toward him in his hospital bed. He squirmed under their gaze and turned his eyes toward the curdling clouds outside his window.

"Listen," Papaw said, "I ain't got but an hour 'fore I have to be back at work, so we best get this train movin'."

The social worker nodded her head, picked up her papers, and they got to work making a Safety Plan. Mamaw and Papaw agreed to only allow Christy Goodman to have supervised contact with Jacob. They agreed to only allow sober communications. They agreed to ensure Jacob went to school and the doctor. They agreed to take Jacob to counseling, which would be provided free of charge. They agreed to provide for Jacob until he could safely return to his mother's care.

"Now, listen," Papaw said, the pen poised in his hand, his name not yet signed to the Safety Plan. "I love my daughter, but she's got a serious problem. We ain't had nary a thing to do with her since the last time she stole from us. She took a checkbook and put all kinds of hurtin' on our finances. I ain't allowin' her back in my house. These here supervised visitations need to take place elsewhere."

The social worker, Melissa Atwell, was already nodding her head.

"It might be a little bit before she's out, but we can do the visits at the office or at Archer Park or at McDonald's," she said. "Wherever is convenient for y'all."

Papaw nodded, but still did not sign his name.

"I don't want anybody to get the idea that this is a permanent thing," he said, his eyes moving from the social worker to Jacob then back to the social worker. "We ain't far from retirin' and I done raised three young 'uns and I don't intend to raise another'n."

Jacob could see the social worker cringe and the word "unwanted" popped up in his head.

"This is a temporary situation, Mr. Goodman," Melissa Atwell, the social worker, said. "We'll be going to court on Monday for the Temporary Removal Hearing. We'll work with Judge Hershel on a timeline for reunification."

Papaw Russell's eyes returned to Jacob. They were beady and hard and looked sharp enough to peel paint from the walls.

He sighed, then signed the papers.

-

"Ye know what they charged yer momma with?" Papaw Russell said from the driver's seat.

Jacob stared blankly out of the window.

"Huh? Answer me, boy."

"What?" Jacob said.

"Drunk 'n' disorderly, possession of *drugs* and paraphernalia, resisting arrest, assaultin' a police officer, *and* child endangerment and neglect."

He let loose a sharp bark of laughter.

"Jaysus Christ!" Papaw Russell said. "They went to that rattrap trailer y'all were staying in and found all sorts of drugs too. They got her in that cell with a bail so high she won't see the light of day 'til a soft-hearted judge says so."

"She's gotta take parentin' classes, substance abuse classes, anger management classes, and do a year's worth of community service once she's released," Mamaw Melinda said.

A new knot formed in Jacob's stomach and he felt hot, Judas tears fill his eyes.

*I hate her*, Jacob thought. *I hate her! Why couldn't she be a normal mother? Why?*

*Sure she's yer momma*, the bald man had said, *but she's still a cunt.*

They rode the rest of the way harping on his mother. Jacob focused on the wind whistling by outside Papaw's rusty S-10, holding his breath and squeezing his fists together, willing himself to not cry.

-

Jacob looked up at the slowly turning ceiling fan above him. It squeaked and rocked with each rotation of the blades. The couch he lay on was hard and lumpy. The quilt covering him was patched with crucifixes and doves. He was crying as quietly as he could.

*Whimpering like a kitten*, the voice chided him. *Like a little defenseless, useless kitten.*

Jacob covered his face with one of the throw pillows and bit down hard on the rough fabric. He could barely stifle the scream of rage and impotence.

He wanted to tear down the walls of his grandparents' old trailer. He wanted to gouge the eyes out of a puppy. He wanted to stomp on a doe's head until it felt like the meat of a pawpaw between his bare feet. He wanted to stop crying and fall forever.

Jacob found sleep just as the dawn reared its murky head over the ridge opposite Black Branch.

-

Jacob stared down at the open maw of the mineshaft. He heard the infant calling from miles below. The cries, though not words, became words in the dream.

"Help me," the cries said.

"Please, don't leave me down here," the unborn child pleaded.

Jacob wanted to run away from the hole but he saw his feet were cinderblocks. He felt the ground giving way under them, the hole of the mineshaft becoming larger, darker, a black hole slowly pulling Jacob toward the reverberating cries of Tanya Miller's unborn baby.

Jacob woke crying.

Papaw Russell was staring down at him with disgust.

"Quit yer blubberin' and come get some cereal," he said. "I gotta get you to school since we ain't made arrangements with the bus yet."

Jacob sat up, wiped his eyes with his sweaty palms. When he looked again, Papaw had disappeared into the back of the trailer.

-

Jacob was pulled out of home economics and taken to the principal's office. The ruddy detective, the cop, Kevin Thomas, sat in one of the two chairs in front of the principal's desk.

"Have a seat," Principal Williams said.

Jacob sat down beside the cop.

"This is Detective Thomas," Principal Williams said.

"We're acquainted," the cop said. "Aren't we, Jake?"

Jacob barely contained the cringe at the sound of his name.

The detective, the cop, Kevin Thomas, turned in his seat and smiled his red-faced smile.

Jacob nodded.

"Good, good," Principal Williams said. "Well, I know you've had a rough go of things as of late. I'm sorry and I want you to know we're here for you. We care about you and your family and want to make sure you're okay. Okay?"

When neither adult spoke, Jacob nodded his head.

"We all want what's best for you," Principal Williams said. "Detective Thomas here has a few questions he needs to ask you and you need to be absolutely honest with him. Think you can do that?"

*Not a word*, the voice said.

Jacob nodded his head.

"Good, good," the principal said. "I'm going to step outside and do a little paperwork and let you two talk. Is that alright with you?"

Jacob nodded again.

"Okay then," Principal Williams said, pushing himself up from his chair and crossing the room to the door. "Y'all just holler if you need anything."

The door closed behind him, leaving Jacob alone with the detective, the cop, Kevin Thomas.

"I need to ask ye some questions about a couple of different things," Detective Thomas said. "Some of them aren't going to be fun questions but I need ye to tell me the God's honest truth. Can ye do that?"

Jacob nodded, not trusting his voice. He felt on the verge of more Judas tears and hated himself for it.

*Not a word*, the voice said again.

"Ye know what drugs are?"

It wasn't really a question.

"Now not all people that use drugs are bad. We can agree on that, can't we?"

Jacob nodded.

The detective's face was redder than a tomato. Jacob couldn't help but steal glances at the shiny skin on the man's forehead and at the sides of his closely cropped head.

"Now yer Momma isn't a bad person," the cop said. "I don't want ye to think that I think that. Okay?"

His mother's voice yelled in his head: *I ain't ruinin' what I got left of my credit cos yer a fuckin' freak!*

His penis, though well on its way to mending with the medicines and cream the doctor from the ER gave him, twinged painfully.

"Have ye ever seen yer mother use drugs?" the cop asked.

Jacob immediately shook his head.

"Never?"

Jacob shook his head.

"Have ye ever seen her act different?" the cop asked. "Like she was havin' a hard time talking or seemed really, really tired?"

Jacob shook his head again.

"Never seen her with different colored snot or giving herself shots with a needle?"

"No," Jacob said.

"I see."

*Not a word*, the voice said.

The cop stared at him.

"I see," he said again.

The detective, the cop, Kevin Thomas, drummed the index finger of his right hand on the wooden arm of the chair.

"Are ye being straight with me? Ye know it's against the law to lie to a police officer, don't ye?"

Jacob nodded, holding the cop's stare.

Several moments passed in silence. The cop's radio crackled and he turned his head toward the sound the way a dog will when you're speaking to it. He nodded to himself and turned a knob of the radio and the hissing static died down.

"Remember the last time we talked? At yer school?" the detective, the cop, Kevin Thomas, asked.

Jacob nodded.

"I was askin' ye about Tanya Miller," he said. "How well do ye know her?"

"Not well," Jacob said.

"Uh-huh, that's what I thought," the cop said. "So y'all weren't close? Not dating or friends or talkin' or anything like that?"

Jacob shook his head and shuddered at the same time. In his head he saw SAHB in the hideout hacking away at the meat and bones. He saw himself drop each piece down the mineshaft, a crooked smile on his rapturous face.

"What about her cousin, Rodney Tackett?" the detective, the cop, Kevin Thomas, asked.

*what Rodney Tackett done / what Rodney Tackett done*

"Do ye know him well? Are y'all friends?"

Jacob shook his head.

The cop watched him for a long time. Jacob wanted to squirm but he forced himself to remain still.

*Not a word*, the voice said.

The cop seemed to intensify his gaze, his eyes becoming hard little cigarette burns in his red face.

"He's a bully," Jacob said at last. "He doesn't like me."

The cop smiled the smile of those hearing what they wanted to hear.

"That's what I thought."

The spare bedroom at his grandparents' house was stuffed full of things. There were boxes of unopened restaurant utensils, a chest of Chester's old dog toys, stacks of old newspapers and magazines, mostly *Floyd County Chronicles and Times*, *Good Housekeeping*, and *Southern Living*. There was a twin bed somewhere under all the piles of junk, but Jacob couldn't find it.

The social worker, Melissa Atwell, was sitting at the kitchen table. She was filling out the paperwork for Jacob's temporary removal hearing and Kinship Care placement. Jacob sat between his grandparents on the other side of the table. He watched the social worker's hand as she wrote. She had beautifully long fingers and a clear coat of fingernail polish on all ten of her well-manicured fingers.

When Jacob blinked, he saw SAHB using those hands the way he used Tanya Miller's.

"As I said yesterday," the social worker, Melissa Atwell, said as she wrote, "reunification is the goal. This is a temporary placement until we can assure the family's safety and stability. Okay?"

Mamaw Melinda made a nonverbal noise of acknowledgement then sipped from her cracked coffee cup. It read: *On the eighth day God made secretaries*. Chester sat on her lap napping; Jacob wondered what the dog, Chester's, skeleton looked like.

Papaw Russell was on his fourth cigarette of the meeting.

"I just need y'all to sign here saying that you won't allow any unsupervised contact between Christy and Jacob," the social worker, Melissa Atwell, said, "and you won't allow any contact if she appears under the influence."

"Uh-huh," Mamaw said, signing her name at the bottom of the page that read: Safety Plan.

Papaw puffed his cigarette and signed his name without comment. Jacob could tell by the puckered look on his grandfather's face the man was not impressed by the social worker and her Safety Plan.

"At the Temporary Removal Hearing tomorrow, Judge Hershel

will more than likely sign off on placement in your home," the social worker, Melissa Atwell, said, "and he'll set a date out for the Adjudication Hearing. That's the one where he'll make a ruling in the family court case. The criminal ruling will proceed in Circuit Court and those findings may change our case depending on what happens."

*Rulings,* Jacob thought. *What a word. To rule on something. To rule over something. To rule all. Mrs. Horace should use that one someday.*

Jacob looked out the window framing the neighbors', Jim and Debra Varney's, little shotgun house in the morning light like a painting. There were three bronze stars and a great hulking metal sun hanging on opposite sides of the front door that glinted in the morning sun. For no reason at all, he hated those three stars and that smiling sun. He hated the red painted door too.

Jacob watched an orange tabby cat clean itself on the cracked cement front porch steps.

*Mine,* he thought. *Mine.*

"Lots of families go through situations like these," the social worker, Melissa Atwell, said. "I'm not going to sugar-coat it for y'all: Christy has a long way to go. It's an uphill battle but it's not impossible, especially not with familial support."

"Support?" Papaw spat. "Ain't we puttin' 'im up? Ain't we feedin' 'im? Ain't we sent her to the rehab twice already? Support, my ass! We're about used up on support."

The social worker, Melissa Atwell, carefully avoided Papaw's burning eyes.

Jacob could see Papaw shaking with emotion.

"Ain't she done stole us blind already?" Papaw Russell said. "How many times have we bailed her out? Given her money for a ride to rehab? Or to the methadone clinic? Or the pain clinic? Which she always used jus' to get plastered. That's all she does: get plastered. She might as well be a drywall board."

"Stop it, Russell," Mamaw Melinda said. "Hush all that. The boy's sitting right here."

"Ye don't think I know that?" Papaw said, turning his craggy head toward Jacob. "He needs to hear it. That's the only way he'll learn not to fall into the same troubles as his momma. Ye hear me, boy?"

Jacob nodded.

*trouble / in a family way*

# BIRTH OF A MONSTER

*sure she's your momma / but she's still a cunt*

She deserves to be in jail, Jacob decided. She deserves it.

He could tell by the way the social worker was acting that she thought so too. She was too formal, too stiff with the niceties.

"Here's your copy of the Safety Plan," the social worker, Melissa Atwell, said. "And here's a copy of the Emergency Protection Order. After the hearing, I'll have y'all come down to the office and we'll get the rest of the Kinship Care and insurance paperwork filled out so we can get Jacob to the doctor and dentist and all that. Okay?"

She didn't wait for a response but efficiently packed up her paperwork in a leather binder.

"I best be getting on," she said from the open door. "I thank you for the coffee, Melinda. Good afternoon, Russell. Jacob."

*Unfit mother*, that's what the courts would call his mother Jacob knew. *Unfit.*

He wanted to deny it, but he knew it for truth the second the term popped into his head.

Without a word, Papaw Russell left for his workshop, a carport he'd sided with rusted sheets of aluminum, before the front door had closed behind Melissa Atwell, the social worker.

Jacob sat at the kitchen table for some time, watching his grandmother tidy up the kitchen.

*She's so old*, he realized.

It'd been nearly a year since he'd last seen his grandparents. Time seemed to be moving faster for them than it was for Jacob; they'd aged so much and he thought he'd aged so little.

He hadn't known his mother had stolen from them more than once. He didn't know his grandparents had put her through rehab. Jacob wondered which stint it had been. He distinctly remembered his mother "going away" three separate occasions.

*There'd probably been even more*, Jacob thought, *that I wasn't old enough to remember.*

Jacob wanted to cry. This made him angry.

*Weakness*, he thought. *A family of weakness.*

Jacob pushed himself up from the table, left the kitchen. He threw himself down onto the uncomfortable couch that was his bed now and cried into the cushions.

Jacob ran through the woods, tears stinging his eyes, letting the branches and briars slap and rip at his arms and legs. He ran until he was afraid his lungs would explode. When he could run no farther, he stopped, hands on his knees, panting.

He pictured his mother in a little concrete jail cell and wanted to scream and to laugh all at the same time.

*She deserves it. She deserves to be locked up.*

Jacob reached a hand into the waistband of his black sweatpants, Walmart, and felt his penis, then his testicles. The swelling was gone but they were still a little bit tender. The medication the doctor gave him was working. For this he was thankful.

-

Jacob couldn't sleep. The couch was uncomfortable and the room was stuffy. He sat up, rubbed the crust from his eyes, then turned on the ancient television. It started with a strange whirring sound and a field of static that eventually dissolved into the anchors of the eleven o'clock news.

". . . still missing. Police are asking anyone with information on the sixteen-year-old's disappearance to come forward or call—"

Her picture was on the screen now, Tanya Miller's. It was a yearbook photo: stiff, unnatural, but toothy.

Jacob stared at the blurred image on the crappy television with his mouth hanging open, his foul breath hot and heavy in his nostrils. He didn't think the picture did her justice at all.

*Must be from her other school,* Jacob thought. *She wasn't at Floyd County for picture day.*

Seeing her smiling face, so unnatural with the gaudy blue background, unnerved Jacob.

*That's not how she looks!* he wanted to scream.

He saw her as from above—the shower scene. The suds in her blonde hair. The painted nails of her hands working and working and working.

He remembered the feel of her hand around him, the last breath she released like a sigh of ecstasy when he'd finished. She'd finished, in a way, at the same time.

*Her last breath / the first of my new life*

Jacob smiled.

*Mine*, he thought. *Mine.*

Jacob lay back on the couch and let sleep drape over him like a heavy blanket.

-

# BIRTH OF A MONSTER

He was falling, but Jacob wasn't scared this time. He knew he was dreaming though he could feel the wind whip his cheeks.

The child was really crying now. An angry, agonized frenzy of wails, blubbers, and screeches. The sound bounced off the stone walls as he fell, so heavy and so close Jacob thought the sounds almost tangible.

*Shut up!* His mind screamed at the child. *I'm sorry but shut up!*

*Help me!* the wordless cries demanded. *Help me!*

Jacob woke to find he'd pissed himself. One of the lumpy couch cushions was soaked.

Papaw Russell was standing over him, the kitchen light lighting up behind his head like a halo.

Chester stood and watched Jacob at Papaw Russell's side. Jacob wanted to scoop out the dog's little beady eyes.

"Jaysus Christ," Papaw Russell hissed. "And if all that screamin' and cryin' weren't enough, ye had to go and piss the couch too?"

Jacob wanted to cry. He didn't, but it was a close thing.

"Git yer ass up and into the shower," Papaw Russell said. "Didn't yer mother potty train ye, boy?"

For a second, Jacob was sure Papaw Russell was going to hit him, but the moment passed without violence. Jacob almost wanted the strike to come. He felt he deserved it somehow.

Jacob rose on shaky legs, felt the hot dampness, and cringed.

*What if that baby is still alive down there?*

Jacob knew it was an impossibility but couldn't figure out why he kept dreaming and hearing the plaintive, angry wailings.

"Go on now," Papaw Russell said. "Go clean yerself up. I'll take care of this got damn mess."

# CHAPTER NINETEEN
## STERILE

**THE VARNEYS, JACOB'S GRANDPARENTS'** neighbors, kept massive rose bushes at each of the four corners of their little house. Mamaw Melinda said the Varneys won prizes for the roses a few years back and the Varneys were quite proud of them still, though they didn't enter them into any more competitions. The flowers were blood red and bobbed like nodding heads in the breeze. Jacob waited until both Jim and Debra left for work then he stepped between the flaking siding of the house and the rose bush on the back corner of the house and waited on their orange cat to smell the can of tuna he'd left open in the yard.

The cat came sniffing off the front porch and approached the can hesitantly. It had a pink collar with golden tags wrapped around its orange neck. The cat sniffed the can then the stick supporting the snare. It went back to the tuna and, as soon as it began licking, Jacob sprung the trap.

---

The hike to the hideout was shorter than it had been from the pink trailer at Thompkins' Trailer Court. Jacob carried the dead cat— Mindy, the nametag read—over his shoulder like a bath towel. He was surprised and amused to find himself whistling, but he was such a happy boy sometimes.

---

Jacob carefully stitched Mindy's, the cat, orange, bloody hide into the motorcycle wheel's flat rubber tire. He'd taken the tire from an abandoned singlewide at the backend of Thompkins' Trailer Court.

*Like a setting sun,* he thought, running the fingers of his left hand along the soft fur. *Just like a setting sun.*

Jacob hung the creation on the wall above the little pedestals, *where a sun goes.*

He thought the snakeskin interlaced through several of the wheel's spokes was just the perfect touch, *a bit of shade / like an eclipse.* The cat, Mindy's, pink color was clasped to three spokes near the bottom left quadrant of the creation.

*Like a lens flare*, he thought.

Jacob smiled watching SAHB drape the furless body of Mindy, the cat, over the red heads of the roses, *all in my mind / all in good time*. He couldn't wait for the Varneys to find the *flotsam* of his most recent creation, Mrs. Horace's Word of the day, *floating wreckage of a ship or its cargo: floating debris*. He felt like something prickly, a cactus or thorn bush, barbed and angry, wanting to inflict himself onto others.

His jaw ached; how long had he been grinding his teeth? He swore he could feel the damp powder of them sitting on his dried tongue like a spoonful of cinnamon, *something sweet / something bitter*.

-

Jacob slipped back into his grandparents' house through the front door, which let into the living room and the couch on which he slept. He kicked off his filthy miss K-Swisses but didn't bother removing his clothing. He sat down on the uncomfortable couch and fondled the cat, Mindy's, rectangular nametag, luxuriating in the etched lettering.

*Mine*, he thought, lying onto his back.

*Mine*, he thought, putting the tag into his mouth.

*Mine*, he thought, slowly grinding it between his teeth.

-

"Listen here, Jacob," Mamaw Melinda said. "Ye might've been able to go 'round dirty as sin when yer staying with yer mother, but it ain't gonna fly here."

Jacob sat up on the couch and rubbed his eyes. He smelled himself and knew he should feel embarrassed, but he didn't. Besides, a shower sounded pleasant.

"Yes, ma'am," he murmured, the cat, Mindy's, nametag stuck between his cheeks and the bottom row of his teeth.

"Annunciate, boy," she snapped. "I won't have ye mumblin' in this house."

Jacob half-turned away from this grandmother and spit the cat's nametag into his hand, then pocketed it.

"Leave your clothes outside the bathroom door and I'll get 'em warshed with ours later on."

Jacob pushed himself up from the couch and stretched, then made his way down the hall to the bathroom, where he stripped naked and studied himself in the mirror while the shower got hot. He was much skinnier than he'd ever remembered being. He could see his ribs clearly now. If he held himself still and studied the hollow under his left breast, he could see his heart beating like some small bird under a thin strip of cloth.

Jacob set his stiff clothing outside the bathroom door then got in the shower.

-

Jacob, wearing the plush towel around his waist, went back into the living room and retrieved a change of clothes from the black backpack he'd stolen from Walmart, then returned to the bathroom. He wiped the steam from the mirror and studied the face staring back at him. The cheeks were hollow, sunken in, the eyes seemed overly large and vacant. He could almost make out his skull's grin through the skin.

*Such a Happy Boy*, he thought. *God, I just can't help it, now can I?*

Jacob dressed, then hung his towel over the door of the shower to dry.

The bathroom was spotless. Jacob leaned over the mirror and popped a handful of pimples on his face and neck, speckling the clear surface of the glass with white, yellow, and a little bit of red.

-

A sheriff's car was parked in front of the Varneys' house when the bus let Jacob off at the end of Black Branch. The cat, Mindy's, body was still hanging from the rose bushes. One of the two sheriff's deputies was staring at the furless corpse with his camera held dumbly in his hands. The other was writing something down in a little notebook as Mrs. Varney cried beside him. Mr. Varney sat in one of the two rocking chairs on the porch, smoking a cigarette. He watched Jacob walk up the drive, then the walkway, with hard, unblinking eyes.

Jacob unlocked the front door of his grandparents' house with the key they'd given him and felt Mr. Varney's eyes on his back like a hot spotlight.

Jacob closed and locked the door behind him. He flung his backpack, Walmart, onto the couch and peeked out the front window. The cop was taking photos of the cat's skinned body on the gigantic rose bushes. Jacob saw the skinning in Fast-Forward X2 Mode, fileting knife, Roger's Bait 'n' Tackle, gliding like scissors across wrapping paper.

-

"Get warshed up for supper," Mamaw Melinda said.

"I am washed up," Jacob said.

Mamaw turned away from the stove and looked Jacob up and down.

"Git yer ass to the bathroom and do a little scrubbing," she said. "Ye can be cleaner than that, by Gawd."

Jacob tried to see what his grandmother saw but didn't. He made his way to the bathroom anyway. He turned on the hot water and masturbated into the cascading stream thinking about Tanya Miller's last breath, her hand wrapped around himself, his palm on the soft skin around her knuckles, those painted nails glinting like the splashing water under the 60-watt bulbs over the bathroom mirror.

They sat down to dinner at the scuffed but clean table. Jacob wasn't hungry. He almost never was anymore, but he ate what was given.

The three of them ate in silence. Jacob caught each of his grandparents stealing glances at him throughout the meal.

Jacob watched his hands work, fascinated at their dexterity. They'd been studying evolution the past few days in school and, for the first time in longer than he could remember, Jacob had been interested.

"Damn shame about the Varneys' cat," Papaw said after a time.

Jacob looked up from his hands and saw both of his grandparents watching him, closely. He forced himself to sit still and not squirm.

*They don't know a thing*, the voice said. *Keep your head.*

Jacob chewed the bit of country-fried steak then swallowed.

"What happened to Mi—" Jacob faked a cough. "'Scuse me. What happened to the Varneys' cat?"

Neither Mamaw Melinda nor Papaw Russell answered him right away. Jacob looked first at his grandfather then his grandmother, who quickly looked away.

"I saw the sheriff's car over there when I got off the bus," he said.

They watched him.

He forced a forkful of the gravy-covered meat into his mouth and began chewing.

"Something kilt it and strung it up on their rose bushes," Papaw said.

Jacob swallowed the half-chewed steak. It nearly choked him but he forced it down.

"That's terrible," Jacob said, after a time.

Papaw Russell looked from Jacob to Mamaw Melinda and back again.

"Well," he said.

Mamaw Melinda shook her head and looked down at the napkin in her lap.

Papaw Russell made a disgusted sound and pushed himself up from the table. He left the kitchen without another word.

-

"Don't ye leave the yard," Papaw told Jacob the following morning, which was a Saturday. "I don't care where yer little friends live or whatever. Ye don't leave this property, ye hear me?"

Jacob nodded his head sullenly. He went into the living room and flung himself down onto the couch and used the remote to turn the television on.

"The community is shocked by the appalling death of one Prestonsburg family's pet cat, Mindy."

Jacob adjusted the volume on the remote, but Papaw had heard and stepped into the living room.

"Melinda!" he shouted toward the back of the house. "Get up here and see this. The Varneys're on the tube!"

He strode over to the couch.

"Scoot," Papaw Russell demanded.

Jacob made room for him on the couch.

Sheriff Lawless was on the screen, his muttonchops catching the bright sunshine under his huge Stetson hat. A microphone bobbed and dipped into the shot.

"Not sure if it 'twer an animal that done it," the sheriff said, "or not. We're still looking into the matter."

"Jaysus Christ," Papaw said. "Melinda! Git in here!"

"I'm right here, Russell," Mamaw said from the entrance to the hallway. She was leaning against the wall, watching the television over Papaw Russell's and Jacob's heads.

"The family is heartbroken over the loss of their eight-year-old tabby cat, Mindy."

"She was every bit a part of this family," Debra Varney cried. "Who would do such a thing?"

"Who indeed?"

The television now showed a well-manicured news anchor sitting at a shiny desk.

# BIRTH OF A MONSTER

"Mindy is the thirty-third missing or killed animal in the Prestonsburg area this year. Authorities are unsure what's causing the disappearances but more than a few residents have their guesses, which range from the macabre but plausible all the way to the downright fantastic.

"Everybody wants to laugh when I say there's a Big Foot but just look at the sheer number of pets that've gone missing this year. Only a superior hunting creature could account for numbers this high."

*Hun-ter.*

Jacob recognized the man on the television. He lived just off Front Street and had had a Doberman Pinscher that Jacob poisoned with antifreeze. He'd used the skull of that dog—he'd already forgotten the animal's name—for one of his earlier creations.

*A failure,* Jacob remembered, grinding his teeth. *One in a long line of failures.*

"EKTV has reached out to Animal Control but no comment was provided."

"Well," Papaw Russell said as the news moved on to local sports.

"Well," Mamaw Melinda repeated.

Jacob could feel their eyes on him. He chose to ignore them and change the television with the remote control.

-

Jacob got off the bus, nearly the last kid on the thing after an hour and half of riding, and walked up the last bit of hill to the end of Black Branch where his grandparents and the Varneys lived at the top of the knob. Jacob was breathing hard. He felt slightly dizzy from skipping breakfast and lunch. He stopped in front of the Varney household and smiled at the rose bushes. Then he used his key and entered his grandparents' house.

He had the place to himself for about an hour. During this time, Jacob masturbated into the bathroom sink rubbing the polished blue and white thumbnail between his right index finger and thumb, thinking about the sound of that last breath, imagining her hand, Tanya Miller's, around himself, forcing her to finish the job he started. He closed his eyes and breathed through his clenched teeth, imagining the sound as the sound of her last breath.

When he'd finished and opened his eyes, panting, Jacob was shocked to see his grandmother standing in the open doorway of the bathroom, her face a study in horror and disgust.

"Sor—" he started but Mamaw Melinda slammed the bathroom

door shut.

Jacob watched himself wither in his left hand, then turned on the water as hot as it would get.

The waiting room was mostly empty. A younger couple sat with a small child across the room near the entrance.

"Jacob," a voice called.

Jacob and his grandmother got up and followed the nurse back into an examination room where she took Jacob's vitals and asked question after question. When the nurse was finished she left Jacob and Mamaw Melinda alone in the little room. It was very quiet; neither spoke.

Jacob wished his grandmother had stayed in the waiting room. He wanted to ask the nurse or the doctor how long a baby could live inside a dead mother. He heard the crying child all through the night before and he felt jumpy and tired.

There were two quick knocks on the door, then it opened and a young doctor entered.

"Good morning," the doctor said, sitting down on the rolling chair and pushing himself to the computer beside the examination table. "How're we feeling today, Jacob?"

Jacob shrugged his aching shoulders.

"Okay," he murmured.

"Good, good," the doctor said, his eyes on the computer screen. "Let's see here. You were seen at the ER last week for your . . . penis injury."

The doctor looked at Jacob for the first time. Jacob thought he could see traces of amusement and scorn there.

"How're you healing?"

"Okay," Jacob said.

"Well, we're gonna have to have a look," the doctor said. "Grandma, would you mind stepping out into the hall for a moment?"

Mamaw Melinda nodded, got up from the plastic chair, and left the room.

When the door closed, the doctor asked Jacob to drop his pants.

"Have you had any pain lately?" he asked, putting on examination gloves that reminded Jacob of the gloved hands from the Cadaver Lab.

Jacob wondered if this man had ever worn another person's skin like a glove.

"Yes," Jacob said.

"Have you been masturbating?" the doctor asked, pulling his rolling chair up to the examination table.

Jacob's first instinct was to lie, but the voice in his head told him to tell the truth.

"Yes," he said in a near whisper.

"That's okay," the doctor said, taking Jacob's penis in a light pincher grip between his index finger and thumb. "Masturbation is perfectly normal at your age."

Jacob thought about homo habilis, *the handyman gets handsy*, using flexible fingers and budding thumbs to problem solve.

"The thing is," the doctor said after having Jacob turn his head and cough, "with an injury like yours, you're going to want to give your body time to heal. You understand?"

The doctor looked at him with a gravity Jacob didn't feel belied the question and, though he didn't understand, he nodded his head.

"Good," the doctor said. "You're healing well but you're going to need to lay off the masturbation for a while. Say three weeks. Can you do that?"

Jacob nodded his head though he knew it was an impossibility. He masturbated three or four times a day. He'd snuck out of home economics the previous day to masturbate in the handicap bathroom, which was the least frequented in the east wing.

"If you don't give yourself time to heal," the doctor said, "I'm afraid you might have some permanent damage. You could become sterile. Do you know what sterile means?"

Jacob shook his head though he did.

"Sterile means that you won't ever be able to conceive children. Do you want children one day?"

*What a question*, Jacob thought. He'd never given it a thought.

*Of course*, the voice in his head answered.

*Do I?* he wondered.

"Go on and pull your pants back up," the doctor said, rolling his chair back to the computer.

-

*Sterile*, Jacob had borrowed Mrs. Horace gigantic dictionary, *1: failure to bear or incapable of producing fruit or spores; failing to produce or incapable of producing offspring; incapable of germinating; neither perfect nor pistillate; 2: unproductive of vegetation; free from living organisms and especially pathogenic microorganisms; lacking in stimulating emotional or intellectual quality.*

Jacob could become sterile if he didn't stop masturbating. That's what the doctor told him. Despite this fact, Jacob did not stop. He couldn't. In fact, his masturbation increased after his visit with the young doctor.

-

Mamaw Melinda's car was parked under the carport when Jacob got off the bus. He found her in the kitchen, sitting at the table, her worn, leather Bible opened next to a steaming cup of coffee. Chester, the Jack Russell Terrier, was asleep in her lap. She didn't look up or greet Jacob when he entered. He walked past the doorway to the kitchen and made his way down the darkened hall to the bathroom.

*Something's not right*, the voice told him. *Play it cool.*

Jacob pissed, masturbated quietly into the sink, then washed himself off with scalding hot water.

When he entered the living room from the hall, Jacob saw the nametag sitting on the coffee table. The late afternoon sun shone through the window of the front door and glinted off the teeth marks he'd bitten into Mindy the cat's nametag.

*She found it*, he knew. *Oh God. She knows.*

-

They didn't talk about it. For this, Jacob was both thankful and remorseful. Part of him, *the crazy part*, the voice in his head called it, wanted to confess to Mamaw Melinda. Part of him wanted to tell her about Mindy, the cat, about all the other named and nameless animals. Tanya Miller included.

*Keep your mouth shut*, the voice said. *Or you'll really be in trouble.*

She didn't call him to supper that night. Jacob watched his grandparents eat in silence from the couch in the living room. Long after they went to sleep—they shut and locked their bedroom door, with Chester inside—Jacob, standing in the thin light from the stovetop, ate two slices of white bread to quiet his rumbling stomach.

-

"Do you think we could make a little more progress on getting the spare bedroom tidied up for Jacob?" the new social worker, Kim Cady, asked Jacob's grandparents.

Papaw Russell huffed.

Mamaw Melinda coughed softly into her fist.

"Are there any other options for the boy?" she asked the social worker.

"What do you mean?" Kim Cady asked.

"Like other places he could stay."

Jacob watched the studied way his grandparents avoided both his eyes and the social worker Kim Cady's.

"We're gettin' on in years," Mamaw Melinda said. "And we're jus' not sure we're the ones who should be takin' care of 'im."

"We cain't watch him all the time," Papaw Russell said. "He doesn't listen to a thing we tell 'im."

Jacob, sitting at the round kitchen table with the three adults, felt invisible.

*I'm right here*, he wanted to scream.

"He's secretive and goes off on his own all the time," Mamaw Melinda said.

"We cain't keep 'im in the house," Papaw Russell said. "We think he had something to do with the Varneys' cat."

"We cain't be sure," Mamaw Melinda added quickly, "but we do know we cain't keep 'im any longer."

The social worker, Kim Cady, looked like she'd swallowed something sharp.

"Jacob, could you give us a minute?" she asked him, her eyes not finding his, but looking at something just over his left ear.

Jacob nodded, went out the kitchen door into the side yard.

The social worker spoke with him outside next to her white sedan.

"Jacob, what's going on?"

He didn't know how to answer her.

"Your grandparents think you might've had something to do with the neighbors' cat being killed. Is that true?"

That detective, Kevin Thomas, had asked Jacob to tell him the God's Honest Truth. Jacob wondered what kind of truth the social worker, Kim Cady, needed. He didn't feel like he had any truth but the hunting in him, so he didn't say anything.

"Lord," the social worker sighed. "Do you like living with your grandparents?"

"It's alright."

"Well, if you'd like to stay here, you're gonna have to start following their rules."

*ruling / rules & the rulers*

"Okay?" the social worker, Kim Cady, asked.

*Say okay*, the voice said.

314

"Okay," Jacob said.

"Good," she said, opening the driver's side door. "I'll see you soon. Be a good boy."

-

"Come here, Chessie," Mamaw Melinda cooed.

The Jack Russell Terrier, Chester, jumped up into Mamaw Melinda's lap, its pink tongue lolling out of its lightly panting mouth.

Jacob watched his grandmother stroke the dog behind its ears. He watched her change the channel.

"Why're ye staring at me, boy?" she asked after several moments.

"Sorry," he mumbled, turning his head back to the glow of the television.

"Up next on the seven o'clock news round-up," the news anchor said, "police are still looking for any tips or leads regarding the missing teenager from Prestonsburg. Tanya Miller was last seen—"

"That social worker said the police wanted to ask you a few questions about that missing girl there," Mamaw Melinda said.

She was watching him now. He forced himself to sit perfectly still though he wanted to squirm. It felt like it was written across his forehead: *I Did It.*

Jacob made a noncommittal noise.

The Jack Russell Terrier, Chester, growled at Jacob when he looked at it.

"Hush now, Chessie. She said that little girl's cousin has been making a big stink about you," Mamaw Melinda said. "Don't be surprised if one of them state police boys comes to talk to ye at school."

Jacob wanted the dog's head. He could see the outline of its skull through all the fat and fur and thought it would sit perfectly on the body of the groundhog he'd strung up on display two days ago.

-

Jacob ran through the forest laughing. The moonlight playing off his naked body looked like it was shimmering when he glanced at it.

When he heard the baby crying, he ran through the forest crying. All the stars in the sky looked like *impetuous* eyes, Mrs. Horace's Word of the day, *1: marked by impulsive vehemence or passion; 2: marked by force and violence of movement of action.*

-

The dog was a sucker for pepperonis. Jacob stole a package from Walmart and began feeding them to the dog whenever his grandparents weren't watching, trying to win the dog's favor. After three days,

# BIRTH OF A MONSTER

Jacob found he was "in like Flynn."

"Come here, Chessie," Jacob whispered, imitating the lilt on the nickname his grandmother always used.

The living room was completely dark, save the pale glow of static from the television. It was three o'clock in the morning. Jacob had cracked his grandparents' bedroom door, lured the Jack Russell Terrier, Chester, from his bed at the foot of the four-poster his grandparents shared, led him down the short hall with the open package of pepperonis. Now came the tricky part.

Jacob knelt down on his knees on the carpet and held out a pepperoni.

"Come here, ye little shit," Jacob whispered calmly. "I'll show ye wanted. I'll show ye care. Kinship care. I'll show ye."

As the dog reached for the treat, Jacob slipped the noose around its neck and pulled it tight.

"Chester! Chester? Chester!"

His grandmother's frantic calls woke him. He'd gotten back to the little house up Black Branch just before daylight. He'd made quick work of the dog, skinning him alive and putting him on display. He'd left the nametag and collar back at the hideout. He didn't want to risk his grandmother finding another set of tags, especially this one.

"Jacob, what have ye done?" Mamaw Melinda was standing over him, looking down. "Where's Chester? Where is he?"

*Play it cool*, the voice said.

Jacob couldn't see her face well in the early light. He sat up, turned on the lamp beside the couch, and rubbed his eyes.

"What's wrong with Chester?" he asked, then yawned.

He stretched his arms above his head, not full extension but enough to show how he'd been asleep.

"He ain't here," Mamaw Melinda said, her voice quiet and hard. "What've ye done with him? I'm not playing no games with ye. Where is my dog?"

"I don't know," Jacob lied.

Mamaw Melinda's hands were on her hips, her feet a shoulder's length apart.

"Jacob Hunter Goodman," she said slowly, "ye best tell me what ye done with my dog and ye'd better not have harmed a hair on

Chester's little head. I swear I'll beat ye black and blue. I don't care what that social worker says about it neither."

Jacob made himself flat, sterile. He spoke in a cool monotone.

"I don't know where yer dog is Mamaw Melinda," he said.

She shivered. Jacob saw it start somewhere low in her back and work its way up until her head rocked from side to side with it.

Jacob wanted to smile but the voice reminded him to "play it cool" and he kept his face as blank as stone.

"Oh God," Mamaw Melinda said, fleeing the living room.

-

Papaw held him down over his lap. Jacob could've broken away, Papaw wasn't that much stronger than he was, but something kept him still.

*Take it*, the voice said.

Papaw whipped the belt against Jacob's backside. His black sweatpants, Walmart, weren't much protection but Papaw still yanked them down before he struck Jacob again.

"What did ye do, ye little freak?" Papaw hissed.

Jacob could almost hear the old man's jaw's creak from his clenched teeth.

Papaw Russell brought the leather belt down against Jacob's bare ass.

There was a tickle in the back of Jacob's throat. He coughed into his hand.

"Where's Chester?" Papaw hissed, slapping Jacob's ass with the belt again. "What did ye do to Mindy?"

Jacob's throat tickled even worse. He began giggling.

Papaw let the belt fall with a muted thud to the carpet.

Jacob pushed himself off his grandfather's lap and stood. His throat was itching and the only way he could seem to scratch it was laughter, so he laughed.

"Ye sick little freak," Papaw whispered. "What've ye done?"

Jacob couldn't help but laugh; he was such a happy boy sometimes.

-

"Git yer ass in the car," Mamaw Melinda said.

"Where're we goin?" Jacob asked.

"Just git in the fuckin' car," Papaw Russell said.

Jacob got in the backseat of Mamaw Melinda's sedan. His grandparents took the front two seats and his grandmother started the

317

engine. They drove down Black Branch in a charged silence.

Mamaw Melinda's cellphone rang. She picked it up with one hand, steered with the other.

"It's her." Mamaw Melinda handed the cellphone to Papaw Russell, who answered the call.

"We're on our way down there now," he said. "No. No. Stop. Listen, we cain't do it. Just cain't. Ye be down there or the boy will be there on his own. We cain't do it no more."

Papaw Russell ended the call without saying bye.

*They're giving you up*, the voice said.

Jacob felt several things but forced himself to sit still and watch nighttime Appalachia whirl by from the backseat.

"Wait in the car," Mamaw Melinda said.

Jacob watched his grandparents get out and walk over to the only other car in the parking lot. Kim Cady, the social worker, got out and greeted them with an uneasy expression on her face.

Jacob couldn't hear what they were saying but he could tell it was bad from the social worker's reaction.

Papaw stalked away from the social worker, Kim Cady, and stomped across the parking lot back to the car. He threw open Jacob's door.

"Git out," he said.

Jacob undid his seatbelt and stepped out into the cool air. He could hear the Big Sandy bubbling by the lower parking lot of the social services building.

"What's happening?" Jacob asked, then he cringed. He wished he hadn't spoken. Something about asking that question made Jacob feel weak.

"Ye ain't stayin' with us any longer," Papaw said. "Come on."

Jacob followed his grandfather across the blacktop to the social worker and his grandmother, who wouldn't meet Jacob's eyes.

"Jacob," the social worker, Kim Cady, said. "What's been going on?"

Jacob shrugged his shoulders and was ashamed to feel tears sting his eyes.

*Keep it together*, the voice said. *Don't give them the satisfaction of seeing you cry.*

"We'll bring the Medical Passport Book and his things tomorrow," Mamaw Melinda told the social worker. "We're sorry but we gotta do what's righ—best for us."

Jacob and the social worker watched Mamaw Melinda and Papaw Russell walk back across the parking lot to Mamaw Melinda's sedan in silence.

-

Jacob spent the night in a place called the Crisis Stabilization Unit on the outskirts of town. He was given a peanut butter and jelly sandwich and a bag of potato chips then sent to bed. The little twin bed was much more comfortable than the lumpy couch at his grandparents' house.

-

The social worker, Kim Cady, picked Jacob up from the Crisis Stabilization Unit in the morning. She took him through the McDonald's drive-thru for breakfast then, instead of school, Jacob was taken back to the social services building. He rode the elevator up to the fourth floor with the social worker then sat in a small conference room by himself for some time.

Jacob was given a pad of paper and a pen. He began sketching out the details of his next creation. He had the Jack Russell Terrier, Chester's, head and could proceed once the groundhog finished starving to death.

The social worker and another woman, her supervisor, Cynthia Caldwell-Paige, came into the conference room with two binders and two cups of steaming coffee.

"I'm sorry you weren't able to remain with your grandparents," the social worker's supervisor, Cynthia Caldwell-Paige, said. "But our actions always have consequences."

Jacob wanted to smile when he thought about his next creation, the one he'd loosely sketched on the notepad.

*Does it matter what you've done after you've gone?*

His grandparents had given him up, Jacob knew this, but he didn't feel one way or the other about it. He'd live somewhere else just about the same as he'd live there. He'd still have his creations, his displays, the outline of something so large he couldn't quite grasp it yet. All the creations, though satisfying at times, were starting to feel like practice for something larger, more substantial.

"Are you listening?" Kim Cady, the social worker asked.

Jacob looked up from the notepad, then nodded.

"Do you feel angry?" the supervisor asked.

"No," Jacob lied.

"We'd like you to start talking to somebody, a therapist, about how you're feeling and what's going on in your life," the social worker said.

"How does that sound?" the supervisor asked.

Jacob shrugged his shoulders.

*It doesn't matter*, he thought.

"Sure," he said.

"We're finishing up the paperwork for your foster care placement right now," the social worker said. "I think you're gonna like staying with the Faraways. They're good people."

-

They took him back to McDonald's for lunch. They ate in the restaurant looking into the empty Play Place.

-

Jacob was set in an empty office for most of the afternoon. Though they'd shut the door, the walls in the governmental offices were so thin he could nearly make out entire conversations from the social worker, Kim Cady's, office, the next one over. He caught nearly every word exchanged between the social worker and a woman with a pronounced lisp.

"They jus' came down here and gave the baby up?" the woman with the lisp whispered loudly.

"Uh-huh," Kim Cady said. "Said he killed their dog. You remember what I tol' you about that cat at their neighbor's place? Said they think he skinned them *both* alive."

*Fast-Forward X2 Mode / the cutting the cutting the cutting*

"Jaysus fuckin' Chriss!"

"'A real sicko,' they said," the social worker, Kim Cady, whispered. "I'm hopin' the court order'll speed things along. You can see it in him. He's angry. So angry."

"I saw his little . . . drawing. I'm ah be praying for the Faraways."

"Strict as they are, they might be just what the boy needs."

-

"Researchers now believe that early man began to evolve thumbs during the Pleistocene."

Jacob was riveted to the images on the pull-down projector screen. A fairly hairy man-like creature was shown hunched forward over a pile of bones. The next slide showed the creature raise a stone above his head. The next showed the man-like creature holding a bone at a tilted angle, allowing the bone marrow to flow down into his upturned mouth.

"Homo habilis, or the Handy Man, used sharpened rocks and even small hand axes and other tools to facilitate their diet. Researchers think Homo habilis is the first toolmaker."

Jacob heard the other kids snicker every time the narrator used the word "homo" but he easily ignored this.

How could they not see how important this was? This hairy, ugly creature, a distant cousin of the human being, as the video stated several times, helped us develop "opposable thumbs and dexterous fingers," without which all our hands and fingers would be good for was picking lice off each other from the jungle treetops.

Jacob tried to imagine the long road of evolution from the uncouth creature on the screen, hairy knuckles and hairy face, to the perfection of Tanya Miller's long, slender fingers with glittery painted nails.

*It took so long for* that *moment to arrive,* Jacob thought. *It took millions of years for* that *moment to occur.*

He was thinking about her last moments, Tanya Miller's hand wrapped around his own, which was wrapped around himself working and working until he'd finished just as that last puff of air left her open, wrecked mouth.

Jacob felt himself stiffening under the table.

"Bone marrow provided a high-energy supplement to Homo habilis' diet."

Jacob wished he'd brought Tanya Miller's blue and white thumb nail with him but he knew that wasn't a good idea. He'd kept it hidden in his tacklebox with the rusted spinnerbaits and popeye jigs in the hideout.

The more Jacob thought about it, the more he came to agree with the bald man, Randall Adkins: it was a man's world. The video helped prove this. Our male ancestors evolved thumbs and dexterous fingers through our innate sense of animality, *hunters working on prey.*

*Hun-ter.*

Jacob remembered how difficult it had been to dismember her, Tanya Miller. Now he imagined how much more difficult it would've been if he didn't have opposable thumbs and flexible, strong fingers.

*It would've been nearly impossible,* he thought.

He imagined himself as hairy like the humanoid creatures on the screen, working at Tanya Miller's smooth, nearly hairless body with a sharpened rock. He felt his pants squeeze tighter against his growing erection.

The slide switched to one of a woman's hands. She wore bright red nail polish on all ten of her shining fingernails.

Jacob gaped at the screen, his mouth hanging open, drool slowly dribbling over his crooked bottom teeth onto his dry, cracked lips.

"Jacob Hun-ter Goodman is in foster care because even his mother doesn't love him," a voice whispered from behind.

Jacob turned, along with half the heads of the class, to see Rodney Tackett smiling a smile that did not touch his hard, brown eyes.

"Jacob *Hun-ter* is in foster care because nobody in his family loves him," the bully, Rodney Tackett, said.

Hun-ter.

"Cos he's a freak!" Rodney Tackett whispered so loudly he was at the normal level of speech.

Jacob felt cold, clammy. He wished he had skipped school but it was harder now that the foster father, Marcus Faraway, drove them to school every day in his ancient minivan.

*Ignore the bully*, the voice said.

Jacob resisted the urge to turn and face Rodney Tackett, the bully.

*what Rodney Tackett done / what Rodney Tackett done*
*You got back at him*, the voice said, *remember?*

Looking at the beautiful hand on the projector screen, Jacob couldn't help but remember, and remember in Fast-Forward X2 Mode. His penis moved in the black sweatpants, Walmart.

"Even yer grandparents hate ye, fuckface," Rodney Tackett, the bully, said.

"Mr. Tackett, is there something I can do for ye?" Mrs. Grant, the substitute teacher, called from the front of the room.

"Ye hear me, *Hun-ter?*" Rodney Tackett yelled. "Nobody loves ye! Freak!"

*Hun-ter.*

"I know ye killed Tanya, faggot!" Rodney Tackett screamed. "This freak fucks dead animals! He killed my mom's cat!"

Jacob kept facing forward, refusing to flinch at the nearness of the bully's voice or the spit that hit him in the back of the neck, so he didn't see the fist coming. An all-encompassing dull thud sounded from everywhere and he saw floaters dancing like television static. His head thrust forward into the desk and he saw even more stars. Then the fist hit him in his left cheek, just below his closed eye.

"Stop that!" Mrs. Grant squawked, rising up from her chair. "Stop it right now, Rodney Tackett!"

Jacob was knocked to the cool, tiled floor. His head was pounding now without the fists' help. The bully, Rodney Tackett, kicked Jacob in the crotch. Hot, electric pain flashed like lightning strikes. He kicked Jacob in the head.

*pain pain / & more pain*

The bully, Rodney Tackett, was screaming with a crazed vehemence. Jacob couldn't make out any complete sentences.

Jacob squeezed his penis and testicles between both of his hands, hard, trying to use a newer, lesser pain to offset the prior massive one. It wasn't working.

"Fuck ye, ye fuckin' freak!"

The bully, Rodney Tackett, kicked Jacob directly in the teeth. Jacob felt one of his upper teeth break off and hit the back of his throat. He choked and nearly swallowed it.

The bully dropped both of his knees down onto Jacob's chest with enough force to knock the air from Jacob's lungs.

"I burned yer shitty little clubhouse down, faggot!" the bully, Rodney Tackett, screamed just before he started pummeling Jacob with both of his closed fists.

*The hideout!*

"I stomped on all yer faggoty animal dolls too!"

*My creations!*

"Stop it!" Mrs. Grant yelled from very near.

The beating stopped suddenly. Jacob opened his eyes, which he could see were both beginning to swell, and saw the substitute teacher grappling with the bully, Rodney Tackett.

Jacob saw the number 2 pencil, the one he'd sharpened with the Case knife, Ace Hardware, the one he'd been using to alternately take down notes of things that interested him and draw a woman's severed hand with great detail, lying on the ground within reach.

*Take it*, the voice said.

*Use it*, the voice said.

Jacob grabbed the number 2 pencil, Walmart, and swung it with all his force at the bully, Rodney Tackett's, right leg. It caught him directly in his Achilles tendon—Jacob felt the brittle, sharpened point snap—and ripped through until the number 2 pencil, Walmart,

# BIRTH OF A MONSTER

came out the other side of the bully, Rodney Tackett's leg. The blood came quickly, as did the screaming.

## CHAPTER TWENTY
## A FUTURE WITH THE LORD

**"YOU'RE GONNA LIKE PASTOR CLARK,"** Marcus Faraway said. "He's no nonsense and gets straight at the heart of things."

Jacob looked out the window at the squat brick building in front of the minivan. He hadn't been able to make it back to the hideout to see if what the bully, Rodney Tackett, had said was true. The boy had lied so often Jacob assumed he was lying now. It made the future burning of the hideout a possibility though and that made Jacob nervous.

"I'll go get ye signed in then I'll wait in the lobby for ye," the foster father, Marcus Faraway, said, putting the vehicle in park.

Jacob read the sign in front of the building and cringed: His Shining Light Mission.

The foster father, Marcus Faraway, turned off the van and removed his seatbelt.

"Well, come on, Jacob," he said, opening his door. "It's almost time for yer appointment."

Jacob followed the foster father up the concrete walk wishing he were deep in the woods on a hunt.

The bald man, Randall Adkins', words came into Jacob's head: *Hunting is righteous. Hunting is sacred. Hunting is man's safety valve, shit ass.*

Jacob hadn't been able to kill a thing since entering the Faraways' foster home. They had schedules for each child placed there. Jacob had chores and blocked off time for his schoolwork. He hadn't been allotted any "unstructured free time," as some of the other foster kids had been. He hadn't "earned it" yet, which required a week straight of "commendable behavior."

The office had a few plastic chairs and a chest of children's toys. Jacob took a seat and let the foster father, Marcus Faraway, talk to the woman behind the glass window. He picked up a National Geographic and flipped through the pages without really seeing a thing.

The foster father laughed at something the woman behind the glass said, then said something that made the woman laugh.

# BIRTH OF A MONSTER

Jacob's mother popped into his head and he wondered why he should think of her now. She was still locked up as far as he knew. She'd also refused visitation with Jacob. The social worker, Kim Cady, said it was because Christy didn't want Jacob to see her in jail, but Jacob knew this was bullshit. The bald man had hightailed it once the police and social workers got involved and she blamed him for this. Jacob knew this just as he knew the sun rose in the morning. He'd pay for this whole situation one day. He knew that too.

*Does it matter what you've done after you're gone?* Jacob wondered.

He was thinking about Chester, the Jack Russell Terrier.

"Come on back, Jacob," a pompous voice said.

Jacob looked up from the magazine at the short, fat man he guessed was Pastor Clark. The man's face was flushed red and blotchy and he wore a khaki suit that shone at the knees and the elbows.

Jacob dropped the magazine back in the rack and made his way past the foster father and the pompous fat man led him deeper into a shabby office.

"Sit down," Pastor Clark said.

Jacob sat down and looked at the man's nameplate on his desk: Honorable Pastor Clark B. Dennison.

*Honorable?* Jacob wondered what that meant but not enough to ask.

"How're you feeling today, Jacob?"

Jacob thought about it.

"Okay," he said.

"Good, good." Pastor Clark smiled.

Jacob forced himself to remain flat, affectless, though in his head he watched Such A Happy Boy smash the nameplate against the smiling man's face.

"I hear you had a little trouble at school recently," Pastor Clark said. "Want to tell me about it."

*No,* Jacob almost answered.

"A bully picked on me," Jacob said. "Rodney Tackett did."

*what Rodney Tackett done / what Rodney Tackett done*

Jacob saw SAHB swing the sharpened number 2 pencil, Walmart, saw the point break as it entered the bully's right leg. He saw it in Fast-Forward X2 Mode several times before he became aware of the silence in Pastor Clark's office.

326

"What were you just thinking about?" Pastor Clark asked.

"Nothing," Jacob said too quickly.

"Nothing? It certainly looked like something you seemed to enjoy thinking on."

Jacob remained quiet.

"Why do you think that boy—what did you say his name was—Randall? Why do you think Randall was picking on you?"

"It was Rodney Tackett," Jacob said. "Randall Adkins is the bald man."

"The bald man? Who's the bald man?"

Jacob didn't know how to answer—*mom's boyfriend? friend? pimp?* He kept quiet.

"I see," Pastor Clark said after a time. "Well, let's start over then, shall we? My name is Pastor Clark Dennison. I'm a preacher and counselor and run this little operation. We work with families and children in the foster care system."

Jacob thought the man was animatronic. He went on for several moments, *the spiel / spills.* Jacob wasn't listening. He watched the man talk, a bit of white goop forming at the corners of his mouth. Jacob saw several places on the man's cheeks and neck that he missed shaving. Jacob didn't have to shave yet but he couldn't wait to use the sharp blades on the smooth skin of his face and neck.

"So you see," the pastor, Pastor Clark, finished, "we're here for you. You and kids just like you."

*There ain't nobody like me,* Jacob thought and smiled.

The pastor smiled back.

"Good," he said. "Now that we're comfortable, let's talk a little, shall we?"

When Jacob didn't say anything, the animatronic pastor went into another of his canned speeches.

"Appalachia has its problems, God knows," he said. "Poverty, drugs, wickedness, sin. The Lord knows."

The man laughed and Jacob couldn't remember hearing a faker one.

"Like so many people here in Appalachia, you haven't been considering the future. Your future."

Jacob felt like he'd been sucker punched. The man was right. Jacob hadn't considered his future. He'd been so caught up in the present, the foster care placement, the lack of hunting, the long absence from the hideout, that he hadn't thought further than the current day.

"Did you know you have a future?" the preacher, Pastor Clark, asked. "You do. You have a future with the Lord."

-

Christian Talk Radio was the only thing that filled the silence of the van ride back to the foster home.

Jacob thought about what the preacher, Pastor Clark, had told him to do: keep a journal. The thought had never crossed Jacob's mind. It never would've if he hadn't been forced to go to counseling twice a week.

*A journal,* Jacob thought, picking at the corners of the first page of the composition notebook the preacher, Pastor Clark, had given him. The idea made him think of his days stacked up like stones on a riverbank. Each one a day passed. A night spent.

Jacob thought journaling wasn't a bad idea. He'd keep the one the preacher-man, Pastor Clark, wanted him to keep, the one about what he wanted out of life, the goals he'd then make and the steps he'd take to achieve those goals, and another, *his journal*, the *real* one, the one about the hunting, the creations, the displays, the outline, the real life he knew he couldn't tell another living soul about.

*Yes, I'll keep a journal,* Jacob thought, smiling.

-

Jacob started on the real one first. He stole a composition notebook from Walmart. It looked identical to the one the preacher had given him except it was red. He'd stolen a red ballpoint pen as well.

The first lines he wrote in his journal were: I hear that lone babe's cry every night.

-

"Come on back," Pastor Clark said.

Jacob followed the fat man back to his office.

"Have a seat."

Jacob sat, his journal, not the real one, in his lap.

"I see you brought your journal like I asked you to," the preacher, Pastor Clark, said. "I thank you."

Jacob reached the journal out to the preacher, who shook his head and waved the composition notebook away.

"We can just talk about what's in your journal, can't we?"

Jacob set the notebook back down, nodded.

"What do you want from life?" the preacher asked.

Jacob thought about it. He wanted to spend every night hunting and working on his creations. It made him feel actually alive.

"Well now, whatever it was you thought of just now, I'd bet, *if* I were a betting man, it didn't include much if anything about the Lord, now did it?"

Jacob shook his head.

"That's because you haven't heard the news, boy."

The preacher was smiling. He made a big show of holding up one finger with his right hand and leaning over to open a drawer in his desk with his left.

"But I have a gift for you," Pastor Clark said, his right hand dipping behind the desk and coming back up with a leather-bound book. "The Good News!"

Jacob took the book from the preacher, noticing a series of skintags on the man's second chin.

The title on the cover was embossed, filled with gold foil, and read: Holy Bible.

-

The foster father, Marcus Faraway, was beaming when Jacob emerged from the inner quarters of His Shining Light Mission.

"Well now," he said, "what've ye got there?"

Jacob could tell the man knew what he had and was just making a show of it.

"That's the God's Honest Truth right there, Jacob Goodman."

"Amen," the receptionist said.

"Amen," Pastor Clark said, then closed the door.

-

Jacob read of the rape of Dinah and rejoiced at the simplicity of the story. The woman was wanted, the woman was taken, the revenge was exacted. He imagined himself, Such A Happy Boy, and one cohort armed with swords, taking the men of the city, as they lay recovering from their two-day-old circumcisions. He imagined himself smiling as he looted and burned and raped and stole, all of it justified, all of it *sanctified*, Mrs. Horace's Word of the day, *1: to set apart to a sacred purpose or to religious use, 2: to free from sin; 3A: to impart or impute sacredness, inviolability, or respect to; 3B: to give moral or social sanction to; 4: to make productive of holiness or piety.*

Jacob wanted to feel holy. He wanted to feel sanctified.

-

Jacob read the story of Cain and Abel through twice before setting his Bible on the cheap little nightstand next to his twin bed.

He imagined himself as Cain, the first born of Eve, the world's first murderer, the third person to have been cursed by God. What a being. What a life.

*Cain slew Abel,* Jacob sang in his head. *Cain tilled fields of blood / furrowed the sodden soil / not his brother's keeper / but his brother's reaper reaped / only blood and was marked.*

Jacob enjoyed reading the Bible he was given at His Shining Light Mission, and his foster parents typically left him alone when they saw him reading it. When he went to bed at night, he regarded his scars and fading bruises as marks from God, just like Cain's.

Jacob imagined his mother as Eve—stupid, tempted, fallen. He almost had pity for her, but then he remembered women weren't complete persons. *They came / from a rib.*

Sarah Faulkner was older than Jacob, making her the oldest of the four foster children in the Faraway home. She was around Tanya Miller's age. Jacob hated her immediately. Sarah Faulkner was stuck-up and Jacob could tell she thought she was better than him because she had a Kinship Care placement in the works, while he had nothing to look forward to except the unlikely return to his mother's custody. She was seventeen, pregnant and showing.

They washed dishes side by side and Jacob whispered things to her. Things he'd read in the Bible. Things he'd heard about unmarried pregnant girls. Things he'd seen in his head. Things he'd write in his journal that she wasn't capable of understanding. She never told on him but she gave him the dirtiest of looks.

Jacob snuck into the room she shared with the other foster daughter, Jenny, almost every night and watched her sleep while he touched himself. He put his nostrils over her open mouth and breathed in her exhales. He wished he'd taken more time with Tanya Miller, *blue / white*, and felt her last breath the way he felt Sarah Faulkner's when she was asleep.

The night before the court hearing that would determine Sarah Faulkner's placement, Jacob crept into her shared room and breathed in her sleeping breaths. He carefully stroked her dark hair on the pillow, taking a loose strand and pocketing it. He traced the curve of her pregnant belly with his hovering hand. He wanted to know what it looked like inside. He wanted to see the little unborn child and hold it in his hands.

Jacob went through her underwear drawer and took three pairs, one green, one red, and one white and stained a dirty brown in the crotch region, feeling it was his just desserts for the taking of a female from his household.

"There's a lot happening in there, isn't there?" Pastor Clark asked.

Jacob looked up from the Bible in his lap at the preacher, now his court-ordered counselor.

"Yes, sir," Jacob said.

And he meant it. He'd been reading the Bible every day and most nights since it was given to him, and he was enthralled with the amount of violence he found there.

"What've you been studyin' lately?"

This was the way he phrased the question at each of their counseling appointments. Pastor Clark meant the Bible, not Jacob's schoolwork.

"Lot's wife looking back and getting turned into a pillar of salt."

"Ah, that's a powerful one, is it not?"

Jacob nodded his head. He could see it in the movie screen in his head. The fight, the flight, the last glance back at the holy destruction of the wicked city of Sodom, then POOF! a woman-sized salt block.

"He offered up his two daughters to the wicked men of the city to rape."

"Instead of the angels."

Jacob nodded.

"But how did he know they were angels?"

"He knew."

Jacob waited for more to the preacher's response, but there wasn't any.

*Take it as it is*, the voice said.

*Commands / & combat Commandments*

*Don't look back, what a rule*, Jacob thought. *Such sound advice, but so hard to follow.*

Jacob opened his journal and read what he'd written about the story to the preacher.

Lot's wife looked back and God turned her into a pillar of salt. When I look back I feel frozen, stuck just like that.

"Frozen," the preacher, Pastor Clark, said. "That's about it, ain't it? When we spend all day reveling in the past. Worryin' ourselves to death with our pasts."

# BIRTH OF A MONSTER

*Does it matter what you've done after you're gone?*

"It's best we reflect on things we're not proud of only to a certain extent. We all live in the material world, the world of sin. It's all around us, sticky, clinging, attaching itself to us all despite our best intentions."

Jacob was seeing all the sin of the world like a *miasma*, Mrs. Horace's Word of the Day, *1: a vaporous exhalation formerly believed to cause disease; also: a heavy vaporous emanation; 2: an influence or atmosphere that tends to deplete or corrupt; an atmosphere that obscures.*

He wondered how much of it was his.

How much of it was Tanya Miller's? The bully, Rodney Tackett's?

Jacob felt confused.

*Don't look back*, the voice told him. *Keep moving forward.*

"I can tell you're a very serious boy," Pastor Clark said. "I know you've been through a whole lot of . . . stuff. Life can seem overwhelming, but just remember, the Good Lord doesn't give us burdens we cannot carry."

Jacob thought he could hear the crying of a small child.

"Let's leave on a positive note, shall we?" the preacher asked this question at the end of every one of Jacob's appointments. Not one time did he expect a response. "Turn with me to the Book of John, Chapter Four, Verse Seven."

Jacob opened his Bible and read along with the preacher, Pastor Clark.

"Dear friends, let us love one another, for love comes from God. Everyone who loves has been born of God and knows God."

Jacob stepped out into the sunshine and felt dirtied by the cars passing by the parking lot. He felt all the world's sins filling his eyes and lungs. He wished he could live inside the stories from the Bible instead of this modern world of school and bullies and detectives and foster homes. He felt he could understand the Bible more than he could understand the world in which he lived. With the Bible, all you had to do was believe in God and do what he told you to do. It was that simple. If someone took something from you, you avenged yourself. Eye for an eye.

Jacob heard the baby cry again. It took all of his concentration not to flinch at the sound and seek its source. He knew there wasn't a child near him, but the cry came from the open maw of the mineshaft.

*Don't look back*, he told himself. *Don't become a pillar of salt.*

Jacob went straight to his chores when they returned to the Faraways' foster home. He always did the bare minimum, washing most of the crud from the dishes but not taking extra time when the dish called for it. He felt like a machine running low on oil. He was moving but, if he stopped, he was afraid he wouldn't be able to start back up again. He finished the dishes, moved on to sweeping and mopping the small kitchen.

His infection had completely cleared but he still felt a pang of electric pain from time to time, usually after masturbating. He'd taken the last of the antibiotics—he'd required two doses to rid himself of the infection—three days ago. He felt worlds better without the fever. When he thought about the past few weeks everything seemed to speed up into a blur faster than Fast-Forward X2 Mode.

*Don't look back*, he told himself again. *Beware the pillar of salt.*

Jacob finished his chores and rushed back to the Bible and his twin bed.

The cry of the baby woke him. Jacob sat straight up in the bed and was immediately aware he was covered in sweat. His chest heaved like he'd just run a five-minute mile.

The child cried again.

Jacob's body jerked violently at the sound.

The child cried again.

Jacob, shaking, began to cry as quietly as he could manage.

Rodney Tackett's suspension ended and the bully returned to school. He began following Jacob, hobbled up on his crutches, his right leg in a medical boot.

"I know it was ye," the bully, Rodney Tackett, hissed at the back of Jacob's head. "I don't care if nobody believes me. I know it was ye 'n' I'm ah gonna make ye pay, freak."

Jacob went immediately to the first teacher he saw, Mrs. Horace, and told her he'd been threatened by Rodney Tackett and that he was scared. His affect was flat, which he couldn't help.

The bully, Rodney Tackett, was visible at the end of the hall, his awkward movement on the crutches helping the teacher, Mrs. Horace, and Jacob see him easily despite the crowded hall.

"Mr. Tackett!" Mrs. Horace shouted.

The bully stopped and turned around.

"Come here!"

The bully took his time about it.

"Yeah," he said.

"Did you just threaten Mr. Goodman here?"

Rodney Tackett, the bully, bore two fiery holes into Jacob. There was a rage there, Jacob could see it and was sure Mrs. Horace could as well. Jacob wanted to stomp on the bully's head the way the bald man had stomped on that doe's head, just like crushing the meat of a paw-paw between your toes.

"Earth to Mr. Tackett," Mrs. Horace said. "I need you to wipe that dirty look off your face and look at me. Right now, mister!"

The bully finally looked away from Jacob.

"What's your deal, Mr. Tackett?" Mrs. Horace asked, her hands on her hips. "You just get back from suspension and already itching for another fight?"

The bully looked down at his booted foot.

"No, ma'am," he muttered.

"What was that?"

"No, ma'am."

"Good. Well then," Mrs. Horace made a clucking noise in her throat. "If there's no more ill will, which I can see quite clearly to be the case, then why don't we shake hands and move on with our afternoons. Shall we? Shake hands?"

Jacob extended his left hand.

The bully made a face and swatted Jacob's left hand with his right, then took Jacob's right hand and jerked it up and down two quick times. The bully then brushed by him on his crutches, moving in uneven jerks.

"Well then," Mrs. Horace said.

Jacob watched the teacher walk down the hall with clenched fists but an expressionless face.

-

The bully was following him. Jacob was mindful of his surroundings in the woods, well-learned of its sounds, its feel. Jacob could feel the bully moving with difficulty up the steep trail.

Jacob smiled, then climbed even higher.

-

Jacob stepped off the trail, crouched, and waited, straining with all his concentration to listen. Did he hear the click and thump of the

# A.S. COOMER

crutches? He waited nearly ten minutes but heard nothing. He rose to his feet and started back up the mountain.

The bully, Rodney Tackett, was waiting for him at the burnt out remains of the hideout. Jacob could see him sitting on his ass, the leg with the boot extended straight ahead of him.

*Oh God, he did it.*

The baby cried.

The next thing Jacob was aware of was the fact that he was running, full-on sprinting down the mountain path toward what was left of the hideout. He hit the flat ground and picked up his pace.

The bully had enough time to get to his feet and ward off Jacob with his crutches. Jacob paced around the bully, feeling like a hyena, feeling like a wolf, feeling nothing remotely like himself. He wanted to reach out and rend the bully's flesh. He wanted to scratch out the bully's eyeballs and piss in his eyeholes. He wanted to kill the bully, but he couldn't get past the crutches. He grabbed one and was quickly whoomphed with the other.

Jacob gave it up, his hands clutching his knees, his chest heaving. *Fucker!* he yelled in his head. *The fucker! Kill 'im!*

"See?" the bully taunted, sure of himself, absolutely full of himself. "Tol' ye. Tol' ye I burnt it down."

Jacob renewed his attempts to get to the bully, but only for a moment. It was pointless. Blinded by rage, he'd been stupid to think he could overtake the bully, Rodney Tackett, who was much larger and stronger than he was even with the lamed foot, by sightless rage. He'd have to take him unawares.

*The Creations*, he lamented. *The quilt! The outline! Gone. All gone.*

Jacob felt zapped. He let himself fall to his haunches, keeping the bully in his sights, but examining the smoldering remains of the hideout.

"Ye fucking freak!" the bully spat. "Ye really did kill her, didn't ye?"

Jacob didn't answer.

"Didn't ye?" the bully's face was flushed; veins rose up in his forehead and neck as he screamed. "I'll fuckin' kill ye! Kill ye!"

The bully stepped to swing the crutch at Jacob's head, but nearly toppled over when the boot got caught in a gnarled root protruding up from the sandy soil. Jacob easily avoided the blow and put more distance between himself and the bully.

335

"Why?" the bully was crying in his impotent rage now. "Why, got damn it?"

Jacob could see the telling white of bone winking out of the ashes in some places.

*Maybe some of the skulls and bones are still usable*, Jacob thought.

He'd have to find another time to come back, some time the bully wasn't here making his life hell.

*It looks like the burnt out remains of the mineshaft*, Jacob thought, hearing the baby's faint echoing cries.

"Ye sick fuck," the bully cried. "I'll make sure ye never have a moment to yerself again. I'll follow ye everyday 'til I kill ye, cos I will, I will kill ye one day, Jacob *Hun-ter* Goodman. I will kill ye dead."

Jacob remembered stabbing the bully, Rodney Tackett, with the number 2 pencil, Walmart, and wanted to feel that feeling again.

*It's so easy to be bad*, he thought.

The preacher man was right, *Pastor Clark was right. It's so damn easy to be bad.*

Jacob wanted to dent the metal braces of the crutches with the bully's skull.

The bully was staring at Jacob, his breath ragged but slowing. Jacob listened to the air suck in and out of his open, gaping mouth. Jacob imagined jingling the bully's loose teeth in the palm of his hand, *like dice / so nice.*

*It's too damned easy to be bad.*

Jacob turned and started for the path at a trot.

"Get back here!"

The bully shouted and screamed, but Jacob could only hear the cry of the baby he'd left at the bottom of that mineshaft.

-

Jacob opened the Bible at random and read.

Ephesians, chapter five, verse twenty-two through twenty-four: Wives, submit yourselves to your own husbands as you do to the Lord. For the husband is the head of the wife as Christ is the head of the church, his body, of which he is the Savior. Now as the church submits to Christ, so also wives should submit to their husbands in everything.

*Wives should submit to everything*, Jacob read.

He flipped to another section at random.

Genesis, chapter three, verse sixteen: Unto the woman he said, I will greatly multiply thy sorrow and thy conception; in sorrow thou shalt bring forth children; and thy desire shall be to thy husband, and he shall rule over thee.

Jacob turned the pages again.

Genesis, chapter two, verse twenty-two: And the rib, which the Lord God had taken from man, made he a woman, and brought her unto the man.

*Women aren't even complete*, Jacob thought. *God made them from used parts, one of Adam's ribs. No wonder they don't make much sense.*

Jacob stared at his hazy reflection in the night-filled window.

-

The days stacked up like unopened boxes. Jacob learned the routines and schedules of his new home, the Faraways' foster home. He learned when he could sneak off and when he couldn't.

-

The hideout was a total loss. The stained, sticky floor was the only thing remaining and it was scorched and mostly burned as well.

*what Rodney Tackett done / what Rodney Tackett done*

Jacob took to the woods and left his creations on display in several prominent points in the unmarked trails crisscrossing the hills like healed suicide scars. It gave him a sense of pride to come up the steep incline and see the body of a buzzard with the arms and tiny hands of a raccoon and the head of a housecat. The creations stood out against the backdrop of the forest like they were meant to be there—collectively—every bit as much as they did individually. They moved with the fading light of the sun and seemed to jerk and sway under the moon's pale glow.

-

The bully, Rodney Tackett, was waiting for him after school. The bully was no longer on crutches but he moved gingerly in his clean Nike Air Max tennis shoes.

*This is gonna be a problem*, he thought. *How am I gonna shake him now that he's off the crutches?*

Jacob tightened the straps of his backpack, Walmart, and set out across the rapidly emptying student lot at a trot, heading for the woods beyond. The final bell rang its last time, clanging disharmoniously out into the clear afternoon.

Just before slipping into the tree line, Jacob stole a look over his shoulder and saw the bully hurrying after him with a pronounced limp.

*Shit.*

337

# BIRTH OF A MONSTER

Jacob wanted to thrash the forest around him in his impotent rage. The bully was going to follow him, just like he said he'd do, and now how was Jacob supposed to hunt with the bully trailing him? How was he supposed to work on his creations with Rodney Tackett tailing him everywhere he went? Jacob took a left onto a smaller trail, this one avoiding several of his creations he'd put on display from the hemlocks and white oak trees, not wanting the bully to discover and destroy them.

Jacob increased his pace, hearing the bully, Rodney Tackett, stumble and cuss through the briar patch Jacob had just expertly snuck through. He stopped for a moment and listened to the bully cuss.

"Got damn it! Shit!"

Jacob smiled and set out on a jog, knowing the bully wouldn't be able to catch up.

-

He ran until his lungs felt on fire. He unslung his backpack, Walmart, stooped down on his haunches, and let the air rush in and out of his open mouth. He listened but did not hear any footsteps in his wake. The sun was gone; the sky a pale simmer boiling on toward darkness. The air was much cooler now that the sun had sunk. Jacob watched his breath materialize in front of his face then disappear.

Jacob was ruminating on how easy it was to be bad.

*Pastor Clark's always telling me how easy it is to be bad,* Jacob thought, *and he's right. But that last verse he read to me yesterday is so confusing.*

Romans, chapter twelve, verse two: Do not be conformed to this world, but be transformed by the renewal of your mind, that by testing you may discern what is the will of God, what is good and acceptable and perfect.

*If God has a plan and made each of us in His image, then why doesn't this include what I am and what I do?*

Jacob was thinking of his creations.

*I do have a knack for this stuff,* he thought. *I mean if I came to it naturally, isn't that good and acceptable and perfect? Doesn't that mean God made me and gave me these talents? To hunt and kill and create?*

*Thou shall not kill.*

The Bible seemed full of these inconsistencies. What was Jacob supposed to do? Turn his back on the only thing that felt natural and right?

*Hunting is righteous. Hunting is sacred. Hunting is man's safety valve, shit ass,* the bald man had said and Jacob now fully believed him.

Jacob trapped a raccoon and skinned it alive. Its screams pierced the night like a lone siren's wailing.

-

The classroom was empty through the little pane of glass on the door. Jacob tried the knob. It was unlocked, so he entered, pulling the door shut behind him. Mrs. Horace's classroom didn't look as big when it was empty of children. He went over to the chalkboard and started breaking each piece of chalk.

The Word of the Day was *iniquity*: *1: gross injustice: wickedness 2: a wicked act or thing: sin.*

Jacob broke the halved chalk into even smaller pieces.

*Den of iniquity* was a term Pastor Clark had used for boys of his age running around in packs and doing drugs. Jacob wondered what it'd be like to run in a pack like wolves. *It must be demeaning to have to rely on others*, he thought. Jacob much preferred keeping to himself. He was often disappointed, but he only had himself to blame and that made it a little easier.

*Or did it?* he wondered.

Jacob lifted a piece of broken chalk to his mouth and tasted it.

"What're you doing in here?" a sharp voice asked.

Jacob dropped the chalk from his lips, felt a string of pasty spit dribble down onto his pimple-covered chin.

"Jacob Goodman, what're you doing in here?"

Mrs. Beasley stood in the doorway, looking at him with both of her hands on her hips.

"Were you eating that chalk?"

She stepped into the room and looked from the piece of chalk on the tiled floor to Jacob then at the dozens of broken pieces lining the chalkboard.

"Why on earth would you sneak in here just to break a bunch of chalk?"

Jacob hadn't thought about it, he'd just seen the empty room and acted, so he kept quiet.

"Hateful thing," Mrs. Beasley said. "Why would you want to break all of Mrs. Horace's chalk? Answer me!"

Jacob's silence seemed to grate on her, which made Jacob want to remain all the quieter.

"Come on then, Mr. Silence," Mrs. Beasley said. "Let's go talk to Mr. Harold. It'll be detention again, I suppose."

# BIRTH OF A MONSTER

The foster father, Marcus Faraway, loved his after-dinner toothpicks. It was one of the few things the foster family splurged on: mint-flavored toothpicks. While Jacob and the other three foster children went about their after-dinner chores, cleaning up the kitchen and living room and doing laundry, the foster father, Marcus Faraway, sat at his place at the head of the table and read the newspaper while picking his teeth with the mint-flavored toothpicks.

Jacob waited until all the lights in the foster home went out. He waited until he could hear nothing but soft snores and the ticking of the cuckoo clock at the end of the hall and got up and made his way on bare feet to the kitchen. He found the box of toothpicks and picked them out, one by one, and snapped them in half. He was nearly halfway through when the kitchen light suddenly came on.

The foster father, Marcus Faraway, stood squinting in the bright light at Jacob.

"What're you doing?" the foster father asked, then he saw. "What? Why?"

Jacob thought about telling Marcus Faraway it was just so easy to be bad, but he decided against it.

He took the whipping without flinching or crying. Spankings, though not new to Jacob, were not nearly as bad as what he'd experienced in the past.

Jacob raised his hand and, when Mrs. Horace called on him, asked to use the bathroom. When he wasn't sleeping, Jacob liked to roam the halls. With the foster father driving him to school, Jacob found skipping full days to be a thing of the past. He hadn't decided if he was going to dip out and not return to class yet. He thought he'd go take a look at the book fair now that it was empty during classes, opening only for the periods in between, and make his decision down there. Plus, there might be something worth stealing.

Jacob found he was taking things all the time now. He didn't even think about it anymore. If there was something placed within his reach and nobody was looking, he'd steal it. It didn't even have to be anything good or of use to him. He stole several Chapsticks, pencils, pens, folded notes, baseball cards, toys, anything and everything. Every time the foster family, the Faraways, took him with them shopping, Jacob stole candy bars and magazines and comics and even a bottle of Stetson cologne, which he now put on every day.

The book fair was in the auxiliary gym, just off the backside of the cafeteria, quiet now that it was between breakfast and lunch periods. Jacob found the doors unlocked. There was a circle of fold-out tables loaded with stacks of books and stuffed animals and Legos and Build-Your-Own Model sets. Jacob languidly made his way from table to table, taking a plastic T-Rex that fit in his front pocket, a pocketbook of jokes, and a sticky hand.

The front table had a small lockbox with the key sitting in the keyhole. He opened it, saw several rows of bills rubber-banded together—*has to be at least a hundred dollars here, more probably!*—and a set of car keys. Jacob put the keys next to the T-Rex in his pocket. He saw several checks under the larger of the bills, which Jacob immediately began to rip to pieces.

Then he got an idea, which caused him to smile. On the lined paper showing sales, Jacob picked up the pen and wrote: Rodney Tackett. Then: My Prancing Pony book. Jacob finished ripping up the last of the checks, then took the box with him back the way he came. He stopped every fifteen feet or so and left a handful of bills and pieces of ripped-up checks on the floor. He made a perfect little path directly to the bully, Rodney Tackett's, locker, where he stuffed the remaining ten and twenty-dollar bills through the slats.

Jacob then went back down the hall, into the auxiliary gym, and out of the back doors to the row of dumpsters. He retrieved the lighter from his pocket and set a halved check on fire and set it, blazing, back into the lockbox. Once a good little fire was raging inside the lockbox, Jacob opened the lid of the dumpster nearest him and threw the box inside. There was a whooshing sound then flames began licking the midmorning air.

He forced himself to walk back through the open back door of the auxiliary gym, down the hall, and back to class. He handed the teacher the hall-pass without a trace of emotion on his face, but imagining a smile, *a smile a mile long*, in his head.

-

"It was Jacob Goodman, I swear!"

Jacob heard the bully screaming from behind the closed door as he approached. Mrs. Horace was escorting him to the principal's office. She knocked on the door and the bully, Rodney Tackett, stopped screaming and cried loudly.

The door opened and Principal Williams' dour face greeted them. "Have a seat, Mr. Goodman," he said. "Thank you, Mrs.

Horace."

The vice principal was leaning against the windowsill beside a police officer. The bully was sitting in one of the two chairs in front of the desk. Jacob sat down in the other.

"What's going on here, Jacob?" Principal Williams sat, slamming the door shut.

Jacob thought the bully looked overly righteous with his slanted sneer and wet eyes.

The vice principal pushed himself off the windowsill and put both of his clenched fists down on the tabletop.

"He asked ye a question, boy," Vice Principal Harold said.

"I don't know," Jacob said.

"Which one of you started that fire in the dumpster?" Principal Williams asked. "Huh?"

"Or was it the both of ye?" the vice principal asked.

"I had nothin' to do with it," the bully shouted. "I tol' ye. He's a psycho! He killed my momma's cat!"

"He did what?"

"Killed a cat?" the cop asked.

Jacob kept his face blank.

"He did! He killed Tanya too!"

"Stop it, Rodney!" Vice Principal Harold said.

"Hush now, Rodney," Principal Williams said.

The room sank into an unsteady silence. Jacob listened to the bully gulp breaths, tears and snot tracing clear lines across his face.

*Mine*, he thought, staring at the bully, *what Rodney Tackett done / what Rodney Tackett done.*

*Mine*, he repeated in his head. *Mine.*

-

Jacob read the Bible during his long days in in-school detention.

He flipped to the book of Peter and read: Do not repay evil with evil or insult with insult. On the contrary, repay evil with blessing, because to this you were called so that you may inherit a blessing.

*The bully's death will be a blessing. In this, I am holy.*

*what Rodney Tackett done / what Rodney Tackett gonna get?*

He turned to the first book of Samuel, sixth chapter, and read of God killing fifty men because they looked into His Ark.

He wished he still had the hideout. Jacob wished he could make people disappear. Then he thought of her, Tanya Miller.

*Tanya Miller / Fast-Forward X2 Mode*

*blue white / white blue*

*I kind of did*, he realized. I made her—*Tanya Miller / Tanya Miller*—disappear.

Jacob let the book open at random and read: Blessed is the man who destroys you as you have destroyed us. Blessed is the man who takes your babies and smashes them against the rocks!

*I will kill Rodney Tackett*, Jacob decided. *I will lure him out into a trap and I will kill him.*

Jacob smiled down at his Bible despite the faint crying he couldn't help but still hear.

*He has bullied me too long. I will not allow it to continue.*

Jacob wished he were alone so he could say the words out loud. They felt so powerful reverberating around in his head. They felt as heavy as etched stone tablatures too.

He turned to the Book of Matthew, fifth chapter, read and felt vindicated: Happy are those who are persecuted because they are good, for the Kingdom of Heaven is theirs.

Jacob smiled down at his Bible. He was just such a happy boy sometimes.

-

*Heaven is mine*, Jacob thought.

He waited for the bully in the hallway after the last bell, pretending to go through the things in his locker until he felt Rodney Tackett's hate-filled eyes on him. Then he shut his locker, adjusted the straps of his backpack, Walmart, and set out down the hall toward the exit.

"Freak!" the bully called out.

Jacob pushed open the doors and the bright sunshine felt good on his face. He briefly closed his eyes and savored the moment before starting across the parking lot at a jog. Just before he stepped into the woods he stole a glance over his shoulder and saw the bully following him at a trot.

*Good*, he thought. *Today's the day Rodney Tackett pays for what he did to me.*

A phantom pain pinged wildly in his groin and, for a moment, Jacob was sure the infection had returned to his crotch.

Jacob took the path that led over the first ridge behind the school and the second branch that led off toward the little valley with the burnt-out remains of the hideout. It was a good two-mile hike to the place where Jacob hid the trap: the place where the slope of the trail met the bottom of the valley. Jacob adjusted his speed to a brisk walk and put some space between the bully and himself.

The woods were filled with afternoon sunlight, which came down in long slants from the angle of the soon-to-be setting sun. Jacob felt the rays splash across his face and smiled. The woods always held such wonder and comfort to Jacob.

Somewhere not far off, farther down the trail, Jacob heard the bully fighting his way through the thick huckleberry bushes, cursing and huffing loudly.

*Not much further*, Jacob realized, seeing the path down the ridgetop to the little valley and the burned down hideout.

He'd never tried one of his traps on a human. Jacob had a moment of fleeting panic the trap wouldn't work, but it passed quickly.

*If it doesn't*, Jacob thought, *there are other means.*

He had the hatchet, Walmart, in his backpack, Walmart. The rope from the trap was stolen from Ace Hardware, which Jacob had hidden under similarly colored leaves, pinecones, and pine needles. He stepped over the rope and out into the clearing. He stopped and watched the bully descend the steep slope.

"Ye forget yer little clubhouse was burnt, faggot?" the bully yelled, his breath heavy as he worked his way down the path. "Huh? Forget I burned it to the fuckin' ground?"

Jacob kept his face expressionless though the corners of his lips wanted to curl up into a smile.

"I'm thinkin' it's high time I beat yer ass, freak," Rodney Tackett said, his right foot landing directly in the center of the trap. "Not like last time. This time it's jus' a good, old-fashioned ass-whippin—"

The trap sprung, whipping the bully off his feet. Jacob watched Rodney Tackett's head bounce off the sandstone then he was hanging upside down with a little cloud of dust from the sudden motion settling all around him.

"Wha—" he stammered.

Jacob watched the young pine bow with the weight of the bully, but it did not snap. The bully twirled four feet off the ground. He tried using his hands to find some purchase on the sandy soil beneath him but it was just out of reach.

Jacob walked slowly over to where the bully hung.

"Well, then," he said, smiling down at the bully. "Mine."

-

"I'll fuckin' kill ye!" the bully, Rodney Tackett screamed.

His voice bounced around the little valley. Jacob turned around and around, dust kicking up from his miss K-Swisses, laughing. The bully's voice echoed around the little valley.

"Let me down right this fuckin' moment," the bully's voice was getting higher as he continued. "I mean it, freak! Let me down right now!"

Jacob walked over the hanging bully, who was desperately trying to keep Jacob in view and his shirt from covering his face, and punched him in the stomach. Jacob felt all the air rush out of the bully with the blow.

*Jesus but that felt good*, Jacob thought.

He punched the bully again, this time on the side of his ribcage.

The bully made a strangled sound in his throat as he tried to scream without any air in his lungs.

Jacob pulled the bully's shirt over his face, then punched him in his white belly.

"Stop it!" the bully shrieked, when he could find the air to scream. "Stop it! Quit!"

Jacob kicked the bully directly in his head, which was still covered by his shirt. The blow sounded hollow. Jacob was delighted. He kicked the bully, Rodney Tackett, there again, then again.

-

The bully woke with a start. Jacob had hogtied him with the same rope that'd trapped him to begin with and set him in the center of the stained, sticky, and scorched floor of what was left of the hideout. The bully tried to speak but Jacob had stuffed most of the bully's shirt into his mouth.

"Rodney Tackett," Jacob said slowly, the words feeling awkward and unseemly on his tongue. "Rodney Tackett."

The bully stopped struggling when he heard his name. His eyes came to focus on Jacob and Jacob was delighted to see fear there.

*Good*, the voice said. *Make him pay for what he done.*

*what Rodney Tackett done / what Rodney Tackett done*

"Ye hurt me," Jacob told the bully. "Ye hurt me real bad."

The bully struggled against his bindings but Jacob had triple-knotted the rope. There would be no getting out of them.

"Ye ever read the Bible, bully?" Jacob asked.

The bully continued his struggles against the rope.

"Huh? I just started and I can't seem to get enough of the Good

News," Jacob said. "Take Matthew five-ten for example: Blessed are those who are persecuted because of righteousness, for theirs is the kingdom of Heaven. Isn't that nice?"

The bully was more focused on freeing himself than listening so he kicked him in the head. Not hard, just hard enough to get his attention.

"Or if that's not speaking to ye, what about John fifteen-eighteen: If the world hates ye, keep in mind that it hated me first."

Jacob dropped to his haunches to be closer to the bully.

"And ye do, don't ye?" he asked. "Hate me. Ye really do, huh?"

The bully's face flushed bright red as he struggled against his bindings.

Jacob thought the little floor sitting in the middle of the clearing kind of looked like a stage.

*a little pagan alter / out in God's country*

Jacob took out the Case knife, Ace Hardware, and made a show of opening it before the bully. At the sight of the knife, Ace Hardware, the bully redoubled his efforts to break free from his bonds.

Jacob made a tsking noise and leaned in closer to the bully with the blade extended.

"Ye don't want me to cut ye, that it?"

The bully nodded his head and yelled something unintelligible behind the shirt in his mouth.

"Don't want me to cut ye like I did Tanya Miller?" he asked, lifting the shirt from the bully's face.

At the sound of his cousin's name, the bully, Rodney Tackett's, face blanched and his struggles ceased.

"Well, here's the thing," Jacob said, "I think I'm supposed to regardless of what ye want. The urge is in me and God made me in His Image. I think that means I'm supposed to do what I'm supposed to do."

The bully pissed himself. Jacob watched it happen and smiled.

"'Bless those who persecute ye; bless and do not curse,' the Bible says," Jacob said. "I'm going to bless ye, Rodney Tackett. I'm going to give ye the blessing of death. Living is a curse that I'll help ye break."

Jacob poked the bully's cheeks with the edge of the Case knife, Ace Hardware. A droplet of blood bloomed on the blade then ran down the bully's tear-slickened cheeks. Jacob poked the bully's other cheek.

*Looks like he's bleeding tears,* Jacob thought, wiping the blade on his pants and returning it to his front pocket.

*Purify,* the voice said. *Settle up the bully's sins.*

Jacob walked over to the edge of the stained, sticky floor to the backpack, Walmart, and removed the rusty hacksaw he'd stolen from shop class.

"Ye destroyed most of my other tools," Jacob told the bully, "but I took this yesterday and I doubt it'll ever be missed."

Jacob held up the hacksaw for the bully to see. The rust glinted dully in the afternoon sunshine.

"Do ye believe in God?"

Jacob crouched down at the bully's side.

"Do ye?" he poked the bully in the stomach with the blunt side of the hacksaw.

The bully vigorously nodded his head.

"That's good. Have ye read the book of Psalms?"

The bully yelled something behind the shirt.

"The Lord tests the righteous, but His soul hates the wicked and the one who loves violence," Jacob said. "Ye hurt me. Ye remember what ye did?"

The bully was crying now. Snot and tears were smearing alongside the blood from both of his cheeks.

"Beloved, never avenge yourselves, but leave it to the wrath of God, for it is written, 'Vengeance is mine, I will repay,' says the Lord."

Jacob leaned in close to the bully's face and whispered, "I am the wrath of God."

The bully, Rodney Tackett, passed out. Jacob had never seen anybody faint before and relished the moment, replaying it immediately in his head in Fast-Forward X2 Mode and wishing the bully would wake back up so he could make him pass out again.

Jacob wondered if there was a point, *when you cut so deep,* that you absolutely couldn't remain conscious. He must be getting close to that point.

The bully woke up and screamed. Then he blacked back out.

Jacob couldn't help but smile; he was such a happy boy sometimes.

-

SAHB didn't bother returning the bully's t-shirt to his mouth after he puked it out. SAHB stopped sawing to watch the twin streams of vomit erupt through both of the bully's nostrils, then the shirt seemed to jerk in the bully's mouth and it was forced out by more vomit.

The bully screamed. No words, just a plaintive wail before passing out again.

SAHB went back to sawing, which he hadn't remembered to be such slippery work.

-

"God help me! Help!"

"Have I not commanded ye? Be strong and courageous."

"Stop this! Oh God!"

"Do not be frightened, and do not be dismayed, for the Lord yer God is with ye wherever ye go," SAHB told the bully, whose left leg was still clinging somehow to the hip joint.

The bully dry-heaved then lost consciousness again.

Jacob dropped the hacksaw and separated the leg with his hands. He looked at the cracked, cut bone clasped firmly in his blood-covered hands.

*Humans evolved thumbs to get to the marrow*, Jacob thought. *We made tools to make it that much easier.*

A verse he read during detention popped into his head.

"The heart of man plans his way, but the Lord establishes his steps."

-

Jacob cut the bully's arms and legs off and put them in two trash bags that he duct-taped closed.

"For I know the plans I have for ye, declares the Lord, plans for welfare and not for evil, to give ye a future and a hope."

Unintelligible screaming.

"God has abandoned ye to me."

-

Jacob did not notice the moment the bully died. There'd been screaming but even that stopped eventually.

*Maybe there is an amount of pain a body can endure before consciousness must be lost. A point just before death where you're in limbo, purgatory.*

Jacob found it strange how unlike a person the bully's body felt. It was just meat and bone. Stringy bits of fat and pools of gelatinous blood and other liquid matter.

Jacob found he could carry all four bags of the bully, Rodney Tackett's, body at one time. He thanked the lord for this blessing.

He'd only have to make the one trip to the mineshaft.

Halfway up the mountain, one of the trash bags got snagged on a bramble. Jacob set the other three down to carefully undo the briar. When he bent back down to retrieve the other three bags, the first broke, spilling Rodney Tackett's disembodied arms onto the sandstone.

Jacob stooped and picked up the bully, Rodney Tackett's, left hand, which had the front portion of the ulna still attached.

*Look how pitiful his hands had been*, Jacob thought. *Not as developed and dexterous as these.*

Jacob marveled at the workings of his fingers in the moonlight.

*Use your shirt*, the voice said.

Jacob took off his shirt and used it to carry the bully, Rodney Tackett's, arms and hands up the mountain path to the mineshaft. He watched each piece slip into darkness, smiling broadly. He felt giddy, nearly laughing out loud.

## CHAPTER TWENTY-ONE
## A HANK WILLIAMS SONG


**BARBARA AVA FINDLEY WAS NEARLY** late to the morning case roundup. By the time she made it to the boardroom, there weren't any chairs left. She leaned against the wall near the back, not peeved because Sergeant Ellis had made her a detective the week before, after five long years of uniform patrol, and she still felt she had to earn a place at one of the tables beside the other detectives in the room.

"Yipee-ki-yay, cowboys," Sergeant Mark Ellis said, entering the room.

He saw Barbara and froze.

"And cow . . ." he paused, "woman."

All the eyes in the room turned to Barbara and she hated herself for it but felt her face flush crimson. She forced herself to give the Sergeant a nod of acknowledgement.

*Cowwoman?*

There were a few snickers and Barbara tried not to hear any of the catcalls and snide remarks. She'd thought the promotion to detective would've eliminated all this, but if the first week was any gauge, she'd never climb out of the muck of being a woman on the police force.

"Alright, boys," the Sergeant said, stepping behind the small podium at the front of the room. He opened a manila folder and pulled out some pages.

"And girl," some wiseass chimed in.

"Yes, yes," Sergeant Ellis said. "And girl. Listen, we got a lot to get through so let's quit fiddlin' sticks, huh?"

He looked across the room at Barbara when he said it. She felt new blood blanket her face.

Roger Bailey and Dougie Hall thought this was particularly funny. They each added their twist for the cops around them to enjoy.

"Alright. Enough," Sergeant Ellis snapped. "Let's get to it."

The briefing went by quickly with Sergeant Ellis assigning a pharmacy stakeout to Barbara and her new partner but longtime mentor, Hank Henry Gray. Hank had been there for Barbara since her first days on patrol, helping her through all the hurdles that come with being a newly minted officer of the law and the ones that came with acclimating to the life.

"Fill Gray in whenever he decides to make his presence known," Sergeant Ellis said, scanning the room for Hank and not finding him present.

There were childish oohs and aahs and somebody, she thought it Dougie Hall, sang "sitting in a tree K-I-S-S-I-N-G" to much guffaws and knee slapping.

"Pipe it," Sergeant Ellis said, but his normally craggy visage was tinted with the hint of a smile. "That is all. Dismissed."

Barbara waited until the rest of the room had cleared, overhearing the comments she was meant to hear but refusing to acknowledge a single one.

"Sergeant Ellis? Can I have a word?"

"What is it, detective?" Sergeant Ellis asked, not looking up from the podium, where he was returning the papers to the manila folder.

"Ferrell and Smith just caught that homicide from yesterday," Barbara said, trying to take some of the eagerness out of her voice. "Does that mean I'm next up?"

"You'll get your cases, don't you worry, Findley," Sergeant Ellis said. "Just do the work assigned to you."

With that, he left Barbara standing in the empty room.

Barbara waited for her partner in the parking lot, wishing she had a pack of cigarettes. She'd stopped smoking twice now, this time for the past month without any hiccups. The unmarked car pulled up to the curb and Hank rolled down the passenger side window.

"Ready?" Henry Hank Gray asked.

Barbara got inside.

"Miss anything in briefing?" Hank asked.

Barbara shook her head.

"Not really."

"You sure?"

"Yep."

"Okay. Then off to Righteous Drugs?"

Barbara nodded.

"Righteous Drugs."

Hank eased the car into the light traffic on Highway 62, heading away from town.

"You sure there's nothing bothering you, Fin?"

Only her partner and her foster family used the nickname and the familiarity of it at that moment was just the thing Barbara did not need. She felt tears sting up into her eyes and she forced them away.

*Stop being a baby*, she told herself. *Toughen up! So the boys treated you like a little girl. So they make fun of you and have zero respect. Get over it. That's how it is. That's how it works.*

"Fin?"

She sniffed loudly and cleared her throat, forcing her voice a little lower and hating herself for it.

"Yeah, I'm good. What held you up this morning?"

"Ah, the deflection. Nice," Hank said, turning off 62 onto the Bypass. "Gabriella couldn't find her lucky sweater. Spent all morning going through the laundry room."

"Oh, man," Barbara said.

She'd seen the mess that was the Gray family's laundry room. With three children and two working parents, the room was a constant wreck.

"Tell me about it," Hank said, backing the unmarked car into a spot at Righteous Drugs.

They both stared out at the bustling pharmacy and sighed.

"And we wait," Hank said.

"Yep," Barbara said.

The tip had been right. They didn't have to wait long. The white cargo van pulled up to the side door and a man in a khaki uniform got out. He stretched then went around the building to the front door and entered the pharmacy.

"There's our delivery of prescription drugs," Hank said.

A red Dodge Dart pulled into the spot to the left of the cargo van.

"And there's our would-be robber," Barbara said. "Robbers, I should say."

There were two people in the Dart but neither Hank nor Barbara could see them clearly because of the glare of the sun on the Dart's windshield.

"What's this?" Hank asked as the Dart's passenger side door

opened and a man got out. He took a quick scan of his surroundings then walked around to the backside of the van.

"This is it," Barbara said.

The man was holding something in both of his hands.

"Crowbar!" Hank and Barbara said at the same time.

Then they were out of the unmarked car and sprinting across the asphalt. The driver of the Dart, Barbara now saw that it was a woman, began honking its horn in rapid successions of threes.

*Honkhonkhonk! Honkhonkhonk!*

They split at the front of the van, Hank going left, Barbara right. The man was still wrenching at the locked backdoors of the delivery van, trying his best to make a quick job of it or so high he hadn't heard the Dart's honking.

"Freeze!" Hank yelled.

"Put it down!" Barbara said.

The man spun toward Hank, who was closer, and swung the crowbar. Barbara was in the middle of holstering her weapon so she could retrieve and use the taser when it happened. She nearly dropped the gun. She'd got it caught somehow on the holster, *like an idiot*, one hand going for the taser, the other the gun.

Hank dodged the crowbar and smacked the top of the man's hand with the butt of his gun, which sent the crowbar clanging across the pavement.

The man screeched in pain.

Barbara used the moment to look down, get the gun in the holster, settled the taser back in its place, and retrieve the handcuffs from her belt. She kicked the back of the man's right knee, which dropped him to his knees. She was just getting ready to handcuff the man when Hank yelled.

"Secure the driver! I've got 'im."

*Idiot*, Barbara thought. *Secure the driver. Rookie mistake, Barbara!*

The woman behind the wheel was gunning the gas, the engine revving wildly, and jerking at the steering wheel but she'd seemed to have forgotten she was in park. Barbara threw open the driver's side door and yanked the woman out of the car, which had been slightly awkward for both of them because the woman had been wearing her seatbelt. Barbara had to reholster her weapon, undo the belt buckle, then throw the woman onto the asphalt.

She dropped her left knee onto the woman's back, retrieved the cuffs from her belt once again, and got both of the woman's track marked arms behind her and cuffed.

"What's going on?"

The driver of the cargo van and an employee of the pharmacy were standing on the sidewalk, the side door open behind them.

During the scuffle, the Dart had been thrown into neutral. Barbara, oblivious to this, wasn't aware of the car slowly rolling away from the crime scene like a guilty perp. She only realized what had happened after all the honks and the squealing of tires.

"Jesus, Fin," Hank said over the shoulder of the perp.

The Dodge Dart had rolled down the slight decline of the parking lot, right through the intersection, and into the ditch of an empty field about two hundred yards from where they all stared, stunned, in the Righteous Drugs parking lot.

The couple blubbered and cried their laments to each other in the backseat on the drive to the Hardin County Detention Center while Barbara cursed herself up and down for getting overly excited.

*Like always. You're always one step ahead of yourself, Barbara. You gotta learn to take each step as it comes.*

She also needed to stop being so negative. That's what her therapist had to keep reminding her, *twice a month at $150 an hour.*

But wasn't that negative too? To worry about the price tag of your mental health?

"Everything alright?" Hank asked for the second time that day.

She nodded.

"Yep."

They rode in silence, listening to the would-be robbers' declarations of love and remorse.

"How's Kenny and Luanne?" Hank asked.

"They're good," Barbara said, though she'd been so busy, wrapped up in the new promotion, she hadn't visited her former foster parents in the last few weeks.

"I been meaning to stop by," Hank said. "Say hi, how are ya, shoot the shit."

*Me too,* Barbara thought.

"Ye should," she said. "They'd love to see ye."

*Ye,* she heard her own eastern Kentucky accent and cringed. It was one of the other things they all dogged her for, that and being a woman.

"Stop beating yourself up over there," Hank said, pulling into the jail's turnoff. "We're both good. They're good. We're good."

Barbara nodded. While she hadn't violated any departmental policy, she'd been dimwitted and unobservant. She chided herself once again: *idiot!*

Hank put the car in park.

"Well, since we're good, let's get good and gone."

The couple, seeing the familiar surroundings of the house of detention suddenly became combatant with the officers. Barbara was kicked twice, once in the sternum and once in her right breast.

*That'll leave a mark*, she thought as she reached inside the car and grabbed a handful of shirt.

She got the woman out of the car bucking and kicking. Then, out of nowhere, the woman was holding an uncapped needle in both of her handcuffed hands. She spun in a circle warding off Barbara and several of the guards who'd heard the commotion and come out for assistance.

"Jesus! Where'd she get that?"

"Didn't y'all pat her down?"

"Did you check her?"

"That's a fuckin' dirty needle, y'all!"

Barbara had patted her down, did a thorough search, she'd thought.

*But then how does she have a weapon?* she thought. *She must've had it down the crack of her ass is all I can come up with.*

The woman was hit with the taser. One of the guards did it. She dropped like a sack of potatoes, the needle skittering across the floor to land near a drain.

Barbara let the guards scoop her up and restrain her, now that the fight had been zapped clean out of her. Barbara wondered if she should've tasered her herself? Had she been slow, yet again, in her in-the-moment thinking?

They started in on the endless paperwork.

-

"Fin. Hey Fin, you alright?" Hank asked for the third time that day.

"Yeah. Sorry. Tired, I guess," she said, then she saw the clock on the wall. "Shit. I gotta go. I'm already late for date night."

"Uh-oh," Hank said.

"Uh-oh is right."

"P-Boy gonna be pissed?"

P-Boy was Hank's nickname for Barbara's husband of three

years: Perry.

"When is he not?"

There was an awkward silence.

"Where're y'all goin' for dinner?" Hank asked.

"Supposed to go to that new place in the square."

"Flywheel?"

"No, the Italian place."

"Oh. Yeah, I heard that place was nice."

"I'm already gonna be late if I leave now."

"See ya tomorrow. Take it easy on yerself."

"Ye too," Barbara said then cringed. "I mean you have a nice night and I'll see ye tomorrow."

"Jesus."

"Bye."

Barbara pulled into the parking lot, luckily found a close spot, and entered the restaurant already fifteen minutes late. She told the hostess of their reservation and was told their table was waiting.

Perry wasn't there.

"Care for a drink while you're waiting?"

"No, thank ye," Barbara said. "He shouldn't be too long."

The phone took a few moments to refresh the map but it eventually showed Barbara that her husband was at the La Quinta Inn near the interstate.

*What? Why?* They hadn't been getting along lately—*when had they ever really, Barb?*—but Barbara didn't think that meant he was at the La Quinta Inn because he was having an affair.

*Did she?*

He'd been so distant lately.

*Call him*, she thought. *'N' if he lies about where he is, then ye'll know.*

*No. Quit being so negative. If he's there, he's there on business.*

*At the La Quinta Inn?*

"Start ya off with a drink, while ya wait?"

Barbara looked up from the phone. The waitress was young and blonde.

"Rye and ginger ale," Barbara said. "Please."

Barbara refreshed the screen.

*La Quinta Inn & Suites.*

*Shit.*

The drink came.

*He's been so . . . aggressive when he's not distant*, she thought. He'd nearly lost his shit when she told him she couldn't make the Mulberry Club's luncheon in his honor last week. *Or was that the week before?*

*Jesus, Barbara. You're working too much.*

That's definitely what Perry would say.

Perry hated that Barbara was a cop. At first, when they'd only been on a handful of dates, he'd thought it was cute. Endearing, even, but that hadn't lasted long. He'd been trying to get her to quit for the entire past year.

"Another rye and ginger ale?"

Barbara nodded, not looking up from her phone.

He'd acted like he was going to charge her then, she remembered. Like some white-collared bull. He'd stomped his feet, his face red, red, red, waved his clenched fists around in tight, angry, little circles.

Not that Barbara was scared of him and didn't think she could defend herself. She could. Her job taught her plenty. Her upbringing too.

*But he'd been so angry*, she remembered, sipping the bourbon. Like he wasn't but one half-step away from losing all control and wanting to hurt her. She'd seen it in his rage-filled eyes, which showed more white than was normal.

*Me. Me. Me*, the eyes shouted. *It's all about me!*

Barbara realized she was appalled by her husband's recent behavior.

*Might makes right and all that*, she thought. *What trash! And if he's cheatin' on me, I swear to God . . .*

*But you've been so busy*, she thought. *You've been working all the time, rarely having time for him, definitely not cooking and cleaning and helping out much around the house.*

*Is that my job too?*

She felt she was only home to sleep and bathe. The place was just barely above a wreck and that was nearly all thanks to Perry.

*Who earns the Big Bucks, as he often says. Perry Who Earns the Big Bucks Finley better not be cheating on me. That's the last thing I need, a detective who can't even uncover her husband's infidelities. I'll be the laughingstock of the department.*

*You care more about what other cops think than you do about whether your husband is having an affair.*

*Oh shit.*

Barbara had to bite her lower lip to keep the tears at bay.

# BIRTH OF A MONSTER

*I will not cry in this restaurant,* she told herself. *I will not cry in this restaurant.*

Her phone rang and she flinched, nearly spilling what was left of her second drink.

"Perry," she said. "Where are ye?"

"I'm still at work, babe," he lied. "I got stuck. You at the restaurant? I'll be there in ten."

Barbara ended the call, set the phone on the table and just sat there staring at it for several moments.

*So he's cheating on me.*

*I wonder who she is?*

*I bet it's his secretary.*

*You would think that.*

*He would love that power over her. He wishes he had it over me now, but he doesn't and he knows it. That's why he's so distant, and when he's not, it's why he's so angry. Your job isn't supposed to be as important as his is.*

*Shut up!*

"Would you like another drink, ma'am?"

"No," Barbara said, forcing a smile on the waitress. "Just the bill, please."

-

Barbara pulled off Highway 62 onto the feeder road that ran parallel with the interstate. The La Quinta Inn came into view and she pulled into the parking lot, scanning for Perry's Land Rover. Spotting her husband's green SUV, Barbara backed into a spot that gave her a view of the hotel and the Land Rover. She pulled up Perry's location on her cellphone again. Her husband's blue dot was nearly atop the one that showed her own location.

*He's still here,* she thought, *or, at least, his phone still is.*

Movement caught her eye and Barbara looked up from the glow of her cellphone and watched her husband and his secretary exit through a side door that let out into the parking lot. Everything seemed to slow. Barbara heard blood rushing through her ears and the sound of her stunned, open-mouthed breathing in the silent car as she watched her husband walk his secretary, Steffanie Phelps, to a silver Lexus, where he wrapped his arms around her and held her in a long embrace. Barbara watched her husband and his secretary kiss, then he opened the door for her and she got inside the Lexus.

Barbara felt like somebody was sitting on her chest. Her breathing was labored.

358

Perry shut the door of the Lexus and smiled down into the window. He turned around languidly, as if he had all the time in the world, and strode across the asphalt to his Range Rover, his hand slipping into a pocket of his jacket and returning with his cellphone. He tapped the screen as he walked then raised it to his ear.

Barbara's phone rang, startling her enough to make her jump.

Perry unlocked the Range Rover and disappeared behind the tinted windows.

Barbara saw that it was Perry phoning her. She hit the silence button and let the call ring until it went to voicemail. The Range Rover started and her phone rang again. This time she answered it.

"Hello."

"Hey," Perry said. "I got hung up at work. I'm so sorry. I'm leaving the office now."

"Okay."

Barbara's lips didn't feel under her own control. They felt foreign, controlled by unseen strings and unseen hands.

"Order us an appetizer and I'll see you in five minutes."

"Okay."

"See ya soon, babe. Love ya."

"Okay," Barbara said.

The call ended and Barbara watched her husband's Range Rover pull out of the parking lot behind his secretary's Lexus.

Barbara pulled into the driveway feeling her numbness slip away like a name written in the sand. In its place was a rage tinged with sadness. She slammed her car door shut and walked up the path to the front door on wooden legs. It took her three tries to unlock the door.

Inside, she stood in the darkened front room for a second, listening to her breathing.

*The bastard.*

*The cheating bastard.*

She unlocked her phone and pulled up Erick Rammie's contact info in her phone. She hit the call button.

"Rammie's Lock and Alarm. This is Erick."

"Erick. Hi. It's Barbara Findley with EPD."

"Hi Barbara. What can I do for ya?"

"I need to change my locks. ASAP."

"I can do that now. What's the address?"

Barbara had worked with Erick Rammie on a number of

occasions during her five years on the force, changing locks for evictions and victims of domestic violence. The man was always professional and timely. His van pulled into Barbara's drive not ten minutes later.

Her phone buzzed again. She saw that it was Perry calling for the fifth time. She hit the ignore button, set her phone down on the coffee table next to her drink, and turned up the volume on the Chris Isaak record.

Perry hated Chris Isaak, calling him a "crooner wannabe." When she saw Perry's Range Rover pull into the drive, Barbara closed all the blinds and curtains and turned the volume up even louder. She watched the front doorknob jiggle then jerk as Perry tried to unlock it with a key that no longer fit. Then he knocked.

"Barbara?" he called from the other side of the door.

Barbara put her hot face against the cool door but did not respond.

"Barbara!" Perry called. "Unlock the door."

"*San Francisco days*," Chris Isaak sang. "*San Francisco nights*."

Barbara's phone buzzed on the coffee table. She walked across the room and picked it up, saw that it was Perry calling, and set it back onto the coffee table. She picked up her drink and drained it.

The bourbon was making the room warm and fuzzy. It all seemed kind of funny, in a sad way.

The detective didn't know her husband was having an affair. The mechanic's wife is stuck taking the bus.

It wouldn't be a Chris Isaak tune though.

She picked up the MP3 player and scrolled through the artists.

*This song, this one right here, would be more of a Hank Williams song.*

She hit shuffle and set about making another drink.

After that was done, she decided that she best give the man some sort of explanation if he was too dimwitted to put one and one together and see that it's two. She picked up her phone and texted: *Best try getting a room at the La Quinta Inn and Suites.*

She hit send.

The knocking and hollering stopped.

Barbara pushed open the sleek modern doors of the courthouse and stepped into the brisk morning sunshine feeling like she could either puke or shit at any moment. She hadn't been this hungover in . . .

ever. She'd never in her life been this hungover.

*And Lord did you show it*, she thought. *I can't believe you let this affect your job.*

She wanted to cry but knew that was completely out of the question. Not in uniform, not at the courthouse, not on duty, and, particularly not after that botched testimony.

How had she gotten so slipped up in Craymoore's slippery words? She hadn't let his sideways questioning slip her up since she was a rookie.

"Fin!"

*Shit. I just want to be alone*, she thought.

"Hey, Fin! Wait up," Hank called.

Her head was pounding at the temples and a cold sweat seeped steadily out of every pore on her body. She stopped on the sidewalk and waited for her partner.

"What the fuck was that, Fin?"

"It was as bad as it felt then."

"Yeah, I'd say that didn't feel too good," Hank said.

They stood silent for a moment.

She knew he was waiting her out, that old interrogation method, the tried, the true, but she couldn't stop herself for breaking the silence.

"I'm sorry I fucked that up," she said. "I had a rough night last night."

"Want to talk about it?"

"No."

"Ten-four. Let's go get some lunch."

Barbara nearly gagged at the pain of nodding her head.

They sat in one of the back booths of the little diner and ordered coffees.

"And a water," Hank said, looking at Barbara.

His eyes felt hot and searching.

"Cut the third degree."

"Wanna tell me what's going on?"

Barbara couldn't seem to get comfortable in the cramped little booth. She readjusted her sitting position, then turned a bit.

"Fin."

"Perry's cheatin' on me," she said, her voice low, rushed, and embarrassed. It'd nearly come out a single word: perryscheatinonme.

Her mind had to patch it together and she saw it as if written on a chalkboard: *Perry's cheatin' on me.*

"Shit," Hank said. "Shit."

Hot, heavy tears spilled over onto her burning cheeks. She shook with the effort of not allowing the dam to break.

"Yeah," she said, then cleared her throat, which felt choked and claustrophobic suddenly. "Shit."

The coffees came. The waitress, feeling the tension, said she'd be back in a moment to take their order but Hank stopped her and ordered for the both of them.

"Two bacon cheeseburgers, two fries, two pieces of pie after."

The waitress took the menus and left.

"I'm sorry," Hank said. "You're sure?"

Barbara wanted to scream.

"Ye have to ask me that?"

"I'm sorry."

"Yeah, me too!"

She needed to cool down. She felt like a boiling forge.

*Hot and cold*, she thought. *Hot and cold. Just like a* woman.

She spat the word out, in her head, the way so many people in her life spat it, like it was something unsavory or undercooked.

Hank watched her for a few moments.

"You talked to Luanne?" he asked, finally.

Barbara shook her head and had to close her eyes. She felt shaky. *Hot and cold*, she scolded. *Keep it together, Barbara.*

"You should."

"I know," she said. "I will."

"Today."

Barbara stared off over Hank's shoulder, willing the food to come, for this moment to end.

"Today, Fin. Okay?"

She nodded her head and swallowed down a sob that felt almost too sudden to stop. It turned into a hiccup of sorts.

"It's just that they never cared for him much," Barbara said, flinching with each word she hadn't intended on speaking. "Perry. They told me once that they thought he was shallow, egoistical, stuck-up."

"Damn," Hank said.

"Nail on the head, huh?"

She'd probably feel better with a little food in her system. She hated to admit it, but she felt better having talked a bit.

There was another long, painful silence then Hank seemed to come to a decision and switched gears.

"So, Marks may be reconsidering the plea arrangement after your little fudgie this morning," Hank said, "but I doubt it's changed anything in the eyes of the jury so we're probably still okay. He'll sign the agreement tonight or tomorrow morning."

The food came and, somehow, Barbara managed to eat every last bite.

The sun was intense despite the lukewarm temperature of the day. Barbara still had on her sunglasses as they entered the police station. She nearly walked right into her husband.

"Barbara," Perry said, taking hold of her left arm at the elbow. "Barbara."

She pushed his hand off her arm roughly.

"Get yer hands off of me," she hissed.

"Let's go to lunch," Perry said, on his face a placating smile. "And talk about things."

Hank moved to Barbara's right side.

"We just had lunch, P-Boy," Hank said.

"I didn't ask you, now did I, Officer Gray?" Perry said and Barbara saw him for who he was for the first time: *a spoiled brat.*

*A rich, spoiled, little brat. Always assuming he'll get his way. Always assuming he can talk or smile out of the mess he's made getting what he wants.*

"At my job, Perry? Really?"

Perry had both of his hands in the air, palms facing her, and a smile on his smooth face, but Barbara thought she saw a dawning recognition of his precarious position in his bright, blue eyes.

"We need to talk about this," like he was talking to a client. "We just need to talk about it."

"Get out of here," she whispered.

"Come on, Perry," Hank said, stepping forward.

He took Perry by the arm.

"Get your fucking hands off me!" Perry shouted. "This coat costs more than you make in a day, officer."

*Even the way he says 'fucking' is bratty*, she thought. *The way he calls Hank officer to demean him while sounding so patronizing.*

"Ye gotta go," Barbara said, hating him. "Now."

Hank let go of the silk blazer and Perry made an exaggerated show of dusting it off.

Perry looked at Barbara one last time, then turned and left the building.

Barbara was fuming now. She turned and saw that everybody had stopped what they were doing and were watching her. Her face was burning bright red, she could feel it.

Her phone buzzed in her pants pocket. She retrieved it and saw that it was Perry calling.

She spun on her heels and stalked to the door.

Hank called, "Don't!"

Fin stomped across the parking lot to Perry's Range Rover.

"Ye have the fuckin' nerve to come to my job!" she shouted, throwing open the driver's side door. She pointed a shaking finger in his face. "After what ye've been doin'?"

"Barbara," he kept saying. "Barbara. Barbara, Barbara. Barbara, please."

She called him a "motherfucker" and a "bastard" and a "little boy." She yelled herself hoarse, which didn't take long. Plus, her headache was coming back with a vengeance.

Barbara took a step away from the Range Rover and slammed the driver's side door shut. She took a shuddering breath, then another, then turned and walked across the parking lot. She could feel all the eyes looking out of the huge glass windows of the police department. She kept waiting for Perry to get out of his SUV, but he didn't.

She opened the door and everybody present looked at her. She pursed her lips, getting ready to say something acidic, but the moment passed and everybody went back to what they were doing before all the commotion.

Barbara made her way to her small office, avoiding all eye contact.

*Jesus fucking Christ. I can't believe he came here. I can't believe I freaked out like that. Jesus Christ. I made a scene out there.*

She closed her door, but there came a knocking before she could even sit down.

"What?" she yelled.

The door opened and Hank came in.

"Easy," he said, shutting the door. "The lew just told me he wants to talk to ya. You need to calm down. Just take a few breaths."

Barbara hadn't realized how hard she was breathing until now. *Easy does it. Breathe.*

She closed her eyes, breathed in through her nostrils. Counted to five. Exhaled through her open mouth. She went through one of the grounding techniques she'd learned in foster care. *What do you smell?* The fragrance plug-in, cinnamon and apples, the rye whiskey on the back of her tongue, dripping hot and bile-like in her throat and stomach, and Hank's cologne.

*Okay*, she thought. *Okay.*

She opened her eyes.

"You alright?"

"Yes," she said.

*Fake it 'til ye make it. How many times had she told herself that?*

"Thomas wants to see ye. Best not keep the lew waitin'."

Barbara waited exactly five seconds after Hank left her office, then she rose on shaky legs and walked down the hall. Lieutenant Thomas' door was shut. Barbara knocked twice.

"Come in."

*Time to take your medicine*, she thought.

She turned the knob and stepped inside.

"Gray said ye wanted to see me, sir?"

*Here it comes.*

"I've got a missing-persons for ya."

*Oh.*

"Mary Ann Gregory's a bartender at the B.A.T.," Lieutenant Thomas said. "Worked her Saturday night shift. Didn't show up for her Sunday. That was last week."

He handed over the case files.

"Thank ye, sir," she said.

*Correctly, Barbara.*

"Thank you, sir," she said carefully.

Lieutenant Thomas said, "That's all, detective."

# CHAPTER TWENTY-TWO
## EATPRAYLOVE123

**THERE WAS A QUICK RAP** at the door and it opened before Jacob or his foster father, Marcus Faraway, could respond. A young male doctor in a white coat entered.

"Good morning," he said, extending his hand first to the foster father then to Jacob. "I'm Dr. Riley."

"Marcus Faraway, foster father," the foster father said.

"Jacob Hunter Goodman," Jacob murmured.

"Well, Jacob, we got the results back from the CAT scan and x-rays and it's not all bad or all good," Dr. Riley said, sitting down in the rolling chair and wheeling himself up to the computer. He typed in a few things and read silently for a moment.

*not all bad / not all good*

Jacob thought the doctor looked every bit as young as the doctors he'd spied on back at the Cadaver Lab in Pikeville.

"So there's nothing left in there," Dr. Riley said. "The x-ray and CAT scan showed no debris or splinters so we're all clear there, but the infection damaged the epididymis. You're healing up nicely but the chances are high that you're going to be sterile as a result of that prolonged infection."

Jacob heard the foster father's breath catch then release.

"Sterile?" Jacob asked.

The doctor nodded, turning his eyes back to the screen.

"We could run a semen analysis for confirmation but with the severity of the injury coupled with the prolonged infection, I'm almost positive you'll never be able to procreate."

Jacob heard a baby cry and forced himself not to flinch at the nearness of the sound.

*Sterile*, he thought. *What a clinically cold word. Sterile.*

The doctor was moving on, asking questions the foster father answered, and typing and clicking away on his computer.

*Does he even care?* Jacob doubted he did. *How many patients did this doctor see a day? I'm nothing more than another number. This one with*

366

*unfortunate news. One in a long line of 'em, all in a day's work.*

Jacob forced his face to remain expressionless as the child's crying intensified. He knew without having to check that neither the young doctor nor the foster father heard the cries. They were coming from a long way off to sound so near, that made him feel alone in the small examination room with the two adults.

*I'll never be able to have children of my own,* Jacob realized.

He hadn't thought of having kids of his own, hadn't thought about a serious relationship with a woman, for that matter, but now that it was off the table, he felt cheated.

"Just have a few things to finish up here," the doctor said as he typed.

The room was quiet except for the clicking and clacking of the doctor at the computer.

*What lasting change can I have on the world now?*

The question appeared out of nowhere in Jacob's head. He felt shaken by it. He forced his face to remain expressionless but he wanted to scream and cry, smash the doctor's computer to bits.

*What Rodney Tackett done.*

Jacob felt something tear open in his chest. A hole as hot and dark as the one the bald man showed him, the one that took her body, Tanya Miller's, and the bully's too.

*What Rodney Tackett done.*

Jacob had gotten his revenge on the bully but he still lost somehow.

"Well, let's take you up front and get you checked out. I'll see you in a year for your checkup," the doctor said, rising from the roller chair and leading them from the examination room.

*What lasting change can I have on the world now?*

Jacob wanted to knock down every last stupid painting hung on the wall. He wanted to kick holes in the drywall and bust all the fancy light fixtures. The hole opening up in his chest was filled with rage. He forced himself to put one foot in front of the other and follow the foster father. He forced his face smooth and unreadable.

-

Jacob couldn't help but be bad. There was just too much opportunity for him not to be. The substitute teacher left her purse open and on the desk. Jacob walked over, saw the car keys sitting in the open purse, and took them. He didn't think about it. He just saw that no one was looking and he took them.

He skipped Home Economics and went prowling the faculty parking lot. He kept hitting the lock button until one of the cars, a bland sedan, beeped. He got inside the car and looked around, found nothing worth taking, so he decided to leave his mark. He unpocketed the Case knife, Ace Hardware, and started in on the seats. He was leaning over the console, the knife deep in the seat cushion of the passenger side, when the shadow fell across his vision.

"What are you thinking?" a voice outside the car asked.

Jacob looked up from his work and saw a teacher standing outside the substitute's car looking in on Jacob and the shredded interior.

"Get out. Now!"

Jacob recognized the teacher's face, he thought she taught a grade or so below him, but didn't know her name. He carefully folded the knife up, making sure the teacher saw him do this, then opened the driver's side door and stepped out.

"What're you thinking?" the teacher asked.

Jacob shrugged his shoulders.

*It was just too easy to be bad sometimes*, he thought.

-

"Since you're suspended," the foster mother, Teresa Faraway, said, "you'll be spending the day with me at the Twin Oaks."

Twin Oaks was the nursing home where Teresa Faraway worked.

Jacob didn't acknowledge the statement.

He'd go where they wanted him to, but he'd only do what he wanted. He felt parts of himself hardening and wasn't sure he could stop them from solidifying. All the world felt like a mold and he was being shaped by it despite his best efforts.

"Some time around the elderly might be just what you need," the foster mother said.

-

The floor was dirty. Jacob noticed it right away because he was trying not to look at all the old people. He was revolted by them, the elderly, all that extra, sagging skin and the weird spots and shapes on the skin, *oh God that skin!*, that stretched like ancient leather or hung in lumpy folds like sad scarecrows.

"This is Mary," the foster mother, Teresa Faraway, said. "She works the front desk. Say 'hi' to Mary, Jacob."

Jacob, avoiding all eye contact, said, "Hi."

"Thanks, Mary," the foster mother said after the door was

unlocked.

"You brought your bible and your homework?" she asked.

"Yes, ma'am," Jacob said.

She nodded. "I don't want to hear a peep nor see hide nor hair of you, Jacob Hunter Goodman. I'm still absolutely flabbergasted by your behavior. You're lucky they only suspended you. If I were that teacher I'd press charges and if I was that principal I would've expelled you. I would've."

Jacob believed her. The foster parents had given him separate, and collective, dress downs over the incident with the substitute's car, to which Jacob was also forced into community service.

The foster mother unlocked a door that let into a small windowless office. She went over to her desk and unslung her purse. She walked around to the other side of the desk, unlocked a bottom drawer with a key from her lanyard, and deposited her purse inside. She locked the drawer.

"You sit down here," the foster mother said. "And you get right to work. The computer is locked. Don't try to unlock it. Do all of your homework and then go straight to the Bible. I mean it."

Jacob nodded; his face blank, unfeeling.

He waited a slow count to thirty, *Miss-iss-ippi*, thinking in slow strokes from his fileting knife, Roger's Bait 'n' Tackle, then he got up from the desk and unlocked the door.

-

The hall was empty of people in scrubs. Jacob knew they were the only ones he had to watch out for, everybody else in this place was useless, *inert*, Mrs. Horace's Word of the Day, *1: lacking the power to move; 2: very slow to move or act; 3: deficient in active properties; especially: lacking a usual or anticipated chemical or biological action.*

Jacob peeked into the next room, saw it was another office, then moved farther down the hall. The next room he came to was a double room, two beds separated by a drape. Only one of the beds had an occupant. Jacob stepped into the room. The wall was decorated with pinned holiday and birthday cards, children's drawings of turkeys and snowmen, and pictures.

Jacob ignored the occupant of the bed and went straight to the photographs on the wall. He'd stolen a permanent marker from Mrs. Horace's desk before he was suspended. He began to draw beards and mustaches and penises on the photographs.

"What're you doing?" an ancient, papery voice asked.

Jacob didn't bother with a response. Once he'd finished with the photographs, he saw nothing else of use in the room so he left.

The next room was also a double room. There were two occupants in the room and someone in street clothing visiting. Jacob stepped quickly away from this room.

The next, yet another double room, had two occupants only. Jacob entered. There was a little shelf lining the wall of the bed on the left. There were framed photographs, books, and knickknacks on the shelf. He ignored the voice asking who he was and what he was doing there and telling him to put down the photograph he picked up. Jacob looked at the beautiful woman in the black and white photo. The picture looked ancient. The woman's smile looked pained, like she had to hold it for an extended utterance of Cheese!, but Jacob could tell she was pretty.

He turned to the woman in the bed. She was ancient, every bit as old as the photograph, Jacob slowly saw. He tried to unsee the age, search for the fox in the photograph in the pile of wrinkled skin and thin hair.

*Fast-Forward X2 Mode but in reverse.*

"Put that down," the old woman said.

Jacob looked down at the photo then at the woman, then back again.

His face crinkled as if he'd just smelled something off.

*Come to think of it, it does smell terrible in here,* Jacob thought.

"Ye stink," he told her.

"Put that down," she sounded so winded with the effort.

*Pitiful.*

Jacob tossed the photograph onto the ground. The glass shattered dully.

"Now why would you go and do a thing like that?"

The question had taken so long Jacob felt like hopping with aggravation.

"Shut up!" he hissed at her.

He took out the sharpie and went over to the little pushpin board beside the bed.

"Get away from there."

Jacob read one of the cards: *Thinking of you on your birthday. Love, Alex & Anna & Paige.*

*Asinine,* Mrs. Horace's Word of the Day, *1: extremely or utterly foolish or silly; 2: of, relating to, or resembling an ass.*

Jacob took out the sharpie and wrote: I can't wait til you die. I hope it's soon.

Jacob wrote a similar message on another card, this one from last Christmas.

He looked across the little room, the separating curtain was drawn back, at the bundle of bones in the bed. He saw the slow rise and fall of the chest. The head was a shrunken thing, the eyes set so far back it reminded Jacob of a rotting Jack-o'-lantern.

He turned back to the complaining, ancient woman before him.

"How?" Jacob asked her.

"You aren't supposed to be in here," each word sounded like it was taking seconds off her life.

"Ye disgust me," Jacob hissed.

There was a pitcher of water on the bed's tray. Jacob picked it up and held it over the woman, a smile spreading across his face. He slowly poured the entire pitcher onto the covers at the woman's middle.

"What?" the woman's dismay wasn't much louder than her aggravation.

Jacob wondered what her pain would sound like.

The bedsheets were completely soaked from the water.

"Ye done pissed yerself," Jacob whispered. "Poor old coot cain't keep it in. Best get ye changed."

The woman's frail arms put up only the weakest of fights. Jacob tore the papery gown off in one quick rip. He let it flutter to the dirty floor next to the broken picture frame.

She didn't even try to cover herself up. She was looking for the nurse call button. Jacob saw it hanging off the left side of the bed, well out of her reach. He couldn't stop looking at the woman's ancient tits. They reminded Jacob of the spent condoms he sometimes saw in the student parking lot.

He reached forward and pinched the overripened grape of a nipple. The woman jerked away but Jacob was stronger. He pinched the other, a disgusted smile on his face.

"Stop!" she whispered.

Jacob mocked her.

Jacob threw back the soaked sheets and gasped. He was shocked by the amount of unruly pubic hair. He laughed, doubling over himself, trying his best to stay quiet. It was so comical.

*the jungle / all dried out*

# BIRTH OF A MONSTER

*tropic rot & decay*

He reached forward and pulled a tuft of the pubic hair free. It was thick and coarse. He felt like gagging and laughing at the same time. He let the pubic hair drop onto the floor.

He became suddenly serious.

"Ye disgust me," he said again.

The woman said something that sounded to Jacob like "peanut butter" and it was all he could do to keep from laughing again. The woman reached over the side of the bed and retrieved the call button.

Jacob left.

-

There was a nurse in the hall. Jacob made sure his face remained completely blank.

"There's a woman in there upset," Jacob said. "I's walkin' down the hall and heard the hollerin' and carryin' on. I think she's crazy."

The nurse's smile was more grimace than a smile.

"You're . . ." she flicked her eyes toward the door. "Teresa was looking for you. You're Jacob, right?"

Jacob nodded.

"She was naked," he said.

"What?"

"The old lady in there," Jacob said. "She didn't have no clothes on. And it looked like she pissed herself."

The woman nodded twice then went into the room.

-

Jacob ate the bland lunch sitting on the tray in front of him. He chewed until it was mush then he swallowed. He didn't even see what it was he was eating. The cafeteria was full and loud but Jacob felt all alone. He finished the last bites, then pushed the tray away and returned to his notebook.

I feel empty, hollowed out.

Sometimes I feel an absolute panic and fear drape itself over me like a blanket or a shroud and I feel trapped in my own body.

Jacob felt it then, sitting in the cafeteria writing in the composition notebook he stole from Walmart, the real journal, not the one he kept for Pastor Clark.

I feel so scared sometimes that it makes me angry. Today's another rollercoaster day, I feel sad then

372

angry. Such sweeping changes that I can't control.

Jacob felt a little better writing it down.

-

Jacob took a seat near the window and sat down. He got out his geometry book, his journal, and the Bible, His Shining Light Mission. He opened the geometry book at random, then positioned it on his desk to make it appear he was working on homework. He opened the composition notebook, the real journal, and read over his last entry.

Fast Forward X2 Mode. Such a Happy Boy did all the heavy lifting.

Two gone by my hands. My opposable thumbs and dexterous fingers. The gaping maw swallowed them piece by piece.

As he read, Jacob saw the scenes in the screen in his head. He watched SAHB and Tanya Miller. The blue and white nails of her pliable hands. *Oh God those painted nails.* Then he watched SAHB and the bully, Rodney Tackett. The dismemberment and the trash bags. The moonlit carrying of the bags along the lonely mountain path. Jacob saw each piece slip into the darkness of the burnt-out mineshaft.

Jacob was smiling when the bell rung and detention was over.

-

Jacob woke from another nightmare of the endlessly crying baby. In the dream he ran the ridges and hollows of the mountains trying to get away from the sound but it followed him, getting louder with each step he took until the weight of the infant's cries pressed down on him from everywhere like an oppressive heat.

He was covered in sweat. He threw the cheap covers off his body and swung his legs over the side of the bed, then rubbed the crust from his eyes. He saw that it was still dark. The twin bed on the other side of the bed was still, his foster brother was fast asleep.

Jacob knew he wouldn't be able to fall back asleep. Not after that dream.

He left the small room and made his way, quietly, down the hall to the living room, where the Faraways kept a PC on a small desk in the corner. Jacob sat down at the computer and turned it on. He'd been given the password for the guest account on the computer, *EatPrayLove123*, but the computer was still logged into the Faraways' account. He opened up the internet browser and nearly fell out of the chair at the images that were displayed on the screen. A woman was mostly naked, clad in crotchless leather and chains. There was a black ball gag stuffed into her mouth and her eyes were slit in ecstasy or intense pain, Jacob couldn't tell which. Each of her nipples had metal clamps glinting in the harsh overhead lighting. Her arms were tied behind her back and she hung from the ceiling by meat hooks punctured through the skin of her back.

*Oh God.*

Jacob scrolled down and studied each photo closely. The woman was penetrated with several different objects as she hung helplessly from the ceiling, bound and gagged. One photo was shot from underneath and behind the woman and Jacob saw that her fingernails were painted a bright red. He felt the breath in his chest catch.

*Oh God.*

There was a studded paddle. Several shots of the spanking and the bleeding. Snot and sweat ran down the woman's face. Then there was a man in the shots, also clad in leather and chains. He licked and bit the woman all over her body. He then pulled her hair, pinched and twisted her breasts. The last photo was of the man smoking a cigarette through the hole of his leather mask. Jacob saw several cigarette burns across the woman's sweat-slickened body behind him.

*What is this?* Jacob wondered. *Was Marcus Faraway looking at this.*

Jacob couldn't imagine anybody else in the foster home bringing up something even remotely like this. He was the oldest child in the home now. The other two were years younger. And he couldn't imagine Teresa Faraway sitting at this little chair pulling up what Jacob now couldn't look away from.

His penis was as hard as a rock.

He forced his eyes away from the bright screen and scanned the darkened living room. He reached over to the coffee table and retrieved the box of Kleenex.

-

He couldn't stop himself from getting out of bed and sneaking down to the computer. He tried but he couldn't do it. He opened the internet browser and started clicking.

*Lord, the clicking.*

*Breasts and vaginas and assholes and painted nails and stretched, open mouths.*

Jacob was smiling and touching himself. He'd tried watching videos but the internet way out here was terrible. He found a few sites that had the picture galleries of the pain he wanted, needed to see. He zoomed in on the hands, *those goddamn painted nails*, and panted.

-

Jacob couldn't stop masturbating. He jerked one out every chance he got. Shower: check. Bathroom sink: check. Computer chair: of course. Hall closet: yep. Kitchen sink: also check.

Jacob, in his click-click-clicking every night, stumbled onto auto-erotic asphyxiation and raced down the shadow-ladened hall as quietly as his need could allow. He took an extension cord from the mudroom and quickly wrapped it around his neck. He started beating off, pulling the extension cord tighter around his throat.

*This isn't gonna work*, he thought.

He stepped inside the hall closet and pulled the door closed. He looped the extension cord over the closet rod then dropped down to his knees. He held the cord tight with his right hand and worked himself with his left.

*Oh yes / blue white*

*Tanya Miller / Tanya Miller*

His eyes were squeezed shut. Floaters danced in his vision. Just as he was reaching his climax, the closet rod came crashing down on his head, forcing him to headbutt the closed door. He moaned, then covered himself up as soon as he was able.

He saw the bent metal arm right away and bent it back into place. He then set the rod back into place and returned all the fallen jackets to the rod. Jacob rolled up the extension cord and returned it to the place between his mattress.

-

There was a crash from the hall. Jacob put down the Bible, His Shining Light Mission, and strode across the room and into the hall. The foster mother, Teresa, was bent down in front of the hall closet.

Jacob walked over to where she knelt. The foster mother looked up from the pile of jackets for a moment, saw it was Jacob, then went back to the pile.

"Dang pole just fell off on me," she said.

"I saw Jeremy and Deedee playing in there yesterday morning," Jacob said immediately.

"Well," she said.

"Let me help ye with that," Jacob said, stooping and taking the pole from the foster mother's hands.

He put it back on the arms, saw the one he'd bent had bent

downward again. He corrected it then stepped aside to let the foster mother rehang her coat.

"Thank you, Jacob."

"Welcome," he said smiling.

-

Jacob forced his breathing to slow and stepped inside the darkened master bedroom. He could see the outline of the bed but not the shapes there. He took his steps carefully and made his way to the bathroom. He found the drawer and reached a hand inside.

There was a soft groan from the sleeping foster father.

Jacob froze until he could make out the sound of their breathing then felt the cold glass and plastic containers until he felt one that just felt right. He then shut the drawer and snuck back out of the room.

Back inside his room he made a little tent under his covers with his knees and painted the nails of his right hand with his left in Cashmere Crimson. He didn't wait for it to dry before using the hand to masturbate.

-

Jacob came to hate the smell of fingernail polish remover.

-

Cashmere Crimson.

Golden Bliss.

New York Nights Black.

Pink Lady.

Red Rose Red.

Heavens Above White

-

Jacob had both of his hands bound together. Each of his ten fingernails had been painted in Glitteriffic Tinman. He had his dick in his hands and was working it as roughly as he could. He grunted at the pain but was nearing the end and kept at it. The flashlight under his chin illuminated the painted nails working. He heard something from outside the covers and quickened his pace.

"Jacob!" a woman's shrill voice said, then the covers were ripped away and the overhead light winked on.

"Oh God!" the foster mother shrieked. "What in the hell?"

Jacob came looking into her face, shooting hot ropes into his bound hands.

The foster mother turned around and fled.

"Get in here, Jacob Hunter Goodman," the foster mother screamed from the front of the house. "Right this instant."

Jacob wiggled his hands free of their bonds. He wiped them on the outside of the cheap comforter, then pulled up the sweatpants, Walmart. The younger foster child, Jeremy, was sitting up in his bed staring at Jacob with wide, dumb eyes. Jacob wanted to hit him, but he didn't. He got out of the bed and walked across the room.

"Right this instant, Jacob!"

Jacob walked down the hall, feeling both sticky and wet inside the sweatpants, Walmart.

He entered the living room holding his hands behind his back.

"What on God's green earth were you doing in there, Jacob Hunter Goodman?" she yelled. "Huh? Looked like some pretty sick stuff, mister!"

Jacob, despite his best efforts, felt his face blushing.

"You're not going to turn into no sicko pervert," the foster mother yelled. "Not in this house. No sir-ee. Let me see them hands. Now!"

Jacob slowly brought his hands out from behind his back. He held them palm upwards.

The foster mother acted like she was going to touch him then thought better of it.

"Turn 'em over!" she snapped.

Jacob turned his hands over. The glittery nails glinted under the overhead lighting. He couldn't help himself, he turned them slowly under the light, fascinated by the glittering.

"That my nail polish?" she shrieked. "You sick little boy! Don't you ever go through my things! Don't you ever!"

She slapped him with her open hand. It stung enough to bring tears to his eyes. She slapped him again.

"Don't you ever!" she screamed.

Jacob expected one final blow, but the moment passed and the foster mother just stood there looking at him, panting.

"I'm gonna tell Kim about this," she said after a long time. "Pastor Clark too."

Jacob hated the pang of remorse he felt at the preacher's future knowledge of his misdeeds. He didn't give a shit if the social worker knew. He was already in foster care, what's the worst they could do? Move him to another foster home?

*It doesn't matter*, the voice said.

*You're right.*

"You know what?" the foster mother asked.

Jacob didn't know what so he didn't say anything.

"You better just leave that nail polish on if you want it so bad," she said. "You better just go on and wear it to school for all to see. See the weirdo you are. Sicko. Pervert."

Jacob thought the foster mother, Teresa, was working herself up to strike him again but she wasn't. She was just trying to wound him with her words. Jacob understood this but still felt the sting of embarrassment and shame.

"What is wrong with you?" the foster mother asked.

Jacob didn't say anything. He couldn't look away from his glitter-painted nails.

-

"You know we're gonna have to talk about it," the school counselor said. "The incident with the ropes and nail polish the other night."

Jacob looked out the window, willing his face to remain expressionless, *blank as a canvas / blank as a canvas.*

"Why did you tie your hands together?" the counselor asked.

She waited him out.

He shrugged his shoulders.

"Okay. Why did you paint your fingernails?" the counselor asked.

Again, Jacob shrugged his shoulders.

She waited.

"I don't know," he said.

"You don't know or you don't want to say because you're afraid of what I might think?"

"I don't care what ye think."

"You don't?"

Jacob shook his head.

"What about your foster mother, Teresa?" the counselor asked. "Do you care what she thinks?"

Jacob shook his head. "Nope."

"What about your mother?"

Jacob felt the words like a slap.

*Sure she's your momma but she's still a cunt.*

"Where did you learn to tie your hands up like that?"

As much as he hated the bald man, Jacob found himself wondering where he was. He wondered if the bald man even cared that

Jacob's mother was still in jail. He doubted it.

## CHAPTER TWENTY-THREE
## TERRIBLE TIMING

**"WANT A CUP OF COFFEE?"** Luanne Shepherd asked.

Carefully avoiding her former foster mother's eyes, Barbara Findley nodded her head and pulled up a chair to the scuffed kitchen table. She watched Luanna Shepherd pull the carafe from its place and fill a Kentucky Wildcats coffee mug with steaming black coffee.

"Still two sugars?"

"Uh-huh."

The clinking of the spoon in the cup seemed overly loud in the quiet kitchen.

"Here ye go," Luanne Shepherd said, passing the steaming cup to Barbara.

"Thanks, Lu."

Luanne sat down with her own cup across the table from Barbara.

"What's going on with ye?" she asked.

Barbara fought back the stinging of tears.

*Keep it together, Barbara*, she told herself. *You can't be blubbering all the time. Relationships end every day. You can't let yourself fall apart just because your marriage is.*

But she wanted to cry and be comforted by the woman she felt closest to in the entire world, the woman she thought of as her mother whenever she heard the word "mom" or "mother."

"Well?" Luanne Shepherd asked. "What's got a hold of yer tongue?"

"Work . . ." Barbara began but her voice betrayed her, it was higher than it should be and felt on the verge of breaking.

"Work, my foot," Luanne Shepherd said. "Tell Momma Luanne what's wrong. Come to Jesus now."

At the sound of the words "Momma Luanne" Barbara broke like a cracked levee, tears spilling down onto her hot cheeks. The foster mother's trademark "come to Jesus" statement put her over the top. The room blurred as her eyes filled with more tears.

*This is so embarrassing*, she thought.

"Perry's havin' an affair," she said, her voice just above a whisper.

She panted trying to keep the sobs from racking her shaking body.

"Oh baby," Luanne Shepherd said. "He isn't! He cain't be!"

Barbara nodded her head.

"Oh the rotten shit," Luanne Shepherd said. "The spoiled rotten little shit."

Barbara felt torn. She'd always known Momma Luanne didn't care for Perry but to hear her mother figure call her husband a "spoiled rotten little shit" made her at once defensive and vindicated. The ugly head of truth made her speak.

"We never should've gotten married," Barbara said. "Y'all were right about him."

The words both freed and shackled Barbara. Hearing them aloud, she knew she'd never be able to forgive Perry. She felt the weight of a wasted three years. All the work of the relationship felt like grains of sand slipping between her grasping fingers. She hadn't been able to steer her thoughts toward life after Perry until this moment.

She sobbed.

Momma Luanne came across the table and held her.

"Not even three years," Barbara said bitterly. "Not even three years and it's all crumbling."

"Some cakes are like that," Momma Luanne said. "They look solid from the outside but crumble as soon as ye go to pick 'em up . . ."

"He doesn't support me. He's always trying to get me to quit the force and find some nice little job at HR somewhere. A desk-jockey. A paper-pusher. That's what he wants me to do."

"Oh honey."

"He also thinks I'm demented for not wantin' children," Barbara said, speaking faster, feeling that all the words had to come out now or they'd be stuck inside her forever. "He can't understand that I really, positively don't want any children. He looks at me like I'd stepped on his toes on purpose every time it comes up."

She sucked in a lungful of breath and willed herself to continue. *Think Band-Aid, Barbara*, she told herself. *Just get it out of ye.*

"He wants kids so bad," she said. "My IUD is about ready to need removing, it's been eight years, and he keeps pushing me to not get another'n. He asks me how long it's been in from time to time so I know he's just counting down and hoping I forget about it. You know what he told me?"

"What, baby?"

"He said I wasn't a 'proper woman' because I don't want to have kids," Barbara said, breaking out into a sob. "A 'proper woman' would want to stay at home and raise babies. A 'proper woman' would be content to make dinner every night and clean up afterwards. A 'proper woman' would keep the house clean without complaint."

Her tears were hot and slippery. She wiped them away but seemed only to smear them around.

"I hate cookin' and cleanin'!"

"I know ye do, baby," Momma Luanne said with a smile.

Barbara couldn't help but return it. They'd had row after row about chores when Barbara had been living in the Shepherds' home with the revolving door of other foster children. She'd aged out of the system in Momma Luanne and Poppy Kenny Shepherd's home.

"He said somethin' must be wrong with me for not wanting those things," Barbara said. "Is there somethin' wrong with me?"

Momma Luanne shook her head.

"Not a thing a piece of pecan pie won't fix," the older woman said, pushing herself up from the table. She got the pie from the fridge and served them each a piece with a dollop of whipped cream.

"I don't know what I'm gonna do," Barbara said after a time.

"Ye'll get on," Momma Luanne said.

Barbara felt like crying with happiness hearing the sentence.

"Ye'll get on," Momma Luanne said again.

They ate their pie in silence for a time.

"To top it off," Barbara said, "mother dearest was just picked up on drug charges again."

"Oh no. I thought Melissa was doing better."

"Nope. She got popped somewhere in Knott County with possession, paraphernalia, disorderly, evading, and more."

"Jesus God."

"And you know what next week is?"

There was a brief pause as the older woman thought about it.

"Oh no," Luanne Shepherd said.

"Yep. What terrible timing."

The next week marked the third anniversary of Barbara's biological father, Clayton Johnson's, drug overdose.

"Oh, Barbara, I'm so sorry, honey," Momma Luanne said, setting her fork down and patting Barbara's hand.

"I know it's probably paranoid but I can't help waiting for Bailey and Hall to use it all against me at the department: Perry's affair, both my biological parents' drug issues, all of it. They're always biting and mean and I can tell they don't want me to succeed." Her laughter was derisive. "Can you imagine? Wanting someone to fail?"

"It takes a lot of energy to be so hateful," Momma Luanne said. "They won't keep it up. Ye'll prove yer worth, just ye wait and see. Ye'll outlast 'em."

The foster mother hugged her former foster child.

"Thank you," Barbara said, closing her eyes and squeezing the older woman tight. "I love you."

"I love you too."

## CHAPTER TWENTY-FOUR
## JUST DESSERTS

**JACOB WAS PAST HIS CURFEW.** He knew it and didn't care.

*The Faraways can fuck off.*

They weren't his real parents. They couldn't tell him what to do.

Jacob looked around the empty woods but still felt watched. He knew this was a paranoid feeling but he couldn't help but feel some unseen eyes on his back everywhere he went. He also couldn't help but feel the hills were tainted now somehow. They felt dirtied up, not as soothing as they'd been before.

*Before what Rodney Tackett done.*

*Tanya Miller / Fast-Forward X2 Mode*

*the bully gets his / just desserts*

Jacob wondered if it was easier to feel alone in the city. All those tall, unseeing buildings and faceless herds of people. He thought of himself as a wolf and saw himself prowling the city in his head.

He wouldn't have to go to the therapist's once a week if he was alone in the city. He wouldn't have to see Pastor Clark and submit to his condescension and disappointment.

*And disgust,* Jacob thought of the preacher man's fat shining face and the slanted hint of a sneer it wore.

*Everybody thinks they're better than me.*

The woods felt close despite the barren boughs.

*They think it, but it's not true. They'll see. I'll show 'em.*

Jacob wanted out of his skin. He wished he could zip it on and off like a onesie.

He stopped walking and unslung the backpack, Walmart, and took out the can of silver spray paint, Ace Hardware. He retrieved the rag from his back pants pocket. He held the stiff, stained cloth over the nozzle of the spray and sprayed for several seconds. Then he slapped the cloth over his nose and inhaled, deeply.

*Oh. Yes.*

Jacob closed his eyes and took another long breath.

He'd show everybody. *Soon.*

First he wanted to play with his foster siblings.

He was beginning to like being the oldest foster child in the home. It gave him a certain power over the younger ones. He was learning he could get them to do things, things that weren't on the chore list, things he just wanted them to do because he wanted to see them done.

"Take her shirt off," he'd said on several occasions.

"Strip 'er down," he told them and had been obeyed.

Jacob was only doing chores at face value, whenever the foster parents, *the cunts*, were watching. The younger ones did all his chores for him now. They did them without complaint too.

He waited until Jeremy Bevins was finished with his afternoon chores then cornered him in their shared bedroom.

"Let's go down to the Corner Pump 'n' Pay," Jacob said.

The younger boy gave the older a wary look but nodded his head. "Come on."

They walked the half-mile in mostly silence.

"Look," Jacob said as they rounded the corner and the convenience store came into view, "I need ye to get me a few things while we're in there."

"I don't have any money."

"I know ye don't."

The younger boy gave him an exasperated look.

"Well, what then?"

"Ye're gonna take 'em."

Jeremy Bevins' face blanched.

"I . . . I don't . . . I mean I cain't . . ." he stammered.

"It's nothing too hard, quit bein' a baby."

The younger boy closed his open mouth.

Jacob mimicked the boy's voice and made it even more babyish.

"I just want a porno mag and some nail polish," Jacob said, stopping and putting both of his hands on the smaller boy's shoulders. "Ye can do that, cain't ye. Just a single magazine and a little bitty bottle of fingernail polish."

"What magazine is it?" the boy said, looking down at his off-brand sneakers.

"It's called *Bound and Gagged*," Jacob said, smiling. "It's on the top shelf, first row, second or third from the end. It'll have a blackened cover except for the name: *Bound and Gagged*."

"*Bound and Gagged?*" Jeremy Bevins asked. "What's that one about?"

"Pain and pleasure," he said. "I'll meet ye back at the home."

"You're not goin' in with me?" the boy looked terrified.

Jacob leaned in close.

"No, I ain't," he said. "Yer a big boy and can handle a simple thing like this on yer own, cain't ye?"

"I, uh," the boy swallowed. "I can do it. No problem."

"Good," Jacob smiled.

He said the one thing they all yearned to hear.

"I'm proud of ye," Jacob lied.

Jacob started back for the house as soon as the child pushed in the door of the convenience store, wanting to laugh out loud but forcing himself to merely smile instead.

The foster mother's phone was ringing.

Jacob knew it had to be about Jeremy and slipped into the kitchen where the foster mother had been sitting at the kitchen table working out her checkbook, to listen.

"Hello," the foster mother, Teresa Faraway, said. "It is. Yes. What? Are you serious? Jeremy took what?"

Jacob leaned against the doorjamb.

"You've got to be kidding me," she said into the receiver.

The foster mother's eyes found Jacob's. He smiled at her blandly. She did not return the gesture.

"I'll be here. I'm so sorry," she said, ending the call.

"Jacob Hunter Goodman, you had something to do with this."

Jacob didn't say anything.

"Well?"

Jacob shrugged his shoulders.

"Jesus Christ! I cain't deal with this," the foster mother said, pushing herself up from the table. "I'm tellin' the social worker. I'm sorry but I can't deal with this. You're sick, you know this right? *Bound and Gagged Magazine?* Sick! Perverted!"

Jacob let the smile curl further; he was such a happy boy sometimes.

Jeremy ratted Jacob out to the uniformed sheriff's deputy who responded to the shoplifting call. Jacob could tell by both the cop's face and the foster child's.

"Ma'am," the deputy said to the foster mother when she answered his knock on the door.

"I'm so sorry," the foster mother said. "I think he was put up to it by this one here."

Teresa Faraway pointed at Jacob.

He felt his face sting as the eyes turned in his direction.

*Stay calm*, the voice said. *Don't speak unless spoken to.*

"Well, boy," the deputy said, gently pushing the younger foster child into the house. He stepped in behind him.

"I'm gonna need a word with yer other boy," he said, indicating Jacob.

The foster mother nodded.

"You want me to leave y'all alone in here so you can talk to him?" she asked.

The sheriff's deputy nodded.

"That'd be fine."

The foster mother ushered the younger foster child into the kitchen, but just before she disappeared from the room, she turned and spoke to Jacob.

"Not smiling now, are ya?"

Jacob felt a surge of hatred for the woman as she turned and left the room. He could hear her scolding Jeremy and had to keep his face from smiling.

"What's yer name, boy?" the deputy asked.

"Jacob."

"Jacob what?"

"Jacob Hunter Goodman."

"Ye go by Jake?"

Jacob shook his head.

"Listen, Jake," the deputy said. "That one in there told me ye put him up to this. Is that true?"

Jacob didn't respond.

"I asked ye a question."

Jacob wanted to run away from the man's searching eyes. The deputy towered over Jacob and the things on his belt squeaked when he moved. He leaned over, his face and massive shoulders taking up most of Jacob's view.

"I know ye got that little boy in there to steal that dirty magazine and that nail polish for ye," he said.

Jacob read the man's nametag to avoid meeting his eyes.

Deputy Greene.

"How'd ye like to take a ride down to the jail in the backseat of my cruiser, huh?"

Jacob stared at the walkie-talkie receiver pinned to the man's shoulder. It crackled and buzzed softly.

"I asked ye a question."

Jacob shrugged his shoulders.

"What'd ye want with a magazine like that?"

Jacob shrugged his shoulders.

"I didn't take it," he said.

"I know ye didn't take it. Ye got the other boy to take it."

Jacob didn't reply.

"What's with the fingernail polish?"

*blue / white*

"Ye some sort of fairy? Like to get all prettied up?"

Jacob saw his own nails shining and glinting in the light of the flashlight under his covers.

The foster mother returned to the room.

"Would you like a cup of coffee, Deputy?"

The man kept his gaze on Jacob for several moments before he answered.

"No, thank ye, ma'am," Deputy Greene said. "I best be getting on, unless there's anything else I can do for ye."

"No, I thank you," the foster mother said. "And I'm sorry about all this."

The deputy grunted.

"I'd keep an eye on this one," he said, placing his beefy pointer finger into Jacob's sternum. "He don't say much but I've got a feeling he's up to no good."

The foster mother nodded.

"He's lucky they're not pressing any charges for shoplifting," Deputy Greene said. "Ye know that, boy? Yer lucky you didn't get that other boy sent to juvee for this. Yer lucky I don't take ye there my own self."

Jacob studied the man's shining boots.

"Well," the deputy said.

"Well," the foster mother replied.

The sheriff's deputy turned on his heels and opened the front door.

"Y'all have a good night," he said over Jacob's shoulder to the foster mother.

"And ye stay out of trouble," Deputy Greene said to Jacob. "I mean it."

Jacob nodded his head.

---

"Why'd you put him up to it?" the foster mother asked again.

Jacob shook his head.

"I didn't have anything to do with it," he said, his face blank, showing nothing.

"He said you did."

Jacob shrugged his shoulders.

"You've got no excuse? You're just going to stand there and lie to me about it?"

Jacob didn't respond.

"Get on to bed then, if you're gonna lie. No supper. No television," the foster mother said. "You can read a little from your Bible. Might find something about not stealing in there while you're at it."

---

Jacob flipped the Bible open at random and read from the second book of Timothy: everyone who wants to live a godly life in Christ Jesus will be persecuted . . .

*Don't I know it.* Jacob thought.

He flipped several more pages and read: Blessed are you when people hate you, when they exclude you and insult you and reject your name as evil, because of the Son of Man. Rejoice in that day and leap for joy, because great is your reward in heaven.

Jacob felt vindicated. He closed the Bible and feigned sleep, a faint smile on his pimply face.

---

Jacob laid awake long after the rest of the household was asleep. When he was sure everyone was sound asleep, he got up, crept into the kitchen, and made himself a ham and cheese sandwich with the last of the deli meat in the fridge.

After he'd finished the sandwich, he washed it down with several long swallows of milk directly from the carton.

---

"You know stealing is a sin, don't you?" Pastor Clark asked.

Jacob nodded his head.

*Here we go*, he thought.

"And pornography is a sin too," the preacher said. "Using others like you did is sinful too, Jacob."

The preacher just stared at Jacob from across the cluttered desk for several moments.

"Let's find us a starting place, shall we?" he asked.

Jacob shrugged his shoulders.

"For all have sinned and fall short of the glory of God," Pastor Clark said. "Can we not agree on this?"

Jacob thought about it.

*Everybody's surely sinned at least once in their lives*, he thought.

Jacob nodded his head.

"Now I'm not going to waste a bunch of our time trying to get you to confess to putting your foster brother up to stealing those dirty magazines and that nail polish. I know you did it. You know you did it. We can move on from there."

*We can / move on.*

"I'm not trying to patronize or insult you," Pastor Clark said. "I'm trying to change the way you look at the world. I can see you're so full of hate, ate up with it. You got to move beyond your hatred to find God's shining light. Our petty feelings get in our way too."

The pastor picked up his Bible. He had a page marked with a piece of paper, he opened the book and read.

"Who shall separate us from the love of Christ? Shall trouble or hardship or persecution or famine or nakedness or danger or sword?"

He looked over the book, across the desk, at Jacob.

"Our own actions can separate us from the love of Christ too," he said. "Are you going to let your own trouble and hardship keep you from God's love?"

Jacob didn't know what to say.

"I didn't make him do nothin'," he said, after a few moments.

The preacher answered him immediately.

"And you will know the truth, and the truth will set you free," Pastor Clark said, closing his Bible.

-

The Faraways kept a deep freezer in the single car garage attached to their house. Jacob took the chains he'd stolen from Ace Hardware and sprayed them and the padlock, also stolen from Ace Hardware, with the water hose just outside the garage. Then he set the dripping chains and padlock into the deep freezer.

He'd skipped school, slipping off into the woods after the foster father dropped him off. By the time he'd made it back to the Faraways' he had two hours before the other foster children got off the bus.

Jacob was sitting on the couch in the living room when two of the three other foster children entered the house. Jeremy Bevins wasn't present; he'd been given community service as a diversion for the episode with the magazine and nail polish.

Thomas Miller and Deedee Simmons were both several years younger than Jacob, both in middle school. They were instantly wary when they found Jacob home alone and waiting for them.

"Ye guys ever smell paint?" Jacob asked, a broad smile on his face. He sprayed the cloth and held it over his face, breathing in the pungent silver paint.

Both of the younger foster kids shook their heads.

"Ye gotta try it," Jacob said, uncovering his face and feeling the instant rush of the high. "Here."

Jacob took Deedee Simmons's hands and put the can of spray paint and cloth in them.

"What ye do is spray a little into the cloth," Jacob said, moving the younger child's hands for her. "Like this. Then ye hold it over yer nose and smell. Try it."

"I'm not sure—"

"Try it," Jacob demanded.

Reluctantly, Deedee did as she was told.

Jacob's face creaked from the expanding smile.

"See?" Jacob said. "Pretty fun, isn't it?"

"I feel weird," Deedee giggled. "Funny."

"Yer turn," Jacob said, taking the cloth and canister of spray-paint from Deedee.

Thomas Miller, a year or two younger than Deedee, shook his head and tried stepping away but Jacob caught him by the arm.

"Yer not scared, are ye?" Jacob asked.

Thomas Miller shook his head but didn't say anything. He avoided Jacob's eyes.

Deedee was giggling.

"He's scared, isn't he?" Jacob asked her.

She giggled. "I think so."

"Yer not a pussy, are ye?" Jacob taunted the younger kid. "Just try it. If you don't like it, ye don't have to do it again."

The boy shook his head.

"Deedee likes it, don't ye?" Jacob asked.

Deedee was smiling but she looked slightly uncomfortable.

"Here, have another," Jacob said, spraying into the cloth and hold it for the younger girl to take.

Jacob held the cloth over Deedee's face and she breathed deeply.

"Oh," she sighed, her eyes rolling back in her head momentarily. She started giggling again.

"See?" Jacob said, turning to Thomas Miller. "It's fun. Makes ye happy."

Jacob reached down and took the younger boy by the shoulder and pulled him a little bit closer.

"Here," Jacob said, letting go of the boy to spray some more paint into the cloth. "I'll help ye. All ye got to do is spray a little into the cloth, like this, then hold it over your nose and smell it."

Jacob held the cloth over the boy's face against his weak struggles. The boy eventually had to breathe and, after he did, Jacob removed the cloth. A bit of silver was streaked across the bridge of Thomas Miller's nose.

"See? Ain't so bad, is it?"

The boy's smile was crooked.

Jacob sprayed more onto the cloth and held it over Thomas's face. The boy breathed in, his face now showing a slanting smile.

"See? I'm just trying to help y'all have a good time," Jacob said.

Both of the younger children looked at each other, saw the bits of silver paint on their faces, and laughed.

"Who wants more?" Jacob asked.

They both smiled and huffed more paint when Jacob offered.

"Hey, what'd ye say we play a little game?" Jacob asked.

Thomas Miller and Deedee Simmons both heartily assented in slurred words and fresh giggles.

"Y'all wait right here," Jacob said. "I'll be right back."

Jacob left the children laughing and high in the living room and made his way through the house into the Faraways' single-car garage. He opened the deep-freezer and retrieved the chains and padlock, Ace Hardware, both hard and cold and frozen together. He left the chains and the padlock, Ace Hardware, in his little bedroom, pocketing the padlock's golden key, and made his way back into the living room.

-

"Here, have a little more," Jacob said, handing the stiff, wet cloth to Thomas Miller.

Deedee Simmons was sitting cross-legged on the carpet, smiling up at the slowly spinning ceiling fan.

Thomas Miller huffed the paint.

"Lookie here," Jacob said.

It took a few moments for the younger children to focus on Jacob. He held up a small golden key.

"Let's play a game. I'm going to leave this key on the coffee table and y'all will have to race to be the first to get it and unlock the padlock. What'd y'all say?" Jacob asked, smiling. "Want to play a game?"

"Sure," Deedee Simmons said.

"Sounds fun," Thomas Miller said.

Jacob smiled and said, "Let's go back to the bedroom."

The two younger children followed Jacob down the short hall to the small bedroom Jacob shared with Jeremy Bevins. Jacob shut the door behind them.

"Clothes are cheating," Jacob said.

"What?" both children asked.

"Clothes are cheating in this game," Jacob said. "Ye can't have on any clothes in this game. It's against the rules."

Thomas Miller took off his shirt clumsily. Deedee, watching Thomas, followed suit.

The children stood in their underwear in the dimly lit room. Jacob sprayed the cloth and passed it to Thomas Miller, who huffed then passed it to Deedee Simmons, who also huffed some more paint.

"Alright, turn around and put yer hands together like ye's praying," Jacob commanded.

The children did as they were told, giggling all the while.

Jacob bound each of the younger children's hands together with rope he'd stolen from Ace Hardware.

"Put yer backs together," he commanded.

Giggling, the children did as they were told. Jacob then lifted the freezing chain from the carpet and looped it around the children, who flinched and bucked against the cold metal. Jacob wrapped the chain, Ace Hardware, around the children four times then padlocked it shut.

"I don't like this," Deedee Simmons said.

# BIRTH OF A MONSTER

"It's too cold!" Thomas Miller said.

"The object of the game is to get out of the chains and rope," Jacob said. "The key is sitting on the coffee table."

Jacob sprayed more paint into the cloth then breathed it in deeply. A drip of paint dropped from his nose onto his upper lip and he licked it off.

Jacob then shoved the bound children to the floor. They began to cry and struggle against the rope and the chains, Ace Hardware.

Jacob laughed watching the bundled lump of flesh and chain and rope on the dingy carpet.

"Ye've got about an hour and a half before the Faraways get home," Jacob said. "Plenty of time to get to the living room and free yerselves."

"Let us out!" they screamed.

Jacob walked over to the bedroom door, opened it, and stepped into the hall. He took one last look at the younger children and smiled. He turned off the overhead light and the room sank into shadows, the only light coming from the closed blinds.

"Good luck," he said, pulling the door closed behind him.

Jacob smiled as they screamed from the closed bedroom. He walked down the hall back into the living room, the paint canister and the cloth in his hands. He plopped down onto the couch and huffed some more paint, the golden key gleaming in the fading afternoon light pouring in through the living room window.

The screams eventually became wails then crying. Jacob couldn't handle the crying. It sounded too much like the crying he still heard emanating from the mineshaft.

*Tanya Miller / & her unborn baby*

Jacob went back to the Faraways' garage, retrieved two tennis balls, and two pet collars from his collection. He tried opening the door to the bedroom but Thomas and Deedee were on the floor just inside it, blocking it from opening.

"Y'all havin' fun?" Jacob called. "Move back 'n' I'll open this door."

He heard motion from inside, sniffling and thumps.

Jacob opened the door and flipped on the overhead lights. The children were still on the floor, their eyes squinted under the light. They hadn't made any progress with their bindings.

*Good*, he thought.

He leaned forward and took Deedee's soft chin in his hands.

"Here," he said, opening the Case knife, Ace Hardware, and putting a slit into each of the tennis balls. "Open wide."

Deedee Simmons actually opened her mouth for him. Jacob stuffed one of the tennis balls into her mouth and kept it in place with one of the pet collars, this one without a nametag. Her muffled cries warned Thomas of what was to come even though he couldn't see what Jacob was doing.

Jacob had to use the Case knife, Ace Hardware, to pry open and keep open the younger foster child's mouth. Jacob put in the tennis ball then tightened the collar, this one with a nametag reading: Blackie, then rose to his feet.

He smiled down at his work.

*such a / happy boy sometimes*

Jacob was sitting on the couch when Teresa Faraway, the foster mother, arrived home from work. The can of silver spray paint and the stained, stiffened cloth were sitting right out in the open on the coffee table. Jacob had been dozing, the house peaceful and quiet after the younger children cried themselves into silence from the back of the house, and the foster mother's key in the door had woke him.

For a fleeting second, Jacob thought the sound was the younger kids unlocking the frozen padlock. He smiled when he saw he was temporarily alone in the living room.

The key turned in the lock and the door opened.

The foster mother froze when she saw Jacob. Jacob could feel the dried paint all over his face, could feel it drying and clogging up both of his nostrils.

"Jacob?" she asked.

Jacob nodded and his head felt like a hollowed-out drum, one marble rattling around in there, and he giggled.

The foster mother looked wary and concerned.

"What's so funny?" she asked. "What's all over your face?"

Jacob couldn't help it, he giggled. He felt his body shaking with some strange hilarity he knew he wouldn't be able to control much longer.

"Where's everybody else?" the foster mother asked.

There were screams and a long, plaintive wail from the back of the house.

# BIRTH OF A MONSTER

Teresa Faraway, the foster mother, took another look at Jacob and, in it, Jacob saw disgust, fear, and hatred all intermingled and present. The foster mother left the front door standing open as she rushed to the rear of the house.

Jacob sat on the couch looking at his hands, which were clasped together in his lap. The social worker had come with a state trooper. Jacob was told to sit on the couch and not move while the social worker and the state trooper talked with the foster mother and both of the foster children Jacob had restrained. He could hear their voices through the thin walls of the house but not well enough to hear individual words. He could hear their tone of voice and Deedee Simmons's constant crying.

After a time, the social worker came into the living room.

"Jacob, can I sit beside you and talk a little bit?" she asked.

Jacob scooted over and the social worker sat down beside him.

"I work with Kim Cady,," the social worker said. "I'm the social worker on-call, meaning I handle all the calls after normal business hours. Okay?"

"Okay."

*Stay calm*, the voice said.

"My name is Tara," the social worker said. "Tara Jacobs."

Jacob made sure his face remained blank.

"What happened here this afternoon?" the social worker asked.

Jacob didn't know what to say, so he didn't say anything.

"How'd your foster brother and sister get tied and chained up?" she asked. "Did you have something to do with that?"

Jacob studied the thumbs of each of his hands. They were strong and flexible. He thought about his ancestors breaking bones to get to the nutrient-rich marrow inside.

"Jacob?"

Jacob saw a bit of fingernail polish he'd missed removing on his left index finger. He tried scratching it off with his right thumb.

"This is a very serious matter," Tara Jacobs, the on-call social worker, said. "I need you to pay attention and answer my questions."

"Jacob Hunter Goodman." The foster mother's voice was angry and shrill and came from just inside the hall. "You sit up and pay attention to what this woman is telling you."

There were heavy footsteps from the hall and the state trooper emerged into the living room. Jacob saw his gun shining in its holster on the trooper's belt. Jacob wondered what it felt like to hold a gun like that. He bet they were heavy.

"Why'd you tie them up?" the social worker asked.

Jacob shrugged his shoulders.

"Why weren't they wearing clothes?" Tara Jacobs asked.

Jacob shrugged again.

"You answer her!" the foster mother shouted. "You answer her right this minute."

Jacob kept his gaze on his hands. He saw them in Fast-Forward X2 Mode dismembering the bully. He saw his hands drop the bully down into the mineshaft piece by piece, the darkness yawning upwards and taking whatever it was given without sound or complaint.

The trooper crossed the small living room and came to a crouch in front of the couch. Jacob couldn't avoid looking at the man.

"You need to open that mouth of yours and speak up," the trooper said. "You're about to be in a world of trouble if we don't get some answers right quick."

"It was a game," Jacob said quietly.

"What?" the foster mother shouted. "A what?"

"It was a game," Jacob repeated.

"A game?" the social worker asked.

"Game?" the trooper repeated. "What kind of game were y'all playing?"

"Where'd those collars come from? Huh?" the foster mother was screaming now. Teresa Faraway's face was full of blood and twisted in anger and disgust.

The trooper shot her a look and pointed toward the end of the hall.

"Go on back and check on them others," the trooper commanded.

The foster mother did as she was told but shot Jacob a fierce look beforehand.

"You're out of this house, Jacob Hunter Goodman," the foster mother said. "You're out!"

Jacob didn't mind leaving the Faraways. He had a few hiding places but felt no real connection to the place aside from that. The way the foster mother brandished his removal from the home did not sting the way he supposed she thought it would.

Not for the first time, Jacob wondered what a sense of home felt like.

Jacob could hear the foster mother and the foster father all the way from the kitchen.

"I want him out," the foster mother yelled. "Now!"

"He cain't stay here," the foster father said. "Not now. Not after this!"

Through the walls, Jacob heard the placating tones of the social worker and the stern voice of the trooper drowning out the foster mother.

"Pack up your things," the social worker said.

It was like magic. Jacob was alone in the little bedroom, then the social worker, Tara Jacobs, was standing just inside the doorjamb looking down at him. Jacob couldn't read her face, not completely. There was just so much going on there: disgust, sadness, *dismay*, Mrs. Horace's Word of the Day, *1: to cause to lose courage or resolution (as because of alarm or fear); 2: upset, perturb*, and annoyance. Then she was turning and, in her departing, he smelled her: perfume and cigarettes.

It didn't take but a minute. He had so few things to pack. His three changes of clothes, the tacklebox, the two composition notebooks, the ballpoint pen, Tanya Miller's blue and white thumbnail, tucked into the baconing waistband of his stained underwear, and the Bible, His Shining Light Mission.

Jacob hated the intense fear he felt when he saw the state trooper's car out in the drive. His legs carried him, but only just barely. The social worker led him to her vehicle, and Jacob hated himself for the shaky sigh of relief that escaped his lips. He sat in the passenger seat and they rode in silence through the gloomy evening. The trees, now devoid of their leaves, looked like skeletal fingers reaching up, some with suspicion, others in supplication. The social worker gave up on conversation not even five minutes into the drive. She turned the car radio to a religious station.

"The path to the Lord can be long, boys. The path to the Light can be filled with dark, brothers. The Way is war every day. The war a personal cross to bear, each and every one of us. Made in His image and suffering for Him in His image."

The social worker rolled the window down and smoked a cigarette, the hand on the steering wheel tapping along with a cadence in the preacher's stream of words. Jacob reached down and touched the Bible, His Shining Light Mission, and felt goosebumps ripple across his body.

"Blessed are those who are persecuted because of righteousness, for theirs is the kingdom of heaven. Let me repeat, brothers and sisters: for *theirs* is the kingdom of heaven. We all suffer, y'all. We got them demons 'n' devils in the world out there. We've all got a skeleton or two hangin' 'round our closets. We've all suffered and sinned, yes! We all suffer, yes!, but *ours*, yes!, is the kingdom of heaven. Ours, y'all! Ours! *Yes!*"

Jacob smiled.

Jacob set the trash bag containing his belongings on the front desk and watched as the woman in scrubs went through them. There wasn't much: his black backpack, a mostly empty tacklebox, the Case knife, Ace Hardware, a few changes of clothes, his two notebooks, and the Bible, His Shining Light Mission.

"Can't let you have the knife," the woman said, setting it aside. "Or the tacklebox. We'll keep your things locked up in the front room. You can have them when you leave."

Jacob watched the woman as she wrote but couldn't get his eyes to focus. He was still rolling the words "residential," "treatment," and "facility" around in his head and felt fuzzy all over. He heard the words "locked facility" and felt his throat constrict, making him burp suddenly.

"Excuse you," the woman said, looking up momentarily from the tacklebox. "You can't be carrying around lures neither. Hooks."

She reached into a large drawer and pulled out a pair of sweatpants and a plain white t-shirt.

"Here's your duds," she said, then pointed to a door. "You can change in there. Bring me back your street clothes. Go on, now."

Jacob did as he was told.

"You can keep your Bible," she said, pushing the book across the desk.

"Thank ye," Jacob said.

Kim Cady, the social worker, Tara Jacobs, the other social worker, and Cynthia Caldwell-Paige, the social workers' supervisor, and Jacob sat at the scuffed conference table.

"I'm not sure what to tell you," Cynthia Caldwell-Paige said.

Jacob was indignant.

"I demand to be placed back with my momma," Jacob yelled.

"Quit hollerin'," Kim Cady said. "Right now!"

Jacob was panting. He couldn't hunt in the facility. He'd nearly had Tanya Miller's thumbnail taken away from him. He couldn't handle it anymore.

"I cain't be here," he whispered. "I cain't. I just cain't."

"You'll have to," Cynthia Caldwell-Paige said. "That little stunt you pulled with the chains and dog collars nearly got you charged criminally. Criminally, not this family court stuff, No, crimin-ally. Let it sink in."

Jacob tried, but couldn't.

"I cain't be here any longer," he said.

"You've got less than a year" Tara Jacobs said. "Buck up, buck-aroo."

I will begin these letters, these letters to all the children I'll never have, by saying the world is suffering. You were born, or not, and that's its own kind of suffering, to suffering and can expect only suffering from life, for that is what it is.

Jacob's left leg bounced as he wrote.

The Bible is the only thing seeing me through these hard times, boys. James 1:12: Blessed is the man who remains steadfast under trial, for when he has stood the test he will receive the crown of life, which God has promised to those who love him.

"Chow time, boys!"

Jacob put away his red notebook, the one he thought of as **Letters to My Children**, slipped it between his sheet and his mattress, then made the bed. He hid it even though he didn't have to. He was allowed to have a notebook of his own, it wasn't against the rules. But he did. He was used to hiding things. He still had some things hidden around the hills around Prestonsburg.

I'm surrounded by sadists and sickos, he wrote. I hear all about their twisted life stories during group therapy every single day. Their abusive fathers. At least they had them. Their cold, loveless mothers. Last I heard, Momma was still in jail pending trial. Heard the social worker say she was facing ten years with all the drug charges. Serves her right. Children, do not allow your selves to go down the road of drugs. I've been in toxicated and look where it got me! Writing you these letters in the juvenile detention center.

"Lights out!"

Jacob scribbled faster.

I miss hunting the most.

All of the lights winked out.

Jacob felt tears sting his eyes and willed himself to not sob.

-

"Take your medicine."

Jacob took his medicine. He *always* took his medicine.

-

"You need to start thinking about your future," the social worker said.

It made him remember Pastor Clark for the first time in a long time.

"If I was you, I'd go the stipend route," the social worker said, pushing the brochure across the table. "You qualify and all you have to do is keep a C average. You can go to trade school too. Learn electrical or welding or something."

*Welding,* Jacob thought. He saw sparks shooting off in his head.

-

*Trust me that it's better this way, little one.*

Jacob had taken to calling Tanya Miller's unborn baby, which he didn't hear crying every night, just most nights, "little one" because he felt a strong kinship with it. He felt fatherly toward it and thought his **Letters to My Children** would be imparted to it somehow.

You should all be comforted to know you'll never have to inhabit a world so full of evil and sin. So full of hate, hate, hate, HATE. I know you may come to feel robbed of the lives you didn't get the chance to live, My Children, but I strongly feel it is best this way. The world is too far gone. The end must be nearing. Rest easy, My Children. Rest easy and I'll join you one day soon in the Kingdom of Heaven.

-

The medicine makes me numb. Numb numb numb. It's like my brain is soaked in a soft cottony gauze and I can't shake it. I want to hunt still but not nearly as bad as I just want to go to sleep. Sometimes I want to go to sleep and just not wake up, just like you, My Children. Just like you. I often feel like the only sane person in an insane world. All these people are living these fake lives, lives that don't count, lives that don't matter. Like sheep, really, the lot of them. Not like me, my children, not at all like me. I can almost see the outline sometimes, when all these medications let me think my own thoughts. I can almost see it now, something like Fast Forward X2 Mode and Crystal Cubism. Something blurred but with definite shape and boundaries.

These days stake up like ash in a fireplace coming in flurries or hissing into the night. I feel sad, then the beginnings of an anger that never quite bubbles to the surface. Sometimes, often actually, I wish I could feel the pure burning fury of anger again.

-

The social worker helped Jacob get the trailer rented. She showed him how to open a checking account and how to balance the checkbook. Jacob knew he should be thankful but the *perfunctory*, Mrs. Horace, *1: characterized by routine or superficiality: mechanical; 2: lacking in interest or enthusiasm,* manner in which she imparted her knowledge made him resentful.

He was overjoyed to be on his own. The singlewide trailer up Black Dog Branch was in terrible condition but it was all his own. The rent and utilities were even covered by the state. It didn't have any furniture but the social worker said she knew a place that would deliver him some second-hand furniture the day after tomorrow.

Jacob slept like a baby on the sleeping pad he stole from Walmart.

-

He felt in-tune with himself when he took the Adderall his therapist had prescribed him. He could think clearly and think clearly quickly. He felt like the best possible version of himself when he took an extra dose.

Jacob took to the welding with vigor. He was a perfectionist and often ruined the first and second drafts of his projects due to hours of welding and rewelding, overworking the metals and melting most of it away.

Jacob began making metal sculptures instead of ruining his welding projects. He made strange layers of shapes doing his best to think both in terms of Crystal Cubism and Fast-Forward X2 Mode. Each of his sculptures were a strange mashup of half-animal/half-human creatures, often with multiple arms and hands. When asked about them, Jacob referred to them as "angels" or "creations." He overheard one of his teachers chuckling with a student.

"More like a demon than an angel!" the student whispered.

How they both laughed.

Jacob paid them no mind. He was on his own again. He was making art. He was hunting.

-

"I think you should switch majors," Jimmie Honaker, the art professor said.

Jacob had been asked to bring three of his sculptures to the small student gallery for display. He'd just brought the second in, a small piece with human face-like features on a prickly body that somehow looked both like a bear and a bison. Jacob set the sculpture down.

"I appreciate ye asking me to display a few of my creations," he said, keeping his face blank, empty.

"I think you could go places with your art," Jimmie Honaker said. "If you switch majors and start putting in longer hours and focusing on your composition."

"I'm going to have to make money to support myself soon," Jacob said, echoing the social worker's words even if he didn't completely understand or care. "I might be able to minor in art."

The professor sighed.

Jacob went back for the third sculpture, which had the body of a falcon or some other bird of prey and three humanoid heads in varying displays of emotion: happy, sad, and fearful.

Jacob didn't see the point of an art degree but a minor would be covered by the state so he agreed. He made study after study of Jean Metzinger's *Two Nudes, Two Women*. Some with charcoals, some with pen, but most with metal.

-

He'd run out too quickly too many months in a row and now Stacie Duggens, his therapist, was "having reservations" about his medicine and "beginning the tapering process." Jacob was getting less of the medicine and hating her for getting him hooked on it and himself for being so weak, so without the prerequisite moral fortitude. The long hours he spent in the shop welding were more trying without the Adderall.

Jacob stopped taking his other medications so the Adderall he took would have a heightened effect. He took to only having a single

# BIRTH OF A MONSTER

meal a day for the same reason.

Beer and liquor were wonders. He found he could walk into most of the gas stations and liquor stores and purchase alcohol without having to show his identification card—the social worker was helping him get a driver's license. Jacob loved getting drunk, which was easy to do on a mostly empty stomach.

The world is dark and lonely, My Children. I shine a light from the machine and bring new creations into it but it still feels so unreal sometimes. The sculptures, though pretty, though done with growing mastery and accomplishment, pale in comparison to what I fear not do.

Jacob was having visions of human flesh and metal.

It is trying, living with so much suffering.

Metal and bone and skin and gristle.

Jacob drank himself into oblivion to avoid seeing what his mind showed.

*on / display*

Jacob opened his eyes and saw that it was midmorning. His head was pounding.

*How many beers did I drink last night?*

It felt like a cat threw up in the back of his throat. He'd bought a thirty-pack after class that afternoon. He doubted a beer was left.

He rolled off the bed—the social worker had got it for him—and sat perfectly still, forcing himself not to retch or shit. He rubbed his sleep-crusted eyes. When he opened them again, Jacob saw that all ten of his toes were painted red.

"What the . . . ?"

He reached down to see if what he was seeing was real and noticed all ten of his fingernails were painted bright red too.

"Jesus," he whispered.

Jacob had no recollection of painting his nails or having red fingernail polish anywhere in the singlewide.

"Yer Christy's boy," the man said.

Jacob was unsure if this was a good thing for the man to point out at that moment so he said nothing.

"How much for five?" Jacob asked.

"They're ten apiece."

Jacob passed the man the money then took the handful of blue pills.

"Thanks," he said, turning to leave.

"Sure. Hey," the man said, "how's yer momma doin'?"

Jacob stopped and turned around. "She's locked up," he said.

"I know," the man said. He opened his mouth to say something else, closed it, then opened it again. "Ye know I used to date Christy," the man said, "from time to time."

Jacob didn't want to have this conversation. He'd known many men to date his mother. More men than he'd care to remember.

The man waved a hand. "See ye around," he said.

Jacob stepped off the front porch and made his way toward the road. It was a half-mile walk down the county road to Black Dog Branch. He put one of the pills on his tongue and dry swallowed it.

Things were warmer with Xanax. Xanax was a gentle blurring of all the hard lines in small doses. It was outright bliss the more you did. No wonder his mother loved it so much.

Jacob pushed open the cheap door to his trailer and stepped into the darkened living room. His tacklebox was sitting open on the secondhand coffee table where he left it. All the different-colored collars looked festive in the gloomy trailer. He'd been hunting nearly every night.

Jacob set the pills on the table and began crushing them with the bottom of his lighter. When the four pills were powder, he used his food stamps card to line them up. He used a rolled-up dollar bill to snort one of the lines.

Everything felt better for a while.

-

Jacob woke up and knew he'd almost died. He was sitting in the little closet of the master bedroom, his chin almost touching his chest, the rope around his neck. He pushed himself up, easing the tension of the rope, and knew his neck was bruised by the pain he felt. He didn't remember setting up but he knew what he'd been doing: using a rope to choke himself while he masturbated.

Jacob lifted the rope over his head, then cleared his clogged nostrils. Blue lined his fingernails. He felt the dried snot and powder on his upper lip, could taste it in his dry mouth.

Jacob made his way to the trailer's tiny kitchen and opened the fridge. He retrieved a beer and popped the top, drinking half as he made his way back to the living room. He sat down on the couch the social worker had found for him. He looked down at the table. There was half a line of Xanax left. Jacob picked up the dollar-straw and snorted it.

*I could've strangled myself,* Jacob thought. *I could've died.*

He felt nothing. He finished the beer and went back to the fridge for another.

Jacob walked out under the bright moonlight, sure he was invisible, leaving the shadow-laden forest behind him. With the bedside lamp on inside the trailer, Jacob could make out the couple inside. The woman was rubbing cream on her face. She was in an oversized t-shirt and nothing else. Jacob could make out the twin ridges of her breasts in the mirror. The man was already in the bed, under the covers, his face half-mooned and tired looking.

Jacob stepped closer to the window.

The woman was talking. He watched her mouth move but could only hear a feminine murmur. Jacob didn't wonder what she was saying. He assumed it was something *asinine,* Mrs. Horace Word of the Day, *1: extremely or utterly foolish or silly; 2: of, relating to, or resembling an ass.* Most everything women said was asinine.

The next trailer down was the last in the lot and a good thirty yards away. Jacob took several large swigs from the Thunderbird. He could feel the alcohol rushing through his bloodstream, especially in his ears. Jacob thought it sounded like how he'd heard the ocean described.

Jacob circled the double-wide. All of the lights were out except for the one above the stove in the kitchen. Jacob noted that there was a vehicle parked out front: a red S-10. This meant there was probably someone inside.

He set the Thunderbird down on the porch. He tried the front door and it was unlocked. He stepped inside and retrieved the pen-light he'd stolen from the University of Pikeville Medical School. He clicked it on and immediately shut it off when he saw the sleeping female on the couch.

*Shit!*

*Stay calm,* the voice said. *She would've cried out if she woke up and saw you.*

Jacob forced his breathing to slow.

He replayed what he'd just seen in his head in Slow Motion. She was young, his age or a bit older, dark-haired, and overweight. Jacob had seen the ham hock arms and then couldn't unsee them in his mind.

*Fat slob.*

He walked over to where the girl slept, his hand slipping into the waistband of the sweatpants, Walmart. He stood over the sleeping girl for several minutes, his hand steadily working. He was sweating now. He could feel it trickling down his spine, dropping down into the crack of his ass.

Jacob finished onto the threadbare carpet beside the couch. The girl did not so much as stir. He took the crucifix off the wall on his way out.

-

Jacob couldn't stop staring at the woman's bulging stomach.

*Definitely preggers*, he thought. *Super preggers.*

The woman, in her mid-thirties, Jacob guessed, had a distinct waddle when she walked. She took the bowl of ice cream she'd just eaten into the kitchen and set it down into the sink.

*She's 'bout to pop!* Jacob thought, watching the stomach bounce and sway.

Jacob knew the woman lived alone in the little trailer, off all on its own off the county road about three miles away from his own, because he'd watched her house for a week straight. Her mother and a woman Jacob guessed was a social worker—she looked the part anyway—visited the pregnant woman during the day but she had no visitors for the past five nights.

The pregnant woman walked back into the living room, the glow of the television making her momentarily a pale blue. She sat down heavily and Jacob watched her ringless hands begin to knead and rub the bulging stomach.

*Unmarried and pregnant*, Jacob thought, *another wasted life.*

The woman fell asleep, the back of her head resting on top of the couch, her mouth hanging wide open.

The front door was locked but the bedroom window slid open soundlessly. Jacob took his steps as carefully as the Thunderbird would allow. He nearly fell over a house slipper, catching himself on the paneled bedroom wall.

*Get it together*, the voice said.

Jacob breathed in through his nose, then let it out through his open mouth, then he stepped into the hall. The glow of the television lit up the entire trailer. Jacob stepped soundlessly through the kitchen into the living room.

The woman's belly was uncovered, the t-shirt bunched just under her swollen breasts.

Jacob could feel the child crying before he heard it. All the hair on his body seemed to rise with a static hiss and he nearly jumped when the baby cried out.

*Keep it together*, the voice said. *It's only in your head.*

The woman snored softly.

The baby cried again, angry and echoing.

Jacob ground his teeth, doing his best to not hear the baby's cries, *Tanya Miller's baby's cries*, his left hand dipping into the sweatpants, Walmart, without conscious thought. He worked at it harder and harder until he came suddenly all over the woman's exposed stomach. He jerked and spilled more onto the couch and carpet.

Jacob kept waiting for the woman to wake, but she didn't. He pulled his pants up and stared down at the thick mucus-like mess he'd left on the woman's stomach. It glowed silver momentarily then the image on the television changed and it glowed golden.

The child cried from the mineshaft miles away. Jacob ground his teeth.

Jacob wondered if any of the semen would seep through the stretched-thin skin and affect the baby inside. He hoped it could.

*Sterile the normal way maybe*, he thought, *but not this way. This is different.*

Jacob unlocked the front door and closed it silently behind him. He picked up the bottle of Thunderbird and drained it. He flung the empty off into the woods where it hit the ground with a dull thud. He felt holy somehow, shrouded in moonlit invisibility.

*I'm invisible*, Jacob thought, smiling. *I am the desert. I am the seabed.*

-

Jacob thought about raping the pregnant woman often. He saw it in his head in Fast-Forward X2 Mode. The voice in his head told him not to though, so he didn't.

*There's too much that could go wrong*, the voice said. *The woman lives too close. She's got people that would notice her missing.*

Jacob needed more pills. He'd run out.

Casey Gladwell and Steven Douglas lived a few trailers down from Stephen. He'd bought off them before but he didn't have any money right now.

Jacob watched their trailer from the woods beyond. Through the cracked blinds he could see the kitchen table, littered with drugs and paraphernalia, and the couple. They were gearing up to go out, Jacob could tell because they were both wearing jackets. Jacob stepped deeper into the woods and waited.

He planned on stealing the pills as soon as they left. It was cold but Jacob had Thunderbird and a Goodwill jacket. He crouched when the porch light came on and Casey Gladwell and Stephen Douglas emerged. Jacob watched them climb inside the lifted Dodge Ram.

As soon as the taillights disappeared into the night, Jacob rose on his unsteady legs and made his way across the small yard. He nearly tripped over the last stair on the front porch but was able to catch himself just in time. He tried the front door even though he'd watched Steven Douglas lock it.

He took a half-step away from the door and kicked it with all his might. The lock broke through the thin jamb and the door swung open, the doorknob embedding itself into the wall. Jacob stumbled into the trailer's living room and fell headlong over the coffee table. He hit the foot of the couch and got a rug burn on his left cheek. He sat up, shook his head, momentarily saw two television sets across the room, then just the one.

He pushed himself to his feet and made his way over to the kitchen table and the drugs. There were three prescription bottles, two of them were unlidded. Jacob didn't bother trying to read the labels. He opened each one and squinted inside. The first pills were oval-shaped and white. The second bottle was full of circular yellow ones. The third was the jackpot, nearly a third full of 1mg Xanax tablets.

He popped one immediately.

He used the bottom of the prescription bottle to crush up another. There was a cut plastic straw on the table. Jacob used it.

Light poured into the living room and Jacob realized with horror that the lifted Dodge Ram had pulled back in front of the trailer.

*Shit! Move!*

Jacob, Xanax bottle in hand, ran to the front door. He could just make out two shapes stepping around the shining high beams.

"What the fuck!" Steven Douglas yelled.

"They're still in there!" Casey Gladwell shrieked.

There was a hollow pop then something smacked into the wall beside Jacob.

*Move*, the voice said. *Back of the house. Now!*

Jacob ran through the trailer to the back bedroom. There was a window unit blocking the window.

*Shove it out of the way.*

Jacob ran across the room and threw all his weight into the air conditioner. It dropped from the window with a crash.

There was yelling from the front of the trailer.

Jacob threw himself through the open window. He thumped down onto the cold ground beside the air conditioning unit. He pushed himself up and started running for the woods. There were several more hollow pops and Jacob heard something whizz by overhead. He put his head down and forced his feet to remain un-tangled and moving.

-

It took him twenty minutes to work his way slowly, quietly back to his trailer.

*Stupid*, the voice said. *You don't shit where you eat. You shouldn't have tried to rob somebody that lives this close.*

The sirens wailing in the distance had helped distract Steven Douglas and Casey Gladwell, who abandoned their pursuit of Jacob and rushed into their trailer at the first sound of sirens.

*Probably gonna hide all they can before the cops arrive.*

Jacob slipped into his trailer and pulled down the cheap blinds.

-

Cops were crawling the mountainside. Jacob saw their headlights and search beams combing the area. He sank away from the window and popped two Adderalls, washing the pills down with a large swallow of Southern Comfort.

*Keep it together*, the voice said.

*You're safe in here*, another said.

*No, you're not.*

*Yes.*

*No.*

Jacob listened to the gravel crunch under tires outside his trailer.

*Oh God! They're here and they know!*

Jacob shook.

The car moved away from Jacob's trailer.

*Thank God!*

Jacob heard voices outside his trailer.

*Shit!*

411

There was a loud knocking at his door.

"Sheriff's Department!" a loud voice yelled. "Sheriff's Department!"

Jacob put the bottle of pills under the couch.

"Coming!" he said.

His tongue felt strange and alien in his mouth. It was moving around moving from the backs of his front teeth down to the undersides of his lower lip then back up again. His hands were working each other and he felt his skin beginning to crawl.

*Open the door*, the voice said.

Jacob felt his face twitch. He waited until he was sure he had complete control over himself then he unlocked and opened the front door of his trailer.

A uniformed sheriff's deputy stood with one hand resting on the butt of his holstered gun and the other holding a flashlight. He shined the beam up into Jacob's face.

"Sheriff's Department, how're ye doin'?" the deputy asked.

"Fine," Jacob said carefully.

"Anybody else with ye?"

Jacob swallowed, an action that seemed to take a very long time to complete.

"No, sir."

"Ye sure 'bout that?"

Jacob nodded, his head feeling jerky and unnatural in its movement.

"Had anything to drink this evenin'?"

Jacob's first instinct was to lie. He flinched then forced his expression to remain slack, blank.

"Yessir," he said.

"How much would ye say ye've had to drink?"

"A lot."

"Been here all evenin'? Been out anywheres else drinkin'?"

Jacob shook his head.

"No, sir," he said. "Had me a few bottles of Thunderbird here at the house."

"I see," the deputy said, finally removing his light from Jacob's eyes. "Sir, I'm gonna need ye to go back inside and go to sleep. We've had a shooting out here tonight. Ye probably slept right through it."

Jacob reached a hand up to his face, making sure it was smooth, empty.

"A shootin'?" Jacob asked. "Who got shot?"

"We're working on that," the deputy said. "Go on back inside now."

The deputy turned to leave.

*Don't*, the voice said.

"Wait," Jacob called.

*Shut up*, the voice said.

"Let me he'p y'all," Jacob called, feeling the sudden need to not let the cop disappear.

*He doesn't know my secrets but I have to make sure*, he thought.

"Sir, go back inside yer trailer."

"I can he'p ye'ns," Jacob said, hearing the slurring of the words despite his best efforts to the contrary. "A shootin', ye said? Jesus Lord!"

The deputy put his hands on Jacob's shoulders and spun him around.

"Git back to yer trailer before I arrest ye for PI."

Jacob stumbled but did not fall. He steadied himself against the cold metal siding of his rented trailer.

"Now, I live here got damn it," Jacob said, fighting uselessly against the anger. "Ye cain't be comin' up here and touchin' me at my house-trailer."

*Don't get angry*, the voice said.

*I cain't help it.*

Jacob spun on unsteady legs and nearly went down on the uneven sidewalk.

"Git back inside," the deputy snapped.

"Fuck ye, ye cock-sucking motherfucker," Jacob screamed.

*Stupid*, the voice said.

"That's it," the voice said.

There was a cracking sound then everything went black.

Jacob woke in the back of the police cruiser with a pounding headache. The night-shrouded world blurred by in the window. Jacob blinked back tears and forced himself to sit up straight in the seat despite his hands being handcuffed together behind his back.

Why couldn't he just have listened to the cop and went back inside the trailer?

Jacob felt so tired despite the Adderall. He leaned against the cool window and fell back asleep.

There was a slight echo to everything in the Floyd County Detention Center, as if every sound bounced off all the concrete and metal before making its way to your ear. There was someone hollering not far off, something about a peach pie, it sounded like.

Jacob opened his eyes, looked around the drunk tank, then closed them again. He wasn't alone but he might as well have been. The other three people were on the opposite side of the room but they weren't paying Jacob any mind. One of the men's shirts was shredded and barely covered his massive beer belly.

*I gotta get out of eastern Kentucky*, Jacob thought. *I can't keep living like this.*

His head was pounding and he wished he'd had a Xanax or even a beer. He closed his eyes and decided to sleep until they cut him loose.

Jacob was released hours later. By that time, the poison headache had burned down to a low simmer. He was processed and given his court date paperwork and, before he knew it, Jacob was blinking under the harsh afternoon sun. He'd been given the opportunity to make a phone call but who could he call?

Jacob put one foot in front of the other and started walking toward his little trailer up Black Dog Branch feeling his time in eastern Kentucky had come to its end.

*Louisville is a big enough city to get lost in,* Jacob thought. *There's enough bigness to hide in. The urban jungle. Urban hunting. I can transfer my welding classes to the community college there.*

Jacob walked the four miles smiling, glad to be unencumbered under the sun.

## CHAPTER TWENTY-FIVE
## GOOD RIDDANCE

**JACOB MET WITH HIS CLASS** counselor and completed all the required paperwork to transfer his classes to the Jefferson County Community College in Louisville. The social worker helped him find an apartment and get a new caseworker in Louisville. The social worker also helped him find a cheap efficiency unit near the community college's campus that the Office of Student Affairs got him a voucher for.

Jacob boarded a Greyhound bus with Tanya Miller's blue and white thumbnail as the only belonging on his person. His few other belongings were stored in a trash bag in the storage bins below. He watched the hills of eastern Kentucky slip by and wished them good riddance.

*Louisville will be better*, Jacob told himself. *There'll be more people, more anonymity, more freedom.*

Jacob was nearly halfway through the welding program. The class counselor ensured him he'd be done and certified within a year if he kept at it.

The new social worker helped Jacob obtain his driver's license. Jacob picked up a few apprentice welding jobs he could work on in the shop on campus and began saving for a vehicle.

Jacob worked hard at his classes and on his creations. He found the art department of the community college receptive to his sculptures and was allowed to put several of them on display. They were stark and sleek things now that he was welding with proficiency and know-how. His angels were monstrous things full of righteous terror. Wings and beaks and claws and hard, unsmiling faces.

Jacob spent most of his considerable free time working on his sculptures. When he wasn't working on his art or studying, he got drunk or high. Mostly he got drunk. He was still scared from his arrest and was keeping clear of drugs aside from the Adderall, which he was prescribed and often ran out of long before his script was up for refill.

Jacob earned his initial certification in welding not long after moving to Louisville. He expedited the process by taking several classes at the Elizabethtown campus, about forty-five minutes south of Louisville. It was a much smaller town than Louisville, but Jacob found a bar that suited him: The Bourbon and Ale Tavern, known around town as the B.A.T., "the Bat," everyone called it. He started his nightly ramblings there after welding classes.

Jacob drank cheap bourbon and beer until he ran low on funds then he'd get a bottle or two of Thunderbird and hit the streets. Prostitutes were easier to come by in Louisville than Elizabethtown but he liked the B.A.T. because it was the kind of place where women became prostitutes. It was the steppingstone to a lower plane of existence. A purgatory of barflies and wastrels and terrible acoustic cover bands.

*A real dump*, Jacob thought, pushing himself up from the bar.

It was the kind of place where a person could be overlooked, forgotten.

Jacob missed the rideshare back to Louisville and knew he'd be spending the night somewhere in Elizabethtown, which he was fine with. He'd catch a ride back to Louisville tomorrow after class. He'd slept in parks overnight a few times since he'd relocated to central Kentucky. The night was cool but not cold and Jacob had brought several of his new knives, all stolen from the hunting section of Academy Sports in Louisville. He took to the night, *on a hunt*, and began looking for unlocked doors and windows.

-

Jacob slipped into the squat, single-story house near Valley Creek through the unlocked backdoor. It led into a small kitchen. There was a light on over the stove. Jacob walked over to it and turned it off. He listened to the quiet house for several moments then clicked on the penlight he'd stolen from the University of Pikeville Medical School.

He searched the cabinets for pills but didn't find any in the kitchen. He tried the living room next. No luck. He found the bathroom and opened the mirror but there was only aspirin and Benadryl. He made his way back into the hall and down toward the two bedrooms. One was a child's room. Jacob could tell from the pictures hanging on the door. He peeked his head in and saw the small bed and the sleeping child in it, not much older than a toddler, Jacob judged by the size of it.

The bedroom door at the end of the hall was cracked. He eased it open and slipped inside, clicking off the penlight. He waited while his eyes adjusted to the darkness. He could hear someone breathing softly from the bed.

Jacob held his breath and clicked on the penlight. A woman was sleeping alone in the bed. She was in the middle of the bed, so Jacob assumed she was used to sleeping alone. He could see both of the woman's hands. They were outside the covers, crisscrossed at the elbow, hugging a pillow. Her nails were painted a rich mauve. Jacob moved the light over the woman's hands, carefully shielding part of the beam from her face with his own hand.

*Those painted nails.*

There wasn't a ring on the woman's finger.

*Another sinful woman,* Jacob thought.

He moved to the dresser and went through the woman's clothing. He took a pair of green panties and smelled them deeply before cramming them into the front left pocket of the sweatpants, Walmart. He turned back to the bed and nearly screamed. The woman had turned silently onto her side and was facing him. He thought for an instant she'd awoken, but a gentle snoring assured him she hadn't.

I feel adrift sometimes, My Children, Jacob wrote. I feel alone in a sea of sin. I feel like the lone shining light in an endless darkness. I read the Bible every day, My Children. I feel the urge to hunt almost every minute of every day. The kill being held higher than all else. The hunt and the kill are holy.

Jacob had read: *I am sending for hunters to chase you down like deer in the forests or mountain goats on inaccessible crags.*

God had sent hunters in the past.

*Wherever you run to escape my judgement, I will find you and punish you,* the Bible said.

Jacob felt deeply in his heart that he was one of God's hunters.

God wouldn't have made me this way if he hadn't intended to. Just like he would've given you life, My Children, if it'd been in His plan. I hear your cries and I weep. I hear your cries and I don't think I can go on sometimes. But I put my trust in the lord and

417

# BIRTH OF A MONSTER

*He guides me. Proverbs 3:5 6: Trust in the Lord with all your heart and lean not on your own understanding; in all your ways submit to Him, and He will make your paths straight.*

There were so many pets and other animals in the city. There were so many unlocked doors and open windows.

-

They called her Candy. Jacob had heard them, johns, *I shoulda named ye John, boy, one in a lo-o-ong line of 'em*, and her fellow whores all call her that: Candy.

Jacob didn't have any money but a crazy-haired man had given him a fake fifty-dollar bill in the streets earlier that day. It was a dollar-shaped advertiser for a tent revival happening later in the month. Jesus Christ was on the back, the halo a brighter shade of green than the rest of the fake bill.

Jacob waited until Candy was alone then he stepped into the light.

"Hey, baby," she said when she saw him. "Lookin' to party?"

*Party. Ha.*

Jacob nodded his head.

"Money's up front, hon," she said, extending a hand.

She had on fake nails and they were hot pink.

Jacob felt weak in the knees. He reached into the front pocket of the sweatpants, Walmart, and got the fake fifty. He passed it over to the whore, watching her hands closely as she took the bill. She held it up to the streetlight then jerked her head back in his direction.

"Get the fuck outta here," she hissed.

As Jacob ran away, her laughter hit his back like buckshot.

-

Jacob earned his certification in welding. On the day he went in to pick up his paperwork, four of his sculptures were on display in the student-run art gallery on campus.

Jacob thought they stood out like their own perfect islands in a sea of imposters' art. His four pieces, the four angels, were perfect islands of beauty and homage. He was immensely proud of them.

-

Jacob received two pieces of mail within a day apart. One was a summons for a rescheduled court date—he'd missed the first—and the other was a letter from the state terminating his scholarship program due to his pending criminal charges. He smiled; he'd already earned his certificate.

*And they can't take it away from me.*

Jacob crumpled each paper up and tossed them into the garbage. He resolved to forgo checking the mail from then on.

-

"The woman was arrayed in purple and scarlet, and adorned with gold and jewels and pearls, holdin' in her hand a golden cup full of abominations and the impurities of her sexual immorality," Jacob whispered to himself.

Jacob thought they walked the roads like lice on fur, the harlots, the whores. They walked by the neon signs proclaiming Happy Hour, they swayed by signs reading Hourly Rates. Louisville was full of them, the walkers, the harlots, the whores.

Jacob liked to sit on the benches and just watch them. There they'd stand in little packs of two or three, sometimes with a man but mostly it was an all-girl's affair. Jacob watched them walk up to the cars that stopped so suddenly. He watched them talk then climb inside. He watched them walk back a short time later.

*Lice*, Jacob thought. *Whores.*

"And behold, the woman meets him, dressed as a prostitute, wily of heart," Jacob quoted to himself.

Jacob waited until she was alone then he took her from behind. He quickly overpowered her and choked her into unconsciousness and dragged her behind a dumpster, out of view.

"And if yer hand causes ye to sin, cut it off," Jacob said, removing the knife, Academy Sports, and cutting the woman's gaudy outfit off her limp body. "It is better for ye to enter life crippled than with two hands to go to hell, to the unquenchable fire."

Jacob groped the unconscious woman roughly. Then grabbed and pulled her left nipple away from her body.

"And if yer foot causes ye to sin, cut it off," Jacob said. "It is better for ye to enter life lame than with two feet to be thrown into hell."

Jacob cut.

The woman came screaming back from the depths of unconsciousness but Jacob quickly sent her back down.

-

Jefferson Memorial Forest was Jacob's favorite place in Louisville. By far. It was huge, the sign said 6,500 acres of near wilderness just southwest of the city. There were plenty of places to put the pieces of a person. There was a patch of ground that stayed pretty damp near Bee Lick Creek that was easy to dig in too. Jacob made use of this area often.

Jacob was drunk. He felt the Thunderbird coursing through his veins, causing him to hiccup periodically. He was still learning Louisville but he knew vaguely where he was: the southside. He wasn't too awfully far from Jefferson Memorial Forest.

The homeless woman was asleep under the overpass high up the concrete embankment. Jacob could see the ragged rise and fall of her chest under the army surplus blanket. Jacob could also see his breath and wondered how people could sleep outside in weather like this. He slowly, quietly made his way up the steep concrete embankment to where the woman lay.

The dog Jacob hadn't spotted raised its head as he approached.

"Woah, easy," Jacob whispered.

The woman stirred but did not wake.

There were several concrete cinderblocks lying around. The woman had used five of them to make a ringlet for a small campfire, which had burned down to ashes.

Jacob picked up one of the cinderblocks and cleared his throat.

The woman opened her eyes and it took her several moments to register what she was seeing.

"What're you doin'?" she asked blurrily.

Jacob smiled down at her with the cinderblock raised high above his head. He brought it down over and over again until the woman did not move. She lay crumpled, bleeding under the blanket. The dog had scampered a few feet away and crouched, shaking and crying softly.

Jacob was panting and blood flecked. He smiled at the dog.

"Here, boy," he cooed. "Come here, boy."

The dog growled low in its throat and moved out of Jacob's reach. Jacob crouched and circled the dog, the bloody cinderblock raised in his left hand, his right out, beckoning the dog to come.

After a time, it did.

Jacob smashed the empty Thunderbird bottle against the building as he exited the alley. The euphoria of the hunt was wearing off and he wasn't sure where he was any longer. After he killed the homeless woman and her dog under the overpass, he'd drank another bottle of Thunderbird and walked, aimlessly. He'd felt invisible but now he wasn't so sure.

He came out of the alley and there was a crowd milling about half a block down the street. They were crowding the sidewalks of a squat brick building. Jacob walked a little closer, keeping close to the buildings, hoping to see but remain unseen, and noticed two distinct groups present: the smaller group were all wearing orange vests and seemed to shield the building from the other group, which held signs and chanted in unison.

The sun was lightening the sky in the east. He could just read one of the signs.

**They Kill Babies Here!** it read.

*Woah*, Jacob thought. *What have I stumbled onto?*

Jacob nearly tripped over the sidewalk as he made his way closer. He ran forward a few awkward steps and caught himself on a lamppost. He held fast to the post, the world seeming to surge and sway with his drunkenness. He blinked, hard, hoping to steady his swimming vision.

*Get it together*, the voice said.

*This is interesting*, Jacob thought.

He leaned forward and squinted, reading more of the handmade signs.

**Stop Killing Children!** one read.

**LWC = Louisville Women Child-killers**

**Smile! Your Mom Chose Life**

He was speaking before he even realized he'd approached the crowd.

"What's this about?" Jacob cringed at the slurring of his own words.

*Man, I'm drunk.*

"They're killing babies in there," an older man said.

"Yeah! That's the last abortion clinic in the state," a woman said.

*The last abortion clinic in the state*, Jacob thought. *Wow.*

He turned and looked at the ugly little building. It looked so nondescript, gave no inkling to what went on inside.

"They kill little babies in there?" he asked.

There was a chorus of responses.

"Sure do."

"The devils!"

"Demons!"

"Murderers!"

Jacob heard the baby crying all the way from the mineshaft in eastern Kentucky.

"They kill babies here?" he asked.

"Yes!"

"They do!"

A car pulled up to the curb of the building. Several orange vest-clad people made their way through the yelling crowd to the car. The window rolled down and words were exchanged. The passenger and driver's side doors opened and two women got out. The Orange Vests formed a protective circle around them and walked them past the protestors into the brick building. The protestors shouted and held up their signs.

"You've got options!"

"Don't let them kill your baby!"

"Jesus loves you!"

Jacob could feel their hatred bubbling just under the surface. It felt like rising oil in boiling water. Jacob found himself buoyed from his drunkenness on their rising tide of exclamations. There was a sense of common purpose and Jacob felt swept up in it.

"You oughta come to our meeting tonight," a man said, passing Jacob a handout.

Jacob took the paper and carefully folded it and put it in the pocket of the sweatpants, Walmart.

-

The meeting took place in the basement of an old church. The sign out front read: Dominion House. The stairs were close and rickety. Jacob took them carefully. He'd had a bottle of Thunderbird and popped an Adderall as well, making him feel simultaneously shaky and loose. He was nervous about being around people but he'd felt something in the crowd protesting outside the abortion clinic, something righteous and hate-filled he could identify with.

There were several people in the basement already. They all turned and welcomed him as he entered.

"Welcome, brother," a man in stained, greasy bib overalls said.

He extended his hand to Jacob, who clasped it and shook. The grip was strong and firm.

"Thank ye," Jacob said.

"Welcome to Dominion House," the man said, releasing Jacob's hand. "Want a cup of coffee?"

"Sure."

Jacob followed the man to a little foldout table.

"The meeting'll start here in a few," the man said. "I'm Josiah, by the way. Josiah Powers."

The man poured the coffee and handed the cup, black, to Jacob, who immediately took a careful sip.

"Thank ye," he said.

"Saw ya at the protest yesterday morning, friend," Josiah Powers said. "I'm glad to see ya here."

"Thank ye," Jacob said. "Do they really kill babies at that place?"

"Ya better believe it," Josiah Powers said.

The people began taking their seats. Jacob hadn't noticed the flood of bodies in the room until now. The place was bustling with people.

"Take a seat, y'all," a voice boomed from the front of the room.

"Come on, let's get us a seat," Josiah Powers said.

Jacob followed the man and sat in the metal fold-out chair next to him.

The meeting began with a prayer for every life lost to the deviltry of the Louisville Women's Clinic and a request for reprisal.

"Give us the strength to put an end to this abomination in your name, amen."

Amens rippled across the basement like wind on a flag.

"We have a new member in our midst," the man at the front of the room said. "We welcome you. Why don't you stand up and introduce yourself."

All eyes turned to Jacob.

He felt his face flush a hot red and rose on shaky legs.

"Hello," Jacob said. "My name is Jacob Hunter Goodman."

"Hello, Jacob," the room replied in unison.

"I saw y'all out there protesting yesterday," Jacob said. "One of y'all gave me a handout and here I am."

"We're glad you're here, Jacob," the man said from the front of the room. "We're always looking for new faces to turn towards the light of the Lord. Aren't we, y'all?"

"Yessir!"

"Praise him!"

"We're always happy to see another potential soldier of God, aren't we?"

"Amen!"

"Praise be!"

Jacob sat back down next to Josiah Powers, who smiled warmly at him. Jacob didn't know what to do or what to think. He'd never been made to feel so welcome in his entire life.

The meeting was a blur of excited speech and exclamations. It was over before Jacob knew it. The people were filing up the stairs, a few were helping break down the fold-out chairs, some were standing in little groups of four or two, talking.

Josiah Powers set his folded chair against the wall and walked over to where Jacob stood next to the coffeepot.

"Ya new to town?" he asked.

Jacob nodded. "Pretty much," he said. "Been here for a few weeks now."

How long had it been? Jacob had a difficult time keeping track of his days.

"Lookin' for any employment?" Josiah Powers asked.

Jacob, who'd finished his welding program just four days ago, nodded his head again.

"Yessir," Jacob said. "I just got my certification in welding from the community college."

"That's great!" Josiah Powers said. "I own a little scrap yard over by Jefferson Memorial Forest. I do need some welding from time to time but mostly I'm looking for somebody to stay on and watch over the place at nights. Been having some vandalism and theft."

Jacob smiled.

"Something you'd be interested in?"

"Yessir."

-

The little camper wasn't tall enough to allow Jacob to stand. He had to crouch forward when inside. It was relatively clean and warm though.

Jacob stepped back out into the scrap yard.

"What'd ya think?" Josiah Powers asked. "I know it's not much, but it's free and it's dry. I've got a little gas generator we can run in and get ya a space heater for the colder nights."

The camper sat in the middle of the junkyard. Jacob looked around at the stacks of crushed and dilapidated cars and trucks and scrap metal.

"Ya can come and go as you please, just make sure you're here most of the nights to keep the hoodlums from stealing and setting fires," Josiah Powers said. "Everything is cash, under the table, off the books. We're not much for taxes at Dominion House."

Jacob extended his hand and the older man took it and shook it.

"When can I move in?"

"Anytime ya please."

"Got a machine here?"

"Got a Howard Electric, but it ain't much."

Jacob nodded, smiling. He'd worked with worse.

-

Jacob attended every Dominion House meeting, often riding with Josiah Powers in his little Mazda pickup. He'd never felt a sense of community before. There were so many open, smiling faces turning his direction and two-armed embraces with emphatic declarations that "it's so good to meet you!" that Jacob had to force himself to relax. He focused on slowing his breathing and releasing the tight hold he held over his entire body.

They preached of God's Second Coming. The End Times. They preached about the immoral world, the myriad ways we've disappointed God, who made us with love in His Image. Jacob listened to the Bible stories he'd read and heard them as if for the first time amongst so many like-minded people. He felt bathed in a warm pool of light and couldn't wipe the smile from his face if he'd tried.

When he wasn't at a Dominion House meeting or protest, he was working on his sculptures at Powers' Scrap 'n' Metal. So far, Josiah hadn't said a thing about them. Jacob molded great giant creatures out of bumpers and car doors and front hoods and crumpled gutters and scrap metal. The welder wasn't the best he'd ever worked with but it wasn't half-bad. Jacob popped Adderall and worked until he felt he'd drop. Only when the sun lightened the starless sky did he put down the welder, Powers' Scrap 'n' Metal, and allow himself an hour's reading of the Bible before sleep, staved off for as long as possible, finally came.

The creations were definitely angels. Maybe not Angels with a capital A but they were angelic forms of some sort. Jacob saw them taking shape as he worked, saw his arc welder as the divining light, the breath of life on but crude clay, and felt nearly sinful for how godly it made him feel to create.

*From nothing / heavenly bodies*

They had multiple arms, eyes, hands. They were single curving eels. They were multi-headed sirens singing mournful songs into the night. They were serpentine nude figures in an endless tangle. Above all, they were *religious*.

-

"I noticed ya walkin' all the time," Josiah Powers had said earlier that morning. "I've got that Mazda, it's in pretty good shape. Just needs a new transmission put in is all. I'd sell 'er to ya cheap if'n yer interested."

Jacob was.

*Just think about how much easier hunting will be with wheels*, he thought. *Good Lord! I'll have Jefferson Memorial Forest filled 'fore too long.*

*Maybe you could dispose of them here in the junkyard somehow*, the voice said.

Jacob looked around. The place was immense, acres of rusted car bodies and huge piles of jagged scrap metal.

He smiled as he walked the grounds.

*One of these cars is bound to have a transmission that'll fit that Mazda*, he thought.

-

She's pregnant and unmarried. No ring on those pretty fingers of hers anyway. I'll see where she lives, My Children, and then we'll know. Today she walked with the grace of a sunset.

-

He hung up his treasures on the inside of the camper: necklaces, car keys, earrings, one nose-ring, bits of cloth and hair. All the fingers and nails were in the tacklebox, Jenny Wiley State Park. He'd lost count already. There weren't many victims, not yet, but there'd been many fingers. He was fascinated with them, the index particularly recently; it was so stately, the index finger. It signaled the great change in the hand, the first in a series on the form of the finger. The thumb being a wartime invention that came later.

All the trophies and treasures were starting to resemble a great beaconing hand, he thought. Something both prophetic and placating but gone before he could really even see it.

Jacob's creations were increasing in their attention to detail. The normal welder's helmet didn't offer the level of magnification he needed. He recalled the jeweler and watch repairman's magnifying glasses he'd stolen from Tackett's Jewelry and Watch Repair. He wondered if he could attach a pair of them or something similar to the front of the welder's helmet for enhanced vision.

I couldn't help myself, My Children, I followed her all around the Elizabethtown campus today. She's as big as a house and showing and I thought I was being careful but I guess I was overeager. I saw her coming out of the administrative building and the way her legs supported the extra weight she carried in her belly was too *mesmerizing* not to follow, Mrs. Horace. Word of the day, 1: hypnotic induction held to involve animal magnetism; 2: hypnotic appeal. I lost myself in her movements, following in her wake like a dazed dog, tongue unrolled and hanging.

I've watched her tending bar too, her belly bumping up against the crates of light beer at the B.A.T., her shirt always showing some stain where her pregnant belly brushed up against something, salt, lemon rind, beer foam. I know she's not in welding but she's full time at the community college because I see her almost every day. I can't tell you, My Children, how hard it is not to take her when she's alone.

I followed her to her car in the parking lot today and she spun on her heels and faced me. I had nowhere to turn in the desert of parked cars so I took the verbal lashing like a penitent dog.

*Fucking creep!* she hissed. *Stop following me around!*

I was so embarrassed, My Children, but thankfully the parking lot was mostly empty. I nodded my head several times to show just how penitent this dog was then scurried off with my tail between my legs promising myself that I'd get her, make her mine. Soon.

## CHAPTER TWENTY-SIX
## A BED IS A BED IS A BED IS A BED

**"I MEAN, I HATE TO** say it, I really do, but I took a risk, a big risk, capital R Risk in marrying you," Perry said, worrying the knot of his tie.

"Ye what?" Barbara was dumbfounded. "A risk in marrying me? What's that supposed to mean?"

"Don't play dumb, Barb, it's not your style," Perry said. "You know exactly what I mean. People with as different backgrounds as us rarely end up married happily ever after."

"Yer saying ye took a step down to marry me?" Barbara had to keep her voice low to keep from screaming. "Is that what yer telling me?"

"You know what I mean, don't play dumb."

"I'm not playing dumb," Barbara whispered, afraid she was going to start screaming again. "Maybe I'm too dumb to realize ye lessened yerself by marrying a former foster kid. Maybe if I came from money I'd be able to keep up with these blue-chip disappointments ye seem to be carrying around about me."

"Don't be hysterical," Perry said. "We can either discuss this like adults or try again when you're not so hysterical."

*Hysterical*, Barbara thought. *I'll show you hysterical.*

She picked up a ceramic coaster and slammed it down on the coffee table, snapping it in two.

"Jesus Christ," Perry yelled. "You're acting like a hysterical bitch right now."

Barbara broke another coaster. She picked up a halved portion of coaster and threw it against the wall where it shattered and fell in a dozen pieces to the floor.

"I know you can't help it," Perry said, his tone now placating. "You're a woman. You're subject to tempests but you really need to learn how to control your emotions."

Barbara felt on the verge of unintelligible screaming. She'd always had a temper and Perry knew how to push her buttons, always had.

*Keep it together, Barbara*, she told herself. *Ask him to go.*

"I need ye to leave," she said, focusing on controlling her breathing. "I can't be around ye right now."

"We need to have an adult conversation about this."

"Ye need to go. Now."

Barbara thought Perry was going to say something snarky and she clenched her fists, ready to take the barb.

"I'll go," Perry said after a long moment, "but we still need to discuss this. Like adults. No screaming. No breaking things."

"Ye need to go," Barbara whispered through clenched teeth. "And don't come back."

"I'll go," Perry said, slipping his arms into his silk jacket, "but this isn't over. We'll work this out, trust me. Plus, you know you can't afford this place without me. Not on that pitiful cop's paystub."

Barbara felt her nails bite into the palms of her hands. She knew if one of them didn't leave immediately she'd lose it, so she brushed past Perry and slammed the front door closed behind her. She stalked across the front walk to her car and got inside. She breathed in through her nose and let out the air through her open mouth. Her hands were shaking but she got the car started just fine. She backed out of the drive and accidentally gave it a bit too much gas. She peeled out of the neighborhood grinding her teeth.

*Stuck up prick*, she thought. *The fucker!*

Barbara wasn't paying attention to where she was driving. She was just trying to put as much distance between Perry and herself as she could. She pulled into the parking lot and found a space before she even realized where she was: the La Quinta Inn & Suites.

Barbara couldn't help it; she began to sob.

When she regained control of herself, Barbara called her former foster mother, Luanne Shepherd.

"Hello?"

"Luanne, I . . ." Barbara had to take a breath before she could continue. "I need a place to stay. Can I—"

"Of course," Luanne said. "Come on over. We had pot roast tonight. Got plenty leftover."

"Thank you," Barbara said. "Thank you."

Barbara ended the call and put the car back in drive but kept her foot on the brake, staring at the vacancy sign.

# BIRTH OF A MONSTER

For all his talk of money, Barbara wondered why Perry had taken his secretary to the La Quinta Inn & Suites and not the Hyatt House or someplace nicer like the Galt House in Louisville.

Convenience?

*Stop dwelling on it*, Barbara told herself. *A bed is a bed is a bed is a bed.*

She let off the brake and pulled out of the parking lot.

-

Luanne and Kenny were waiting for her when she pulled in. Luanne wrapped her warm arms around her and pulled her close. Barbara didn't bawl, not exactly, but she cried a bit in the comforting embrace of her former foster mother.

"There, there," Luanne said, rocking them both. "It's okay."

*It's not though*, Barbara thought. *My marriage is falling apart.*

Kenny hugged her next.

"Hey," he said in his gruff voice. "Am I gonna have to go out there and wring Perry's little pencil neck?"

Barbara smiled and shook her head.

"Ye hungry?" Luanne asked.

Barbara, surprised, found she was.

-

Barbara spent the night on the couch—there were new foster children in the Shepherd's home, her old bedroom was no longer hers—staring up at the flood light's yellowed lines on the ceiling, trying not to cry too loudly.

*I'm gonna put all of myself into finding that missing woman*, she told herself. *Get my head off of Perry and back into the job. The job will get me through this.*

Barbara lay awake long into the night trying not to think of her crumbling marriage but thinking about it anyway.

## CHAPTER TWENTY-SEVEN
## HOW CLEAN A DEATH CAN BE

**CANDY WAS WORKING THE LONELY** stretch of Dixie Highway just south of Louisville called the Strip. There were half a dozen strip tease joints and beer halls along the road. The whore wore a wig as she passed under the neon Miller High Life sign outside Ricki's Tattle Tail's Gentlemen's Club, a bit of her natural, brunette hair hung out the back like a coon tail hat.

Jacob pulled into the empty back parking lot of Tattle Tail's and put the Mazda in park. He watched the whore, Candy, unsling her purse and begin searching for something inside. Jacob stepped out into the night and closed the door silently. He slipped into the tree line and silently made his way closer to where the whore stood, now lighting a long, skinny hand-rolled cigarette.

*Mine*, he thought, watching the red ember burn brighter as she took a drag. *Mine.*

She'd scorned him for the fake fifty. Jacob remembered how small that made him feel.

He waited until Candy turned back to the street to watch a car pass slowly by then he took her from behind, dragging her off her feet and deep into shadow-laden forest.

-

Jacob hunted nearly every night. Driving up and down the strip in the Mazda pickup looking for the ones that were easy for most people to forget: whores, homeless, wastrels. He picked up whores for their services and let many of them go free afterwards feeling *magnanimous*, Mrs. Horace's Word of the Day, *1: showing or suggesting a lofty and courageous spirit; 2: showing or suggesting nobility of feeling and generosity of mind.*

Hunting wasn't always about killing. Sometimes hunting was about stalking and patience.

Jacob often remembered the way the bald man hunted, putting out the salt block and picking off the deer as they stood still, licking and oblivious. Jacob marveled at how clean a death could be.

Sometimes hunting turned into killing and killing turned into disposing of unwanted parts. Jacob found a cloth truck bed cover that fit the Mazda pickup and this made transporting the unwanted remains easier.

Not all of them had identification but several did. Jacob kept their driver's licenses and photo IDs as if they were a new type of collector's trading cards: Beatrice Pottsfield, Stacie Martinez, Regina Thomas, Heather Findley, and Valerie Fuller.

Candy turned out to be Cynthia Wells. She also had a bottle of Xanax in her purse.

Jacob pinned the cards up in his camper in the junkyard, where he took his meals and snorted the Xanax, staring at them. The outline was beginning to take shape in his mind again and he marveled at how often artistic vision changed. The outline on his little wall in the camper was morphing into something new again. He added to it nearly every night, patient and dutiful, *a servant / to the art.*

-

Jacob pulled up to the curb and honked his horn. The whore waddled over to the passenger-side door and hung in the open window.

"Hey, baby," she cooed like a pigeon. "Lookin' for a good time?"

Jacob nodded. They agreed on an act and a price. The whore climbed inside the Mazda.

Jacob liked to talk to them while they blew him. He told this one she wasn't special, that nobody loved her, that she was worthless. She didn't even slow her pace.

"Have ye ever been pregnant?" he asked.

She took him out of her mouth and held him in her little fist.

"What was that, daddy?" she asked.

"Have ye ever been pregnant, whore?" he asked.

She rolled her eyes.

"What's that matter?"

Jacob put his hand over hers and started it working. He forced his face to remain blank, empty.

"Just answer the question, whore."

"Yes."

"Got any children?"

"You want this blowjob or not?" she asked.

He did. Jacob let her finish and let her live. Sometimes he felt so *magnanimous.*

-

Listen and consider yourselves lucky, My Children. Lucky you don't have to reach your hand into the muck of this life and live with the stains. Consider yourselves lucky to have never been born into a world drenched to the teeth in sin. A world baking under the heat of a loveless sun completely oblivious to your toil, My Children.

My Children, I find strength and refuge in the Bible and in hunting. The bald man was right: a man has got to hunt. It's his safety valve. If he doesn't hunt he'll eventually kill everything he sees, comes into contact with. That's why I hunt those that God doesn't love, the sinners, the scum. The way a catfish feeds off the bottom, so do I cleanse this world of sin one wasted life at a time.

Flipping at random, My Children, and the Bible hits the nail on the head again: 1 Peter 5:10: And after you have suffered a little while, the God of all grace, who has called you to His eternal glory in Christ, will Himself restore, confirm, strengthen, and establish you.

I do the Lord's work, My Children.

---

Jacob was drunk. He needed to sober up. He knew the whore in the back of the Mazda was dead—he could see a small trickle of blood under the rear bumper—but in his drunken state he kept waiting for her to start screaming.

*Get it together*, he told himself. *She's dead. She can't cry out. You're just drunk.*

How many cans of beer on top of the two bottles of Thunderbird had he drank? Six? Seven? He'd been stalking this one, another whore, for days—three, to be exact. He'd finally got her alone tonight and made quick work of her. Then he'd driven her, dead in the back of the truck bed, wrapped in an old tarp under the cloth truck bed cover, back to Powers' Scrap 'n' Metal and he couldn't quite understand why.

He popped an Adderall and washed it down with the dregs of an old bottle.

The crispness began to come back into the world. So he'd driven drunk with a dead whore in the back of the truck, so what? He didn't get caught.

He needed to get rid of her body but he didn't feel like taking the truck out to Jefferson Memorial Forest despite how close it was.

433

Jacob stepped into his camper and added the whore's necklace, a cheap golden goose, to the wall of trophies, *show / what's there to display*, then stepped back into the coolness of the night.

The stacks of crushed cars rose up into the blue-black, starless sky. Morning was hours away. The Howard Electric welding machine caught his eye and the idea sprang into his mind: encase the whore in the creation.

His hands began to shake at the thought of it. It was perfect, Jacob saw, putting life into the creations. He'd cut the whore up, put her inside, and weld it all closed. He thought of all the animal skins he'd sutured back in the hills of eastern Kentucky.

*All that child's play at creating.*

Jacob smiled, thinking about how far he'd come.

—

"They're lookin' for a more reliable welder at Rubbish Management," Josiah Powers said.

Jacob flipped the welding machine off and tipped his modified welding helmet up off his face.

"Yeah?" he said.

"The guy they got, Wallace Skaggs, is what you'd call unreliable," Josiah Powers said, then leaned in closer, conspiratorially. "He's got a bit of a drug problem but ya didn't hear that from me."

Jacob had seen the purple and green trashcans and garbage trucks all over the city. Rubbish Management was the main garbage collection agency in Louisville.

"You'd be doing mainly welding but you'd also drive a truck when somebody called in," Josiah Powers said. "Ya know Brock, Brock Sither from Dominion House? He's high up in management so it'd be no problem getting you on. Interested?"

Jacob nodded.

"Ya can still stay on here, watching the place at night," Josiah Powers said. "I'll introduce ya to Brock at tonight's meetin'."

Jacob nodded again then pushed the welding helmet back over his face.

"I'll let ya get back to it then."

Jacob waited for the man to mention the circle of creations just outside the camper, but he didn't. Jacob watched the wiry man study each of the creations for a moment before walking across the dirt to the little trailer that served as Powers' Scrap 'n' Metal's office.

Jacob laid the metal filler in the seam and made his pool, closing the last seam of the hooker at the base of the three-headed cat-like angel. He stepped back and admired his work.

It'd taken him the rest of the previous evening and most of the early morning hours to cut up and encase the whore in the metal sculpture. Jacob was tired. He turned off the welding machine and removed the helmet, squinting in the bright daylight. The sun glinted off the three-headed angel and Jacob marveled at the smoothness of his seams, the cleanness of the design, the lithe limbs protruding upward, heavenward, beckoning.

-

Rubbish Management's offices were inside an immense warehouse down by the river. Brock Sither, an officious man in his late forties, showed Jacob around on his first day.

"Here's where you'll be set up most days," Brock Sither said, showing Jacob the welding section of the warehouse.

As soon as the man could, he passed Jacob off to an underling and disappeared into the office space of the warehouse. The man, Jacob didn't bother learning his name, showed him how to operate a garbage truck and let Jacob drive around the vast lot and practice using the truck's automated side-loader.

Jacob liked being high up in the garbage truck. It made him feel above it all, all the trash and sin on the streets. He liked the rough-sounding idle of the diesel engine and the idea of being out in the city on his own too.

-

Jacob took over the routes of whoever called in, and somebody always seemed to be calling in. There was always welding work to be done back at the warehouse too. Wallace Skaggs, a surly man on his best days, was a slow worker and the welding projects backed up and Jacob was often asked to stay overtime and play catch-up. He didn't mind. He thought of the welding work as practice for the creations. Plus, he was earning quite a bit of money, almost enough to buy his own welding machine, something a little more powerful than the Howard Electric back at Powers' Scrap 'n' Metal. He had plans for larger creations and he'd need equipment able to keep up with his ideas.

Jacob learned the ins and outs of his new job slowly. He'd always been a slow learner.

He drove the routes and picked up the trash. There were several more monied neighborhoods where there were still housewives, women kept up by their men to stay home and play homemaker. Jacob ignored the children and their toys scattered about but he couldn't help but notice all the women's glossy painted nails.

*red / blue*

*blue / white*

Jacob wanted to collect all of them. He saw his tacklebox lined with nails, each compartment stocked with nails and fingers in perfectly lined rows. He made mental notes of which women lived where and came back at night to look into their windows. If their doors were unlocked, he prowled their homes, going through their things, taking what he wanted. Jacob's little camper in Powers' Scrap 'n' Metal was littered with his treasures.

Over time, Jacob was found to be a hard worker and, above all else, reliable. He was given more and more responsibility until he spent most of his days on his own, working without the constant eyes of a manager.

*Only God can judge me*, Jacob thought.

There were missed deadlines but most of the blame came down on Wallace Skaggs because he was the senior employee, which Jacob knew he held against him. The man was barely civil when they had to work in close proximity.

*He sees me as a threat*, Jacob thought. *Fuck him. I am a threat.*

-

Wallace Skaggs was messed up. Jacob could tell right off when the man pulled into the lot in his red Ford Ranger with the matte camper shell on top and got out as if pulled by a stiff wind. He threw the driver's side door closed and nearly lost his balance.

"Mornin'," Jacob said.

The man muffled a response that was lost on Jacob.

Wallace Skaggs walked across the lot in a wide arc, nearly stumbling over his own feet. When the man had disappeared into the warehouse, Jacob walked across the lot and studied the camper shell attached to the man's truck. He thought it'd fit the Mazda just about perfectly. It had been spray-painted a matte gray some time ago. There weren't any windows.

-

Jacob waited until Wallace Skaggs turned off the welding machine and took off his helmet to mop his sweat-covered face then stepped out of the shadows.

"I'd like to buy that camper shell off ye," Jacob said.

"What?" Wallace Skaggs asked, startled.

"That camper shell on yer truck, I'd like to buy it off ye."

The man spat on the concrete.

"It ain't for sale."

"Still."

The two men looked at each other in the dim light of the warehouse.

"Ain't for sale," Wallace Skaggs said, taking off the welding helmet and dropping it on the workbench. "I'm goin' on break. You can finish this one."

The man bumped his shoulder into Jacob's in passing.

-

Jacob clocked out early and waited in the Mazda just around the corner from the lot's entrance. Wallace Skaggs pulled out into the quickly darkening dusk in his red Ford Ranger. Jacob followed him at a distance a few blocks west before Skaggs parked the truck in front of a rundown house. Jacob watched the man get out of his truck and enter the house. He was inside maybe ten minutes and when he reemerged from the house Jacob saw he was high. He walked back down the concrete sidewalk to his Ranger in uneven, slow steps as if he were walking carefully through heavy, deep snow.

The man got back into his truck but it didn't start it right away. The man huddled forward in the interior with the lights off. A few moments later, a cloud of smoke billowed from the cracked windows. Then the truck started and Jacob followed Skaggs another few blocks to another rundown house. This one he parked in the driveway of and got out and again seemed to be buffeted by some strong, unseen wind.

Jacob got out of the Mazda, looked for anybody paying attention, and made it to the front porch just as Skaggs was unlocking the front door.

Wallace Skaggs did not notice Jacob until it was too late.

-

Jacob, using a wench at Powers' Scrap 'n' Metal, transferred the gray camper shell onto the Mazda. He then climbed inside and ripped off all the fabric lining. With the interior of the shell only metal and plastic, Jacob knew it would be easier to spray out.

-

"You seen Skaggs?" Brock Sither asked.

Jacob shook his head.

"Well, when he comes in, tell him to come see me in the front office," Brock Sither said.

Jacob nodded, then pushed the helmet back into place to cover his smile.

—

"Nice camper shell," Josiah Powers said.

"Thank ye," Jacob said, flipping the welding machine off.

"Where'd ya get it?"

"Wallace Skaggs at work."

"Huh. Seen him around lately? Brock Sither was asking around about him."

"Nope."

The man adjusted his weight from his left foot to his right.

"I got some paint in the back if you're wanting to cover over that gray."

"No, thanks."

"Well," Josiah Powers said, lingering.

*He wants to ask me something but he's afraid to,* Jacob thought. *I just want him to go away.*

"How's the job at Rubbish going?" Josiah Powers asked.

"Fine," Jacob said.

"Well."

"Well."

"See ya at the meeting."

Jacob put his modified welding helmet back on and went back to work. He was welding several concentric lines into the torso of the angel, giving it a fur-like quality. He stepped back, removed the helmet, and observed his work.

*Good,* he thought.

—

Dominion House meetings were lively. People perished in the spirit, hitting the floor like sacks of potatoes and rolling around gibbering in tongues. Jacob had waited and waited to perish in the spirit. He wanted to be struck down by the Lord and be overcome by the experience but it did not come.

Jacob knew it was only a matter of time. God had a plan for him. In the meantime, Jacob thought it felt so nice to have a community like Dominion House. He was surrounded by fellow Christians, people there to put their egos aside and delve into the Word of God.

Jacob had attended every Dominion House meeting, the

Monday, Wednesday, and Saturday nights, as well as the Sunday morning. The church was unlike anything Jacob had been a part of before, not that he'd been a part of many things. He felt as close to at-home around other people as he could get. He attended potlucks and Sunday dinners and church socials. He'd even twice turned down offers of dates from other church members.

Through Dominion House, Jacob began to show his art in religious-minded galleries around Louisville and Jeffersonville, Indiana. People were immediately enthralled with Jacob's creations or they instantly hated them. Jacob could care less what the people thought of them.

*They're an act of prayer*, Jacob thought. *These creations praise and revere the Lord, fuck anybody who couldn't understand that.*

Jacob was asked to provide an artist's statement. He wrote: These works were created to honor God the Almighty.

He could tell by their faces some people didn't believe the works were religious in the slightest.

-

The television was wheeled to the front of the room and turned to WGAS channel 11 just as the graphics displaying the intro to the news program ended.

"Tonight on Your Local News," the television blared, "reports of missing women all across Kentuckiana. Is there a serial killer on the loose? New Metro budget cuts come to a crisis. An artist makes art for God. The Wildcats take on the Cardinals at the KFC YUM! Center. What to expect in Your Local Weather Forecast."

Several hands patted Jacob on the back.

"It's so neat to know a real artist!" someone nearby said.

"All in the glory of God," someone else said.

Jacob allowed himself a smile—a proper, dour thing—and nothing more. His face felt tight with the tension of it.

"I read the *LEO Weekly* piece, Jacob," Brock Sither said, taking his hand and shaking it. "Great stuff. Great stuff. Glory be."

"Glory be," Jacob said, feeling a blush begin to rise.

The television switched from the news anchors to a reporter standing outside Powers' Scrap 'n' Metal in the harsh light of day.

"Jacob Hunter Goodman isn't your typical artist, if there even is such a thing," she said. "His art has higher aims. Instead of personal expression, Goodman's art is deeply religious. His work has been called 'grotesque' and 'horrifying' but the artist claims each of his creations serves the Lord Jesus Christ."

There were several still images of angels Jacob had on display throughout the city. There were several shots of angels in Gallery East, his most recent showing. The camera switched to a shot inside Powers' Scrap 'n' Metal, the lens trained on the little circle of sculptures next to the RV. It lingered on the one filled with the whore and Jacob thought for sure that everybody knew. He was sure of it for a long moment, then the camera showed the reporter and Jacob felt relief wash over him.

*Of course they don't know,* he thought.

"Jacob Hunter Goodman grew up in impoverished eastern Kentucky but learned welding when he moved to Louisville."

The television showed Jacob squinting in the sun.

"I learned weldin' at Jefferson Community College," he said.

"Goodman, who welds and drives a garbage truck for Rubbish Management, makes his sculptures here at Powers' Scrap 'n' Metal just off the Gene Synder Freeway, where he lives in this RV."

The television showed the exterior of the little camper. He hadn't allowed them inside.

"I get a lot of extra scrap from Rubbish," Jacob said through the tinny speakers of the television, "not valuable stuff, just scrap, and I work on everything here."

"Goodman is the night-watchmen here at the junkyard, a job that gives him plenty of time to read the Bible and work on his sculptures, which are selling like hotcakes all over the city."

"How do you feel about your recognition for your art?" the reporter asked Jacob earlier that morning.

"All glory be to God," Jacob said. "But now, O Lord, ye are our Father; we are the clay, and Ye are our potter; we are all the work of Yer Hand. Isaiah Sixty-Four Eight."

There was a chorus of Amens around the basement of Dominion House, then applause and several utterances of "Praise be."

"You can catch Goodman's latest showing at Gallery East now through the end of the month."

Jacob's face twitched with the effort of keeping his face expressionless, blank.

-

"You seen Wallace?" Brock Sither asked.

Jacob shook his head but remembered the cutting in Fast-Forward X2 Mode. He remembered how he thought killing a grown man would've been harder than it had been.

"No, sir," Jacob said.

Brock Sither shook his head.

"Always a problem with that one," he said. "Can you cover the welding jobs until he shows back up?"

"Yessir."

"Good, good," Brock Sither said. "Congratulations on the art stuff. I'm looking into one of your angels for our sitting room. The one green one with two heads?"

Jacob knew exactly which one Brock Sither was talking about. It was on display in the foyer of Dominion House and had a dead hooker sealed up in it. Not Candy but one of her streetwalking friends. There was to be a new showing at Dominion House of Jacob's work in a week. The phones had been ringing at Dominion House ever since the TV piece and the *LEO* article inquiring about Jacob's art.

"You've sold several already this week, haven't you?"

Jacob nodded. He'd donated every penny of the five thousand dollars to Dominion House. He told himself he'd buy a new welding machine with the money from the next sale, then go back to donating all the money to the church.

"Say, isn't that camper shell on your truck Wallace Skaggs'?" Brock Sither asked.

"Yessir," Jacob said. "He sold it to me. Cheap."

"Huh," Brock Sither said, sighing. "Well, you send him my way if you see him."

"Okay."

-

"Are angels supposed to be so scary, Mommy?" the child asked.

Jacob saw the way the child looked at the three-headed angel: a mixture of awe, shock, and, underlying everything else, fear.

"I'm not sure, honey," the woman replied, not taking her eyes off Jacob's creation.

Jacob couldn't help but feel like he'd returned to the scene of some crime. He hovered in the foyer of Dominion House, watching all the people look at his sculptures. The crowd had been so big this opening night they had to have someone at the door counting heads coming in and heads going out so the fire department didn't show up and shut the showing down.

There was somebody asking about purchasing in bulk for the

# BIRTH OF A MONSTER

Ronald McDonald House. A billboard attorney was asking about custom design and offering to "throw a big check" Jacob's way for a sculpture of himself in Jacob's style. Jacob didn't turn him down outright but he told the man in the silk suit he only made religious art.

The centerpiece of the showing was a towering giant of an angel. It stood around seven feet tall and had three sets of arms. There were tiny wheelhouse wings on its back and its eyes were black pits. He'd made the two rows of teeth with sharpened tin. The price tag was eight-thousand dollars. He'd let the church help dictate the prices after the first few sold at a church-sponsored auction.

The centerpiece sold early in the evening just as Jacob decided he'd had enough socializing for the evening. He slipped out the back door and made his way around the block to the parked Mazda. He had several new pieces in the works back at Powers' Scrap 'n' Metal and he felt like hunting.

## CHAPTER TWENTY-EIGHT
## A MAN TO TAKE CARE OF HER

MITCHELL RISNER WAS GREASY. BARBARA had heard stories about the way he ran his businesses, making employees work off the clock, forced overtime, special privileges for the beautiful, all those sorts of things, and when she sat down across the little table from him at the B.A.T., Barbara believed every word of the rumors. The man had oily black hair on a balding head. His smile was somewhere between lewd and sinister.

"She was preggers," Mitchell Risner said. "I don't know if they told you that, sweetheart, but Mary Ann was knocked up. Four or five months preggers, I'd say."

Barbara wrote that information down.

"She worked Saturday night but didn't show up for her Sunday shift."

"She miss much?"

"Never," Mitchell Risner said, smiling. "She's the most dependable person that works here."

"Did anything out of the ordinary happen Saturday night?"

The man shook his head.

"The place was pretty full," he said. "It was a decent night for the place, lots of regulars and new faces."

"Got any video?" Barbara said, pointing her pen up at the hanging camera above the bar.

"Nope," he said. "We erase the tapes every Sunday. Saving space means saving money, honey, you know what I mean?"

The way he said honey made Barbara's skin crawl.

"Now, listen, honey, I gotta wrap this up," Mitchell Risner said. "I gotta find me a new head barkeep. This place ain't gonna run itself."

The man winked at her.

"Looking for a job?" he laughed.

Barbara did her best to keep the disgust off her face.

He said, "Look, my best guess is that Mary Ann finally wised up

443

and quit wastin' her days in college, her nights bartendin', and finally found herself a man to take care of her."

Barbara stuck around after Mitchell Risner left and interviewed the bar staff as they arrived for their shift. She learned Mary Ann Gregory was a model employee and that she was well-liked by everybody who worked at the B.A.T.

The dishwasher was an older man with broken blood vessels blooming around a nose that had been broken at least once. Barbara spoke with him last, in the back of the bar, near the large sink of dishes.

"Everybody liked her if they're doing what they's supposed to be doing," he said. "You might want to talk with Allison Rogers if you're looking for anybody with bad blood."

Barbara wrote the name down.

"Got a phone number or address for me?"

"She's in jail," the dishwasher said. "Hardin County Bed 'n' Breakfast."

Barbara drove down to the jail and asked for Allison Rogers. A short time later she was led into a small, windowless room with a metal table and three chairs. She was told to sit and wait and, after a time, a guard brought a thin woman into the room and sat her down in one of the metal chairs across the table from Barbara.

"Allison Rogers?" Barbara said. "I'm Detective Barbara Findley. EPD."

"What'd you want?"

"I want to ask ye a few questions about a former coworker of yers, Mary Ann Gregory."

The woman made a disgusted face.

"That stuck up bitch is why I'm in here," Allison Rogers said.

Barbara flipped back to her notes.

"I talked with the front desk sergeant and he said ye were here for possession and forgery," she said.

The woman rolled her eyes.

"Listen, I was a few days late on my rent and my landlord was giving me a hard time," Allison Rogers said. "I had a Tuesday night shift with Miss Goody Two Shoes and I lifted a few bucks from the register when she wasn't watching. I was gonna pay it back with my next check. I just needed to get even with the landlord before he threw me out, which he was threatening to do."

The woman was so skinny Barbara thought she could almost see the skull under the thin skin. She had little sores on her lips and neck. She scratched at several more in the crooks of her arms.

"So I took about forty, fifty dollars thinking it'd be no big deal, but the bitch wouldn't let me count the drawers out at the end of the night and she caught the missing dough."

"So what happened?"

"What do you think happened?" Allison Rogers snapped. "I got canned. They didn't file any charges against me. Thank God. But I got fired all the same. I hope something bad did happen to Miss Goody Two Shoes. I had to write some bad checks after I got fired, that's why I'm in here."

Barbara finished her notes and saw that the skinny woman was getting agitated.

"What about Leslie, huh?" Allison Rogers asked. "You've got all the time in the world to come up here and ask questions about Little Miss Goody Two Shoes Gregory, but y'all ain't sent one person looking for Leslie. Not a one. Have you?"

"Who?"

"See?" The woman seemed vindicated. "You don't even know who she is."

Barbara tapped on the door, signaling for the guard.

"She's got a record. That's why y'all don't give a shit about her."

The guard opened the door and told Allison Rogers to stand.

"Thank ye for yer time," Barbara said.

"Fuck you," Allison Rogers said. "Get out there and find Leslie."

The guard led the thin woman away.

Barbara wasn't surprised when she returned to her office and was assigned the Lindsey Leslie missing persons case.

-

Barbara found out Lindsey Leslie was a thief and not a particularly good one. She'd been fired from the Dollar General, Bub's Café, and the BP filling station on Mulberry for stealing. She had a lengthy and spotty record too: drug possession, domestic battery, petty theft, tampering with evidence, fleeing, public intoxication, and on and on.

Barbara interviewed Cynthia Leslie, Lindsey Leslie's mother, at her trailer near the Valley Creek Reservoir. She was an alcoholic in the final stages. The woman had been plastered drunk but was able to give Barbara a few of her daughter's friends' names. She also informed Barbara that Lindsey Leslie used to work at the B.A.T. but had been fired for stealing.

It didn't take long to see that all of Lindsey Leslie's friends were drug addicts. They all had shifty, heavy-lidded eyes and covered arms. Several were high during their interviews, but Barbara learned Leslie was last seen at the B.A.T., where she still went to get shit-faced despite being fired from the place, last Wednesday, where, according to all reports, she was, you guessed it, completely shitfaced. Lindsey Leslie was so drunk that she was 86'd that night.

Daniel Heath, a shifty-eyed man, was a fount of information.

"She came over to my place Tuesday night all strung out," he said from behind the little desk of the cellphone case kiosk he operated at the Towne Mall. "Sayin' she'd taken a pregnancy test and it came back positive. Sayin' all kinds of crazy shit about how I was the father."

"Are you?"

"I ain't the only one that's fucked her," Daniel Heath said. "You looking for that information, you're gonna need a bigger notepad than that."

"She must've been pretty sure if she came to ye with that information."

"I don't think I was her first stop," he said, "or her last. She was messed up. Looking to use the whole pregnant thing to score. You knocked me up, the least you can do is give me a little on the side."

"Why'd she come to ye to score? You're a businessman, are ye not?" Barbara pointed at the cellphone cases displayed around the kiosk.

"I've been known to help people get things a time or two."

*Why does he look so satisfied with himself?* Barbara wondered. *Men're always so self-satisfied even when they're in the wrong.*

"I thought that would be the end of it," Daniel Heath said. "But she showed up at the B.A.T. the next night all sorts of fucked up. She came in yelling that she was knocked up and that I was the father. In front of the whole damn bar."

"What did ye do?"

"I denied it, of course," he said, smiling. "They tossed her out not ten minutes after she got there. She was higher than a kite, she was."

"Ye find something for her after all?"

The smile never left his face.

"Nope," he said. "She's pretty good at finding what she's looking for even when she doesn't have the money to pay for it. You know what I mean?"

Barbara thought she did.

"Look, if she hasn't showed up around town," he said. "It might be because she found somebody to take care of her little problem, you know?"

Barbara got the information and checked out Daniel Heath's alibi. It checked out.

-

Barbara did some searching and found, in the entire state of Kentucky, there was but one licensed, legal abortion clinic. It was forty-five minutes north of Elizabethtown in Louisville. She found the number on the web and tried calling but couldn't get through.

She got the address and checked out of the office for the afternoon.

-

The knobs looked bearded with the stubble of leafless trees as Barbara drove north on I-65. She kept the radio off and the passenger side window was cracked just a hair. She felt her mind peacefully numb for the first time in several days. She was tired, she'd slept horribly every night since she'd locked Perry out of the house.

She found the squat brick building and parked on the street. There were three people hanging around outside, wearing orange vests that said: Clinic Escort Volunteer. One of them was at the side of her vehicle before she'd even shut the door behind her.

"Afternoon, ma'am," the volunteer said. "Care if I escort you into the building."

"Do I need one?"

"Well no, but that's why we're here, just in case you do want an escort."

Barbara heard the chanting then.

"Don't kill kids! Don't kill kids!"

"Jesus Christ," Barbara said, seeing the protestors for the first time.

They stood about twenty yards away from the building, waving signs and fists in the air. Barbara read: *They Kill Babies Here!* And: *Choose Life!* And: *Abortion is Murder!*

Barbara walked down the sidewalk toward the building and the protestors. Another volunteer in an orange vest came over and walked between the protesters and Barbara.

"Murderer!"

"Don't do it!"

"You've got options!"

"God loves you!"

*All these angry voices*, Barbara thought. *It must be so hard to work with this going on just outside your door.*

Barbara stood under the little portico and turned to the crowd. She counted fifteen protestors. An ugly man on the edge of the group was staring at Barbara intently with dark, hard eyes. He wasn't holding a sign or raising his fists. He was just standing there, staring at her. She felt goosebumps ripple across her arms. She held his eyes for a moment then turned and stepped inside.

-

The man working the front desk was young and had feminine features. When Barbara identified herself as a detective from the Elizabethtown Police Department he said, "You go, girl!" and offered up a high-five.

In the fifteen minutes Barbara was inside Kentucky's last abortion clinic she learned Lindsey Leslie had sought their services in the past but not recently and that Mary Ann Gregory had never been one of their patients.

When she stepped back into the street, the man that had creeped her out was no longer protesting in the street. She chided herself for feeling unnerved by this.

## CHAPTER TWENTY-NINE
## THE EYES OF THE LORD

**"THEY KILL BABIES HERE!" THEY** shouted.

Jacob had helped make the signs: LWC = Losing Women's Christianity; My Unplanned Pregnancy is Now a Student at Louisville; Pro-Life; Satan Works Here!; The Only Choice is Right vs. Wrong.

There was something catching in the pumping of fists and the raising of numerous voices. Jacob felt his hair stand up on end.

*This is my first real protest*, he thought.

The sign he held above his head read: **Women Deserve Better Than Abortion**. There was a picture of a dead fetus underneath the bold text.

Brock Sither had the bullhorn.

"Stop killing babies!" he chanted.

The twenty or so of them echoed: *Stop Killing Babies!*

Jacob could almost see the black cloud hanging over the Louisville Women's Clinic. He thought he could feel the evil pulsating from the squat brick building.

A car pulled up to the building.

"Here comes another sinner!" Brock Sither yelled.

The chanting picked up its intensity as the orange vested volunteers made their way over to the car. Two women got out and were escorted the twenty-five yards to the building. They had to walk directly in front of the Dominion House protesters. Jacob could tell by the women's body language which one was seeking the services of the Louisville Women's Clinic and which one was there offering moral support. One of the women was crouched so low Jacob half-expected her to drop to her knees right there on the sidewalk and beg God for forgiveness.

*Fat chance*, Jacob thought.

The Call of Jeremiah was what they discussed earlier that evening at the Dominion House meeting. It sprang to Jacob's lips now.

"Before I formed ye in the womb I knew ye, before ye were born

449

# BIRTH OF A MONSTER

I set ye apart; I appointed ye as a prophet to the nations."

Brock Sither heard Jacob and echoed him through the bullhorn.

"Before I formed you in the womb I knew you, before you were born I set you apart; I appointed you as a prophet to the nations!"

With each raised voice, the woman seemed to shrink within herself, bringing a smile to Jacob's face. The pace of the little envoy heading for the clinic's front entrance slowed as if some unseen weight came to rest on the pregnant woman's shoulders.

*Whore of Babylon*, Jacob thought, *take your medicine.*

He thought he could just make out the raised tummy on her. For a startlingly vivid moment, Jacob saw himself over the woman with a bloody knife.

*I could save that unborn child*, he thought. *I can save the babies they kill here. I can save these wayward mothers too. I can serve God and hunt. Hunt and serve.*

Jacob watched the two women disappear inside the clinic with a smile on his face.

-

My children, I have seen the light. It is bright and it is illuminating. There is a dark stain on Louisville's soul and I think I can help God remedy it. All these lost souls, little unborn baby souls thrown against the black altar of the Louisville Women's Clinic can be redeemed. In death I can father these children, I can shepherd these little souls to their celestial home. These sinful women I will put before God Almighty to do with as He sees fit. Home, my children, I will be sending all these souls homeward. My way is sure, I am the hand of God. Deuteronomy 32:39: See now that I am He; there is no God besides Me. I bring death and I give life; I wound and I heal, and there is no one who can deliver from My hand.

-

"Gone are the days when the Jezebels of the world have sole control of social media. Gone are the days of the minions of Satan ruling the internet," Brock Sither said into the microphone. "With Dominion House's Pro-Vision 15:3, we step into the new paradigm of religiosity in the social media world. It's time God's light shone in the darkness of the internet."

There was applause from the congregation.

"Proverbs 15:3 says, 'The eyes of the Lord are everywhere, keeping watch on the wicked and the good.' We are nothing if not eyes for the Lord. We are nothing if not God's watchdog warning of the evils of entities such as the Louisville Women's Clinic."

There was more applause. The screen behind the podium showed a woman's smiling selfie. Her full name, social media handles, address, and phone number were listed under the photo. There was a dramatic sound effect of something heavy slamming down and a banner appeared over the woman's head: *Profiles of the Wicked*.

"Pro-Vision 15:3 will highlight key persons in the struggle for Louisville's soul with our *Profiles of the Wicked*. We'll publish names, addresses, and phone numbers of LWC's employees, volunteers, and *patients*. We'll list everyone involved in our *List of Killers*. We'll put volunteers' and patients' places of employment on blast in a page on the site entitled *Accomplices*," Brock Sither said. "We'll make it hard on these women to kill their innocent little children. The children that God gifted them."

*Yes we will*, Jacob thought.

"We'll need volunteers to get this project off the ground and running."

Jacob raised his hand immediately.

"So you'll be following the women once they leave the clinic," Brock Sither told the small group of volunteers. "Find out where they live, where they work, everything. Take the best photos of them you can get without being seen."

Digital cameras were passed out. Jacob studied his, found the "on" button, looked through the lens, snapped a photo of Brock Sither.

"We'll do all the actual posting," he said. "Y'all will be our content gatherers. We've already brought in an IT guy who's redesigning the DH website with our new focus."

"So we're not supposed to approach them with their sins?" Deanna Cole asked.

Brock Sither shook his head.

"No, we'll be doing that on the website," he said. "The idea is for y'all to silently, secretly gather the content for the site. The site will be the horn of the Lord."

Deanna Cole nodded her head.

"Understood," she said.

# BIRTH OF A MONSTER

"We'll start tomorrow," Brock Sither said. "The plan is for y'all to take turns following the women after they leave the clinic. Jacob will be one; Deanna: two; Smithey: three; Greg: four; Leanna: five; Georgie: six. Keep your cameras on you and take more photos than you think you'll need. The more content, the better. Just stay hidden and watchful. We're the eyes of the Lord."

-

Jacob watched the woman climb behind the wheel of the F-150 and fire up the engine. Jacob zoomed in with the camera and took a shot of her puffy, tear-streaked face then put the camera aside and started the Mazda. As the F-150 pulled out into traffic, Jacob followed.

At a stoplight, Jacob snapped a photograph of the F-150's license plate. Sither hadn't mentioned taking photos of the license plate but the more content, the better. Jacob followed the woman, the *patient*, seven and a half miles to a comfy, cookie-cutter neighborhood. He snapped photos of the woman parking and exiting the vehicle. He zoomed in on the front door, getting shots of the woman unlocking the door with the house number clearly visible in the frame.

Jacob knew that was all that was required of him. He could put the Mazda in drive and pull away, but he didn't.

The more content, the better.

-

The house was dark. Jacob exited the Mazda, camera strap around his neck, and walked up the driveway to the side of the house. He walked briskly and surely, not looking around but wanting to. The dead winter grass crunched under his boots. He opened the fence and entered the backyard.

*The eyes of the Lord are everywhere*, he thought, *keeping watch on the wicked and the good.*

The backdoor was unlocked. Jacob stepped inside and pulled the door closed behind him. The light above the stove showed him he was in the kitchen. He stepped into the hall and made his way to the front of the quiet house. The hall ended in a small living room. There were stairs leading upwards near the front door. Jacob stopped at the front door and unlocked the deadbolt then carefully climbed the stairs to the upstairs portion of the house. There were three doors at the head of the stairs: two closed doors and a bathroom in between.

The carpet muffled his steps. Jacob tried the door on the right side first. It was a bedroom that had been converted into a little office. There was a desk with a computer and two bookshelves crammed with books. He left the door open and made his way to the other bedroom door.

He eased the door open and stood for a moment listening, waiting for his eyes to adjust to the darkness. He saw the bed and a single shape in it.

*Good*, he smiled.

Jacob crossed the room and went through the dresser. He took a pair of silky underwear and stuffed them in the front pocket of the sweatpants, Walmart. He hovered over the sleeping woman, the *patient*, for several minutes just breathing in her smell. He took the dildo from the top drawer on his way out.

"We made the news, brothers and sisters!" Brock Sither told the congregation.

The television was on but silent beside him. Brock reached over and unmuted it.

"Tonight on Your Local News," the male anchor said. "A local church is making national news with their aggressive new approach to abortion shaming."

There was a spatter of applause then the entire room was whooping and hollering, Jacob included.

"Behold I have come to do your will!" Brock Sither yelled into the microphone. His tinny voice came out distorted through the hanging speakers.

"Amen!" Jacob yelled.

*Get control of yourself*, the voice said.

Jacob felt blood come into his face. He forced his face to become blank, expressionless.

"A local church is pushing the boundaries of accepted internet decorum through religious shaming."

"Shame on them!" a woman shouted.

"Shame!" they echoed.

"Dominion House, a local Christian church based out of Louisville, recently made headlines for the avant garde sculptors of one of its members is now making headlines because of its website www.pro-vision1513.com and its *Profiles of the Wicked*."

There were several whoops and two yeses.

Jacob saw four different women's homes in his head in shadow-laden Fast-Forward X2 Mode. He paused the mental image of the sleeping pregnant woman from Pioneer Village, asleep and uncovered, her skin broken out in droplets of sweat. Jacob went to her home nearly every night now, now that he'd found her. She lived alone, was unmarried, and seeking services from Louisville Women's Clinic. They'd featured her in the last *Profiles of the Wicked* and her employer had fired her. He couldn't stop himself from watching her while she slept.

"—who said she was fired from her job at Card 'n' Al's Doughnut for seeking the services of LWC, which often include abortion into the second trimester."

*Serves her right*, Jacob thought, seeing himself clad in the black sweat suit, Walmart, his left hand steadily working under the waistband, his right hovering over the woman's sweat covered stomach with the filet knife, Roger's Bait 'n' Tackle. He saw himself pull the knife away just as he came.

Jacob passed several of the houses of the Wicked in the routes he drove for the drivers that called in sick. He slowed by each of them, recalling the chill of the night and the warmth of the houses, the smell of the women, the stink he couldn't get enough of, their soft underthings.

"The church has also created social media accounts on all the major platforms to further shame those they refer to as simply *The Wicked*."

How many doors had been unlocked? How many windows?

*How easy it is getting inside*, he thought.

He'd chosen her, the one, one of *The Wicked*, and planned on taking her life in His name that evening.

"Holding company names like hostages on their page entitled *Accomplices*," the reporter said. "The church must be provided with documentation that the company has terminated the employee they label as *Wicked*. WGAS-11 has documented four company names that were listed as *Accomplices* but have since been removed from the list. See who after this message from our sponsors."

"In His name!" Brock Sither shouted. "Amen!"

"Amen!" Jacob screamed. "A-*men*!"

-

How many times had he simply watched through the windows? People would do every despicable thing they do behind closed doors right out in front of the window for all the world to see. He'd seen all the sex acts he thought possible through Louisville and

Jeffersonville's dirty but open windows.

Jacob preferred going inside but it was always a risk. He tried to be careful but sometimes he couldn't stop himself, couldn't control what his hands and nose and tongue just had to do.

He'd planned on taking her tonight, the night before her scheduled appointment at the Louisville Women's Clinic, but she was putting on a little show for him at the moment. She had her dildo out and was working it along the outside of her pink panties. Jacob watched her as she went about it, wondering what she was thinking.

*Is she even capable of thought?* he wondered. *Or is she rubbing one out thinking about the murder she plans on having committed under His damning eyes in the morning?*

After she'd finished—Jacob had a go at it himself—she went to sleep. Jacob watched her sleep for nearly an hour before entering through her unlocked back door. He walked over to the calendar and took out his penlight, University of Pikeville Medical School, and the permanent marker, Walmart, and wrote *Proverbs 15:3* in the square of the next day's date.

-

She was sleeping outside the covers. Jacob assumed she must have intense hot flashes because she was rarely under her covers when he came to her each night. He had the knife in his left hand, the penlight in his right. He stepped into the room and forced himself to stand still and slow his breathing.

*Take yer time*, he told himself. *Enjoy the moment.*

Jacob clicked on the penlight but had most of the beam obscured by his fingers.

*Shit!*

There was an extra shape in the bed. He extinguished the light in a hurry and crouched.

*Calm down*, the voice said. *They didn't wake.*

It was true. After a moment, Jacob heard their gentle breathing.

*Okay*, he told himself. *This changes the plan.*

*Proverbs 16:2: Commit to the Lord whatever you do, and He will establish your plans.*

*I will take one from the Louisville Women's Clinic tomorrow*, he told himself. *I will leave this one here for another night.*

-

The parking garage was around the corner from the Louisville Women's Clinic. It was old and poorly lit. Jacob pulled the Mazda

455

into a parking spot facing the entrance/exit and killed the engine. It was early, but he didn't have to wait long.

He watched three vehicles pull into spots and park, each having at least two people inside. He needed his prey to be alone, *the lamb / separated from its mother.*

An older model Saturn pulled into the parking garage, one of its headlights out, a lone female behind the wheel. He stepped out into the brisk morning at a crouch and snuck over to where the woman sat in her idling parked car. He shielded himself from her view with the pickup she parked beside. He waited, forcing his breathing to stay even and calm, until she opened the door and got out.

Jacob thought he'd seen her enter the clinic earlier the week before but from his angle he couldn't quite tell until she reached skyward, stretching. Then he recognized her as Margaret Hatfield. Dominion House was in the process of getting her *Profile of the Wicked* ready for release. Jacob hadn't been assigned to gather information on her but he knew another member of Dominion House had been.

*Mine*, he thought, stalking around the corner of the car, still at a crouch.

He waited until she'd come around the car, big pregnant belly protruding out in front of her, heading for the exit signs, before springing up behind her. He wrapped his left forearm around her throat and lifted her off her feet, dragging her, choking, toward the Mazda. Her fingernails bit into his wrists but he had no problem overpowering the woman, who was several inches and pounds smaller than himself.

"Please!" she hissed with the last of the air in her lungs.

Jacob held her inert body in his right arm and opened the camper shell, Wallace Skaggs, and threw her inside, disgusted to see she'd pissed herself. He felt himself but he was dry. He locked the hatch and the tailgate then climbed back inside the Mazda and pulled out into the morning traffic, smiling.

Josiah Powers closed the scrap yard on Mondays, so Jacob had the place to himself. He parked the Mazda next to the RV and stepped out into the bright sunshine. The day was brilliant and cloudless but deceptively cold. His breath plumed out of his nostrils like wispy ghosts.

He walked over to his semi-circle of creations. The sculptures were in various forms of completion. The one he planned on working on today, a great limbed praying mantis looking thing with four sets of large bulbous eyes, was ready for the harlot, Margaret Hatfield, and her unborn child.

Jacob got the welding equipment ready then slipped into the RV to pop two Adderall and retrieve a bottle of Thunderbird from the mini fridge. He stepped back into the sunshine feeling happier than he had in a long time.

A verse popped into his head as he made his way around the Mazda to the back of the camper shell and he spoke it out loud, "Let the morning bring me word of yer unfailing love, for I have put my trust in Ye. Show me the way I should go, for to Ye I entrust my life."

Jacob unlocked the hatch of the camper shell then the tailgate. The woman, Margaret Hatfield, was still unconscious. Jacob reached inside and put his hand on her pregnant belly. It was warm and more solid feeling than Jacob had expected. He lifted the woman out of the truck and set her in the middle of the semi-circle of creations.

*surrounded by angels / driven to His will*

Her fingernails were painted red and felt warm all over. The sun felt like a watchful, ruminating eye beating down on Jacob's skull. He was smiling as he put the modified welding helmet over his head and another verse came to him.

"Therefore, I urge ye, brothers and sisters," Jacob said over the unconscious woman, "in view of God's mercy, to offer yer bodies as a living sacrifice, holy and pleasing to God—this is yer true and proper worship."

Jacob retrieved the filet knife, Roger's Bait 'n' Tackle, then covered his face with the welding helmet. He knelt down over the woman, everything magnified through the jeweler's lenses he'd put in the helmet, and cut her clothing off. He marveled at her body for some time, his right hand slipping into the sweatpants, Walmart.

Everything felt heightened. His breathing was quick but even and he felt sweat prickle across his body despite the temperature. He could smell her stink and heard the bald man's voice in his head repeating *cunt stink* over and over in soothing tones of supplication.

*I'm doing God's work*, Jacob told himself. *I am but His hand. I am the desert, the seabed.*

Jacob sunk the filet knife, Roger's Bait 'n' Tackle, into the woman's chest just below her left breast. He watched her eyes open wide, the scream dying on her lips before it could escape. He watched her face through the magnified lenses as she died.

His lips felt tingly as he spoke aloud, "For whoever wants to save their life will lose it, but whoever loses their life for Me will save it."

Jacob pulled the knife free from the woman's breast and crouched over her inert body. He started cutting into her rounded stomach.

*I am life*, Jacob thought. *I am death.*

"I'm coming, my child," he whispered. "Hang on, poor little one. I am coming."

Jacob lifted the small, unmoving fetus from the open stomach. He cut the cord and studied the little boy in his hand. It was tiny—Jacob had seen puppies larger than the boy—and blue in hue.

"My son, ye're serving Him in yer death," Jacob said. "For if the blood of goats and bulls and the ashes of a heifer sprinkled on those who are ceremonially unclean sanctify them so that their bodies are clean, how much more will the blood of Christ, who through the eternal Spirit offered Himself unblemished to God, purify our consciences from works of death, so that we may serve the living God!"

Jacob's hands were slick with blood but he held the dead child firmly. The blood shone dully under the bright sun. Jacob had made a small pile of kindling near the newest angel. He set the child down on top of the kerosene-soaked pile.

Jacob liked the way the world looked through the modified welding helmet. He lifted the kerosene container and poured it over the child. He knelt before the little pile of sticks and lit it.

"He said, 'Take now your son, yer only son, whom ye love, Isaac, and go to the land of Moriah, and offer him there as a burnt offering on one of the mountains of which I will tell ye,'" Jacob said, watching in enlarged detail as the flames licked the small, blood-soaked body.

Jacob felt invigorated, awash in heat and energy. He waited until the child was mostly burned then lifted up the bundle of bones and sinew and put it inside the trunk of the newest angel.

"Rest easy, my son," he said before welding the opening closed.

They'd needed a crane to hoist the angel onto the bed of the Josiah Powers' flatbed truck. It was Jacob's most elaborate creation to date, standing nearly ten feet tall with wide, reaching arms and shiny, sharpened talons. Each of the mantis eyes were as large as human skulls.

The man from Gallery East was with them at Powers' Scrap 'n' Metal, oohing and ahing at the mantis angel and the unfinished works in the semi-circle near Jacob's RV. Jacob noted how the dried dirt soaked up most of the blood and the puddle that remained looked more like spent oil than anything else.

"A masterpiece!" the man kept repeating. "You're a genius, Mr. Goodman! A genius!"

# CHAPTER THIRTY
## NO HANDS

**BARBARA CAUGHT THE JANE DOE** homicide as soon as she clocked in. Sergeant Ellis was waiting at her desk.

"We've got a female head, bits of hair and skin still on the skull, a torso, one breast removed, one left arm, no hand, and two legs," Sergeant Ellis said. "All found by one lucky jogger early this morning, which is what you get for exercising at such an ungodly hour."

Barbara smiled but it was a pained thing. She never could get used to joking about bodies the way the other cops did, especially when it was a female.

"The guy didn't take it well from what Stevens said," Sergeant Ellis said. "Threw up all over the place and couldn't stop crying."

Barbara nodded.

"Where at?" she asked.

"Down at the Buffalo Lake walking trail," he said. "Coyotes had dug them up from a shallow grave and it sounds like buzzards had a turn with them too."

Barbara parked her car and followed the uniformed officer to the spot. It wasn't far off the path but the woods seemed to close in on you as soon as you stepped off the path, creating a decently secluded area. Barbara could see how desolate it would look at night. She shivered in her jacket.

She studied each piece of the body, directing the photographer to snap shots as she worked.

*What kind of monster is this?* Barbara wondered. There were several stab wounds on the torso and the left breast had indeed been cut completely off and taken away from the body.

There was a tattoo of Taz the Tasmanian devil just above where the left hand should've been. They closed down the park and searched the entire wooded area. They found two more cut-up pieces of bodies. There were no hands with any of the arms.

460

The dental records for the head came back as belonging to twenty-three-year-old Teresa Skyler. Barbara quickly learned she was another drug addict with several arrests for possession and paraphernalia that frequented the B.A.T. The two additional bodies came back as belonging to Mary Ann Gregory and Lindsey Leslie. The ME told Barbara the time of death was probably the day of each of the women's disappearance. They'd been killed somewhere else and dumped at Buffalo Lake. Each of the women had been pregnant.

The media was on it quickly. There were helicopters from the bigger news stations in Louisville circling the area, shooting the cops and ME teams as they worked. There were also four news vans and four sets of reporters working the little trail's parking lot.

Barbara heard the news on the radio on her way back to the department.

"The Derby City Butcher, believed to be responsible for at least seven deaths in the Kentuckiana area, seems to have moved south from Louisville down I-65 to Elizabethtown. Elizabethtown police have uncovered human remains at Buffalo Lake Wildlife Habitat walking trail near the intersection of I-65 and the Bluegrass Parkway. It is believed the bodies are the work of a serial killer in the area. Derby City Butcher Task Force Leader Mitchell Skeeters told the public to use caution around strangers—"

Barbara turned the radio off as she pulled into the parking lot. She was tired and numbed by her morning working the park. She hadn't eaten anything for breakfast and had worked through lunch.

Sergeant Ellis was waiting for Barbara when she got back to her office.

"Well, LPD is sending down two of their own claiming your bodies are theirs," he said.

"What?"

"The Butcher task force is pulling weight and they've got the LPD commissioner behind them."

"This is my case, Sarge," Barbara said.

"I know it."

"Well, what're we gonna do?"

"You're gonna work the cases just as you would normally," Sergeant Ellis said, "and you're going to keep your head down and give them what they want."

Barbara's stomach growled.

"This is mine, Sarge," she said.

"I know it," he said. "We'll hold primary on the case but I'm not sure for how long. You're gonna have to work fast on this one."

"What've you got?"

Barbara looked up from her computer at the man standing in the doorway to her office.

"Mitchell Skeeters, LPD Homicide," the man said, stepping inside and pulling the door shut. He didn't offer his hand.

"Listen, this is my case," Barbara said. "Y'all can assist but I'm running point. Period."

The man smiled.

"Of course," he said. "That's until we find anything linking this back to us, then we're taking control."

The two cops stared at each other across Barbara's cluttered desk.

"Well."

"Well."

"We'll get y'all set up in one of the conference rooms. We've got a mess of CCTV footage to go through. How many you bringing on with ye?"

"Three."

"Okay. Well let's get y'all set up and get to work."

"Yes, ma'am."

The man hadn't stopped smiling.

"Is something funny?" Barbara asked.

"No, ma'am."

"Ye can quit with the ma'am business."

"Sure."

Barbara showed Skeeters to the conference room and tracked down the IT guy to get the four LPD detectives up and running.

"There're three cameras on this stretch of I-65 and one on the on-ramp to the Bluegrass Parkway." Barbara motioned to the shots displayed on the screen behind her. "We're thinking our guy could've pulled over to the shoulder of I-65 or the on-ramp to the Bluegrass and got into the park that way. The fence lining the highway had been cut—clean, purposeful cuts."

"What's the ME say?"

"ME said that all the bodies had been killed elsewhere and

transported to our spot."

Skeeters gave one of his detectives a knowing look.

Barbara ignored it and changed slides. The screen showed the on-ramp to the Bluegrass Parkway. Several cars made the wide arcing turn off of Interstate 65 onto the Bluegrass Parkway.

"We've got a window now that we've got the ME's report," Barbara said. "So we don't have a mountain of footage, more like a molehill. Let's divvy up the highway camera footage and see if we can find our man."

With help from IT, the detectives began going through the footage.

Barbara left the Louisville detectives in the conference room and went back to her office.

Perry had emailed her departmental address. She opened it and was in the process of reading it when there was a knocking at her door. She quickly minimized the window and looked up to see Skeeters smiling down.

"We got something."

"Already?"

"We work fast at LPD."

Barbara followed Skeeters back into the conference room. They'd pulled up one of the cameras on the screen at the head of the room. It showed all four lanes of the interstate as well as the beginning turnoff to the Bluegrass Parkway. Skeeters walked over to one of the laptops and clicked away. Barbara watched a light tan sedan pull over onto the shoulder of the interstate. It was nighttime, few vehicles were on the road. A man got out, walked around the car to the trunk and opened it. He knelt inside and retrieved several black trash bags. He walked off the shoulder of the road, down the embankment to the fence lining the interstate. He tossed the bags over the fence and reached into a pocket of the dark sweatshirt he was wearing and took out something. He leaned over the fence and cut each strand of metallic wire before stepping through and picking up the trash bags and disappearing into the woods beyond.

"When was this?" Barbara asked.

"Last Tuesday," one of the detectives said.

"Can we get a clearer picture of the guy?" Barbara asked.

The IT guy walked over to Skeeter's laptop and sat down. He clicked and typed for a few moments then the image on the screen rewound and zoomed as the man opened the sedan's trunk. His face was blurred but they could tell he was a white male in dark sweatpants and sweatshirt. They could, however, clearly make out the license plate number.

"Run it," Barbara said, calmer than she felt.

"Yes, ma'am," Skeeters said.

The plates came back to a Russell Whitehead, a resident of Shepherdsville who'd reported the car stolen from the Elizabethtown Community College's campus two weeks ago. The car's description, the plate numbers, and the VIN number, pulled from the DMV, were circulated through the department and the state police.

They had an interagency hit almost immediately. The car had already been found by a Sheriff's Deputy out at an abandoned rock quarry in rural Hardin County, near Stephensburg. It'd been torched.

Barbara drove out to see it. The interior was a total loss.

*No way any fingerprints are coming out of this*, she thought, walking around the blackened sedan. The trunk was standing open and was scorched. She got a uniform to cordon off the area and started looking around. Not far from the car near the rock quarry's green lake, an oil drum stood out like a sore thumb. Barbara walked over to it and toed it. It felt full.

She radioed for the uniform to come over and assist her in opening the oil drum. He brought over a crowbar and pried the lid off. The smell of lye was overwhelming. Barbara gasped at the body crammed into the oil drum. It was surrounded by gravel and lye. It'd been partially dissolved by the lye. Half the face was missing but Barbara could tell it was a female inside.

She called it in.

## CHAPTER THIRTY-ONE
## HEAVEN AWAITS


**"POLICE SAY THE REMAINS OF** twenty-four-year-old Sandra Burke of Jefferson County were found at Fulcrum's Rock Quarry in rural Hardin County. Has the Derby City Butcher moved out of Louisville? Find out tonight on Your Local Six O'Clock News."

Deanna Cole shut off the television and turned to Jacob, who was stacking chairs in the corner.

"Want to go get a milkshake or something?" she asked.

Dominion House had been featured in another primetime newscast for their Louisville Women's Clinic protests. Jacob thought this piece had focused more on the fact that LWC was Kentucky's last licensed abortion clinic than Dominion House's crusades against it.

Jacob fought the urge to see if they were looking at him in suspicion after that last bit on the TV before Deanna shut it off. One part of him was sure it was emblazoned on his forehead: GUILTY. The other part of him was sure he was invisible, that he would never get caught because he was God's vengeance serving out His will and shepherding His Children off to Heaven.

"No," Jacob said, adding another chair to the stack.

"Oh, okay," Deanna Cole said, her voice sounding small.

They worked in silence.

Deanna Cole's getting annoying, Jacob thought. The woman had asked him to accompany her to eat on four separate occasions now. Jacob didn't want the woman's extra attention. He was already having a hard-enough time at keeping his face blank, expressionless. He felt he was tearing in two, so sure of himself when he was hunting, killing, creating, and then, at the drop of a hat, so completely unsure of himself and *paranoid*, Mrs. Horace Word of the Day a few short years ago, *1: characterized by or resembling paranoia or paranoid schizophrenia; 2: characterized by suspiciousness, persecutory trends, or megalomania; 3: extremely fearful.*

He felt her looking at him at various points in every meeting. She always sat close to him, if not directly at his side, then usually in either a seat in front of him or, most frequently and to Jacob's great chagrin, behind. He felt her eyes boring into the back of his head, the side of his face, his hot, burning ears.

She was waiting for him in the parking lot, though he'd purposefully stayed after to help clean as slowly as he'd allow himself to, hoping she'd be gone.

"How about we go back to my place and have coffee and talk about Brother Henry's sermon?" Deanna Cole said.

She was leaning against the camper shell, Wallace Skaggs, on the Mazda.

Jacob forced himself to take a breath before answering.

"No," he said, "thank you. I'm not looking for a relationship."

A moment ticked by.

"Right now, at least," he said. "Okay?"

She nodded her head, her eyes large and wet and searching.

"Why don't you like me?" she asked.

"I like you," he lied.

She smiled. Jacob thought it a lurid thing, her smile. It showed too much teeth and, coupled with her leering eyes, made her look like a harlot more than anything else. He brushed by her and unlocked the Mazda.

"Good night," she said.

"Night."

Jacob drove around aimlessly for some time, his thoughts jangling around like loose change in his skull. The night came on and he needed gas. He filled up somewhere south of town, a forgotten stretch of back city with boarded-up shotgun houses and abandoned factories, their rows of broken windows yawning like infected teeth in gaping mouths.

He felt too jittery to hunt properly. He kept getting distracted by his racing thoughts so he drove back to Powers' Scrap 'n' Metal, deciding he'd spend the evening working on the angels. He unlocked the gate, pulled through, and was in the process of closing and locking the gate when she stepped out of the shadows under the security light.

"Hi," Deanna Cole said.

"What're ye doing here?"

Jacob was stunned to see her. Had she been following him? Or had she been here waiting on his return? What if he'd hunted and killed and brought home a corpse?

He was suddenly furious.

"Why are ye here?"

"I want to spend time with you," she said, smiling. "We don't have to do anything. Just be together. I want to watch you work on your sculptures. I won't make any noise or nothing."

*Stay calm*, the voice said. *Keep your calm.*

Jacob breathed in air through his nostrils and let it out through his clenched teeth.

"I need ye to leave right now," Jacob said carefully.

"I'm not leaving until you tell me what you hate so much about me." She was crying and smiling at the same time. It unnerved Jacob. "Tell me. Tell me!"

Jacob breathed slowly.

"I don't hate ye," he said. "I'm tired and I don't like being watched."

"Why won't you go on a date with me?" she asked. "Do you have a girlfriend already? Who is she?"

"I don't have a girlfriend," Jacob said. "I'm not looking to date anyone right now. I'm really focused on the creations."

*And the hunting.*

"Well fine," she said, her lower lip pouting out below all those white teeth. "We don't have to date. I just want to be your friend. You can't say no to that, can you?"

He found he couldn't.

-

The intensity of the protests outside the Louisville Women's Clinic was startling. Jacob could only get to one or two protests a week now that he was full-time at Rubbish Management. There were nearly thirty Dominion House members present this morning.

Jacob accepted the sign Deanna Cole handed him and read it out loud, "The Devil Works Here."

Deanna Cole smiled up at him then turned and joined in the chanting.

Jacob mouthed along with the words.

"What do we want?"

"Life!"

"When do we want it?"

"Now!"

"Who runs the Louisville Women's Clinic?"

"Satan!"

Jacob held the sign above his head. A reporter took his picture.

She came alone. Jacob watched her slowly pass the protestors in her purple PT Cruiser, her eyes as wide as dragstrip tires, park, then get out. She kept her head down but shot looks up at the protestors. There was something in her face Jacob needed to see again.

Jacob watched the volunteer escorts wrap their arms around her, putting their bodies between the patient and the protestors. Jacob wished he could get that close.

Her belly stuck out in front of her as she was whisked away by the orange-vested escorts.

"Whore must be due soon!" Deanna Cole shouted up at Jacob.

Jacob doubted that. He guessed she was probably somewhere near the beginning of the second trimester.

The woman entered the clinic and the protestors returned to their posts.

*She's mine*, he thought. *I'll follow her when she leaves here. See how it goes.*

"The lot is cast into the lap, but its every decision is from the Lord," Jacob whispered out loud.

He was smiling. Deanna Cole happened to turn around and smiled up at him.

The purple PT Cruiser pulled into the driveway. Jacob parked the Mazda quickly and watched the pregnant woman enter the darkened little house. He watched the lights come on in the front room, then a room toward the rear Jacob assumed was the small house's only bedroom. He got out of the Mazda and stalked around the PT Cruiser and crept up onto the front porch. The neighborhood, which was well on the skids, half the houses empty and boarded up, was asleep, quiet.

Jacob put his hand on the doorknob, willing it to be unlocked. It was. He pushed in the door with his shoulder and stepped into the living room of the woman's house. He had the filet knife, Roger's Bait 'n' Tackle, in his left hand, his right clenched into a fist. The woman wasn't in the room. Jacob closed the door then walked across the room.

He heard a shower running in the back of the house. He made

his way through the small kitchen into the hall beyond. There was no light in the little hallway, nor was there a window. Jacob felt his way along the wall toward the light coming out of the open bathroom door.

*I am the desert*, Jacob told himself. *I am the seabed.*

He felt himself harden imagining the killing in the hot shower steam. He stepped into the bright lights of the bathroom. The shower was empty.

"What the—"

He turned around and there she was, naked and pregnant, her face a surprised O of alarm. Jacob was on her before she could scream.

-

Jacob wrapped her up in the hall runner, securing the bundle with stretched bungee cords. He leaned her against the wall and looked around the house. When he returned to the living room a small puddle of blood had formed at the foot of the rug.

*Better move her before the mess is too much to clean up*, the voice said.

Jacob nodded his head, then lifted up the heavy bundle. He opened the front door and peeked outside. The neighborhood was quiet, the streets empty. The streetlights were off but the dusk was settling on toward night and Jacob figured they'd light up soon. He carried the dripping rug down the front porch steps to his waiting truck. He opened the back hatch and put the bundled rug inside the camper shell, Wallace Skaggs.

He walked back up the walk and into the house. He found a bottle of Pine-Sol under the kitchen sink and used it along with a roll of paper towels and the clothes he cut off her body to clean up his mess. He put the bloody remains in a plastic grocery bag and pulled the door shut behind him. He tossed the bag into the camper shell with the body.

He felt prying eyes on him but, when he scanned the area, he saw no one. He started the Mazda just as the streetlights came on.

-

Jacob pulled into Powers' Scrap 'n' Metal and closed the gate behind him. He backed the Mazda up to the most recent creation and killed the engine. He stepped out under the rising moon and stretched, his back popping and creaking. He walked over to the angel and studied the welds. He left the lifted left arm and the chest region open for this kill. The baby would go in the trunk of the angel, bits of the woman would go in the left arm.

Jacob walked around to the side of the main building and retrieved the modified welding helmet and the thick, stained gloves. He walked over to the Howard Electric and flipped it on.

He still felt eyes on him. He turned around slowly, taking in everything around him, but saw no one.

*You're being paranoid*, the voice said. *No one is here but you and God. Get to work.*

Jacob opened the hatch of the camper shell and hoisted the runner rug out and carried it to the semicircle of creations. The angel closest to completion, the one Gallery East had already requested Jacob let them show, was a metallic hunter green. Most of the metal had come from an ancient, battered AMC Gremlin. The angel seemed to glisten under the glow of the junkyard's security lights.

Jacob thought about the recent sales of the creations and the thousands of dollars he was able to donate to Dominion House because of it.

"Every man shall give as he is able, accordin' to the blessing of the Lord your God that He has given ye," Jacob said, putting the helmet on. He used the Case knife, Ace Hardware, to cut the bungees off the bundle. He used his foot to unroll her out of the rug. Blood was smeared all across her naked body. Her stomach looked pooched and deflating. Jacob wondered how long a baby could live inside a dead mother.

He put away his Case knife, Ace Hardware, and retrieved his filet knife, Roger's Bait 'n' Tackle, ignoring the warning bells clanging in his head. He still felt unseen eyes on him, watching his every move. He couldn't help but steal a glance over his shoulder back at the gate as he worked. He saw no one.

*Focus on the work*, he told himself.

He made his incision in a straight line beginning a few inches above the bellybutton.

*I'm coming, My Child, to set you free. Heaven awaits.*

He held the little body up in his gloved hands.

"But when Jesus saw it, he was indignant and said to them, 'Let the children come to me; do not hinder them, for to such belongs the kingdom of God,'" Jacob said, setting the child into the open trunk of the green, metallic angel.

Jacob sealed the dead fetus inside first.

-

Jacob was asleep in the camper late in the morning when there was a knocking at the door. He felt immediately trapped inside the small confines of the camper. He threw the covers off and palmed the Case knife, Ace Hardware.

He opened the door and harsh sunlight flooded inside. He used his right hand to shield his eyes.

"Jacob," a familiar female voice said.

Jacob blinked in the brightness.

"Yes?" he said stepping down into the dirt barefooted.

Deanna Cole stood before him, alone.

"Jacob," she said again.

"Yes," he said, forcing his voice to be bland, expressionless. "What do you need?"

"I saw . . ."

Jacob's eyes had adjusted to the brightness of the sun and now he could see that she appeared stricken, pale in the bleaching sunlight.

"What is it?" he asked.

"I saw you," she said. "Last night. I saw what you did."

Jacob reeled as if socked in the face. The air rushed out of his lungs.

*I knew I felt somebody watching me*, he thought.

"I saw you kill that woman," Deanna Cole said, seeming to take courage with each word she spoke. "And I couldn't agree with your actions more. Catherine Hensley had an abortion scheduled for next week. The whore."

A long moment passed in silence. Deanna Cole was smiling at Jacob.

*What do I do? Kill her? Did she tell anybody else?*

"I was assigned Catherine Hensley by Brock. I followed her after she left the Women's Clinic yesterday with my camera. Her *Profile of the Wicked* was scheduled to go live tonight."

*Stay calm*, the voice said.

"I was getting ready to get out of my car for some close-ups through the window last night when I saw you take to the night like a shadow," Deanna Cole said.

She took a step closer to Jacob, her smile widening.

"It was really something to watch you," she said.

Jacob noticed the camera hung around her neck for the first time.

"I got some of it on film," she said. "I thought you were just

471

getting some in-depth footage at first, but then I saw the knife and knew. Just knew."

Jacob felt like running. He felt like reaching out and knocking this woman down.

*Stay calm*, the voice repeated.

"I got most of it," she said, lifting the camera off her chest momentarily. "You were something to behold. You were so . . ."

Deanna Cole looked all around them as if the word she was searching for was in their immediate vicinity.

"What did ye see?" Jacob asked.

Deanna Cole looked into his eyes and smiled.

"I saw you doing the Lord's work."

Another long moment of silence passed between them. Jacob felt sweat break out across his body.

*She knows. Oh God she knows. What do I do?*

One part of Jacob felt relieved that another person knew what he'd done. The other part wanted to simultaneously run away and lash out at this woman and her camera.

"Look," she said, handing Jacob the camera.

He took it with shaking hands.

"It's okay," she said, smiling. "You were like a ghost last night. It was really something."

Jacob looked into the little screen. He saw the night-shrouded neighborhood. He saw the house. Then he saw a darker blackness in the shadows that the camera homed in on. Jacob watched himself ease open the front door and slip inside.

He looked up at the woman. She was smiling and nodding her head.

"Go on," Deanna Cole said. "Watch."

*Show / what's there to display*

The next series of photographs were taken through the back-bedroom window, which gave a long view into the bathroom beyond. Jacob watched the woman root around in a drawer and saw himself enter the bathroom beyond, his back to the woman and the camera. The next photograph showed the woman turn and walk through the bedroom out into the hall. Deanna Cole had snapped another shot just as the woman saw the intruder in her home. She stood completely straight, her hands coming to rest protectively around her middle. Her head hunkered down on her neck.

"Deanna—"

"Just look," she said.

The next shot showed Jacob turn on his heels and see the woman behind him. The camera zoomed in and Jacob saw his own smiling face in lurid detail. The next shots were the murder, the filet knife, Roger's Bait 'n' Tackle, going in and out with a steady smoothness of motion. The smile never left Jacob's face.

He looked up from the camera's little screen at Deanna Cole. She was smiling up at him, beaming.

"I know what you did and why you did it," she said, "and I couldn't agree with you more."

Jacob felt rocked.

"You're doing the Lord's Work," Deanna Cole said. "There's nothing to be embarrassed about."

*Embarrassed?* Jacob wondered if that was what he was feeling. He felt so many things at the moment that he was having a hard time deciphering between emotions. He was angry at being confronted with photographs. He was scared the knowledge of what he was was now in the hands of a woman that had a crush on him. He was terrified she'd already told somebody else. He felt a great weight, his burden, come untethered to hang precariously above his head, waiting to come crashing down at any moment.

"I want to help you," Deanna Cole said, smiling. "I want to assist you. We can do the Lord's work together."

A partner? The thought was *ludicrous*, Mrs. Horace's Word of the Day, *1: amusing or laughable through obvious absurdity, incongruity, exaggeration, or eccentricity; 2: meriting derisive laughter or scorn as absurdity inept, false, or foolish.*

His scorn must've showed on his face because Deanna Cole's visage abruptly changed.

"Why not?" she demanded. "If you can go out and kill, why can't I?"

Jacob forced his face to become expressionless, blank.

"Don't think I can do it? Well, believe me," she said, "I can do it. No problem. Not with these *whores*."

She nearly spat out the word.

"Plus, it'd be much easier on you with an extra set of eyes and hands."

Jacob still held the camera. He looked down into its screen to avoid her searching eyes. He watched himself kill Catherine Hensley with the filet knife, Roger's Bait 'n' Tackle, the blood looking more black than red.

The next series of photographs were taken through the fence of Powers' Scrap 'n' Metal. Jacob saw himself cut the fetus from the dead woman's body and hold it dripping in his gloved hands. He watched himself place the dead child into the angel and seal it inside. He watched himself hack the woman into smaller bits and insert her into the gigantic arms of the green angel.

"You're an artist," Deanna Cole said. "I want to help you. Let me."

Jacob wanted to dash the camera to bits but didn't think this would rid him of the problem.

"Who have ye shown these to?" he asked.

"Not a soul," she said instantly, lifting her chin under the sun.

After a moment she said, "I swear."

Jacob didn't know what to say. He held the camera in his shaking hands.

"The pics are on that card," Deanna Cole said, pointing toward the card slot on the back of the camera. "You can do what you want with it. I didn't make a backup and I didn't share it with anybody else. Nobody knows but me."

*And God*, Jacob thought.

He passed the camera back to Deanna Cole.

"I don't need a partner," he said. "Forget what ye saw."

She looked like he'd slapped her.

"You have to let me help you," she said, stepping closer.

"No I don't," he said, turning away from her.

"Listen to me," she said. "There are others in Dominion House that'll help too. Think about it! A whole new realm of worship, of carrying out His will!"

Jacob felt unnerved by the thought.

"You're a true artist," she said. "We could help you create bigger and more elaborate sculptures. Think of all the harlots we could help you with. I've always wanted to learn how to weld. We could carry out these holy sacrifices as a group. We could form a higher community, a purer form of worship."

Jacob tried to walk away but she followed him, her mouth never stopping.

"I saw the way you held that baby last night," she said. "I know you're capable of such gentleness. Let me help. I need to help you. Please."

Jacob walked over to the little shed where Josiah Powers kept a bunch of tools.

"'How good and pleasant it is when God's people live together in unity,' it says," Deanna Cole said. "Think of all we could do together!"

Jacob stepped into the small shed and kept his back to Deanna. He picked up the clawhammer.

"For where two or three gather in my name, there am I with them," she quoted. "The Lord wants us to work together. He does!"

Jacob spun on his heels with the clawhammer hidden between the crook of his arm.

He stared into her eyes, hard. For a fleeting second, he could envisage it: a group dressed in black sweatpants, Walmart, coming down on a house together from all angles, the harlot defenseless and easily overpowered. He saw the group crowded around the body, each taking a piece like communion. Then he saw the hell that is other people and showed Deanna Cole the clawhammer.

"Jacob, don't," she whispered. "I'm your friend. Let me be your friend."

Jacob, hating himself for it, raised the hammer then brought it down. The camera hit the dirt with a tiny, broken sound. He hit Deanna Cole with the hammer over and over again, feeling his eyes well with tears.

*I must go it alone. There's no room for another. This is the way.*

The sunlight shone down on the crumpled body. Jacob walked over to the Howard Electric and turned it on.

-

Jacob wept as he sealed Deanna Cole into the green angel, his tears dripping down his cheeks behind the welding helmet. His thoughts swam like a drunken mariner, at one moment sure he'd done the right thing, the only thing, then the next he felt he'd just made the biggest mistake in his life.

*I could've had a family*, he thought. *I could've let others in.*

He thought about Dominion House and how he'd felt a sense of community for the first time.

*Now that's gone.*

He felt calmer as he worked, more sure of himself as he welded the arms closed.

"For what credit is it if, when ye sin and are beaten for it, ye endure? But if when ye do good and suffer for it you endure, this is a gracious thing in the sight of God," he said from inside his welding helmet.

"The Devil works here!" the crowd chanted.

Jacob lifted his sign and mouthed along with the rest of them.

"Stop killing babies!"

The protesting crowd was the biggest Jacob had seen. There were many familiar faces, people from Dominion House, but also many faces Jacob didn't recognize and everybody was in a frenzy. Jacob saw lots of bared teeth and too much white in everyone's eyes.

The police were present as well. Jacob saw them right away and guessed they had at least one undercover in the crowd.

Jacob felt his stomach drop.

*This isn't gonna work anymore*, Jacob realized. *I can't hunt here like this anymore. The police are here. The protesters are getting too riled up.*

Jacob watched the vehicles pull up to the Louisville Women's Clinic and the pregnant women get out. He watched the orange vested volunteers escort them inside.

*I need to be that close*, he thought.

He saw the woman earlier in his route. She wasn't a Rubbish Management customer but most of the families on her street were. She had hot pink-painted nails and dyed blonde hair.

*Mine*, he thought when he first saw her.

*Mine*, he thought when he saw her pregnant belly.

She didn't have a ring on her finger and Jacob guessed she lived alone in the little duplex. There was only one car parked on her side in the morning and again when Jacob drove the truck back by her place in the late afternoon.

He waited until the sun went down then drove the Mazda to the duplex and parked in the street. He watched the house, taking slugs from a brown-bagged bottle of Thunderbird until all the lights were turned off. He waited another hour then got out of the Mazda and walked around the duplex. The blinds were drawn on most of the windows but several of the slats were bent and he could see the darkened outlines of things inside.

He went to the front door and tried the knob but it was locked.

Jacob walked around the house to the back and tried that door but it too was locked.

*Shit*, he thought.

He went to the side of the house and tried the bathroom window. He got the screen off easily and the window was unlocked. He slid it up quietly and hoisted himself up and inside. He stepped down onto the closed lid of the toilet seat then the tiled floor.

The blood rushed in Jacob's ears, a giant whooshing sound he was almost sure would give him away. He clicked on the penlight, University of Pikeville Medical School, and made his way into the hall outside the bathroom.

"Who's there?" a scared voice called from ahead.

Jacob clicked off the penlight and froze.

"Who's there?"

Jacob turned and ran through the bathroom. He dove through the window, catching the heel of his left foot on the pane of glass in the process. He heard the window crash down onto the tile behind him as he hit the ground hard on his right shoulder. He thrust himself to his feet and ran across the little front yard to the Mazda.

Lights were coming on within the duplex as Jacob started the engine. He kept his headlights off until he was out of the neighborhood.

-

"Fuck!" Jacob screamed inside the cab.

He punched the steering wheel three times in rapid succession.

"Fuck!" he screamed again.

*Calm down*, the voice said. *Slow down. Don't get pulled over.*

Jacob slowed the Mazda and checked his side mirrors expecting to see blue lights but he didn't.

*It's okay*, the voice said. *You didn't get caught. You'll just have to find someone else.*

He saw the blonde in his head, pregnant with pink painted nails. *Shit.*

Jacob directed the Mazda toward Dixie Highway.

*I'll take a whore*, he decided. *Not the ideal kill but a man's got to hunt.*

-

Jacob pulled the Mazda onto the shoulder of the road and honked his horn. The whore sauntered across the street to his open window.

"Hey, baby," she said. "Looking for some company?"

Jacob nodded his head, squinting out into the darkness, trying to see if the belly the whore had was fat or pregnancy. He hoped the latter.

"I know a place real close," the whore said. "Want to use the back of the truck here?"

Jacob nodded again.

"Forty dollars for anything your heart desires."

*payin' for power / is all*

The whore walked in front of the headlights and Jacob watched the pooch jiggle.

*Fat*, he decided. *Oh well. Beggars can't be choosers.*

He reached across the cab and unlocked the passenger-side door. The whore climbed inside.

"It's up here on the right," she said.

*I shoulda named ye John, boy, / one in a lo-o-ong line of 'em*

Jacob followed the whore's directions to a dead-end street lined with abandoned factories. He put the truck in park and reached under the seat for the filet knife, Roger's Bait 'n' Tackle.

The whore saw the knife and froze, her eyes wide and glassy in the light of the Mazda's gauges.

"Please," she whispered. "Don't."

Jacob smiled.

"Are ye pregnant?" he asked.

The question seemed to stun her.

"It's okay to lie to me," Jacob said. "I wouldn't expect anything less from a harlot."

-

When it was over, Jacob drove the body to Jefferson Memorial Forest, pulling the truck onto the shoulder of the entrance to avoid the closed gates. He found the spot he'd used for all the whores and homeless women and parked. He stepped out into the brisk darkness feeling better but not great.

A great gnawing need to kill unmarried pregnant women made the kill less fulfilling. He'd still enjoyed it very much but the spiritual aspect of shepherding his unborn children to the Great Beyond was what he craved, needed.

As he dug the shallow grave, Jacob debated on using Dominion House's *Profiles of the Wicked* for victim selection. They were all guaranteed to be pregnant and seeking abortions but with the police presence at the LWC protests it seemed risky. He thought about the orange vested volunteer escorts and wished he could get as close to the women as they did.

*Why don't you switch sides?* the voice asked.

Jacob dropped the whore into the hole and began covering her up.

Dominion House had tried to protest the volunteer escorts' weekly meetings at the Starbucks but had been asked to leave by management. Jacob decided to attend the meeting and go from there.

"Commit to the Lord whatever ye do, and he will establish yer plans," Jacob recited, putting the last of the dirt on the whore.

-

"Welcome everybody," the gray-haired woman said. "I see a few new faces and I welcome each of you."

Jacob sipped his coffee.

"Now I want to say right up front that this is a difficult thing we do each day," the woman said. "When you zip up your orange vest you are going to be derided and ridiculed by all the pro-lifers and zealots. The protests have gotten rather extreme as of late."

There were several exclamations and sounds of affirmation.

"LWC's had to bring in law enforcement for fear of violence," she said. "Violence is always a possibility with these people."

Jacob could believe it.

"Putting on this orange vest is a sign that you care about women's rights," the woman said, lifting an orange vest in the air. "Putting this on means that you care about a woman's right to choose what happens to her body."

Jacob forced his face to remain blank, expressionless. Inside he was sneering.

"The police aren't always able to assist and a lot of the time it's just going to be you and the patient. You'll be the buffer, the bodyguard standing between these women and the *monsters* that want to tear them down."

The woman gave Jacob a pointed look as she said the word: monsters.

*Good*, Jacob thought. *Let them get this out of the way.*

"This is an important function," she said. "Not a game we play, switching sides whenever the wind blows."

All the heads turned toward Jacob. He forced his face to remain expressionless but was appalled to find his face reddening despite his best efforts to the contrary.

"I'll start the signup sheet," the woman said after what felt like a year.

The meeting was breaking up, each person leaving after signing up for a time to escort. Jacob was left with a time slot four days away by the time the paper made its way to him.

Jacob signed, got up, walked over to the trash can and tossed in his nearly full coffee.

"Excuse me," the woman said. "Sir?"

Jacob turned and faced the older woman.

"I've seen you on the other side of the line," she said. "What made you decide to come to this meeting?"

Jacob made sure his face was expressionless before answering.

"We all make mistakes," he said. "I hate the sin, not the sinner."

"I've seen you on the TV," she said. "You're that artist who makes the metal sculptures, aren't you?"

Jacob nodded.

"Religious art, right?"

Jacob nodded again.

After a moment, she said, "I'm glad to see you here today."

"I'm glad to be here."

"I hope you're here for the right reasons."

*reasons / are subjective*

"I am," he said.

The woman studied him without speaking for several long moments.

"Good," she said finally.

She left Jacob smiling at the trashcan.

*In like Flynn*, he thought.

-

Jacob took two more prostitutes that week and one homeless woman, allowing him to finish the green angel. He started a silver and blue, four-headed angel immediately after. He attended another Orange Vest meeting and, though he still felt several glares and hard stares, the gray-haired woman who appeared to be in charge smiled at Jacob, seemed to accept him, which went a long way with the others.

After his first shift escorting the women inside, he was fully accepted by the group.

-

Jacob was working on one of the angels when Josiah Powers tapped on his shoulder. He cut the power to the Howard Electric and lifted the modified welding helmet off his face.

"Could we, uh, talk for a minute," Josiah Powers said.

"Sure," Jacob said, setting down his tools and removing the long, heavy gloves.

"We've seen ya with the Orange Vests," he said. "What in the world are ya doing?"

Jacob let a smile come over his face.

"Hate the sin, not the sinner," Jacob said.

"They kill babies there. Babies!"

Jacob still felt cheated that the belly on the prostitute had just been fat. He needed to rescue more of His Children. He felt this urgently.

"I know it," Jacob said. "But the Good Books says, 'Therefore welcome one another as Christ has welcomed ye, for the glory of God.'"

Josiah stood there shaking his head.

Jacob picked up the gloves.

"Is there anything else?"

The man spat in the dirt and walked away.

Jacob felt so above them all, the Dominion House people that had shouted at him, called him vile names, accused him of assisting murder.

*If only you knew how I served Him,* Jacob thought. *How I usher My Children to the Great Beyond. How I make the harlots clean in death.*

With both of his hands now gloved, Jacob flipped the helmet back over his face, then flipped the Howard Electric back on.

-

"Traitor!" they jeered when they saw Jacob in his orange vest.

"Murderer!" they chanted.

Jacob kept his face blank, expressionless and avoided all eye contact with the protestors.

A car pulled into a spot on the street and Jacob's radio crackled.

"Goodman, you're up," the walkie talkie said.

Jacob strode over to the parked car just as the driver's door opened.

"Hello," Jacob said to the wide-eyed woman. "I'm Jacob. I'll be yer escort this morning."

"Okay, thanks," the woman said, pulling her heavy frame from the car. "Give me a hand, won't ye?"

Jacob took hold of the woman's beefy arms and helped her climb to her feet.

"Thank ye," she said.

Jacob wanted to crinkle his nose at the woman's raunchy smell. He saw her gigantic belly but wouldn't have guessed she was pregnant if she hadn't pulled up to the abortion clinic. He would've just thought she was extremely obese.

*She must be nearing two-hundred and fifty pounds*, he thought, closing the door behind her.

He held onto her arm and walked her down the sidewalk past the protestors and uniformed police officers to LWC. There were several flashes as someone snapped photos of Jacob and the woman as they passed.

*Pro-Vision 15:3*, Jacob thought.

"The eyes of the Lord are everywhere, keeping watch on the wicked and the good," Jacob said.

"What?" the woman asked.

"Nothing," Jacob said. "Nothing at all. Here ye go."

Jacob released the woman's arm as she came to the entrance to the Louisville Women's Clinic.

"Have a nice day," Jacob said.

The woman turned to him and said, "Thank ye," then disappeared inside.

Jacob returned to his post, doing his best to ignore the chants and name calling from the protestors. He felt like a pillar of salt standing rigid, waiting for the next patient to arrive, like he'd looked back at his time with Dominion House—he hadn't attended a meeting in two weeks—the way Lot's wife had looked back at Sodom. He missed the feeling of comradery and community more than he'd dare admit to himself.

*I am the Hand of God*, Jacob thought, stilling himself. *I am God's flaming sword.*

He imagined gutting the fat woman he'd just escorted. He saw himself standing over her huge body and lifting the fetus out of her open stomach. He smiled to himself, waiting for her to reemerge from the Louisville Women's Clinic.

# CHAPTER THIRTY-TWO
## #DERBYCITYBUTCHER

**"THEY'RE NOT TECHNICALLY TAKING THE** case from you," Sergeant Ellis said. "They're bringing you on to the Butcher task force. You should be happy about this."

Barbara was pacing the Sergeant's office.

"You won't be lead but so what? You're still on and this could be big for you," he said.

"They only brought me on because I'm a female," Barbara said.

"That may be," Sergeant Ellis said, tapping his desk with his fingers, "but they still brought you on. You get to stay on and work this one 'til it's done or the task force is disbanded. You should consider yourself lucky. Hall and Bailey are miffed they didn't get asked on."

Barbara nodded her head.

Of course, what he was saying was true but having the point taken away still stung. Barbara hated the idea of taking orders from Mitchell Skeeters.

"Is there anything else, Findley?"

"No, sir."

Barbara walked back to her desk, clenching and unclenching her fists.

*They took the case away because I'm a female and assigned me to the task force for the same reason,* Barbara thought. *I'd never have been assigned the case if the news stories and hashtags hadn't put "the gender thing," as Mitchell Skeeters had called it, at the forefront of the conversation about the Derby City Butcher.*

#worthathoroughinvestigation

#ourwomenareworthfinding

#findoursisters

And more were all trending on Twitter in the Kentuckiana area and nationally. Last night's featured piece of journalism was an interview with several Louisville area prostitutes, their faces blurred to conceal their identity, who all said the police have known about the Derby City Butcher for some time but had been dragging their feet because a good portion of his victims had been hookers, a population the police didn't feel particularly interested in protecting and serving. Several homeless people were believed to be missing too but it was harder to determine if they'd just moved on or if they'd been taken by the Butcher.

#derbycitybutcher was trending nationally and several of the big twenty-four-hour news companies were running lead pieces. Barbara had her photograph taken more times in the past three days than she'd ever had. She spoke briefly to a reporter from the *Courier-Journal* and was interviewed by WGAS-11.

"There's our media princess," Bailey called from a desk in the bullpen.

There was a spattering of faux applause.

"Yipee-ki-yay, cowgirl," Hall said.

Barbara kept her head down and didn't take the bait.

*They're just jealous they didn't make the task force*, she told herself.

"Hashtag you go girl," Hall said. "Find the Mother Fucker!"

That's what some of the cops had taken to calling the killer: the Mother Fucker.

Barbara had been asked how she felt about the Derby City Butcher's task force being all male and she'd carefully side-stepped that question by saying it wasn't, that she was on the task force, and that she'd work hard to find out who was killing so many women in the area and that's what the task force was dedicated to doing as well. The news had run a special feature on her being a female in the man's world of policing. She hadn't asked for it, hadn't wanted such a piece to air, but she couldn't do anything but play the hand dealt.

"Yeah, yeah," she said, walking by Hall and Bailey to her office. She shut the door behind her.

She checked her cellphone and saw three missed calls from Perry. He'd texted her several long messages too. She scanned them.

*. . . I can't take this anymore . . .*

*. . . I'm so sorry but . . .*

*. . . I love you so much, Barbara . . .*

*. . . please let me come back home . . .*

She didn't answer any of the messages or return his calls. She put her cellphone in the top drawer of her desk and unlocked her computer. There'd been two more bodies found across the river in Jeffersonville and that meant including their police in on the investigation, a job Skeeters had put on Barbara. She answered emails and shared documents and reports for an hour or so before getting up from her desk and seeking out her partner in his office.

"Hank, wanna get some fresh air?" she asked.

He looked up from some paperwork.

"Yes, ma'am," he said. "Give me five minutes."

She nodded and headed for the big conference room, where the task force had set up shop in Hardin County. There were several detectives and cops from other agencies working at laptops. She walked over to the corkboard and looked through the pictures of victims. There were eleven vic pics tacked onto a map of the area, indicating where their bodies had been found.

She looked at each of the photographs, taken from social media or provided by family members, studying the faces of the women and bringing up the grisly images of their remains.

*I'm going to find this fucker*, she told herself. *I'm going to put a stop to this.*

Then she noticed the photograph of herself that had appeared in yesterday's *News Enterprise* was tacked to the corner of the map. Pig-tails had been drawn on top of her head and liquid had been drawn dripping down her mouth and chin.

*Media Whore* was written across her forehead.

*Bastards*, she thought, ripping the newspaper clipping off the board.

"Barb, you ready?"

She turned around and Hank was there.

"Sure," she said, crumpling the paper in her fist. "Let's go grab a coffee."

"Sounds good."

"You have a makeover recently, Findley?" Bailey asked as they crossed the bullpen.

"Are you the one calling me a media whore?" she asked, tossing the crumpled clipping onto the desk he sat behind.

Bailey carefully unfolded the paper and smiled.

"If the shoe fits," he said, "I suggest wearing it."

For a second, Barbara considered jumping across the table and clawing the detective's eyes out.

"Come on, Fin," Hank said.

They walked through the bullpen and out of the front entrance into the parking lot.

"Fuck those guys," Hank said. "They're just jealous they didn't make the task force."

Barbara nodded her head but didn't trust her voice just yet. She was too angry.

"Saw ya on the TV last night," Hank said as they stepped into the sunshine.

Barbara felt a stab of embarrassment. She didn't like all the attention she'd been getting in the media. She'd had emails to speak to women's groups around the area she'd respectfully declined. She'd been asked to speak at two elementary schools as well.

She'd watched the news special last night too, saw herself looking slightly dour and tired as she answered the reporter's questions. They'd asked her several questions about her personal life—*You're married right? What's your husband think of your job?*—that she'd made immediately known was off the table.

"Do you have any advice for girls wanting to be police officers?" the last question of the segment had been.

"Law enforcement isn't for everyone," she'd said, "but if your heart is in it, then follow it."

She kept waiting for Hall and Bailey to use that last line to goad her.

"Vibe or Starbucks?" Hank asked.

"Let's go to Bubs," she said.

"Sounds good."

They drove in silence the short distance to Bub's Café. Barbara could tell Hank wanted to ask her something but he kept quiet and she silently thanked him for this. She just wanted to be near someone she trusted that wouldn't pry and poke fun at her. She wanted to talk about Perry but knew she wouldn't, couldn't, not yet.

She parked the car and they entered the restaurant, ordered coffees, and sat looking at everything but each other.

"Well," Hank said.

Barbara cleared her throat.

"How're things going on the Butcher task force?" he asked.

"Fine. They got me playing concierge for the most part," she said. "Forwarding memos and reports with Indy and answering phone calls."

"Damn."

"Yeah, but I got access to the rest of the case files and, man, is this big," she said. "This guy is a monster. You should see some of these bodies."

"What's he using?"

"A blade," she said, seeing the crime scene photographs in her mind's eye. "Cut most of them up afterwards too."

"I heard there's something about hands," Hank said.

Barbara nodded and sipped her coffee.

"Most of the vic's left hands were missing from the dump sites."

"Weird."

"Uh-huh."

"What's Skeeters think?"

"That his shit don't stink."

"Aside from that."

"He thinks it's probably two people working together."

"Two?"

"Cos there're prostitutes and homeless women as well as up-standing citizens in the mix."

"Hm."

"I think it's one guy," Barbara said. "One rabid dog."

"That needs putting down."

Barbara nodded.

"Most of the vics were pregnant but not all."

"Why do ya think he's choosing pregnant women?"

Barbara shrugged her shoulders.

"Think he's got mother issues?"

"Who doesn't?"

The waitress came over and asked if they were going to order any food with their coffee. They ordered cheeseburgers and French fries.

"How're things with Perry?" Hank asked when the waitress left.

Barbara felt her face color.

"I changed the locks."

"I see."

They drank coffee for some time in silence.

"Well if ya ever want to talk about it," Hank said, looking into Barbara's eyes, "I'm here."

She had to look away. She was scared she'd tear up if she didn't.

"Thanks," she said, watching an old man scratch his protruding stomach at the table beside theirs.

The cheeseburgers came and they ate, talking mostly about the Butcher. Hank took the check, insisted on paying, so Barbara left the tip. On the way out, the waitress stopped Barbara with a hand on her arm.

# BIRTH OF A MONSTER

"I just want to thank you," she said.

"For what?" Barbara asked.

"For working on catching the Derby City Butcher," the waitress said. "Those men don't care, not really, but I saw you on the TV and I can tell that you do. I know you're gonna catch the bastard killing all these women. I just know it."

## CHAPTER THIRTY-THREE
## LAVENDER AND VANILLA

**JACOB FOLLOWED HER GREEN SATURN** sedan home, at a distance, from the Louisville Women's Clinic, where she attended her appointment alone. He scanned his mirrors constantly, looking for a tail, but saw nobody following him. He parked the Mazda on the road a few houses down and watched her get out of the car and waddle up the stairs to the two-story brick house.

She walked with a tired determination, not bothering to look at her surroundings. Jacob wanted to rush out in the fading light of the afternoon and take her. He had to force himself to sit still in the Mazda and wait for sundown.

The neighborhood was quiet and nobody paid Jacob any mind. He watched the house through the front windshield as dusk fell, alternately popping his knuckles or tapping a frantic beat on the Mazda's steering wheel. He hadn't been able to kill in two nights and thought he was going to lose his mind. He felt all this pent-up energy bubbling out of him. His thoughts skipped across the surface of his mind like a rusted nickel flicked across a frozen pond.

When full dark came, Jacob opened the door and stepped out into the night. Pulling the black hoodie, Walmart, down low over his face and making his way around the pregnant woman's, Helen Lewis, Saturn and up the little walkway to the house. He saw her sitting on the couch in the front room, watching television, a pint of ice cream and a spoon in her hands. Jacob watched her there for some time, taking in the way her stomach sat pooched on her lap like a sack of oats, the way her red-painted nails moved in the glow of the television.

Eventually, Jacob moved along the side of the house toward the back, where he found the backdoor unlocked. He stepped inside and slowly, carefully made his way through the darkened kitchen into the hall. He found a hall closet and stepped inside and pulled the door partially closed, leaving just a crack that peeked out into the glow of the television on the wall opposite the closet.

The woman's cellphone rang and he heard her sigh deeply before

489

answering it.

"I don't want to talk about it right now, Troy," she said. "No, no. No. No! I said I don't want to discuss it right now. I'm tired."

Jacob sank a little deeper into the closet as he heard the floor creak and groan as she made her way across the living room into the hall. She walked past the closet and Jacob breathed in her smell and wasn't surprised to find it was lavender and vanilla.

*lavender and vanilla / vanilla and lavender*

He thought of her, *Tanya Miller / Tanya Miller*, for a few moments, listening to the woman talk on the phone.

"No," she said. "I don't want you to come over and no, I don't think you should have a say in this. It's my body. It's my choice. No! I told you: I don't want to talk about this tonight. I'm tired and getting ready to go to bed."

Jacob crept forward in the closet and pushed the door outward a hair. He could just see Helen Lewis' back at the kitchen sink; Helen Lewis who was seeking an abortion well into her second trimester according to her *Profile of the Wicked*. She turned away from the sink and Jacob eased the closet door closed.

He listened to her walk by in the hall and reenter the living room. For a while, the only sound was the television. Jacob bent his legs and stretched his back.

*I'll take her when she goes to bed*, he decided.

Thirty minutes later there was a knock at the front door.

*Shit!*

"Goddamn it!" the woman, Helen Lewis, said. "I told you I don't want to discuss this tonight. I'm tired and cranky."

"I can't help it," the man, Troy, said. "I just can't stand the thought of you ending this pregnancy. I'm the father. I should have some say in what happens."

"Bullshit! You have no say; it's not your body, it's mine."

"But I helped make that baby. It's my DNA in there too."

"It doesn't fucking matter. And I don't want to talk about this right now!"

"Well tough titty! I do! And I think the situation calls for a conversation, not a rash decision only taking into account your feelings."

"My feelings?"

There was a charged, silent moment.

"I'm not up for this right now. I'm going to bed. You can sleep on the couch if you're intent on staying but I feel like a whale and want the bed to myself."

"Fine," Troy said, "but we're discussing this first thing in the morning. I'm not leaving until you give me a conversation."

"I don't owe you a conversation. It's my motherfucking body!" The woman's voice broke.

Jacob's breathing sounded overly loud in the quiet that followed. He forced himself to remain perfectly still, hearing the blood rushing in his burning ears.

"I know you care about your job, but this is bigger than that. This is the start of our family. Our child, Helen, *our* child. You can't turn your back on that, can you? You can't be so career-minded to end the life of this child, can you?"

Helen Lewis was crying now. "I told you I didn't want to talk about this right now!"

"That's not the way life works. Difficult conversations come and you have them. You don't wall up and turn your back on them."

Jacob cracked the door, trying to get a peek at the couple, but the angle was wrong and he didn't risk fully opening the closet.

"Did you go to your appointment today?"

"You know I did."

"I can't believe you kept it. They kill babies there. Are you going to let them kill ours?"

"Stop it! Just stop it right now! I can't take this."

Jacob listened to her sobs.

"Don't you touch me. Get back. I don't want you to touch me right now."

"Please," the man cooed. "Calm down. It's alright."

The woman cried and Jacob thought he heard the man sniffling as well.

*I wish he'd hurry up and leave,* Jacob thought, his back aching from the awkward hunched over position the closet forced him into.

"I'm going to bed," Helen Lewis said. "You can sleep on the couch if you want, but I meant what I said. I feel like a whale and I'm taking the bed to myself."

"That's fine," Troy said. "Let's sleep on it. We'll talk again in the morning. I love you."

"I love you too, even if you're a hard-headed bastard."

They laughed softly together then the floor creaked as the pregnant woman walked down the hall, past the closet, and into the back bedroom.

After a few moments, the television was turned off and the house sank into darkness and quiet. Jacob waited for what felt like hours before easing the door open and stepping out into the hallway, the fileting knife, Roger's Bait 'n' Tackle, in his left hand. He hadn't planned on a man being present but his need was overwhelming and he knew he couldn't leave without killing the unmarried harlot. He saw those painted nails and bulging stomach and felt a need to get to her quickly.

*Deal with the man first*, the voice said.

Jacob made his way into the living room and saw the man curled up on the couch, sleeping. He leaned down and pressed the blade against the man's throat.

"Don't make a sound," he whispered.

The man bolted awake, his eyes wide and white in the darkness. Jacob forced the man to roll over onto his stomach and secured the man's hands behind his back with duct tape, Walmart. He then looped the duct tape through the knot, making a leash of sorts.

"Move," he hissed.

The man thumped off the couch onto the floor on his knees. Jacob held the duct tape leash hard and high, forcing the man to hunch forward. Jacob pressed the tip of the filet knife, Roger's Bait 'n' Tackle, against the man's carotid artery and leaned forward to whisper in the man's right ear.

"Make one sound and I'll gut ye like a pig," Jacob told him. "Make one move without my saying so and I'll make ye watch me gut yer whore girlfriend."

The man was shaking and sweat ran down his brow into his eyes. Jacob watched him blinking and blinking on his knees and felt sorry for the woman for choosing such a weak man to procreate with.

"Let's go," Jacob hissed, pushing the duct tape leash forward.

Jacob led the man down the hall to the back bedroom on his knees. It was a long, slow process but it made Jacob feel good, powerful.

Once inside the darkened bedroom, Jacob pushed the knife into the man's throat until a thin trickle of blood bloomed in the darkness.

"Make one sound and ye're both dead," Jacob whispered.

Jacob flicked on the penlight, University of Pikeville Medical School, and took quick stock of the room. There was a glass of water on the nightstand. The woman was snoring, the cover flung off.

Jacob could see the sweat on her face.

*Night sweats*, Jacob thought, putting the penlight back in the pocket of his sweatpants, Walmart.

He forced the man forward until his face was pressed against the hardwood floor.

"Don't move," he hissed.

Jacob retrieved the glass of water from the nightstand and took a drink. He then moved the man until his back was parallel with the floor. He set the glass on the small of the man's back.

"If this glass falls off yer back, ye're dead and she's dead," Jacob whispered. "Got it?"

The man nodded his head and started to speak but Jacob jabbed him in the back of the neck with the knife and he whimpered then quieted.

Jacob walked over to the bed. The man began to whimper again and Jacob held one finger to his lips and made a quiet shushing sound. The glass was still balanced on the man's back. Jacob ran the knife over the length of the sleeping woman's body before letting the dull side of the blade run the arc of her belly.

The woman woke with a start.

"Troy?" she asked into the darkness.

Jacob smiled down at her.

"Oh my God!" the woman cried. "Troy!"

Jacob was on her before she could move, pinning her arms down with his knees.

"Move and ye die," he said. "Whore."

The woman ceased struggling. Jacob reached over the side of the bed and turned on the lamp on the nightstand.

"Helen Lewis," Jacob said, smiling.

"Don't," Troy Isaacs said from the floor. "Please."

"Please," Jacob mimicked.

"What'd you want?" the woman asked.

"I'm here to save yer immortal soul, whore."

Jacob reached down between the woman's legs and rubbed the front of her underwear.

"Stop," she cried. "Please."

Jacob felt himself grow hard.

There was a clunk and Jacob looked over to see the glass roll away from the man on the floor. The man had risen up on his knees, his hands still taped behind his back, and was staring up at them with wide, frightened eyes.

"I told ye not to move," Jacob said, angry.

He leaned forward and pressed the knife against the woman's throat.

"Move or scream and yer little boyfriend gets gutted."

Jacob got off the bed and picked up the glass, which hadn't shattered when it hit the hardwood. He kicked the man in the stomach and forced him to lie flat on his stomach on the floor. There was a little bathroom off the side of the room and Jacob refilled the glass with water then returned to the bedroom. He took a long drink of water and returned the glass to the small of the man's back.

"Last chance," Jacob said. "If this cup hits the floor again, ye die and she dies slowly."

The man was crying now, snot and tears galore.

Jacob returned to the bed and cut off the woman's clothes.

"I'm here, My Child," Jacob whispered, his lips brushing against the woman's pregnant stomach. "I'm here."

"What do you want?" the woman asked. "There's money in my wallet. Take it. Just don't hurt me."

"Money? Ye think I want money?" Jacob laughed. "I'm here to save yer soul."

"Please," the man said from the floor.

"Shut up!" Jacob screamed. "Shut the fuck up!"

He turned back to the woman and smelled her.

*lavender and vanilla / vanilla and cunt stink*

Jacob couldn't help himself. He pulled down the sweatpants, Walmart, and handled himself with his right hand, the left still holding the knife against the woman's throat. He climbed back on top of her. He directed his hardened penis against her but couldn't make an entrance. The pressure grew and grew until he came, shooting his load on her shaking stomach.

"Jesus," the woman whispered.

Jacob hated her so intensely he forgot himself for a moment. The next thing he knew he was staring down at her open throat.

There was a crash as the glass shattered on the hardwood floor. The man slammed his shoulder into the doorframe as he tried to flee. Jacob caught him in the hall, grabbed hold of the duct tape leash and tackled him to the floor, punching holes in his back with the filet knife, Roger's Bait 'n' Tackle. He carried the bleeding man back to the bedroom and threw him on the bed next to the dead woman.

He thought about tying him up, but by the way the man was bleeding, Jacob didn't figure he'd last long.

"Ye're a failure, Troy," Jacob said.

The man was conscious but slipping.

"Ye failed as a man," Jacob said. "Ye failed as a protector. Ye failed at selecting a proper woman."

Jacob began cutting the fetus out of the woman's stomach.

"The last thing ye need to know before ye meet yer maker is that I am the father of this child, not you. This child is mine."

Jacob lifted the dripping fetus above his head.

"Rest easy, My Child," he said.

Jacob woke from the dream covered in sweat. He'd been staring up at Heaven from the palm of a great flaming hand. Flames flickered all around him, lapping at his bare, exposed skin. The flames, though painful, purified him somehow. He rolled out of the little bed in the camper and got dressed. He stepped into the main room of the camper and looked at the wall of treasures. There were dozens of identification cards and driver's licenses and necklaces and rings and hair barrettes. He sat down at the little table and opened the tacklebox and ran his fingers on the thumbs and fingernails he'd collected.

His phone buzzed. He picked it up and saw that it was Rubbish Management calling.

"Hello."

"Goodman, this is Rogers," Demarcus Rogers, one of the foremen at RM, said. "We don't need you today."

"Okay."

"It's looking like we won't need you tomorrow either. Orders from higher up."

Jacob pictured Brock Sither in his head, the man's brow furrowed, his rich man's mouth dour and expressing disapproval, the look he'd given Jacob from across the protest line.

*They're going to fire me,* Jacob thought. *For not attending Dominion House meetings and for escorting the pregnant women. If only they* knew.

*They had a chance to,* the voice reminded him. *Deanna Cole wanted to form a new branch of Dominion House, one that wasn't afraid to get their hands dirty doing the Lord's work.*

Jacob hung up the phone and set it on the Formica table.

"If the world hates ye, know that it has hated Me before it hated ye," Jacob said out loud.

# BIRTH OF A MONSTER

*Well I'm free to work on the angels all day then*, he thought.

He'd encased the Helen Lewis fetus in the trunk of one last night. He'd driven from the woman's house across town with the bloody child wrapped in a towel in the seat next to him, a bottle of Thunderbird between his knees. He remembered most of the work he'd done the previous evening but he'd had three bottles of Thunderbird and popped two Adderall and things got kind of blurry toward the early hours of morning.

Jacob stepped outside into the harsh sunlight. He walked over to the semicircle of sculptures and studied his work.

*Not bad*, he thought, *especially considering how drunk I was.*

He'd left the woman, Helen Lewis, and the man, Troy Isaacs, where they'd died. He walked through the killing of the woman step by step in his head, savoring the smells and the blood.

*Shepherding the flock onward*, he thought. *My Wives, My Children.*

Jacob put on the gloves, then the helmet, and got to work.

-

Gallery East picked up three of the angels on a flatbed truck and transported them to the gallery for his next showing. Jacob knew he was finished with angels for the time being. The great flaming hand kept coming to him in his dreams. He could almost see it every time he closed his eyes: the palm facing upwards, the fingers slightly curled as if balancing something unseen and heavy on the palm. He always envisioned the hand in flames, the metal shining and glistening in the heat.

Jacob walked through the junkyard seeking out the right materials. He found the hood of a 1969 Dodge Polara that was mostly intact. He'd use that for the base of the palm. He found the crumpled remains of several motorcycles and saw they'd make great fingers if he disassembled them and welded them just right. He wondered if he emptied their gas tanks and refilled them with torch fuel if they'd burn like the flames he saw in his visions.

He was gathering his supplies when Josiah Powers came out of the singlewide trailer that served as the scrapyard's office.

"Jacob," he called. "A word."

Jacob set down the metal and took off his gloves.

"Yes."

"Why aren't ya at work?"

"They called and said they didn't need me."

"Uh-huh. Brock is pretty tore up about what you're doing."

"I know it."

"Why don't ya quit this escort business? Can't ya see you're playing a part in the killing of children?"

"Hate the sin, not the sinner."

"Don't give me that. We've been good to ya," Josiah Powers said. "We've given ya jobs and a place to stay and ya repay us by going behind our backs and assisting LWC to carry out their heinous atrocities. Why? Answer me that. Just why?"

"Blessed are those who are persecuted for righteousness' sake, for theirs is the kingdom of Heaven."

"There's nothing righteous about what the Louisville Women's Clinic is doing. They're letting these women kill babies. *Babies*. And you're helping them. Why?"

Jacob looked up at the oppressive sun, then down at the dirt.

"Beloved, do not be surprised at the fiery trial when it comes upon ye to test you, as though something strange were happening to ye," he said. "But rejoice insofar as ye share Christ's sufferings, that ye may also rejoice and be glad when His glory is revealed. If ye are insulted for the name of Christ, ye are blessed, because the Spirit of glory and of God rests upon ye."

"Ya can quote all ya want but I still don't understand what you're doing. Brock doesn't either and I think he's gonna give ya the boot if ya don't stop escorting those whores."

Josiah Powers nodded once then turned and went back inside the trailer.

Jacob wondered how much longer he'd keep his job at Powers' Scrap 'n' Metal. He didn't think long.

*I'll cross that bridge when I get to it*, he thought. *The Lord doesn't give us loads we can't carry.*

Jacob cracked open a bottle of Thunderbird, put on the long gloves, and went looking for more materials for The Hand of God.

"Humble yerselves, therefore, under the mighty hand of God so that at the proper time He may exalt you."

-

The sculpture was nearly two stories tall now. Jacob had to use the scissor lift and the crane to work on it. Despite the cool temperature, sweat ran in rivulets down his back and under his arms. Every time Jacob blinked he saw the arc of the welding machine. He'd gotten each of the crumpled motorcycle frames in place but left their seals open for his prey, the victims, His Children, and His Wives.

Josiah came out of the front trailer every so often to watch Jacob work. Jacob did not sleep for three whole days, popping Adderall and washing it down with Thunderbird as he worked on The Hand of God. It eclipsed anything he'd made previously in both size and detail. Jacob put creases in the palm by welding on several car and truck spoilers at slanting angles. Each of the five fingernails was a motorcycle frame and gas tank filled with torch oil and topped with tiki torch wicks.

Jacob lit them, removed the welding helmet, and stepped back to see the effect. The flames were small but it was exciting to see the vision slowly coming into fruition. The Hand of God would take some time but it was definitely coming along. Jacob took another Adderall and went back to welding the dahlia-like pedestal at the base of The Hand.

*I'll put My Children in the fingers*, Jacob thought. *And My Wives in the palm.*

He left the seams open for them, planning on hunting soon.

-

The car pulled up to the curb, Jacob's walkie talkie informed him that it was his turn, and he was there before the driver's door opened.

"Good mornin'," he said to the small woman.

"Morning," she mumbled.

The protestors were so loud Jacob read the woman's lips more than heard what she said.

"This way," he said over the raucous crowd.

Jacob put himself between the woman and the protestors. He saw several camera flashes and looked at the crowd to see a video camera, *red eye unblinking / watching*, following his progress up the sidewalk. His initial reaction was to shield his face but he didn't. Instead, he forced his face to remain blank, expressionless.

Jacob held open the door for the woman to pass into the building then returned to his post in front of the protestors. For a second, he thought he saw Deanna Cole holding a sign and chanting but on closer examination he saw it wasn't her.

*How could it be? I killed her.*

Jacob was a little drunk, not enough to be noticeable, but he'd downed a bottle of Thunderbird on the drive to the Louisville Women's Clinic.

-

"Come in here," Josiah Powers called from the open front door of the trailer. "I need to show you something."

Jacob took off the helmet then the gloves and walked across the dirt to the trailer. He stepped up and into the darkened interior.

Josiah was standing behind the counter, his hands working at the ancient computer there.

"Take a look at this," he said.

Jacob walked around the counter and looked into the computer screen. He saw himself wearing an orange vest and leading a woman, the squat brick building of LWC in the background.

*WICKED*, was written in bold letters above his head.

"Ya've earned yourself a *Profile of the Wicked*," Josiah said.

Jacob felt anger rise in the pit of his stomach.

*How dare they.*

"I was against it," Josiah Powers said, "but I was out-voted. Here, go on, take a look."

Josiah Powers moved out of the way and let Jacob sit down at the chair in front of the screen. He used the mouse to click his high-lighted name.

Jacob watched a video of himself leading a woman to the front entrance of LWC. The camera trained in on his blank, expressionless face.

Jacob read what was written out loud.

"Jacob Hunter Goodman works for Powers' Scrap 'n' Metal. He has works of metal sculpture on display at Gallery East, The Louisville Art Center, and several church organizations in the Louisville area. He volunteers to help whores get abortions. What kind of Christian is that?"

Jacob clicked on the link at the bottom of the page and the screen showed a close-up shot of his blank, expressionless face. WICKED ACCOMPLICE was flashing above his head.

"I'm sorry," Josiah Powers said. "I ain't gonna throw ya out, but I think it's time ya start looking for another place to stay. I can't keep ya on with all this. It's bad for business."

"Fear not, for I am with ye; be not dismayed, for I am yer God; I will strengthen ye, I will help ye, I will uphold ye with My Righteous Right Hand," Jacob said.

"Uh-huh," Josiah Powers said. "I'm glad you're holding strong. You're gonna need to take the sculptures with ya when ye go."

-

Jacob went straight to the camper and took two Adderall, swallowing them with gulps of Thunderbird.

*Bastards! The fucking bastards!*

Jacob shook with rage.

*To Hell with them!*

He picked up his Bible and opened it at random. The first place he stopped at didn't apply to him so he flipped several more pages and found himself in Exodus. He read the story of Moses asking God how to deal with the doubts of his people. God commanded Moses to throw his staff down and it became a serpent, which scared Moses and sent him running away. God gets Moses to return to the serpent and convinces him to grab it by the tail, which turned it back into the staff.

Jacob set the Bible on the little Formica table and closed his eyes, smiling. Dominion House was Jacob's staff/serpent. He could lead his people from the slavery of a sinful world. If he could just get his people to follow him instead of Brock Sither, he could lead his people in The Way. He'd failed Deanna Cole, Jacob now saw. Dominion House could be his vehicle for affecting larger change in the world and he'd failed his first test.

*How could I have been so blind?* Jacob wondered.

He flipped the pages and read, "Though he falls, he shall not be cast headlong, for the Lord upholds his hand."

He turned at random again, landed on the exact verse he'd quoted earlier that morning, and read it out loud, "Fear not, for I am with ye; be not dismayed, for I am yer God; I will strengthen you, I will help ye, I will uphold ye with My Righteous Right Hand."

Jacob smiled and knew what he needed to do.

## CHAPTER THIRTY-FOUR
## A LEGAL SEPARATION


**BARBARA PULLED OUT HER CELLPHONE** and brought up Perry's location again. She couldn't help herself. It made her feel weak and vulnerable and conniving all at the same time. She knew Perry had forgotten about the tracking feature or else he'd have turned it off by now. The little icon on her screen showed Perry at the Spring Meadows Luxury Apartments, just off Ring Road.

Barbara had a friend at the DMV pull up Steffanie Phelps' info earlier that morning and knew Steffanie lived at the Spring Meadows Luxury Apartments.

*Fucking your secretary at three o'clock on a Wednesday*, Barbara thought, *How low can you go?*

But she had been working crazy hours for some time now. The job had somehow become more than just a job. It wasn't just a uniform she could take on and off, not that she wore a uniform anymore.

Barbara had more important things to worry about than her cheating husband but she couldn't stop herself from compulsively pulling up Perry's location at every free moment. She had more than her fair share of leads to follow with the Butcher, not to mention the other cases she was working.

*But he's fucking her right now*, Barbara threw her cellphone in the top drawer of her desk and slammed it shut. *Fucking cheating bastard!*

Barbara felt tears well in her eyes but willed them to stay put, to not spill down her lashes and ruin the mascara she'd put on earlier that morning. No, she wouldn't cry for Perry, but she felt if she didn't do something right away, she wouldn't be able to help it. She opened the drawer and retrieved the cellphone. She opened her contacts and scrolled down until she found her lawyer friend Tiff's contact info. She texted: *Hey Tiff, can I ask a favor from ye?*

The reply was nearly instantaneous.

*Of course.*

*Could ye help me change my name? I want to include my maiden name with a hyphen. Barbara Shepherd-Findley.*

*Sure thing. Everything alright, dear?*

Barbara typed out and deleted several responses to this before replying: *Yes and no. Perry is having an affair.*

Her phone rang; Tiff calling in.

"Hey, Tiff."

"That motherfucker is *what?*"

"Yeah, he's cheating on me," Barbara said, "with his goddamn secretary."

"Want me to cut his motherfucking balls off for you?"

Barbara smiled. She loved Tiff, loved how her lawyer zeal for a fight was always present.

"I'm not far from doing it myself," she said. "Ye mind putting in the paperwork for the name change?"

"Not at all. You sure you want the hyphen? You don't want to just go back to Shepherd?"

"No, maybe later," Barbara said. "I want to see how all of this plays out first."

"Got new business cards you're afraid of spoiling?"

Barbara also loved Tiff's sense of humor.

"Ha ha, no, but it would make things a bit strange in the office. Most people just call me Fin or Findley at the department."

"His secretary though?!"

"I know."

"What a fucking loser."

Barbara marveled at how good it felt to laugh.

"I'll get it started this afternoon, hon," Tiff said. "You need anything, you call. You hear me?"

"Thanks, Tiff," Barbara said. "There is one other thing."

"Anything for you, dear."

"Could ye help me file for a legal separation?"

"Of course."

"I don't think I'm quite ready for any of this but I guess I gotta play the hand dealt."

"I'll get the paperwork ready now."

"Thank you. I really appreciate it."

"No problem. You say the word and I'll go break Perry's motherfucking legs."

After she got off the phone with Tiff Shelby, Barbara took off her wedding ring.

Barbara didn't bother with a shower; she was far too tired. She undressed as she made her way to the bedroom, leaving her clothes in a pile beside the bed. She climbed under the covers in just her underwear, goosebumps prickling across her pale skin.

She wondered what Perry was doing at that moment and hated herself for it.

*I'll bet he's at the Spring Meadows Luxury Apartments fucking what little brains his secretary has out of her pretty little head.*

Barbara blinked back tears, willing them not to fall, but they splashed down on the pillows she'd shared with Perry for these last three years. She reached over the side of the bed and retrieved the wedding ring from the front pocket of the pants she'd just taken off. She held it under the glow of the lamp on the nightstand. The band glowed dully in the light and she studied each minute scratch on its outside surface for some time, then the initials engraved on the inside: *BS & PF 2017.*

The tears were spilling freely down her cheeks now. She shuddered, fighting back the sobs she knew were coming.

*Goddamn it, Perry,* she thought. *Why couldn't I be enough for you?*

For one blinding moment, she hated her life, hated her job, hated her failed marriage, hated the stupid golden band in her dry, cracked hands.

Sleep came, but slowly.

## CHAPTER THIRTY-FIVE
## CUT OFF THE SNAKE'S HEAD

**JACOB FOLLOWED BROCK SITHER IN** his BMW at a carefully measured distance in the Mazda, knowing it was the kind of vehicle that stood out because of the primer-gray camper shell, Wallace Skaggs. He'd been following Sither every day for a week now, learning the man's habits and the places he moved between: the offices at Rubbish Management, his home in Cherokee Gardens, the hospital where his wife, Maureen, was undergoing treatment for late-stage cancer, the hotel rooms where he met another member of Dominion House, Diane Johnson, the restaurants they frequented together, and Dominion House itself, where he spent a great deal of time working on Pro-Vision 15:3 and the *Profiles of the Wicked*.

*To get the skin, you have to cut off the snake's head.*

Jacob watched and waited and planned.

He debated on bringing Brock Sither's affair to the attention of the members of Dominion House but didn't know how to go about this or if it would do any real good at converting them to his side.

*No*, he thought. *I'll have to do something else about Brock Sither and Diane Johnson.*

Jacob watched through a window as Sither visited his wife in the hospital, stopping first at the gift shop and buying a gaudy spread of flowers and a box of dark chocolates.

"But a man who commits adultery has no sense; whoever does so destroys himself," Jacob whispered inside the cab of the Mazda.

Jacob followed Sither's BMW across town, where he met Diane Johnson at a Mexican restaurant. They shared margaritas, their hands often touching across the table, their lips curling upwards into smiles of satisfaction and contentment.

Jacob hated them.

They exited the restaurant together but got into separate cars. He followed both of them to the Brown Hotel, where they shared a single room for the night. Jacob considered breaking into the room and killing them both but felt it wasn't quite the right response to the situation. Instead, he drove to a convenience store, bought several bottles of Thunderbird and went back to Powers' Scrap 'n' Metal where he popped a couple of Adderall and put in a little work on The Hand of God, which rose from the dirt some twenty-five feet or so into the air. Jacob could see it over the high fence every time he returned to the junkyard now.

Jacob noted how different Brock Sither and Diane Johnson acted when around other members of Dominion House.

"Nothing is covered up that will not be revealed, or hidden that will not be known," Jacob whispered to himself, sliding the facemask of the helmet down.

He flipped on the Howard Electric and worked on the seams of The Hand's pinky finger, a spot he'd worked and reworked several times now, unable to get it just the way he envisioned it when he dreamed of the flaming Hand.

Jacob felt he had Sither's movements pretty down pat, so he started shadowing Diane Johnson, learning about her habits and locales. He quickly learned she was married too. Her husband worked construction and was a stout, short man. He didn't attend any of the Dominion House meetings, nor did he attend church anywhere else.

*The man doesn't know his wife is a cheating whore.*

Jacob thought about leaving the man some kind of hint or clue as to his wife's infidelity but didn't.

*No, I'll expose them in another way*, he decided.

Jacob worked on the Hand of God and plotted.

## CHAPTER THIRTY-SIX
## A BUSY BOY

**THE PHONE ON BARBARA'S DESK** was ringing when she opened the door. She set down the Styrofoam cup of coffee and picked the phone up.

"Shepherd-Findley," she said.

There was a pause. There was a huff from the other line.

"Goddamn it," Perry said. "I can't believe you're doing this."

I'm *doing this?! I swear to God . . .*

But she did feel a bit of spiteful vengeance when she remembered she just answered Shepherd-Findley to Perry. *Perry*!

"Getting me served with papers like some welfare daddy," Perry yelled. "And at my work? My work!"

The way he said "work" made it sound like his work was worth more than anybody else's.

*The expensive prick*, she thought, then immediately felt bad about it.

*This is your husband*, she reminded herself, *in sickness and in health, for better or for worse.*

"That's just *low!*" he shouted. "Do you know what that does to a guy like me? It makes me look bad. And you know what looking bad does to a guy like me? Well, it loses me business, sweetie. *Bu*siness!"

The way his voice broke at the beginning of "business" reminded Barbara of a goose's startled honk.

Again, she felt bad and hated herself for it.

"This is costing me serious money, babe," he said with a pained calmness.

Barbara listened to him sucking in air through his nose.

"What . . . do . . . you . . . want . . . from me?" he breathed. "It just started," he said in a lower voice that made Barbara immediately held to be a false confidence, the great business bullshitter's confidence. "It was an accident. A mistake. I was confused and lonely. You've been working so much lately, and I felt, well I guess I felt neglected."

"You felt neglected," Barbara repeated with what felt like wooden lips.

"I did, Barbara, downright neglected," he said quickly. "I can't unring the bell, Barbara, but, goddamn it, Barbara, I'm sorry."

*Why's he saying my name so much?*

"Stop saying my name," she told him.

"Let's not treat this situation like children, Bar—" he cleared his throat. "Honey, let's not beat around the bush on this. This is our marriage we're talking about here."

The way he said "marriage" made Barbara think he really meant "business."

"I know it," she said slowly, as if each word carried a separate and heavy weight.

"Well then listen to me," Perry pleaded. "It was an accident. Accidents happen. They don't happen again though; I'm promising you that right now. Let me come home."

Barbara tapped the phone and brought up Perry's icon on the map. He carried on but Barbara had stopped listening. It took it a few moments, the reception in her office was always spotty, but she knew where it'd show her husband. She could picture his Land Rover parked in the VISITOR parking spot in front of the expensive looking apartment buildings. She could picture them walking up the walk lined with sculpted shrubbery hand-in-hand.

"Spring Meadows," Barbara said.

She ended the call before Perry could say anything in return, leaving him hanging there like a teardrop.

She wished she weren't so weak, but Barbara had to take a few minutes before she could get on with her paperwork, the text a jumbled maze of indecipherable words.

*Goddamn it, Barb, pull yourself together. You're a professional*, she told herself. *Act like one.*

She didn't outright cry, and she was once again reminded of the bitter sweetness of little victories. She looked at the clock, willing her twitching face to regain a visage of expressionlessness as she had fifteen minutes before a case review with Sergeant Ellis. And hadn't HR called and left a message saying her new nametag was ready to be picked up?

*That's it*, she thought, *I'll just distract myself until I can deal with these feelings.*

Barbara pushed herself up from the desk, purposefully leaving her cellphone in the top drawer, knowing Perry would be texting up something fierce right about now and she didn't trust herself to not read them and then the goddamn dam would break and she'd have to go to pieces. There'd just be no hope in it not to.

*Get going*, she told herself. *Pick up the new nametag, Shepherd-Findley, then go chat Butcher and bodies with Ellis. Go on, git.*

Barbara received a phone call from Payroll just as she was gathering her things to leave the office for the day.

"You're gonna need to come pick up your check," the woman said. "The direct deposit wouldn't go through. We tried it three times this afternoon."

Barbara sighed, hung up the phone, and made her way to the Payroll and HR offices, where she signed for and received her paycheck.

She drove to the bank and tried to deposit the check through the drive-thru but there was a problem and she was asked to park and come inside. Barbara was ushered into one of the banker's little offices and told that the checking account she shared with her husband had been recently closed.

"Closed?"

"Yes, ma'am," the banker said. "The funds have been moved into another private account."

"I didn't sign off on this."

"The action did not require both account holders' signatures."

"So he just up and drained the account?"

"He moved the funds to another private account, yes."

How could he do this?

"We can set up a new checking account in the meantime, if you'd like."

"I guess that's what I'll have to do."

"We'll have to order you a new debit card for the account."

"Jesus Christ."

"Would you like to cash part of the check in the meantime?"

"I guess so."

Barbara left the bank feeling drained. Her stomach turned over hungrily and she decided to take some of the cash she'd just taken out of her check and get some Chinese takeout from Green Bamboo. She drove along Dixie Highway in a fog, her mind numb and distracted.

*My marriage is a failure*, she thought. *How could Perry be so low?*

They were paving the parking lot in front of the restaurant so she pulled the unmarked cruiser around to the back of the building and parked beside the dumpster. She walked alongside the building to the front and entered. She placed her to-go order and sat in one of the little chairs beside the aquarium that lined the waiting area. She watched the fishes troll the bottom line of the glass enclosure, their little oval mouths opening and closing, opening and closing.

Her order didn't take long to prepare. She paid for it and left with her food in a plastic bag. Halfway out the door, her cellphone rang.

"Shepherd-Findley," she said, cradling the phone between her shoulder and ear.

She switched the plastic bag containing her food to her left hand, using her right to dig in her pants pocket for her car keys.

"Fin," Hank said. "What're—"

There was a hollow thud and a flash of bright light. The next thing Barbara knew, she was lying on the pavement next to the broken Styrofoam container of General Tso's chicken.

*What happened?* she wondered, feeling woozy.

She was roughly moved onto her side and she felt the strap of her purse pull taut then slip free from her shoulder.

*I'm being robbed*, she realized.

She reached for her gun but the man's hands were already at her waist pulling the gun free from the holster.

"Packing heat, lady? That's dangerous business."

The man punched her in the forehead, causing the back of her head to bounce off the asphalt. She tried to look up into the man's face but her vision swam.

"Sorry about your takeout but ya can't make an omelet, ya know?"

Barbara felt hands reach inside her pockets, felt them feel her breasts.

"If I weren't such a busy boy, I'd stay and spend some time on ya, bitch."

Barbara listened to the man's footfalls as he ran away, trying to remain conscious but knowing it was a battle she'd lose. She heard tires peel not far off.

From somewhere very far away she thought she could hear Hank asking if she was alright.

Barbara blacked out.

## CHAPTER THIRTY-SEVEN
## MORE BLACK THAN RED

**"LOOKING FOR A GOOD TIME,** honey?"

Jacob nodded his head, keeping his face blank, expressionless.

The whore got inside the truck. Her stomach was round and Jacob didn't think it was all fat.

"Well, what're you looking for, hon?" she asked once inside the Mazda with the door closed.

"I want head," Jacob told her.

"That's twenty."

Jacob put the Mazda in drive.

"You know a spot, honey?"

Jacob nodded. He pulled the Mazda through the empty streets off onto a smaller service road, then parked in an empty lot in Jefferson Memorial Forest. He stole sidelong glances at her pregnant stomach.

"I take payment up front," she said once Jacob had the Mazda back in park.

Jacob sneered but handed the twenty-dollar bill to her, noticing that her nails were painted hot pink.

He unzipped his pants and leaned his seat backwards. Just before she started, Jacob asked her name.

"Onyx," the whore said, then took him in her mouth.

The quiet cab was filled with the sounds of sucking.

"Choke on it," he commanded.

She feigned the action. Jacob put his hand on the back of her head and forced her head down until he heard her gag. She made a sound of protest he wished she'd never stop making.

"Call me Daddy," he said.

"Daddy," she cooed. "Oh, Daddy."

"Tell yer Daddy ye're pregnant."

He felt her stiffen but she didn't stop.

"I'm pregnant, Daddy," she said, her hand wrapped around his base. "Daddy."

He let her work for some time in silence, pushing her head down just a little farther with each bob.

"Tell yer Daddy ye're pregnant," he said again.

"You gonna let me do this or do you want to just talk?" she snapped.

"Fucking bitch," Jacob said, the smile spreading across his face.

He shoved her head down until her forehead met his lower stomach then he held her down there as she struggled. She vomited, her mouth still wrapped around his penis.

"Fucking bitch," Jacob said, punching her in the back of the head. "Stupid whore."

It was easy overpowering her in the enclosed space. Jacob had her pinned against the console and was inside her before she'd finished gagging. He entered her from behind and it was over in a matter of seconds.

"Oh God," she whispered, crying softly. "Why?"

Jacob punched her in the face. Then again. Her little hands tried to shield her face and he switched to choking her. Her neck was so thin in his hands he felt he could snap it in half with a flick of his wrist. Jacob choked the whore, Onyx, until she was unconscious, then he drove the short distance to Powers' Scrap 'n' Metal.

Jacob laid the whore, Onyx, across the metal palm of The Hand of God, her arms and legs fully extended and tied to the motorcycle fingers. He stared at her through the modified welding helmet, the magnifying glasses showing every impurity of her pale, tattooed skin. He used the trauma shears, University of Pikeville Medical School, to cut off the whore's clothing. He then retrieved the filet knife, Roger's Bait 'n' Tackle, and cut into her pregnant stomach.

The whore, Onyx, woke screaming, but Jacob had her mouth stuffed with most of her cut shirt. He looked up from his incision and watched her wide eyes roll back in her head, then he continued cutting. He couldn't help but stare at the bite marks he'd left on her breasts. He'd nearly severed one of her nipples.

"I'm coming, My Child," he said, returning to the work. "Children are a heritage from the Lord, offspring a reward from Him. Like arrows in the hands of a warrior are children born in one's youth. Blessed is the man whose quiver is full of them."

Jacob held the dripping fetus in his gloved hands, studying it in the magnifying glasses of the modified welding helmet. He reached up and set the child in The Hand of God's middle finger, inside the open motorcycle gas tank. He then turned back to the unconscious woman. Her breathing was ragged and unsteady. She was bleeding out, her blood looking more black than red on the metallic palm.

## CHAPTER THIRTY-EIGHT
## LUNCH MONEY

**BARBARA WAS SHAKEN.**

"Lady," a voice said. "Hey, lady, wake up!"

She opened her eyes and felt immediately nauseous. She turned her head away from the voice and vomited.

"Oh Jesus, lady!"

There were footsteps then everything returned to darkness.

-

When she next woke, Barbara was helped into a sitting position. One of the workers from the Chinese restaurant had a bag of something frozen and was holding it on her pounding head.

"Stay awake, lady," the worker said. "I called for an ambulance."

Barbara looked around her. Everything moved in her vision.

"Phone," she said. "I need to use the phone."

Her cell phone was pressed into her hand. Squinting into the bright screen, Barbara called her partner.

"Hank," she said.

"What happened? You were talking then there was nothing."

"I got robbed," she said.

"Robbed?"

She nodded her head and immediately regretted it. Nausea made her feel like she was floating in an oily sea.

"Where are ya?"

"Green Bamboo."

"I'm on my way."

-

Hank got there just ahead of the ambulance, which was quite a feat because the hospital was just across Dixie Highway from the Chinese restaurant. He helped Barbara to her feet and looked at her bruised head. His fingers gingerly followed the curve of her skull to the large knot on the back of her head.

"I bet your head is pounding, huh?" he said.

She didn't answer.

The EMTs got out of the ambulance and took over. She was taken across the street to the hospital where they diagnosed her with a concussion, stitched up the bleeding lump on the back of her head, and told her to get some rest.

Hank drove her to his house where his wife, Meredith, made Barbara a grilled cheese sandwich and a bowl of hot soup. Barbara nearly cried when Meredith said, "You poor thing."

"I can't believe this happened," Barbara said between bites. "I can't even begin to think about what Bailey and Hall are gonna say about this."

"Ya can't think like that," Hank said across the kitchen table. "That could've happened to anybody."

When Barbara didn't respond, he repeated, "Anybody."

"Etown is just getting rougher and rougher," Meredith said. "That gas station was robbed over off Mulberry just last week and now this."

Meredith Gray shook her head.

"Just can't believe how little Etown is growing Big City Problems."

Barbara ate what she could and thanked Meredith.

"It's no problem," Meredith Gray said. "I'm so sorry this happened to you, hon."

"Thank ye."

Barbara didn't think she'd ever felt so embarrassed.

*My husband is cheating on me and I can't even stop myself from getting mugged*, she thought. *What is my life coming to?*

She wanted to cry and hated herself for it.

*You're stronger than this, Barbara. Get it together. You just need a good night's sleep and this headache to go away and you'll be right as rain.*

"I called it in while you were with the EMTs," Hank said, breaking the silence. "I'll bet it was one of the dopeheads from the rehab facility on the hill there trying to make a quick score."

*If I weren't such a busy boy, I'd stay and spend some time on you, bitch.*

"We made up the bed in the guest room for you, hon," Meredith said. "It's all ready. You look tired."

"I am," Barbara said, trying to smile. "I think I'll go ahead and turn in. Thank y'all for everything."

For a moment, Barbara was sure she was going to break down. She found the strength, some reserve she hadn't known was there, and kept the tears from falling.

"It's no problem," Hank said. "Get some rest."

-

Barbara bolted upright in the unfamiliar room covered in sweat. It took her several panicked moments to recall where she was and why she felt so out of sorts.

*You've been mugged, knocked on the noggin, and you're not at home,* she reminded herself. *Easy, Barb. Easy does it.*

She settled back onto her back, focusing on slowing her breathing.

Bright moonlight was pouring in through the open blinds. Her wedding ring was sitting on the nightstand beside the bed. She hadn't remembered having it on her or taking it off.

*Fucking concussion*, she thought.

She picked up the ring and tears filled her eyes.

*Perry*, she thought.

Barbara couldn't help it, she cried. She cried hard but as quietly as she could, knowing Hank's girls were in the next room over.

-

Early the next morning, after Meredith helped Barbara change the bandage on the back of her head, Hank drove Barbara back to Green Bamboo to get her car. She thought she could still see the greasy spot her spilled food had left on the pavement but she wasn't sure. Her head felt coated in a sluggish gauze. Moving her head quickly made her vision swim and left her dizzy and sick to her stomach.

"Ya sure you're okay to drive?" Hank asked.

She smiled and said she was. She'd been driving since she was twelve, she was sure a knock to her head wouldn't change her abilities behind the wheel. She had too much work to do not to be able to transport herself right then anyhow.

Hank left and Barbara started up the unmarked cruiser. She pulled out onto Dixie Highway feeling a bit better to be on her own for a few minutes. She clenched the steering wheel and tried not to look at the empty space on her ring finger, her wedding band feeling like a burning ember in her front pocket.

*Oh Perry*, she thought, feeling simultaneously sad and mad.

-

"There she is!" somebody shouted from the bullpen.

Barbara kept her head down as she crossed the crowded room to her office.

Bailey was waiting near the water fountain.

"Give me your lunch money, Findley," he sneered, acting like he had a gun in his jacket pocket.

"Nancy Drew and the case of the missing lunch money," Hall called from the bullpen.

The jackals all laughed. Barbara stopped for a second, considered saying something witty, but her head hurt too much for her to think of anything. She shuffled past Bailey and Hall and closed the door of her office behind her. She wasn't in there ten minutes before Sergeant Ellis knocked on the door and entered without waiting for a response.

"What in the blue hell are you doing here?" he asked.

"Working," she said.

"Not after yesterday you're not," he sat down at one of the two plastic chairs in front of her desk. "You're concussed, I hear. That means you need to be home resting. Take the day and we'll see about tomorrow."

"Sarge—"

"This isn't up for debate."

He looked in her eyes and she knew he wasn't going to back down.

"But the Butcher case—"

"We'll work it," he said. "The case can get along without you for one day. Go get some rest. You look like hell."

"Thanks."

"Get."

Sergeant Ellis rose to his feet, gave her a curt nod, then left. She was glad to have him gone because she was experiencing a dizzy spell.

*Maybe I do need a day off,* she thought, her computer screen doubling momentarily before settling back into the single screen.

She picked up the phone on her desk and dialed Hank's extension.

"Gray."

"Would you care to drive me home? Sarge wants me off today."

"That's probably for the best," he said. "I didn't want to say anything but you look like hell today."

"Gee, thanks," she said.

"Ya ready now?"

"Yep."

"Meet ya out front."

Barbara hung up the phone and sighed.

-

Perry's Land Rover was in the drive when they pulled up to the house. There was a van parked behind it.

*What the fuck?*

Schneider Lock & Key, Barbara read on the side of the van.

"Oh hell no," Barbara said.

"Easy, Fin," Hank said, pulling up to the curb.

Barbara was out of the car just as it was put in park.

"What the fuck?" she shouted.

Perry and the locksmith were standing at the front door, the locksmith bent over, working on the lock.

"Barbara," Perry said, smiling. "I'm so glad to see you."

Barbara was across the lawn and in his face before she realized she'd taken a step.

"What happened to your head?" Perry asked, seeing the bandage for the first time.

He reached out a hand to touch her and she slapped it away. She put both of her hands into his chest and shoved him. He stumbled backwards into the locksmith, sending his tools clanging to the concrete.

"Jesus, Barb!"

"What the fuck do ye think ye're doing? Changing the locks?" Barbara shouted. "Ye don't live here anymore! Get the fuck out of here."

"What happened to you?" Perry asked, stepping toward her again.

When he reached out a hand to touch her head, Barbara lost it. She swung a roundhouse that connected squarely with Perry's nose. She felt the cartilage snap under her fist. Blood spurted out of Perry's broken nose.

He crumpled to his knees, holding his nose.

"Get the fuck out of here," Barbara shouted at the locksmith, who looked scared to death.

"Let me put this back together real quick," he mumbled and Barbara saw that he had the front doorknob off and was in the process of replacing it with another.

"Hurry it up," she snapped.

"Jesus fucking Christ," Perry moaned. "You broke my fucking nose."

517

His words were muffled as he held his bleeding face. He rose to his feet and took a half-step toward her.

Barbara wanted to hit him again. She knew she was going to but just as she was winding up another punch she was grabbed from behind.

"Easy, Fin," Hank said into her ear. "Easy."

Her breathing was heavy. She felt like she'd sprinted a mile. She let herself be pulled away from the front porch into the yard.

"Ya better be getting on," Hank called over Barbara's shoulder to Perry. "I can't hold her forever."

Perry said something to the locksmith, who was busy putting the original doorknob back on the front door.

"Fucker!" Barbara snarled. "Ye shit!"

Barbara leaned over, away from Hank, and vomited onto the grass. It steamed in the cool of the morning.

"Jesus," Hank said. "You alright?"

She waved him away with one hand, the other holding back her hair as she retched. When she was finished, she let Hank lead her back to his car. She sat down in the passenger seat and closed her eyes. She sucked in the crisp morning air and tried to calm down.

*The motherfucker was trying to change the locks. The nerve!*

She heard hushed voices and looked up to see Hank talking with Perry on the front porch. Perry had blood all down the front of his shirt, which he was using to staunch the flow of blood from his nose. Hank leaned in and said something to the locksmith, who finished putting on the doorknob and gathered his tools quickly.

Barbara watched the locksmith back out of the drive and leave the neighborhood.

Hank spoke with Perry for some time before he too got inside his vehicle and left. She gave him the bird as he passed.

Hank returned to the car and stood silently beside the open passenger door for a moment.

"Well," he said.

Barbara opened her mouth to say something, but she didn't know what to say so she shut it again.

"Let's get ya inside," Hank said.

Barbara unlocked the front door with her key. Hank followed her inside.

"He's not going to press charges," Hank said.

"He better damn well not," Barbara said, setting her keys in the bowl on the table.

"You can't just hit him," Hank said. "I know he's done ya wrong but that's how ya lose your badge."

"I know it," Barbara said after taking in several shaky breaths. "Thanks, Hank. For everything."

"Don't mention it," Hank said. "That's what partners are for, right?"

Barbara offered up a weak smile and sat down at the kitchen table.

"I guess it's a good thing Sarge sent me home," she said. "If we'd come face to face with the Butcher, I might've torn him to shreds with my bare hands."

Hank laughed.

"Want me to make ya some coffee?" he asked.

"I'd rather have a rye."

"Rye it is."

Hank poured some rye into a cup and splashed in some ginger ale from the fridge. He handed the glass to Barbara.

"Thanks," she said after taking a long draw.

"Get some rest," Hank said.

"I will."

She locked the door behind him, then finished her drink in two gulps. Barbara made another, this time forgoing the ginger ale.

Barbara saw her own mother, pregnant and running, her belly bouncing with each frantic step. She was screaming but the only sound Barbara could hear was a sustained high-pitched ringing. She could read her mother's lips though: *Help! Help me!*

The man was walking and somehow keeping up with Barbara's frightened mother. The long-bladed knife in his hand gleamed in the moonlight. Barbara knew her mother wouldn't make it. There was nowhere to run.

The man's face was shrouded in shadows as he reached out and grabbed a handful of Melissa Johnson's hair and yanked her to the ground. Barbara watched her biological mother raise shaking hands to ward off the knife blows. She watched her mother butchered, trying to scream but finding she had no voice.

Then she was running through a darkened forest. She heard the man's steps behind her, knew somehow that the knife was thirsty, unquenched by the blood of her biological mother. Barbara felt weighed down, sluggish. She looked down to see her stomach was distended, bulbous.

*I'm pregnant!*

She tripped over a root and crashed onto the forest floor. The man with the knife loomed over her and moonlight peeked through the canopy and she saw it was Perry wielding the knife, a demonic smile plastered across his smooth, handsome face. She tried to beg for her life but no words came out of her floundering mouth.

*Please*, she wanted to say. *Don't. Please don't.*

Perry lifted the knife and Barbara woke screaming. It took her several moments to realize she was in her own bed in the house she used to share with Perry.

"Oh Jesus," she cried.

Then she noticed the wetness around her and sat bolt upright. She flung off the covers and saw she'd pissed the bed, something she hadn't done since her first few years in foster care.

"Goddamn it," she hissed, flinging herself up from the wet bed.

She pulled all the bedclothes off the mattress, turned on the overhead fan and adjusted its speed to high.

"I can't believe this," she told the empty laundry room as she stuffed the bedclothes into the washer. "I can't."

The clock on the stove read: 2:37 AM.

She wanted to call Luanne, her former foster mother, but hesitated at the time. She called anyway.

"Barbara? What's wrong?" Luanne's sleepy voice asked.

"I'm sorry, Luanne," Barbara said, tears stinging her eyes. "I just needed to hear your voice."

*I pissed the bed*, she wanted to say but didn't.

"Oh, honey," Luanne said. "What's the matter?"

"I punched Perry," she said. "He tried to get the locks changed at the house and I punched him. I got mugged behind Green Bamboo too."

"What?" Luanne sounded more awake. "Ye got mugged? Are ye okay? Did he hurt ye?"

"I've got a concussion and I had to cancel all my cards and get a new driver's license but I'm okay."

"When did this happen?"

"Day before yesterday."

"And ye're just now telling me?" Luanne sounded more hurt than angry.

"I thought I was alright," Barbara said, crying now. "But I'm not. I'm not alright."

"I'll be there," Luanne said. "Give me ten minutes and I'll be there."

"No, no, no," Barbara said. "I just needed to hear yer voice is all."

She heard the sounds of motion on the other line.

"I love ye, Luanne," Barbara said.

"I love ye too, honey," Luanne said. "I'll be there in a jiffy."

Barbara decided to buy a pregnancy test in the morning. Though she couldn't remember when her last period was, she doubted she was pregnant.

*Better safe than sorry.*

Barbara's robbery made the front page of the *News-Enterprise*: *Cop robbed behind restaurant.* She cringed as she held the paper just inside her front door.

*Great*, she thought. *Just great.*

She flung the paper onto the couch. She made a pot of coffee and put a little rye in her first cup.

## CHAPTER THIRTY-NINE
## IN DEED AND IN TRUTH


JACOB WATCHED DIANE JOHNSON GET out of her car and unlock the front door of Dominion House. Once she was through the door, he stepped out of the shadows and followed her inside. He closed the door behind him and locked it.

He knew he had at least an hour, probably an hour and half until Brock Sither would be finished visiting with his wife at the hospital. If he could convince Diane Johnson that Dominion House needed a change, it would go a long way in convincing Brock Sither.

Jacob walked through the main sanctuary space to the cluster of small offices in the back of the building. Light spilled out from the main office into the hall. Jacob could hear Diane Johnson typing at one of the computers.

After ensuring his face was blank, expressionless, Jacob stepped into the doorframe.

"Diane," he said.

She nearly jumped out of the chair she was sitting in.

"You scared the hell out of me!" Diane Johnson said, her right hand clutching at her throat. "What're you doing here?"

She seemed wary, not happy to see him.

*Not a good start.*

"I need to talk to ye," Jacob said.

Her eyes narrowed and her face soured.

"I've got a lot of work to do," she said. "Shouldn't you be out volunteering to slaughter babies?"

Jacob wanted to lash out at her, wanted to scream, "If ye only knew the work I did for Him ye wouldn't act so snotty."

"It's time for a change," Jacob said after a moment.

"A change?" she asked, dubiously. "I'd say you're in need of one. I can't believe you're escorting those *women* at the Clinic. How could you?"

Jacob cleared his throat.

"Dominion House can be so much more," he said. "Pro-Vision

522

15:3 is an excellent start, but it doesn't go far enough."

She looked at him strangely. Jacob couldn't read what it meant.

"Little children, let us not love in word or talk but in deed and in truth," he said. "Dominion House is pointed in the right direction but ye're a few steps behind. Let me guide ye."

"Guide me? You?" Diane Johnson laughed derisively. "You'd lead us straight to the pits with your escorting harlots. Where is your head, Jacob? I thought you were a stalwart Christian, not some little lamb. Did one of them convince you that what you're doing is kind?"

*She thinks my heart is soft.*

"Well it's not," Diane Johnson said. "It's not kind to kill babies. It's not kind to support sin and sinners. I was actually getting ready to work on your Profile a little more. Add Gallery East to The Accomplices section for showing your work."

"Ye didn't have any trouble accepting the money from the sales of my angels."

"You think you can buy your way back in?" she laughed. "You think you can buy your way into Heaven? 'Do not be deceived: God cannot be mocked. A man reaps what he sows.'"

Jacob wanted to scream. It took a considerable effort to keep his face blank, expressionless.

*Don't you quote scripture at me. Me! The Hand of God!*

"We could be so much more," Jacob said with a careful, even tone. "Follow me. Let me show ye The Way."

How she laughed then. Jacob was sure he'd snap and lash out.

*Calm yourself*, the voice said. *Try harder.*

"What way? Your way of making weird sculptures and escorting whores to the baby slaughterhouse? No thank you."

Her laugh was hard, brittle.

*She doesn't understand. She doesn't see.*

"It's not what it looks like," Jacob said, stepping into the room. "I'm shepherding these women. I'm doing my part to save these children."

"You're not fooling me," Diane Johnson said, crossing her arms across her chest. "You might fool some with that 'hate the sin, not the sinner' BS but not me. You're an Accomplice to murder. And of children! Children!"

*She'll never understand*, Jacob realized. *This is futile.*

"He will repay each one according to his works," Diane Johnson said.

"Let me be judged," Jacob said. "But not by ye. Ye don't understand. Ye have no foresight. I walk The Way. Ye don't know the half of it."

"I think it's time for you to leave now," Diane said, making a show of pushing her chair back up to the computer. "It seems we don't see eye to eye and have different interpretations of what it entails to be a Christian."

She turned her eyes to the screen but Jacob could tell she wasn't seeing anything there. Her demeanor was closed off and wary.

"It's not just words," Jacob said. "It's not just pages on the internet. 'He will repay each one according to his works.' It's deeds that prove yer devotion."

"You need to leave," Diane Johnson said. "You're no longer welcome here."

"It takes sacrifice," Jacob said, taking another step closer. "What do ye know of sacrifice?"

He could tell she was growing afraid. It made him want to smile but he didn't.

"To do what is right and just is more acceptable to the Lord than sacrifice," she said, looking up into his eyes.

"How dare ye quote scripture to me," Jacob yelled. "To me! I am God's Hand!"

She flinched at his sudden rage.

"Go!" she cried. "Get out of here before I call the cops."

"I am not beholden to their law," Jacob said, forcing himself to lower his voice. "I am beholden only to God's law."

Jacob stood over her. She tried to back away but the chair hit the wall and she was stuck. Jacob stood between Diane and the door.

"You're scaring me," Diane Johnson whispered. "Just go. Please."

"Ye need to understand. I walk The Way. I don't just escort those women to their appointments."

He watched understanding dawn on her upturned face.

"That's right. Glory be," Jacob said.

"Don't," she said. "Please. I'm pregnant."

Jacob let the smile spread across his face.

"Is it yer husband's child or Brock Sither's?"

Her head rocked back on her neck as if his words had been a blow.

"How did you know?"

"An excellent wife is the crown of her husband," Jacob quoted, "but she who shames him is like rottenness in his bones."

Diane Johnson started crying. Her shoulders shook and tears spilled down onto her cheeks.

*She doesn't even know,* Jacob thought.

"It's you that's killing all those women," Diane Johnson whispered.

Jacob, smiling, reached down and took a handful of her hair with his right hand. He struck her directly in her shocked face with his left. He hit her two more times before she lost consciousness. He held her up by her hair for a moment before he let the strands slide loose between his fingers and she slumped out of the chair onto the carpet.

"Little children, let us not love in word or talk but in *deed* and in *truth*," Jacob said, toeing Diane Johnson's middle with his left foot.

She did not move.

Jacob went back to the Mazda for the rope, Ace Hardware.

He heard the chirping of her phone as he carried her on his left shoulder out to the Mazda. He set her down in the bed of the truck, the camper shell blocking her from view from the road, and dug around in her pants pockets until he found the phone. He closed the camper shell, locking the hatch and the tailgate, then looked at the cellphone.

She had several text messages from Brock Sither. He didn't bother reading them. He put the phone in his pocket and got behind the wheel of the Mazda. He drove slowly, carefully back to the Powers' Scrap 'n' Metal and backed the Mazda up to The Hand of God.

The phone was buzzing and chirping in his pocket as he unlocked the camper shell. He lifted Diane Johnson, still unconscious, out of the truck and set her on the ridged palm of The Hand. Then he pulled her phone from his pocket and read through the text messages.

Brock Sither was finishing up at the hospital and wanted to know where they were meeting for dinner. Jacob typed in the address of Powers' Scrap 'n' Metal and hit send. Brock Sither called Diane Johnson's phone but Jacob hit ignore, sending the call directly to voicemail. Several texts came in and Jacob replied without reading any of them.

*I have a surprise for you*, he typed. *Hurry.*

# BIRTH OF A MONSTER

Jacob returned the phone to his pocket, a broad smile spreading across his face.

## CHAPTER FORTY
## DESK DUTY

**BARBARA HADN'T FELT MUCH OF** anything when she followed Tiff through the court room through a hulking oak door.

"It won't take but a moment," Tiff said over her shoulder.

"Good, cos I got a lot on my plate this afternoon," Barbara said. She followed her friend down a hall to the judge's chambers.

Tiff knocked on the door and someone inside called for them to enter. Tiff pushed open the door and Barbara followed her inside.

"Afternoon, Judge Thomas," Tiff said.

"Good afternoon, ladies," Judge Thomas said from behind his desk. "Have a seat."

They sat.

Tiff opened her briefcase and retrieved a manila folder. She opened it and handed the document to the judge. Tiff and the judge chatted but Barbara felt distracted, thinking of the Butcher case as well as the stack of paperwork sitting on her desk. She felt impatient to get this over with.

"By signing this document, detective," Judge Thomas said, "you're legally changing your name to Shepherd-Findley."

"Yes," Barbara said.

The judge slid the paper across his shining desk. Tiff handed Barbara a pen.

Out of nowhere, tears stung her eyes. She had to blink several times to keep them from spilling.

*Where'd this come from?* she wondered.

She'd expected to feel nothing and now tears?

*What the hell, Barbara,* she thought. *Keep it together.*

She signed her name.

Tiff signed her name and passed the paperwork back to the judge, who signed his name.

"Well, that's it," Judge Thomas said, "you've officially got your hyphen, Mrs. Shepherd-Findley."

He smiled at her.

"Thank you," she said.

"Not a problem."

Barbara followed Tiff back out into the little hallway.

"You alright, hon?" Tiff asked.

Barbara still felt close to tears and hated herself for it. She nodded her head.

"Good," Tiff said. "I'll walk ya out. This place can be a maze."

They walked in silence through the back halls of the courthouse to the front entrance. A uniformed Sheriff's deputy stood beside the front entrance.

"Barbara Findley?" he asked as they approached.

"Shepherd-Findley," Tiff said, smiling.

"Yes?" Barbara said. "Can I help you?"

"I'm Deputy Harrison with the Sheriff's office. I'm here to serve you with an Emergency Protective Order," the man said, handing a folded series of pages to her. "Sorry, detective, just doing my job."

Tiff took the paperwork from the man and unfolded the pages. She skimmed.

"This is bullshit," Tiff said.

"Perry took out an EPO on me?"

"I'm just here to do the serving," Deputy Harrison said, turning and exiting the courthouse.

"What the fuck?" Barbara said. "What does this mean, Tiff?"

"It means Perry is an asshole," Tiff said. "It also means that you'll have to come back here in fourteen days for a hearing."

"Shit," Barbara said. "Do I have to tell my supervisors?"

Tiff nodded.

"They might already know."

"This means desk duty, doesn't it?"

"I'm sorry, hon," Tiff said, handing the papers to her.

Barbara didn't look at them. She folded the papers and put them in her back pocket.

-

"I'm gonna need your weapon," Sergeant Ellis said after passing the paperwork back to Barbara. "Until the hearing, you're on desk duty."

Barbara nodded, feeling her eyes fill with tears.

*Fuck*, Barbara thought. *Perry, you asshole.*

"The department takes instances of domestic violence seriously, Barbara," Sergeant Ellis said. "I'm not saying you did anything any of us wouldn't have, I'm just saying we got to play this by the book or the public would give us hell."

"I know it."

Barbara willed herself not to cry in front of Sergeant Ellis, but when she got back to her office, she closed the door and broke down, hating herself for it but powerless to stop it.

She blew her nose, then wiped her eyes.

*I've got enough work for fourteen days of desk duty*, she told herself. *Get back to work, Barbara. The Derby City Butcher isn't going to catch himself.*

Her days of desk duty flew by. The Butcher task force and her other cases had a backload of information to process and leads to follow. She spent her days running back and forth between the conference room and her office, making phone calls, answering and sending emails and memos and reports. She had eight hours of mandatory domestic violence video lectures and a week-long, after-hours anger management course online.

Bailey and Hall showed Barbara no mercy. They ragged her every chance they got, calling her "bruiser" or "DV Findley" and "Ronda Rousey." Barbara didn't even consider going to Sergeant Ellis about any of it. She thought it would only exacerbate things and part of her felt she deserved it—some of it, at least. She was a detective for Christ's sake and she didn't even know her husband was having an affair. She often wondered what else she was missing, what else was hiding out there in plain sight.

She met Tiff at the courthouse on the day of the EPO hearing. They'd prepped for the hearing the night before and Barbara knew her job, her one constant, was in jeopardy. She focused on her breathing as they entered the courtroom and found seats. They didn't have long before Barbara's case was called.

Barbara scanned the crowded court room but Perry wasn't anywhere to be seen.

Barbara and Tiff waited as the judge called Perry's name several times, then a small, neat man in an expensive looking suit approached the judge, informing him he was Perry's attorney and his client was not present.

Tiff smiled at Barbara.

The judge listened to the little man for a few moments then called Tiff over. The three of them talked together for some time. Barbara was unable to hear what was said. She reached into the front pocket of her pants and fiddled with her wedding band. She wouldn't wear it, but she found she couldn't not have it on her person. She'd carried it in her pocket for days, taking it out each night and setting it on the nightstand. Every time she woke up in the night, she'd pick up the ring and run her fingers along its smooth, shiny surface.

The judge said something Perry's little attorney didn't like. His face looked pained, then resigned. The judge said something else and Tiff crossed the room to Barbara, smiling.

"The case is dismissed," Tiff said.

Barbara hadn't realized there'd been such a heavy weight on her chest until it was gone.

*Thank God*, she thought.

"Let's go celebrate," Tiff said. "Lunch is on me."

Just outside the courtroom, in the courthouse's anteroom, the little attorney called to them.

"Hold on," he shouted, his voice much lower in register than Barbara expected for his stature.

"Yes?" Tiff asked, pointedly.

"Hello, Mrs. Findley," the little man said. "I'm Lance Pressler, your husband's attorney."

"Mrs. Shepherd-Findley," Tiff corrected him.

"Yes, well," he said. "Mrs. Shepherd-Findley, my client made a mistake withdrawing all of the money from your joint checking account. He'd only meant to withdraw his portion and he apologizes. Here."

The man retrieved a check from his briefcase and handed it to Barbara. She saw right away that it was well short of what it should've been.

"This isn't right," she said, shaking the check at him.

"Well, I'm sorry you feel that way," Lance Pressler said. "If you object to the amount of the check you can call my office and schedule an appointment and we can discuss the matter further. You can also send a complaint through your attorney here but I'm not able to discuss the matter further this afternoon, I'm a busy boy. I've got court in Louisville this afternoon."

The man turned on his heels and strode across the anteroom and out the front doors.

*It's better than nothing*, Barbara thought, folding the check carefully and putting it in the same pocket as her wedding ring.

Back at the department, Barbara met with Sergeant Ellis, who cleared her to return to full duty and gave her her weapon back. She holstered it, its weight a comfort she hadn't realized she needed.

## CHAPTER FORTY-ONE
## THE SCREAMING DIDN'T LAST LONG

**JACOB WATCHED THE BMW PULL** through the open gate at Powers' Scrap 'n' Metal. From his hiding place, Jacob had a clear view of the man's worried face in the glow of the dashboard lights. The BMW's headlights illuminated the base of The Hand of God. Jacob had lit the torches on the five fingers of The Hand and they sent flickering shadows down onto Diane Johnson's naked body, giving the impression of dark stains.

Brock Sither got out of his car, which he left running, calling Diane Johnson's name.

"Diane! Oh my God!" he yelled. "Are you alright?"

Brock Sither ran over to the base of the structure and yelled her name several more times, trying to find a way to climb up onto The Hand. He jumped and grabbed hold of one of the spoilers on the palm but his grip slipped and he dropped back down onto the dirt.

Jacob noted with pride that the motorcycle fingers, though not yet complete, looked like jagged teeth from the ground.

*a great gnashing hulk / barring fang*

"Diane, can you hear me?" Brock Sither called up.

Jacob had stripped all of her clothes off and tied her to the fingers with the hemp rope he'd stolen from Walmart. He'd stuffed her mouth with a dirty rag.

"Oh my God, Diane, wake up!"

Jacob watched the man pat his pockets in a frenzy.

*He's looking for his cellphone,* Jacob knew, quietly moving in the shadows.

Brock Sither turned away from The Hand of God and ran over to his car but stopped short when he saw Jacob, who was wearing the modified welding helmet, the long gloves, and a thick welder's apron.

"Hello," Jacob said, pointing the blowtorch at him.

"Oh God."

Jacob couldn't tell if the man passed out before the flames hit him or if the blowtorch's flames knocked him into unconsciousness. Either way, the man crumpled beside his still-running BMW, his clothes and skin blackened.

The man woke screaming as Jacob doused him in gasoline. He struggled against his bonds but Jacob had tied them tight and most of the skin on the front part of his body had been seared off.

"Why are you doing this?" Brock Sither screamed. "Help! Please, someone! Help!"

"No one will hear you," Jacob said, pouring more gasoline onto the badly burned man.

Brock Sither looked up at The Hand of God and saw Diane Johnson tied there, naked and unconscious.

"Oh my God," he cried.

Jacob stepped onto the scissor lift and rose up until he was even with the palm of The Hand. He stepped onto the metallic structure and pulled out the filet knife, Roger's Bait 'n' Tackle. He leaned over the unconscious woman.

"Stop! Please, don't!"

Jacob had positioned Brock Sither so he had an unobstructed view of the palm.

"God has forsaken ye," Jacob called down.

"Fuck you!" Brock Sither screamed, then he gagged and vomited on himself.

Jacob knelt down over the woman and cut into her stomach.

"No!" Brock Sither screamed. "Stop!"

"Did you know she was pregnant?" Jacob asked, sinking the blade in.

The woman woke screaming, her arms and legs flailing against her bonds, then she passed out again.

"Adultery is a sin," Jacob said, finishing the long incision. "It's one of the commandments, but ye know that."

Jacob reached inside the woman's stomach with his gloved left hand.

"But ye're not a real man of God, are ye?"

"Oh Jesus, what're you doing to her?"

"I'm saving this child," Jacob said, pulling the little mass out of the hole. "I'm sending this woman to her reward, cleansin' her filthy soul, the soul that ye helped tarnish."

"You're sick!"

"I'm holy."

Jacob studied the little fetus in his hand with the magnified lenses of the helmet. It was so small it looked fake to Jacob. He rose and stepped over the crisscrossing spoilers to the ring finger of The Hand. He set the dripping little bundle down inside the gas tank of the motorcycle finger. It looked like a manger to him.

"The Lord preserves all who love Him, but all the wicked He will destroy."

*Rest easy, My Child.*

The woman jerked then lay still. Jacob couldn't tell if she was breathing.

Jacob flipped on the Howard Electric and welded the ring finger closed, ignoring the man's screaming from below. When he was finished, he looked down at the woman and saw she had died.

"For the wages of sin is death," Jacob said, "but the free gift of God is eternal life in Christ Jesus our Lord."

"Oh God!" the man screamed. "Help! Help me!"

Jacob stepped back onto the scissor lift and descended.

"Stay away from me, you psycho!"

Jacob looked down at the man through the magnified lenses of the modified welding helmet, studying the singed flesh in detail.

"Take comfort knowing that I saved that child and that fallen woman," Jacob said.

The man ceased struggling against his bonds.

"The soul who sins shall die. The son shall not suffer for the iniquity of the father, nor the father suffer for the iniquity of the son. The righteousness of the righteous shall be upon himself, and the wickedness of the wicked shall be upon himself."

Jacob picked up the blowtorch and turned it on the bound man. The gasoline ignited and the screaming didn't last long.

Jacob ignored all the sideways stares and glares from the members of Dominion House. He ignored them and waited for his chance to speak.

"Has anybody heard from Brock or Diane?" Stephen Harold asked from the front of the room.

There were no definite responses. Someone asked about Deanna Cole.

"Well, if anybody hears from Brock or Diane, let me know," Stephen Harold said. "I've found some coding bugs in Pro-Vision that needs their attention."

Just as the meeting was coming to a close Jacob rose and walked to the front of the congregation.

"I've got something to say," he said. "I think it's time for a change in Dominion House. The Lord is working through me. He wants you to follow me now."

There were several guffaws and snickers.

*Ignore them*, the voice said.

"So do not fear, for I am with ye," Jacob said. "Do not be dismayed, for I am yer God. I will strengthen ye and help ye; I will uphold ye with My Righteous Right Hand."

Jacob saw The Hand of God reaching upwards, enflamed and immense. He had to make them understand.

"I know several of ye think I've done wrong shepherding those women to and from the Louisville Women's Clinic, but ye don't fully understand. 'My feet have closely followed His steps; I have kept to His way without turning aside.'"

Several members of the congregation got up and left.

Jacob felt shell-shocked.

*They don't understand.*

*Of course they don't understand. When has anybody ever understood you, Jacob?*

*I have to make them understand.*

Jacob felt desperate.

"I am the way and the truth and the life. No one comes to the Father except through me," he shouted.

There were noises of discontent. More members left.

*It's useless*, he thought. *They'll never understand. I'm destined to go it alone. I should've never come here.*

Jacob threw his hands in the air.

*Let all bitterness and wrath and anger and clamor and slander be put away from you, along with all malice*, Jacob quoted to himself. *Be kind to one another, tenderhearted, forgiving one another, as God in Christ forgave you.*

*They don't understand; they can't.*

Jacob walked down the center aisle and out the doors into the cool night.

"Jacob," a voice called from behind him. "Jacob! Wait up!"

It was Josiah Powers.

Jacob stopped and turned around.

"Hey," Josiah Powers said, sounding a bit out of breath. "I know

Brock let ya go, but have ya seen him lately?

*Does he know? He can't know.*

Jacob shook his head.

"What about Diane? Or Deanna?"

The man looked sheepish as he asked the questions and Jacob had to fight the urge to lash out at him with his fists.

*Say something*, the voice said. *Don't just stand there like an idiot.*

Jacob said the first thing that popped into his head.

"There are six things that the Lord hates, seven that are an abomination to Him: haughty eyes, a lying tongue, and hands that shed innocent blood, a heart that devises wicked plans, feet that make haste to run to evil, a false witness who breathes out lies, and one who sows discord among brothers."

Josiah Powers looked perplexed.

Jacob turned and walked across the parking lot to the Mazda.

## CHAPTER FORTY-TWO
## SOMETHING HE SAID

**"LOUISVILLE CRIME STOPPERS."**

"I can't believe I'm doing this, but I'd like to give some information anonymously."

"Sure thing."

"I think y'all need to look into Jacob Hunter Goodman."

"Jacob . . . Hunter . . . Goodman. Okay. What crime do you think this individual is involved in?"

"I think he's been involved in the disappearance of several people."

"Okay. Who's disappearance?"

"Diane Johnson, Brock Sither, Wallace Skaggs, and . . . Deanna Cole."

"Why do you think Jacob Hunter Goodman is involved in these individuals' disappearances?"

". . . something he said to me this evening."

"Can you elaborate?"

". . . not really, no. Y'all aren't going to tell him I called y'all, are ya?"

"No, sir. Your anonymity will be kept."

"Good. I think he's sick. He's the one on the TV making all the crazy angel sculptures out of old car parts and junk down at my scrapyard, er, Powers' Scrap 'n' Metal. He stays in a little camper at the junkyard. Y'all might want to check it out. He hasn't let me anywhere near the inside of it for some time. I think he's hiding something in there."

"Let me get a little information from you, sir, and if an arrest comes from the information you provided you'll be eligible for a cash payment."

"Oh, no. No, that's not why I called. I called because I think this man is dangerous and has had something to do with several of my church members' disappearances. He might be the Butcher even. I don't want to leave my name or anything like that. I just want to make sure y'all look into him."

"The information you provided will be passed along to the authorities."

"Great. Thanks. Bye."

"Sir?"

The line went dead.

## CHAPTER FORTY-THREE
## WHO DOESN'T HAVE A CELLPHONE?

**LAMARCUS TERRY PULLED UP TO** the curb outside Powers' Scrap 'n' Metal and stretched. He'd been following up on the task force's leads all morning and all afternoon and he was tired. He got out of the car and walked around the fence to the singlewide trailer that served as the offices for the place. The door opened just before he could knock.

"Can I help ya?" Josiah Powers asked.

"Detective Terry, LPD. I'm following up on a tip we've received," Detective Terry checked the name in his notebook. "Does Jacob Hunter Goodman reside on the premises?"

"Yes, he does, but he's not here right now."

"When do you expect him to return?"

"That I can't tell ya."

"Do you have a contact number for him? I need to get in touch with him."

"No, sir. He doesn't have a cellphone as far as I know."

LaMarcus Terry blinked.

*Who doesn't have a cellphone?*

"He work for you? You're the owner of this place?"

Josiah Powers nodded. His eyes kept darting over the detective's shoulders.

"He a good employee?"

Josiah Powers nodded his head again, his eyes refusing to meet the detective's.

"Could you give me a description of Jacob Hunter Goodman?"

Josiah Powers flinched.

"Look, I've got a lot to do," he said quickly. "I cain't be wastin' any more time on this. He ain't here right now, so if you're needing to talk to 'im, y'all'll just have to come back later."

Detective Terry opened his mouth to ask another question but the singlewide's flimsy front door was shut in his face.

"Hm," he said, turning away from the trailer and studying the

539

junkyard around him.

There were cars piled on top of each other, nearly two stories tall in some places. There was a ring of strange metallic sculptures in front of a little popup camper. Detective Terry walked over to them and studied them for a long time before walking back to his car and radioing the information into the task force.

# CHAPTER FORTY-FOUR
## GHOST TOWN

**"TERRY SAID THE MAN SEEMED** jumpy," Hank said, taking the exit off the Gene Snyder Freeway. "Shut the door in his face too."

"I'll bet he's the one that called it in," Barbara said. "The caller said Jacob Hunter Goodman might've had something to do with several disappearances, two of which have been reported, two others that haven't been."

She flipped back to the page of her notebook.

"Diane Johnson, Brock Sither, Wallace Skaggs, and Deanna Cole," Barbara read. "Initial look showed they all belonged to one of those fringe churches, *God Hates Fags*, those kind of people, except for Wallace Skaggs, who worked for Rubbish Management. But he hasn't showed up for work in weeks and was canned. The foreman over there hinted that Skaggs had a drug problem but he wouldn't come out and say it."

"Who doesn't on this side of town?" Hank asked as they passed abandoned houses and buildings.

Barbara returned her notebook to her pocket and looked out the window. Several of the boarded-up houses had spray-painted signs reading: *No Copper Here!* and *Keep Out!*

"This is a ghost town," she said. "Perfect place for the Butcher to set up shop."

"Yep."

They drove in silence until they reached the junkyard. Hank parked across the street and they got out.

"It sure is quiet over here," Barbara noted.

Hank nodded.

They walked across the street and up the walk to the singlewide trailer. Barbara knocked on the door. They heard movement from within and, after a moment, the door opened.

"Yeah?" Josiah Powers asked.

"You Powers?" Hank asked.

The man looked all around then back at the detectives.

"Who wants to know?"

"I'm Detective Gray," Hank said. "This is Detective Shepherd-Findley. Mind if we ask you a few questions?"

"It's a free country."

"That it is," Hank said.

"Does Jacob Hunter Goodman reside on the premises?" Barbara asked.

"I tol' that other guy earlier that he does and that ain't changed in five hours," Josiah Powers said. "But he ain't here right now."

"Why does he live in a junkyard?" Hank asked.

"He's like a night watchman," Josiah Powers said. "He makes sure kids and methheads don't break in and steal stuff. Happens more than you'd think."

"I'm sure it does," Hank said. "What's Jacob Hunter Goodman's relation to you?"

"No relation. He used to go to my church is all."

"What church is that?" Barbara asked.

"Dominion House."

"Y'all the ones that protest outside the Louisville Women's Clinic?" Hank asked.

"Yessir," Josiah Powers said. "They kill babies there."

"Uh-huh," Hank said. "What's Jacob Hunter Goodman like?"

"Why don't y'all find out for yourselves," Josiah Powers said. "I expect he should be back anytime now."

Dusk was descending. The light shifted and grew weaker. A whippoorwill called from somewhere nearby.

"I best be getting back at it," Josiah Powers said. "I'm closing soon."

Barbara read the hours hand-painted on the singlewide trailer to the right of the door, checked her watch and saw that Powers' Scrap 'n' Metal was supposed to be open for another half-hour.

"Mind if we wait here?" Hank asked.

"Yes I do," Josiah Powers said. "It's not good for business to have two cops hanging around."

"We'll wait in the car then," Barbara said. "Thank ye for yer time, Mr. Powers."

Josiah Powers grunted and disappeared back inside the trailer.

The two detectives shared a look then walked back to the unmarked cruiser. Back inside the car, Hank spoke first.

"That's our caller."

"Yep."

"Think he meant what he said about suspecting his guy for the disappearances or do ya think he just wants to get rid of a trouble-some night watchman?"

"Guess we'll have to wait and find out," Barbara said. "He sure seemed jumpy."

Hank nodded.

Barbara sipped her coffee, which had gone cold.

"How ya holdin' up, Fin?" Hank asked. "Shit. I'm sorry, should I stop calling you Fin with the whole name change?"

Barbara shook her head and swallowed the cold coffee.

"No, it's fine," she said. "I'm alright. There are times when I'm not, but I guess that's to be expected when your marriage is falling apart, right?"

"Well, you know I'm here if ye ever need to talk," Hank said, turning toward her in the car. "I won't even say anything if you don't want me to. I'll be there just to listen if that's what ya need."

Barbara felt tears sting her eyes and found it hard to meet her partner's eyes but she willed herself to meet and hold them.

"Thank ye, Hank."

"Don't mention it, Shep."

They both laughed.

"I like Shep," Barbara said.

"What about Shep-Fin?"

"Now that's a mouthful."

They watched Josiah Powers drive off toward the freeway.

"Sounds like a garden utensil or something, doesn't it? Could you hand me that, Shep-Fin?"

They laughed. An hour passed in which full dark descended and Barbara finished her cold coffee.

A Mazda pickup with an oversized camper shell turned onto the road. The detectives watched as it slowly pulled up alongside their unmarked cruiser. A man stared out at them, his face expressionless, his eyes hard.

"That's our man," Hank said.

The truck pulled up to the junkyard's gate but the man did not get out. He stared out the open driver's side window at Hank and Barbara.

"What's he doing?" Hank asked. "He gonna run?"

"Looks like he's waiting on us," Barbara said, opening the passenger side door and stepping out into the night. "Let's go have us a little chat."

They walked across the empty street to the idling Mazda. Barbara approached the driver's side, Hank the passenger.

"Jacob Goodman?" Hank asked through the open window.

"Can I help ye, officers?" the man asked, his voice bland.

Barbara thought the man looked familiar. She wracked her brain trying to remember where she'd seen him but she came up empty.

"Got an ID for me?" Hank asked.

The man shook his head.

"Lost it."

"No driver's license?"

"Nope."

"You do know it's illegal to be operating a motorized vehicle without a license, right?"

The man didn't reply.

"Could I see your insurance and registration?" Hank asked.

"I ain't got it transferred to my name yet. I've got the pink slip though."

Barbara shone her flashlight around the interior of the truck. The man gave her a hard look but said nothing.

He slowly reached across the cab and opened the glove compartment and retrieved the papers. He passed them to Hank, who walked to the back of the vehicle to see the plates. He radioed it in. The man turned and stared at Barbara while they waited on HQ to run the information.

Barbara felt goosebumps ripple across her arms.

*Where have I seen this man?* she wondered.

The man locked eyes with her and Barbara felt unnerved by the man's glare. She turned back to looking around in the interior of the truck. It was littered with trash and tools.

Hank handed the papers back to the man.

"Care if we have a look around the premises? We hear you're the night watchman here."

"No, you may not."

"Why's that?"

The man didn't reply. He held Hank's eyes.

"Alright. Do ya know Diane Johnson?" Hank asked.

Barbara watched the man but he didn't react.

"Or Brock Sither?" Hank asked. "Or what about Wallace Skaggs or Deanna Cole?"

The man's face remained blank, expressionless.

"I know them, yes," Jacob Hunter Goodman said. "Why?"

"How do ye know them?" Barbara asked.

"I used to attend church with Brock Sither, Diane Johnson, and Deanna Cole at Dominion House," he said. "I used to work with Wallace Skaggs at Rubbish Management."

"Used to and used to," Hank said. "Why aren't you still going to Dominion House? Why aren't ya still working at Rubbish Management?"

"I had a change of heart," the man said. "I don't work for Rubbish Management anymore because it was taking too much of my time. Time I could've spent workin' on the creations. The sculptures."

*That's where I recognized him*, Barbara thought.

"I've seen ye on the TV," she said.

The man nodded but his face remained unmoved.

"Ye're the guy who makes the strange angels."

The man nodded again.

"Care to let us inside and show us one?" Hank asked.

The man shook his head.

"Why not?"

"There're several on display throughout the city," he said. "You could go to Gallery East and see five of the angels in one place."

"Care if we took a look inside the back of the truck?"

"No you cannot."

"You're making me a bit uneasy, Mr. Goodman," Hank said. "Ya got something to hide?"

The man did not respond. He stared at Hank with an expressionless visage.

"How about we go back to HQ for further questioning?" Barbara asked. "How'd ye like that, Mr. Goodman?"

The man turned toward her. Barbara broke out in fresh goosebumps. The man's eyes were dark and piercing. His face showed no emotion whatsoever.

"We both know ye've got no right to search the premises or my vehicle," he said after a long moment had passed. "I'm going to go inside. I'm on duty tonight. Y'all aren't welcome to follow me."

The man put the Mazda in drive and pulled slowly through the open gate.

Hank and Barbara looked at each other and walked across the empty street to their car.

"That guy gives me the creeps," Barbara said.

"Me too."

"Let's see what we can find out about him."

## CHAPTER FORTY-FIVE
## BAD FRUIT


*FUCKERS!* **JACOB FUMED. HE KICKED** over a trash barrel behind the singlewide trailer. *They have no right! No right to come ask me questions. No right to come to my home and smile at me with their questions!*

*Calm yourself,* the voice said.

Jacob walked over to the gate and looked out at the empty street. The cop's car was gone.

*Good,* he thought, walking back to the Mazda.

Jacob opened the camper shell, Wallace Skaggs, and stared in at the unconscious woman. Her pregnant belly moved up and down as she breathed. He reached a hand inside and placed it lightly on the protruding stomach.

*Soon, My Child. I'm coming to save you.*

Jacob lifted the woman out of the camper shell, Wallace Skaggs, and carried her over to the scissor lift, which stood in front of the towering Hand of God. He lifted them up to the palm and set her down amongst the crisscrossing spoilers.

*I can't believe the fuckers came here. How did they know where to find me? How did they find me?*

*Dominion House,* the voice said. *That den of iniquity.*

"Behold, I was brought forth in iniquity, and in sin did my mother conceive me," Jacob said, tying the woman's arms and legs to the motorcycle fingers of The Hand of God.

*The fuckers! I can't believe they came here. Here!*

*Calm yourself,* the voice said.

Jacob's hands were shaking. He fumbled with the knots, his fingers feeling numbed and stupid. He used the trauma shears, University of Pikeville Medical School, to cut the woman's clothing off.

When he'd finished securing the unconscious woman—*Patricia Huffman* her license read—Jacob descended on the scissor lift to retrieve the Howard Electric. As he picked up the modified welding helmet, he heard a strange sound then a yelp. He turned around to see the woman had somehow managed to escape her bonds and had

547

leapt off The Hand of God. She was limping off farther into the junkyard.

*See what happens when you don't remain calm?* the voice asked. *See?*

*It's fine,* Jacob thought. *Now I get to hunt her all over again.*

Jacob put on the welding helmet but did not lower the facemask. He picked up the filet knife, Roger's Bait 'n' Tackle, and started after the pregnant woman, Patricia Huffman, a smile planted firmly on his face.

She screamed and screamed.

"Help! Someone help me!"

Jacob felt each scream like a soft breath on the nape of his neck. He felt each panicked scream like a caress. He stalked her, taking his time, enjoying the way her naked body jiggled as she limped deeper into the junkyard. He held off on killing her, savoring her ill-fated fleet in the wrong direction. There was no way out in this section of Josiah Power's scrapyard. Jacob stuck to the shadows, smiling, smiling, smiling.

The filet knife seemed to sing in his left hand. It seemed to call out to the woman, a response to her screams for aid.

*I'm coming,* it sang.

"I'm coming, My Child," Jacob whispered. "Don't ye worry none. Daddy's here to save ye."

Piles of crushed vehicles towered over this section of the junkyard making a narrow path that dead-ended in a tall fence. The woman, Patricia Huffman, pounded on the fence and attempted to climb it in vain. She beat her fists against the enclosed mesh and screamed.

Jacob stepped out of the shadows smiling. He lowered the facemask of the modified welding helmet and stepped closer.

The woman turned around and saw him.

Jacob drank the moment in: the way her face crumpled like an empty paper sack, the tears that streamed down her pale cheeks, the twitching mouth that called out for help she now knew wouldn't come.

Jacob took each step slowly. He showed her the filet knife, Roger's Bait 'n' Tackle and her legs buckled under her. She dropped onto the dirt, naked and unconscious. Jacob reached down and lifted her up and carried her back to The Hand of God. He used the scissor lift to bring them level with the palm. He set the woman down and retied her bonds, this time ensuring they were tight.

Jacob made the incision with the filet knife, Roger's Bait 'n' Tackle, and the woman woke screaming. She fought against the rope, Ace Hardware, but this time it held. The woman died as Jacob cut the fetus out of her stomach. He held it in his gloved hands and studied it with the magnified lenses of the modified helmet for some time.

"My Child," he said. "My Child, ye're free now. Go to yer reward."

Jacob set the dripping fetus inside the motorcycle gas tank of the pointer finger, hearing the sound of many children singing at once. He then turned back to the dead woman, Patricia Huffman, and set about cutting her into smaller pieces, humming along with the holy song without words. He put her head inside the gas tank with the fetus then turned on the Howard Electric.

After he welded them inside, Jacob doused the palm of The Hand of God with gasoline. He dropped a match and watched the flames boil and burn off all the blood.

"Do not be conformed to this world, but be transformed by the renewal of yer mind, that by testing ye may discern what is the will of God," Jacob said, "what is good and acceptable and perfect."

*I am The Hand of God. I am God's Flaming Sword.*

Jacob saw the Great Hand reaching down and smiting the world. He saw The Hand commending his work. He heard trumpets and the chiming voices of all his singing children.

Jacob felt his penis stiffen painfully in the sweatpants, Walmart. He ejaculated as he sang.

-

Josiah Powers set the paper down as Jacob stepped inside the little office.

"Mornin'," Josiah said.

"Mornin'," Jacob replied. "Done with the bathroom for a minute?"

Josiah nodded his head and Jacob saw the way his eyes were drawn back to the newspaper.

"You see this?" Josiah asked, nodding toward the paper he'd just set down on the counter beside the register.

"What?" Jacob asked.

"This city is going crazy with all this Butcher stuff."

Jacob kept his face blank, expressionless as he picked up the newspaper. It was an open letter from Pastor Brent Kitchens of Evergreen First Christian Church, a megachurch out in the ritzy Anchorage suburb, addressed to the Derby City Butcher. Jacob forced himself to breathe normally and read slowly.

*It has come to our attention that a wolf masquerading as a sheep is committing great atrocities in our area under the guise of God, attacking a den of iniquity. The Good Book does not condone the actions of this murderer despite what he may be telling himself. Romans 12:9: Do not take revenge, my dear friends, but leave room for God's wrath, for it is written: "It is mine to avenge; I will repay," says the Lord. Taking the lives of these misguided women and their unborn children is a greater travesty than the act in which they were trying to execute on their own. God does not condone any of this madness.*

Jacob wanted to sneer but he didn't. He was keenly aware of Josiah's eyes on him.

"Mind if I take this with me to the bathroom?" Jacob asked, folding the newspaper and tucking it under his arm beside his Bible.

"Go ahead."

Jacob walked through the hall and entered the singlewide's little bathroom, holding the newspaper with the hand not holding his toiletries. He opened the commode, pulled down his pants, and sat. He read on.

*Though the Butcher may think he is ridding the world of as ugly a sin as there is, he must remember what the Good Book says: The commandments, "You shall not commit adultery," "You shall not murder," "You shall not steal," "You shall not covet," and the rest of them are summed up in this one command: "Love your neighbor as yourself." If the Butcher were a real Christian he wouldn't be committing these atrocious crimes against pregnant women. He would reach out a hand and help them see the error of their ways and keep the babies they're so intent on slaying. The Book of Peter tells us: Do not repay evil with evil or insult with insult. On the contrary, repay evil with blessing, because to this you were called so that you may inherit a blessing. Also in the Book of Peter: Finally, all of you, be like-minded, be sympathetic, love one another, be compassionate and humble.*

*I, Brent Kitchens, pastor of Evergreen First Christian Church, along with the following names, condemn the actions of the person the papers dub The Derby City Butcher. We ask that he turn himself into the authorities and confess to his monstrous deeds and ask forgiveness from the Lord Almighty. It's not too late to save the soul of this monster.*

Jacob let the paper fall to the floor beside his feet. He picked up the Bible and saw that his hands were shaking.

*The fuckers! If they only knew that He sanctioned me. If they only knew that I'm The Hand of God.*

Jacob opened the Bible at random, found himself in the first chapter of the Second Epistle to the Thessalonians, and read: *All this is evidence that God's judgment is right, and as a result you will be counted worthy of the kingdom of God, for which you are suffering. God is just: He will pay back trouble to those who trouble you and give relief to you who are troubled, and to us as well. This will happen when the Lord Jesus is revealed from heaven in blazing fire with his powerful angels. He will punish those who do not know God and do not obey the gospel of our Lord Jesus. They will be punished with everlasting destruction and shut out from the presence of the Lord and from the glory of His might on the day He comes to be glorified in His holy people and to be marveled at among all those who have believed. This includes you, because you believed our testimony to you.*

Jacob grunted, his bowels released, and he smiled. He knew what he had to do. He studied the names of the pastors and preachers signed to the letter and the names of their so-called churches. This was divine guidance, Jacob knew. He'd bring God's cleansing fires, everlasting destruction to these false prophets. He was holy, he was sanctified, he was The Hand of God. Jacob felt he could hear the angels heralding his ascension. He knew the metallic angels he made and filled with his Children and Wives joined in the chorus.

-

Jacob tried the doors but they were locked. Carrying the jerry-can of gasoline, he crossed the front walk and walked alongside the building until he found an unlocked basement window. He set the jerry-can on the ground, climbed down into the darkened basement of Evergreen First Christian Church then clicked on his penlight, University of Pikeville Medical School. He scanned the room, ensured it was empty, then reached up through the window and brought down the jerry-can.

He sloshed the gasoline behind him as he walked through the basement up the stairs into the main sanctuary. Jacob went up the center aisle trailing gasoline until he was standing on the raised stage next to the pulpit.

"My brothers," he said in his best preacher's voice. "My sisters. The time has come for a cleansin'. Lord Jesus is revealed from Heaven with His mighty angels in blazing fire."

Jacob soaked the stage, stepped down and made his way along the wall, all the while spilling more gasoline. He walked to the front of the building and unlocked the front doors and opened them. He made his way to the front walk surrounded by the large front yard.

A bit of inspiration came to him then. Jacob stepped off the concrete onto the grass and, remembering a time when he was a kid pissing in the snow, he used the gasoline to write *7 Mt 15-20* in the grass.

He lit a match and dropped it onto the gasoline-soaked grass. *7 Mt 15-20* was quickly singed into the grass and the fire ran up the walk, up the stairs and into Evergreen First Christian Church. Jacob turned and ran for the Mazda.

Back inside the truck, Jacob watched the flames rise through the stained-glass window. He smiled and quoted from the Good Book, "Watch out for false prophets. They come to ye in sheep's clothing, but inwardly they are ferocious wolves. By their fruit ye will recognize them. Do people pick grapes from thorn bushes, or figs from thistles? Likewise, every good tree bears good fruit. A good tree cannot bear bad fruit and a bad tree cannot bear good fruit. Every tree that does not bear good fruit is cut down and thrown into the fire. Thus, by their fruit ye will recognize them."

-

Jacob drove straight to Fern Creek First Baptist. Pastor Timothy Greene had been the second name signed to the open letter to the Butcher. He found another unlocked window and climbed inside, soaking the pews and wooden floors with gasoline. After going through the majority of the premises, Jacob wrote *PS 104:4* in the parking lot and lit another match.

"He makes His messengers winds, His ministers a flaming fire," Jacob said as the flames danced.

Jacob could hear His Children singing as he drove the Mazda toward Jefferson Memorial Forest.

-

Jacob burned down United Church of God on Blevins Road; Pastor Henrick Stanley had also signed the letter. In the small churchyard, Jacob wrote LK 3:16.

"John answered them all, saying 'I baptize ye with water, but He who is mightier than I is coming, the strap of whose sandals I am not worthy to untie. He will baptize ye with the Holy Spirit and fire,'" Jacob called out into the night.

He heard the trumpets sounding off all around him as he drove the short distance back to Powers' Scrap 'n' Metal. The wailing sirens were but a response to the call he initiated.

# CHAPTER FORTY-SIX
## A PRETTY TIGHT TIMELINE

**BARBARA DIDN'T FEEL WELL. SHE** chalked it up to the long hours of overtime and the lack of sleep and food. She hated to admit it, but she was half-afraid to go to sleep now for fear of pissing the bed again.

*I can't believe I did that. An adult woman, pissing the bed like a child. Jesus!*

She felt bad enough to pass along Jacob Hunter Goodman's info to a detective from LPD to look into. She was tired but she didn't want to go home. Barbara walked down the hall to Hank's darkened office and lay down on his couch. Hank had left a few hours ago and she didn't expect him back until the morning. Barbara was just slipping on toward sleep when the image of a pregnancy test popped into her head. She'd planned on buying one that morning but it'd totally slipped her mind.

*What if I'm pregnant?*

*I'm not pregnant.*

*But when was my last period?*

Barbara sat up on the couch in Hank's darkened office knowing she wouldn't be able to sleep now. She decided to get out of the building for some fresh air. While she was out she'd swing by CVS and buy a pregnancy test. She cringed at the thought of purchasing one.

Barbara drove with the radio off, her tired mind mercifully still. She parked, went into the pharmacy, found the "family planning" section, and picked up a First Response because its box looked the most professional. It wasn't as awkward as she thought it'd be paying for it. The cashier scanned the box, put it in a bag, and asked for the money. Back in her car, she put the pregnancy test in her purse. She drove back to HQ doing her best not to think about the possibility of her being pregnant.

*What would that mean for my career? For my failing relationship with Perry?*

Barbara was tired but she didn't have to pee so she made a fresh pot of coffee in her office. Waiting for it to finish brewing, she read the instructions on the outside of the box.

"Two lines means I'm pregnant," she read. "One line means I'm not."

She set the box down and poured herself a cup of black coffee. She sipped it, staring at the pink and white box on her desktop. It felt like it'd take some monumental feat of personal heroics to take the test. She felt panic and fear gnawing at the frayed ends of her consciousness.

*I can't be pregnant*, she told herself. *There's no way.*

But she knew there was. Despite their fighting, she and Perry had an active sex life.

*Shit, maybe because of all the fighting*, she thought.

She stared at the box.

*I can't do this right now.*

She opened the top drawer of her desk and set the pregnancy test inside. She unlocked her computer and tried going through her email inbox but she couldn't focus, thinking about the pink and white box that could change her life forever sitting in her desk. In a rush, she flung open the drawer, grabbed hold of the First Response Pregnancy Test box and rose to her feet, intending to go to the bathroom and take it, but there was a hurried knocking at her closed door. She dropped the box back into the open drawer and slammed it shut just as Hank entered.

"Fin, we've got a serious situation here," Hank said. "Shit, I mean Shep-Fin."

Barbara tried smiling but it was more of a grimace.

"What's up?"

"Fires," Hank said. "Three of 'em."

"What?"

"Remember that letter in the *Courier-Journal?*" Hank asked.

They'd discussed it at the morning roundup.

"Yeah."

"Well, the Butcher hit three of the churches. Burned 'em to the ground. And that's not all."

Barbara waited for the rest of it.

"He burned in Bible verses outside of each of them."

"He what?"

"I know."

"Bible verses? Jesus."

"Let's go," Hank said. "Lieu and the task force are waiting for us in the conference room."

"Accelerant was found at all three churches. The arson investigators said it was probably regular gasoline," Lieutenant Kendrick Thomas said. "Anchorage Middletown Station 1 responded to the fire at Evergreen First Christian Church at 2:35 AM. Okolona 3 responded to the fire at Fern Creek First Baptist at 3:15 AM. Fairdale Fire 1 responded to the fire at United Church of God on Blevins Road at 4 AM."

"Jesus," Hank whispered.

"That's a pretty tight timeline," Lieutenant Thomas said, pulling down the projector screen.

A map of Louisville was displayed with the route mapped out. There were red dots where the burned churches had stood.

"He took Evergreen Road in Anchorage to Shelbyville Road to Hurstborne to Fern Valley Road, where he set the fire at Fern Creek First Baptist," Mitchell Skeeters said. "Then he probably took Grade Lane to Outer Loop to New Cut to Blevins, where he set the United Church of God fire."

The map was a slanting line descending toward Jefferson Memorial Forest.

"At each of the churches he burned a Bible verse into the grass or onto the pavement. At Evergreen First Christian it was 7 MT 15-20," Lieutenant Thomas said.

A picture of the burned letters and numbers appeared on the projector screen.

"That one, for all y'all heathens is the seventh book of Matthew verses 15 through 20," Mitchell Skeeters said. "'Watch out for false prophets. They come to you in sheep's clothing, but inwardly they are ferocious wolves. By their fruit you will recognize them. Do people pick grapes from thorn bushes, or figs from thistles? Likewise, every good tree bears good fruit, but a bad tree bears bad fruit. A good tree cannot bear bad fruit, and a bad tree cannot bear good fruit. Every tree that does not bear good fruit is cut down and thrown into the fire. Thus, by their fruit you will recognize them.'"

"We've got a bad apple here, Sarge," Bailey said.

There were several chuckles and a few eyes rolled.

"The Bible verse at Fern Creek Baptist was Psalm one oh four

four, 'He makes His messengers winds, His ministers a flaming fire.'"

Barbara was in wonder at the deeds of religious lunatics. It seemed like a virus hellbent on spreading itself.

"At United Church of God the message was from the book of Luke, chapter three, verse sixteen, 'John answered them all, saying, 'I will baptize you with water, but he who is mightier than I is coming, the strap of whose sandals I am not worthy to untie. He will baptize you with the Holy Spirit and fire.'"

*This is madness*, Barbara thought.

For some reason, her mind turned to the protestors at the abortion clinic.

"We've contacted the other churches that signed on to the open letter to the Butcher that was printed in the *Courier-Journal* and there haven't been any other arson attempts as of yet," Lieutenant Thomas said. "We've upped uniform patrol in their areas and sent out surveillance teams to stake out the other churches. We've taken the pastors of the three churches the Butcher hit into protective custody for the time being."

"We've divided the map into three grids," Mitchell Skeeters said. "Richards and Hall will take the northern most portion. Rodriguez and Rogers will take the middle. Shepherd-Findley and Gray will take the southernmost area. Y'all see the route, get out and find any cameras you can. There's a ton of gas stations and hotels and businesses along the route. Somebody has footage of the perp driving. Dismissed."

Barbara and Hank walked back to Hank's office.

"Ye driving?" Barbara asked.

"Sure."

"Guess we'll start at the United Church of God and work our way back up to Fern Valley."

"Sounds like a plan."

As they drove, they heard over the radio that several places along the Butcher's route had video and it was being sent to HQ to be processed.

"We'll get a vehicle out of that," Hank said.

Barbara hoped he was right.

They got off the Gene Synder Freeway near the Jefferson Memorial Forest. United Church of God had been a small brick

# BIRTH OF A MONSTER

building surrounded by forest. It was still smoldering and had been taped off. Hank parked the car and they got out. The sun had lightened the sky to the east and they could see the wisps of their breaths in the coolness of the morning as they talked.

"Luke three-sixteen," Hank read.

The letters were scorched in the grass that separated the burned building from the small parking lot.

Barbara flipped back to her notes and read, "He will baptize ye with the Holy Spirit and fire.'"

"This guy . . ." Hank said.

"Monster," Barbara said.

They studied the scene in silence for some time.

Where the parking lot connected with the road, the asphalt had deteriorated into a mud and gravel ditch about three free wide. There were several tire marks there that Barbara took photos of.

Barbara's phone buzzed. She answered it.

"I've got some info on that name you wanted me to run," Detective Terry said. "Jacob Hunter Goodman."

Barbara realized how close they were to Powers' Scrap 'n' Metal and stood straight and still.

"Yeah?" she said. "Go on."

"He's an eastern Kentucky boy," Detective Terry said. "He's got an active warrant out of Floyd County for a missed court appearance for a public intoxication charge. It looks like he was in the foster care system but that'll take a bit more digging. Want me to continue?"

"Yes, I do," Barbara said.

"Ten four."

## CHAPTER FORTY-SEVEN
## SOMETHING FUNGAL


JACOB SMILED DOWN AT THE newspaper and read the headline out loud, again.

"Derby City Butcher burns down three churches."

He translated the headlines out of newspeak into the language he used: The Hand of God cleanses three dens of iniquity. He read about how Louisville was rocked by the burning of the three churches whose pastors had signed an open letter to the Butcher. He read about how those pastors and their families had been taken into protective custody. He read about the increased patrol and sur-veillance of the other churches and smiled.

*Idiots*, he thought.

He felt invincible after burning down the churches. Setting those fires had been gratifying, not as much as the hunt or the kill, but close. The messages had been an inspired touch. Jacob went through the verses in his head before continuing with the article.

The task force, which had been criticized for its past all-male composition, was investigating the disappearances of sixteen women and two men. Jacob smiled when he read the names of Brock Sither and Wallace Skaggs. Each of their families filed missing persons re-ports with Louisville Metro Police. Jacob relived each of their deaths for a moment before putting the paper down on the small Formica table in the camper.

*They'll never catch me*, Jacob thought. *God is protecting me. I am the Hand of God. I am God's flaming sword.*

"But the Lord is faithful, and He will strengthen ye and protect ye from the evil one," Jacob said, crossing the small space to the little bed.

He lay down and felt a satisfied weariness descend on him. He slept and dreamed of fire and blood and skin and bones. He awoke to the smell of something fungal and found he'd ejaculated in his sleep.

# CHAPTER FORTY-EIGHT
## THAT'S OUR BOY

**THE INFORMATION COMING IN ON** Jacob Hunter Goodman kept getting stranger. Barbara learned of the ice-lock situation in foster care from the foster mother. The woman spoke the man's name as if he were the devil himself. She was told Jacob had taken great means to control the younger foster children, getting one of them in trouble for stealing a bondage porno magazine. From a retired family court judge, Barbara learned Jacob was given leniency due to his hard luck background—his mother was a known prostitute and drug addict and there was no father to speak of. Social services had removed Jacob from his mother's care twice before the third and final time in which he aged out of care and enrolled in community college on the state's dime, where he studied welding. He earned his certificate despite the active warrant and the state wanted reimbursement as the criminal charges precluded his eligibility for his higher education. He was allowed to go on attending school and eventually earn his welding certificate by an oversight: Jacob had moved from eastern Kentucky to the Louisville metro area and slipped through the cracks.

"He's our man," Barbara told Hank. "I feel it."

"I think ya might be right," Hank said, shaking his head. "We talked about adopting now that our three are a little older. It really makes ya think twice about it, hearing horror stories like this."

"One Rodney Tackett, who disappeared years ago, screamed to anybody who'd listen that Jacob Hunter Goodman was responsible for the disappearance of his cousin, one Tanya Miller," Barbara read from the memo.

"Hm."

"Hm, indeed," Barbara said. "Neither Tanya Miller nor Rodney Tackett has been located. Also, break-ins and missing pets were reported in all the places Jacob Hunter Goodman resided. He was caught stealing and breaking stuff in every foster home he'd lived in."

"Jesus," Hank said. "If he ain't our guy, he's still a real sicko."

"Yep," Barbara said. "We don't have enough for a warrant, but it's a start. Hopefully a uni will pick him up for the active warrants out of Floyd County."

Barbara was crossing the conference room, heading for the door, when Detective Terry called her name in an excited tone.

"Come look at this," he said.

When Barbara saw the Mazda pickup with the camper shell in the surveillance footage on Detective Terry's laptop she nearly leapt up into the air.

"It's him!" she said, reaching over and hitting the pause button. The video footage was from a gas station in Anchorage and showed Jacob Hunter Goodman pull up to the pump and fill a jerry-can.

"That's our boy," Detective Terry said.

"Yes it is," Barbara said. "Good work, Terry."

"The time stamp on the footage is 2:07AM," Detective Terry said.

"That's enough for your new warrant, Shep," Hank said.

Barbara had to force herself to walk and not run across the conference room toward Sergeant Ellis' office. By the time she'd returned to the conference room, there were several other video footages of the truck driving along the route of the arsons.

With Sergeant Ellis' approval, Barbara put in the paperwork for a search warrant for Jacob Hunter Goodman's truck and camper at Powers' Scrap 'n' Metal.

-

Hank's car was at the front of the convoy that descended upon Powers' Scrap 'n' Metal. He slammed on the brakes just outside the gate and they hopped the closed gate with guns drawn.

"Police! Make yourself known!" they shouted. "Police!"

Barbara saw right away the Mazda pickup with the camper shell wasn't present. The camper sat beside a hulking metal sculpture of a hand. She banged on the door.

"Police! Make yourself known!" she shouted before trying the handle and finding the door locked.

A uniformed policeman appeared with a battering ram and Barbara stepped aside. The officer struck the door with the ram twice and it broke off its hinges and clattered into the dirt after bouncing off the two little steps that led up into the camper.

"Police!" Barbara shouted, stepping inside.

She saw that it was empty right away. Then she saw the wall of objects. She saw photo identifications and necklaces and earrings and assorted jewelry. Then she saw several clumps and strands of long hair and several tacked human fingers. There was a photograph, taken from above, of a young blonde-haired girl showering.

"Oh my God," she whispered.

There was a tacklebox sitting on the small Formica table. She put on latex gloves and carefully opened it. It was full of cut off fingers and painted fingernails.

She felt weak but forced herself not to show any emotion at all. She turned to Hank and showed him the contents.

"Holy shit," Hank said.

There was a notebook labeled **Letters to My Children** in permanent marker on the table beside the tacklebox. Barbara gave it a cursory flip through and saw page after page of cramped, pained penmanship.

"We've got our man," she said. "Let's get the scene processed. Get forensics in here immediately."

She put the notebook back onto the table and stepped down out of the camper.

"Come look at this," Detective Terry called from his position on the palm of the hulking sculpture of the upturned hand.

Detective Terry descended on the scissor lift, helped Barbara up onto it, then raised it back level with the palm. The palm was made of vehicle hoods and rear spoilers. The fingers of the hand were made of motorcycle frames. The thumb was the only finger unfinished, the top of its gas tank cut open and shining emptily under the bright sun.

"There're seal marks on each of the motorcycle gas tanks," Detective Terry said. "I think there might be something in each of them. Can we get the jaws of life over here and crack 'em open?"

Barbara nodded her head.

*This sculpture is massive*, she thought. *This guy had been working on this one for some time.*

When the fire department showed up a half-hour later and opened up the first motorcycle gas tank, Barbara wasn't shocked human remains were found. She was shocked they were fetuses.

They made Barbara do the televised press conference. She stood trying not to tremble in front of the cameras from the local and national stations feeling like the token woman on the force.

"Jacob Hunter Goodman is a person of interest in the series of cases the press has dubbed the Derby City Butcher," Barbara said, surprised at how steady her voice sounded. "We're asking anybody with information to come forward. We've got a dedicated hotline for tips and there're cash rewards for any information leading to an arrest."

Hands darted up from nearly all the press. Barbara chose one at random.

"What did y'all find at Powers' Scrap 'n' Metal when you executed the search warrant this morning?"

"We found human remains on the premises," Barbara said.

She was bombarded with flashes and a cacophony of exclamations.

"That's all I can say about the search warrant," Barbara said. "The investigation is open and ongoing. We're asking the public to be on the lookout for Jacob Hunter Goodman. He's wanted for questioning in regard to several missing persons cases as well as a series of open homicide cases, including the remains we found at Powers' Scrap 'n' Metal this morning. He's also wanted for questioning regarding the three church fires from early this morning."

Barbara gave the press a description of Jacob Hunter Goodman and his vehicle, including license plate number. The boys in IT gave the press a photograph of the vehicle and shared Jacob Hunter Goodman's driver's license photo, which ran on all the networks at 6 o'clock that evening.

# CHAPTER FORTY-NINE
## THE ART OF MURDER

*CLICK*

*Local artist turned serial killer?* WGAS-11 has the latest on Jacob Hunter Goodman, a religious artist thought to be the Derby City Butcher. Is he also responsible for the string of church burnings that rocked Louisville late last night? More on Your Local News tonight.

*click*

*Sculpting murder?* Louisville man known for his strange religious sculptures wanted for questioning in several missing persons and homicide cases. Human remains found at a junkyard where the artist worked on his sculptures. More on the Great 8 at 8.

*click*

*The art of murder?* Does one man's quest for beauty include murder? Tune in tonight for the latest on the Derby City Butcher case.

The news networks re-aired the earlier specials on Jacob Hunter Goodman, the artist. A short special on CNN about Dominion House entitled *The Dominion of Shame* ran that evening with a focus on Jacob Hunter Goodman. It showed the crowd protesting outside the Louisville Women's Clinic. The camera froze and zoomed in on Jacob Hunter Goodman holding up a sign that read: The Devil Works Here.

One station reported Gallery East had sold all of Jacob Hunter Goodman's pieces that morning and mentioned that many serial killers took up art or had artistic leanings. Several of the pieces that had already been sold reentered the market at vastly increased prices.

Several news copters circled Powers' Scrap 'n' Metal, zooming in on the gigantic sculpture of a hand.

## CHAPTER FIFTY
## THE DEVIL WORKS HERE

**BARBARA SAW THE PHOTO OF** Jacob Hunter Goodman holding the sign and froze.

*That's where I recognized him!* she thought. *Jesus Christ!*

She pulled up the Dominion House website and explored the Pro-Vision 15:3 content, including Jacob Hunter Goodman's *Profile of the Wicked*. There were several photographs of Jacob Hunter Goodman wearing an orange vest and escorting harried looking women into and out of the Louisville Women's Clinic.

*Holy shit*, Barbara thought.

Several of their missing women had their own *Profiles of the Wicked* pages.

*He was picking 'em off from both sides.*

Barbara was taken aback at the hatefulness of the website. There were cheesy graphics showing blood dripping off people's names and addresses and phone numbers. Their places of employment were listed.

*What kind of church is this?* she wondered.

She clicked on a link and a closeup shot of Jacob Hunter Goodman holding a sign that read The Devil Works Here filled her laptop screen. He was staring directly into the camera, his face expressionless, empty of any trace of emotion.

Barbara's skin crawled as she stared at the photo, remembering the day she saw him protesting outside the LWC.

*He was right there. That's how he found his prey, then he switched sides like a wolf slipping into sheep's clothing.*

They planted officers in plainclothes around LWC in the slim hope of catching Jacob Hunter Goodman in the act. Barbara feared, with all the media attention, it was highly unlikely to pay off, but they had to cross all their Ts. They sent detectives to Dominion House and the orange vest escorts to find out all they could about Jacob Hunter Goodman and his time with both organizations. Jacob Hunter

# BIRTH OF A MONSTER

Goodman was not known to have any friends. He wasn't known to associate with any of the individuals outside the capacity of their organizations.

Josiah Powers lawyered up and refused to answer any questions.

Rubbish Management said Jacob was fired within his probationary period and did not offer a reason other than "it wasn't working out."

-

Barbara put on latex gloves and opened the notebook labeled **Letters to My Children**. It began when Jacob Hunter Goodman entered foster care. Barbara read the confused and lonely thoughts and felt a sickening feeling in the pit of her stomach as the entries became more sinister. She read about Jacob Hunter Goodman's penis injury and his being told by a doctor that he was more than likely sterile. She read all the obsessive entries about Tanya Miller and her painted fingernails. She read of the young girl's murder and disposal.

Barbara had conflicting feelings raging inside her. On the one hand, she was glad they had their man. On the other, this was a sickness, an absolute madness, that she was finding very difficult to face. It made her physically ill to read the notebook entries. They increased in insanity and violence as they progressed. The boy had tortured animals. He'd prowled the hills of eastern Kentucky killing animals and breaking into houses. He'd fantasized about killing women all while he killed animals and cut and reconfigured them into his *creations*. He'd had grandiose but vague notions of creating some kind of demented quilt out of different animals. There were a few sketches of his creations, strange animals with mismatched parts.

Barbara had to put the notebook on her desk and close her eyes when she read of Tanya Miller's death. Jacob Hunter Goodman had developed some strange alter-ego, Such A Happy Boy, and described the murder with a detachment that made Barbara's stomach knot up.

She had to take a break for a moment. She got up, made a pot of coffee, then went to Hank's office while it brewed.

"This guy is fucked up," Barbara said, "with a capital F."

Hank looked up from his computer.

"Don't I know it," he said, pointing to his screen.

Barbara crossed the room and stood behind Hank's chair and looked down over his shoulder at the screen. It showed a series of photographs from the junkyard. The first was a wide angle of the hand sculpture. The second was a close-up shot of the interior of one of the motorcycle gas tanks. A nearly full-term fetus was balled up and covered in blood inside.

"Jesus Christ," Barbara hissed.

"I know," Hank said, clicking to the next image.

The screen showed a smaller fetus in another gas tank. Then another. Then another. Then one more.

"We interrupted him, at least," Hank said. "The thumb was still open. That means we stopped him from completing the hand."

"Did you see the torches at the top of each motorcycle?" Barbara asked. "It was set up to burn like a goddamn tiki torch."

"Forensics just popped open the palm," Hank said. "It looks like that's where he stuffed all the mothers."

"Jesus Christ," Barbara said. "How many?"

"They're not sure just yet," Hank said. "At least four, probably closer to six."

"Want some coffee?"

Hank looked up from the screen after a long look.

"Yes," he said in a quiet voice.

## CHAPTER FIFTY-ONE
## GET BEHIND ME, SATAN

**THE PANIC ROSE IN HIM.** Jacob tried to swallow it with each slug of Thunderbird. He was somewhere in Indiana. When he'd seen his face plastered on the television screen at the gas station that morning and saw his name printed on the front page of the *Courier-Journal,* he knew the devil was at work. He knew he had to get out of town and fast.

Something pitiful rose up in him when he thought about abandoning the Hand of God, but Jacob felt great Satan breathing on the back of his neck.

*There will be other sculptures,* he told himself.

*The pigs can have that one. I'll make a new one, a better one . . . one day.*

*Be with me, Lord,* he prayed. *Help me flee these demons.*

"The God of peace will soon crush Satan under yer feet," he said, hating the shaky sound of his voice. "The grace of our Lord Jesus be with ye."

He reached over and fumbled with the bottle of Adderall. He turned up the bottle and let two pills fall out onto his tongue. He swallowed them with another pull from the bottle of Thunderbird.

*You need to change vehicles,* the voice told him.

Something swooped quickly in front of the Mazda and Jacob jerked the wheel as he flinched. He barely kept the truck on the highway.

*Was that a demon?* he thought. *It was so fast. God be with me.*

"Get behind me, Satan," he said.

Jacob took the next exit and parked in the back of a truck stop, his hands shaking uncontrollably. He cut the engine of the Mazda and sat with his eyes closed for some time, trying to slow his breathing. His heart felt like it was going to explode in his heaving chest.

*Calm down,* the voice said.

Somewhere nearby a baby was crying.

Jacob knew it was Tanya Miller's and felt that he was coming apart at the seams.

"Please God," he whispered. "Save me from these evil forces."

Jacob woke with a start. He sucked in a mouthful of air as if he'd been submerged for some time. At first, he thought he was still dreaming. Everything was covered in blood and it took him several confused, panicked moments to realize he was inside the Mazda. It looked like it'd been painted for a horror movie scene.

Then he saw that he was naked. He'd pissed and shit all over the driver's seat and himself. His penis was half-erect. His body was sticky with dried and drying blood. He felt himself and did not feel any injuries.

*It's not my blood.*

In the passenger seat was the beheaded corpse of a naked woman. Jacob saw the sloppy attempt at dismemberment and shook his head. He had no recollection of picking up the woman or of murdering her but he didn't doubt he'd done both.

*A man's got to hunt*, the bald man had said.

He reached over and pinched one of the bare breasts and saw teeth marks all over them.

Jacob reached forward and wiped some of the blood off the windshield and saw he was in a heavily wooded area.

*Good*, he thought, opening the driver's side door of the Mazda.

Cool morning air sent goosebumps rippling across his naked body.

*Where are my clothes?*

He stepped out into the woods then turned back and looked at the blood-covered interior of the truck. His clothes and the clothing of the woman were nowhere to be found.

*Where's her head?* he wondered.

Jacob walked around the front of the Mazda, looking all around him, and opened the passenger side door. The headless body fell out onto the grass at his feet. The head was not inside the cab.

"Huh," he said.

He stretched and listened as his back popped in the quiet morning.

*Where am I?*

It looked like the Garden of Eden. Jacob heard water running somewhere nearby. He stood still, listening for some time. He didn't hear anything but nature sounds. He turned back to the front of the Mazda and found his bloody clothing folded on the hood. The front bumper of the truck was crushed in and he saw a clump of hair and a splattering of blood there.

Jacob picked up his clothes and followed the sound of the water down a small path, an animal's path, down to the banks of a large river. He studied his surroundings for some time, not hearing anything but the sound of the river and the calls of several birds. He walked down the gentle bank and waded out into the water. He wiped at his arms and legs and torso, scrubbing the clumping blood off his bare skin. He let his clothes soak and wrung them with his hands.

The water was cold and cleared his head. He dove under and the current pulled him. He kicked his legs but his sodden clothing he held made it difficult to swim. He lost his footing and the current pulled him even farther out toward the center of the wide river. He let go of his filthy clothing and tried swimming back toward the shore but the current was too strong. He was drifting farther down the stream. He was nearly in the middle of the river. He kicked his feet and tried to gauge which shore was the closest. The far bank was also heavily wooded but Jacob saw a great field on down that side, a farmer's field. He decided to swim back to the side in which he'd entered.

A bit of scripture popped in his head as he fought against the current: *So in Christ Jesus you are all children of God through faith, for all of you who were baptized into Christ have clothed yourselves with Christ.*

Jacob felt the water pulling at his naked skin and it felt metaphysical, like the stream was pulling his sins free along with the dried blood. He was briefly pulled under by the current and, when he reemerged, he heard birds chirping and trumpets tooting. The birdsong sounded like words to Jacob. He breathed heavily and strained to hear what they were saying. The closer to the shore he got, the clearer their song became.

"Kill them! Kill them all!" the woods sang. "Kill them all!"

The faces of harlots, whores of Babylon, flashed before his eyes. He saw all the sinful women of his life as he swam. He saw all the screaming, crying faces of His Children as the flames of damnation lapped at their flesh.

*I must save them! Lord help me save them!*

There were many voices singing in the chorus now.

"Kill them all!"

Jacob's feet found purchase and he pushed himself toward the shore, smiling at the growing chorus. He made his way onto the shore, panting, naked, and smiling.

-

It took him nearly an hour to get back to the place where he'd parked the truck. One look inside told him it was a total loss. The blood had dried and the interior looked like an abattoir. The woman's headless body had attracted a buzzing hoard of flies. Jacob walked around the Mazda, opened the driver's side door, and reached inside. He put the truck in neutral and turned the steering wheel as he pushed it toward the river. It was difficult only for the first minute or so then the truck picked up momentum and Jacob stepped aside and let gravity pull the truck down the slope into the river. He watched it splash into the water and slowly drift farther out, carried by the strong current, until it was completely submerged.

Jacob followed an animal's path deeper into the woods, knowing God was leading him in the direction in which he needed to go. The voices were still singing sweetly in his head.

"Enter through the narrow gate," Jacob said. "For wide is the gate and broad is the road that leads to destruction, and many enter through it."

After a long walk, Jacob emerged from the woods at the face of a cliff looking down into the glassy surface of a rock quarry's recycling pond. The rock quarry was quiet save one crow cawing from somewhere just inside the tree line. There was a singlewide trailer at the far end of the quarry. Parked behind the trailer was a battered, old pickup truck.

The sun felt good on Jacob's bare skin. He walked along the edge of the cliff and followed another animal's path down the hill and into the quarry. The rocks were hard and sharp under his feet but Jacob did not flinch. He made his way to the trailer and up the cinderblock steps to its front door. He tried the doorknob but it was locked. Jacob leaned his weight backwards then threw it into the door with all his might. The cheap door buckled on its hinges and the lock broke free from the jamb.

It was dark inside. Jacob stepped in and found the light switch. There was a little desk with a computer, a stained loveseat, a small television, and a pair of overalls hanging from the wall. Jacob walked over to the overalls and put them on. It felt good being clothed again and Jacob wondered if Adam had the same feeling when he covered himself for the first time.

Under the desk, Jacob found a pair of boots only a little too big. He put them on and walked over to the television and turned it on. A woman gradually appeared from the snowy screen and Jacob immediately recognized her as one of the cops that showed up at the junkyard. The screen said her name was Detective Barbara Shepherd-Findley and that the feed was live from Elizabethtown, Kentucky. The woman cop was surrounded by other cops, all men. The woman cop, Barbara Shepherd-Findley, introduced several of them, including the Hardin County Sheriff, then Jacob's picture appeared on the screen. It took the breath out of his lungs. Jacob stared at his driver's license photo and full name. The text on the screen said he was wanted for questioning regarding several missing persons cases and several open homicide cases. A picture of the Mazda then appeared on the screen along with his license plate number.

*She must die*, the voice said. *Kill. Her.*

Jacob could still hear the angels singing, but only barely. Now there was a great chant slowly building.

*Kill. Her. Kill her.*

*She's the antichrist.*

"A voice of one callin' in the wilderness, 'Prepare the way for the Lord, make straight paths for Him,'" Jacob said.

"Jacob Goodman is very dangerous," the woman cop said. "Do not approach him or engage him. If you see Goodman or his vehicle, call law enforcement immediately."

"Children, it is the last hour, and as ye have heard that antichrist is coming, so now many antichrists have come," Jacob said, staring at all the pigs on the screen. "Therefore we know that it is the last hour."

Inside the desk drawers, Jacob found a box of Nutty Bars and ate all of them. He also found a pint bottle of Old Grandad. He took several nips as he ate the Nutty Bars, feeling the bourbon and sugar enter his bloodstream like a warm blanket.

*She must die*, the voice said.

Jacob nodded.

*She must die*, he agreed.

He lifted the bottle to his lips for another drink but stopped himself.

*No, I don't want any more of this. I need to stay in control.*

He screwed the cap back on the bourbon and dropped it onto the top of the desk. Jacob exited the trailer, leaving the front door wide open. He made his way to the backside of the trailer and the pickup truck parked there. The driver's side door was unlocked and the keys were under the seat. The old pickup's engine turned over twice before roaring into life.

Jacob slowed the truck as he approached the old man checking his mailbox. He pulled the truck to a stop, reached across and rolled down the passenger-side window.

"Hey, old man," Jacob said. "Where am I?"

The old man leaned into the open window and opened his nearly toothless mouth but didn't answer right away.

"I'm lost," Jacob said.

The old man nodded.

"You're just outside Shiloh National Military Park," the old man said. "In Hardin County, Tennessee."

The old man flinched at Jacob's sudden laughter.

*Hardin County!* Jacob thought. *Another coincidence? Not on your life.*

Jacob pulled away laughing, knowing God had given him a glimpse of His Mysterious Workings, leaving the old man looking perplexed in the rising gravel dust.

He was still laughing when he came upon the hitchhiker some time later. He slowed the truck and waited for her to approach the truck, suppressing his laughter but unable to wipe the smile from his face.

"Where ye headed?" she asked through the open passenger-side window.

"Hardin County, Kentucky," Jacob said smiling. "Elizabeth-town."

"Care if I hitch a ride to Clarksville?"

"Sure," Jacob said.

The hitchhiker opened the door and climbed inside the pickup. She smiled across the seat at Jacob and reached a hand inside her bag and brought out a bottle of Jack Daniel's.

"Care for a drink?" she asked.

Jacob's smile stretched further across his aching face.

"Trust in the Lord with all yer heart, and do not lean on yer own understanding," Jacob said, taking the bottle. "In all yer ways acknowledge Him, and He will make straight yer paths."

Jacob drank.

## CHAPTER FIFTY-TWO
## PUTTING IT ALL TOGETHER

JACOB PULLED THE PICKUP INTO the backlot of the truck stop and killed the engine. He used a t-shirt from the hitchhiker's bag to wipe up some of the blood from the dashboard and windshield. He tossed the t-shirt into the pickup's bed and unscrewed the license plate. He walked over to an older model Corolla and removed the license plate and put the pickup's where it had been. Then he used the last of his cash to purchase a pair of oversized Aviator sunglasses and a hat that read: Real Men Love Jesus.

He got the Corolla started without setting off the alarm and got back on the highway. He figured he had several hours before the Corolla would be reported missing by the truck stop employee and a different set of plate numbers would be associated with it.

Jacob turned on the radio to an AM news station. They were discussing the Derby City Butcher, making Jacob smile. The woman cop, Detective Barbara Shepherd-Findley, came on the air.

"Jacob Goodman is very dangerous," the woman cop said. "Do not approach or engage him. If you see Goodman or his vehicle, call law enforcement immediately."

Jacob flipped open the visor and studied his reflection for a moment.

*They'll never recognize me,* he thought. *Not until it's too late, anyway.*

The news segment on the Derby City Butcher ended and the news prattled on to the violence in the Middle East. Jacob turned the station to a religious station and half-listened to an excited preacher shunning nonbelievers.

*Kill her,* the voice said. *Kill. Her.*

Jacob saw the woman cop, Detective Barbara Shepherd-Findley, clearly in his mind. He saw her the way he'd see her at the end, her mouth and eyes round O's of surprise and fear. He gripped the Corolla's steering wheel tight between his fingers and smiled at the road ahead.

Jacob got off the highway in Elizabethtown just as full dark was setting in. He passed the police station and pulled into the parking lot of Flywheel Brewing, where he could stare out his window and watch the police station's parking lot. Jacob sat for over an hour before a man stepped out of the station under the glow of the parking lot lights. He recognized him as the man with the woman cop that questioned him at Powers' Scrap 'n' Metal.

Jacob watched the man cross the parking lot and get into an unmarked cruiser. Jacob reached under the dash and got the Corolla started up again then pulled out onto the road behind the cruiser. He followed the man across town to a subdivision on the outskirts of Elizabethtown. The man parked the cruiser in the driveway of a two-story house and got out.

Jacob circled the block once and parked across the street where he had an unobstructed view of the front of the house.

The woman cop, Detective Barbara Shepherd-Findley, pulled up in another unmarked police cruiser not fifteen minutes later. Jacob had to stop himself from rushing out and taking her immediately. He watched her walk up the walkway and knock on the front door twice before opening it herself and disappearing within.

*Kill her*, the voices sang. *Kill her.*

Jacob got out of the car and crept across the street, keeping himself low to the ground and covered by shadows. He walked around the side of the house and peered in the first window he came to, which looked in on the kitchen. A woman, not the woman cop, was preparing a meal. The two cops sat across from each other at the kitchen table, two cups of steaming coffee in front of them.

The woman said something to the two seated cops and they both rose and helped carry the dishes out of the kitchen through a rear hallway that let out onto the back porch where Jacob saw several tiki torches burning around a table. The two cops sat down at the table and the woman went back inside the house and hollered, "Dinner's ready!"

Three children emerged with the woman.

Jacob watched the family eat their dinner from the shadows, hearing every sound the mouths made as they ate.

*I'll take her when she goes to leave*, Jacob thought, creeping back around the house to the Corolla.

Jacob waited an hour. Then another. When the third hour approached and the woman cop still hadn't emerged from the house,

Jacob again exited the Corolla and crept over to the house and peered inside. The two cops were seated around the kitchen table, the children and woman nowhere to be seen. The cops were deep in conversation. Jacob could hear their serious tone of voice but not the words they spoke.

After some time, the cops' conversation came to a conclusion and they got up, depositing their coffee mugs in the kitchen sink. Jacob watched the man place a hand on the woman cop's shoulder. He said something with a solemn smile on his face. The woman cop nodded and returned the smile.

The man led the woman through the kitchen and out of Jacob's view. Above his head, a light came on in an upstairs window. Jacob crept around to the front of the house and, picking his way along an overgrown hedge bush, climbed up onto the front porch of the house. He kept his body low and looked inside the brightened window. Through a crack in the blinds, Jacob could see the woman cop, Detective Barbara Shepherd-Findley, as she undressed in what he assumed was the guest room.

*She's staying the night! Damn it!*

Jacob felt his stomach drop knowing he wouldn't be able to take her.

"In all yer ways submit to Him, and He will make yer paths straight," he whispered to himself.

The woman cop undressed in the light of a bedside lamp. Jacob watched the woman, feeling himself grow hard, until she crawled under the covers of the small bed. Then he turned and carefully made his way off the roof of the front porch and back to the stolen Corolla.

"Fuck!" he hissed into the darkness. "Fuck!"

He reached over and opened the glove compartment and took out the hitchhiker's bottle of Jack Daniel's and took three large swallows.

As the whiskey warmed his stomach, Jacob decided to go back and watch the woman cop sleep. He crossed the street again and again climbed up onto the roof of the porch. When he was in front of the window, he saw that the woman cop had closed the curtains over the cracked blinds. He couldn't see inside at all. The light was still on inside and he pressed his ear against the outer screen and listened. He thought he could make out the woman cop moaning or crying. He strained his ears but still wasn't sure.

*Shit!* he thought.

Jacob climbed off the front porch slowly, his inebriation making him feel slightly dizzy but not enough to throw himself completely off-balance. He crept around the house and tried the back screen door. It was locked but the window beside it slid up without making a noise. Jacob climbed inside.

He smelled the cooking smells of the kitchen as he passed through the darkened room. He turned the corner and found himself in the family's living room. There was a set of stairs ascending to his right. He took them slowly and as quietly as he could. His ragged pulse beat a frenzied tattoo in his ears. He was disoriented by the layout of the house when he made the upstairs landing. There were two doors and two short hallways. He wasn't sure which door or hall led to the woman cop. He tried the first door he came to and it was a closet. The next was the bathroom. The next let in on a room with two small beds and two covered shapes in each.

*The two girls*, he thought, pulling that door closed again.

The next room was the cop's little boy. He turned and went down the other hallway. The first door he opened let in on the master bedroom. Jacob crossed the room and stood over the sleeping shape of the cop and his wife.

Vaguely, he wondered if the woman was pregnant.

He pictured himself stabbing both the sleeping people with the filet knife, Roger's Bait 'n' Tackle, but he knew this was folly.

*Leave them*, the voice said. *Go find her.*

Jacob eased the door closed behind him. The last door opened onto the sleeping woman cop. She slept facing the wall. Jacob crossed the room and knelt over the bed and smelled her hair as quietly as he could.

There was a loud screeching of tires outside the home that sent Jacob flying across the room and out of the door into the hall. He ran down the hall just as lights came on in the master bedroom. He knew he didn't have time to get back downstairs and out of the window in which he'd entered so he threw open the closet door and hid himself inside.

There was a man's angry voice yelling outside the house then the honking of a car's horn several times in rapid succession.

"Barbara!" the voice shouted from outside.

The adults in the house met in the hallway just outside the closet door.

"It's Perry," the woman cop said. "He sounds drunk. Jesus, I'm so sorry, Hank."

"It's not your fault."

"What's going on, Daddy?" a small girl's voice asked.

"Nothing, honey," the cop said. "Go back to bed now."

"Hank?" the cop's wife sounded scared.

"You fucking hypocrite!" the voice outside the house yelled.

There were several more honks.

"You two get out here!"

"It sounds like he thinks we're having an affair," Hank said.

"Oh Jesus," the woman cop said. "I'm sorry about this, Meredith."

"It's not your fault," the cop's wife answered.

Jacob listened to the sound of the adults descending the stairs. When he was sure they'd all left the second floor he opened the door and made his way back to the bedroom the woman cop had occupied. He shut the door quietly behind him. The bedside lamp was on and he could see the room served as an office and guest room. He crossed over to the window, moved the curtains aside with his hand and peered out the cracked blinds. A man had pulled up into the front yard of the house and was reaching inside the open driver's side window to honk the horn.

"Barbara!" he yelled and Jacob could hear how drunk the man was. "Barbara! You two-timing whore! Get out here!"

Jacob heard the front door open and saw both cops step out into the front yard.

"I knew it!" the drunk man yelled. "Y'all thought you were so slick but I knew it!"

"Calm down," the woman cop said. "Ye're drunk."

"So what if I am?" the man said. "I'm not the only one having an affair, it looks like."

Jacob stepped away from the window and something familiar caught his eye on the nightstand beside the bed. There were several pages stapled together and a wedding band sat on top of them. Jacob picked the pages up, letting the ring slide off onto the nightstand, and saw his own handwriting.

*Letters to My Children* was typed in italics at the top of the page.

*The fucking thief!*

Jacob flipped through the stapled pages and saw that several parts had been highlighted. He saw marginalia on nearly every page including names. *Crystal "Onyx" Sadler*, he read. *Mary Ann Gregory. Lindsey Leslie. Jane Doe.*

*They're putting it all together*, the voice said.

Jacob felt his stomach drop.

*The bastards!*

He folded the pages in half and stuck them in the back of his pants.

"Don't lie to me!" the drunk man screamed outside. "I know about you two! Partners? Ha!"

Jacob felt violated knowing his **Letters** had been read. They weren't meant for anybody but His Children.

The woman cop's wedding band gleamed under the bedside lamp. Jacob reached down and picked it up, turned it over several times in the palm of his hand. Then he put the ring in the pocket of the sweatpants he'd stolen from Walmart earlier that day.

*You have to get out of here*, the voice said. *Use the distraction.*

Jacob crossed back to the window and carefully opened it enough to get the screen out of the way. He pulled the curtains around him as he climbed out onto the front porch's roof. The two cops and the drunk man were having words. Jacob didn't focus on what they were saying, just the fact they were still oblivious to his presence. He closed the window and returned the screen to its place. He lay flat on his stomach on the shingled roof and listened for a few minutes. Then he quietly climbed off the roof and made his way around the house, through the backyards, until he was at the Corolla. He crawled underneath and lay there until the scene was over and the drunk man had driven off into the night.

## CHAPTER FIFTY-THREE
## STATIONS OF THE CROSS

BARBARA WATCHED PERRY'S TAILLIGHTS UNTIL they rounded the corner and disappeared from view.

"Jesus Christ," she whispered.

Part of her wanted to call it in. Let Rhonda or Teresa at the call center know her husband was out driving drunk. But she knew she wouldn't. She also knew Hank, being the saint of a friend he was, would let her call the play.

*What a fucking train wreck*, she thought.

"You alright?" Hank asked. "Let's go back inside."

Barbara followed her partner back inside the house. Meredith was waiting just inside the door.

"You okay?" she asked.

Barbara nodded her head, not trusting her voice.

The three adults stood in silence for a moment and Barbara knew she was supposed to say something but she couldn't find the words.

"I'm sorry," she said eventually.

"It's not your fault," Hank said.

Meredith nodded, placed a hand on Barbara's shoulder.

"I'm going to make us some chamomile tea," she said, disappearing into the kitchen.

"That was rough," Hank said. "I'm sorry Perry's being like this."

"I'm sorry he came here and made such a scene," Barbara said. "I can't believe he did this."

"He was drunk," Hank said, shrugging his shoulders.

There was more to it than that but Barbara didn't want to think about it. She wanted to be drunk. She didn't want to have to deal with Perry and her failing marriage.

"I think I'm going to skip on the tea and just go to bed," she said.

"At least take the tea up to the room with ya," Hank said.

They walked to the kitchen together.

"Did one of y'all leave this window open?" Meredith asked, pointing to an open window just off the kitchen.

Barbara and Hank shook their heads.

"Hm," Meredith said, pouring the hot water into the three mugs. "Wonder how it got left open?"

Hank walked over and examined the open window.

"The screen's been popped off," he said.

"You don't think Perry would've tried to get in here, do you?" Meredith asked.

Barbara shook her head. "No, I don't think he'd try breaking in. He was just drunk and looking to make a scene."

"Think one of the kids was trying to sneak out?" Hank asked.

Barbara saw the Grays exchange a look and took it as her cue to go back upstairs.

Barbara thanked Meredith for the tea and left the Grays looking at the open window. She walked up the stairs to the guest room. She shut the door behind her and immediately noticed that the scanned pages of Jacob Goodman's **Letters to My Children** were not on the nightstand. Her wedding band was missing too.

She started turning the room upside down looking for them. She threw the covers off the bed but the pages weren't there. She dropped to her stomach and checked under the bed but they weren't there either.

*What the hell? Where did they go?*

She flung open the drawers of the nightstand but they were empty.

Barbara felt a pang of panic in her stomach.

*How could they just disappear? They were right here. I set my wedding ring on top of them before I turned off the lamp.*

There was a knocking at the door. Hank opened it and stood just outside in the hall.

"What?" Barbara snapped.

Her face flushed red and she felt embarrassed for her tone of voice.

*Calm yourself, Barbara.*

"What's going on in here?" Hank asked, looking at the covers on the floor and the drawers opened on the nightstand. "Everything okay?"

"Yeah, sorry," she said. "I seem to have misplaced . . ."

She let her words trail off, feeling embarrassed at losing both the photocopied pages of evidence and her wedding band.

"HQ just called," Hank said. "Forensics found some things. We should head back."

"Okay," Barbara said, rising to her feet.

"What're ya looking for?" Hank asked,

"Nothing. I'll find it later."

-

"The Hand of God, as Goodman referred to the sculpture in his notebook, is filled with human remains," Mitchell Skeeters said. "Initial reports from the forensic team show that each of the motorcycle gas tanks contains fetal remains while the palm has mostly adult remains. It's looking like the mothers wound up in the palm and their unborn children in the fingers."

There were several noises of disgust and surprise around the room.

"We've got search warrants getting signed right now for all of Jacob Goodman's sculptures on display at Gallery East, Dominion House, and a few other galleries around town. We're looking for a list of all sales to track down the sculptures in private collections. We'll issue a statement to the press about the human remains but we'll keep the fact that many of the remains were fetuses under wraps. Dismissed."

Barbara walked back to Hank's office feeling tired and sad.

"Cup of coffee?" Hank asked.

Barbara nodded and sank down on Hank's couch. Hank poured her a cup and passed her the steaming mug. Hank walked around his desk and sat down heavily in the chair.

"Want to talk about it?" he asked.

Barbara looked up from the mug at her partner, shook her head, and took a sip of the coffee.

"Alright," Hank said. "If ya ever need to talk about it, any of it, I'm here."

"Thank ye."

"No problem."

They drank their coffees in silence for some time. Eventually Barbara got up, nodded at Hank, and walked down to her office.

-

Barbara and Hank were with the party that served the search warrant at Gallery East, which had five of Goodman's angels on display. They were tall, sinister looking creatures made of metal but shaped like mismatched animals. There were multiple heads and several sets of arms and wings, great talons and reaching hands in supplication.

"Jesus, these are hideous," Hank said.

They'd borrowed a jaws of life from the fire department and were using it to wrench open each of the angels. The smell was horrendous. The human remains had been fermenting inside each of the sealed metal sculptures. The photos the forensic team took looked religious within the metal framework of the sculptures, reminding Barbara of the Stations of the Cross.

They found five fetuses, one per angel. There were cut up bits of adults in the angels as well but not full bodies. There was a head in one. Part of an arm in another. A foot in the last one they cracked open. They all appeared to be female.

They had search warrants for two more galleries. They'd issued a statement to the press for owners of Jacob Goodman's artworks to come forward and voluntarily let the police search them or search warrants would be procured. Several art collectors came forward and balked at the jaws of life but none of them refused the searching.

Not one of Jacob Goodman's sculptures had been without human remains.

*Not a single one*, Barbara thought. *Jesus.*

Barbara felt dizzy when she started counting up the man's body count. How could one man be responsible for so many deaths?

The media were having a field day with it all. The Derby City Butcher was national news every night now. Helicopters and press vans followed Barbara and the task force wherever they went. Barbara's lips became numbed mumbling "no comment" and "active investigation" over and over again. The days passed quickly in a blur of evidence tagging and cataloguing. At one point, Barbara felt like a museum curator for the most heinous artist of all time.

She wasn't surprised when the FBI issued a statement on Jacob Goodman and included him in their Most Wanted list. There were talks of getting one of their profilers on the case, but Barbara doubted it'd happen. At least, not yet. There was too much information to process for Barbara to fret about losing the case to the FBI anyway. She put her head down and got to work.

Barbara politely turned down Hank's invitation to dinner and went home after a long day at the office. She just wanted to be alone for a while. She unlocked the front door and turned on the television immediately. She made herself a rye and ginger ale in the kitchen and preheated the oven for a frozen pizza.

# BIRTH OF A MONSTER

While the oven was warming up, Barbara went to the bedroom and changed into sweatpants and a t-shirt, taking sips from her drink all the while.

*I can't believe I lost my wedding ring*, she thought. *Not that it matters much now. And the pages of Jacob Goodman's* **Letters to My Children***. Where had they gone?*

She'd printed off another copy before leaving for the day. She planned on spending the evening reading through it and making notes. They'd already isolated several missing persons cases to it, namely Tanya Miller and Rodney Tackett.

How many more would she find? Time would only tell.

Barbara made herself another drink and put the pizza in the oven. She took her drink to the living room and saw the news had come on.

"Tonight on Your Local News an exclusive interview with the Derby City Butcher's former counselor."

The television showed an overweight man sitting behind a desk smiling at the camera.

"Jacob Goodman, wanted by police in several missing person and homicide cases, went to this man, Pastor Clark B. Dennison for court-ordered counseling when he was in his teens. The Pastor comes forward with information regarding the suspected killer tonight on Your Local News."

"What the hell," Barbara said.

She picked up her phone and texted Hank.

*The Pastor from His Shining Light Mission is on the news*, she texted.

*I saw! Why didn't he come to us?*

Barbara set her phone down on the coffee table and sipped her drink.

The newscast went straight into it. Pastor Clark B. Dennison was shown fixing his hair then quickly putting his hands down and smiling into the camera.

"His Shining Light Mission has been a stalwart in the community for years," he said, "helping at-risk youth and spreading the Good News."

"When did you work with Jacob Goodman?"

"He must've been about fourteen or fifteen years old when he started coming to me for counseling. It was ordered that he attend counseling by the family court judge. His mama was involved in prostitution and drug use and the like. It's really quite common in

584

this part of the state. That's why His Shining Light Mission is so important to the community."

Barbara thought the man was pompous and self-assured, like a TV preacher in the making.

"We've helped hundreds of at-risk youth here in Appalachia," the Pastor said, "but you can't help everyone. Some people are just born evil. Jacob Goodman was like that."

"How could you tell Jacob Goodman was evil, Pastor Dennison?"

"I've got documents showing him as a monster-in-the-making," Pastor Dennison put his hands up. "Y'all don't have to take my word for it. I've got proof."

The pastor reached into one of the desk drawers and pulled out a manila folder and let it plop onto the desktop.

"I've got proof right here," he said. "Not every child is born pure. There are demons in this world around us. We've got to fight the darkness with His Divine Light. That's what we do here at His Shining Light Mission."

*He keeps saying the name of his place*, Barbara thought. *He must be trying to garner donations. I bet he gets some too.*

"What proof are you referring to, Pastor Dennison?"

"I've got Jacob Goodman's journals here. He talks about tying up other foster children and forcing them to do things they didn't want to do. I've got him describing torturing and killing poor little animals in his own writing. He talks about making *his creations* out of all the little animals he killed. These were not just animals from the wild but pets from his neighbors and strangers."

"That's awful. What other kinds of things do the journals discuss?"

"Jacob Goodman talks about his hatred for his prostitute mother a good deal. He discusses an inappropriately named view that he learned from his mother's pimp slash boyfriend."

"What was this view called?"

"You'll have to censor it for television but he called it 'c—t theology'." Pastor Dennison gave the camera a pained smile.

Barbara shook her head then took a sip from her drink.

"What did this view entail?"

"The boy said all women were basically fallen women. They were all lowdown and good for nothing as that was their base nature. The boy didn't have very many positive relationships with the opposite sex and the male guidance he was getting, from individuals like his mother's pimp slash boyfriend, were skewed and painted women in the harshest light."

"Have you given this information to the police?"

The Pastor smiled. "The police haven't asked for it yet."

Barbara unlocked her phone and emailed Detective Terry to prepare a search warrant for His Shining Light Mission.

"Why come on television now, Pastor?"

"You must refute the devil publicly," he said, smiling broadly into the camera. "You must refute the devil and spread the Good News. His will will be done."

"Our next guest on this Special Report is psychiatrist Dr. Lindsey Stafford. Welcome, Dr. Stafford."

Barbara took another drink.

"I can't believe this so-called counselor would break patient confidentiality," Dr. Stafford, a bespectacled woman, said. "And on live television!"

"You must refute the devil publicly!" Pastor Dennison bellowed.

Barbara smelled something burning then remembered the pizza. She rushed to the kitchen but the pizza wasn't salvageable.

—

They got a warrant for Pastor Clark B. Dennison's files on Jacob Goodman. The judge also issued a gag order precluding him from speaking publicly about his former client. Barbara heard through the grapevine that the state was ending their contracted work with His Shining Light Mission. Barbara also heard that the pastor had received a six-figure payment for his television interview.

The pastor was still in Louisville and they set up an interview of their own, this one at Louisville Metro PD HQ. They'd asked him to bring his files and he'd complied.

Barbara and Hank stared at the man from behind the one-way mirror.

"You want first run at him?" Hank asked.

Barbara nodded. She entered the interrogation room and sat down across the small metal table from Pastor Dennison.

"Thanks for coming down to talk with me," Barbara said.

The pastor smiled and nodded.

"My pleasure," he said. "I brought the case files too."

He slid the manila folder across the table.

"Thank ye."

"You're welcome."

"Tell me a little bit more about Jacob Goodman as ye knew him."

The pastor leaned back in his chair and smiled.

"He was a very troubled boy."

"How so?"

"He had issues with his mother on account of her wayward life-style," Pastor Dennison said. "Prostitution and drug and alcohol abuse. I'm sure you know the type."

"Did he ever express any inkling towards violence?"

The pastor sucked in air through his toothy smile. "That's the kicker, isn't it? The boy was obviously going through a great deal and processing it the way a normal child would, or so I thought. In his future journal he expressed the need for a more Christian world, free of lying and drinking and drugging women. I thought he was just referring to his mother, not fixating on women in general. At the time it seemed like a normal processing for a boy going through what he was going through."

"Did he ever express or write about violence?"

The pastor smiled again. "He tended to focus on the more violent passages of the Good Book."

"Could ye give me an example?"

The pastor opened up the notebook he'd brought with him and turned several pages before finding what he was looking for.

"Here's one," he said. "The boy was reading the second book of Kings and wrote out a passage from it. 'And he sacrificed all the priests of the high places who were there, on the altars, and burned human bones on them. Then he returned to Jerusalem.'"

"Why do ye think he'd copy out those lines from the Bible?"

"I think he was drawn to the violence. He also liked the desecration of the priests' altars."

"Interesting."

"Here's another one he was particularly interested in. It's about the Levite and his concubine from the book of Judges. Are you familiar with the passage?"

Barbara shook her head. "Enlighten me."

"Well, the Levite is traveling and stops in Gibeah for the night and is put up by a resident there. That night, a mob of Benjaminites comes wanting to sodomize the Levite. He sends out his concubine and they rape her to death. The Levite then cuts up the concubine and sends pieces of her to the other tribes of Israel."

Barbara didn't know what to say.

"He quoted the passage in full," Pastor Dennison said, sliding the notebook across the table.

Barbara looked down at the pages in front of her and recognized the handwriting from the **Letters to My Children**. The boy had retraced the letters of "cut her limb by limb into twelve pieces" until they were gouged into the notebook paper.

"The future journal is something we do with a lot of the kids we see," Pastor Dennison said. "They're supposed to write about the future they want to come into fruition and start making plans to make that future a reality. A lot of the children of Appalachia are so entrenched in their world of poverty that they can't envision a future beyond it. Jacob Goodman's future journal started out that way but as our sessions continued his entries became more focused on biblical violence than anything else."

"What did ye say to him when ye noticed this trend?"

"I tried to steer him back to the journal's original purpose and for a time he kept to it. I think he might have started another journal to catalogue his violent tendencies but I've got no concrete proof of this. Just a feeling."

"Did ye ever suspect him of violence?"

The pastor's smile tightened. He blinked several times.

"Well, it's hard to say really," Pastor Dennison said. "I mean the foster parents and the social worker told me about the ice lock situation, which I'm sure you've already heard about, but we didn't discuss that. He was moved to another foster home not long afterwards and our sessions ended. He ended up going to counseling at the Mountain Health Regional Center after that, I think."

Barbara asked the pastor a few more questions but didn't get any more information she didn't already have. She took the manila folder and the notebook from the preacher and sent him on his way.

"What do you think?" Hank asked.

"I think the state should've just burned their money instead of giving it to that blowhard."

They laughed because they needed to.

## CHAPTER FIFTY-FOUR
## IN THE TRANSGRESSION


**THE WOMAN AND HER NOISY** two children woke Jacob up. He'd slept in the woods just off a trail by a lake. It took him some time to come to himself and remember he'd parked the stolen Corolla in a small parking lot in front of Freeman Lake in Elizabethtown.

*Hardin County, Kentucky*, he remembered.

He rose to his feet and hid behind a copse of dogwood trees. He watched the woman and her two children walk down the dirt path and followed them at a distance. The woman was pregnant, her belly protruding before her, her gait more a waddle than a walk. She wasn't wearing a wedding ring.

The two children ran before her, squealed at something, then ran back to her. Jacob used their distraction to pass them.

The trail rounded a corner and there was nothing to see but trees and lake. Jacob stepped out into the path.

The woman stopped dead in her tracks, her mouth hanging open in surprise.

"Hello," the little boy said.

Jacob smiled down at him then returned his gaze to the pregnant woman. She looked uncomfortable, scared. She reached down and moved the children behind her.

Jacob's smile stretched a bit further.

"I'm Ritchie and this is my sister, Brooklyn," the little boy said, poking his head around his mother's waist. "This is my mommy."

"Hi, Mommy," Jacob said.

The woman looked like she might scream.

*Kill her*, the voice said. *Unmarried harlot.*

The woman reached into the pocket of her jacket but Jacob was on her before she could even unlock the cellphone in her hand. The startled cries of the children sounded like honking geese.

"What're you doing to my mommy!" the little boy cried.

Jacob pried the cellphone from the woman's hand and flung it into the lake.

"Oh God," the woman said in a quiet, terrified voice. "Please don't hurt me or the children. They're innocent."

*She's right*, the voice said. *The children have no part in this.*

"Make them leave," Jacob whispered into her ear.

He smelled her hair.

"I'll give you whatever you want," the woman said, "just don't hurt my babies."

"Tell them to go," Jacob whispered in her ear, filling himself with her smell.

*lavender and vanilla and cunt stink*

"Ritchie, take your sister on up the path, okay?" the woman's voice was shaky. "Mommy will be right behind you. Go on now."

"Listen to yer mother," Jacob said, smiling down at the children.

The little girl looked to be older than the boy but the boy took her hand and started walking them farther down the path.

They stopped after a few steps and looked back.

"Go on now," the woman said. "Go on and I'll be there shortly."

Jacob slipped behind the woman and reached around and put his hands on her bulging stomach. He rubbed little concentric circles on her stomach, feeling her quiver and shy away from his touch.

*I'm coming, My Child.*

The children rounded a corner and disappeared from view.

"Please don't hurt me," the woman pleaded. "Please, I'll give you anything. Just don't hurt me. I'm pregnant."

"I know."

The woman started crying, her whole body shaking with her tears.

Jacob let his hands explore the woman's body. He pinched and twisted and caressed, taking pleasure in all the woman's little sounds of terror and confusion.

"Whore," he whispered into her ear.

Jacob stuck his tongue in the woman's ear and held her head steady when she tried to move away. He reached into her hair and took a handful and twisted until she was doubled over at the waist.

"Stop! Please!"

"Let the woman learn in silence with all subjection. But I suffer not a woman to teach, nor to usurp authority over the man, but to be in silence," Jacob said. "For Adam was first formed, then Eve. And Adam was not deceived, but the woman being deceived was in the transgression."

Jacob reached his arm around the woman's throat and lifted her off her feet, which kicked out, sending one of her shoes dropping onto the trail. Jacob choked her into unconsciousness and dragged her deeper into the woods.

# CHAPTER FIFTY-FIVE
## 911

**"PLEASE HELP US," BROOKLYN YELLED** at the man running. "Stop!"

The jogger stopped running and took out his earbuds.

"What's wrong?" he asked.

"A man back there took my mommy!" Ritchie yelled, tears and snot now streaming down his face.

"What?"

"A man came out of the woods and threw Mommy's cellphone into the lake and took her," Brooklyn said, tears running down her cheeks.

"He told us to go away and he took her!"

The man unlocked his phone and called 911.

## CHAPTER FIFTY-SIX
## IT'S HIM

**HANK AND BARBARA HAD JUST PULLED** into the parking lot of the Elizabethtown Police Department when they heard the call go out on the radio.

"Two children reported that their mother was taken at Freeman Lake by a man from the woods."

They stared at each other across the cab of the car.

"It's him," Barbara said.

Hank restarted the engine and peeled out of the parking lot with the sirens blaring.

## CHAPTER FIFTY-SEVEN
## DUTCH TILT

**JACOB LOST CONTROL. HE SAW** himself, Such A Happy Boy, biting and punching the unconscious woman. He saw it all as if from above.

*a Dutch tilt / off-kilter attack*

He watched himself rip the woman's jacket and shirt off her body. He watched himself bite her breasts, her arms, her neck.

The woman woke screaming but he punched her back into unconsciousness. He watched himself touch himself.

He saw the smile on his face, Such A Happy Boy, spread further and further. He watched himself rape the unconscious woman. He watched his hands wrap around her throat and he watched himself choke her to death.

Jacob came back to himself when he heard the helicopter flying somewhere nearby. Then he heard the sirens and fully came back to himself and saw the dead naked woman at his feet as if he didn't know how she got there.

Jacob made to flee but he found he was already surrounded. There were cops all over the place. The helicopter hovered just above the tree line over his head.

*Shit! I'm trapped!*

*Stay calm*, the voice said. *Think.*

His mind raced. He couldn't get it to slow down.

"We've got you surrounded," a male voice called out through a bullhorn. "Come out with your hands up."

Jacob could see the woods crawling with police and thought of lice.

"God save me," Jacob said. "Please, God, save me!"

The cops came closer, circling him.

Jacob lifted the woman and held the filet knife, Roger's Bait 'n' Tackle, up to her throat.

"Stay back!" he yelled. "Or I'll cut her throat!"

More cops than Jacob could count were around him.

*Can they tell she's dead? They can't.*

Jacob held the woman as if she were alive. Her bare breasts jiggled with his body's trembling. He could see his bite marks all over her exposed skin.

*I'm sorry, My Child. I have failed you.*

"Stay back!" he yelled.

Jacob backed up until he was leaned against a towering oak.

"I'll gut her like a pig!"

"Put the knife down!"

"Stay back!"

Jacob held the woman tighter against him and felt her body already cooling. He wanted nothing more than to cut His Child from her belly but knew that was out of his reach now.

*God show me the way. Please.*

# CHAPTER FIFTY-EIGHT
## PAINT YER NAILS

**HANK SLAMMED ON THE BRAKES** and the tires screamed. The car came to a stop just behind an ambulance. They both leapt from the car and followed the path down into the woods where they saw several uniformed police officers waiting with guns drawn.

"What've we got?" Hank asked the first uni they came to.

"Suspect matches the description of Jacob Goodman and he's got a hostage. We think she's dead already but we're not certain."

"Jesus."

Hank and Barbara moved farther into the woods. They followed the line of police officers to a spot some twenty yards off the trail in a stand of oaks. They were behind him. Barbara could just make out the man's elbows on either side of the oak tree. They carefully circled around until they were in front of the man and the naked woman in his grip.

Barbara locked eyes with the man as soon as she stepped out into view. The world seemed to stop and her breathing was very loud in her ears. The man looked terrified but fascinated by Barbara. He wouldn't take his eyes off her.

*Oh Jesus.*

Barbara came to within fifteen feet of the man and held her hands up.

"I'm just here to talk, Jacob," she said.

The man seemed to come back to himself at the mention of his name.

"Stay back!" he yelled.

"I just want to talk with ye," Barbara said, her hands still in the air. "Can we talk?"

The man nodded.

"Sure. Say whatever ye want."

"What's it gonna take for us to walk away from this situation, Jacob?" Barbara asked. "What's it going to take to get ye to lay down that knife?"

596

Barbara watched the man swallow. She studied the naked woman he held up against his body. She looked dead.

*Jesus Christ*, she thought, seeing the bite marks.

One of her nipples had nearly been bitten off.

"Paint yer nails," the man said.

"What?"

"I want ye to paint yer fingernails."

Barbara blinked, confused.

"What?"

"I want ye to paint yer fuckin' fingernails," Jacob Goodman said. "Or I'll cut her fuckin' head clear off."

"Okay," Barbara said slowly. "I'll paint my fingernails for ye, if that's what it'll take to get ye to put the knife down."

Barbara heard Hank take a step away and radio the request for fingernail polish in.

They stared at each other for some time without speaking.

"What's with the fingernail fetish?" she asked. "I saw all the fingers and nails in yer tacklebox. I saw the photo of the young girl ye kept all these years. Tanya Miller. What's with yer fascination with painted fingernails?"

Jacob shrugged his shoulders.

The man's hands were shaking.

"Does it turn ye on to see painted nails?"

The man shrugged again.

"Her nails aren't painted," Barbara said, nodding toward the naked woman. "Think ye could let her go since her nails aren't painted?"

"Beggars can't be choosers," Jacob Goodman said.

"How do ye think this is going to end?"

"The way God wills it."

"Okay. What does that look like to ye?"

The man swallowed again. "Paint yer fuckin' nails," he said.

"I don't have any fingernail polish on me, Jacob," Barbara said. "I'm waiting on someone to bring me some. Also, it's against departmental regulation so I'm going to have to get special approval since I'm on duty."

"I want some Thunderbird."

"We can make that happen," Barbara said and nodded at a uniformed officer to her right. "Get the man a bottle of Thunderbird."

The Thunderbird arrived not ten minutes later. Barbara rolled it across the dirt to the man's feet. He bent and unscrewed the cap and drained half of it with four long swallows.

"Where's the nail polish?" the man asked after a loud belch.

"My supervisor is on vacation," Barbara lied. "It's going to take a few minutes to reach him to get approval."

"Hurry it up."

"Why are ya doing this?" Hank asked.

"None of yer fuckin' business, pig," Jacob Goodman spat.

Barbara gave Hank a look and he took a half-step back and remained quiet. After a few moments he disappeared from view.

"What's the end goal here, Jacob?" Barbara asked.

"That's for God to decide," he said, taking another pull from the bottle.

Barbara saw he'd taken a precarious hold of the woman with the bend of his right arm, which held the bottle of Thunderbird. If the woman was alive and woke up, it'd be easy for her to break away, but Barbara couldn't tell if the woman was even breathing. She thought it doubtful. Her face was covered with dirt and debris from the forest floor. She'd been still for so long.

"Do ye believe in free will?" Barbara asked.

"I believe we are free to choose to follow the Lord or face damnation."

"Is God telling ye to hold this woman against her will right now?"

Jacob nodded his head. "This is part of God's plan," he said. "I am the Hand of God. I am God's flaming sword."

"What does that mean?"

"Ye know what I mean. Ye know what I've done. It's all in the name of the Lord. I am shepherding these fallen women and children to God's celestial shores."

Just then Hank stepped back into view and handed Barbara a bottle of candy apple red fingernail polish. She held it up for Jacob Goodman to see.

"It's here," she said. "I'm going to paint my fingernails for ye."

Jacob Goodman took another drink from the bottle of Thunderbird. His grip on the woman was tenuous.

"Get a light on it so I can see it better," Jacob Goodman said.

Hank stepped closer to Barbara and shined a flashlight down onto her hands.

Barbara unscrewed the lid and dipped the brush into the bottle and began painting the nails of her left hand. The man watched in fascination. The knife dipped as he relaxed his hold on the woman to get a better view of the painting of the nails.

Barbara finished painting her pointer finger and moved on to her middle.

The man's mouth hung open as he stared.

As Barbara was finishing her middle finger, two officers tackled Jacob Goodman from behind. The knife flew from his hand and landed at Barbara's feet. She kicked it away and watched the officers get the handcuffs on Jacob Goodman's wrists.

The naked woman had fallen face-first into the dirt and didn't move. Barbara rushed over to her and turned her over and saw that she was dead. She felt for a pulse in vain.

The two officers lifted the man to his knees, his hands cuffed behind his back, his face empty, expressionless.

They stared at each other for a long moment before the officers pulled him roughly to his feet and marched him back toward the trail leading out of the woods.

Barbara could hear the children crying somewhere just out of view.

*Those poor children*, she thought. *Oh God, those poor children.*

# CHAPTER FIFTY-NINE
## FACE GOD

**BARBARA WAS WORKING ON THE** mountain of paperwork pertaining to Jacob Hunter Goodman's arrest when Hank knocked on her door.

"Come in."

Hank stepped inside and shut the door behind him.

"Got a minute?" he asked.

Barbara finished what she was typing then turned her attention to Hank. "What's up?"

"It's about Perry. He's been arrested."

"What?"

"Yeah, a uni picked him up early this morning for a DUI."

"Jesus Christ," Barbara sighed. She put her hands to her temples. "I can't deal with his shit right now."

"That's not all. Police responded to a call at Spring Meadows Luxury Apartments earlier yesterday evening and Steffanie Phelps had a black eye."

"Oh my God," Barbara said. She wanted to scream but she sucked in a lungful of air and forced herself to breathe steadily.

"She didn't want to press charges and Perry had left just before the unis got there so he'll probably avoid a domestic battery charge but the DUI is gonna stick."

Barbara closed her eyes and swallowed. When she opened her eyes again, the room was an impressionistic blur.

*I will not shed any more tears for Perry Findley*, Barbara thought, blinking rapidly at the stinging in her eyes.

"I'm sorry," Hank said.

He reached across the desk and put a hand on Barbara's. She took it and squeezed once, hard.

"Thank ye," she said in a quiet voice.

"If there's anything I can do, don't ya hesitate," he said. "Anything at all. Ya want to come spend a few days with us?"

Barbara shook her head and forced a smile. "No, but thank ye,

Hank. I think I need some time to process all of this."

"Okay, but I'm here for ya. I mean it."

Hank shut the door behind him.

Barbara, hating herself for it, wept. When she could manage it, she picked up her cellphone and texted Tiff Shelby.

*I'm ready to file for divorce.*

-

Tiff Shelby filed the paperwork to start Barbara's divorce the next morning. Lance Pressler, Perry's attorney, upon being notified of the filing, automatically asked for the return of the engagement and wedding rings. Against Tiff's advice, Barbara agreed to return the engagement ring but refused to return the wedding band. She still didn't know where it was. She knew she lost it at Hank's house and had been meaning to get back over there and search the guest room for it.

Lance Pressler petitioned the court to make Barbara pay for the missing wedding band but Judge Hawkins ruled that the rings were gifts. Barbara didn't want the engagement ring any longer so she agreed to return it anyway. She gave the ring to Tiff who passed it on to Pressler.

-

Barbara handed over her gun and keys then passed through the metal detector. She passed through a series of thick steel doors and through a set of barred doors before she was let into a small room with a small metal table and two metal chairs.

"Goodman will be in directly," the guard said.

Barbara took out her tape recorder and her stuffed accordion file folder. She'd finished reading through Jacob Hunter Goodman's **Letters to My Children** late last night and didn't want to interview him but she had to. There were several loose ends to tie up.

The door to the room was opened and Jacob Goodman shuffled in, his hands and legs manacled. The guard walked him to the other side of the table and sat him down in the metal chair, then secured the prisoner's hands to a metal ring in the center of the table.

The man had dark bags under each of his glazed eyes.

"Mr. Goodman," Barbara said.

The man didn't reply.

"I've got a few questions for ye," she said.

The man remained quiet. Barbara looked him over and marveled at how terrible he looked.

# BIRTH OF A MONSTER

*Life behind bars isn't treating him well.*

Barbara pulled a photograph from the accordion folder. It was a shot she'd downloaded from Mary Ann Gregory's Facebook profile.

"Do ye recognize this woman?" she asked, sliding the photograph across the table.

The man looked down at it, his face showing no signs of recognition.

Barbara pulled another photograph, this one of the crime scene at Buffalo Lake. It showed several body parts lying discarded in the dirt. She thought she saw the flicker of a smile play across the man's face but it was gone before she could be sure.

"It's in yer interests to talk to me," she said. "Coming clean would go a long way in regard to leniency of yer sentencing."

The man remained quiet.

She pulled another photograph from the file folder and held it in her hands for several moments. The man looked up from the table and studied the backs of Barbara's hands and her painted nails, she'd painted them in the office that morning. Barbara smiled as she slowly turned the photograph around so the man could see it.

The man's face seemed to curdle.

It was the photograph of the young woman showering they'd taken from the pop-up camper at Powers' Scrap 'n' Metal.

"What Rodney Tackett done," the man muttered. "It was because of what Rodney Tackett done. Make the baby stop crying."

Barbara blinked. "What?"

"The baby!" the man howled. "Make it stop crying."

The man started struggling against his bonds. The metal on metal clanged around in the concrete room. The guard rushed in and took hold of Jacob Goodman.

"Make it stop crying!" the man yelled as the guard hauled him away.

Barbara listened to the man's howls slowly grow fainter.

-

Barbara tried again the next day. The man looked even worse. His hair was disheveled and he had a black eye. The guard fastened the man's chains to the loop in the center of the table.

"I'll be right outside the door, ma'am," he said, closing the thick metal door.

"Are ye ready to talk yet, Mr. Goodman?"

The man didn't reply. He had a twitch that made his eyebrows and the corners of his lips turn upwards in a grimace. The man seemed to be oblivious to it.

Barbara opened her accordion file folder and reached inside. The man followed her movements. She pulled out a series of crime scene photographs. She laid them out on the table facing the man.

"We need to ID these bodies," she said. "We know they're yers but we don't know who they are. Are ye ready to talk?"

The man's face twitched and he sat further back in his chair. His eyes looked to be nearly all pupil, deep black wells without end.

She pulled out several more photos. These showed the Howard Electric welding machine and the modified welding helmet. The man's face twitched and she thought she saw longing there, but only for an instant. She pulled out more photographs: the Hand of God, several of the angels, the trophy wall in the camper.

"Ye need to start talking, Mr. Goodman," Barbara said after a long period of silence.

The man looked up from the photographs and, for a moment, Barbara thought she had him. Then he swallowed and sat back in his chair.

"Are ye really a religious man?" she asked.

She reached back inside the accordion folder and brought out a pocket Bible. She opened the Bible to a spot she'd marked earlier that morning.

"Are ye familiar with the book of Romans?"

The man smiled.

"I see that ye are. Good. Do ye recall chapter two, verse twelve?"

The man's smile stretched further.

"All who sin apart from the law will also perish apart from the law, and all who sin under the law will be judged by the law," Barbara read. "Do ye think this applies to you?"

The man looked like he was going to reply, but the moment passed in silence.

Barbara turned to another place she'd marked in the little Bible.

"Repent! Turn away from all yer offenses; then sin will not be yer downfall."

The man's face twitched. He shifted his weight in the metal chair and Barbara caught a whiff of him. He smelled terrible. She doubted he was going to the communal showers. He probably hadn't bathed in weeks.

"It's time ye start thinking about yer future," Barbara said. "Ye're going to have to pay for what ye've done. Ye're going to need to come clean and ask more than the courts for forgiveness. Ye're going to have to face God."

The man's face broke out in an angry sneer. "Ye know nothing," he said, his voice even but dripping with venom.

"Then enlighten me."

The twitch then a smile.

Barbara felt the hair on the back of her neck rise.

"Something's changed in ye, woman," he said. "I can see the difference."

"What?"

For a second, Barbara thought the man noticed she hadn't painted her nails for the visit.

"Ye're pregnant," the man said.

Barbara felt as if he'd kicked her in the stomach. The air rushed out of her lungs.

"What?"

The man didn't reply. He smiled a knowing smile and turned back to the photographs on the table.

"And ye're missing something, aren't ye, woman?" he said, not looking up from the photographs.

"I don't know what ye're talking about."

"Yes, ye do."

Barbara didn't like the way the conversation was going. She pointed down at the photographs on the table.

"Tell me about the welder's helmet and the sculptures."

After a moment, he did.

-

Back in her office, Barbara opened the desk drawer and stared down at the pregnancy test.

*There's no way he can tell.*

She couldn't remember when her last period had been.

*Jesus Christ, don't let me be pregnant,* she thought, pocketing the pregnancy test and leaving her office. She walked down the hall to the women's restroom. The room was empty and she went inside one of the stalls. She opened the box and peed on the strip. After several silent moments, the test was positive.

-

Barbara felt like a sleepwalker the rest of the day. She stayed in her office with the door closed and mindlessly completed paperwork.

She left a little early and found tears spilling down her cheeks as soon as she was behind the wheel. She cried a little on the drive home, more as she walked up the walkway to the front door, and she completely broke down once the door closed behind her. She made to make herself a rye and ginger ale but found she couldn't uncork the bottle.

*I'm pregnant*, she thought over and over again. *I'm pregnant*.

The idea was ludicrous to her. *Absurd*. She couldn't be pregnant. Not now. Not with the divorce in the final stages. Not with the Butcher trial looming.

"Oh shit," she cried. "Oh shit. Shit."

Barbara had never felt so alone in her life. She wanted to call her former foster mother but found the phone call to be an action beyond her means. She couldn't imagine mouthing the words out loud to another person: *I'm pregnant*.

She knew she didn't want the child but she didn't feel strong enough to go through the process of obtaining an abortion. Kentucky had only one abortion clinic and she'd seen enough of it, the protesters and escorts, to know she wasn't strong enough to go through the ordeal.

*Oh shit*, she thought, crying and crying and crying.

## CHAPTER SIXTY
## NOT GUILTY BY REASON OF INSANITY

**"HOW DOES YOUR CLIENT PLEAD?"** the judge asked.

"Not guilty by reason of insanity."

There was a murmur through the courtroom.

"Order," the judge called.

-

Back in the little anteroom, the lawyer spoke with his manacled client.

"I know you don't agree with it but we're trying to avoid the death penalty here," he said.

Jacob didn't reply. He stared at the short attorney for some time.

"Look, Mr. Goodman, you're going to have to talk to me if we're going to get through this trial. I need to know some things."

Jacob kept his face blank, expressionless. He wanted to scream. All he wanted to do now was scream and scream and scream, but he kept himself quiet. He found some inner strength and kept himself as still as he could manage. His face twitched and he hated himself for it.

"I am your attorney," the smaller man said. "You have to let me in."

-

After a lengthy debate, the trial was moved from Hardin County. The judge didn't think Jacob Goodman could get a fair, unbiased jury in either Hardin or Jefferson County so the trial was moved several counties over to Daviess County, where there were no reported Goodman slayings or disappearances. The magnitude of the crimes was too large and there'd been too much sensational media coverage.

Indiana put in for Jacob Goodman to stand trial there for his killings in Jeffersonville, New Albany, and Starlight, but the courts ruled Kentucky was to have first go at him. This despite the vice president's attempts to pressure the courts to extradite Jacob Goodman to Indiana.

Jacob Goodman fired several attorneys and tried to represent himself but the court did not allow him to do so in fear that the trail would turn into a farce reminiscent of Ted Bundy. It didn't help that Jacob Goodman's face continually twitched. The legal team that eventually came to represent Jacob Goodman had billboards all across the south. They represented him pro-bono as they were anti-capital punishment.

Evidence also postponed the trial on several occasions. Several art collectors refused to turn over Jacob Goodman's angels. One man was arrested and had to pay a fine for disobeying a court order. When the police finally got ahold of these three sculptures, human remains were found in each of them.

Two of Goodman's angels were stolen from evidence and sold on the black market. Theodore Pilgrim, a low-level member of the Louisville Metro Police Department Forensics Team, and another were eventually caught and tried for it.

The media went full-bore crazy. People flocked by the hundreds to the courthouse for the opportunity to get a look at the Derby City Butcher. It was around the clock news on every major network news station. The courtroom filled with women fawning over Jacob Goodman. One woman was arrested for trying to sneak him a knife. As she was tackled and placed in handcuffs she screamed, "I love you, Jacob Goodman! I'm your Carole Ann Boone!" She later gave an hour-long interview to CBS where she professed her love of Goodman and her desire to marry him and have his children.

Jacob Goodman did not show any emotion in court. His face twitched continually but he neither sneered nor frowned.

A straight-to-streaming documentary painted Jacob Goodman as a patsy for a governmental coverup. It was quite popular and several more docuseries sprouted into existence. Most of the series got the facts of the case blatantly wrong and made Jacob Goodman out to be the victim of the liberal media and not a killer at all. Several filmmakers tried to get interviews with Jacob Goodman and the investigative team but the trial was ongoing and they were denied access.

# CHAPTER SIXTY-ONE
## ABSOLUTE DEGRADATION

**THE NEWS COPTER WAS CIRCLING** overhead as Barbara and Hank crossed under the police tape.

"How many have we got?" Hank asked the uniform standing guard.

"Not sure. At least four," the uniformed officer said. "Probably more. It's awful."

Hank had called Barbara not forty-five minutes earlier with the report of another Butcher dumpsite, this one deep in the Jefferson Memorial Forest, near Bee Lick Creek.

Barbara and Hank followed the flashlights through the darkened forest. Barbara thought they looked more like lighthouses as they played around the trees.

"We got a genny and light setup coming," Detective Terry said as Hank and Barbara stepped up to the crime scene. "Should be here any minute now."

"Good deal," Barbara said. "What've we got, Terry?"

"Several bodies," he said, "all cut up. I'm thinking four or five but it's hard to tell. They're pretty far gone."

They studied the area in silence for some time.

They branched out from the first of the shallow graves and found more. Coyotes or some other animals had gotten to some of the body parts. There were no hands to be found anywhere.

"It's him," Hank said.

Barbara nodded, remembering how dark Jacob Goodman's eyes had been when she'd interrogated him. So black and so endlessly deep they'd looked.

*Is he even human?* she wondered. *No human being can do this to another human being. It's inhumane. It's absolute degradation. It's horrid.*

Barbara had seen dead bodies, tons of them, but she still couldn't look at these corpses, cut up and scattered like trash, without shuddering. She felt cold to her soul.

"Let's get it all done as quickly as we can without making a single mistake," she said. "Once the generator and lights get here, photograph everything."

Barbara, for the first time in her career, wished she'd chosen another profession. She stared at the flayed bellies on each of the torsos and held her own, thinking about the baby she still carried.

To Barbara's horror, a copycat murderer sprouted up in Arkansas, leaving a pile of chopped-up women in a field beside a middle school. The fingers were cut off the hands and there wasn't a head present at the dumpsite.

The media went crazy, but the man was caught not two weeks into his rampage and he admitted his inspiration was Jacob Hunter Goodman.

The bodies found in Jefferson Memorial Forest were identified as belonging to Heather Findley, Beatrice Pottsfield, Stacie Martinez, Regina Thomas, and Valerie Fuller. There were several other body parts that did not match any of these women but nothing more could be learned from them due to their decomposition.

Barbara and Hank interviewed Jacob Goodman at the Daviess County Jail, where he was kept during his trial.

"We found your other dumping ground," Hank said.

Barbara slid several photographs from the Jefferson Memorial Forest crime scene across the smooth surface of the metal table.

Jacob Goodman stared down at the photographs and his face twitched.

"What've ya got to say?" Hank asked.

The man's face twitched again but he remained quiet.

"I thought we were beyond this," Barbara said. "Ye talked to me before. What's changed?"

The man smiled at her then his face returned to blandness. "My attorney says I'm not to talk to anyone without him being present."

"Listen," Hank said. "We know it's you. It's just like the Buffalo Lake dumpsite. You've already told us about that one. I don't see any reason for ya to clam up about this one. They're the same. Cut-up women scattered about in shallow graves. What's the difference to ya?"

The man didn't reply.

Barbara leaned across the table until the man looked up into her eyes.

"Want me to paint my nails?" she asked, keeping her voice cool and expressionless.

A great smile spread across Jacob Goodman's face.

-

Jacob Goodman's legal team petitioned the court to move the case to another county, claiming their client couldn't get an unbiased jury with all the publicity. The bodies found at Jefferson Memorial Forest just added more gas to the fire, they claimed.

The judge shot down their request and ordered the trial to proceed.

## CHAPTER SIXTY-TWO
## BAD NEWS

**HANK BURST THROUGH THE DOOR** without knocking and tossed a magazine down onto the desk in front of Barbara.

"Did ya see this shit?" he asked.

Barbara picked up the magazine and saw that it was an issue of *People*. She read the bold print out loud.

"Adam Driver rumored to star in Derby City Butcher movie."

"Fucking sick. It's sick. Disgusting," Hank said.

Barbara let the magazine drop to her desk and shook her head.

"Why on earth would they make a movie about this monster?" Hank asked.

"I don't know," Barbara said.

"Why on God's green earth are these women fawning over him in the courtroom?" Hank asked.

Barbara shook her head.

"He's a monster," Hank continued. "If he weren't in shackles he'd skin them alive and yet they show up to court in low-cut shirts and pencil skirts and flash him 'fuck me' eyes. I don't get it."

"I don't either," Barbara said.

"They're making a summer blockbuster about a serial killer of women," Hank said and laughed. "We're a sick society."

"Yep."

That night, Barbara watched the news and saw that the leading actress, the woman that was set to play her part, had gone missing. The media was supposing all sorts of insanity. They wondered if another copycat had arisen and taken her hostage. Thoughts and prayers were sought.

The morning news the following day concluded the mini drama. The actress had been holed up in a drug house, out of her head, for days. She had a serious cocaine habit apparently. She'd entered rehab and another actress was being sought to play the lead detective in the Derby City Butcher movie. Barbara turned the television off and went to work.

-

The divorce proceeded steadily and got worse as it went. Dozens of emails were exchanged and each one lost a bit of civility. Perry's emails became littered with spelling and typographical errors. Barbara heard that the police were called on several occasions to the Spring Meadows Luxury Apartments on neighbor-reported yelling coming from Steffani Phelps' apartment. No arrests were made and a part of Barbara wondered if that was due to her being on the force.

Perry called her twice, drunk.

"I'm so sorry," he cried on the other line.

"I am too."

And she was too. She was sorry she ever got involved with Perry Findley. She was especially sorry she got pregnant. She almost told him on that second phone call, but she kept it to herself. She wondered if it'd change anything. She didn't think it would. Their relationship had run its course. A baby wouldn't simplify things.

"I'm going to lose my job," Perry whispered.

Barbara could hear the strain of Perry trying to hold back the tears.

"They made me take a leave of absence," he said.

"Maybe they'll let ye come back after the divorce is finalized," Barbara said.

"Maybe they'll let ye come back," he mocked. With the blink of an eye, Perry's tears were tears of rage. "This is all your fault," he spat. "You know that, don't you? This is all your fault."

"Goodbye, Perry," Barbara said, ending the call.

Perry immediately began calling and texting her, leaving drunken voicemails, his voice sounding strangled and wet.

He was picked up for another DUI that evening.

-

Barbara parked the car and took a deep breath. Her hands gripped the steering wheel, her knuckles white from the tension, for a full minute before she killed the engine and opened the door. She stepped out and was met immediately by a volunteer in an orange vest.

"Murderer!" the crowd screamed.

"Baby killer!"

"Sinner!"

Barbara kept her head down and let the volunteer usher her toward the Louisville Women's Clinic's front door.

"This way, ma'am," the volunteer, an elderly man, said. "Don't you worry about those protesters. They're not going to do nothin' but holler and carry on."

There was the flash of a camera in her face, momentarily blinding her. The escort guided her as she blinked away the afterimage of the flash.

Barbara thought about the Derby City Butcher. He'd preyed on women in her situation. He'd been on both sides of the picket line too. An opportunist, a monster.

Barbara stepped inside and breathed a sigh of relief. She could still hear the crowd but faintly. She approached the glass window of the front desk and knocked gently. The glass slid open and a woman in scrubs smiled up at her.

"Hello."

"Hi, I'm Barbara Shepherd-Findley. I have an appointment."

She was given some paperwork to complete while she waited. The paperwork inquired about her marital status and Barbara's thoughts turned to Perry. Should she have consulted with him? It was *his* baby too.

*No*, she told herself. *It's my body; it's my choice. Perry's done making decisions in my life.*

Barbara completed the paperwork, returned it to the woman behind the glass, and sat back down. She picked up a magazine at random from the table but didn't read or see anything in it. She just flipped the pages every so often, her unfocused eyes moving blankly across the glossy pages.

"Barbara?" a voice called from across the room.

Barbara saw another woman in scrubs standing in an open door to the right of the front desk. She set the magazine back down on the table and crossed the room.

"Follow me," the woman said, holding the door for her.

Barbara followed the woman into an examination room where she sat on the paper-covered bed. The nurse took her vitals and asked her several questions about her overall health, then she left Barbara waiting on the examination table. Another woman in scrubs entered the room directly and drew some of Barbara's blood. Barbara stared at the wall, lost in her thoughts, until there was a gentle knocking at the door and it opened. A doctor in a white coat and scrubs entered.

"Hi, Barbara," she said. "I'm Dr. Kronowski. Pleased to meet you."

They shook hands, then the doctor sat down at the computer chair and wheeled herself closer to the monitor.

"So we'll get the results from the bloodwork shortly and determine how far along you are. Can you tell me when your last cycle was?"

Barbara could and did.

They discussed the pregnancy and Barbara expressed her decision to terminate it. The doctor listened and made Barbara feel comfortable. She explained the procedure, pills to induce the abortion, and they set up another appointment for it to take place.

Barbara stepped outside and was bombarded with the protesters' fury. They seemed to lunge at her with their signs of dead fetuses and angry faces. Barbara saw a collage of barred teeth and slitted, narrowed eyes. She was escorted back to her vehicle by the same elderly man, who wished her a good day and closed her door for her.

-

*Bad news*, the text from Hank read.

It was followed by a link, which Barbara opened on her phone's browser. It took her to the Pro-Vision 15:3 website. The page loaded a photograph of Barbara, head down, being ushered into the Louisville Women's Clinic. Barbara read her own *Profile of the Wicked*. She read where the Elizabethtown Police Department was listed as an Accomplice.

"Bastards," Barbara said.

She was shaking with anger.

*How dare they!*

Her phone number and address were listed.

"Jesus Christ!" Barbara said.

Barbara scrolled down and saw a photograph of her house.

She nearly threw her phone.

-

Barbara sat across the table from Perry, lawyers at each of their sides.

"What do you have to say about this?" Pressler asked.

The lawyer slid a printout of the Pro-Vision 15:3 site's *Profile of the Wicked* on Barbara.

Barbara wanted to scream but she forced herself to pick up the page and look at it. Tiff leaned in and whispered, "Don't say anything."

Perry was drunk, everybody could smell him but nobody said a word.

"You're pregnant?" he asked, louder than was necessary.

"That's none of yer business," Barbara said.

"The hell it's not!" Perry shouted. "That's my baby too!"

Barbara hated the hot, angry tears that stung her eyes.

"It's not your decision."

"It should be half-mine."

The attorneys whispered to their clients.

"Don't feed into his bullshit," Tiff said. "Just let him put his foot in his mouth."

"Were you there for police business?" Pressler asked.

Barbara shook her head, not trusting her voice not to be loud and angry.

"So you were there seeking the Louisville Women's Clinic's services?"

Barbara nodded.

"And you don't think Perry should have some say in the matter?"

Barbara shook her head.

"That seems awful cold," Pressler said, "seeing as it took two of you to make that child."

"That doesn't matter at all," Tiff said. "My client's right to seek out medical services is of no concern here."

"I disagree," Pressler said. "I think my client should have a say in the matter."

"It's my body," Barbara said, her voice barely above a whisper. "It's my body, it's my decision. End of discussion."

Perry shoved himself away from the table, nearly toppling over in his chair. He rose on unsteady legs, leaned on the table, and pointed at Barbara.

"I know for a fact that you were drinking at the time when you got pregnant," Perry said. "You probably have to have this abortion because you drowned the kid in rye."

Perry jabbed his finger at Barbara twice more, stomped across the room on unsteady legs, and slammed the door behind him.

# CHAPTER SIXTY-THREE
## SHE PROBABLY DESERVED IT

**NOW ON YOUR LOCAL NEWS:** Christy Goodman, mother of the infamous Derby City Butcher, was murdered in a drug-deal-gone-wrong. Reports are in that Christy Goodman, the mother of alleged Derby City Butcher Jacob Hunter Goodman was slain last night after a drug deal went sour. It was reported to Your Local News Station that Christy Goodman attempted to buy $75 worth of prescription pills and a "dime-bag" of marijuana. Christy Goodman was reported to feel shorted on the amount of drugs provided as well as the type of drugs offered by Marcus "Mack" Stewart of Prestonsburg, who brought Suboxone instead of Roxicodone to Goodman's single-wide trailer in rural Floyd County. The argument escalated quickly and Goodman was shot once in the chest. Mack Stewart fled the scene but voluntarily turned himself into police early this morning, stating the shooting was in self-defense. Jacob Hunter Goodman, when informed of his mother's death, is reported to have said, "She probably deserved it."

Next up on Your Local News: the former foster parents of the Derby City Butcher pen memoir about their attempts at raising the serial killer. *The Devil We Knew* is scheduled for release later this month and a reality show, *Far Away with the Faraways*, is in the works. More after the break.

# CHAPTER SIXTY-FOUR
## THE ANTICHRIST

**BARBARA WALKED UP THE STEPS** of the courthouse thankful this was the last step in her divorce. Tiff briefed her the previous evening over drinks and ensured Barbara she'd be done in plenty of time to get to Daviess County for the Goodman hearing, in which she was scheduled to testify.

Barbara entered the courtroom and approached the front of the crowded room where Tiff was waiting on her.

"Mornin', hon," Tiff said.

"Mornin'."

"Here're are the last of the papers that need signing," Tiff said, passing Barbara a pen.

Barbara signed her name feeling some weight transfer from her shoulders to the documents. She knew she hadn't completely processed her feelings about her divorce but she felt she had to keep herself moving or she'd be overcome by emotional paralysis. She signed and initialed and dated then set the pen on the table.

"That's it," Tiff said, smiling.

"Could ye put in the paperwork to change my name back to Shepherd?"

"Consider it done."

"Thank ye," Barbara said, tears stinging her eyes. "For everything."

"No problem, hon," Tiff said. "How're you feeling after your procedure?"

"Fine," Barbara said, tears spilling down onto her cheeks.

She promised herself she wouldn't cry. She struggled and eventually regained control of herself.

"I'm fine," she told her friend.

They embraced then Barbara left the courthouse and headed for Daviess County.

-

Jacob Hunter Goodman stared daggers at Barbara as she took the stand. There was a constant murmur from the onlookers. Television cameras panned back and forth between Barbara and the Derby City Butcher.

Barbara led the prosecutorial team through her part of the investigation. She described the bodies found at Buffalo Lake and Jefferson Memorial Forest. She described the crime scene at Powers' Scrap 'n' Metal, including the camper where Jacob Hunter Goodman kept his trophies.

Nearing the end of the day, Jacob Hunter Goodman shot up on his feet and started yelling.

"She's the antichrist!" he screamed. "She's a baby killer!"

Barbara watched in horror as the man reached into the seat of his pants, grunted, then flung something across the courtroom at her. Something small and hard hit her in the cheek and fell onto the stand in front of her. Though it was shit-flecked, Barbara could tell right away that it was a wedding band. She couldn't stop herself from picking it up and reading the initials on the interior: BS & PF.

It was her wedding band.

Barbara felt frozen in place. She watched as Jacob Goodman was tackled by the bailiffs and dragged out of the courtroom screaming.

"Why have ye forsaken me?" he yelled. "God, help me!"

She felt all the eyes turn to her and felt her cheeks flush. She tried to wipe away the shit on her cheek but she only managed in smearing it. She was ushered from the stand by Hank and led to a private bathroom in the back.

The judge found Jacob Hunter Goodman in contempt of court and postponed the proceedings until the following day. He apologized to Barbara for the defendants appalling behavior and promised to keep a closer rein on him for the rest of the proceedings.

-

Barbara received a text from a bailiff friend that the jury had reached their verdict. She raced down the Western Kentucky Parkway to Daviess County. She knew the verdict was going to be guilty by the short deliberation time of the jury. She was smiling when she entered the courtroom. She found a seat near the front and didn't have long to wait before the defendant was led to his seat at the table. He stared at Barbara for the entirety of his walk across the front of the court room. Barbara beamed a smile at him and he looked away.

They all rose as the judge entered.

"Be seated," he said. "What does the jury find?"

"We the jury find the defendant, Jacob Hunter Goodman, guilty of twenty-four counts of first degree murder."

There was a ripple across the courtroom. Barbara's face was radiant. She heard the cameras clicking away all around her. She watched Jacob Goodman but he didn't react.

"What does the jury recommend for sentencing?"

"The jury recommends death, your honor," the foreman of the jury said.

Barbara wanted the man to scream and cry. She wanted him to suffer his sentencing but the Derby City Butcher took all of it blankly, without expression.

*We got him!*

A friend from her academy days, Kasey Stumbo, called Barbara later that afternoon.

"I've got some bad news for ye," Kasey Stumbo said. "It's about yer mother."

Kasey Stumbo worked in the prison system now.

"She tried to kill another inmate in a contract hit."

"What?" Barbara asked.

Her mother had been addicted to drugs for as long as Barbara could remember, spending more and more of her adult life incarcerated. Barbara hadn't spoken to her mother for six years.

"Yer mother tried to kill Rebeca 'Shorts' Blackwell in a contract hit but it went awry. She was beaten to death."

Barbara felt like the wind had been knocked out of her.

"It was gang-related."

"My mother was never involved in any gangs."

"No, she wasn't but she was desperate enough for drugs that she took the contract," Kasey Stumbo said. "She was supposed to be paid in Roxies. She was cellmates with Blackwell."

"Jesus."

"I know," Kasey Stumbo said. "I'm awful sorry about it. I wanted ye to hear it from me, not the news."

"Thank ye."

"Don't mention it. Let me know if I can do anything for ye."

Barbara hung up feeling a hollow spot in her chest. She vowed she would not let her biological mother's death negatively affect her life. She was offered a job with LPD as a homicide detective and she planned on accepting it.

## CHAPTER SIXTY-FIVE
## WOMEN ARE THE PROBLEM

**THIS IS YOUR LOCAL NEWS** with this Local News Update: convicted killer Jacob Hunter Goodman is appealing his guilty verdict from death row. Your Local News was granted access to the Derby City Butcher for an exclusive interview.

"You were convicted of killing twenty-four women. Why'd you do it?"

"I've done nothing wrong. I've followed God's commandments. He has set my path and I have not deviated from it."

"God told you to kill all those women?"

"'For I know the plans I have for yoe,' declares the Lord, 'plans to prosper ye and not to harm ye, plans to give ye hope and a future.'"

Reporter: "Why did you kill all those women, Mr. Goodman? Do you have a problem with women?"

"I don't have a problem with women," he said. "Women are the problem."

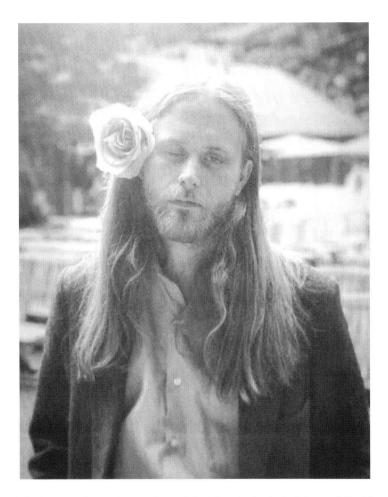

A.S. Coomer is a writer and musician. Books include *Memorabilia, The Fetishists, Shining the Light, The Devil's Gospel, The Flock Unseen,* and others. He runs Lost, Long Gone, Forgotten Records, a "record label" for poetry. He coedits Cocklebur Press.

@ascoomer
www.ascoomer.com
www.ascoomer.bandcamp.com

## Other Grindhouse Press Titles

Printed in Great Britain
by Amazon